STAR WARS™
ADVENTURES
O M N I B U S

COVER ARTIST
DEREK CHARM

SERIES ASSISTANT EDITORS
PETER ADRIAN BEHRAVESH
AND ELIZABETH BREI

SERIES EDITORS
BOBBY CURNOW
AND DENTON J. TIPTON

COLLECTION EDITORS
JUSTIN EISINGER
AND ALONZO SIMON

COLLECTION DESIGNER
JEFF POWELL

ISBN: 978-1-68405-328-5   23 22 21 20   1 2 3 4

STAR WARS ADVENTURES OMNIBUS, VOLUME 1. JANUARY 2020. FIRST
PRINTING. © 2020 Lucasfilm Ltd. & ® or ™ where indicated. All Rights Reserved.
© 2020 Idea and Design Works, LLC. The IDW logo is registered in the U.S.
Patent and Trademark Office. IDW Publishing, a division of Idea and Design
Works, LLC. Editorial offices: 2765 Truxtun Road, San Diego, CA 92106. Any
similarities to persons living or dead are purely coincidental. With the exception
of artwork used for review purposes, none of the contents of this publication
may be reprinted without the permission of Idea and Design Works, LLC. Printed
in Korea.

IDW Publishing does not read or accept unsolicited submissions of ideas,
stories, or artwork.

Originally published as STAR WARS ADVENTURES issues #0–8, 10, 11,
the 2018 Free Comic Book Day issue, and the 2018 Annual.

Chris Ryall, President, Publisher, & CCO

John Barber, Editor-In-Chief

Cara Morrison, Chief Financial Officer

Matt Ruzicka, Chief Accounting Officer

David Hedgecock, Associate Publisher

Jerry Bennington, VP of New Product Development

Lorelei Bunjes, VP of Digital Services

Justin Eisinger, Editorial Director, Graphic Novels & Collections

Eric Moss, Senior Director, Licensing and Business Development

Ted Adams and Robbie Robbins, IDW Founders

Facebook: facebook.com/idwpublishing
Twitter: @idwpublishing
YouTube: youtube.com/idwpublishing
Tumblr: tumblr.idwpublishing.com
Instagram: instagram.com/idwpublishing

VOLUME ONE

01
STAR WARS
ADVENTURES

Writer
LANDRY Q. WALKER

Artist
DEREK CHARM

Letterer
ROBBIE ROBBINS

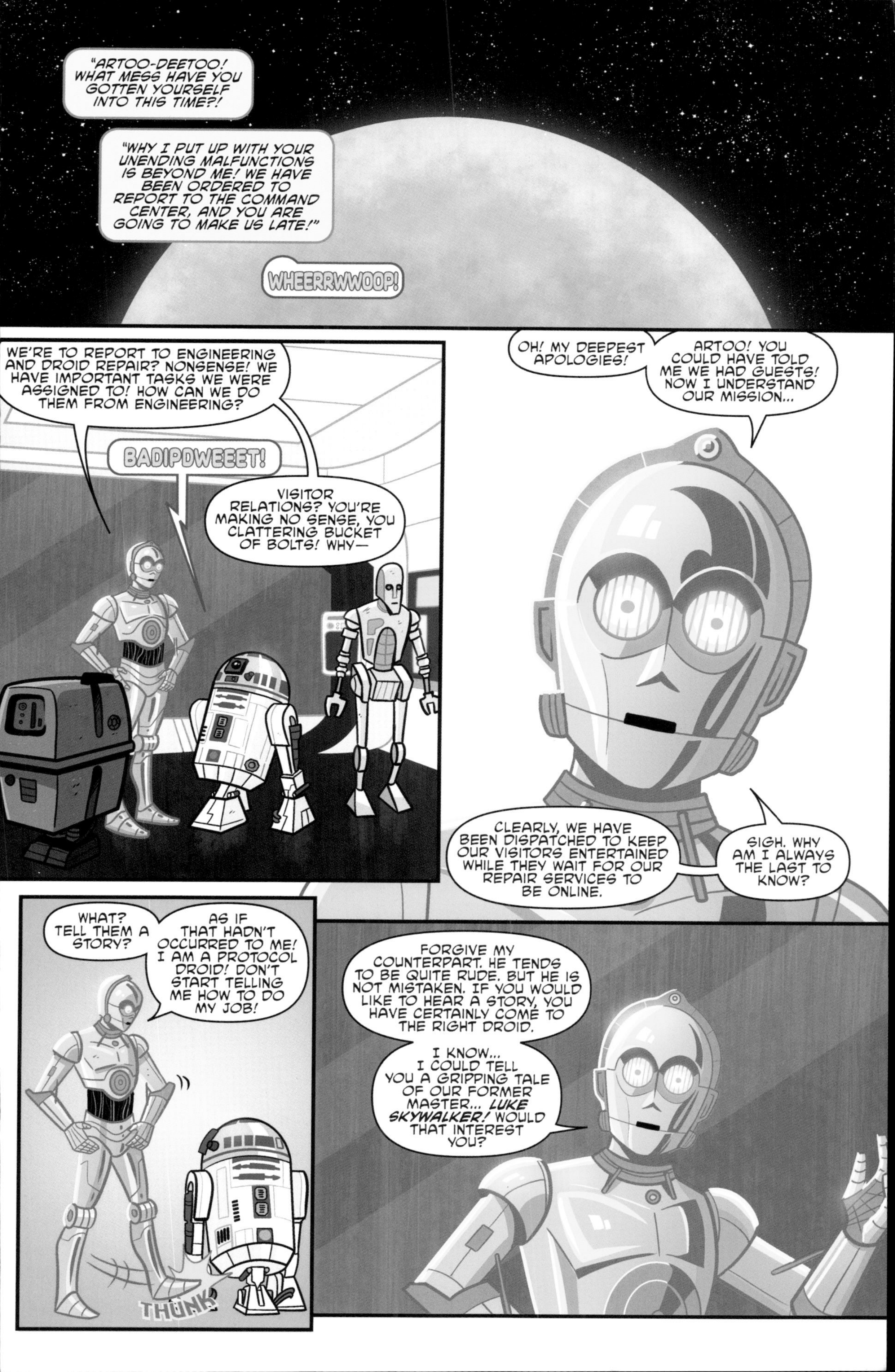
"ARTOO-DEETOO! WHAT MESS HAVE YOU GOTTEN YOURSELF INTO THIS TIME?!
"WHY I PUT UP WITH YOUR UNENDING MALFUNCTIONS IS BEYOND ME! WE HAVE BEEN ORDERED TO REPORT TO THE COMMAND CENTER, AND YOU ARE GOING TO MAKE US LATE!"
WHEERRWWOOP!
WE'RE TO REPORT TO ENGINEERING AND DROID REPAIR? NONSENSE! WE HAVE IMPORTANT TASKS WE WERE ASSIGNED TO! HOW CAN WE DO THEM FROM ENGINEERING?
BADIPDWEEET!
VISITOR RELATIONS? YOU'RE MAKING NO SENSE, YOU CLATTERING BUCKET OF BOLTS! WHY—
OH! MY DEEPEST APOLOGIES!
ARTOO! YOU COULD HAVE TOLD ME WE HAD GUESTS! NOW I UNDERSTAND OUR MISSION...
CLEARLY, WE HAVE BEEN DISPATCHED TO KEEP OUR VISITORS ENTERTAINED WHILE THEY WAIT FOR OUR REPAIR SERVICES TO BE ONLINE.
SIGH. WHY AM I ALWAYS THE LAST TO KNOW?
WHAT? TELL THEM A STORY?
AS IF THAT HADN'T OCCURRED TO ME! I AM A PROTOCOL DROID! DON'T START TELLING ME HOW TO DO MY JOB!
THUNK!
FORGIVE MY COUNTERPART. HE TENDS TO BE QUITE RUDE. BUT HE IS NOT MISTAKEN. IF YOU WOULD LIKE TO HEAR A STORY, YOU HAVE CERTAINLY COME TO THE RIGHT DROID.
I KNOW... I COULD TELL YOU A GRIPPING TALE OF OUR FORMER MASTER... LUKE SKYWALKER! WOULD THAT INTEREST YOU?

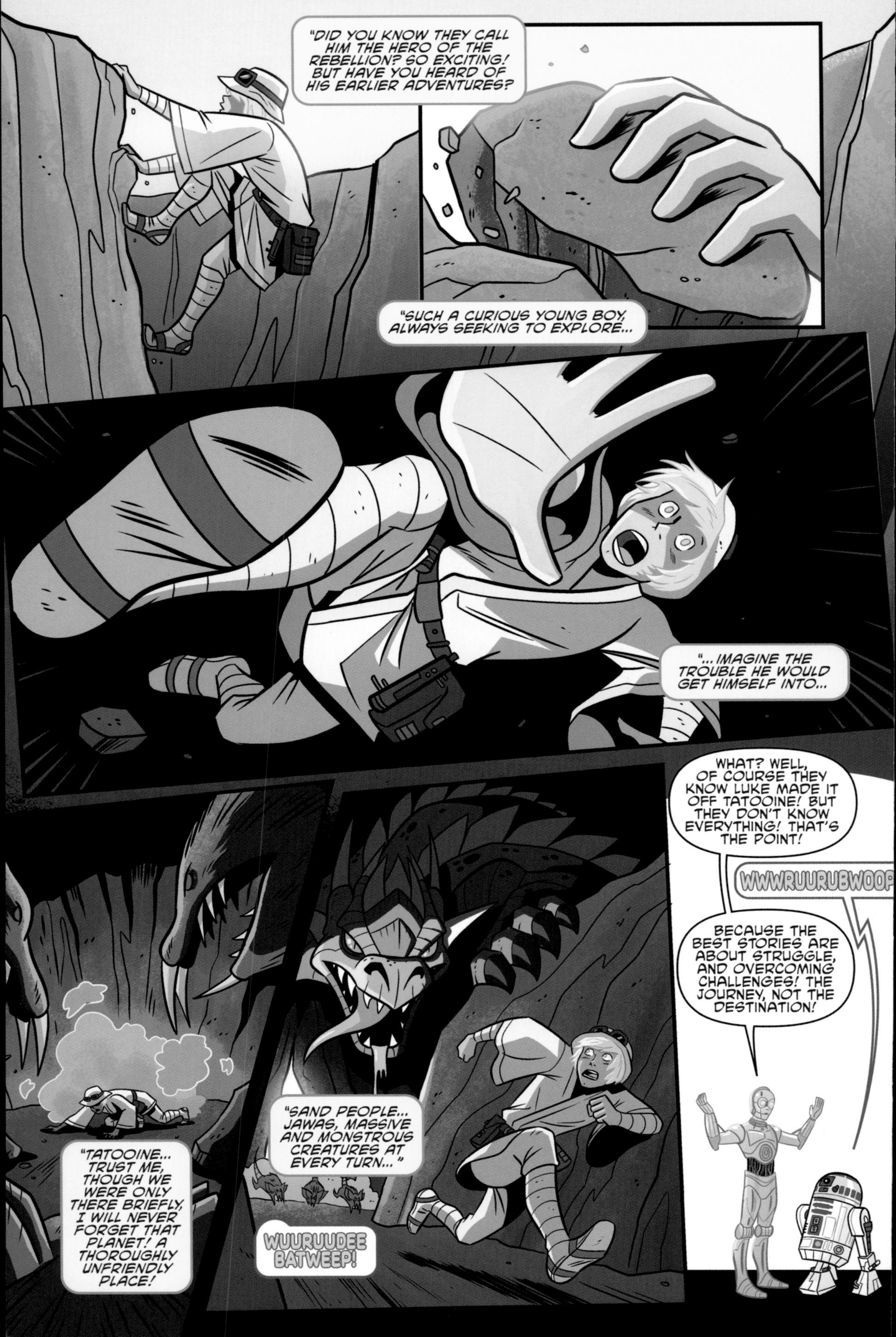
"DID YOU KNOW THEY CALL HIM THE HERO OF THE REBELLION? SO EXCITING! BUT HAVE YOU HEARD OF HIS EARLIER ADVENTURES?
"SUCH A CURIOUS YOUNG BOY, ALWAYS SEEKING TO EXPLORE...
"...IMAGINE THE TROUBLE HE WOULD GET HIMSELF INTO...
"TATOOINE... TRUST ME, THOUGH WE WERE ONLY THERE BRIEFLY, I WILL NEVER FORGET THAT PLANET! A THOROUGHLY UNFRIENDLY PLACE!
"SAND PEOPLE... JAWAS, MASSIVE AND MONSTROUS CREATURES AT EVERY TURN..."
WUURUUDEE BATWEEP!
WHAT? WELL, OF COURSE THEY KNOW LUKE MADE IT OFF TATOOINE! BUT THEY DON'T KNOW EVERYTHING! THAT'S THE POINT!
WWWRUURUBWOOP
BECAUSE THE BEST STORIES ARE ABOUT STRUGGLE, AND OVERCOMING CHALLENGES! THE JOURNEY, NOT THE DESTINATION!

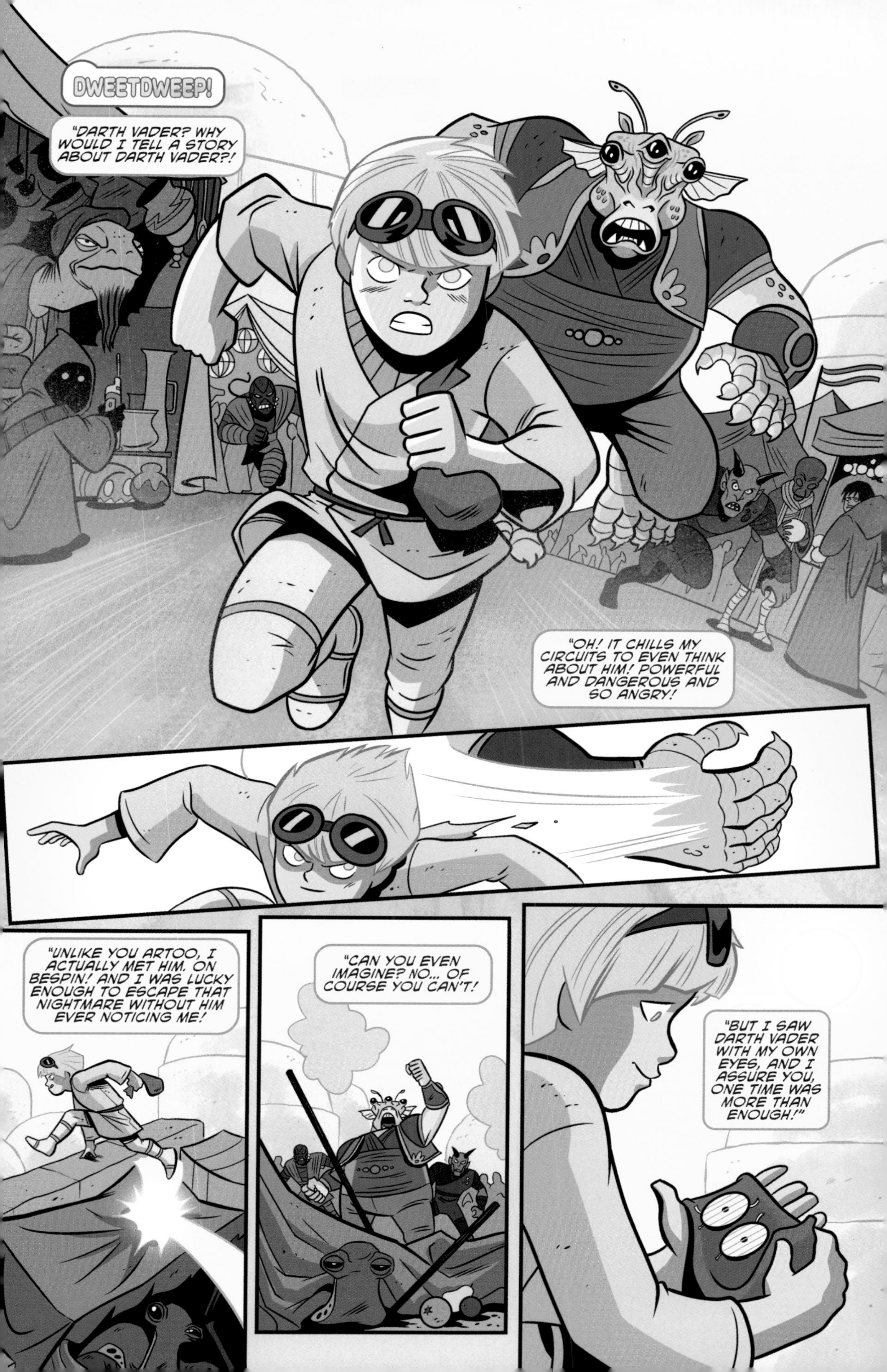
DWEETDWEEP!
"DARTH VADER? WHY WOULD I TELL A STORY ABOUT DARTH VADER?!
"OH! IT CHILLS MY CIRCUITS TO EVEN THINK ABOUT HIM! POWERFUL AND DANGEROUS AND SO ANGRY!
"UNLIKE YOU ARTOO, I ACTUALLY MET HIM. ON BESPIN! AND I WAS LUCKY ENOUGH TO ESCAPE THAT NIGHTMARE WITHOUT HIM EVER NOTICING ME!
"CAN YOU EVEN IMAGINE? NO... OF COURSE YOU CAN'T!
"BUT I SAW DARTH VADER WITH MY OWN EYES, AND I ASSURE YOU, ONE TIME WAS MORE THAN ENOUGH!"

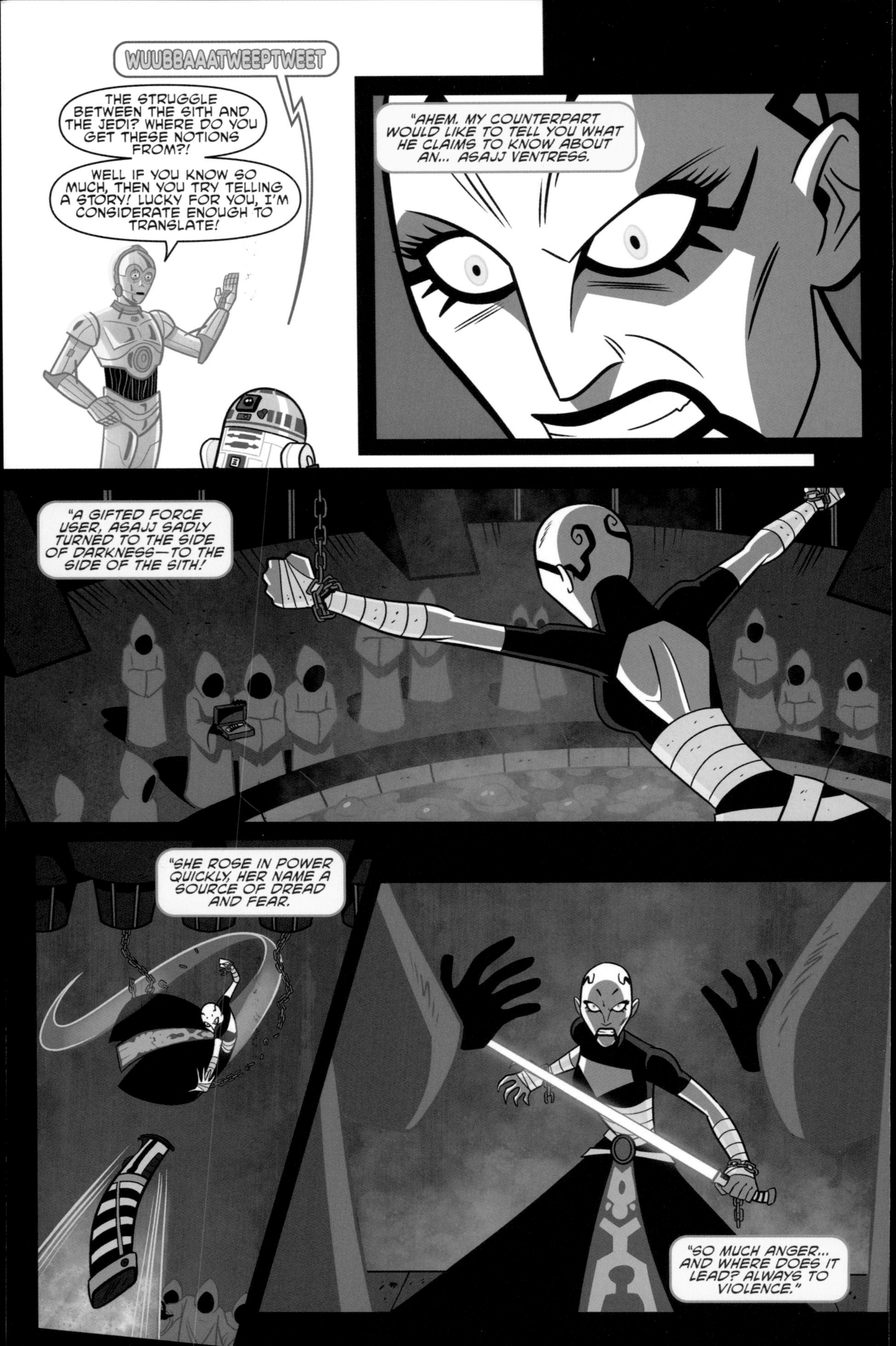
WUUBBAAATWEEPTWEET
THE STRUGGLE BETWEEN THE SITH AND THE JEDI? WHERE DO YOU GET THESE NOTIONS FROM?!
WELL IF YOU KNOW SO MUCH, THEN YOU TRY TELLING A STORY! LUCKY FOR YOU, I'M CONSIDERATE ENOUGH TO TRANSLATE!
"AHEM. MY COUNTERPART WOULD LIKE TO TELL YOU WHAT HE CLAIMS TO KNOW ABOUT AN... ASAJJ VENTRESS.
"A GIFTED FORCE USER, ASAJJ SADLY TURNED TO THE SIDE OF DARKNESS—TO THE SIDE OF THE SITH!
"SHE ROSE IN POWER QUICKLY, HER NAME A SOURCE OF DREAD AND FEAR.
"SO MUCH ANGER... AND WHERE DOES IT LEAD? ALWAYS TO VIOLENCE."

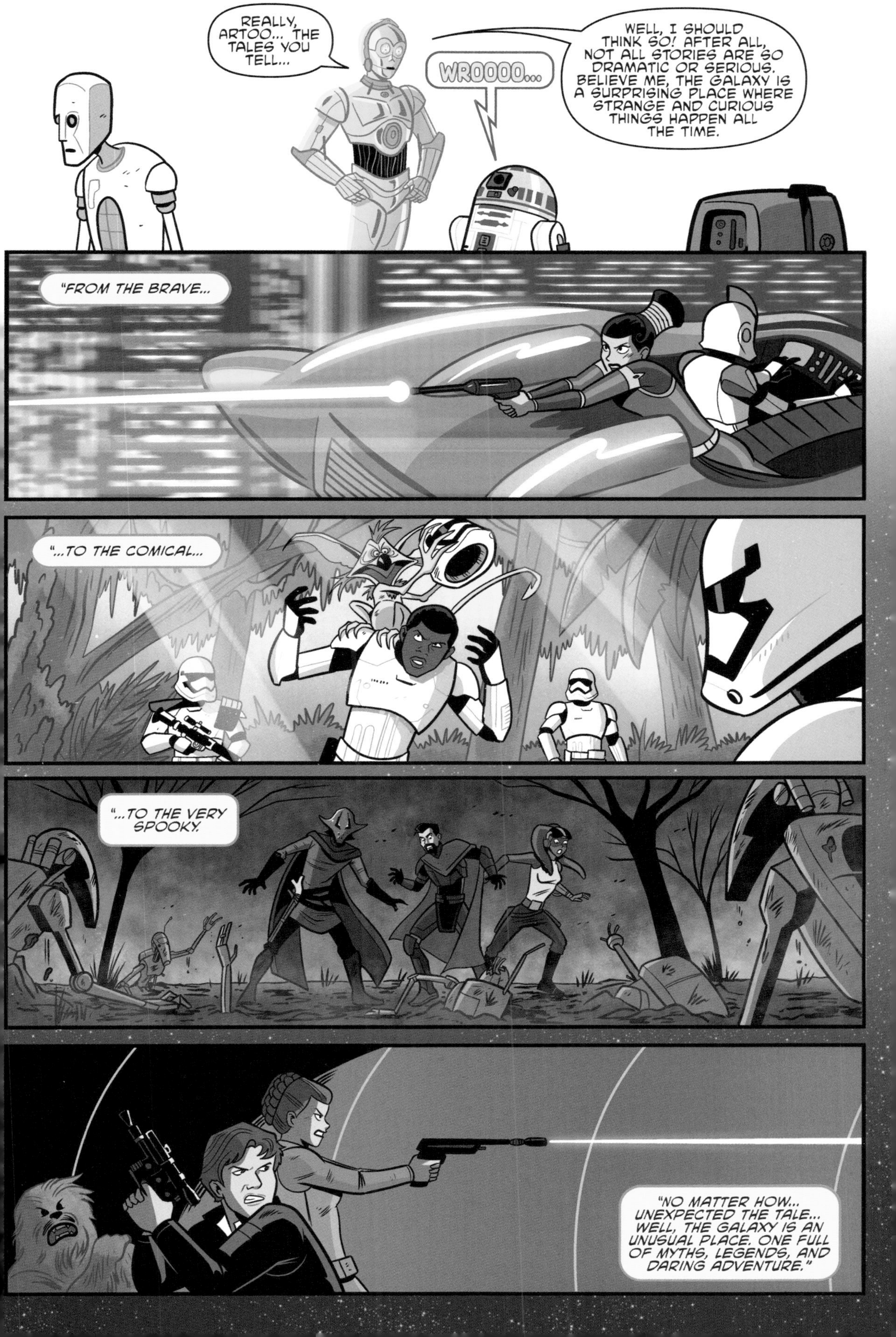
REALLY, ARTOO... THE TALES YOU TELL...
WROOOO...
WELL, I SHOULD THINK SO! AFTER ALL, NOT ALL STORIES ARE SO DRAMATIC OR SERIOUS. BELIEVE ME, THE GALAXY IS A SURPRISING PLACE WHERE STRANGE AND CURIOUS THINGS HAPPEN ALL THE TIME.
"FROM THE BRAVE...
"...TO THE COMICAL...
"...TO THE VERY SPOOKY.
"NO MATTER HOW... UNEXPECTED THE TALE... WELL, THE GALAXY IS AN UNUSUAL PLACE. ONE FULL OF MYTHS, LEGENDS, AND DARING ADVENTURE."

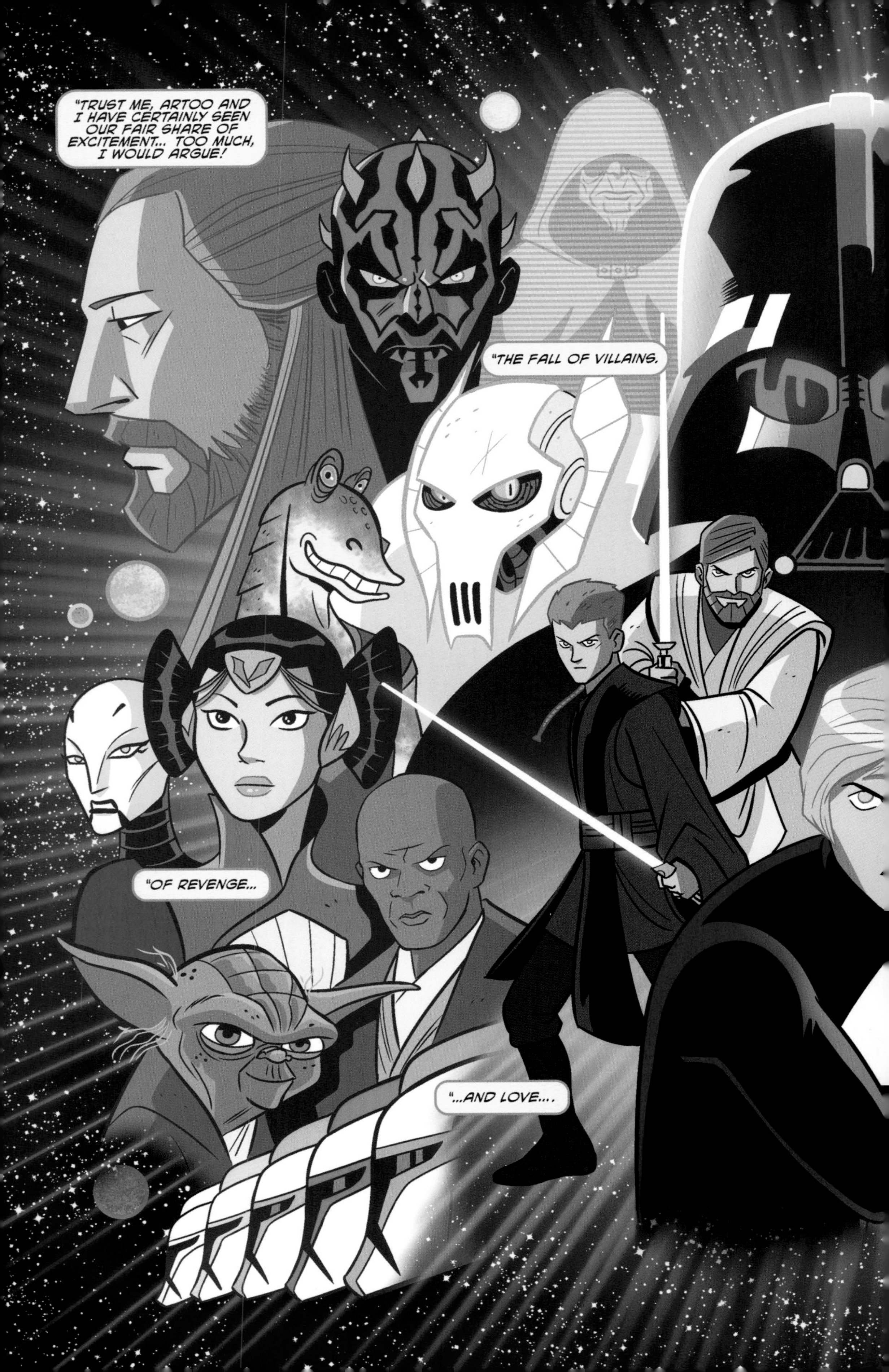
"TRUST ME, ARTOO AND I HAVE CERTAINLY SEEN OUR FAIR SHARE OF EXCITEMENT... TOO MUCH, I WOULD ARGUE!
"THE FALL OF VILLAINS.
"OF REVENGE...
"...AND LOVE....

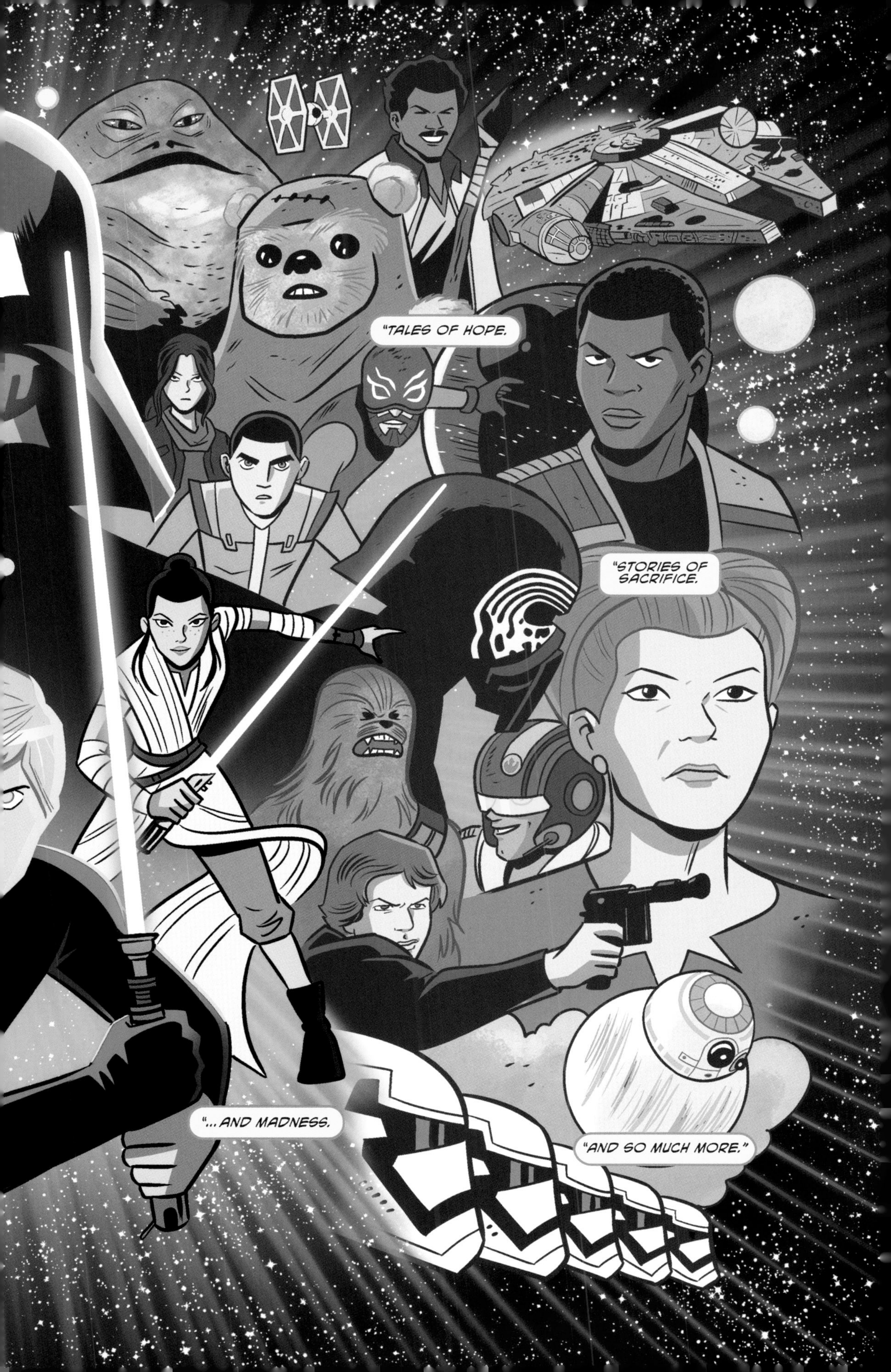
"TALES OF HOPE.
"STORIES OF SACRIFICE.
"...AND MADNESS.
"AND SO MUCH MORE."

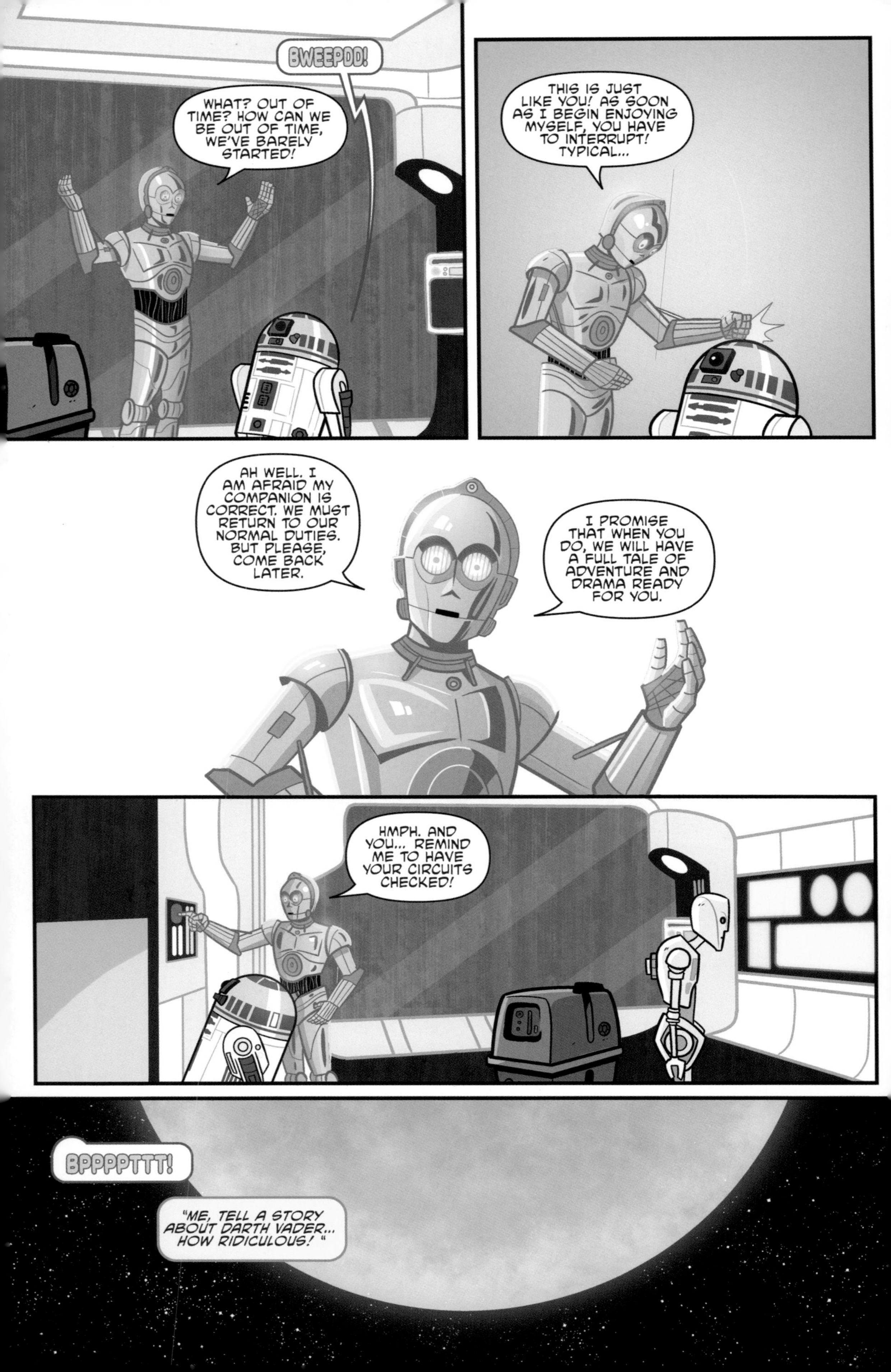
BWEEPDD!
WHAT? OUT OF TIME? HOW CAN WE BE OUT OF TIME, WE'VE BARELY STARTED!
THIS IS JUST LIKE YOU! AS SOON AS I BEGIN ENJOYING MYSELF, YOU HAVE TO INTERRUPT! TYPICAL...
AH WELL. I AM AFRAID MY COMPANION IS CORRECT. WE MUST RETURN TO OUR NORMAL DUTIES. BUT PLEASE, COME BACK LATER.
I PROMISE THAT WHEN YOU DO, WE WILL HAVE A FULL TALE OF ADVENTURE AND DRAMA READY FOR YOU.
HMPH. AND YOU... REMIND ME TO HAVE YOUR CIRCUITS CHECKED!
BPPPPTTT!
"ME, TELL A STORY ABOUT DARTH VADER... HOW RIDICULOUS! "

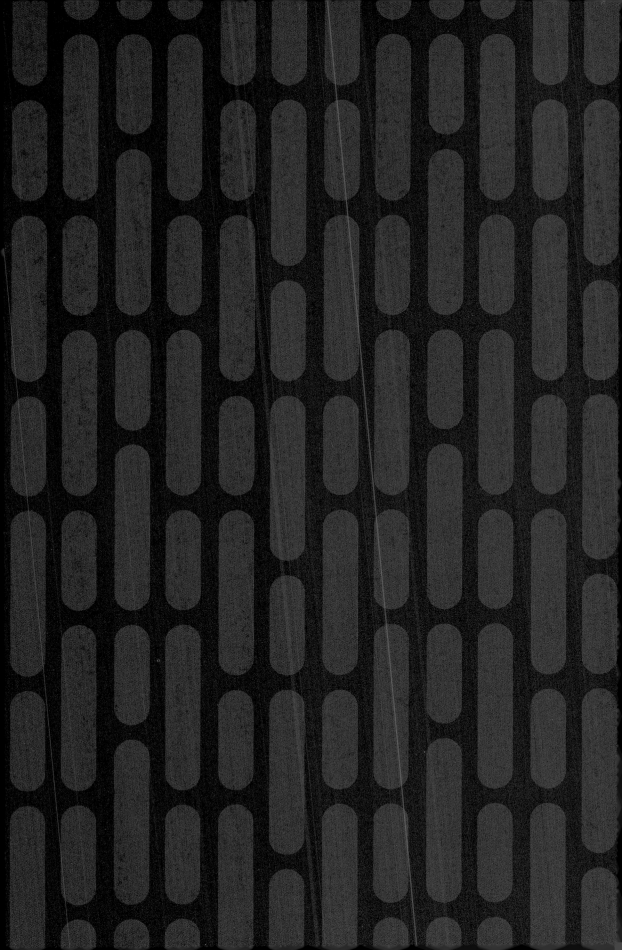

02
BETTER
THE DEVIL
YOU KNOW

Writer
CAVAN SCOTT

Artist
DEREK CHARM

Letterer
TOM B. LONG

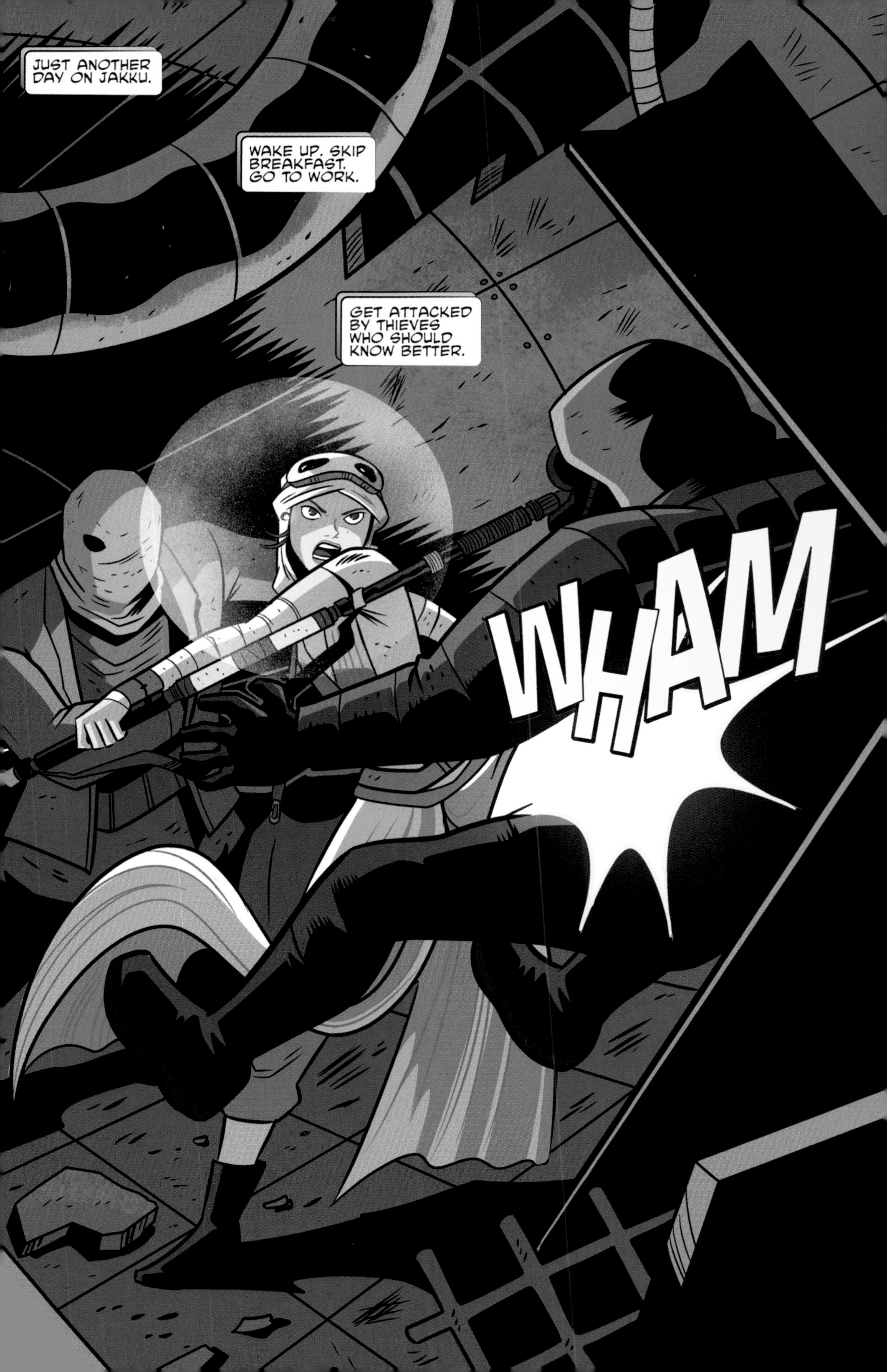
JUST ANOTHER DAY ON JAKKU.
WAKE UP. SKIP BREAKFAST. GO TO WORK.
GET ATTACKED BY THIEVES WHO SHOULD KNOW BETTER.
WHAM

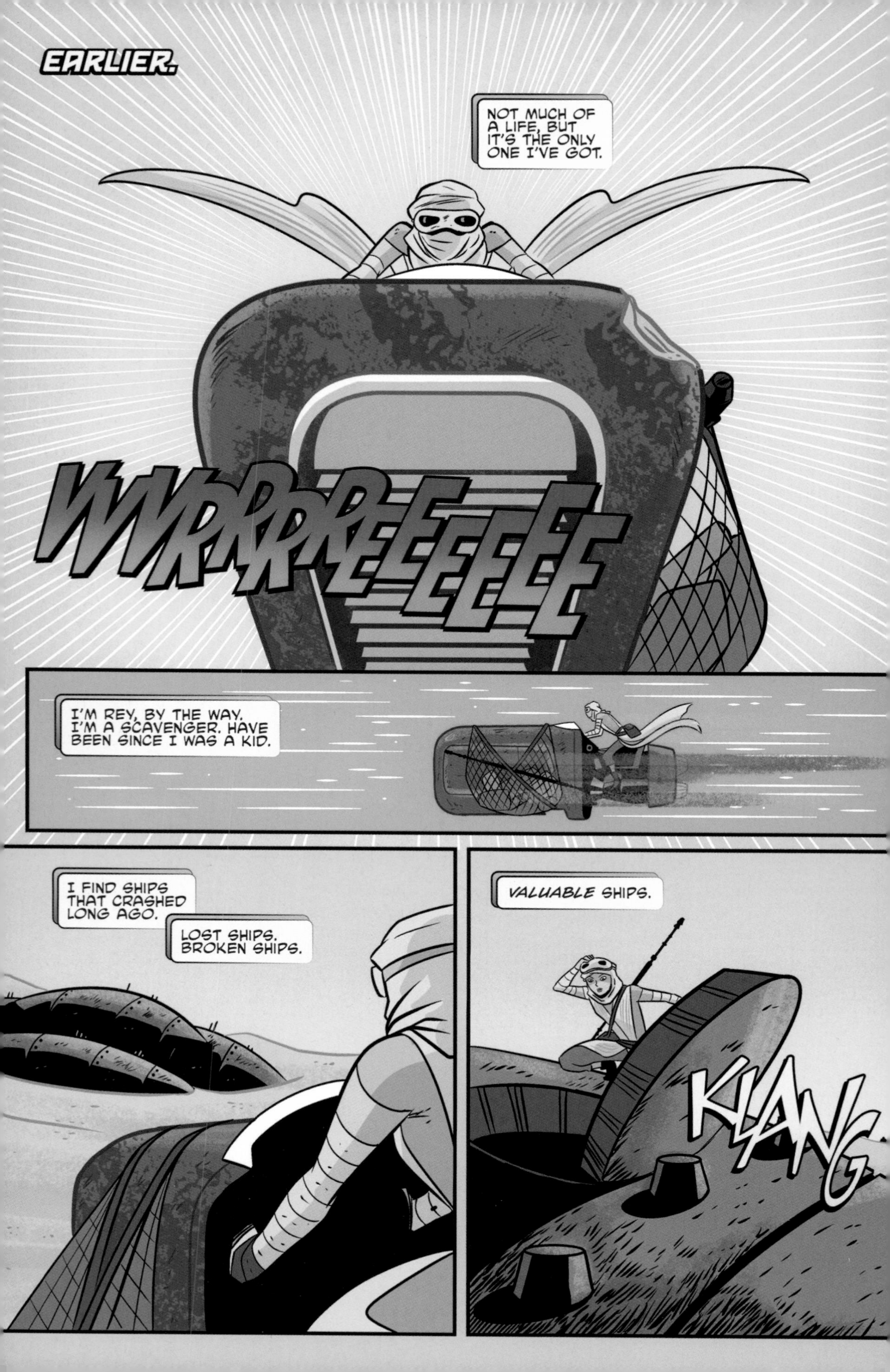
EARLIER.
NOT MUCH OF A LIFE, BUT IT'S THE ONLY ONE I'VE GOT.
VVVRRRREEEEEEE
I'M REY, BY THE WAY. I'M A SCAVENGER. HAVE BEEN SINCE I WAS A KID.
I FIND SHIPS THAT CRASHED LONG AGO.
LOST SHIPS. BROKEN SHIPS.
VALUABLE SHIPS.
KLANG

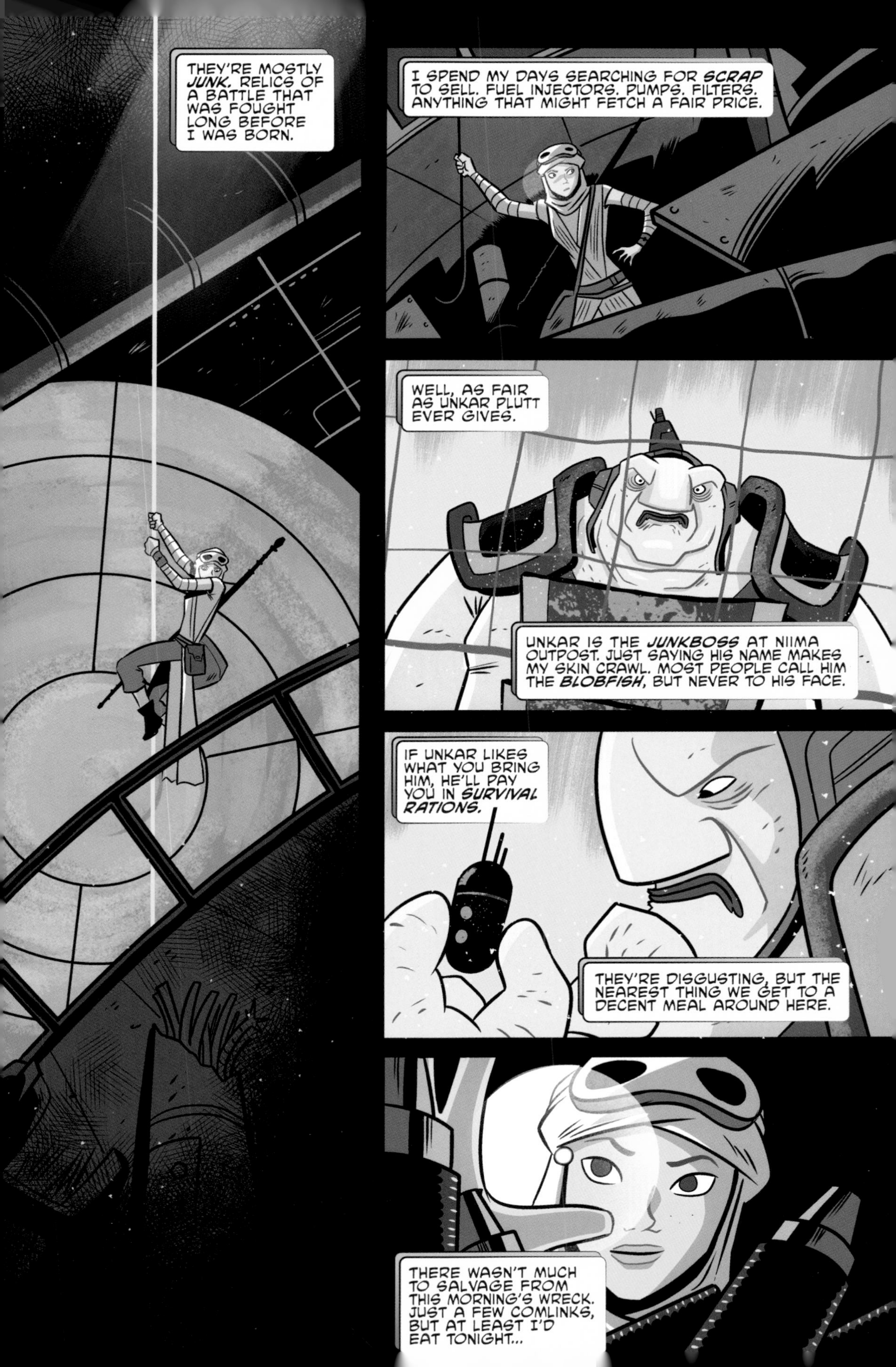
THEY'RE MOSTLY JUNK. RELICS OF A BATTLE THAT WAS FOUGHT LONG BEFORE I WAS BORN.
I SPEND MY DAYS SEARCHING FOR SCRAP TO SELL. FUEL INJECTORS. PUMPS. FILTERS. ANYTHING THAT MIGHT FETCH A FAIR PRICE.
WELL, AS FAIR AS UNKAR PLUTT EVER GIVES.
UNKAR IS THE JUNKBOSS AT NIIMA OUTPOST. JUST SAYING HIS NAME MAKES MY SKIN CRAWL. MOST PEOPLE CALL HIM THE BLOBFISH, BUT NEVER TO HIS FACE.
IF UNKAR LIKES WHAT YOU BRING HIM, HE'LL PAY YOU IN SURVIVAL RATIONS.
THEY'RE DISGUSTING, BUT THE NEAREST THING WE GET TO A DECENT MEAL AROUND HERE.
THERE WASN'T MUCH TO SALVAGE FROM THIS MORNING'S WRECK. JUST A FEW COMLINKS, BUT AT LEAST I'D EAT TONIGHT...

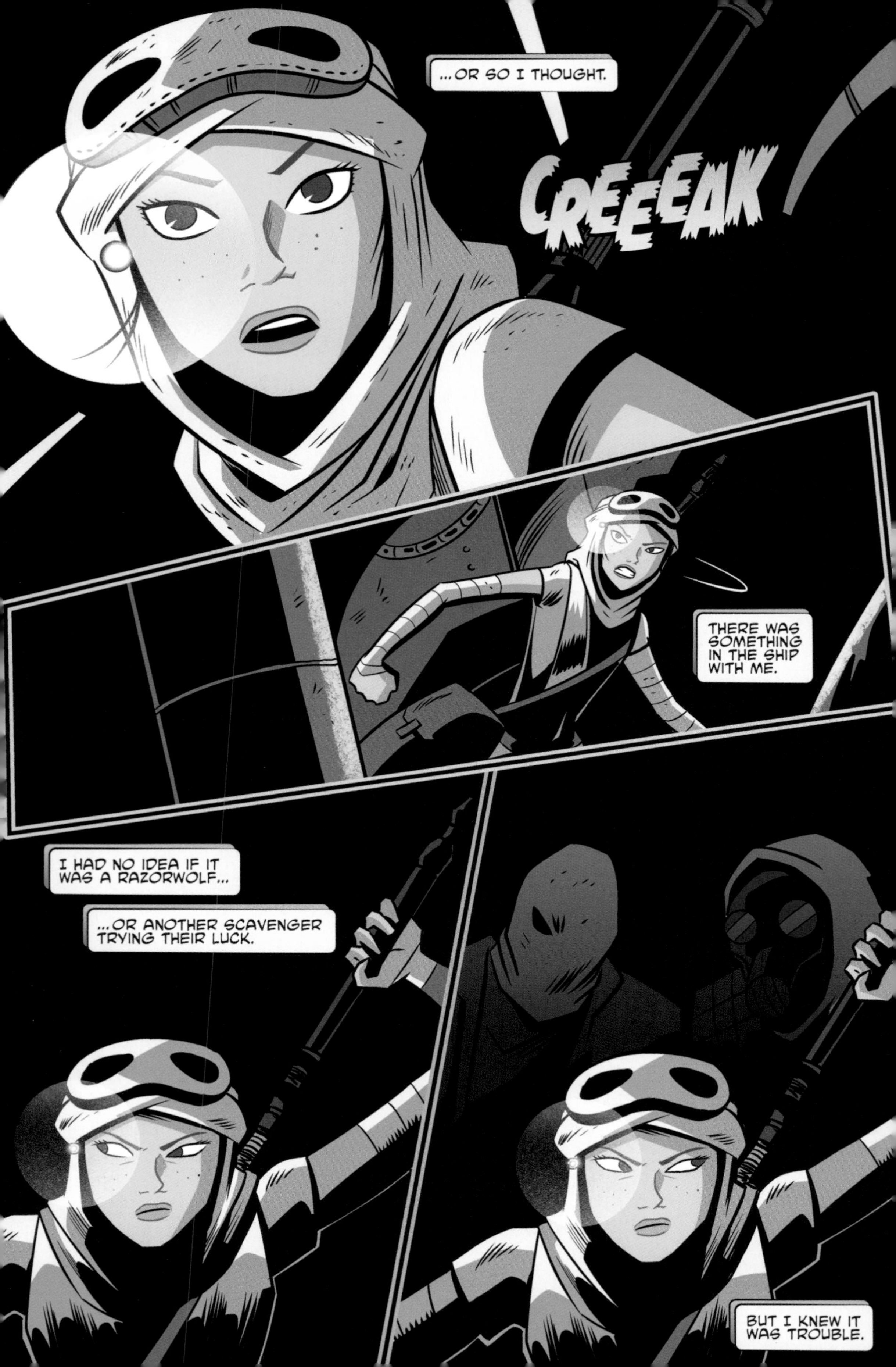
...OR SO I THOUGHT.
CREEEAK
THERE WAS SOMETHING IN THE SHIP WITH ME.
I HAD NO IDEA IF IT WAS A RAZORWOLF...
...OR ANOTHER SCAVENGER TRYING THEIR LUCK.
BUT I KNEW IT WAS TROUBLE.

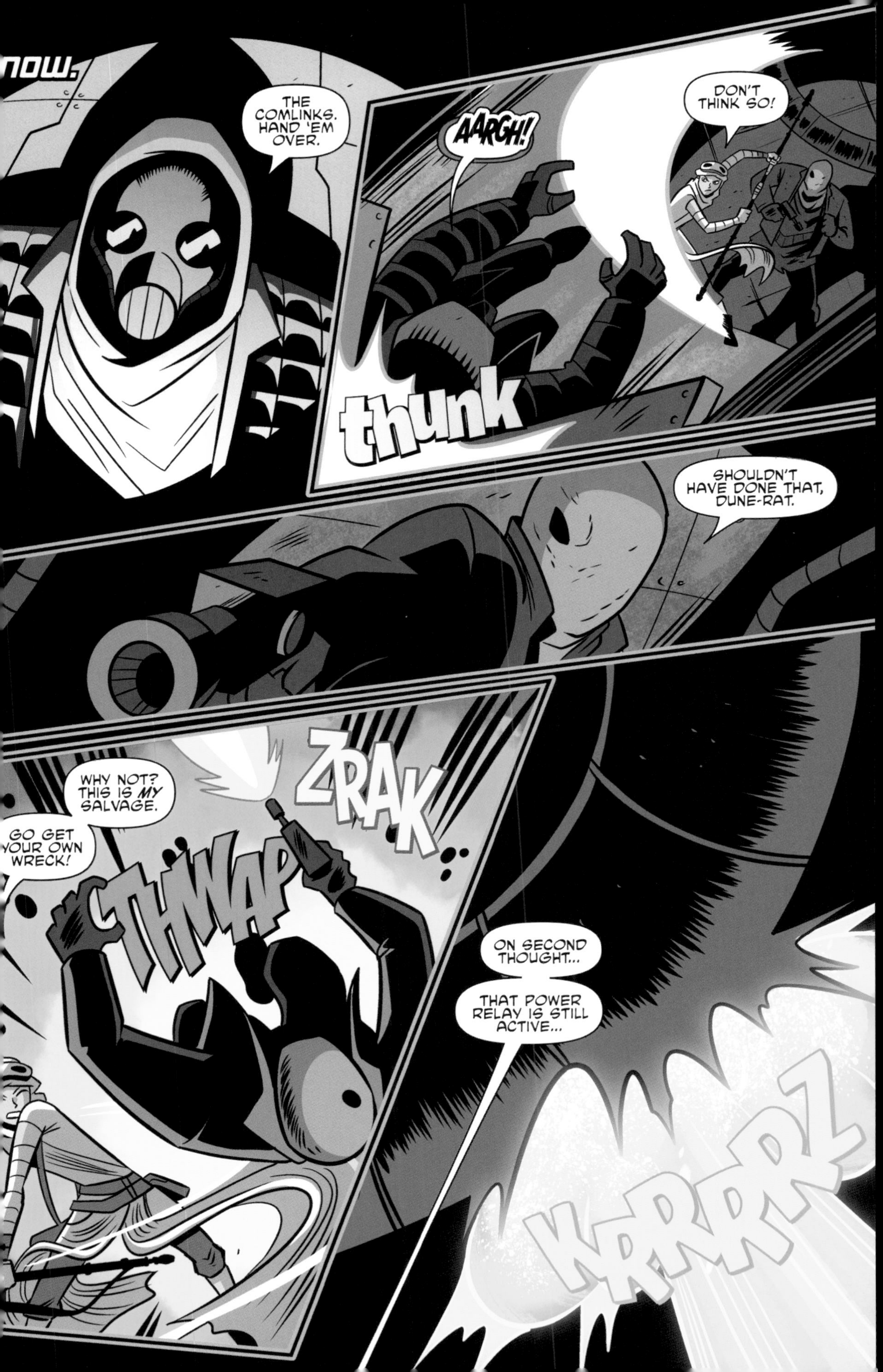
NOW.
THE COMLINKS. HAND 'EM OVER.
AARGH!
DON'T THINK SO!
thunk
SHOULDN'T HAVE DONE THAT, DUNE-RAT.
WHY NOT? THIS IS *MY* SALVAGE.
GO GET YOUR OWN WRECK!
ZRAK
THWAP
ON SECOND THOUGHT...
THAT POWER RELAY IS STILL ACTIVE...
KRRRRZ

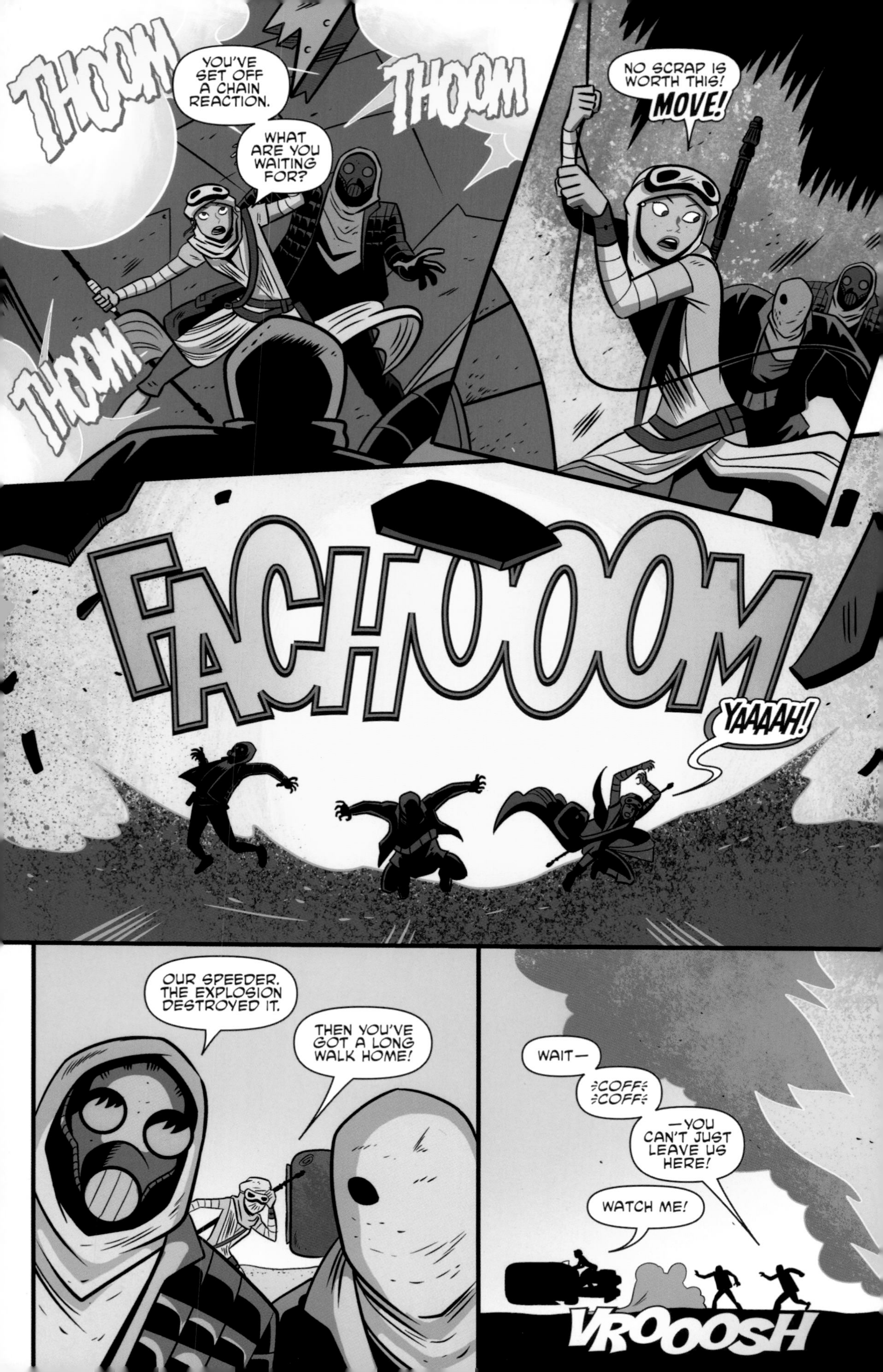
THOOM
YOU'VE SET OFF A CHAIN REACTION.
THOOM
WHAT ARE YOU WAITING FOR?
THOOM
NO SCRAP IS WORTH THIS! MOVE!
FACHOOOM
YAAAAH!
OUR SPEEDER. THE EXPLOSION DESTROYED IT.
THEN YOU'VE GOT A LONG WALK HOME!
WAIT—
COFF COFF
—YOU CAN'T JUST LEAVE US HERE!
WATCH ME!
VROOOSH

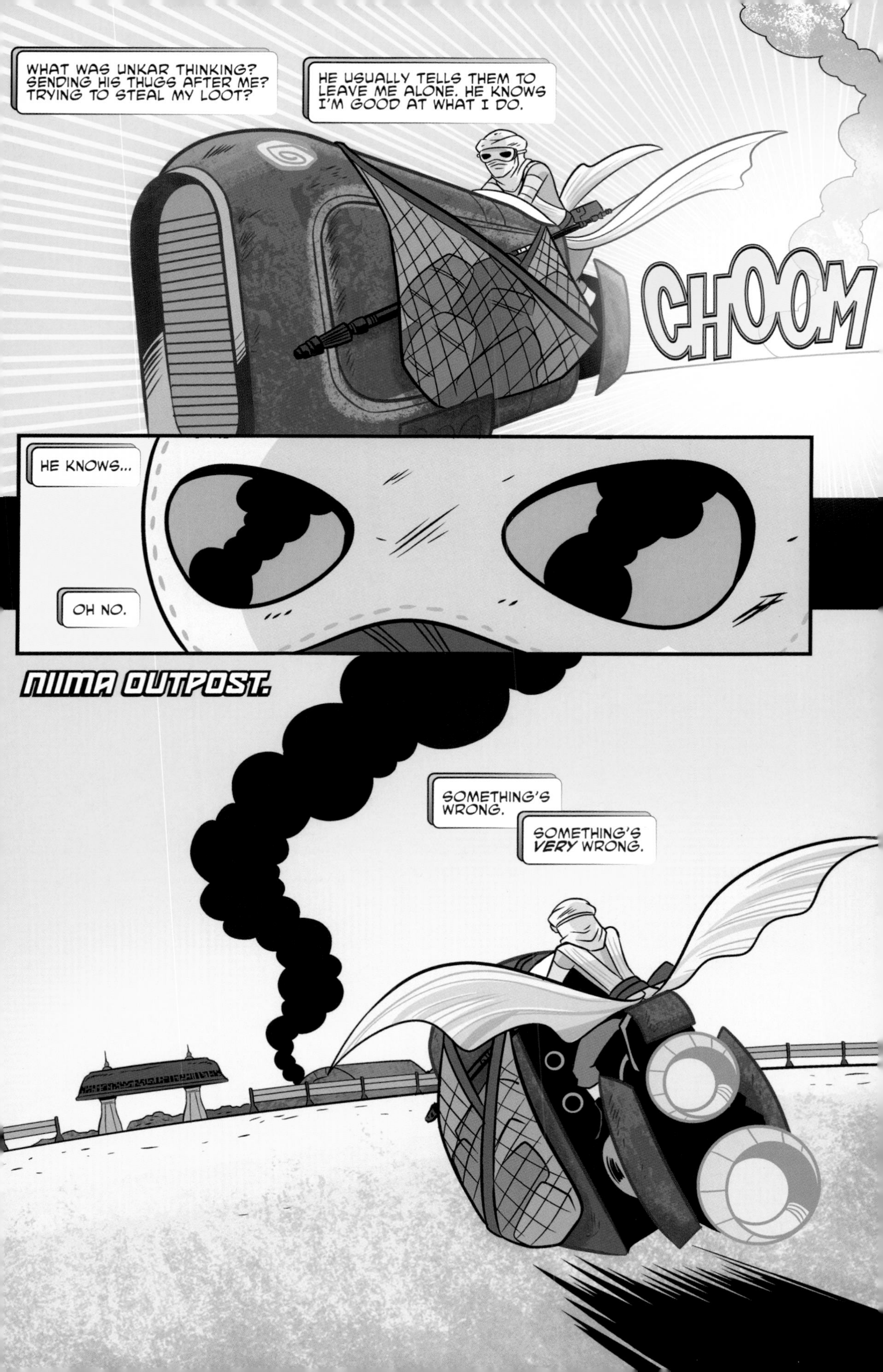
WHAT WAS UNKAR THINKING? SENDING HIS THUGS AFTER ME? TRYING TO STEAL MY LOOT?
HE USUALLY TELLS THEM TO LEAVE ME ALONE. HE KNOWS I'M GOOD AT WHAT I DO.
CHOOM
HE KNOWS...
OH NO.
NIIMA OUTPOST.
SOMETHING'S WRONG.
SOMETHING'S *VERY* WRONG.

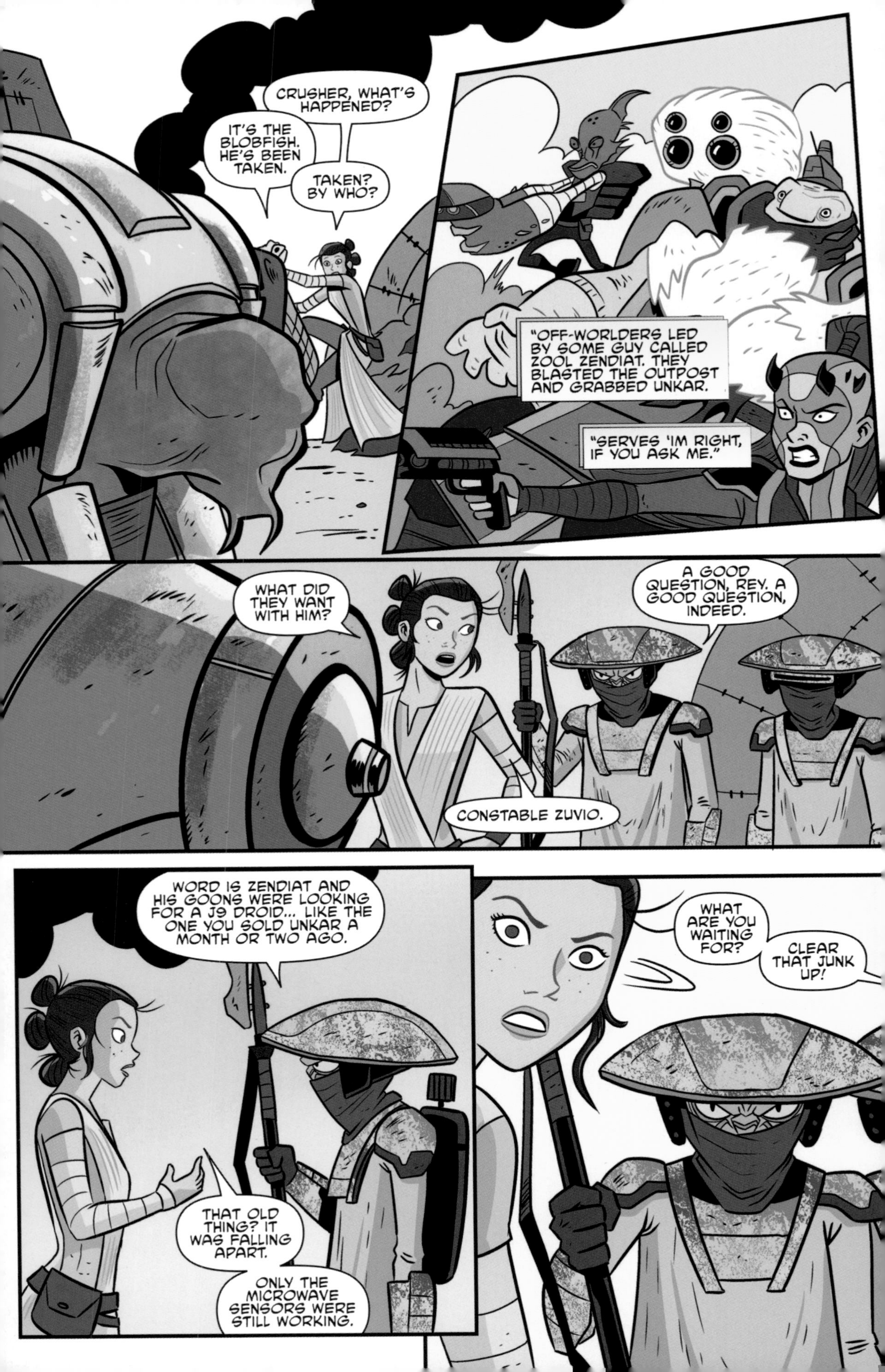
CRUSHER, WHAT'S HAPPENED?
IT'S THE BLOBFISH. HE'S BEEN TAKEN.
TAKEN? BY WHO?
"OFF-WORLDERS LED BY SOME GUY CALLED ZOOL ZENDIAT. THEY BLASTED THE OUTPOST AND GRABBED UNKAR.
"SERVES 'IM RIGHT, IF YOU ASK ME."
WHAT DID THEY WANT WITH HIM?
A GOOD QUESTION, REY. A GOOD QUESTION, INDEED.
CONSTABLE ZUVIO.
WORD IS ZENDIAT AND HIS GOONS WERE LOOKING FOR A J9 DROID... LIKE THE ONE YOU SOLD UNKAR A MONTH OR TWO AGO.
THAT OLD THING? IT WAS FALLING APART.
ONLY THE MICROWAVE SENSORS WERE STILL WORKING.
WHAT ARE YOU WAITING FOR?
CLEAR THAT JUNK UP!

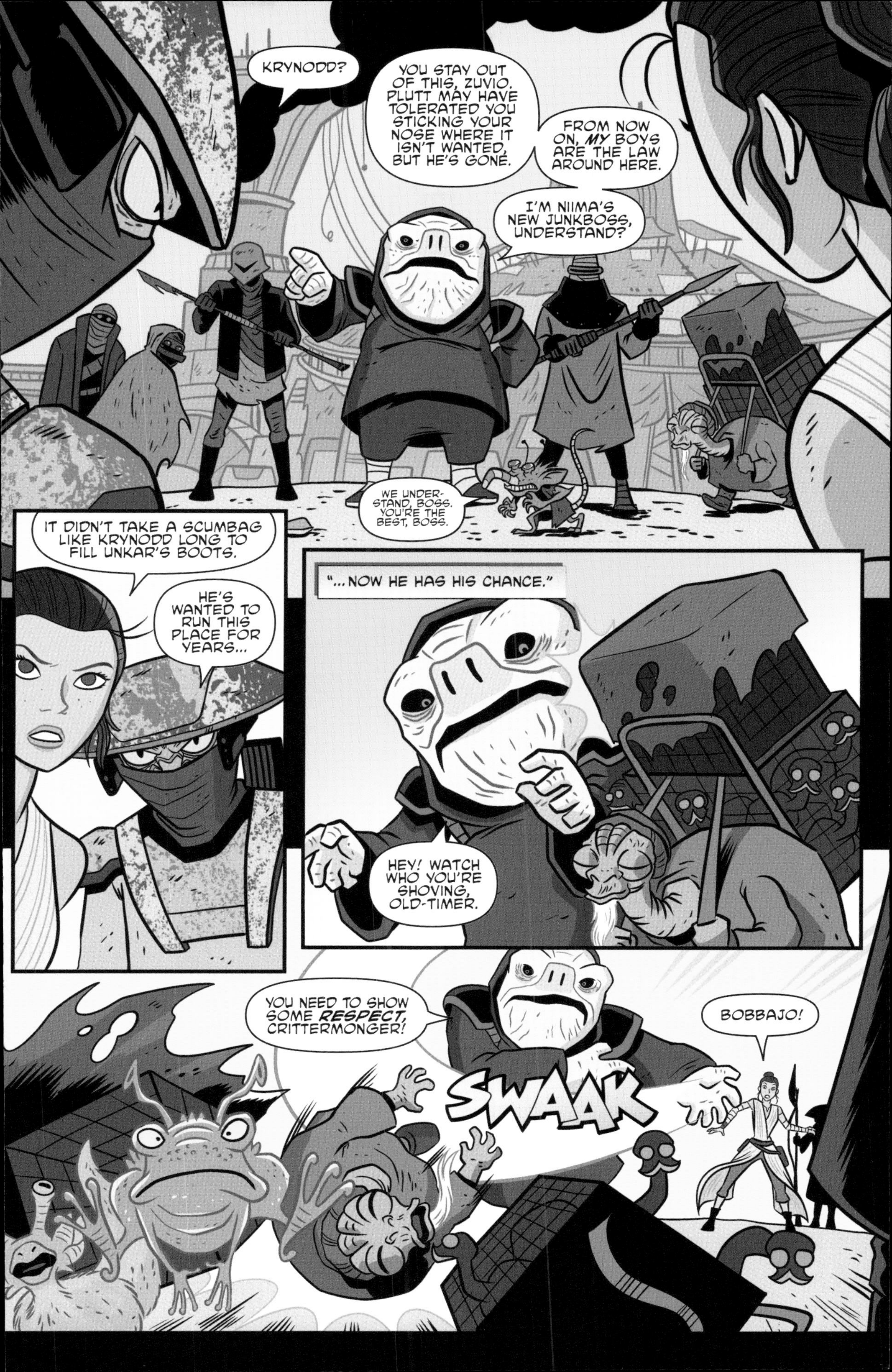
KRYNODD?
YOU STAY OUT OF THIS, ZUVIO. PLUTT MAY HAVE TOLERATED YOU STICKING YOUR NOSE WHERE IT ISN'T WANTED, BUT HE'S GONE.
FROM NOW ON, MY BOYS ARE THE LAW AROUND HERE.
I'M NIIMA'S NEW JUNKBOSS, UNDERSTAND?
WE UNDERSTAND, BOSS. YOU'RE THE BEST, BOSS.
IT DIDN'T TAKE A SCUMBAG LIKE KRYNODD LONG TO FILL UNKAR'S BOOTS.
HE'S WANTED TO RUN THIS PLACE FOR YEARS...
"...NOW HE HAS HIS CHANCE."
HEY! WATCH WHO YOU'RE SHOVING, OLD-TIMER.
YOU NEED TO SHOW SOME RESPECT, CRITTERMONGER!
SWAAK
BOBBAJO!

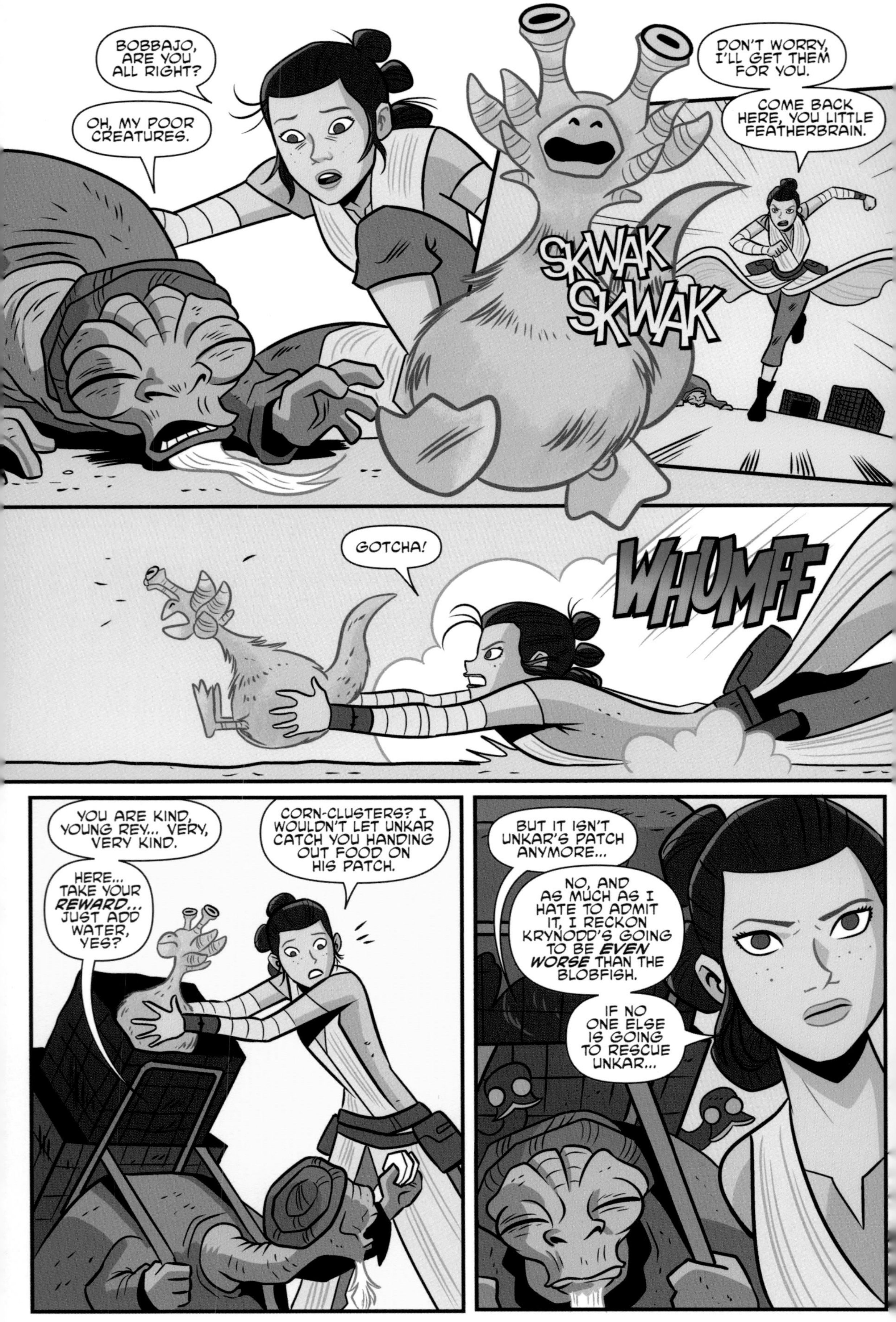
BOBBAJO, ARE YOU ALL RIGHT?
OH, MY POOR CREATURES.
SKWAK SKWAK
DON'T WORRY, I'LL GET THEM FOR YOU.
COME BACK HERE, YOU LITTLE FEATHERBRAIN.
GOTCHA!
WHUMFF
YOU ARE KIND, YOUNG REY... VERY, VERY KIND.
HERE... TAKE YOUR *REWARD*... JUST ADD WATER, YES?
CORN-CLUSTERS? I WOULDN'T LET UNKAR CATCH YOU HANDING OUT FOOD ON HIS PATCH.
BUT IT ISN'T UNKAR'S PATCH ANYMORE...
NO, AND AS MUCH AS I HATE TO ADMIT IT, I RECKON KRYNODD'S GOING TO BE *EVEN WORSE* THAN THE BLOBFISH.
IF NO ONE ELSE IS GOING TO RESCUE UNKAR...

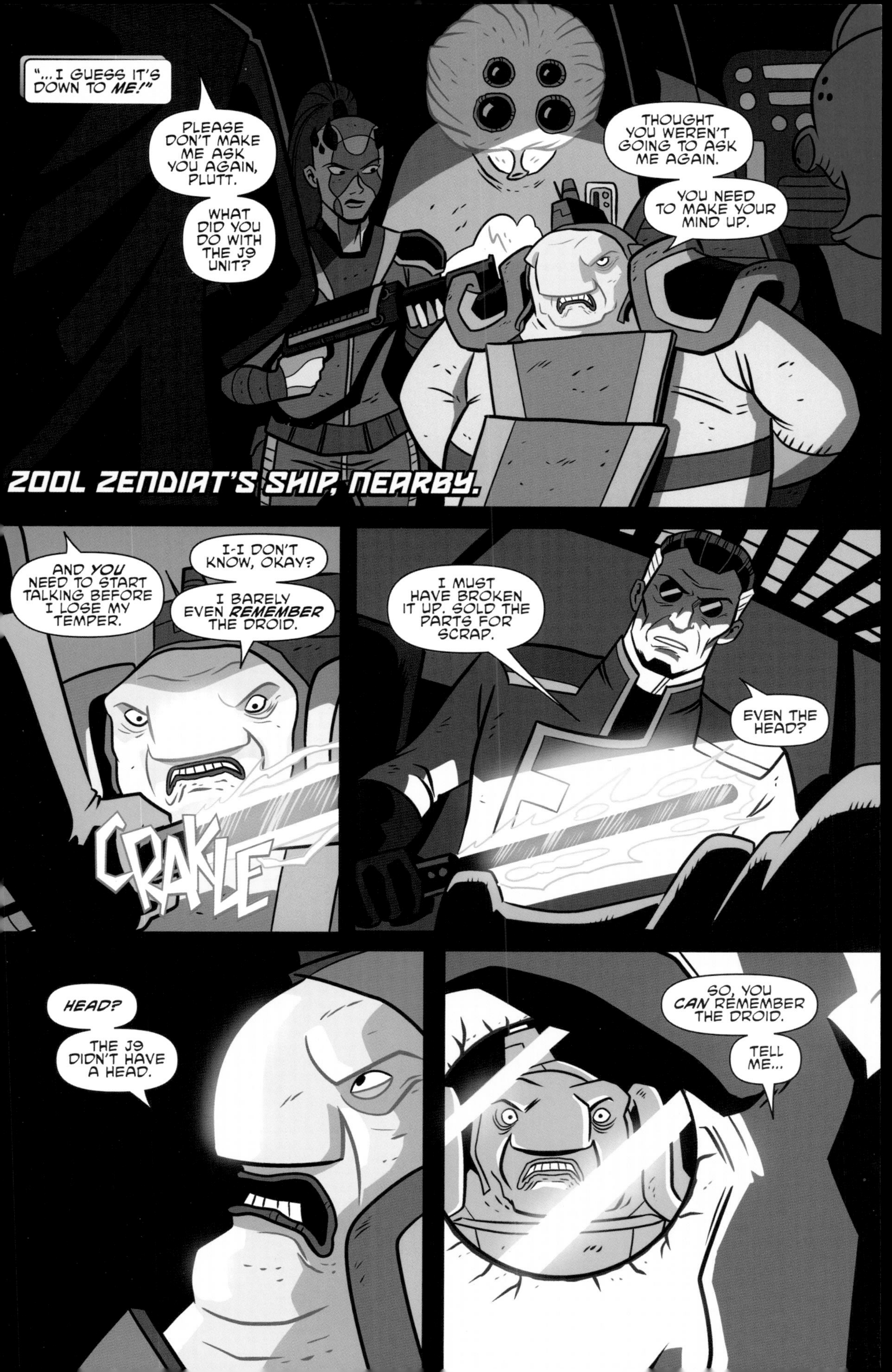
"...I GUESS IT'S DOWN TO *ME!*"
PLEASE DON'T MAKE ME ASK YOU AGAIN, PLUTT.
WHAT DID YOU DO WITH THE J9 UNIT?
THOUGHT YOU WEREN'T GOING TO ASK ME AGAIN.
YOU NEED TO MAKE YOUR MIND UP.
ZOOL ZENDIAT'S SHIP, NEARBY.
AND *YOU* NEED TO START TALKING BEFORE I LOSE MY TEMPER.
I-I DON'T KNOW, OKAY?
I BARELY EVEN *REMEMBER* THE DROID.
CRAKLE
I MUST HAVE BROKEN IT UP. SOLD THE PARTS FOR SCRAP.
EVEN THE HEAD?
HEAD?
THE J9 DIDN'T HAVE A HEAD.
SO, YOU *CAN* REMEMBER THE DROID.
TELL ME...

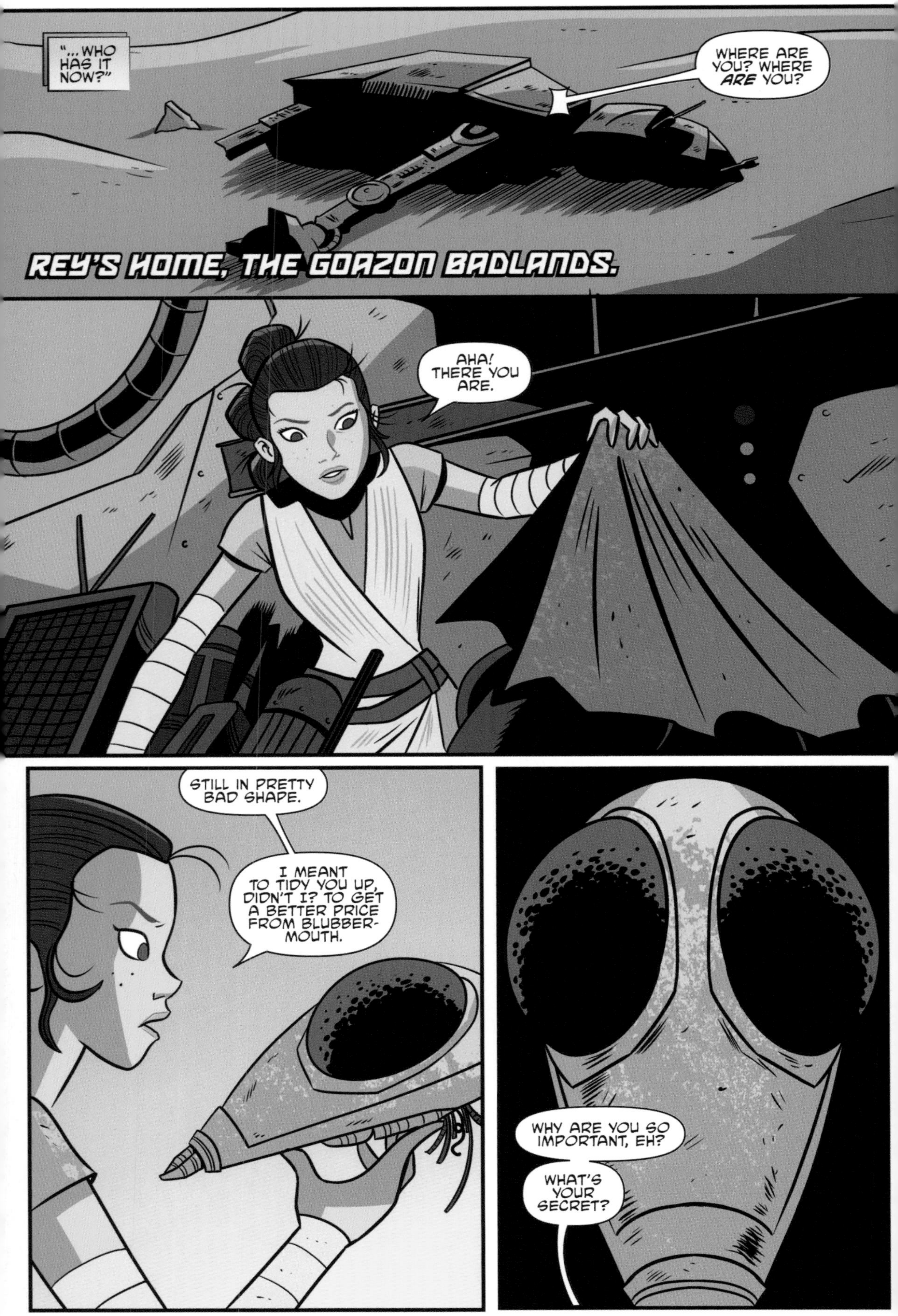
"...WHO HAS IT NOW?"
WHERE ARE YOU? WHERE *ARE* YOU?
REY'S HOME, THE GOAZON BADLANDS.
AHA! THERE YOU ARE.
STILL IN PRETTY BAD SHAPE.
I MEANT TO TIDY YOU UP, DIDN'T I? TO GET A BETTER PRICE FROM BLUBBER-MOUTH.
WHY ARE YOU SO IMPORTANT, EH?
WHAT'S YOUR SECRET?

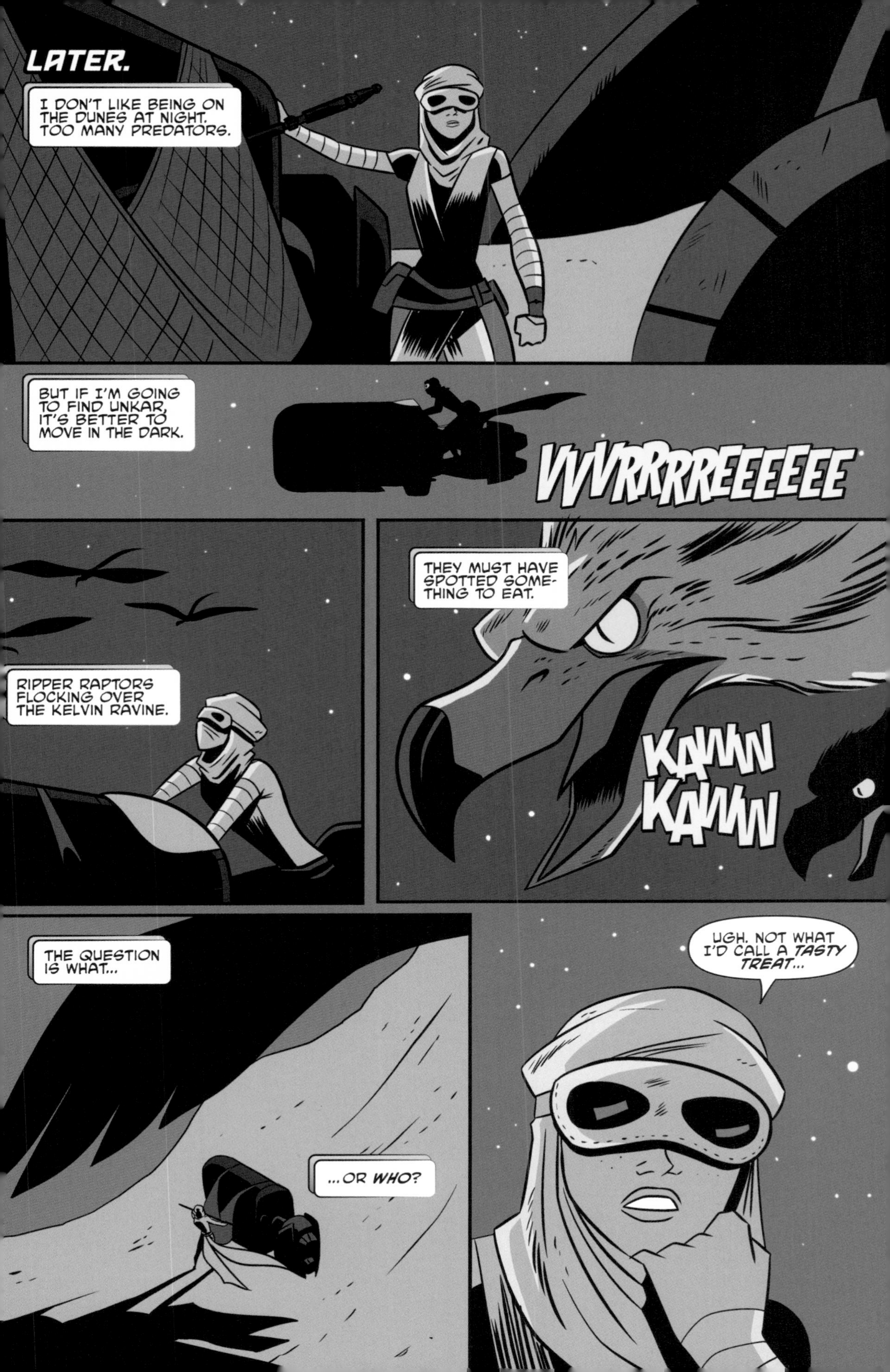
LATER.
I DON'T LIKE BEING ON THE DUNES AT NIGHT. TOO MANY PREDATORS.
BUT IF I'M GOING TO FIND UNKAR, IT'S BETTER TO MOVE IN THE DARK.
VVVRRRRREEEEEE
RIPPER RAPTORS FLOCKING OVER THE KELVIN RAVINE.
THEY MUST HAVE SPOTTED SOME-THING TO EAT.
KAWW KAWW
THE QUESTION IS WHAT...
...OR *WHO?*
UGH. NOT WHAT I'D CALL A *TASTY TREAT*...

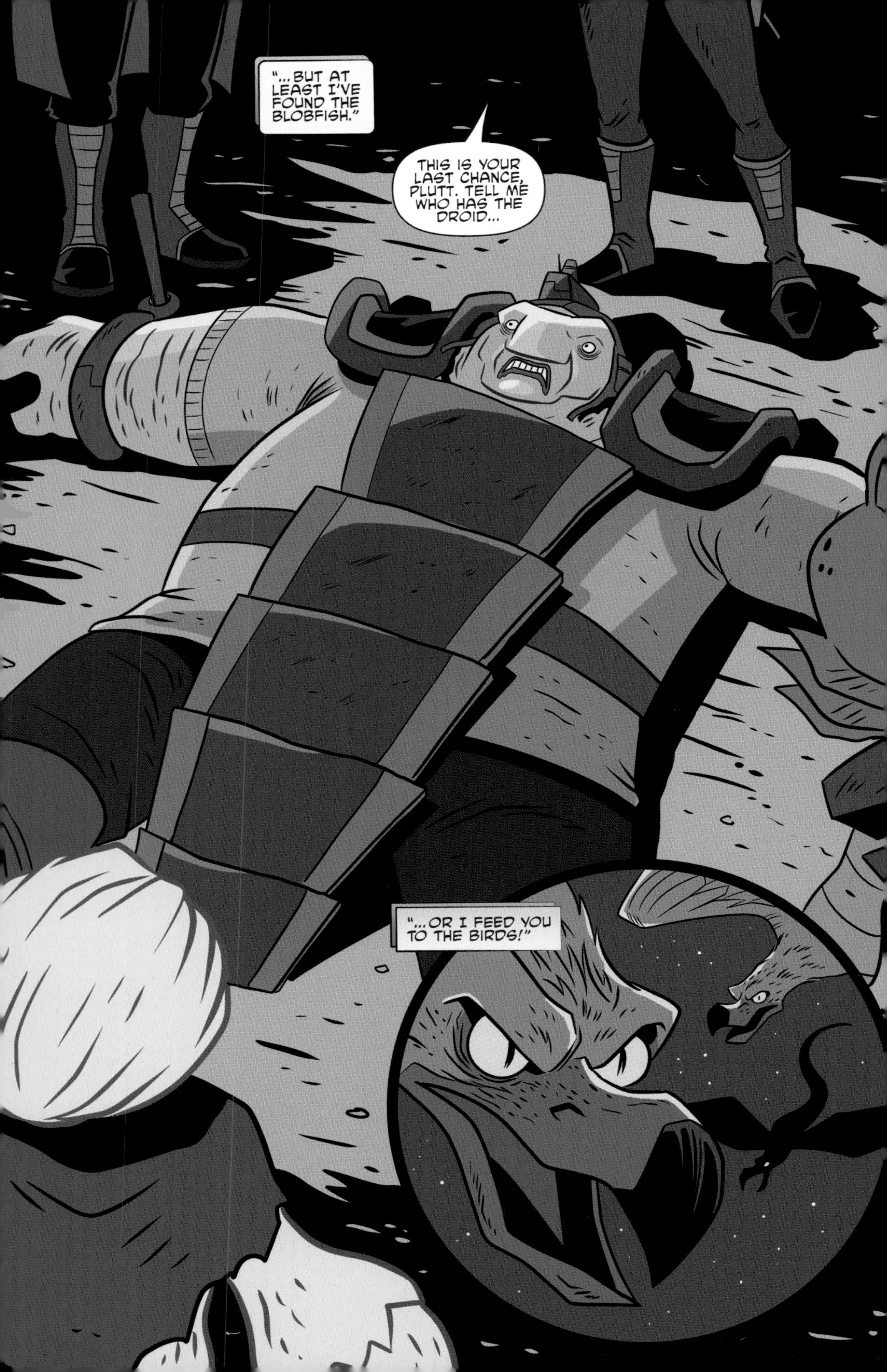
"...BUT AT LEAST I'VE FOUND THE BLOBFISH."
THIS IS YOUR LAST CHANCE, PLUTT. TELL ME WHO HAS THE DROID...
"...OR I FEED YOU TO THE BIRDS!"

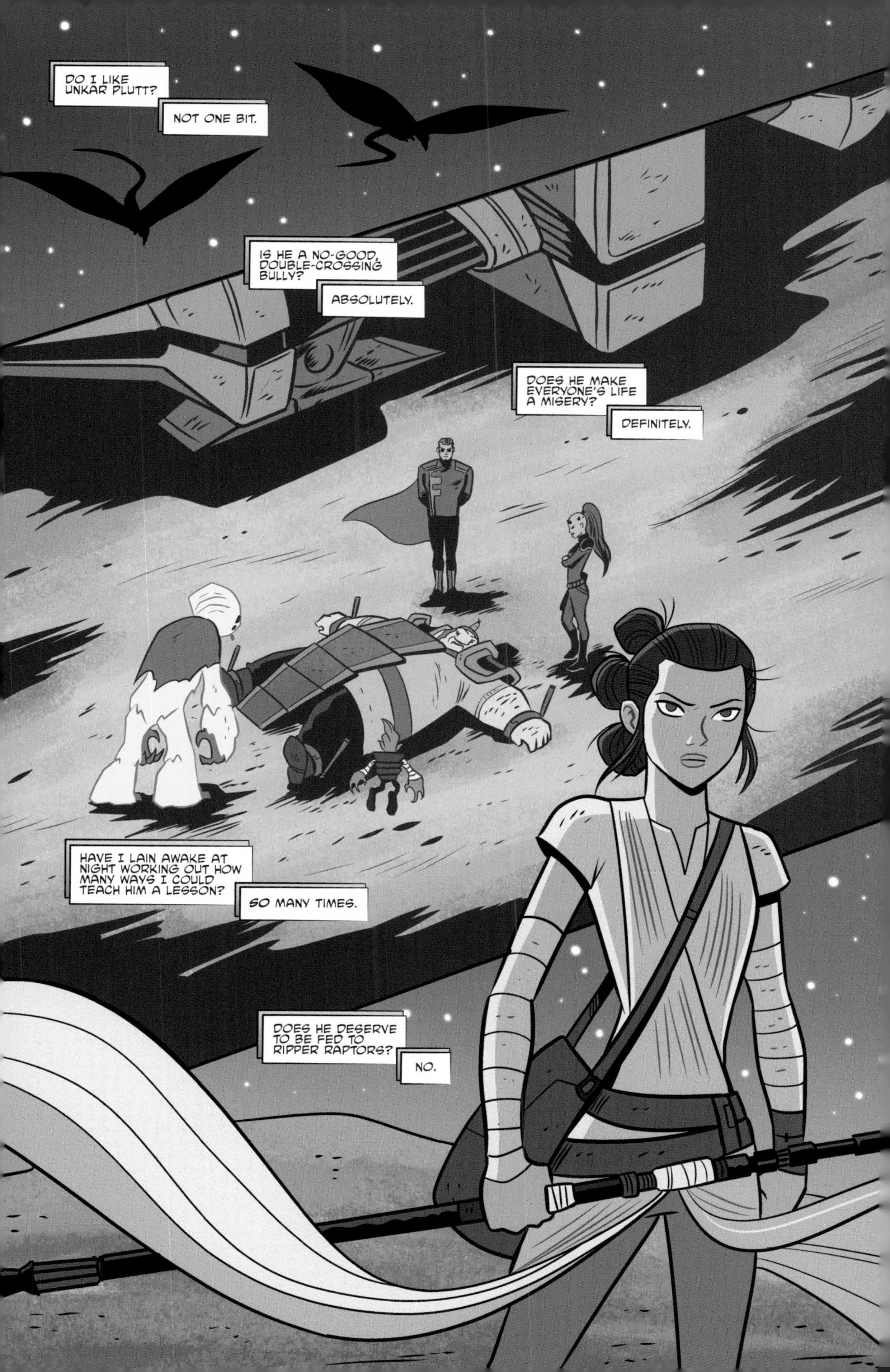
DO I LIKE UNKAR PLUTT?
NOT ONE BIT.
IS HE A NO-GOOD, DOUBLE-CROSSING BULLY?
ABSOLUTELY.
DOES HE MAKE EVERYONE'S LIFE A MISERY?
DEFINITELY.
HAVE I LAIN AWAKE AT NIGHT WORKING OUT HOW MANY WAYS I COULD TEACH HIM A LESSON?
SO MANY TIMES.
DOES HE DESERVE TO BE FED TO RIPPER RAPTORS?
NO.

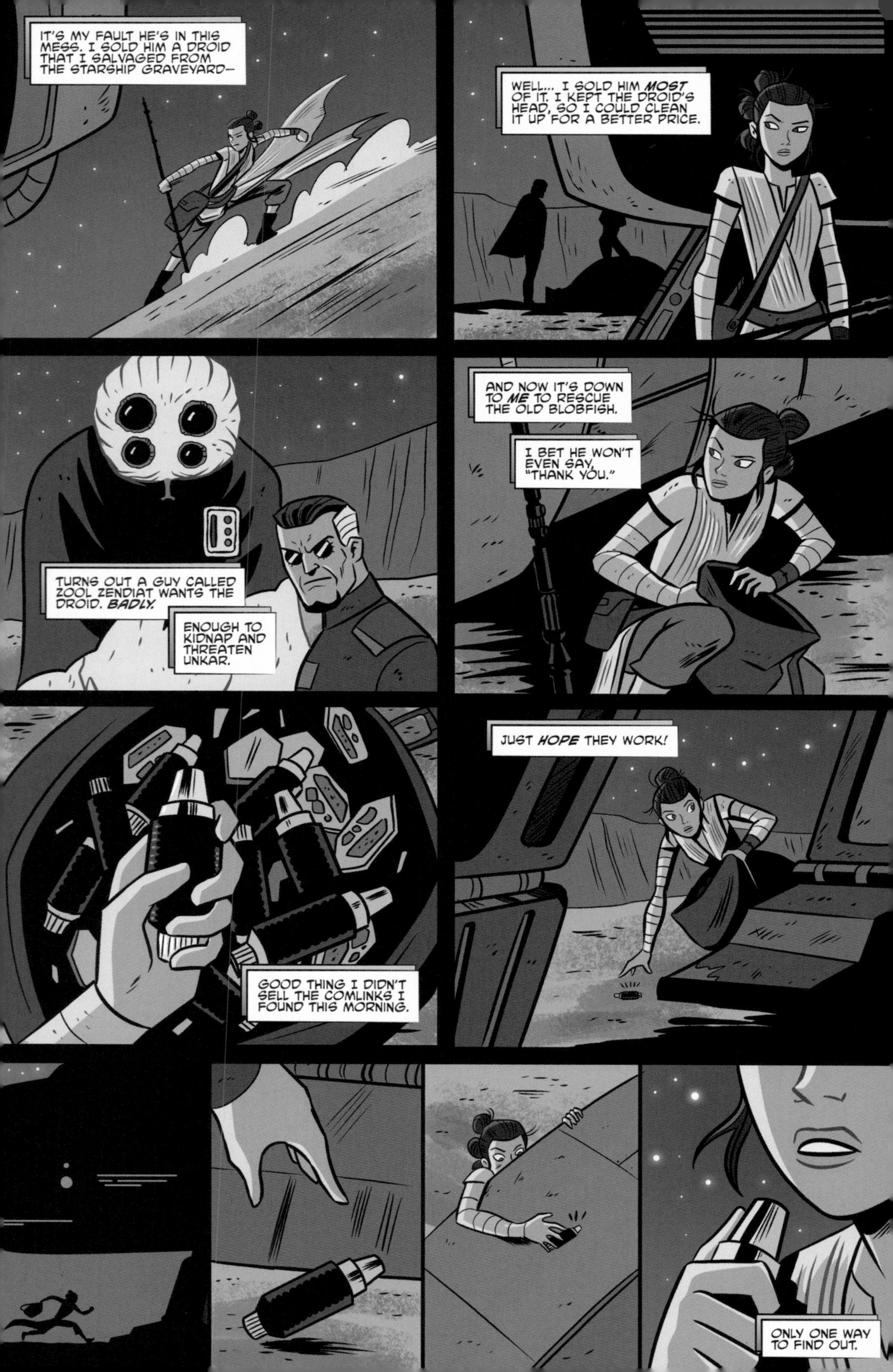
IT'S MY FAULT HE'S IN THIS MESS. I SOLD HIM A DROID THAT I SALVAGED FROM THE STARSHIP GRAVEYARD—
WELL... I SOLD HIM MOST OF IT. I KEPT THE DROID'S HEAD, SO I COULD CLEAN IT UP FOR A BETTER PRICE.
TURNS OUT A GUY CALLED ZOOL ZENDIAT WANTS THE DROID. BADLY.
ENOUGH TO KIDNAP AND THREATEN UNKAR.
AND NOW IT'S DOWN TO ME TO RESCUE THE OLD BLOBFISH.
I BET HE WON'T EVEN SAY, "THANK YOU."
GOOD THING I DIDN'T SELL THE COMLINKS I FOUND THIS MORNING.
JUST HOPE THEY WORK!
ONLY ONE WAY TO FIND OUT.

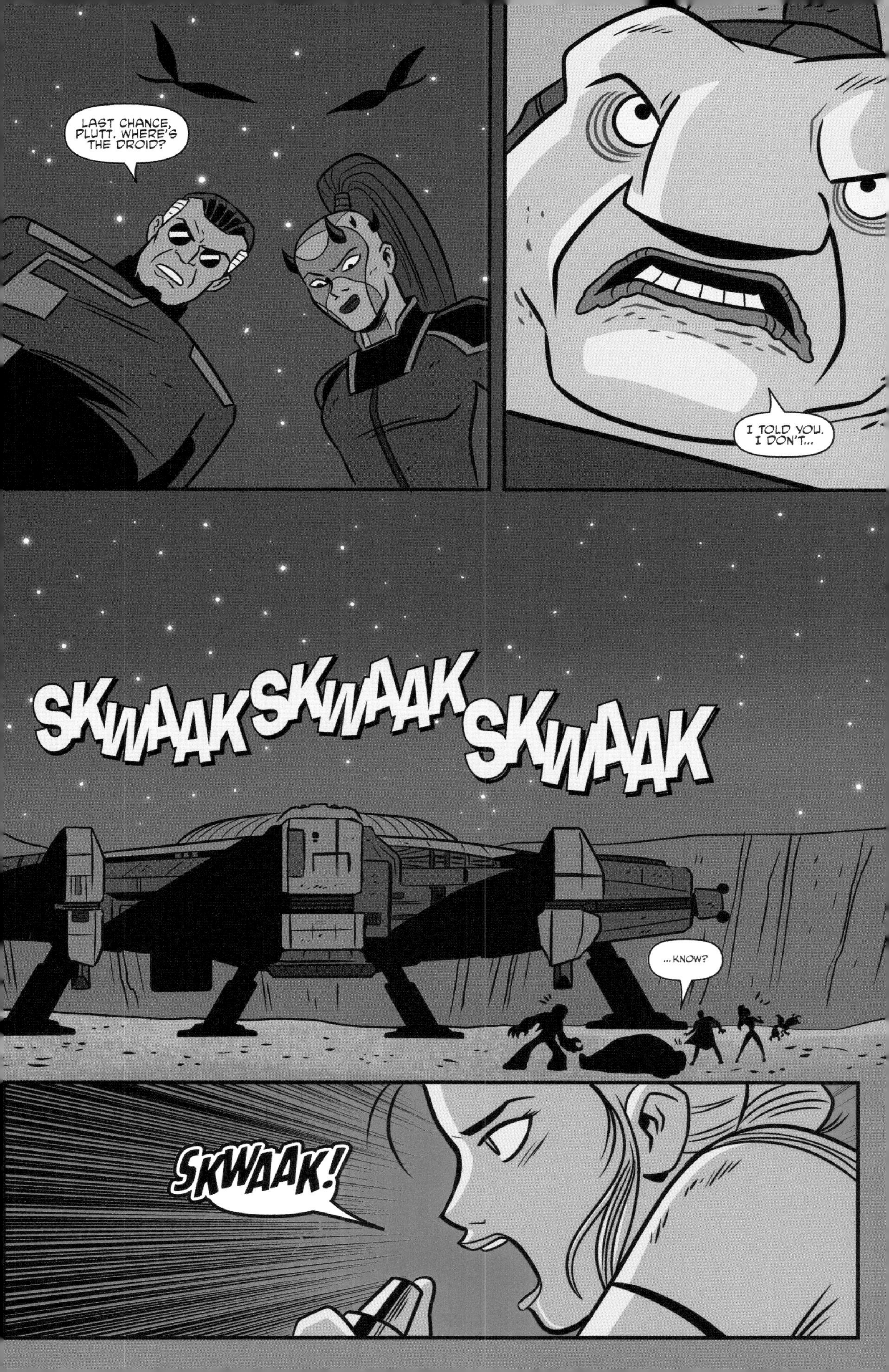
LAST CHANCE, PLUTT. WHERE'S THE DROID?
I TOLD YOU. I DON'T...
SKWAAK SKWAAK SKWAAK
...KNOW?
SKWAAK!

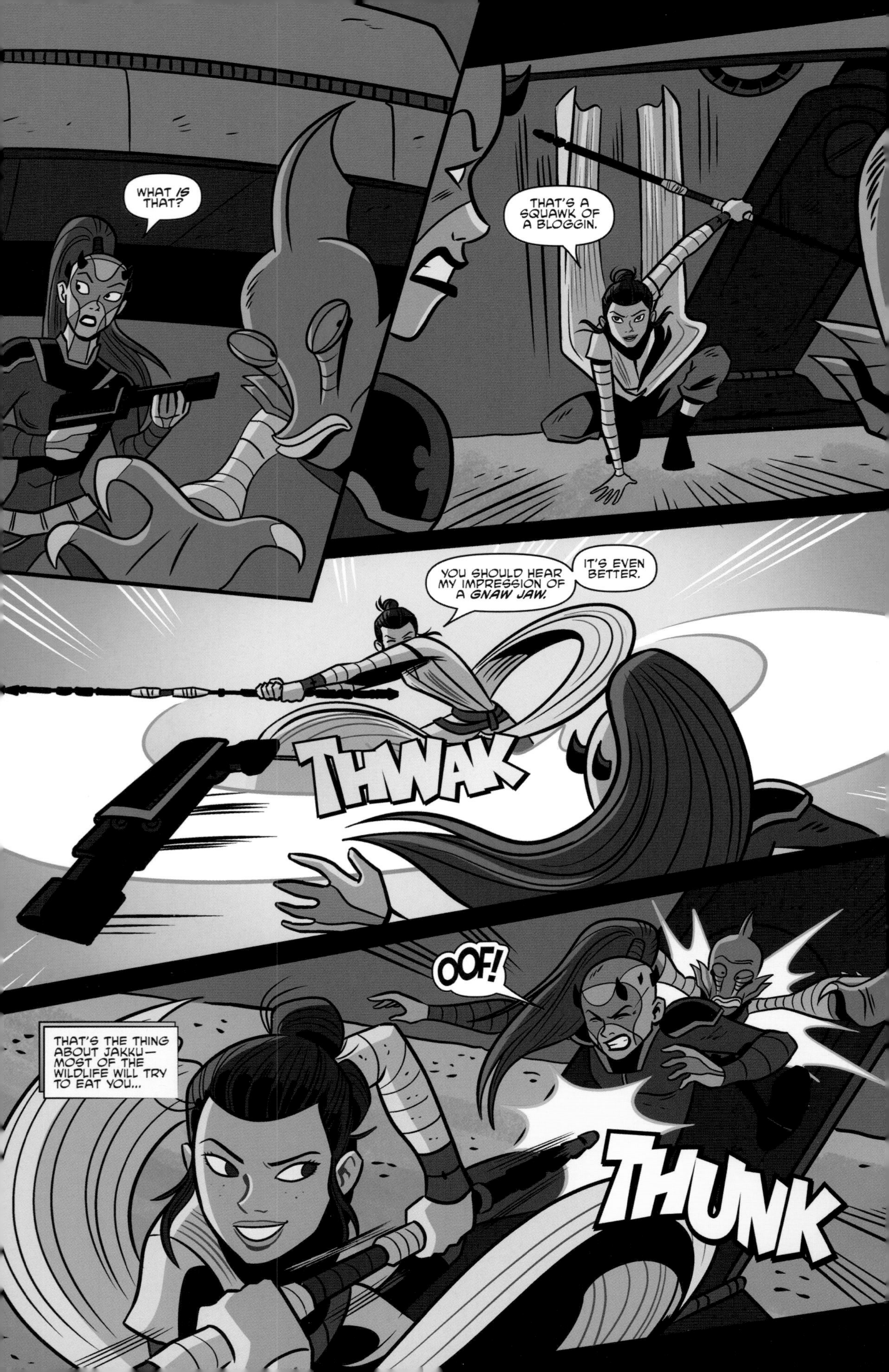
WHAT IS THAT?
THAT'S A SQUAWK OF A BLOGGIN.
YOU SHOULD HEAR MY IMPRESSION OF A GNAW JAW.
IT'S EVEN BETTER.
THWAK
OOF!
THAT'S THE THING ABOUT JAKKU— MOST OF THE WILDLIFE WILL TRY TO EAT YOU...
THUNK

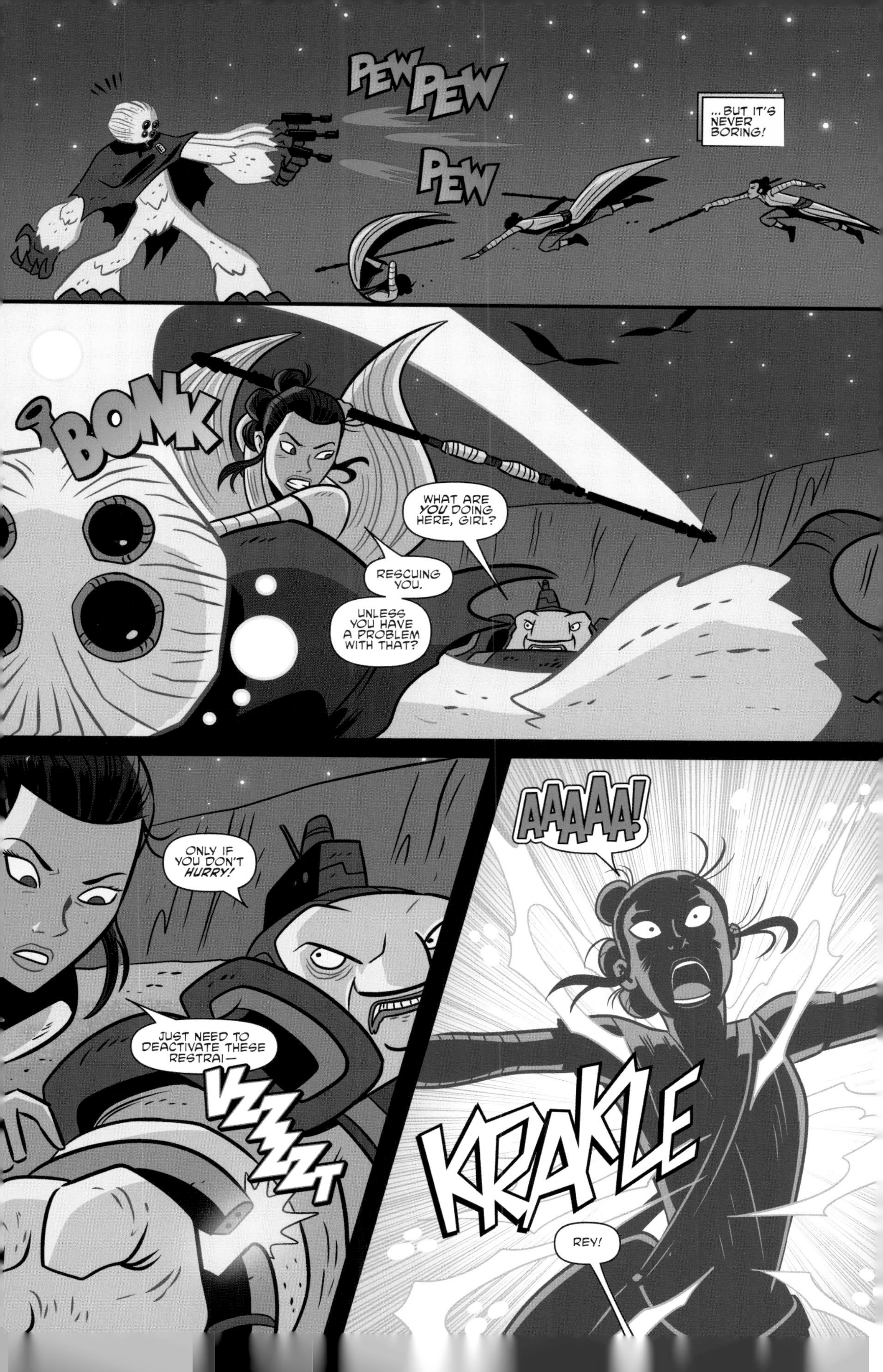
PEW PEW
PEW
...BUT IT'S NEVER BORING!
BONK
WHAT ARE YOU DOING HERE, GIRL?
RESCUING YOU.
UNLESS YOU HAVE A PROBLEM WITH THAT?
ONLY IF YOU DON'T HURRY!
JUST NEED TO DEACTIVATE THESE RESTRAI—
VZZZZZT
AAAAA!
KRAKLE
REY!

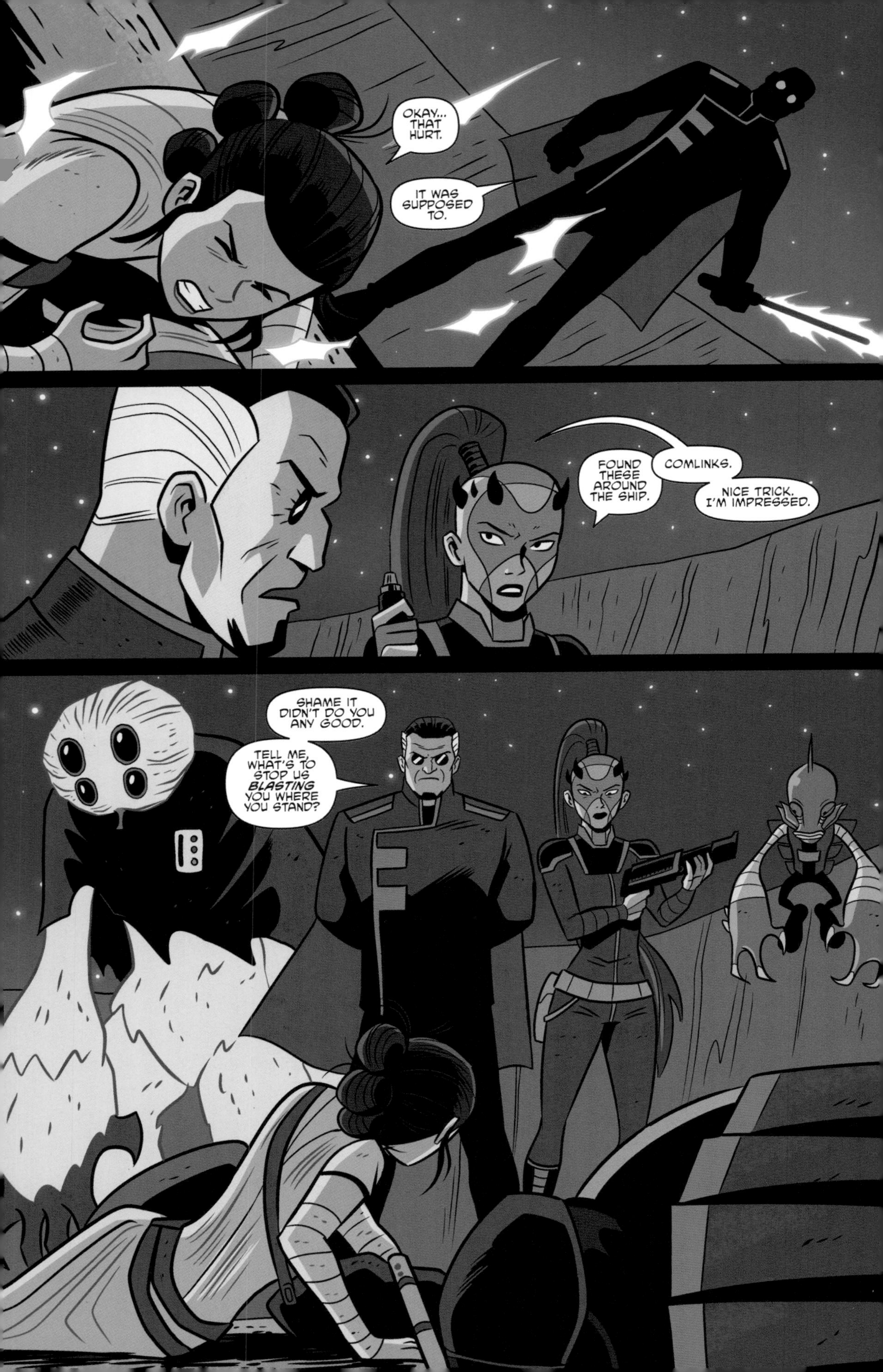
OKAY... THAT HURT.
IT WAS SUPPOSED TO.
FOUND THESE AROUND THE SHIP.
COMLINKS.
NICE TRICK. I'M IMPRESSED.
SHAME IT DIDN'T DO YOU ANY GOOD.
TELL ME, WHAT'S TO STOP US *BLASTING* YOU WHERE YOU STAND?

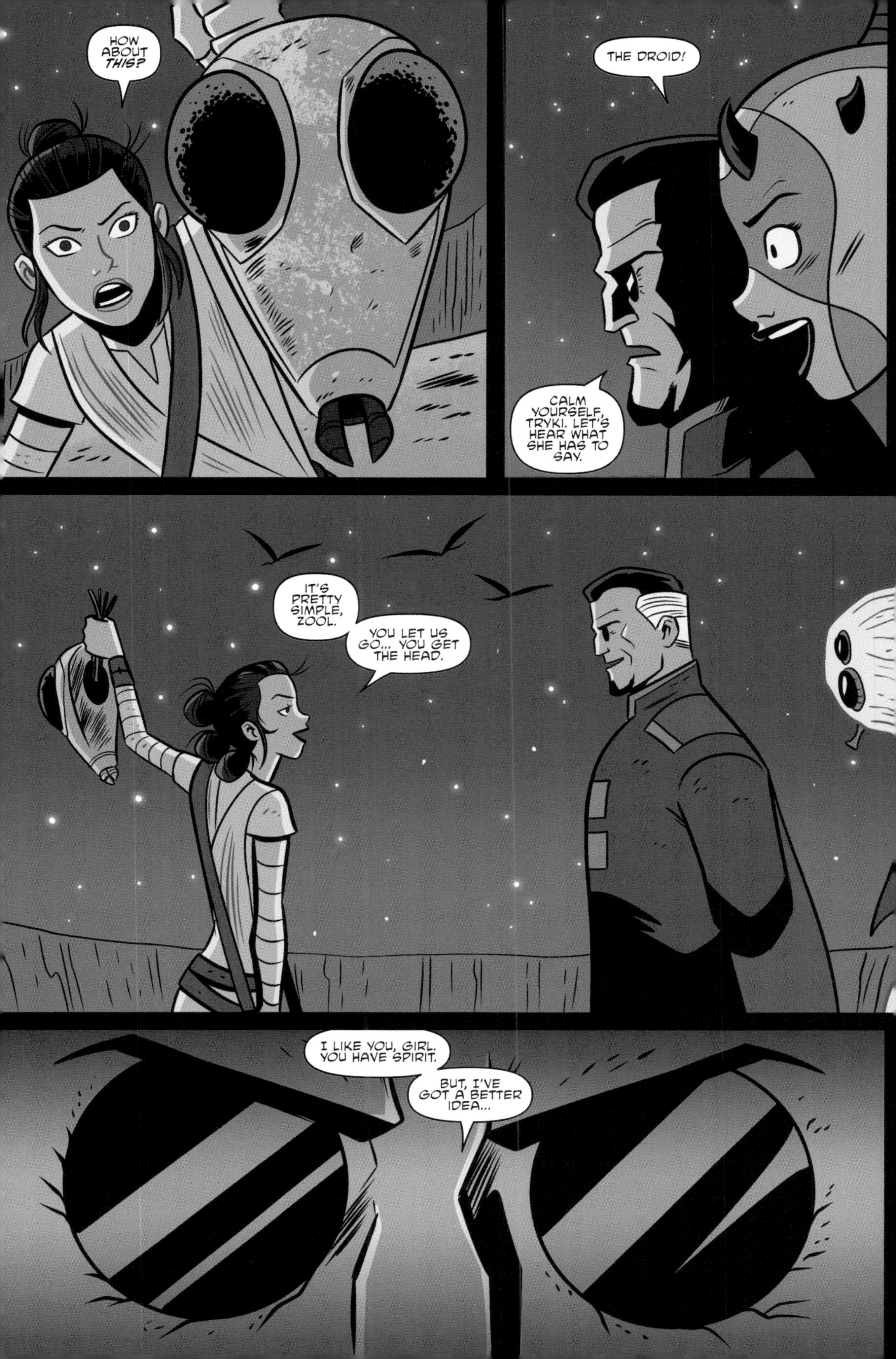
HOW ABOUT THIS?
THE DROID!
CALM YOURSELF, TRYKI. LET'S HEAR WHAT SHE HAS TO SAY.
IT'S PRETTY SIMPLE, ZOOL.
YOU LET US GO... YOU GET THE HEAD.
I LIKE YOU, GIRL. YOU HAVE SPIRIT.
BUT, I'VE GOT A BETTER IDEA...

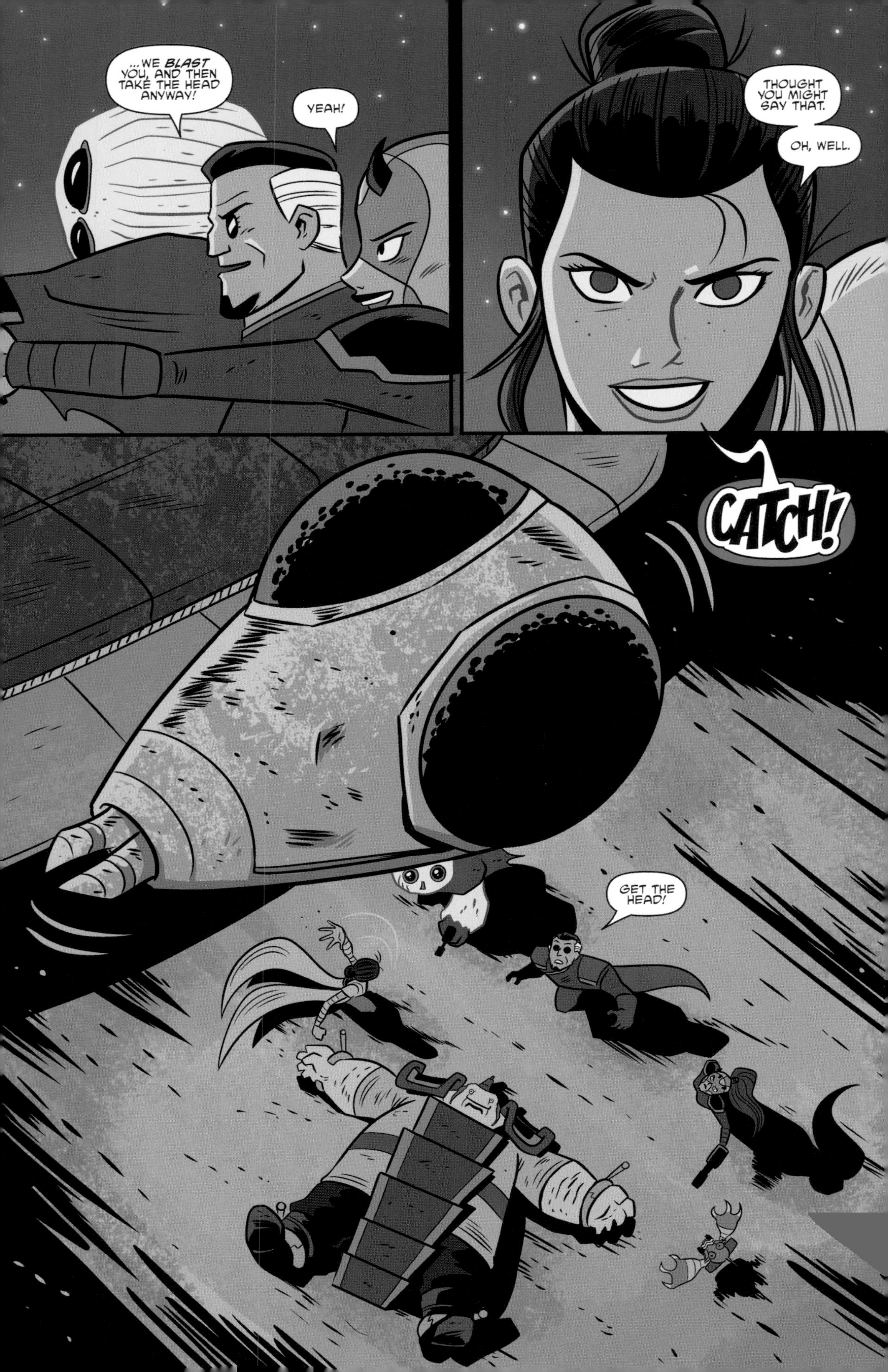

...WE *BLAST* YOU, AND THEN TAKE THE HEAD ANYWAY!
YEAH!
THOUGHT YOU MIGHT SAY THAT.
OH, WELL.
CATCH!
GET THE HEAD!

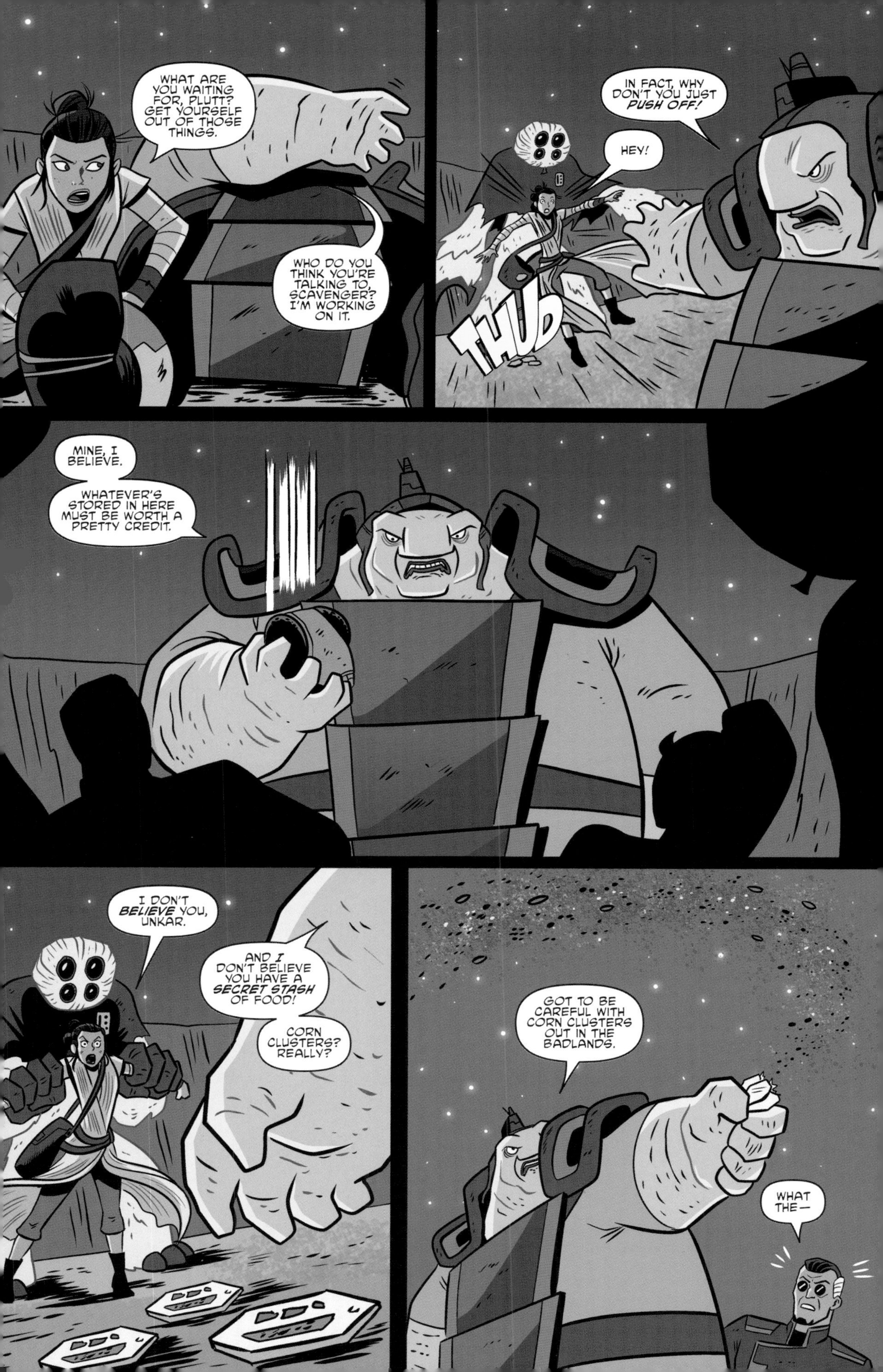

WHAT ARE YOU WAITING FOR, PLUTT? GET YOURSELF OUT OF THOSE THINGS.
WHO DO YOU THINK YOU'RE TALKING TO, SCAVENGER? I'M WORKING ON IT.
IN FACT, WHY DON'T YOU JUST PUSH OFF!
HEY!
THUD
MINE, I BELIEVE.
WHATEVER'S STORED IN HERE MUST BE WORTH A PRETTY CREDIT.
I DON'T BELIEVE YOU, UNKAR.
AND I DON'T BELIEVE YOU HAVE A SECRET STASH OF FOOD!
CORN CLUSTERS? REALLY?
GOT TO BE CAREFUL WITH CORN CLUSTERS OUT IN THE BADLANDS.
WHAT THE—

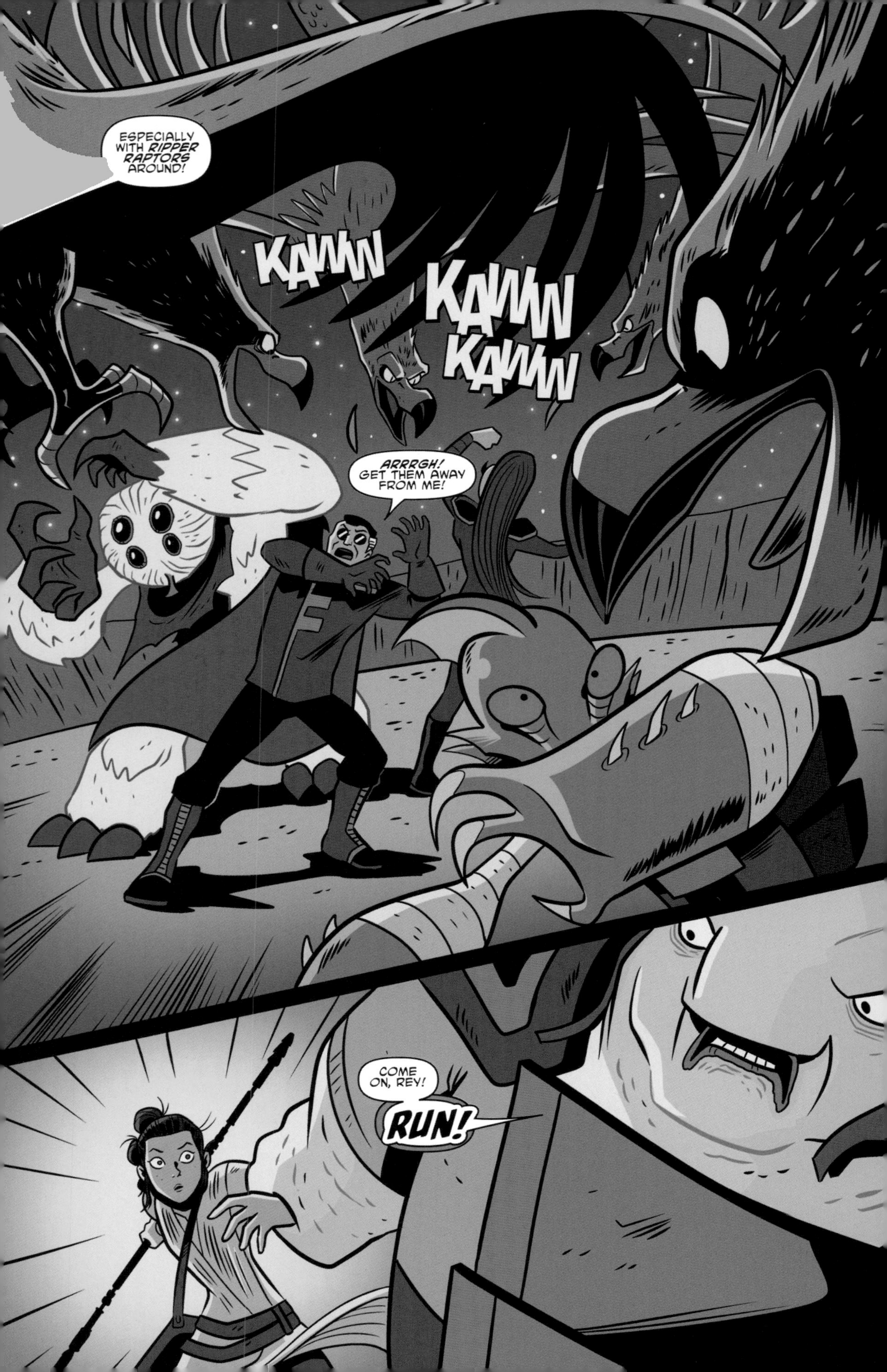
ESPECIALLY WITH *RIPPER RAPTORS* AROUND!
KAWW
KAWW KAWW
ARRRGH! GET THEM AWAY FROM ME!
COME ON, REY!
RUN!

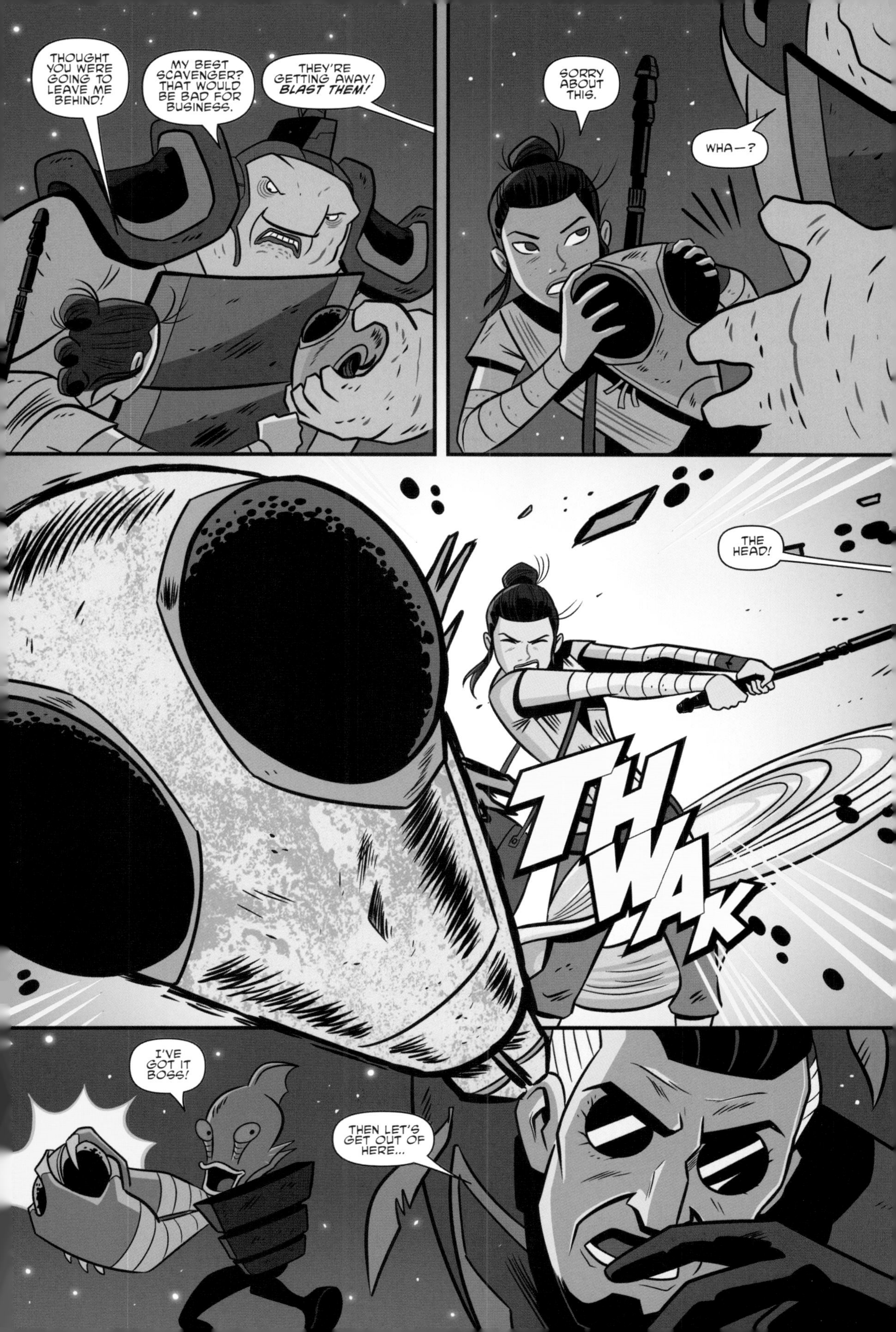
THOUGHT YOU WERE GOING TO LEAVE ME BEHIND!
MY BEST SCAVENGER? THAT WOULD BE BAD FOR BUSINESS.
THEY'RE GETTING AWAY! *BLAST THEM!*
SORRY ABOUT THIS.
WHA—?
THE HEAD!
THWAK
I'VE GOT IT BOSS!
THEN LET'S GET OUT OF HERE...

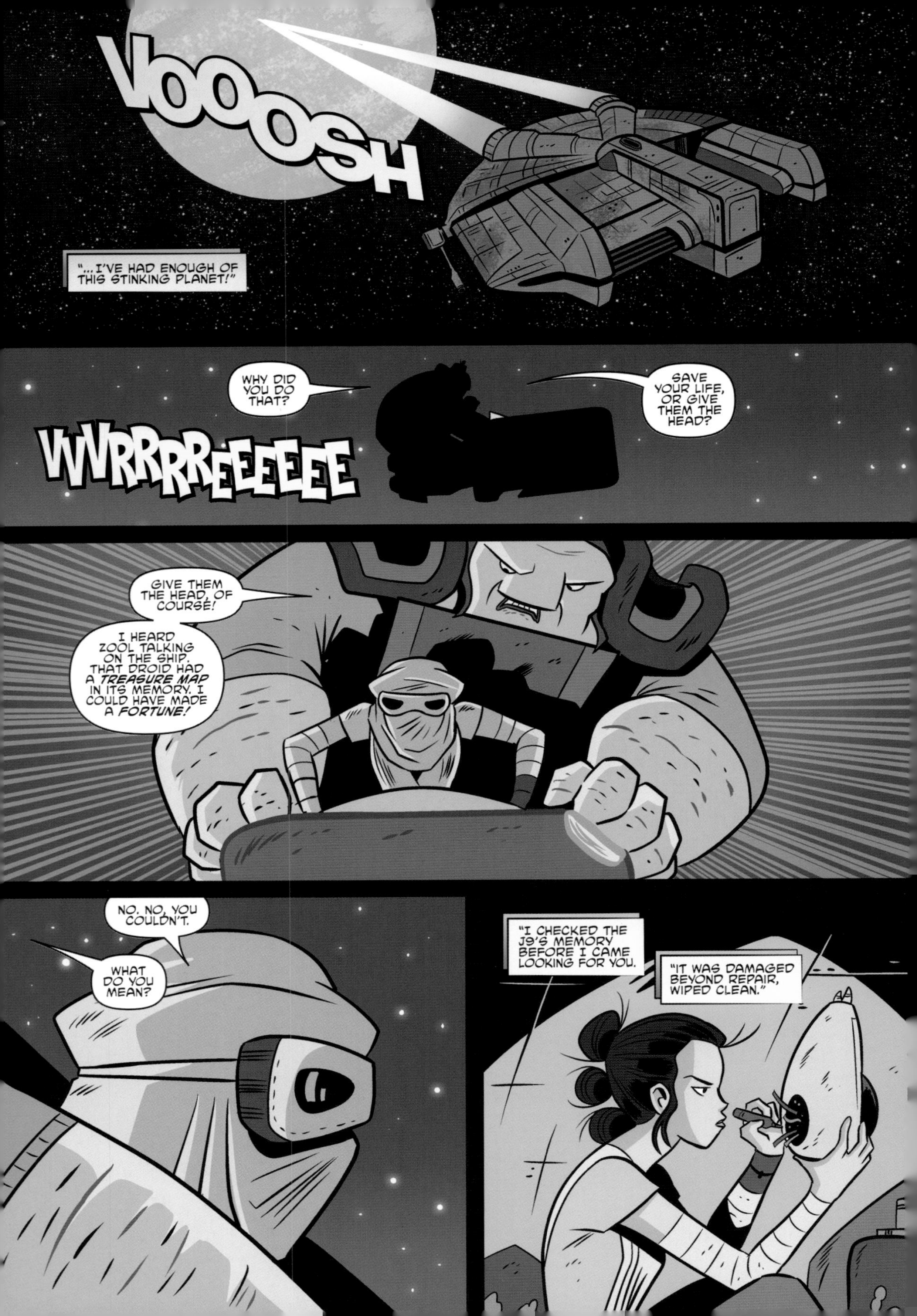
VOOOSH
"...I'VE HAD ENOUGH OF THIS STINKING PLANET!"
WHY DID YOU DO THAT?
SAVE YOUR LIFE, OR GIVE THEM THE HEAD?
VVVRRRREEEEEE
GIVE THEM THE HEAD, OF COURSE!
I HEARD ZOOL TALKING ON THE SHIP. THAT DROID HAD A *TREASURE MAP* IN ITS MEMORY. I COULD HAVE MADE A *FORTUNE!*
NO. NO, YOU COULDN'T.
WHAT DO YOU MEAN?
"I CHECKED THE J9'S MEMORY BEFORE I CAME LOOKING FOR YOU.
"IT WAS DAMAGED BEYOND REPAIR, WIPED CLEAN."

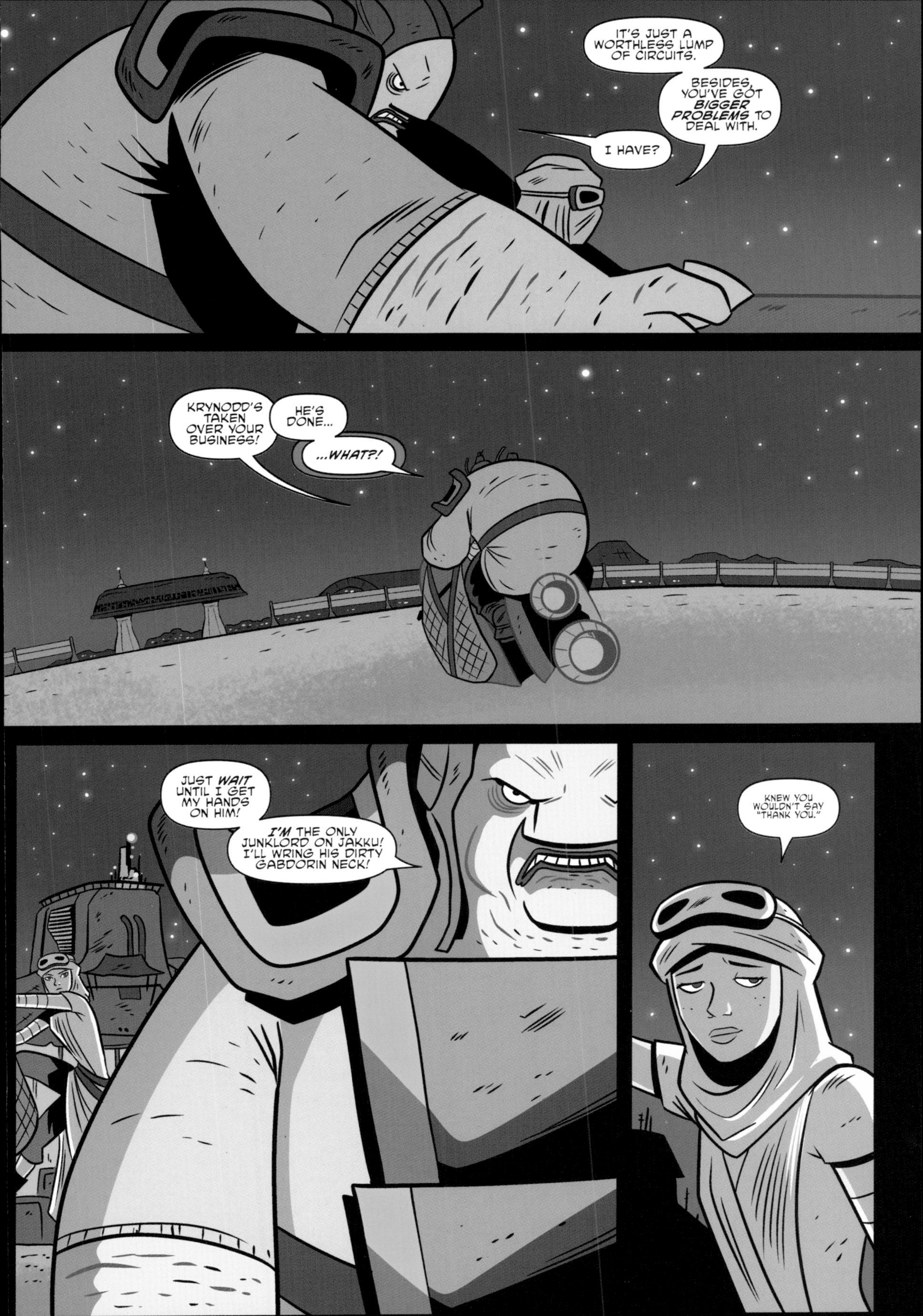
IT'S JUST A WORTHLESS LUMP OF CIRCUITS.
BESIDES, YOU'VE GOT *BIGGER PROBLEMS* TO DEAL WITH.
I HAVE?
KRYNODD'S TAKEN OVER YOUR BUSINESS!
HE'S DONE...
...*WHAT?!*
JUST *WAIT* UNTIL I GET MY HANDS ON HIM!
I'M THE ONLY JUNKLORD ON JAKKU! I'LL WRING HIS DIRTY GABDORIN NECK!
KNEW YOU WOULDN'T SAY "THANK YOU."

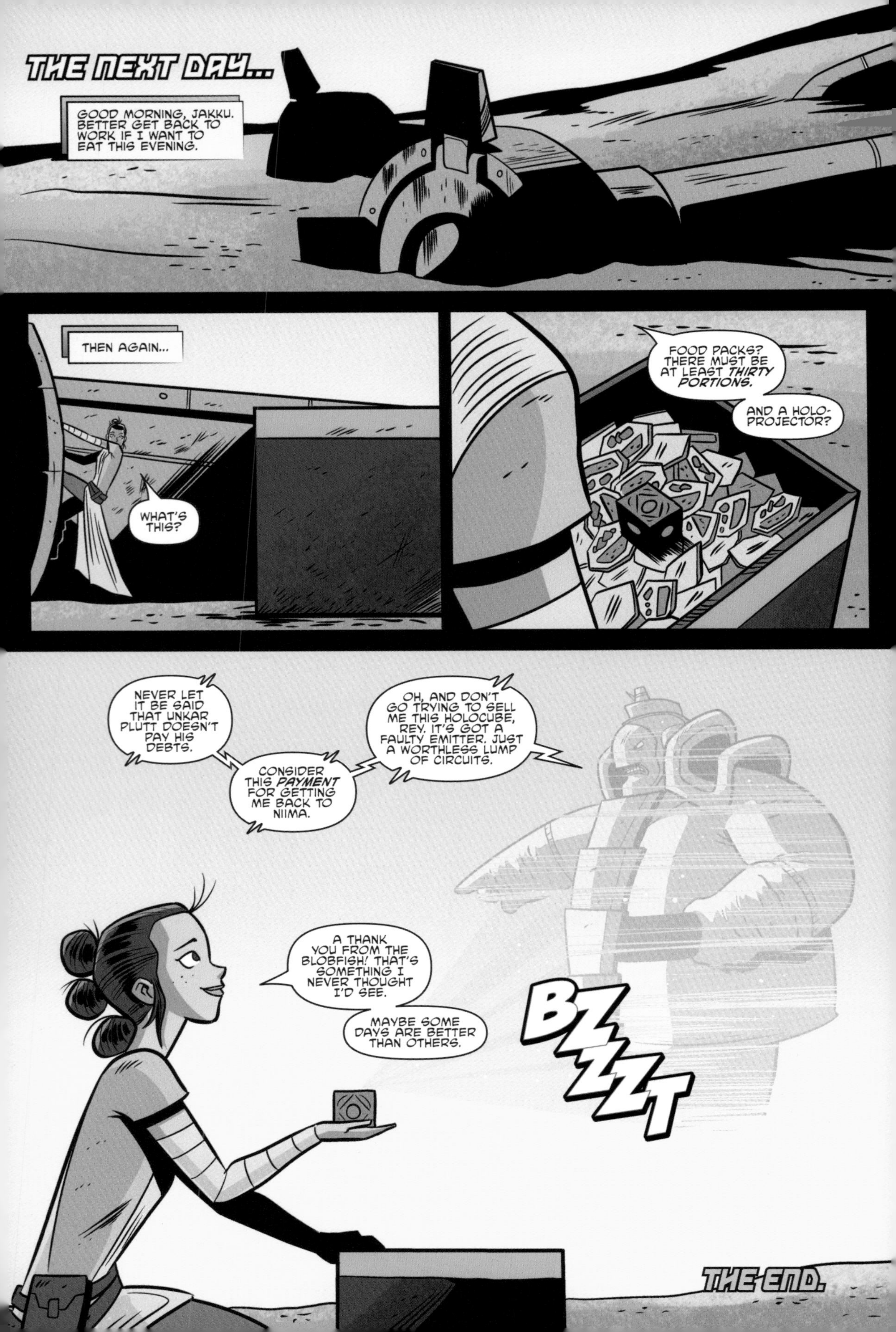
THE NEXT DAY...
GOOD MORNING, JAKKU. BETTER GET BACK TO WORK IF I WANT TO EAT THIS EVENING.
THEN AGAIN...
WHAT'S THIS?
FOOD PACKS? THERE MUST BE AT LEAST THIRTY PORTIONS.
AND A HOLO-PROJECTOR?
NEVER LET IT BE SAID THAT UNKAR PLUTT DOESN'T PAY HIS DEBTS.
CONSIDER THIS PAYMENT FOR GETTING ME BACK TO NIIMA.
OH, AND DON'T GO TRYING TO SELL ME THIS HOLOCUBE, REY. IT'S GOT A FAULTY EMITTER. JUST A WORTHLESS LUMP OF CIRCUITS.
A THANK YOU FROM THE BLOBFISH! THAT'S SOMETHING I NEVER THOUGHT I'D SEE.
MAYBE SOME DAYS ARE BETTER THAN OTHERS.
BZZZT
THE END.

03
STOP, THIEF!

Writer
CAVAN SCOTT

Artist
JON SOMMARIVA

Inker
SEAN PARSONS

Colorist
CHARLIE KIRCHOFF

Letterer
TOM B. LONG

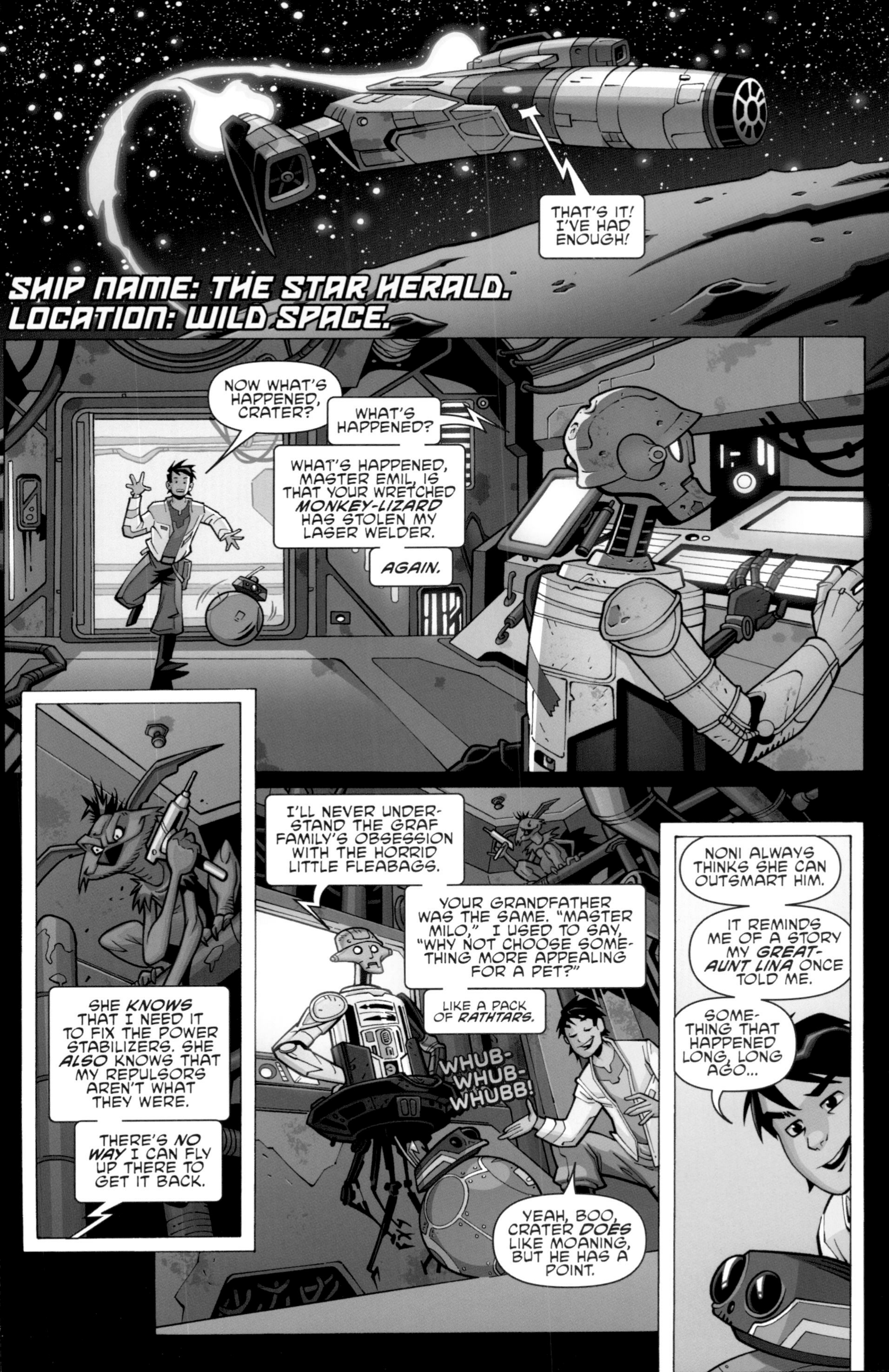
THAT'S IT! I'VE HAD ENOUGH!
SHIP NAME: THE STAR HERALD.
LOCATION: WILD SPACE.
NOW WHAT'S HAPPENED, CRATER?
WHAT'S HAPPENED?
WHAT'S HAPPENED, MASTER EMIL, IS THAT YOUR WRETCHED MONKEY-LIZARD HAS STOLEN MY LASER WELDER.
AGAIN.
SHE KNOWS THAT I NEED IT TO FIX THE POWER STABILIZERS. SHE ALSO KNOWS THAT MY REPULSORS AREN'T WHAT THEY WERE.
THERE'S NO WAY I CAN FLY UP THERE TO GET IT BACK.
I'LL NEVER UNDERSTAND THE GRAF FAMILY'S OBSESSION WITH THE HORRID LITTLE FLEABAGS.
YOUR GRANDFATHER WAS THE SAME. "MASTER MILO," I USED TO SAY, "WHY NOT CHOOSE SOMETHING MORE APPEALING FOR A PET?"
LIKE A PACK OF RATHTARS.
WHUB-WHUB-WHUBB!
YEAH, BOO, CRATER DOES LIKE MOANING, BUT HE HAS A POINT.
NONI ALWAYS THINKS SHE CAN OUTSMART HIM.
IT REMINDS ME OF A STORY MY GREAT-AUNT LINA ONCE TOLD ME.
SOMETHING THAT HAPPENED LONG, LONG AGO...

"...BACK IN THE DAYS OF THE *OLD REPUBLIC.*

"WHEN SHE WAS A LITTLE GIRL, LINA LOVED *DEX'S DINER* ON CORUSCANT. THE BEST *NERFBURGERS* EVER, SHE SAID.

"PEOPLE CAME FROM ALL OVER THE GALAXY TO EAT AT DEX'S.

"*CARTOGRAPHERS,* LIKE MY FAMILY, DOCK WORKERS...

"...EVEN *JEDI KNIGHTS.*

"THE TROUBLE WAS, NOT ALL OF DEX'S CLIENTELE WERE *HONEST...*"

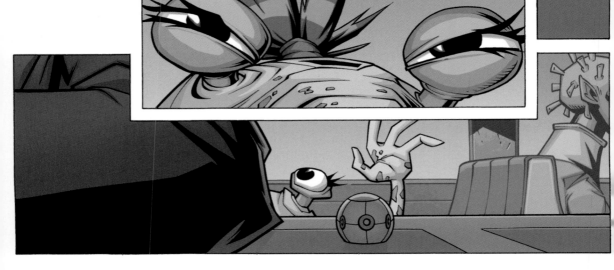

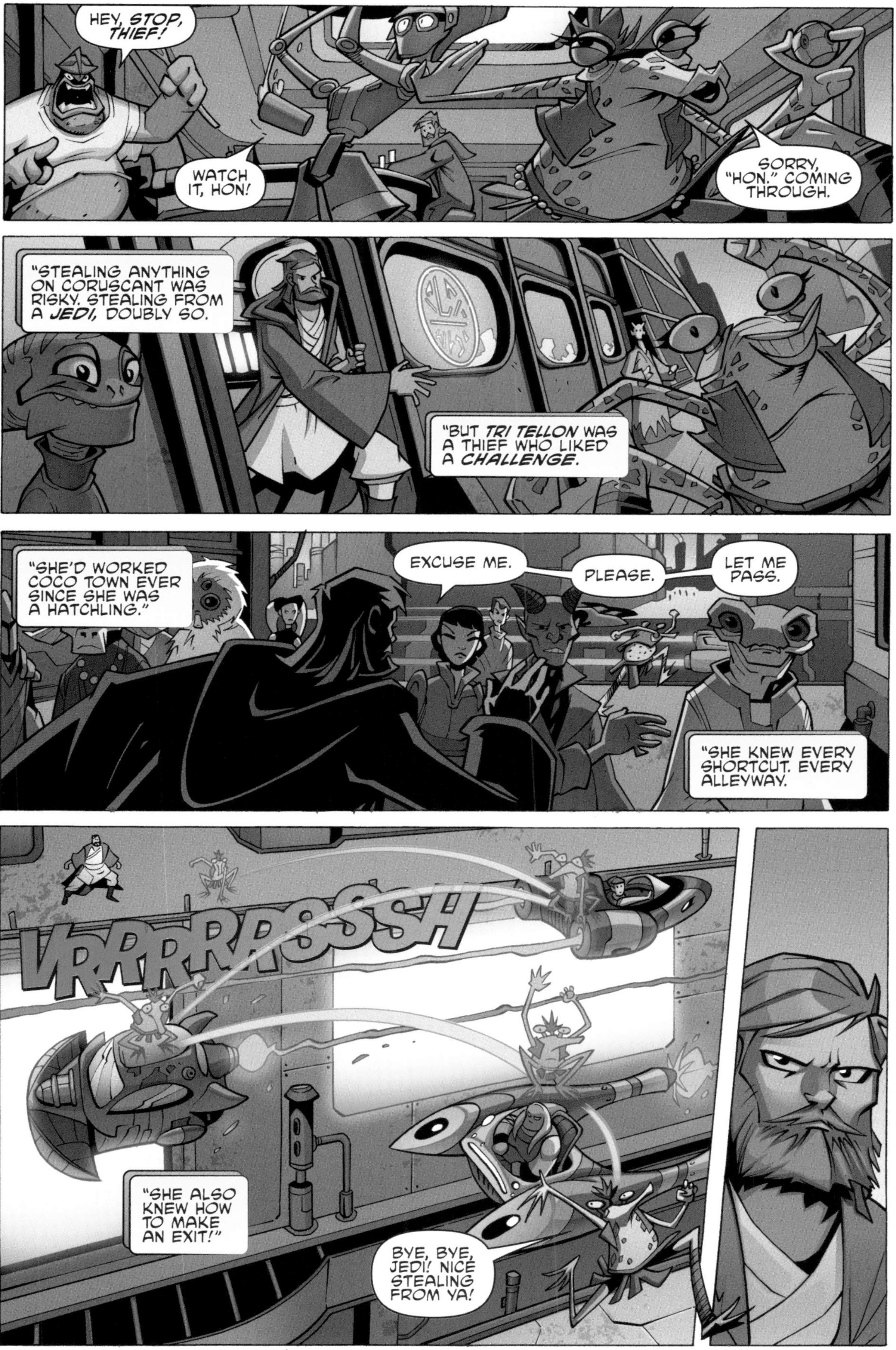
HEY, STOP, THIEF!
WATCH IT, HON!
SORRY, "HON." COMING THROUGH.
"STEALING ANYTHING ON CORUSCANT WAS RISKY. STEALING FROM A JEDI, DOUBLY SO.
"BUT TRI TELLON WAS A THIEF WHO LIKED A CHALLENGE.
"SHE'D WORKED COCO TOWN EVER SINCE SHE WAS A HATCHLING."
EXCUSE ME.
PLEASE.
LET ME PASS.
"SHE KNEW EVERY SHORTCUT. EVERY ALLEYWAY.
VRRRRRSSSH
"SHE ALSO KNEW HOW TO MAKE AN EXIT!"
BYE, BYE, JEDI! NICE STEALING FROM YA!

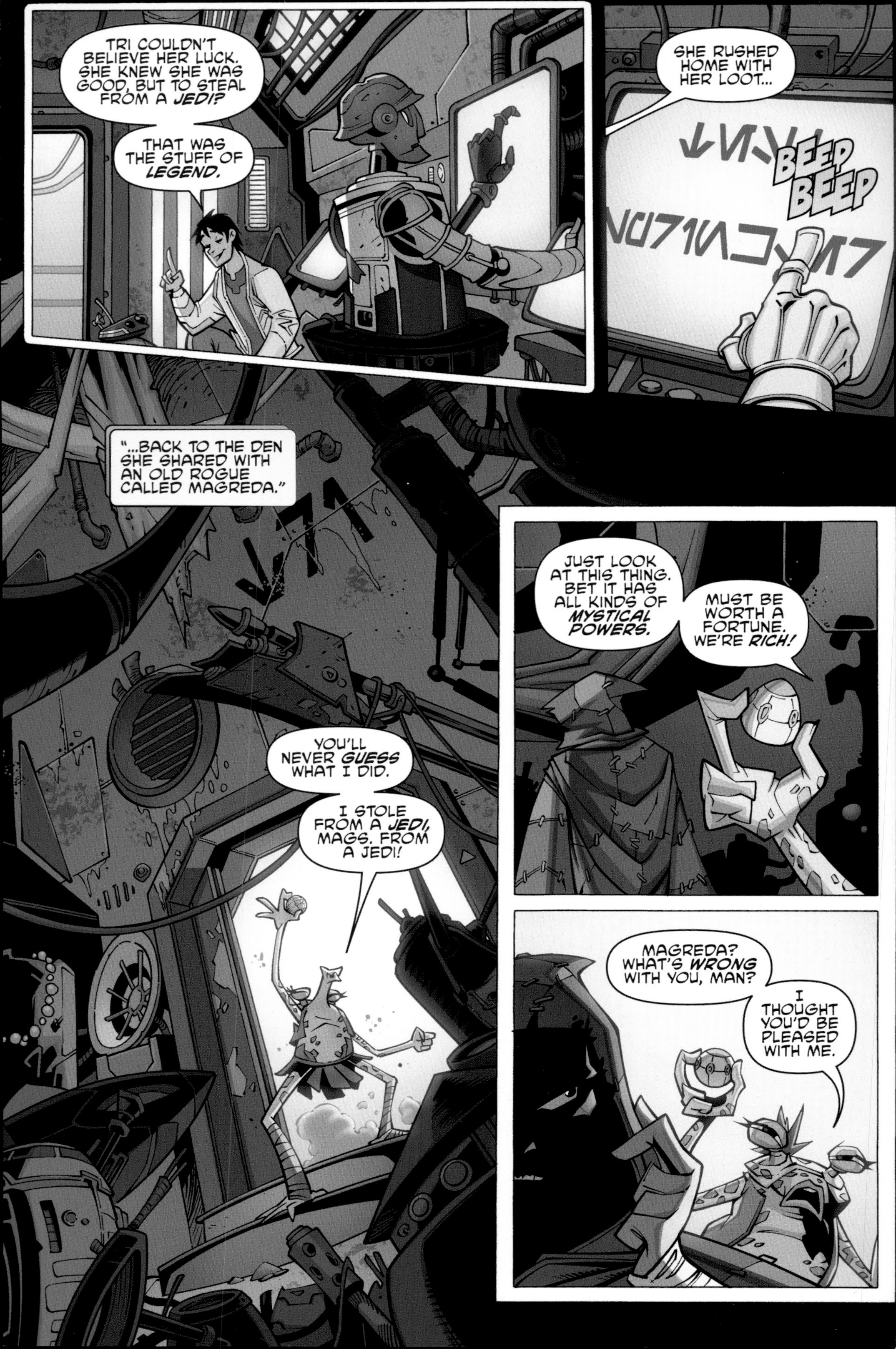
TRI COULDN'T BELIEVE HER LUCK. SHE KNEW SHE WAS GOOD, BUT TO STEAL FROM A *JEDI?*
THAT WAS THE STUFF OF *LEGEND.*
SHE RUSHED HOME WITH HER LOOT...
BEEP BEEP
"...BACK TO THE DEN SHE SHARED WITH AN OLD ROGUE CALLED MAGREDA."
YOU'LL NEVER *GUESS* WHAT I DID.
I STOLE FROM A *JEDI,* MAGS. FROM A JEDI!
JUST LOOK AT THIS THING. BET IT HAS ALL KINDS OF *MYSTICAL POWERS.*
MUST BE WORTH A FORTUNE. WE'RE *RICH!*
MAGREDA? WHAT'S *WRONG* WITH YOU, MAN?
I THOUGHT YOU'D BE PLEASED WITH ME.

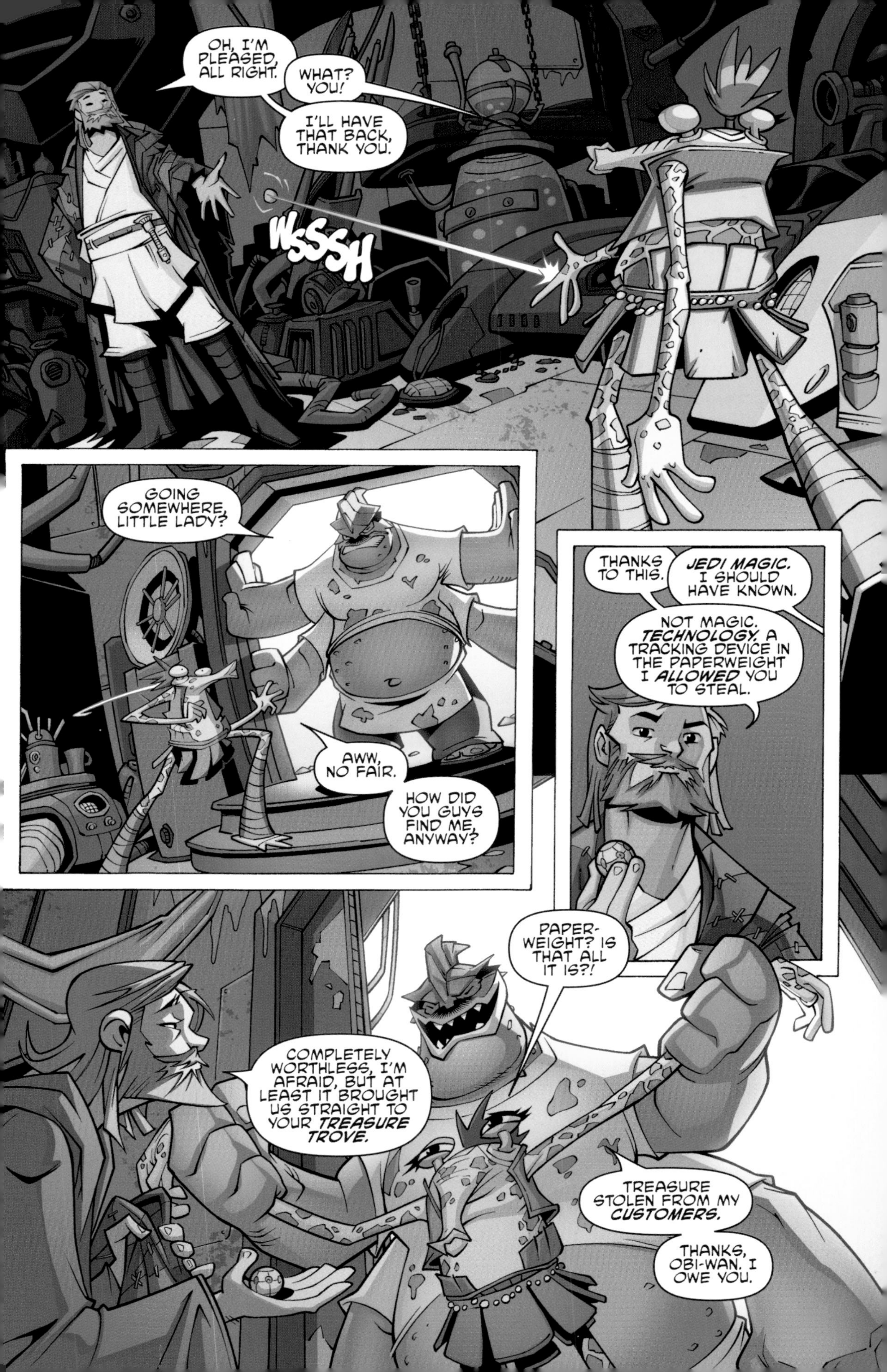
OH, I'M PLEASED, ALL RIGHT.
WHAT? YOU!
I'LL HAVE THAT BACK, THANK YOU.
WSSSH
GOING SOMEWHERE, LITTLE LADY?
AWW, NO FAIR.
HOW DID YOU GUYS FIND ME, ANYWAY?
THANKS TO THIS.
JEDI MAGIC. I SHOULD HAVE KNOWN.
NOT MAGIC. TECHNOLOGY. A TRACKING DEVICE IN THE PAPERWEIGHT I ALLOWED YOU TO STEAL.
PAPER-WEIGHT? IS THAT ALL IT IS?!
COMPLETELY WORTHLESS, I'M AFRAID, BUT AT LEAST IT BROUGHT US STRAIGHT TO YOUR TREASURE TROVE.
TREASURE STOLEN FROM MY CUSTOMERS.
THANKS, OBI-WAN. I OWE YOU.

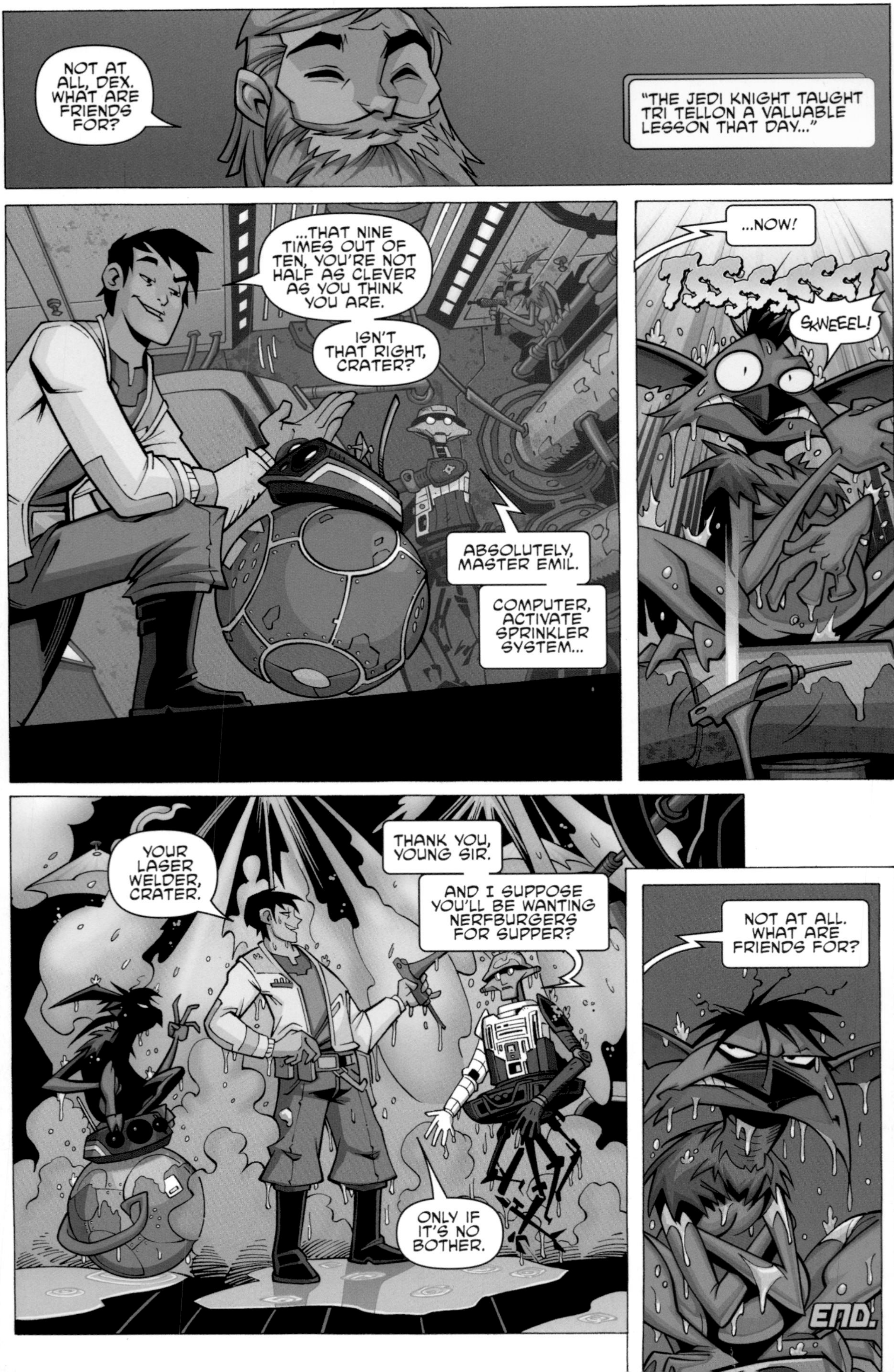

NOT AT ALL, DEX. WHAT ARE FRIENDS FOR?
"THE JEDI KNIGHT TAUGHT TRI TELLON A VALUABLE LESSON THAT DAY..."
...THAT NINE TIMES OUT OF TEN, YOU'RE NOT HALF AS CLEVER AS YOU THINK YOU ARE.
ISN'T THAT RIGHT, CRATER?
ABSOLUTELY, MASTER EMIL.
COMPUTER, ACTIVATE SPRINKLER SYSTEM...
...NOW!
TSSSSSST
SKWEEEL!
YOUR LASER WELDER, CRATER.
THANK YOU, YOUNG SIR.
AND I SUPPOSE YOU'LL BE WANTING NERFBURGERS FOR SUPPER?
ONLY IF IT'S NO BOTHER.
NOT AT ALL. WHAT ARE FRIENDS FOR?
END.

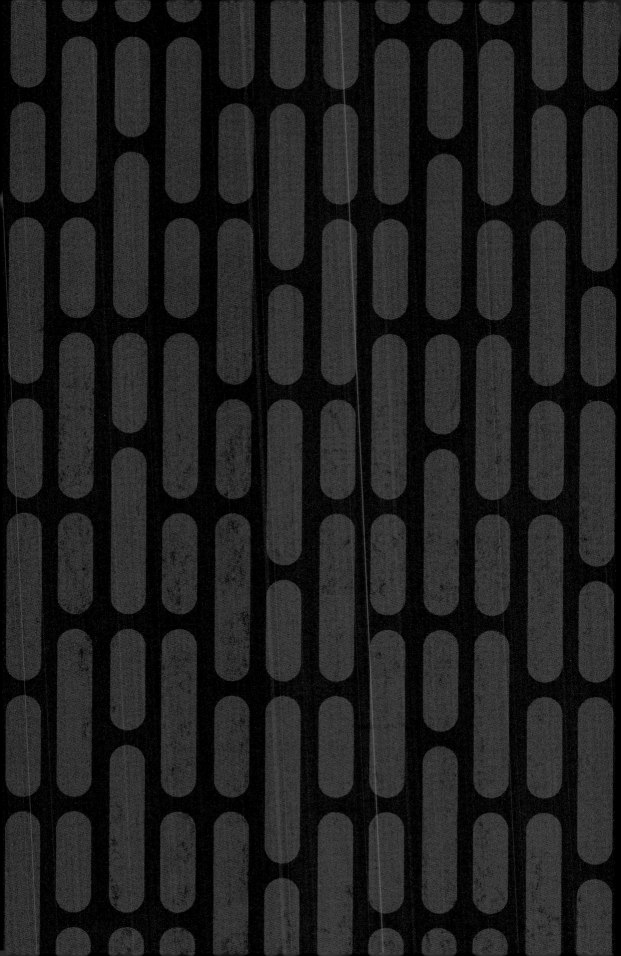

04
THE FLAT MOUNTAIN OF YAVIN

Writers
ELSA CHARRETIER
& PIERRICK COLINET

Artist
ELSA CHARRETIER

Colorist
SARAH STERN

Letterer
TOM B. LONG

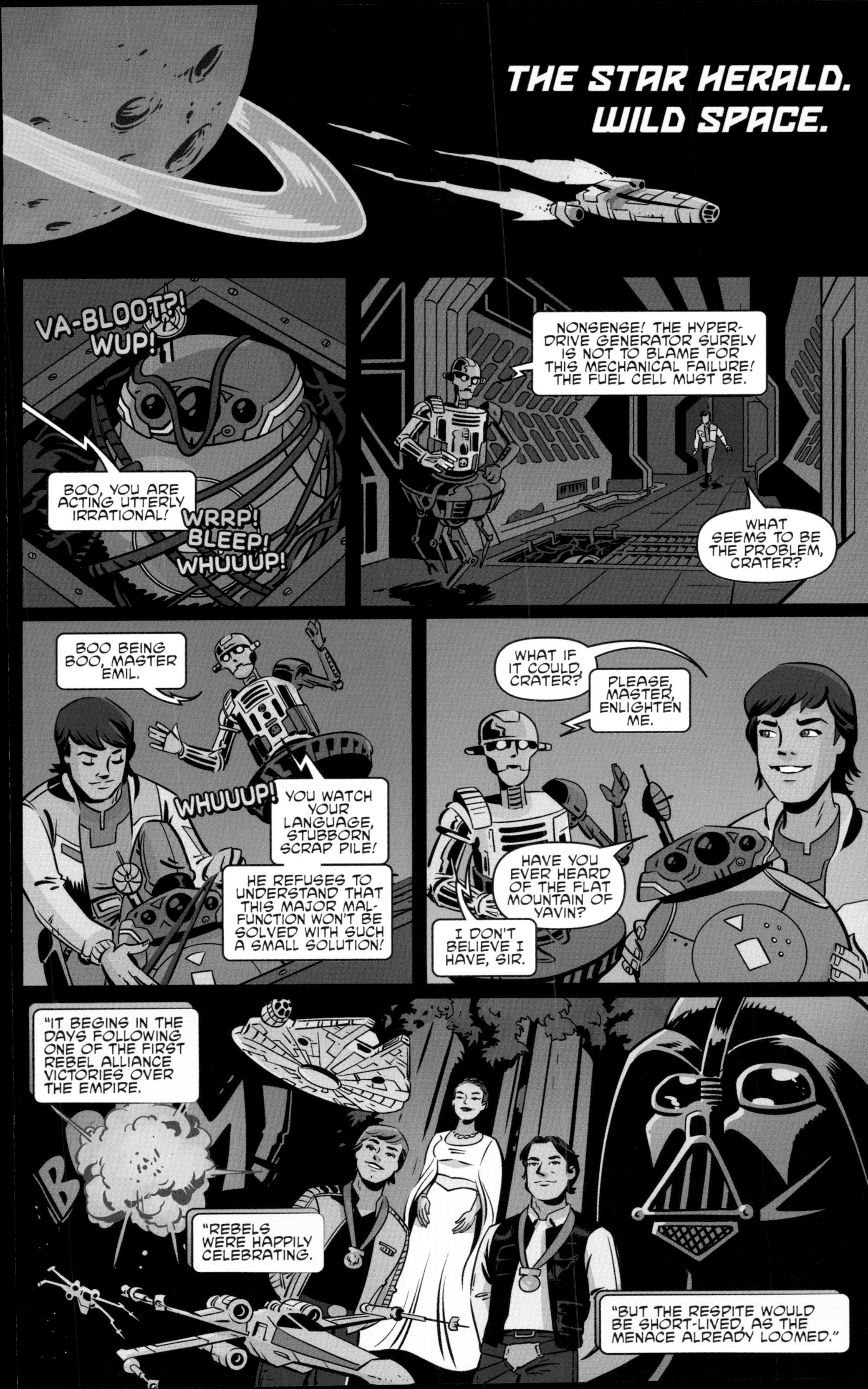
THE STAR HERALD. WILD SPACE.
VA-BLOOT?! WUP!
BOO, YOU ARE ACTING UTTERLY IRRATIONAL!
WRRP! BLEEP! WHUUUP!
NONSENSE! THE HYPER-DRIVE GENERATOR SURELY IS NOT TO BLAME FOR THIS MECHANICAL FAILURE! THE FUEL CELL MUST BE.
WHAT SEEMS TO BE THE PROBLEM, CRATER?
BOO BEING BOO, MASTER EMIL.
WHUUUP!
YOU WATCH YOUR LANGUAGE, STUBBORN SCRAP PILE!
HE REFUSES TO UNDERSTAND THAT THIS MAJOR MAL-FUNCTION WON'T BE SOLVED WITH SUCH A SMALL SOLUTION!
WHAT IF IT COULD, CRATER?
PLEASE, MASTER, ENLIGHTEN ME.
HAVE YOU EVER HEARD OF THE FLAT MOUNTAIN OF YAVIN?
I DON'T BELIEVE I HAVE, SIR.
"IT BEGINS IN THE DAYS FOLLOWING ONE OF THE FIRST REBEL ALLIANCE VICTORIES OVER THE EMPIRE.
"REBELS WERE HAPPILY CELEBRATING.
"BUT THE RESPITE WOULD BE SHORT-LIVED, AS THE MENACE ALREADY LOOMED."

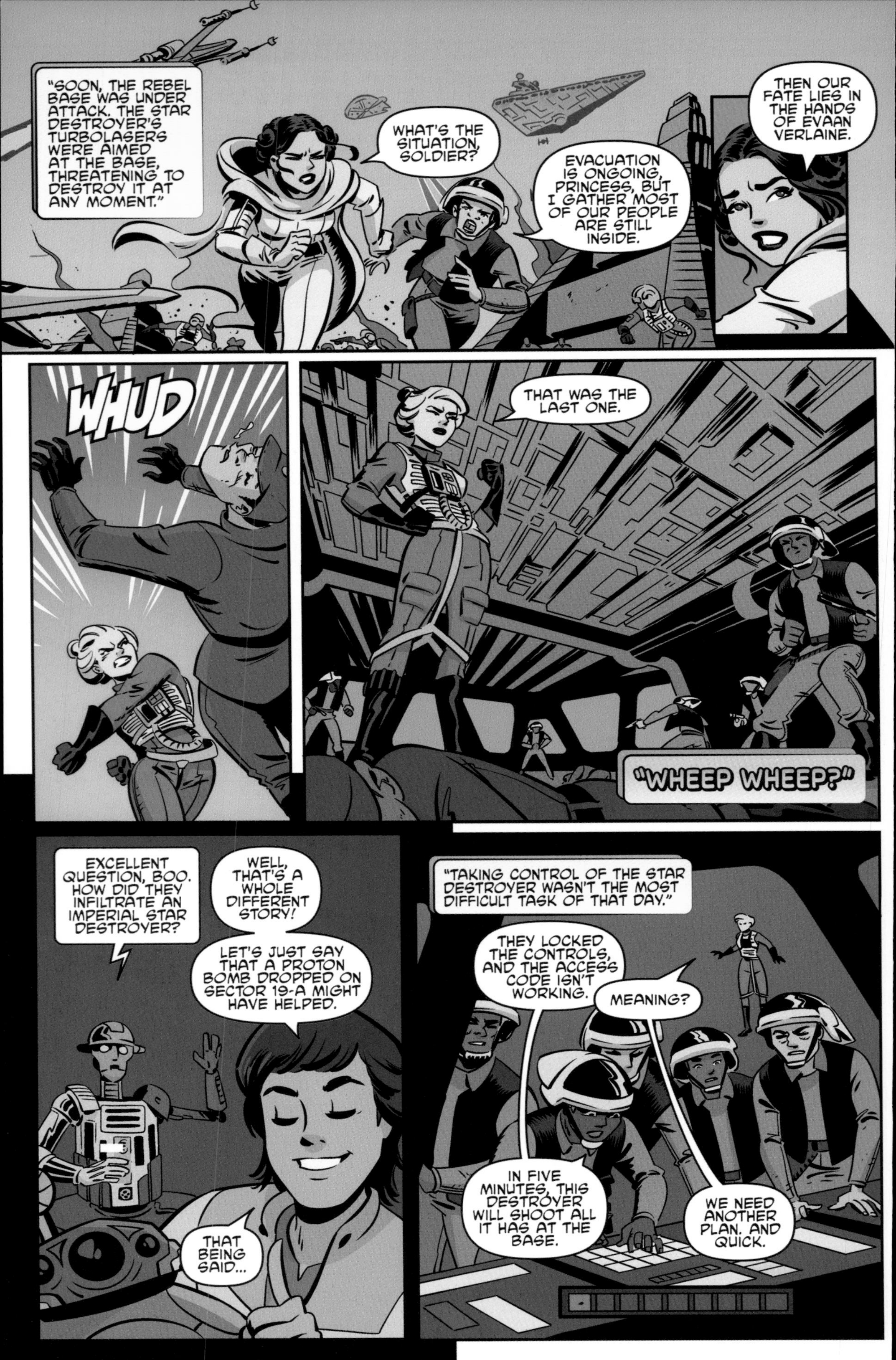
"SOON, THE REBEL BASE WAS UNDER ATTACK. THE STAR DESTROYER'S TURBOLASERS WERE AIMED AT THE BASE, THREATENING TO DESTROY IT AT ANY MOMENT."
WHAT'S THE SITUATION, SOLDIER?
EVACUATION IS ONGOING, PRINCESS, BUT I GATHER MOST OF OUR PEOPLE ARE STILL INSIDE.
THEN OUR FATE LIES IN THE HANDS OF EVAAN VERLAINE.
WHUD
THAT WAS THE LAST ONE.
"WHEEP WHEEP?"
EXCELLENT QUESTION, BOO. HOW DID THEY INFILTRATE AN IMPERIAL STAR DESTROYER?
WELL, THAT'S A WHOLE DIFFERENT STORY!
LET'S JUST SAY THAT A PROTON BOMB DROPPED ON SECTOR 19-A MIGHT HAVE HELPED.
THAT BEING SAID...
"TAKING CONTROL OF THE STAR DESTROYER WASN'T THE MOST DIFFICULT TASK OF THAT DAY."
THEY LOCKED THE CONTROLS, AND THE ACCESS CODE ISN'T WORKING.
MEANING?
IN FIVE MINUTES, THIS DESTROYER WILL SHOOT ALL IT HAS AT THE BASE.
WE NEED ANOTHER PLAN. AND QUICK.

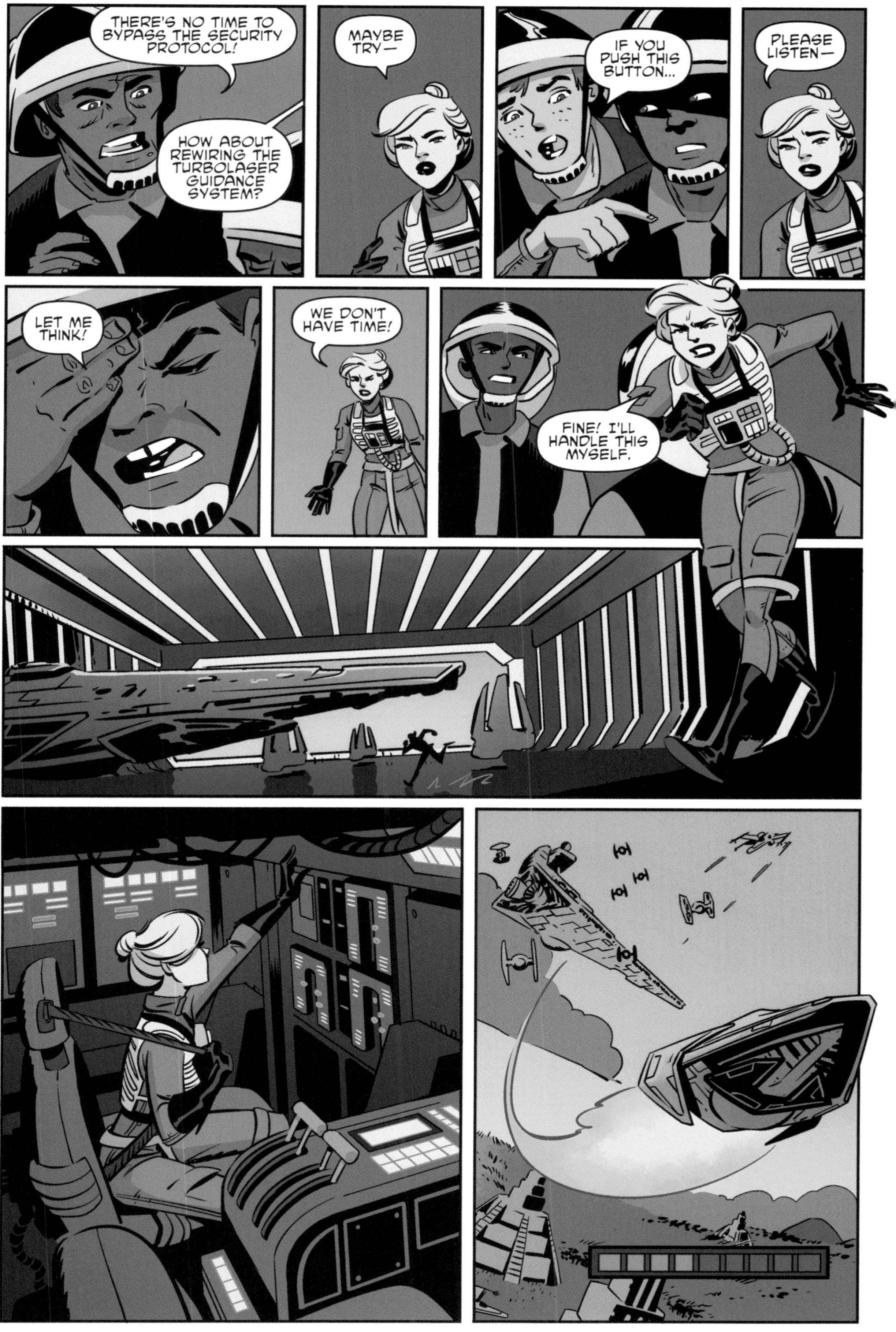
THERE'S NO TIME TO BYPASS THE SECURITY PROTOCOL!
HOW ABOUT REWIRING THE TURBOLASER GUIDANCE SYSTEM?
MAYBE TRY—
IF YOU PUSH THIS BUTTON...
PLEASE LISTEN—
LET ME THINK!
WE DON'T HAVE TIME!
FINE! I'LL HANDLE THIS MYSELF.

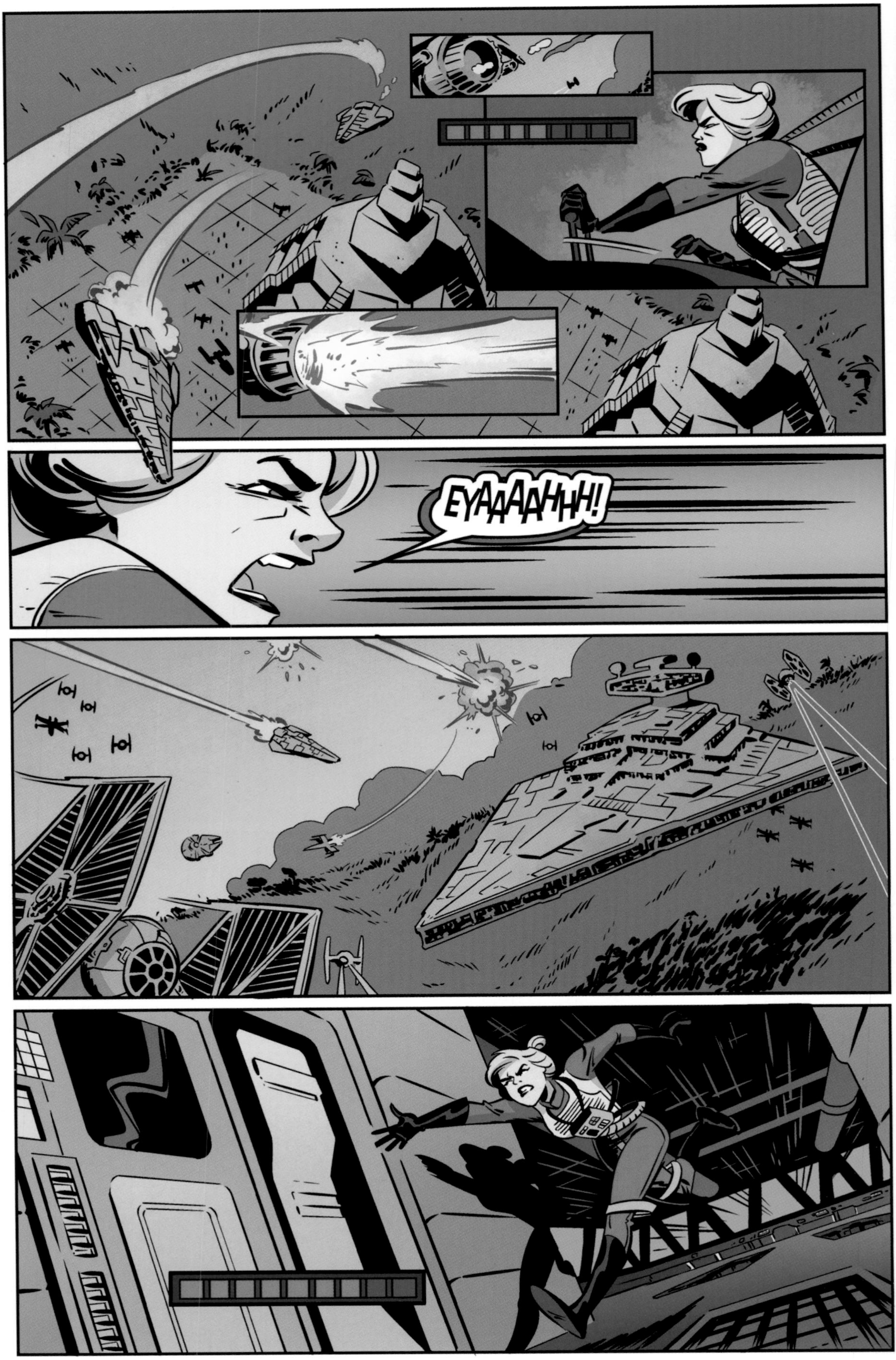
EYAAAAHHH!

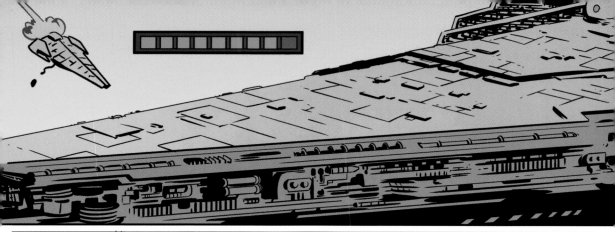

HARDLY EVEN FELT THAT.

IT DIDN'T MOVE. IT'S OVER.

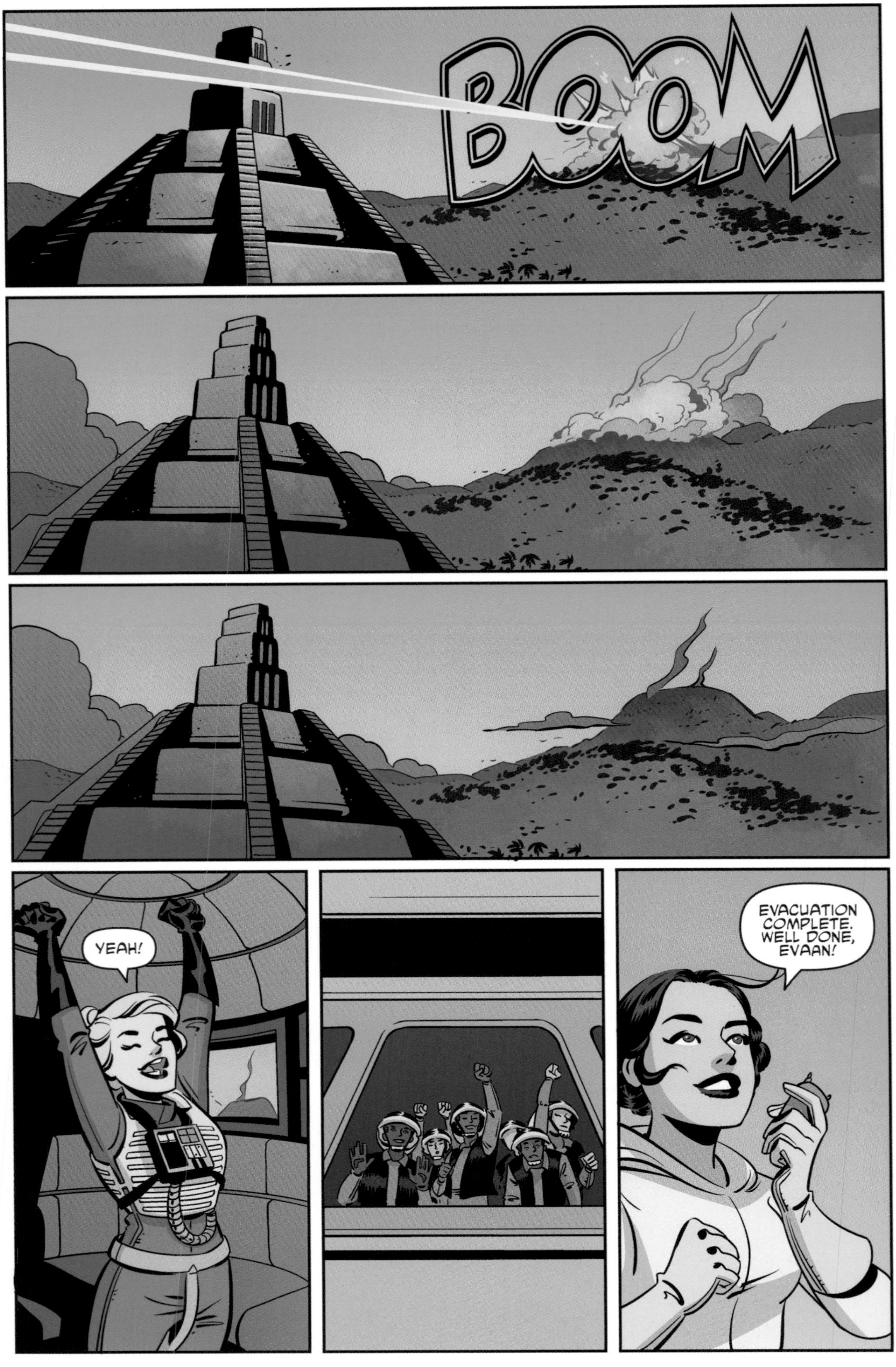
BOOM
YEAH!
EVACUATION COMPLETE. WELL DONE, EVAAN!

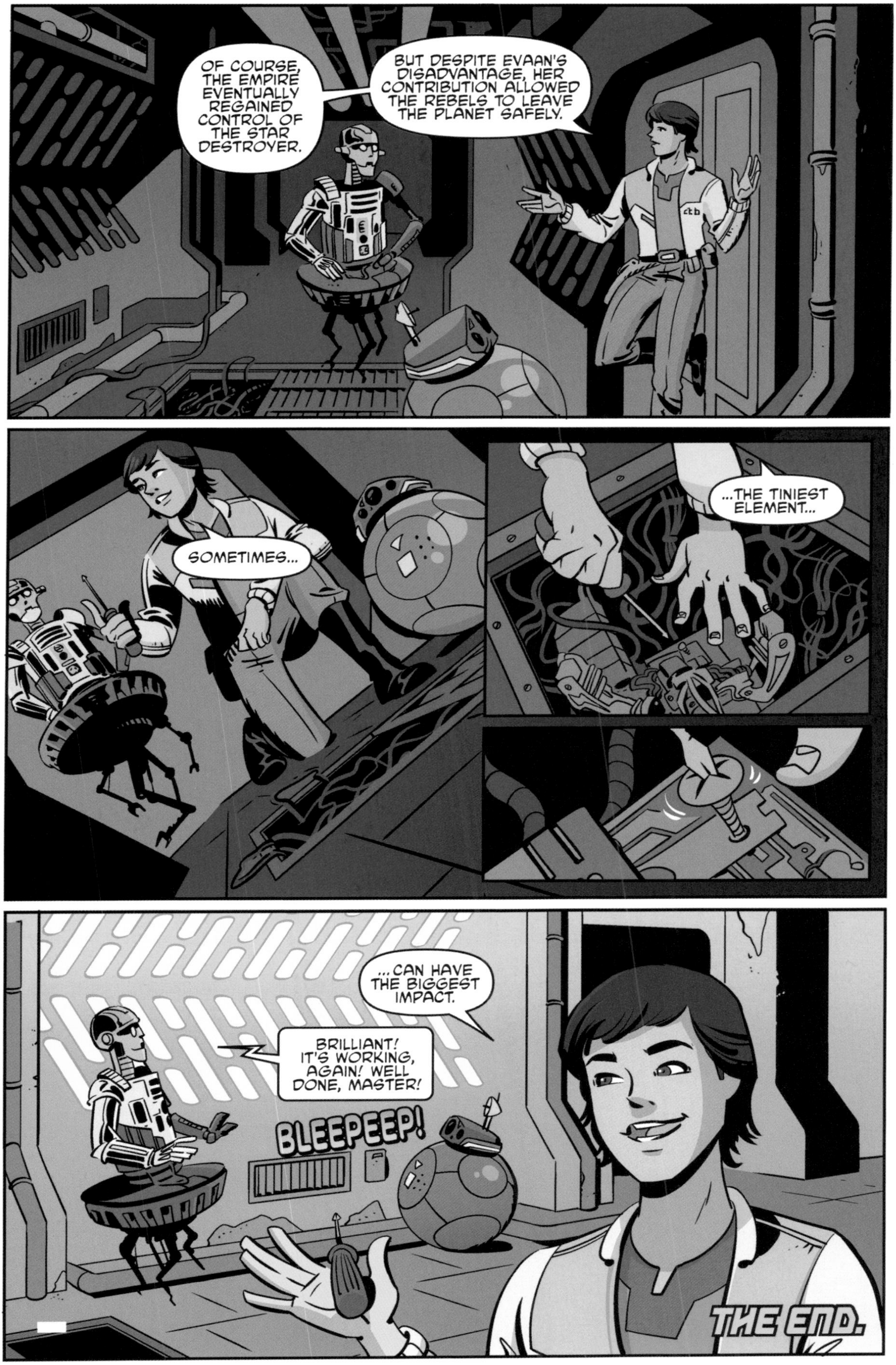
OF COURSE, THE EMPIRE EVENTUALLY REGAINED CONTROL OF THE STAR DESTROYER.
BUT DESPITE EVAAN'S DISADVANTAGE, HER CONTRIBUTION ALLOWED THE REBELS TO LEAVE THE PLANET SAFELY.
SOMETIMES...
...THE TINIEST ELEMENT...
...CAN HAVE THE BIGGEST IMPACT.
BRILLIANT! IT'S WORKING AGAIN! WELL DONE, MASTER!
BLEEPEEP!
THE END.

05
PEST CONTROL

Writer
LANDRY Q. WALKER

Artist
ERIC JONES

Letterer
TOM B. LONG

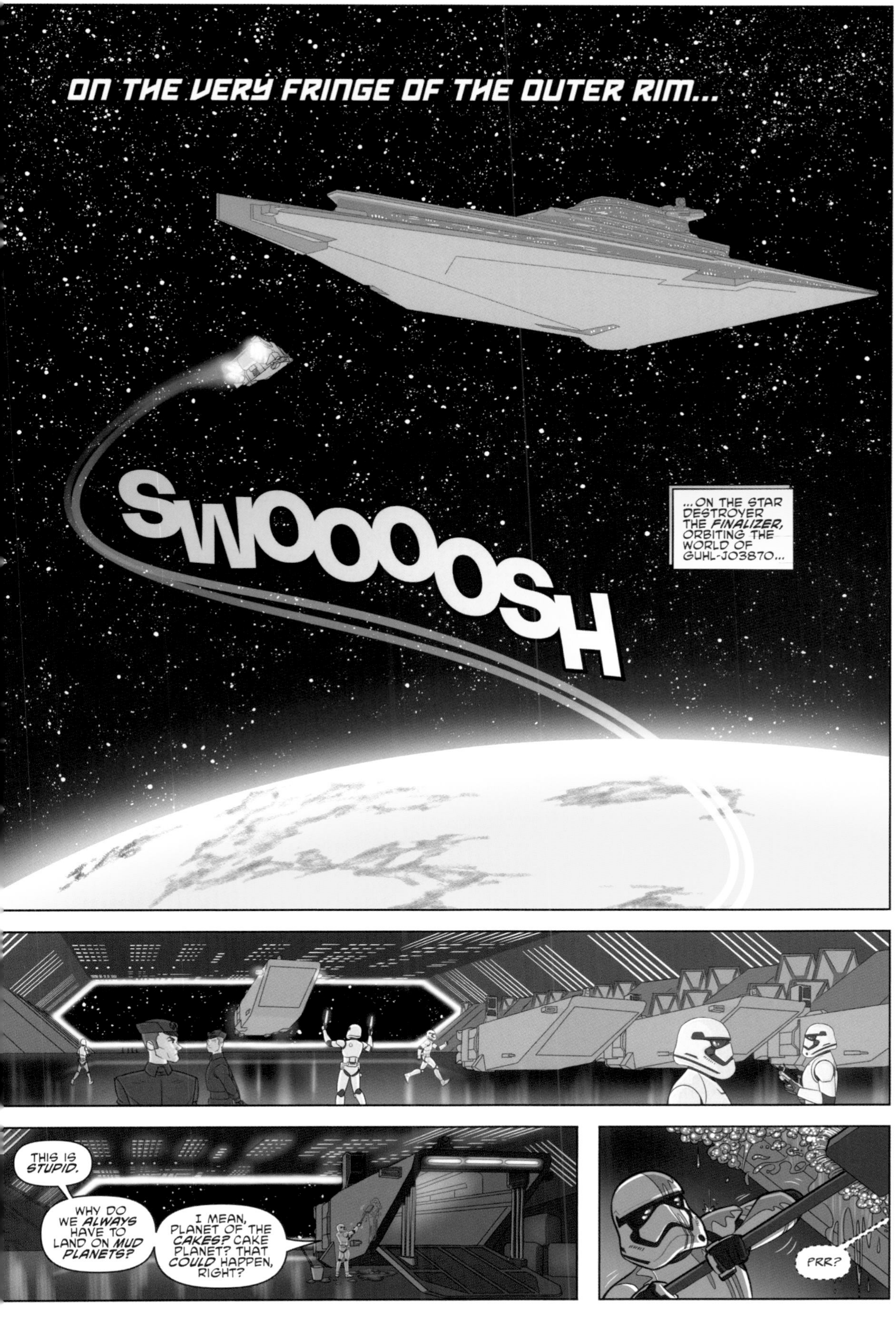

ON THE VERY FRINGE OF THE OUTER RIM...
SWOOOOSH
...ON THE STAR DESTROYER THE *FINALIZER,* ORBITING THE WORLD OF GUHL-JO3870...
THIS IS *STUPID.*
WHY DO WE *ALWAYS* HAVE TO LAND ON *MUD PLANETS?*
I MEAN, PLANET OF THE *CAKES?* CAKE PLANET? THAT *COULD* HAPPEN, RIGHT?
PRR?

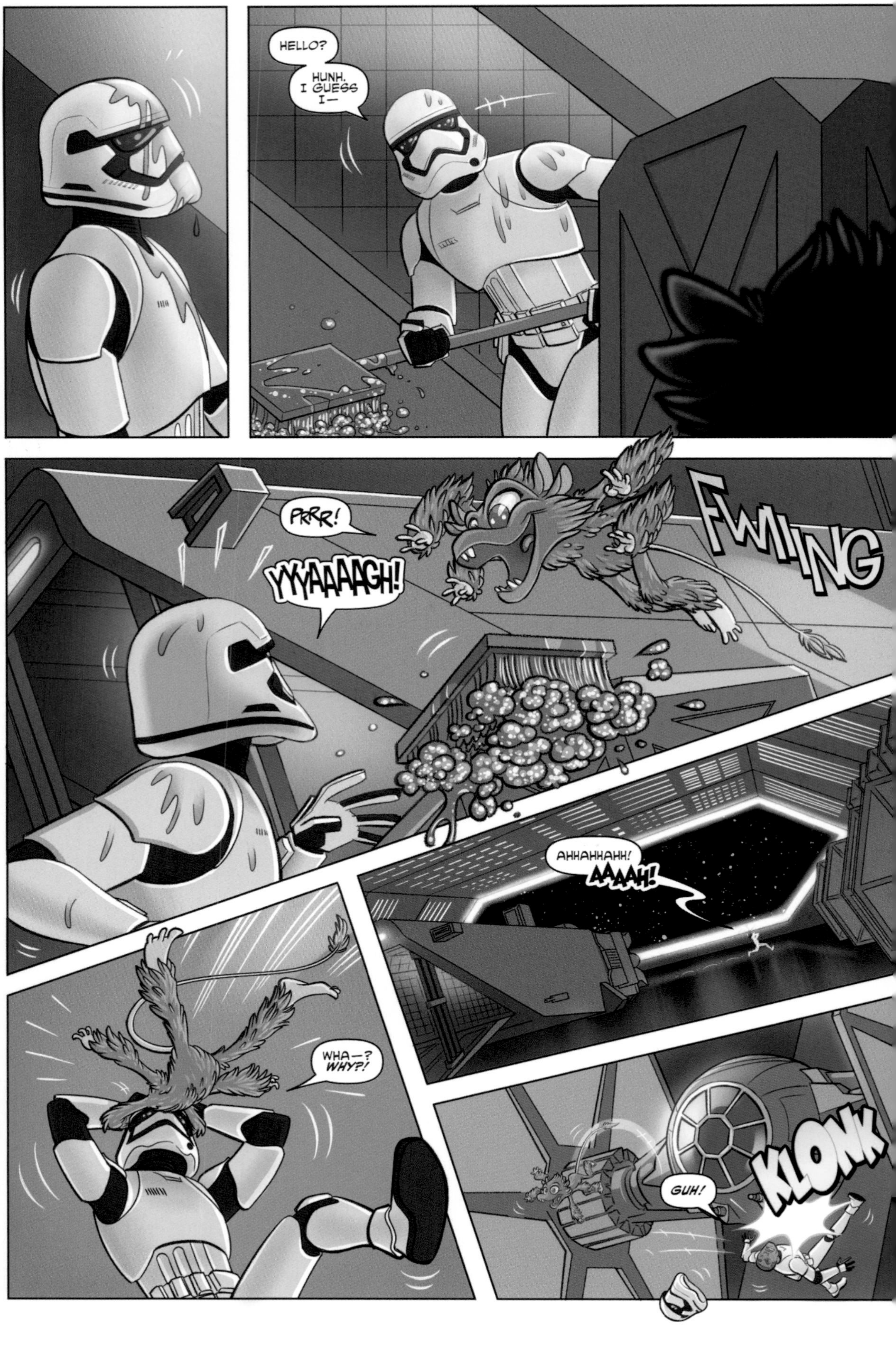
HELLO?
HUNH. I GUESS I—
PRRR!
YYYAAAAGH!
FWIIING
AHHAHHAHH! AAAAH!
WHA—? WHY?!
GUH!
KLONK

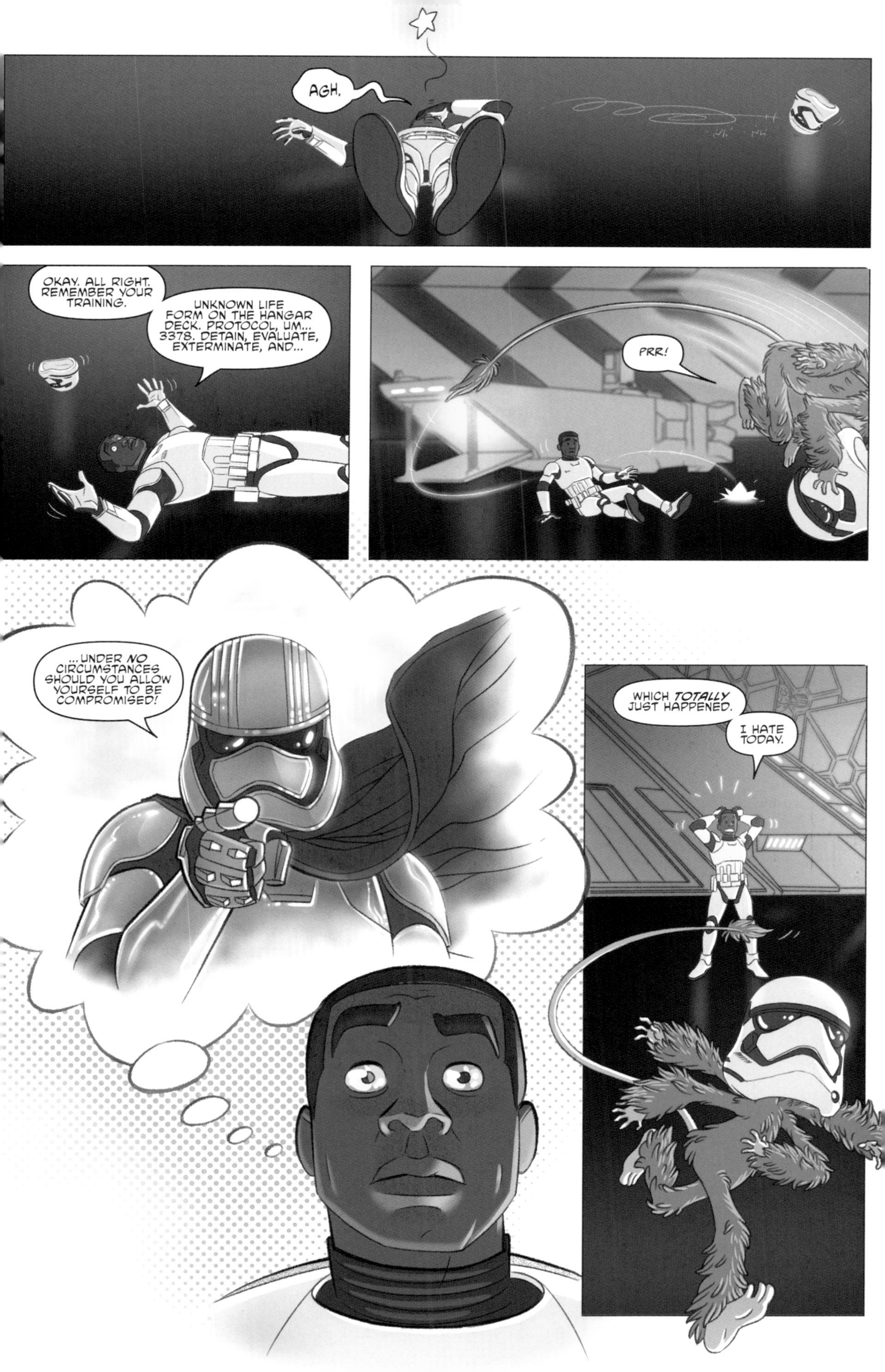
AGH.
OKAY. ALL RIGHT. REMEMBER YOUR TRAINING.
UNKNOWN LIFE FORM ON THE HANGAR DECK. PROTOCOL, UM... 3378. DETAIN, EVALUATE, EXTERMINATE, AND...
PRR!
...UNDER *NO* CIRCUMSTANCES SHOULD YOU ALLOW YOURSELF TO BE COMPROMISED!
WHICH *TOTALLY* JUST HAPPENED.
I HATE TODAY.

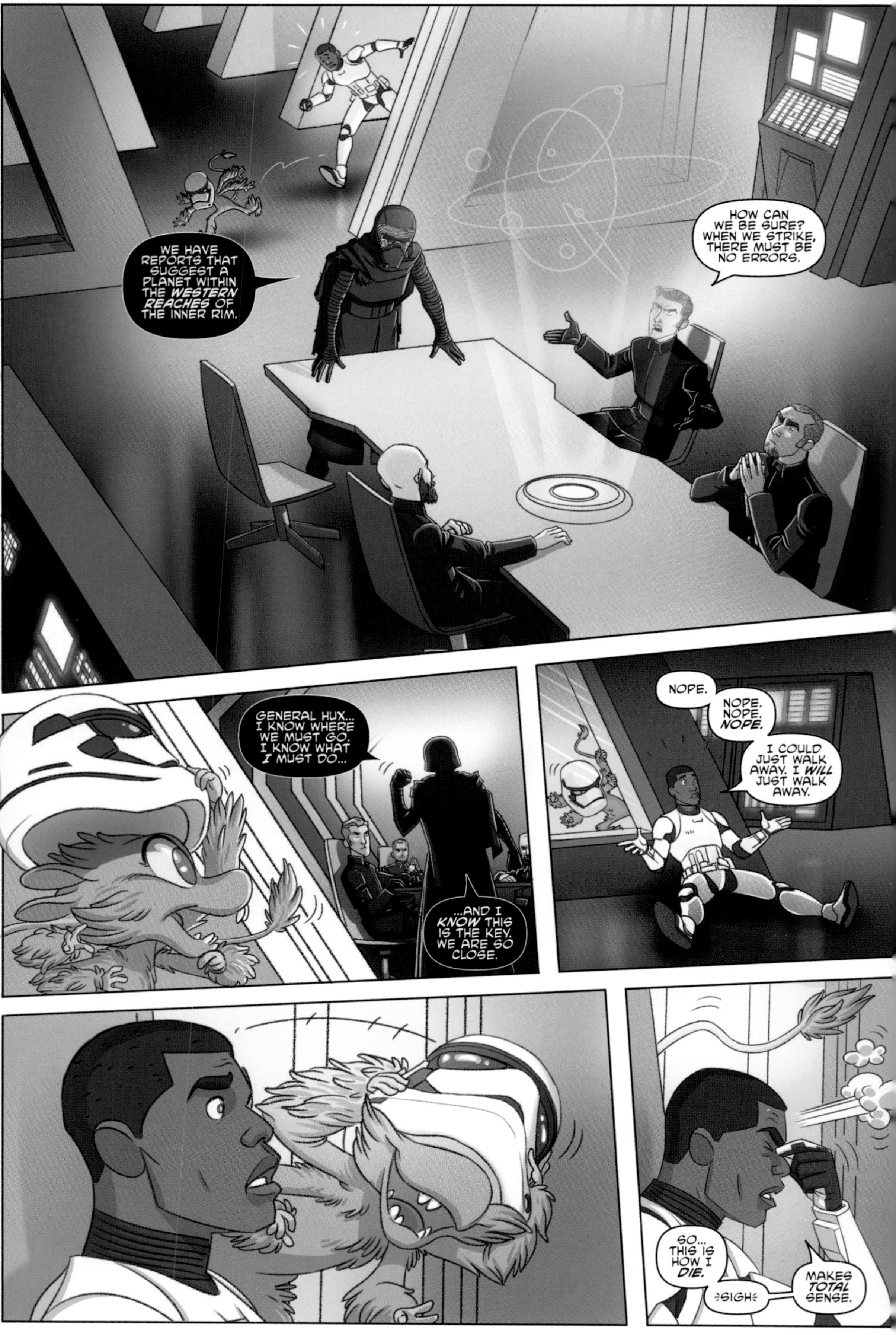
WE HAVE REPORTS THAT SUGGEST A PLANET WITHIN THE WESTERN REACHES OF THE INNER RIM.
HOW CAN WE BE SURE? WHEN WE STRIKE, THERE MUST BE NO ERRORS.
GENERAL HUX... I KNOW WHERE WE MUST GO. I KNOW WHAT I MUST DO...
...AND I KNOW THIS IS THE KEY. WE ARE SO CLOSE.
NOPE.
NOPE. NOPE. NOPE.
I COULD JUST WALK AWAY. I WILL JUST WALK AWAY.
SO... THIS IS HOW I DIE.
SIGH
MAKES TOTAL SENSE.

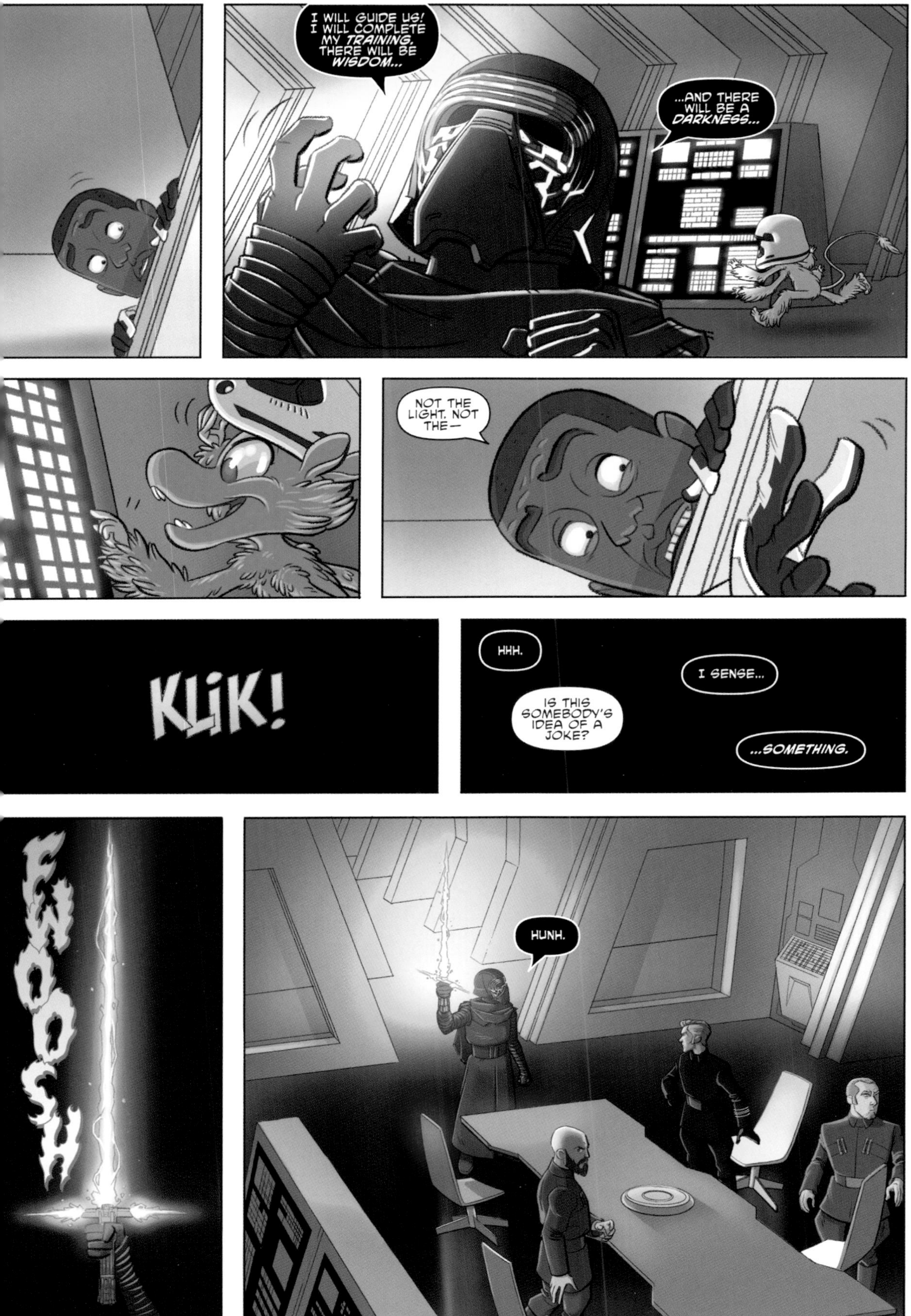
I WILL GUIDE US! I WILL COMPLETE MY TRAINING. THERE WILL BE WISDOM...
...AND THERE WILL BE A DARKNESS...
NOT THE LIGHT. NOT THE—
KLIK!
HHH.
I SENSE...
IS THIS SOMEBODY'S IDEA OF A JOKE?
...SOMETHING.
FWOOSH
HUNH.

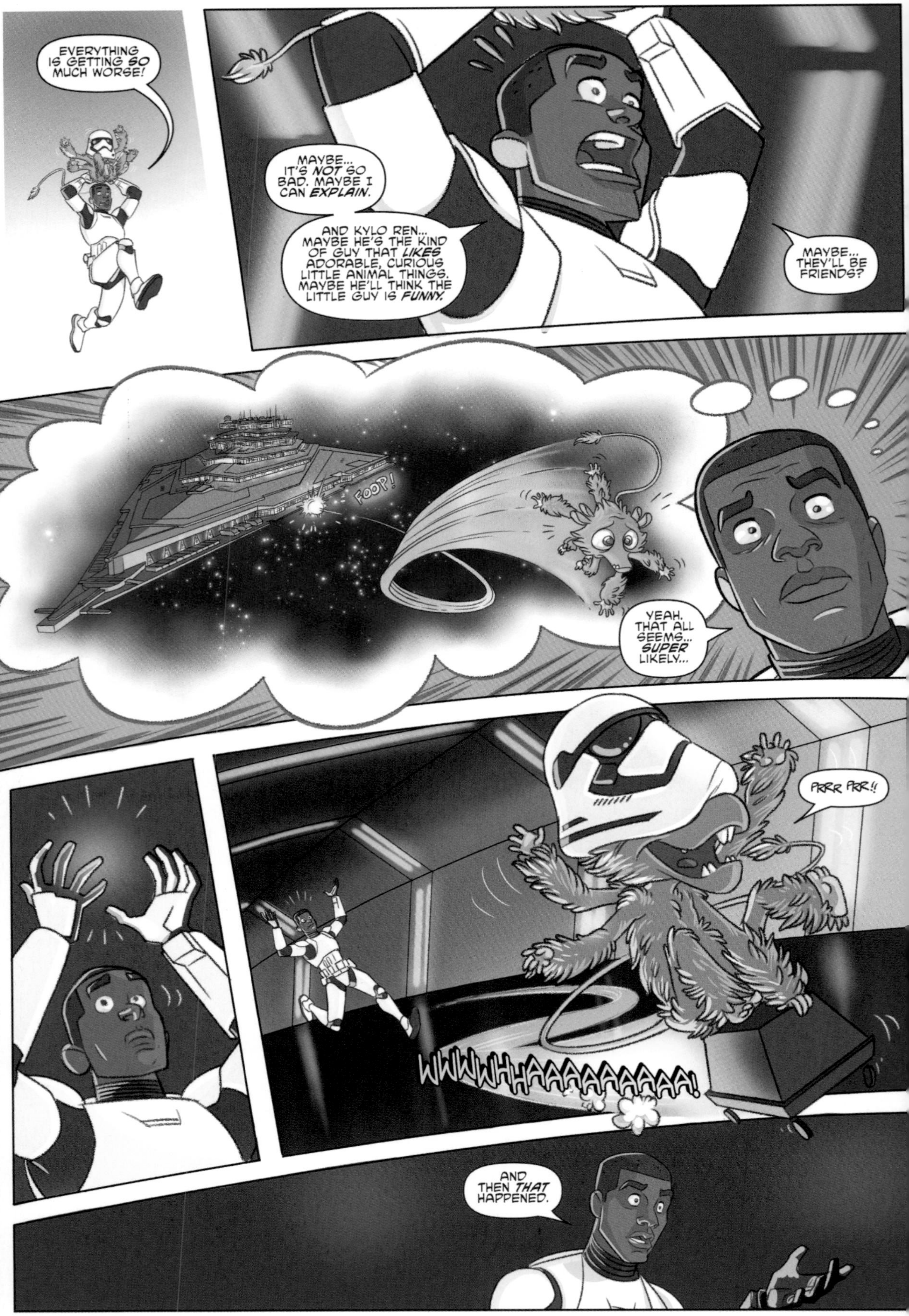
EVERYTHING IS GETTING SO MUCH WORSE!
MAYBE... IT'S NOT SO BAD. MAYBE I CAN EXPLAIN.
AND KYLO REN... MAYBE HE'S THE KIND OF GUY THAT LIKES ADORABLE, CURIOUS LITTLE ANIMAL THINGS. MAYBE HE'LL THINK THE LITTLE GUY IS FUNNY.
MAYBE... THEY'LL BE FRIENDS?
FOOP!
YEAH. THAT ALL SEEMS... SUPER LIKELY...
PRRR PRR!!
WWWWHHAAAAAAAAAA!
AND THEN THAT HAPPENED.

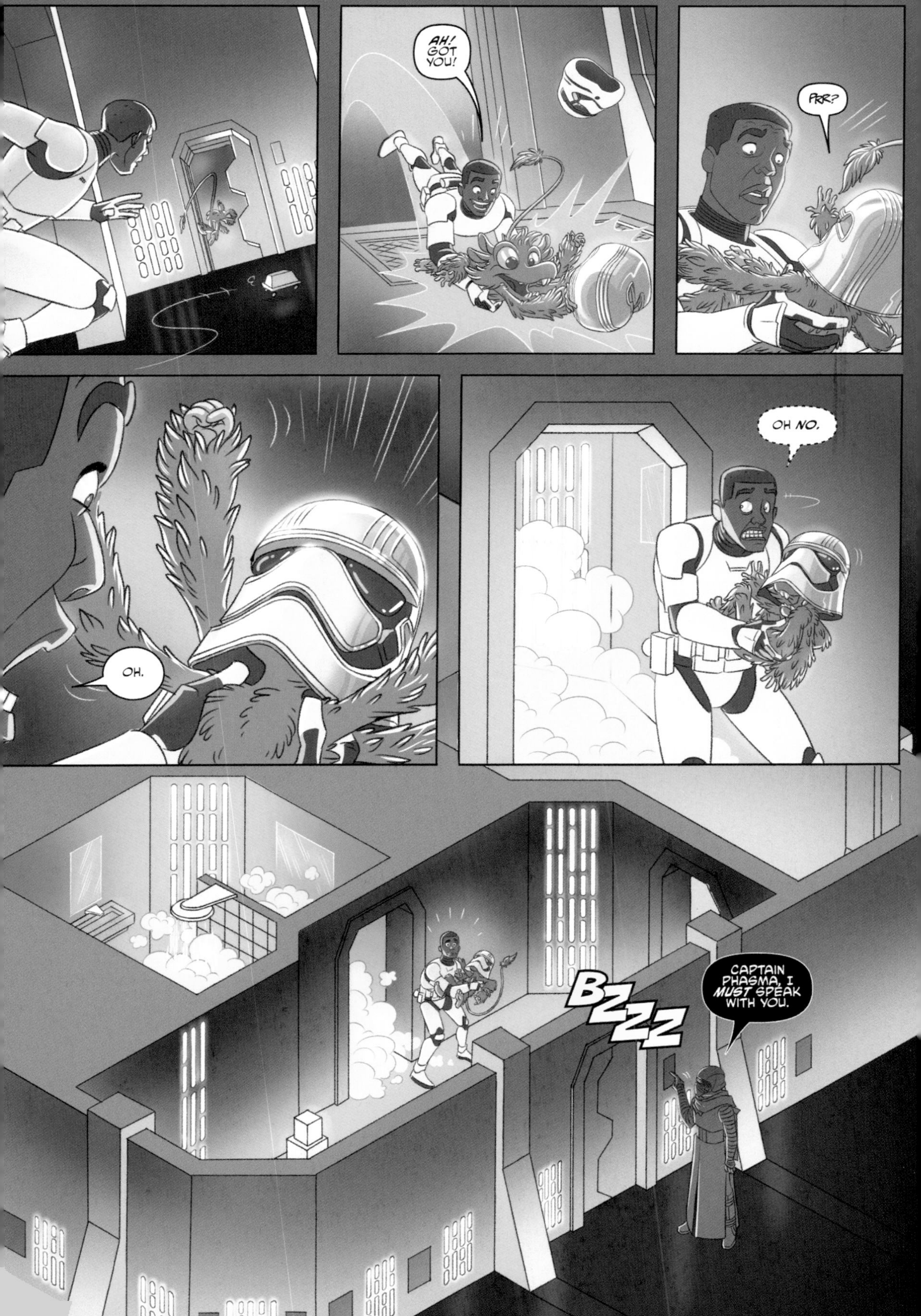
AH! GOT YOU!
PRR?
OH.
OH NO.
CAPTAIN PHASMA, I MUST SPEAK WITH YOU.
BZZZ

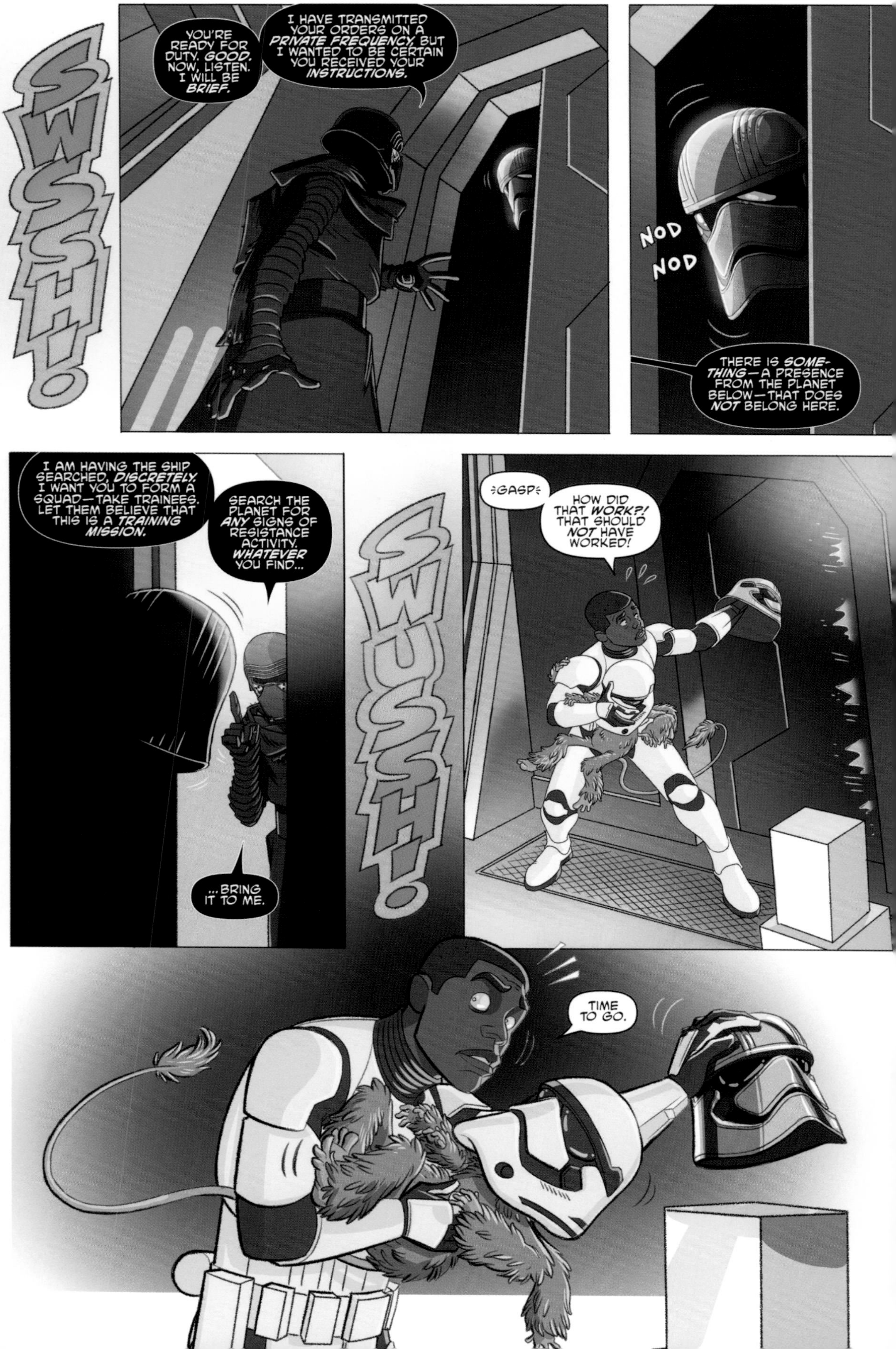
SWSSH!
YOU'RE READY FOR DUTY. GOOD. NOW, LISTEN. I WILL BE BRIEF.
I HAVE TRANSMITTED YOUR ORDERS ON A PRIVATE FREQUENCY, BUT I WANTED TO BE CERTAIN YOU RECEIVED YOUR INSTRUCTIONS.
NOD NOD
THERE IS SOME-THING—A PRESENCE FROM THE PLANET BELOW—THAT DOES NOT BELONG HERE.
I AM HAVING THE SHIP SEARCHED, DISCRETELY. I WANT YOU TO FORM A SQUAD—TAKE TRAINEES. LET THEM BELIEVE THAT THIS IS A TRAINING MISSION.
SEARCH THE PLANET FOR ANY SIGNS OF RESISTANCE ACTIVITY. WHATEVER YOU FIND...
...BRING IT TO ME.
SWUSSH!
GASP
HOW DID THAT WORK?! THAT SHOULD NOT HAVE WORKED!
TIME TO GO.

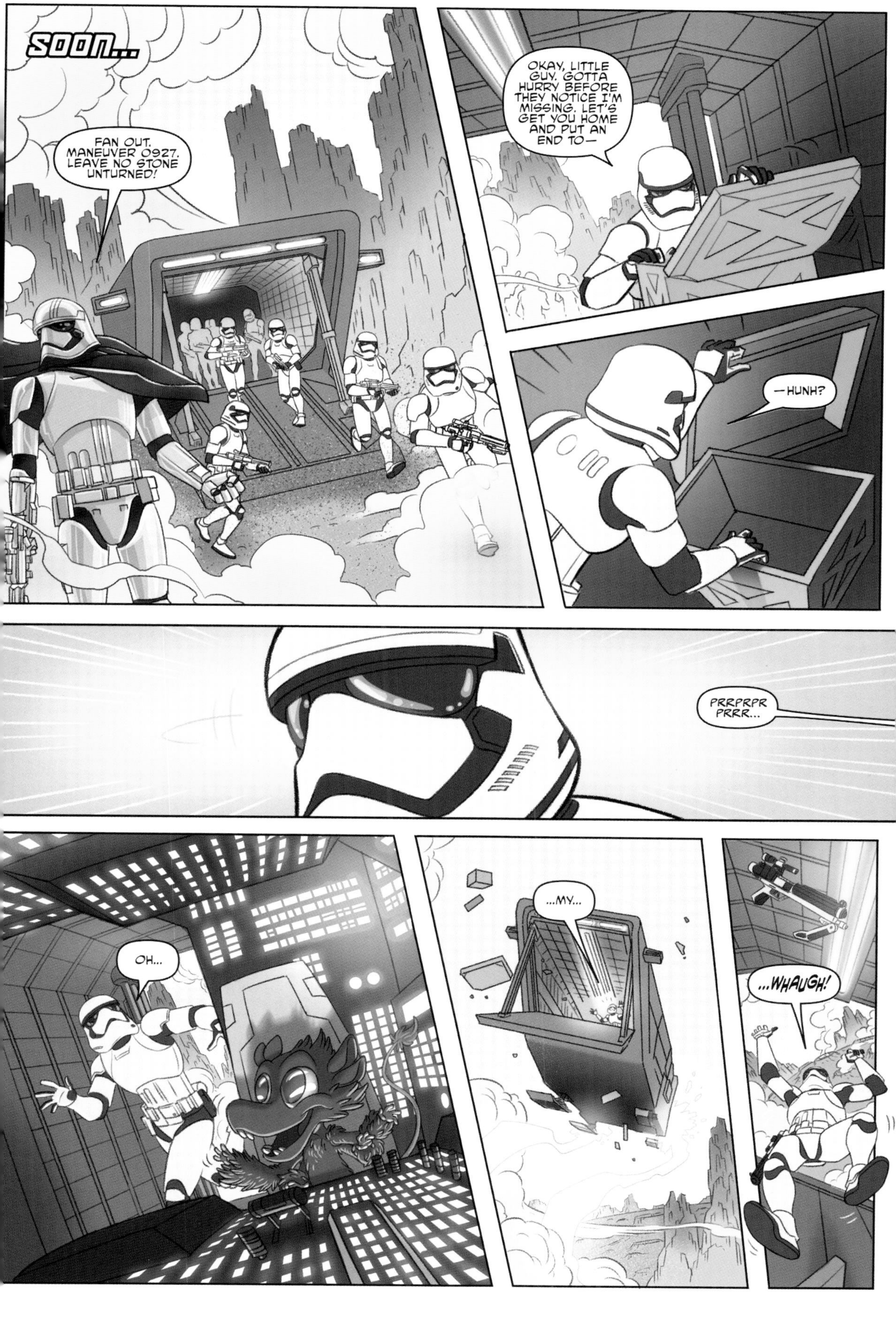
SOON...
FAN OUT. MANEUVER 0927. LEAVE NO STONE UNTURNED!
OKAY, LITTLE GUY. GOTTA HURRY BEFORE THEY NOTICE I'M MISSING. LET'S GET YOU HOME AND PUT AN END TO—
—HUNH?
PRRPRPR PRRR...
OH...
...MY...
...WHAUGH!

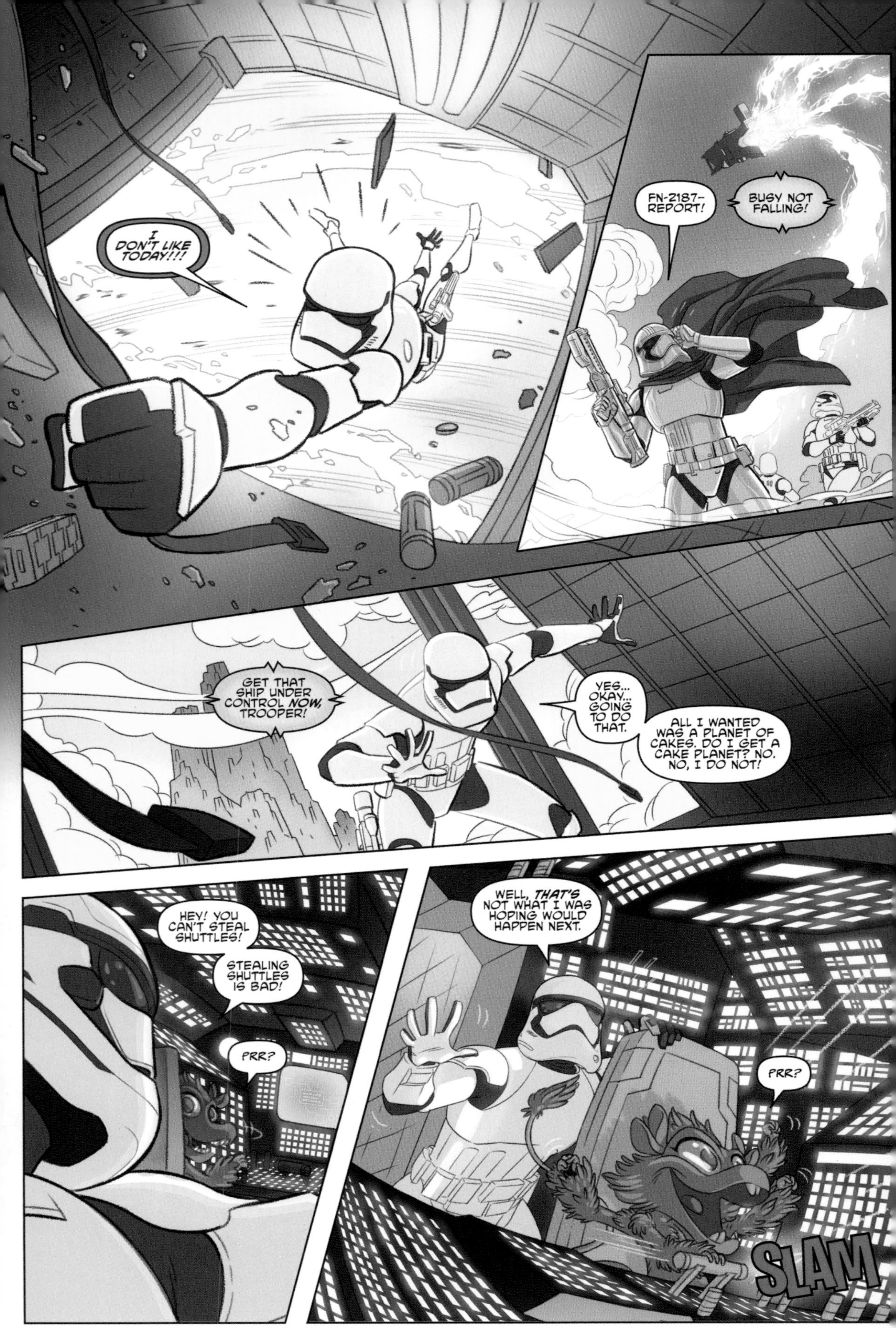
I DON'T LIKE TODAY!!!
FN-2187– REPORT!
BUSY NOT FALLING!
GET THAT SHIP UNDER CONTROL NOW, TROOPER!
YES... OKAY... GOING TO DO THAT.
ALL I WANTED WAS A PLANET OF CAKES. DO I GET A CAKE PLANET? NO. NO, I DO NOT!
HEY! YOU CAN'T STEAL SHUTTLES!
STEALING SHUTTLES IS BAD!
PRR?
WELL, THAT'S NOT WHAT I WAS HOPING WOULD HAPPEN NEXT.
PRR?
SLAM

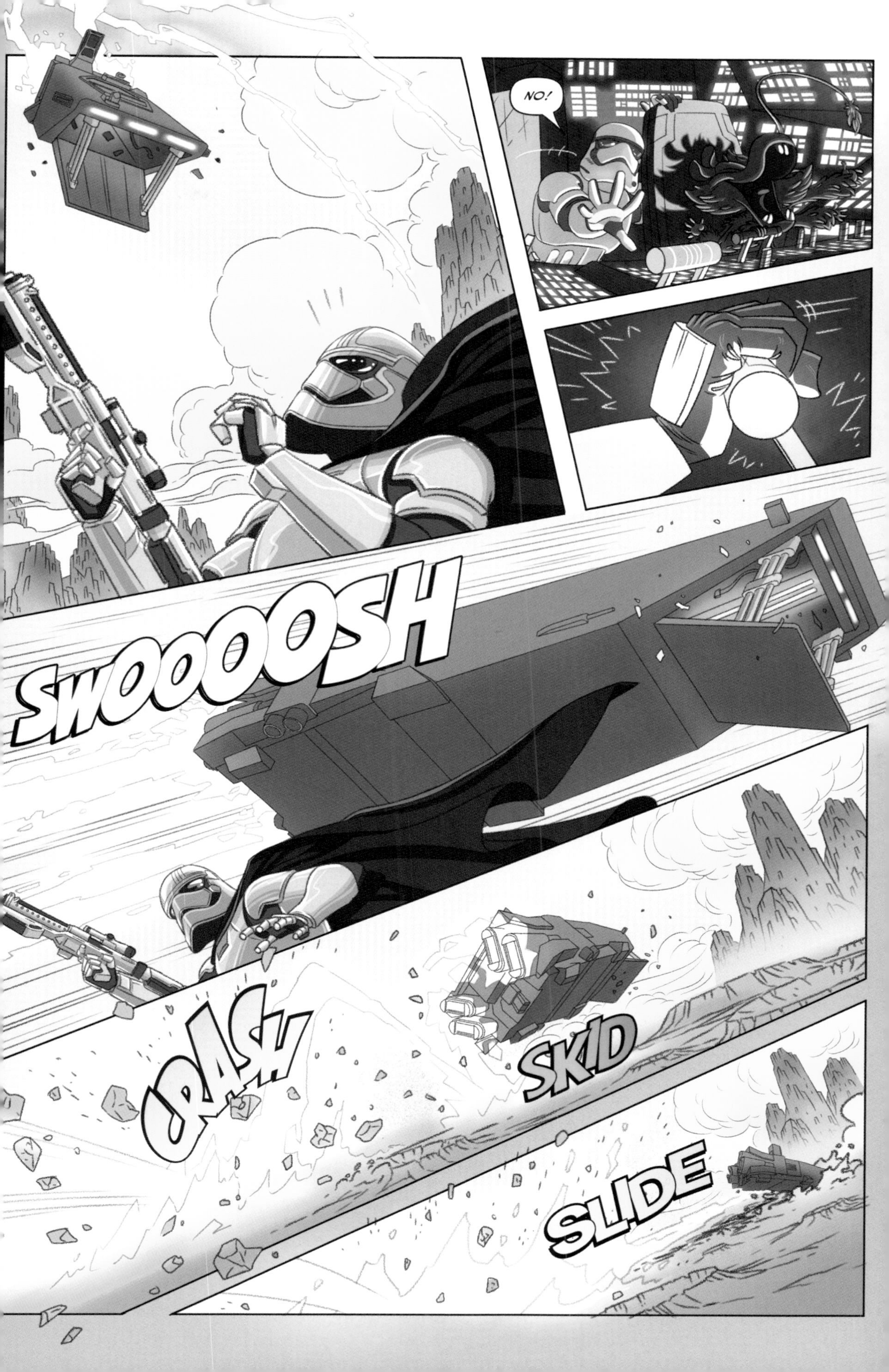
NO!
SWOOOOSH
CRASH
SKID
SLIDE

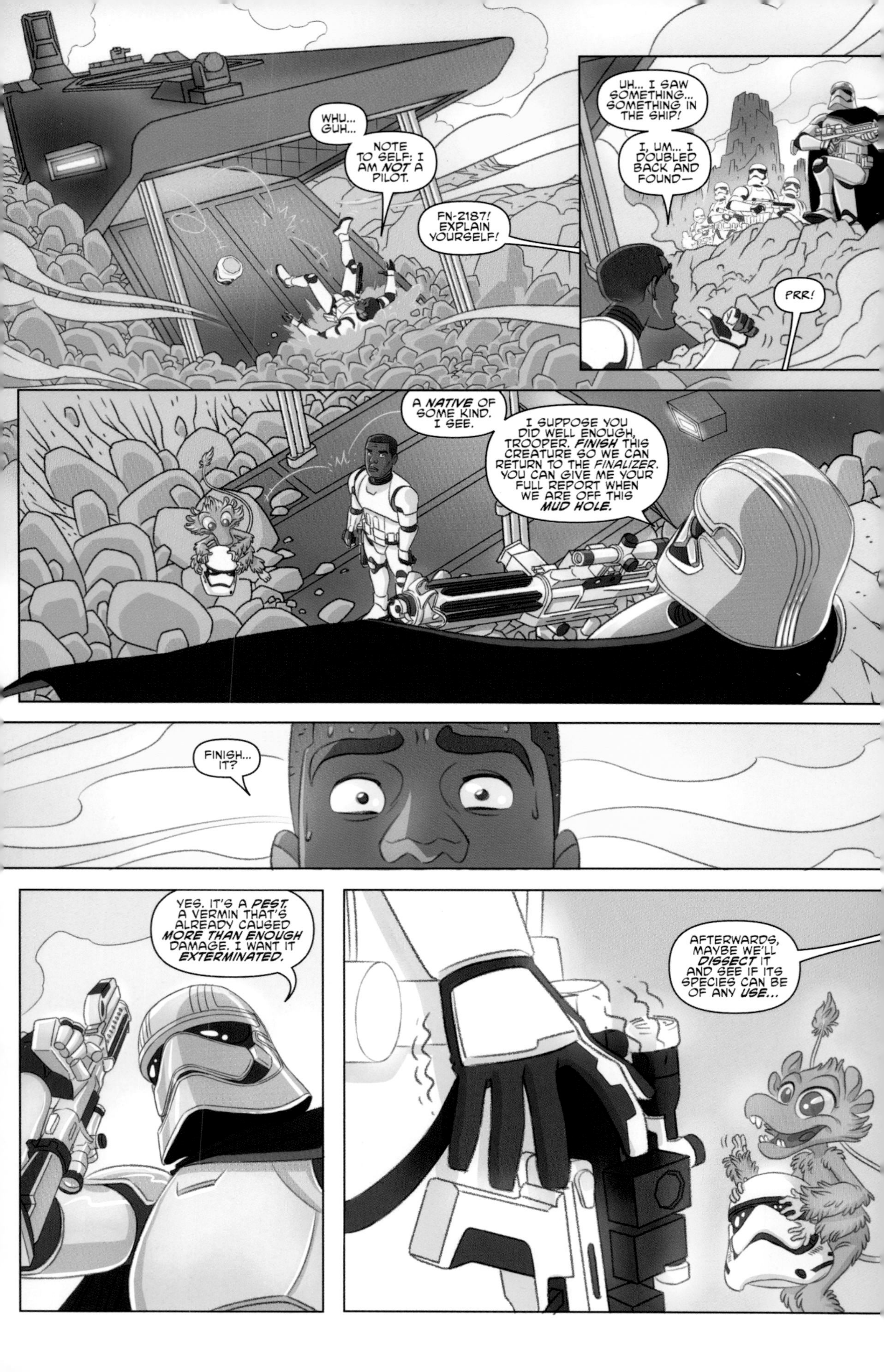
WHU... GUH...
NOTE TO SELF: I AM NOT A PILOT.
FN-2187! EXPLAIN YOURSELF!
UH... I SAW SOMETHING... SOMETHING IN THE SHIP!
I, UM... I DOUBLED BACK AND FOUND—
PRR!
A NATIVE OF SOME KIND. I SEE.
I SUPPOSE YOU DID WELL ENOUGH, TROOPER. FINISH THIS CREATURE SO WE CAN RETURN TO THE FINALIZER. YOU CAN GIVE ME YOUR FULL REPORT WHEN WE ARE OFF THIS MUD HOLE.
FINISH... IT?
YES. IT'S A PEST. A VERMIN THAT'S ALREADY CAUSED MORE THAN ENOUGH DAMAGE. I WANT IT EXTERMINATED.
AFTERWARDS, MAYBE WE'LL DISSECT IT AND SEE IF ITS SPECIES CAN BE OF ANY USE...

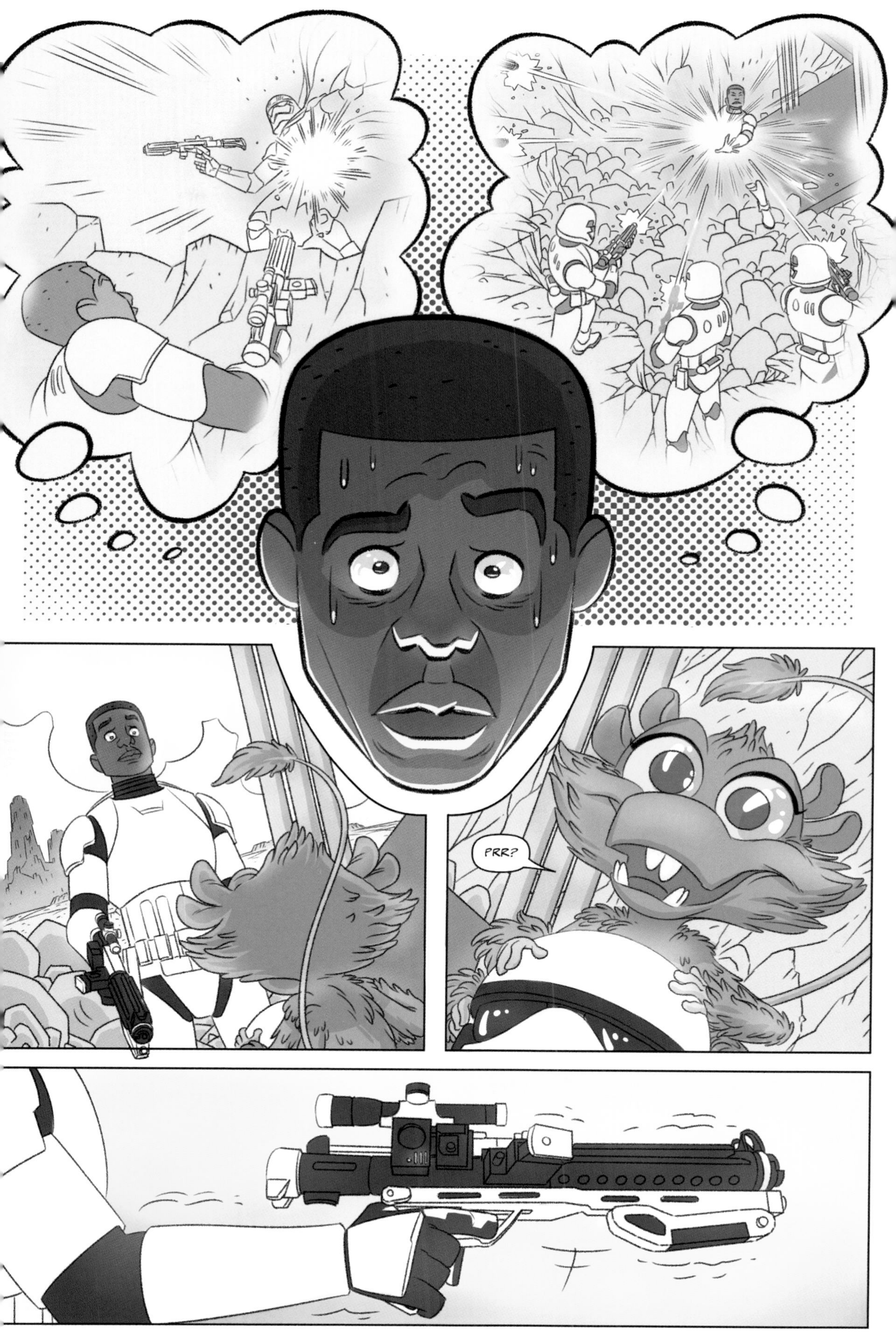
PRR?

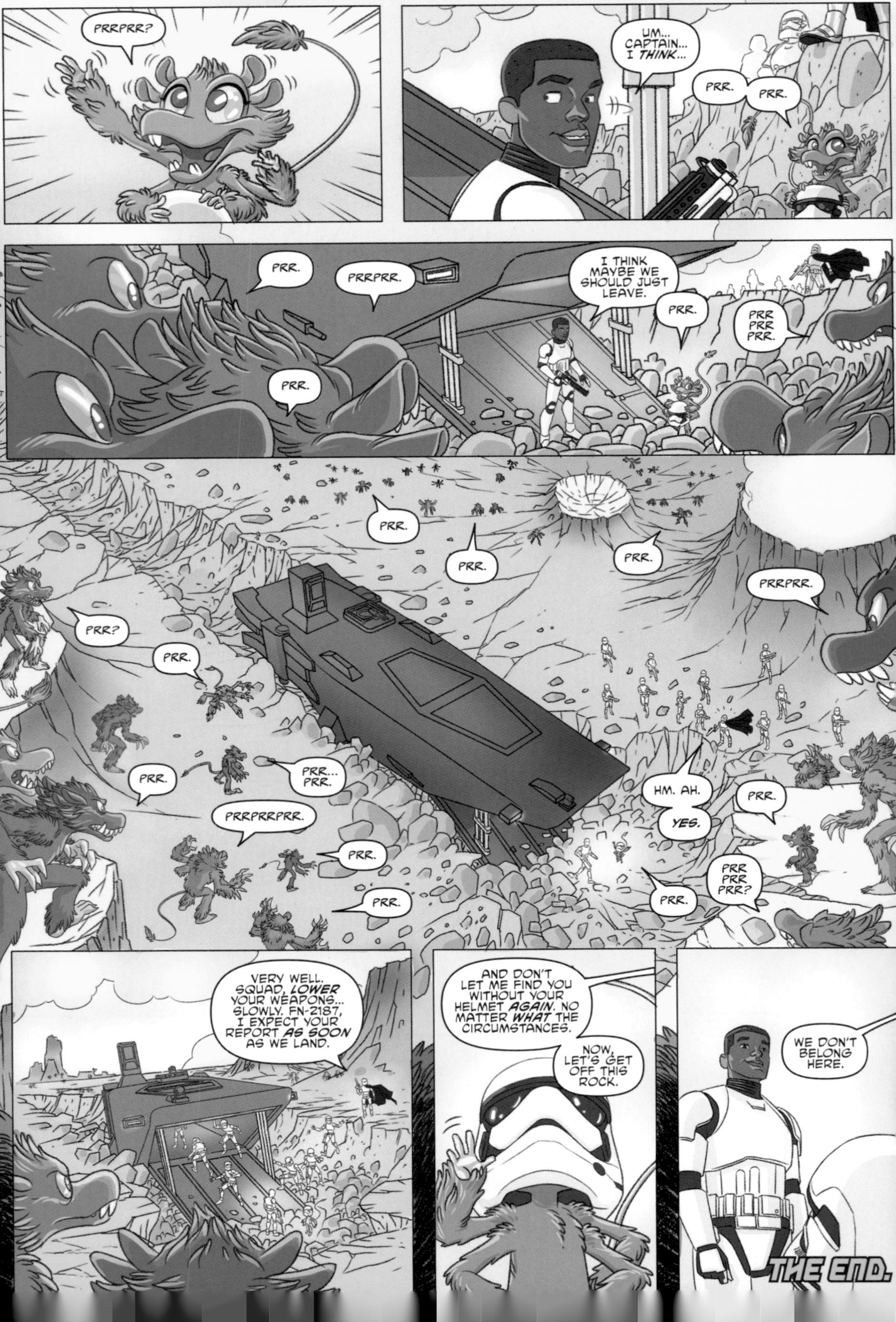
PRRPRR?
UM... CAPTAIN... I *THINK*...
PRR.
PRR.
PRR.
PRRPRR.
PRR.
I THINK MAYBE WE SHOULD JUST LEAVE.
PRR.
PRR PRR PRR.
PRR.
PRR.
PRR.
PRRPRR.
PRR?
PRR.
PRR.
PRR... PRR.
PRRPRRPRR.
PRR.
PRR.
HM. AH. *YES.*
PRR.
PRR.
PRR PRR PRR?
VERY WELL. SQUAD, *LOWER* YOUR WEAPONS... SLOWLY. FN-2187, I EXPECT YOUR REPORT *AS SOON* AS WE LAND.
AND DON'T LET ME FIND YOU WITHOUT YOUR HELMET *AGAIN*. NO MATTER *WHAT* THE CIRCUMSTANCES.
NOW, LET'S GET OFF THIS ROCK.
WE DON'T BELONG HERE.
THE END.

06
THE TROUBLE
AT TIBRIN

Writer
LANDRY Q. WALKER

Artist
ERIC JONES

Colorist
CHARLIE KIRCHOFF

Letterers
TOM B. LONG &
CHRISTA MIESNER

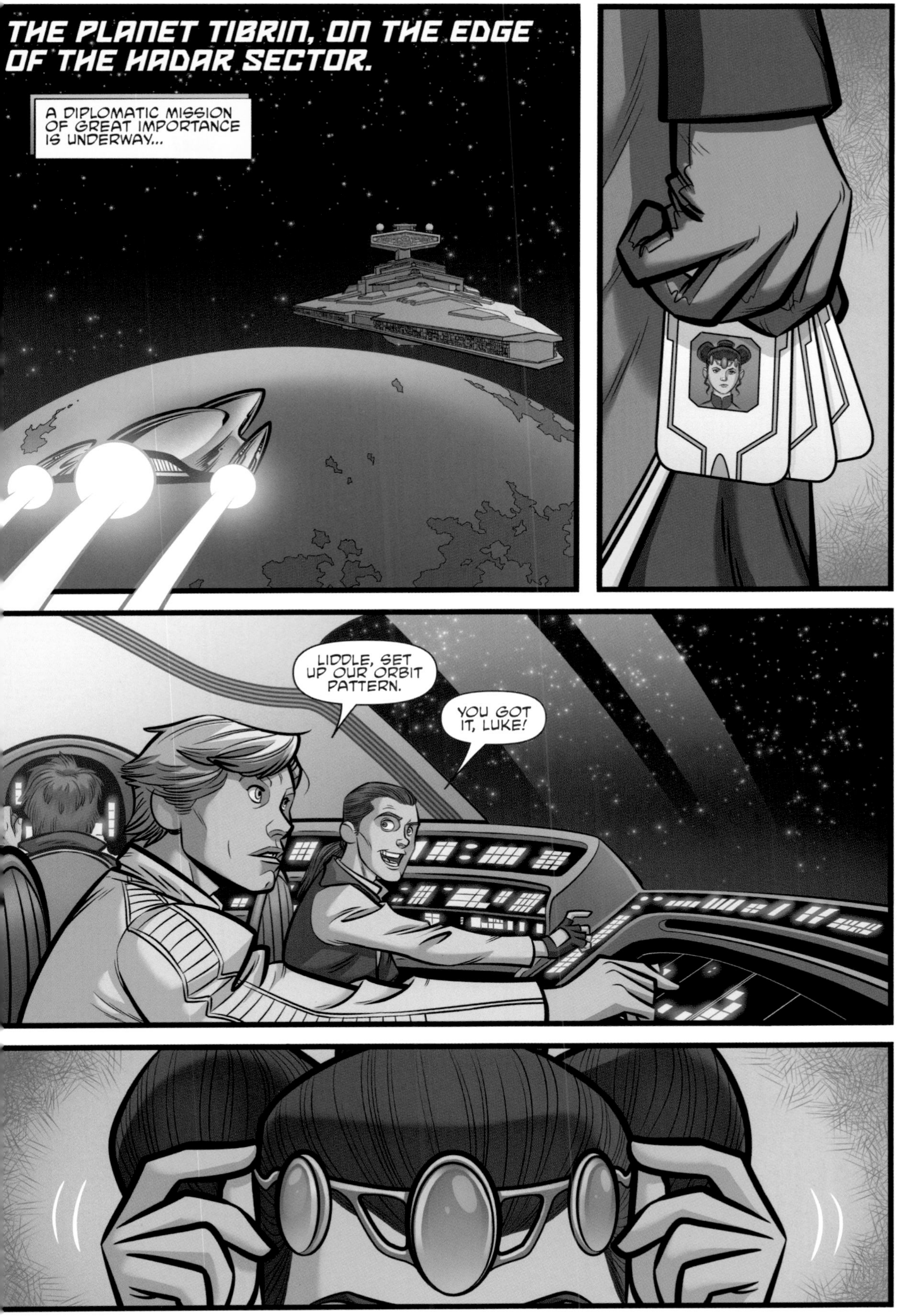
THE PLANET TIBRIN, ON THE EDGE OF THE HADAR SECTOR.
A DIPLOMATIC MISSION OF GREAT IMPORTANCE IS UNDERWAY...
LIDDLE, SET UP OUR ORBIT PATTERN.
YOU GOT IT, LUKE!

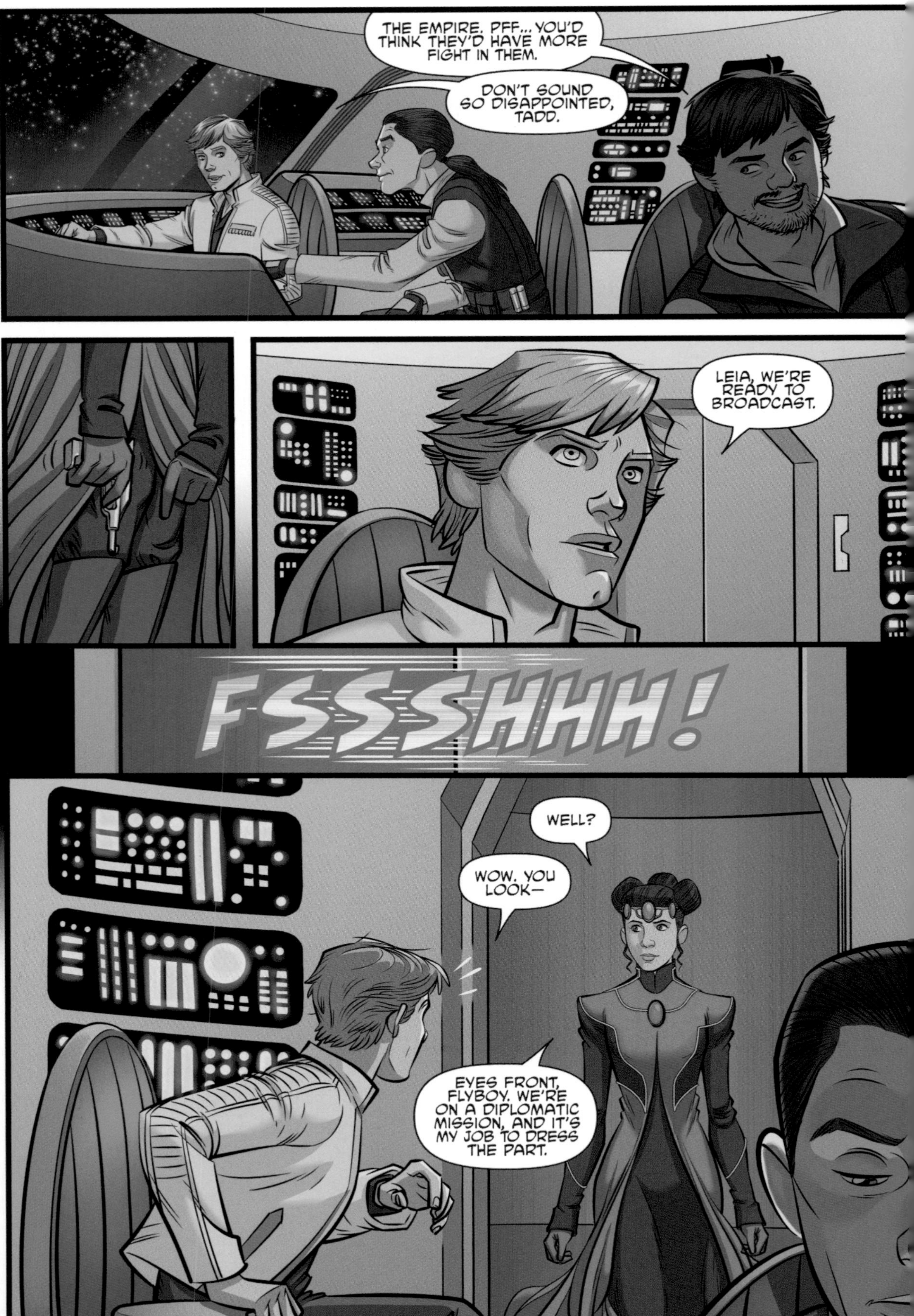
THE EMPIRE. PFF... YOU'D THINK THEY'D HAVE MORE FIGHT IN THEM.
DON'T SOUND SO DISAPPOINTED, TADD.
LEIA, WE'RE READY TO BROADCAST.
FSSSHHH!
WELL?
WOW. YOU LOOK—
EYES FRONT, FLYBOY. WE'RE ON A DIPLOMATIC MISSION, AND IT'S MY JOB TO DRESS THE PART.

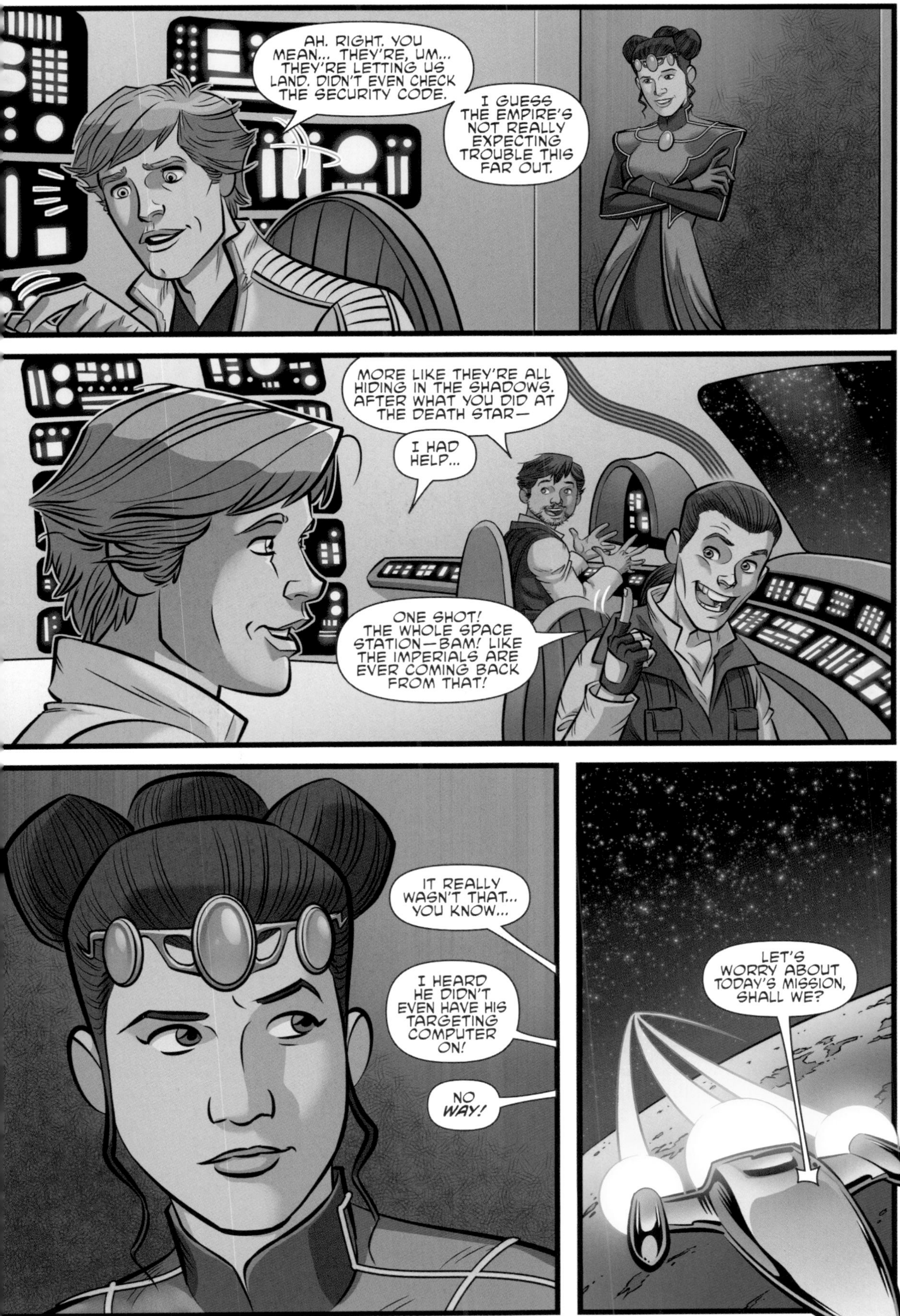
AH. RIGHT. YOU MEAN... THEY'RE, UM... THEY'RE LETTING US LAND. DIDN'T EVEN CHECK THE SECURITY CODE.
I GUESS THE EMPIRE'S NOT REALLY EXPECTING TROUBLE THIS FAR OUT.
MORE LIKE THEY'RE ALL HIDING IN THE SHADOWS. AFTER WHAT YOU DID AT THE DEATH STAR—
I HAD HELP...
ONE SHOT! THE WHOLE SPACE STATION—BAM! LIKE THE IMPERIALS ARE EVER COMING BACK FROM THAT!
IT REALLY WASN'T THAT... YOU KNOW...
I HEARD HE DIDN'T EVEN HAVE HIS TARGETING COMPUTER ON!
NO *WAY!*
LET'S WORRY ABOUT TODAY'S MISSION, SHALL WE?

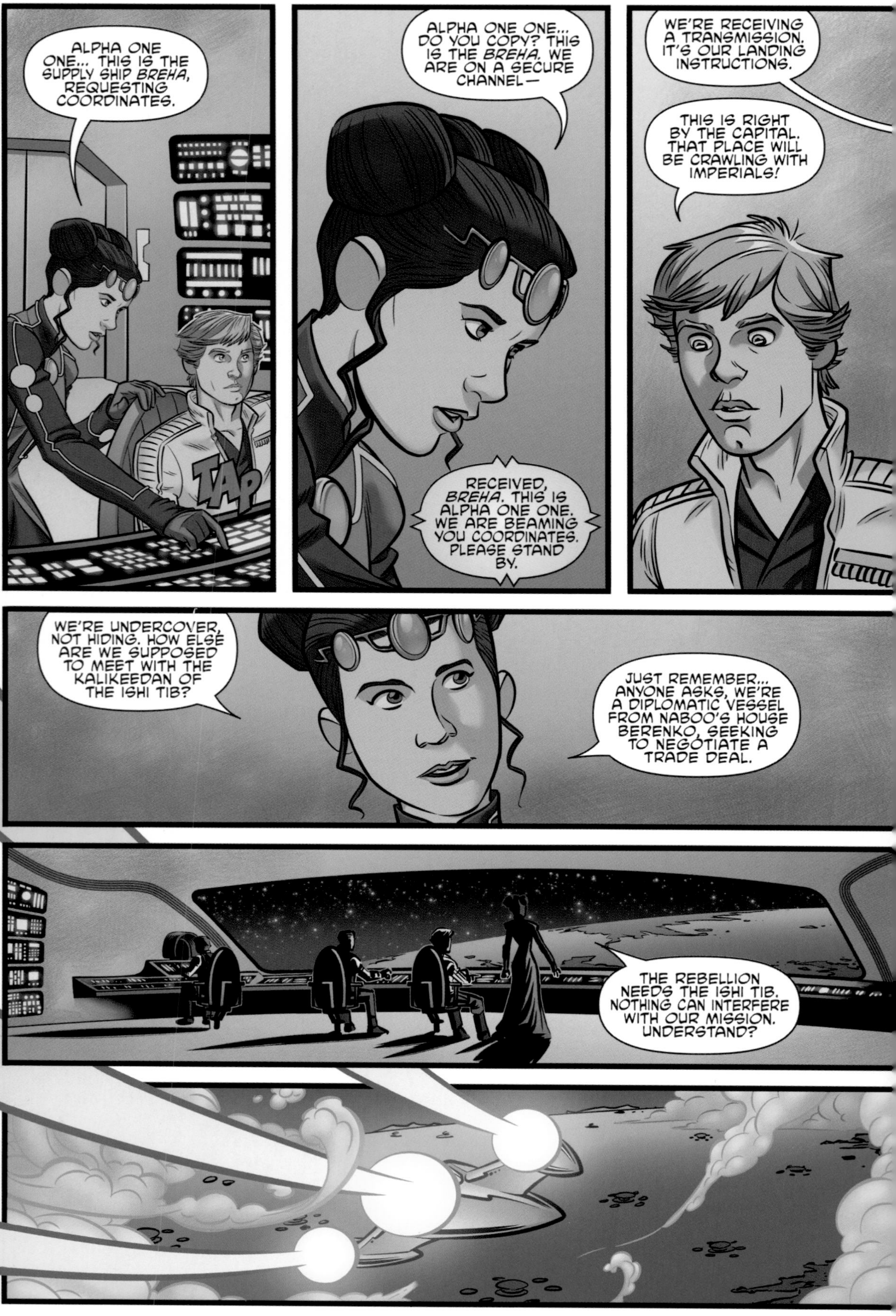
ALPHA ONE ONE... THIS IS THE SUPPLY SHIP *BREHA*, REQUESTING COORDINATES.
TAP
ALPHA ONE ONE... DO YOU COPY? THIS IS THE *BREHA*. WE ARE ON A SECURE CHANNEL—
RECEIVED, *BREHA*. THIS IS ALPHA ONE ONE. WE ARE BEAMING YOU COORDINATES. PLEASE STAND BY.
WE'RE RECEIVING A TRANSMISSION. IT'S OUR LANDING INSTRUCTIONS.
THIS IS RIGHT BY THE CAPITAL. THAT PLACE WILL BE CRAWLING WITH IMPERIALS!
WE'RE UNDERCOVER, NOT HIDING. HOW ELSE ARE WE SUPPOSED TO MEET WITH THE KALIKEEDAN OF THE ISHI TIB?
JUST REMEMBER... ANYONE ASKS, WE'RE A DIPLOMATIC VESSEL FROM NABOO'S HOUSE BERENKO, SEEKING TO NEGOTIATE A TRADE DEAL.
THE REBELLION NEEDS THE ISHI TIB. NOTHING CAN INTERFERE WITH OUR MISSION. UNDERSTAND?

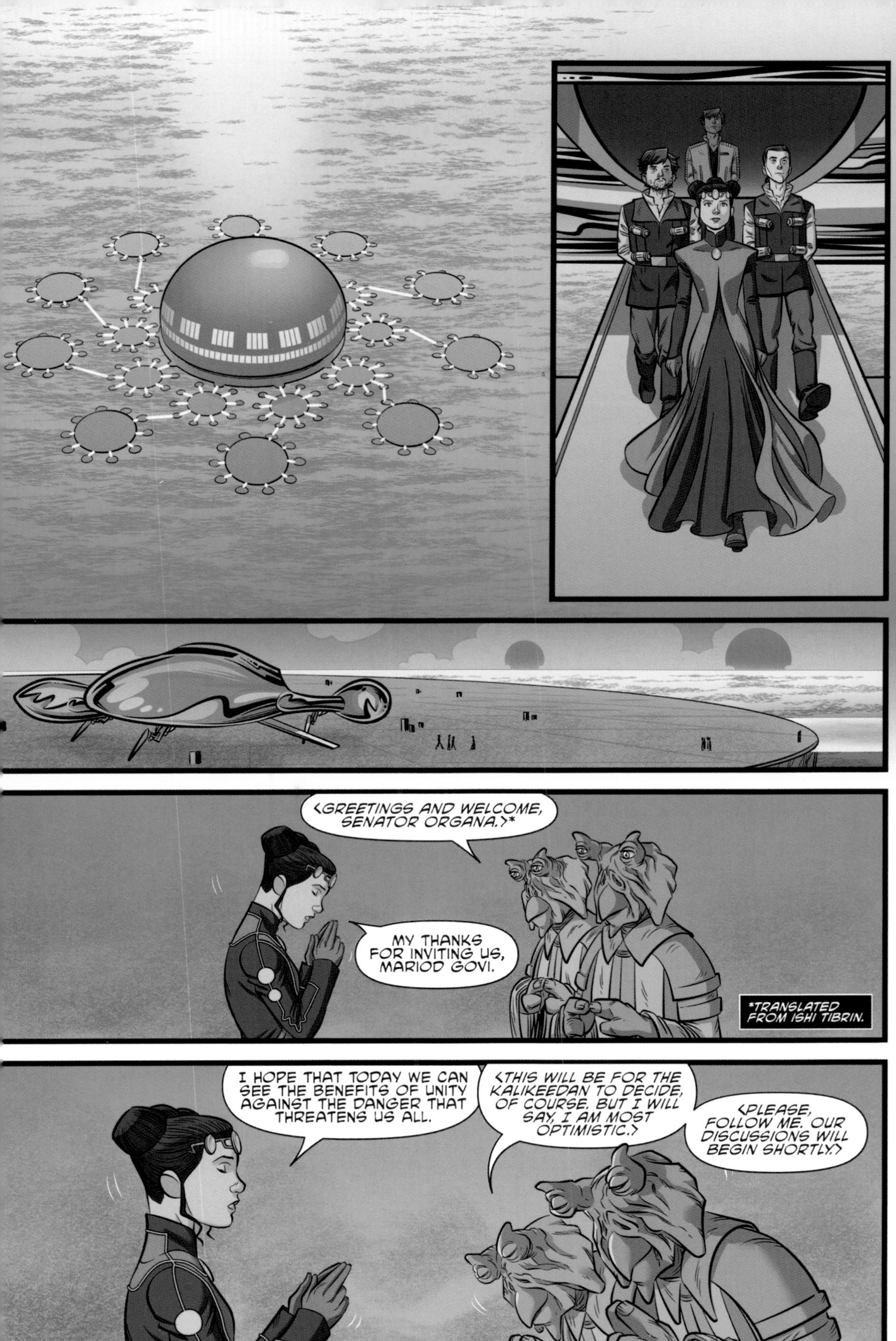
<GREETINGS AND WELCOME, SENATOR ORGANA.>*
MY THANKS FOR INVITING US, MARIOD GOVI.
*TRANSLATED FROM ISHI TIBRIN.
I HOPE THAT TODAY WE CAN SEE THE BENEFITS OF UNITY AGAINST THE DANGER THAT THREATENS US ALL.
<THIS WILL BE FOR THE KALIKEEDAN TO DECIDE, OF COURSE. BUT I WILL SAY, I AM MOST OPTIMISTIC.>
<PLEASE, FOLLOW ME. OUR DISCUSSIONS WILL BEGIN SHORTLY.>

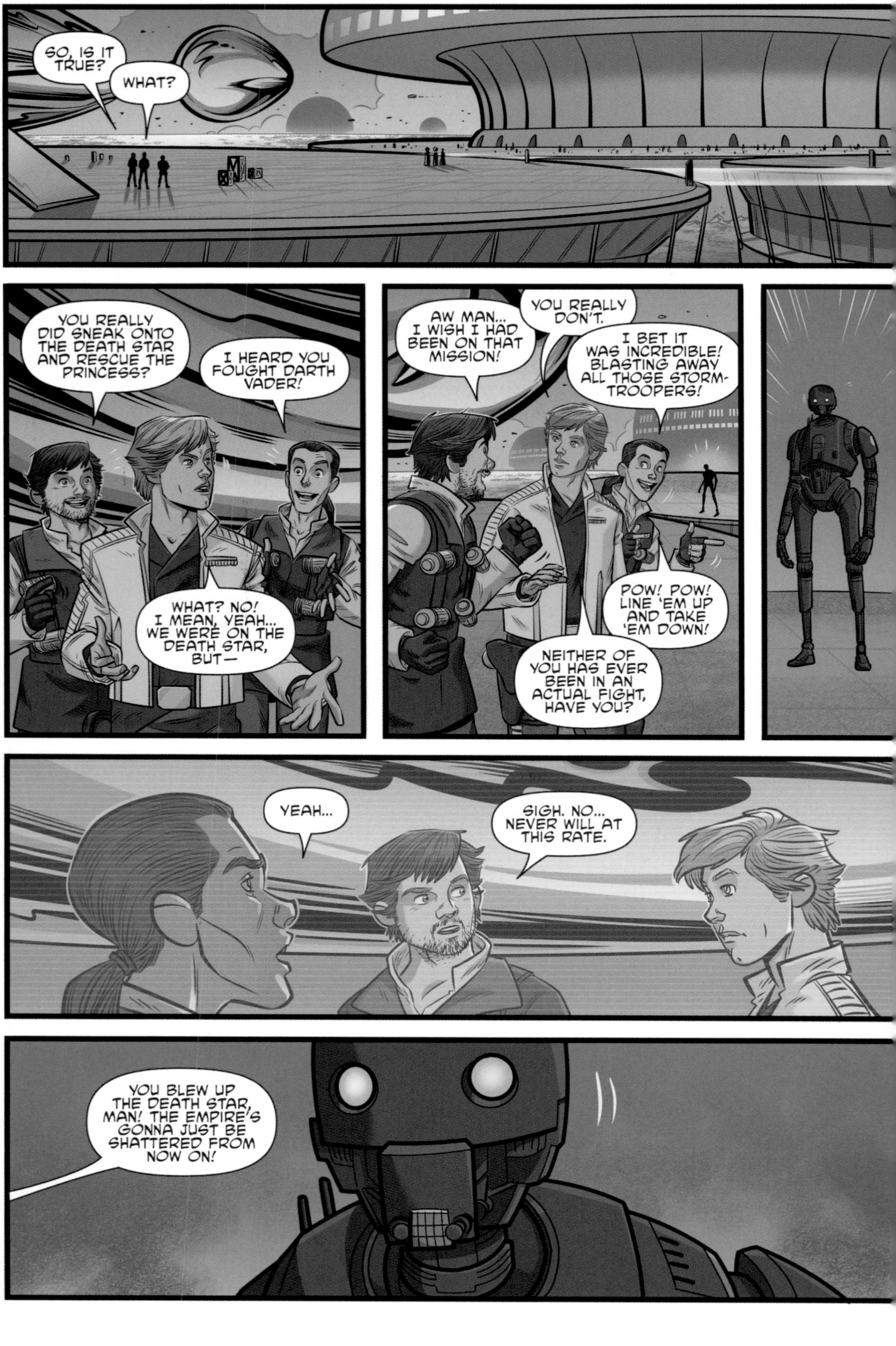
SO, IS IT TRUE?
WHAT?
YOU REALLY DID SNEAK ONTO THE DEATH STAR AND RESCUE THE PRINCESS?
I HEARD YOU FOUGHT DARTH VADER!
WHAT? NO! I MEAN, YEAH... WE WERE ON THE DEATH STAR, BUT—
AW MAN... I WISH I HAD BEEN ON THAT MISSION!
YOU REALLY DON'T.
I BET IT WAS INCREDIBLE! BLASTING AWAY ALL THOSE STORM-TROOPERS!
POW! POW! LINE 'EM UP AND TAKE 'EM DOWN!
NEITHER OF YOU HAS EVER BEEN IN AN ACTUAL FIGHT, HAVE YOU?
YEAH...
SIGH. NO... NEVER WILL AT THIS RATE.
YOU BLEW UP THE DEATH STAR, MAN! THE EMPIRE'S GONNA JUST BE SHATTERED FROM NOW ON!

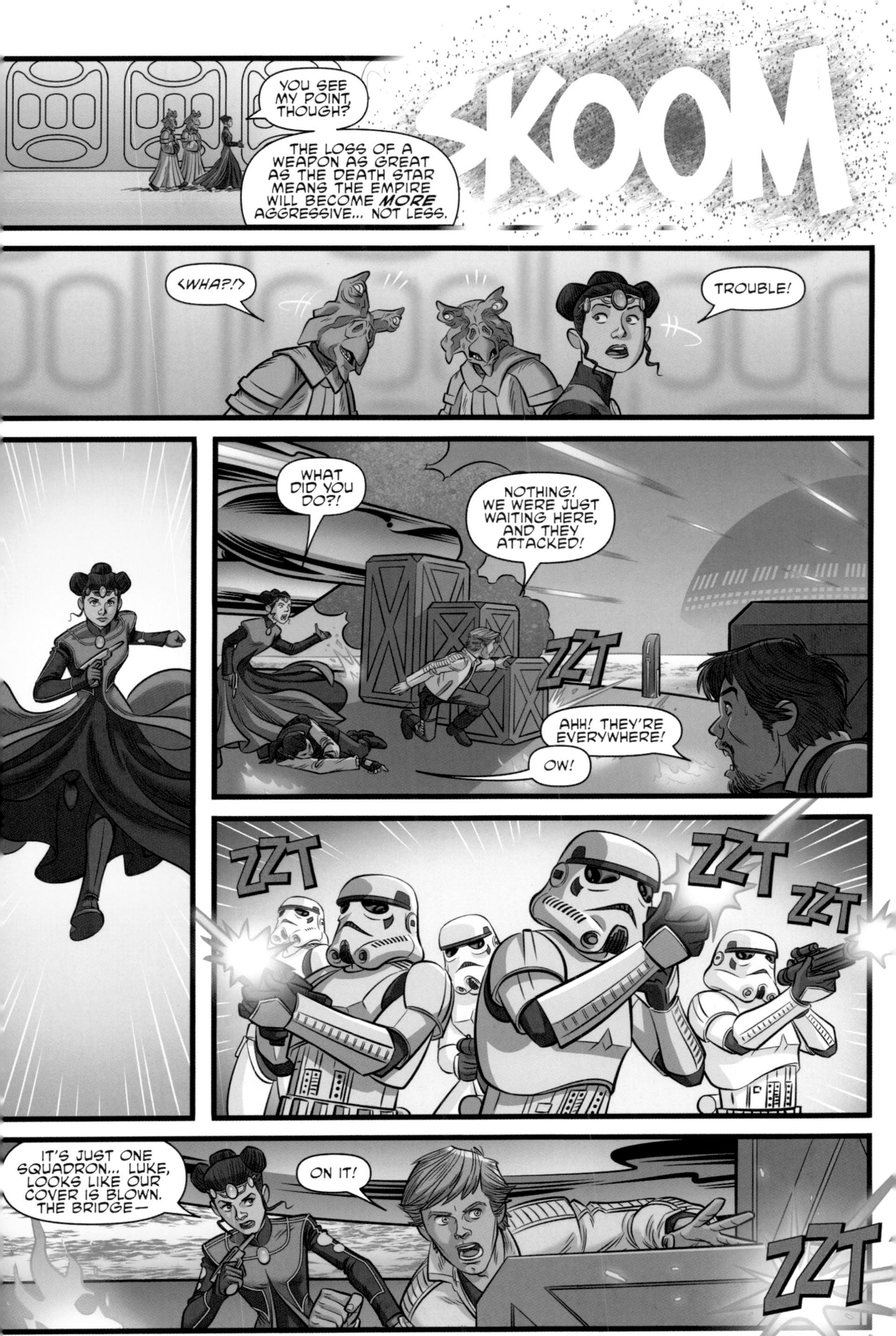
YOU SEE MY POINT, THOUGH?
THE LOSS OF A WEAPON AS GREAT AS THE DEATH STAR MEANS THE EMPIRE WILL BECOME *MORE* AGGRESSIVE... NOT LESS.
SKOOM
<WHA?!>
TROUBLE!
WHAT DID YOU DO?!
NOTHING! WE WERE JUST WAITING HERE, AND THEY ATTACKED!
ZZT
AHH! THEY'RE EVERYWHERE!
OW!
ZZT
ZZT
ZZT
IT'S JUST ONE SQUADRON... LUKE, LOOKS LIKE OUR COVER IS BLOWN. THE BRIDGE—
ON IT!
ZZT

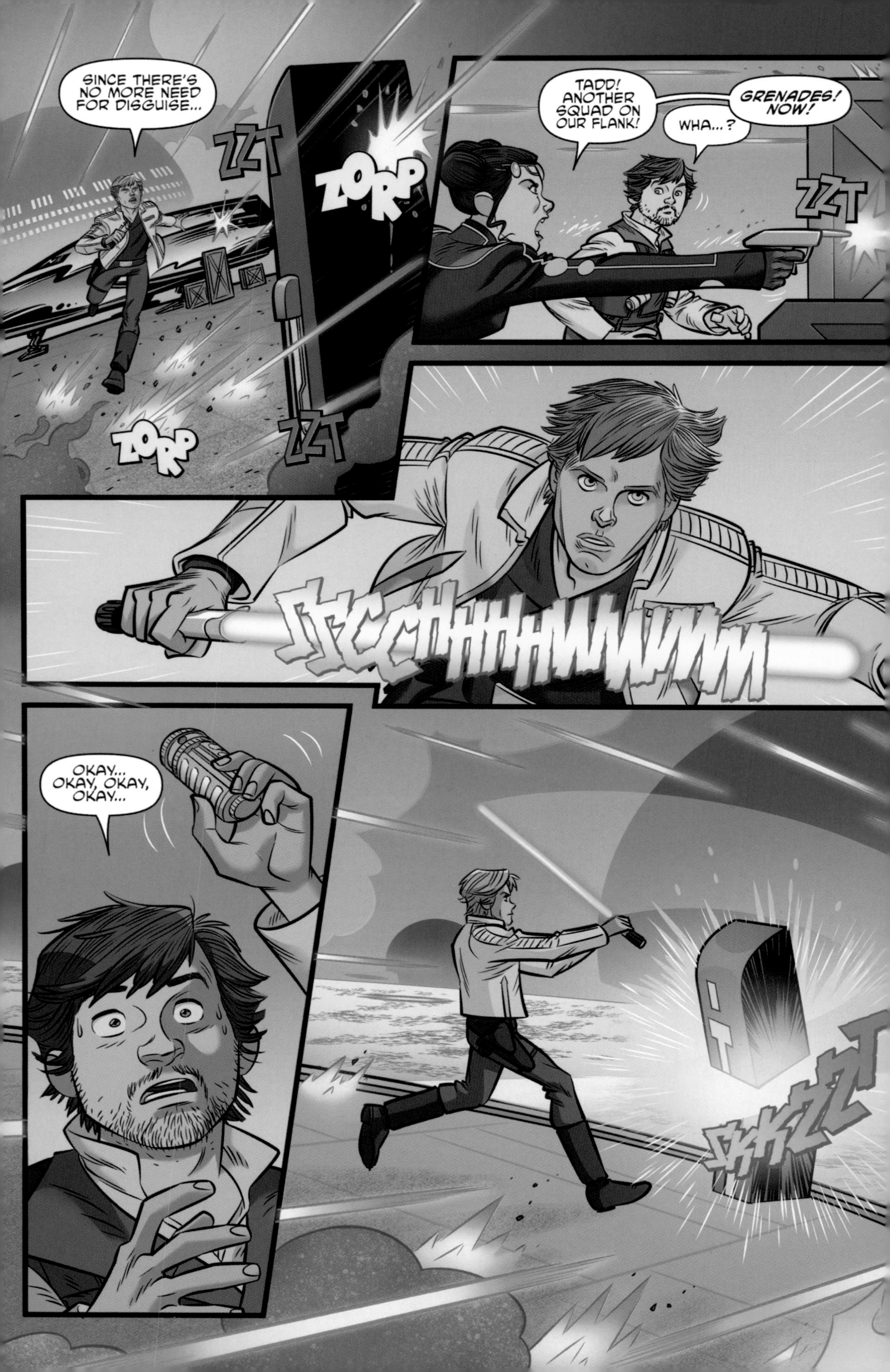
SINCE THERE'S NO MORE NEED FOR DISGUISE...
ZZT
ZORP
ZORP
ZZT
TADD! ANOTHER SQUAD ON OUR FLANK!
WHA...?
GRENADES! NOW!
ZZT
SSCCHHHHHWWWWMMM
OKAY... OKAY, OKAY, OKAY...
SKKZZZT

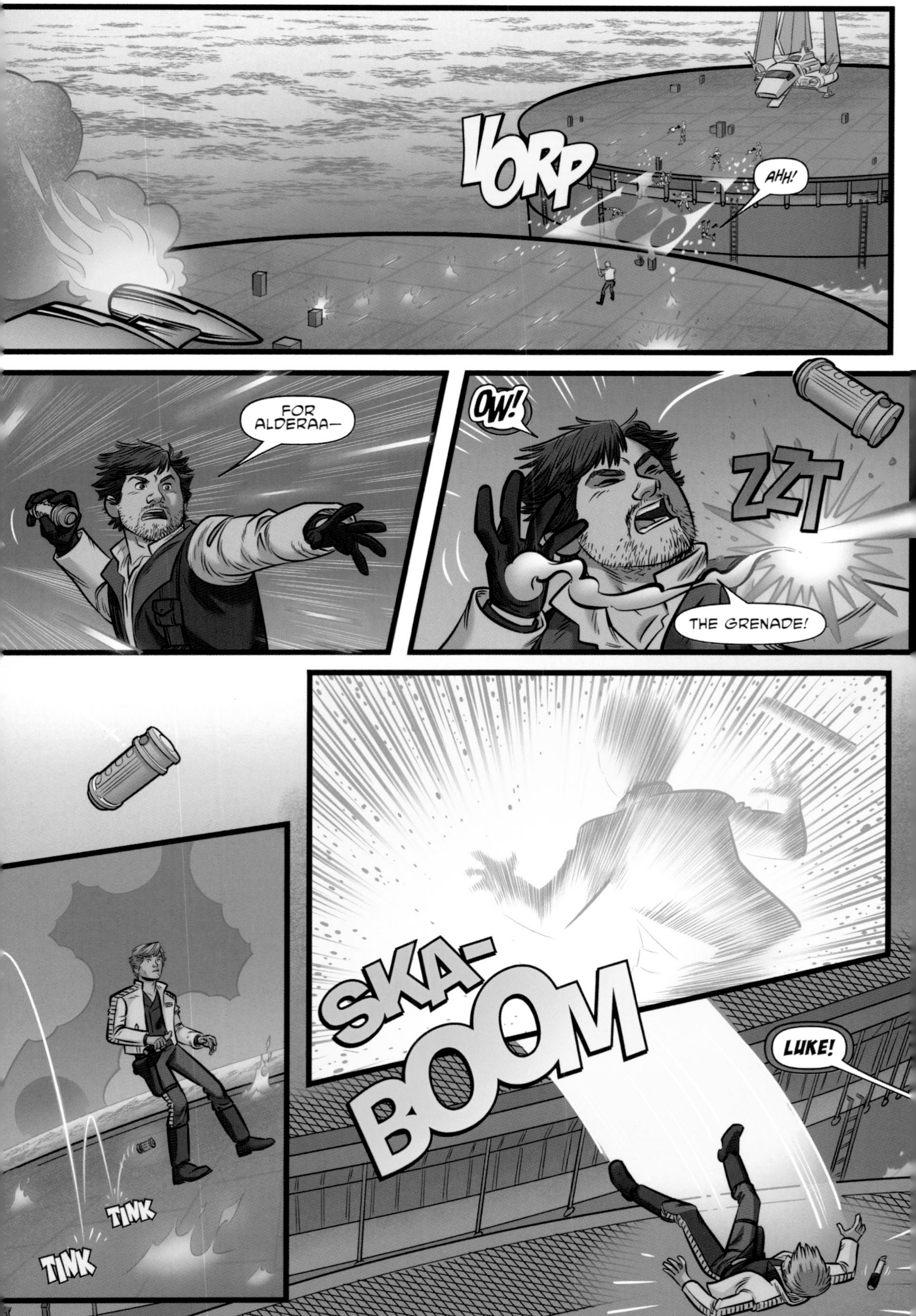
VORP
AHH!
FOR ALDERAA—
OW!
ZZT
THE GRENADE!
SKA-BOOM
LUKE!
TINK
TINK

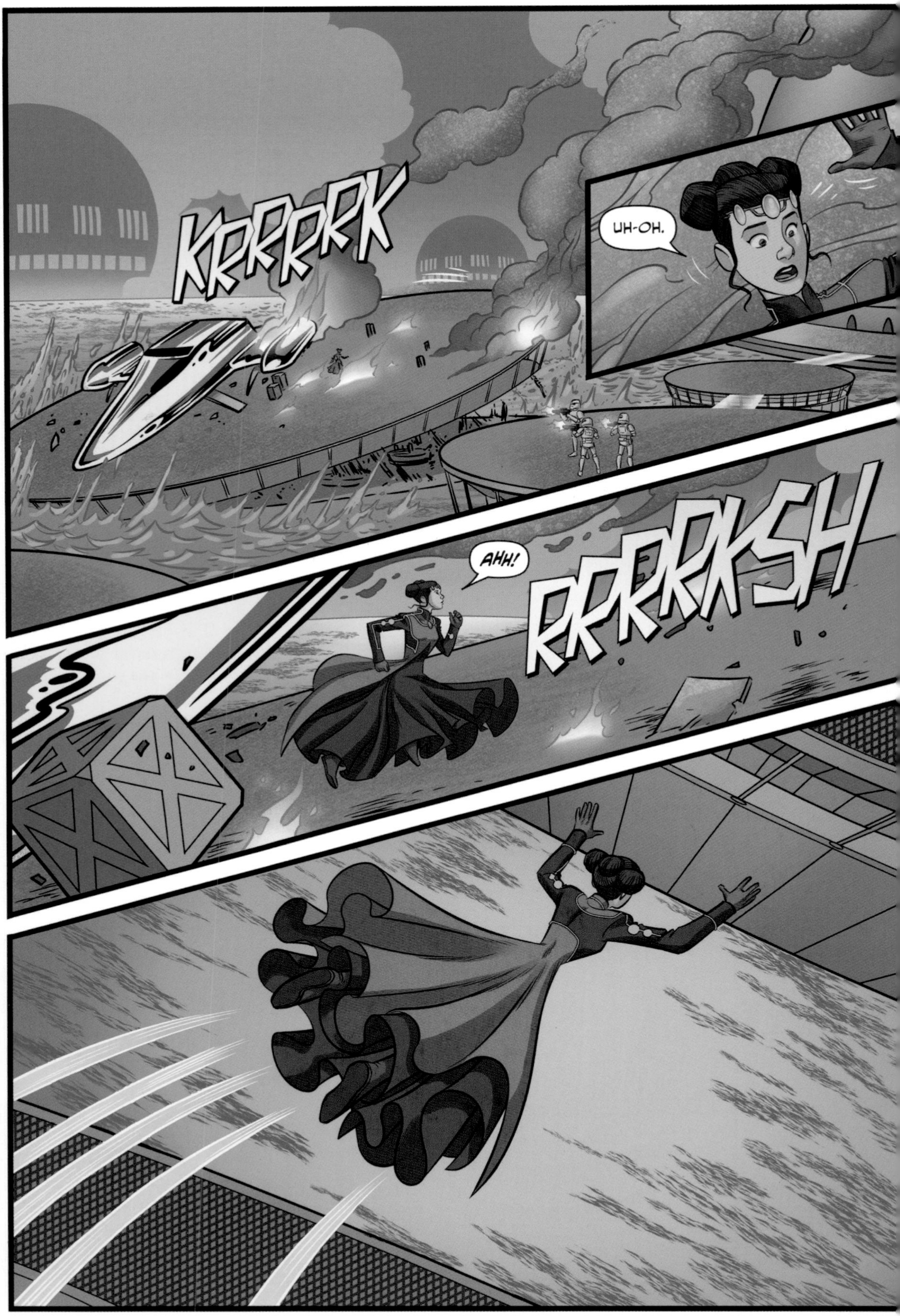
KRRRRK
UH-OH.
AHH!
RRRRRKSH

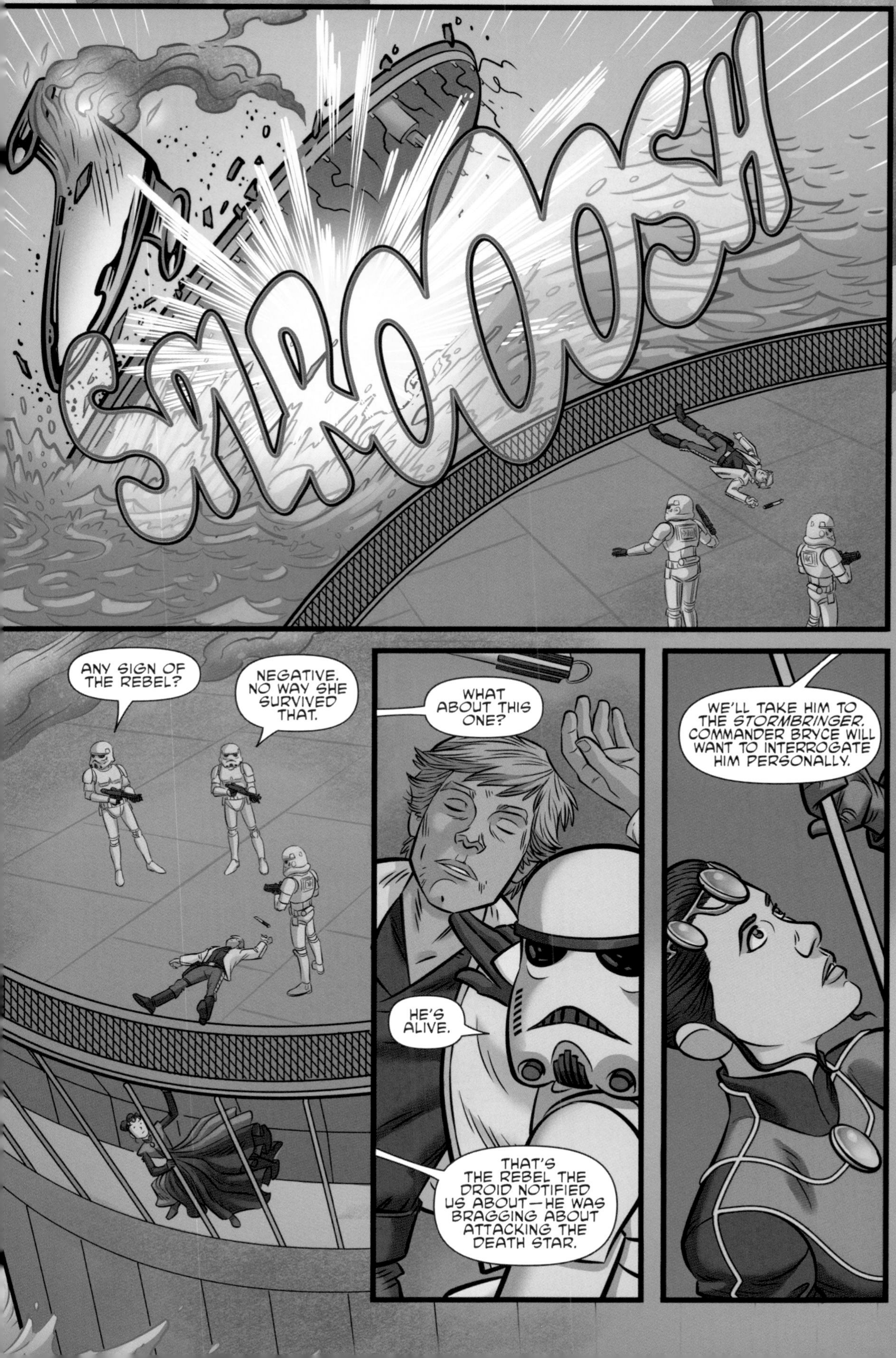
SHROOOSH
ANY SIGN OF THE REBEL?
NEGATIVE. NO WAY SHE SURVIVED THAT.
WHAT ABOUT THIS ONE?
HE'S ALIVE.
THAT'S THE REBEL THE DROID NOTIFIED US ABOUT—HE WAS BRAGGING ABOUT ATTACKING THE DEATH STAR.
WE'LL TAKE HIM TO THE *STORMBRINGER*. COMMANDER BRYCE WILL WANT TO INTERROGATE HIM PERSONALLY.

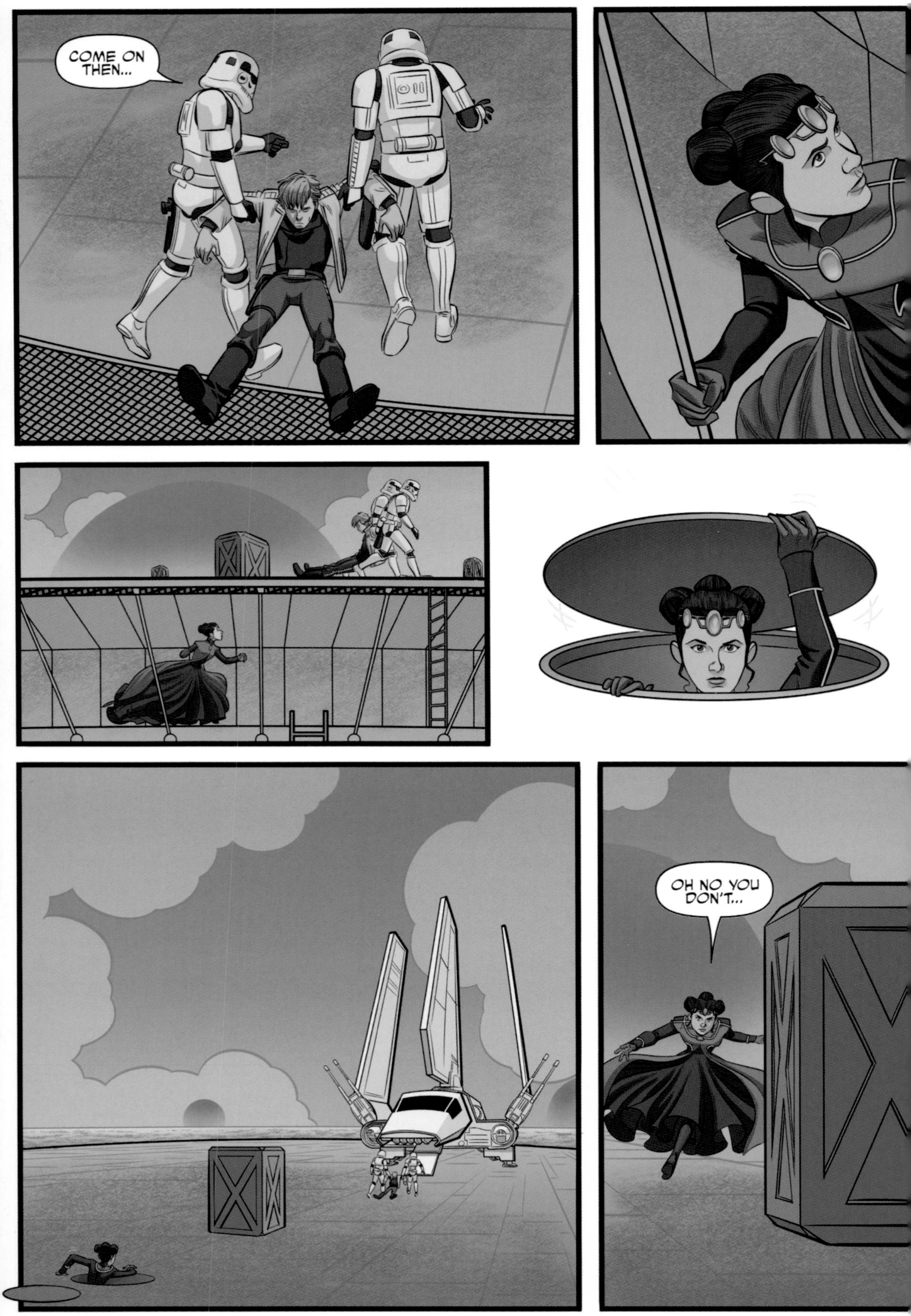
COME ON THEN...
OH NO YOU DON'T...

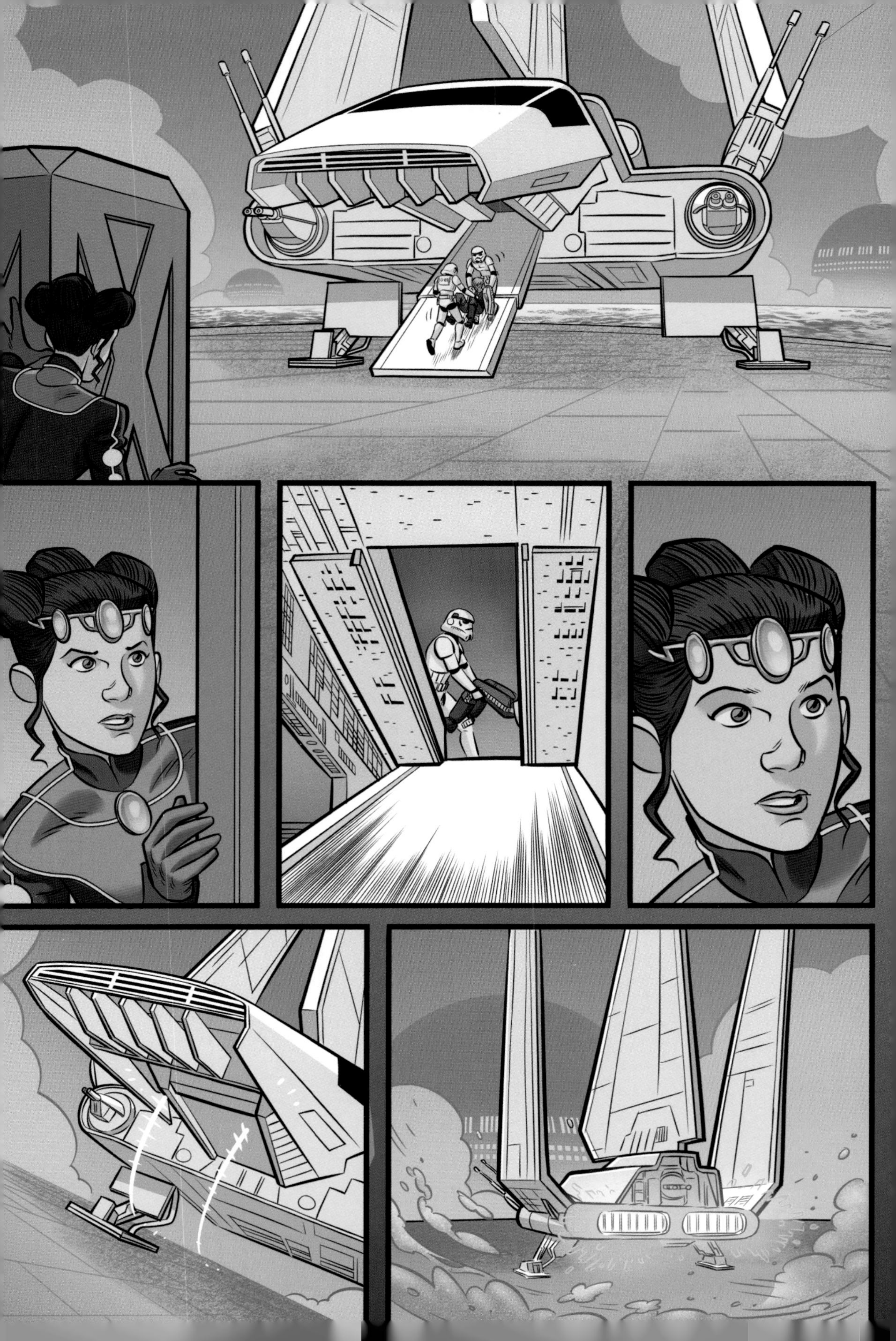

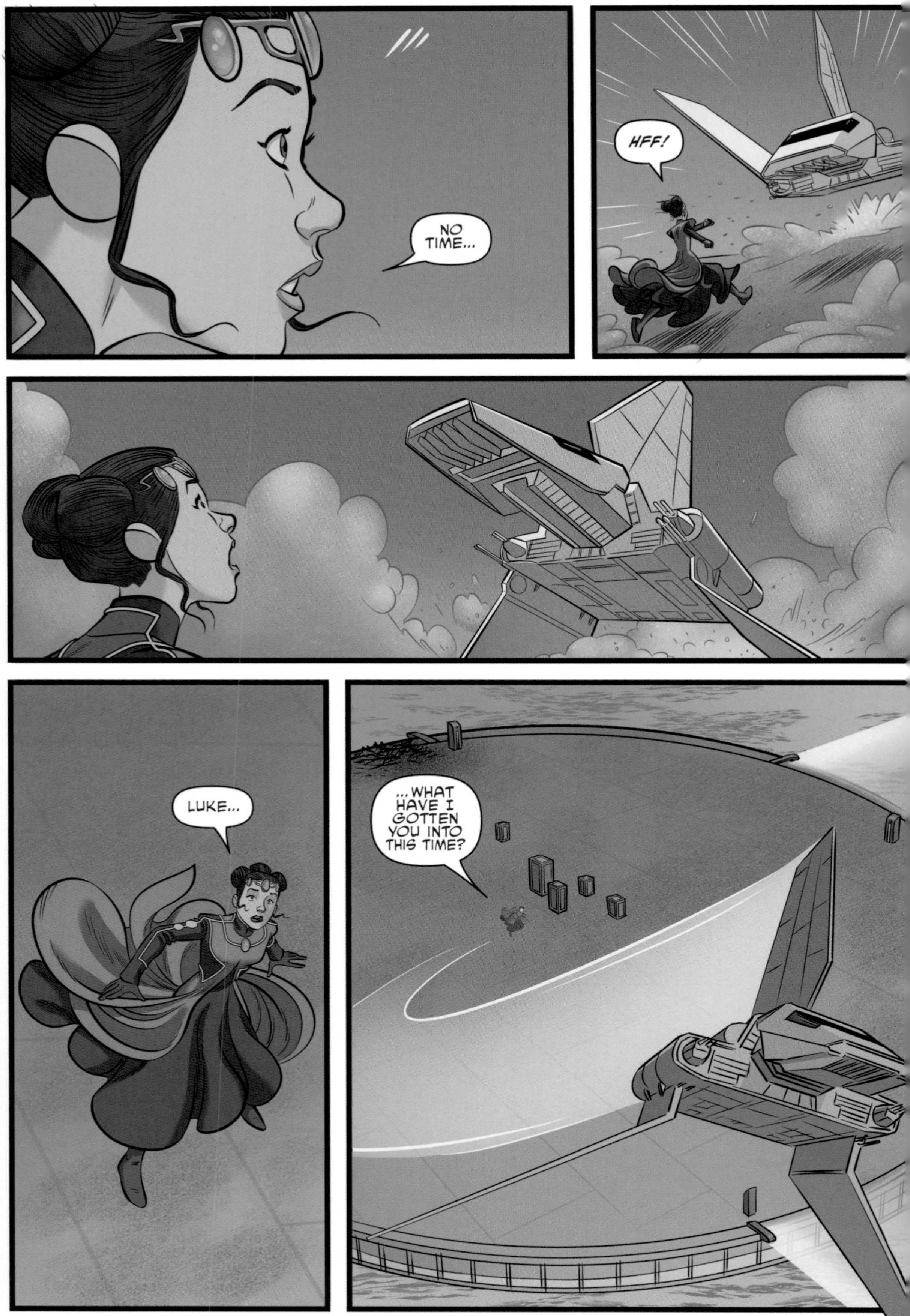
NO TIME...
HFF!
LUKE...
...WHAT HAVE I GOTTEN YOU INTO THIS TIME?

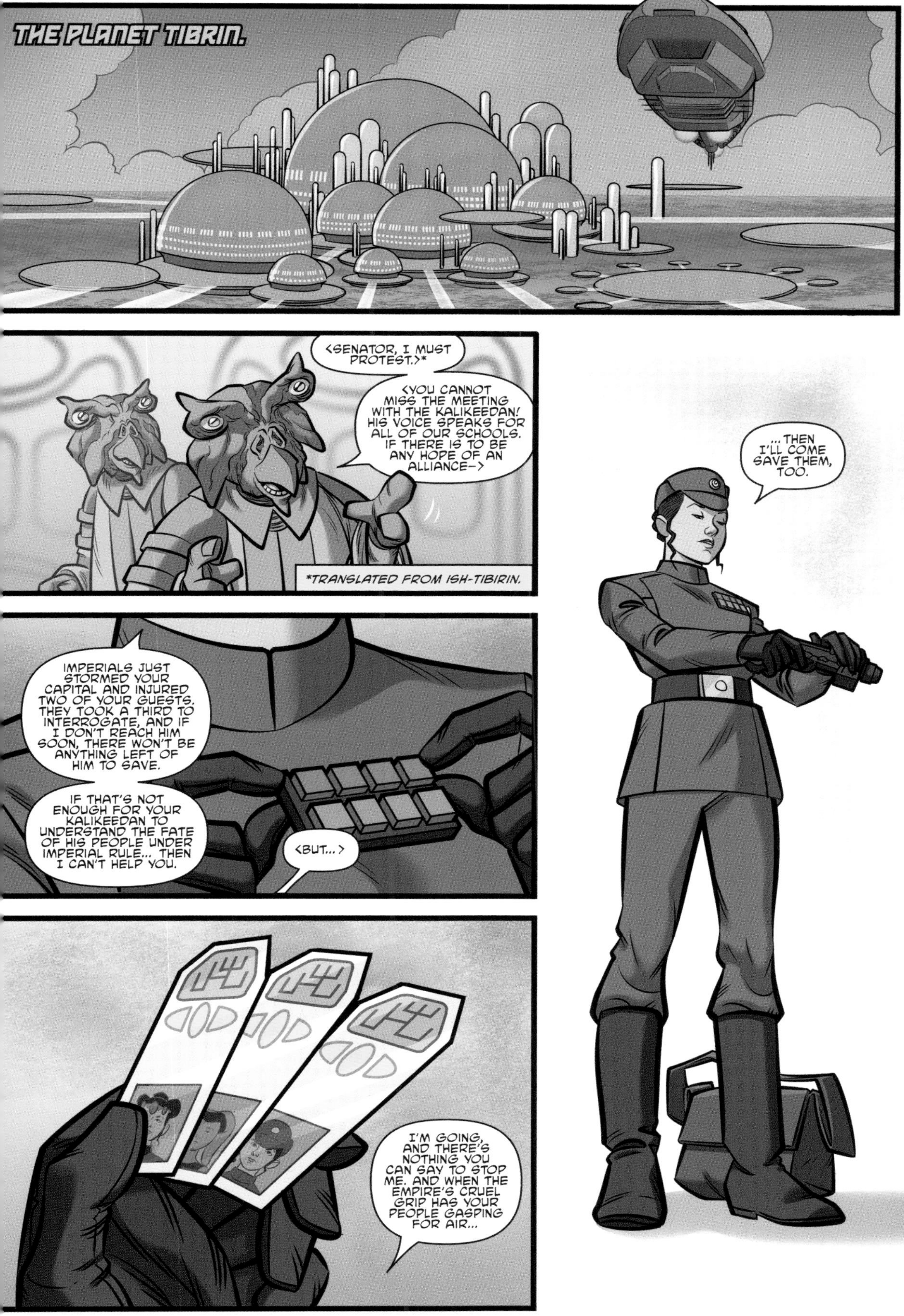
THE PLANET TIBRIN.
<SENATOR, I MUST PROTEST.>*
<YOU CANNOT MISS THE MEETING WITH THE KALIKEEDAN! HIS VOICE SPEAKS FOR ALL OF OUR SCHOOLS. IF THERE IS TO BE ANY HOPE OF AN ALLIANCE-->
*TRANSLATED FROM ISH-TIBIRIN.
IMPERIALS JUST STORMED YOUR CAPITAL AND INJURED TWO OF YOUR GUESTS. THEY TOOK A THIRD TO INTERROGATE, AND IF I DON'T REACH HIM SOON, THERE WON'T BE ANYTHING LEFT OF HIM TO SAVE.
IF THAT'S NOT ENOUGH FOR YOUR KALIKEEDAN TO UNDERSTAND THE FATE OF HIS PEOPLE UNDER IMPERIAL RULE... THEN I CAN'T HELP YOU.
<BUT...>
I'M GOING, AND THERE'S NOTHING YOU CAN SAY TO STOP ME. AND WHEN THE EMPIRE'S CRUEL GRIP HAS YOUR PEOPLE GASPING FOR AIR...
...THEN I'LL COME SAVE THEM, TOO.

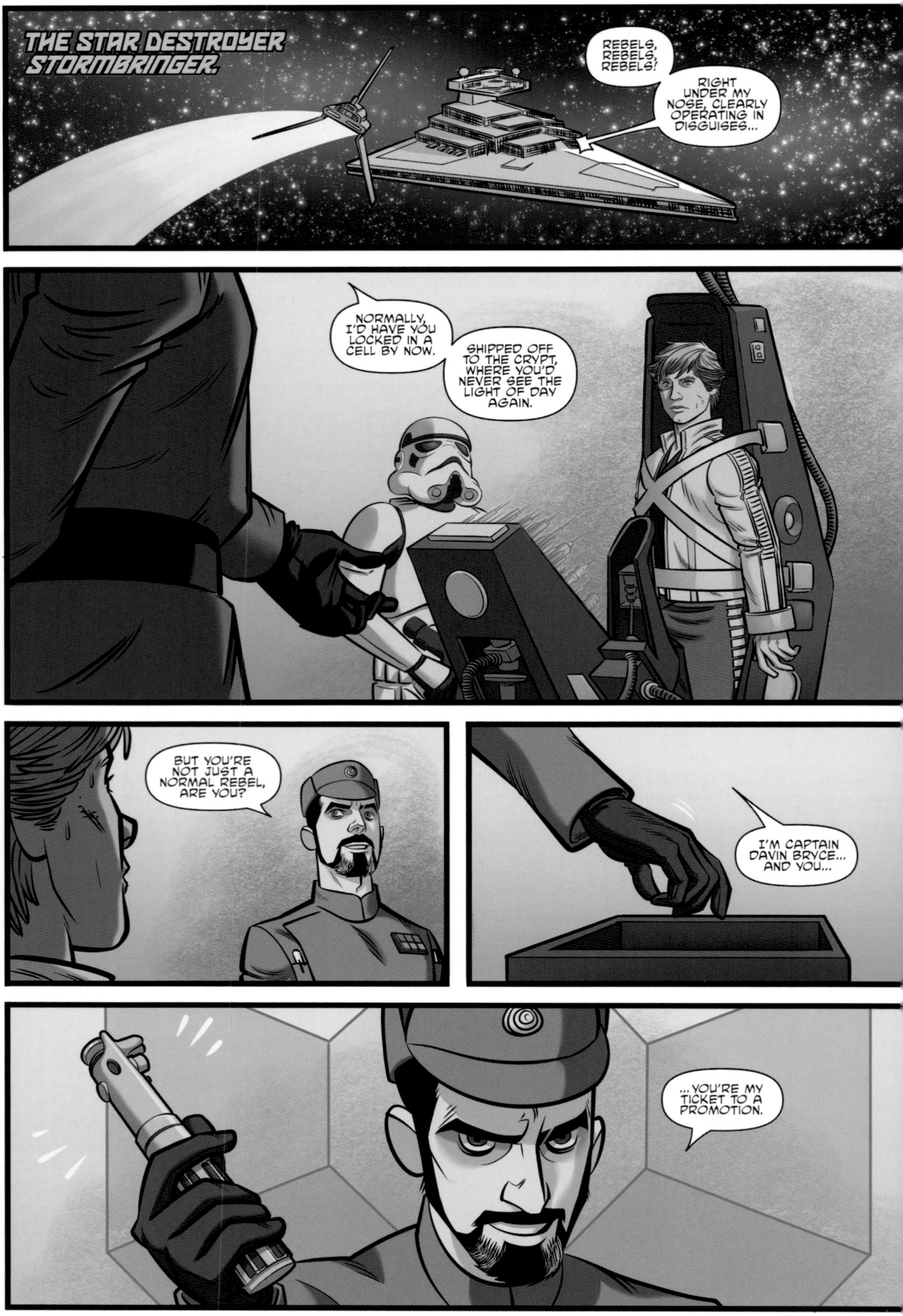
THE STAR DESTROYER STORMBRINGER.
REBELS, REBELS, REBELS!
RIGHT UNDER MY NOSE, CLEARLY OPERATING IN DISGUISES...
NORMALLY, I'D HAVE YOU LOCKED IN A CELL BY NOW.
SHIPPED OFF TO THE CRYPT, WHERE YOU'D NEVER SEE THE LIGHT OF DAY AGAIN.
BUT YOU'RE NOT JUST A NORMAL REBEL, ARE YOU?
I'M CAPTAIN DAVIN BRYCE... AND YOU...
...YOU'RE MY TICKET TO A PROMOTION.

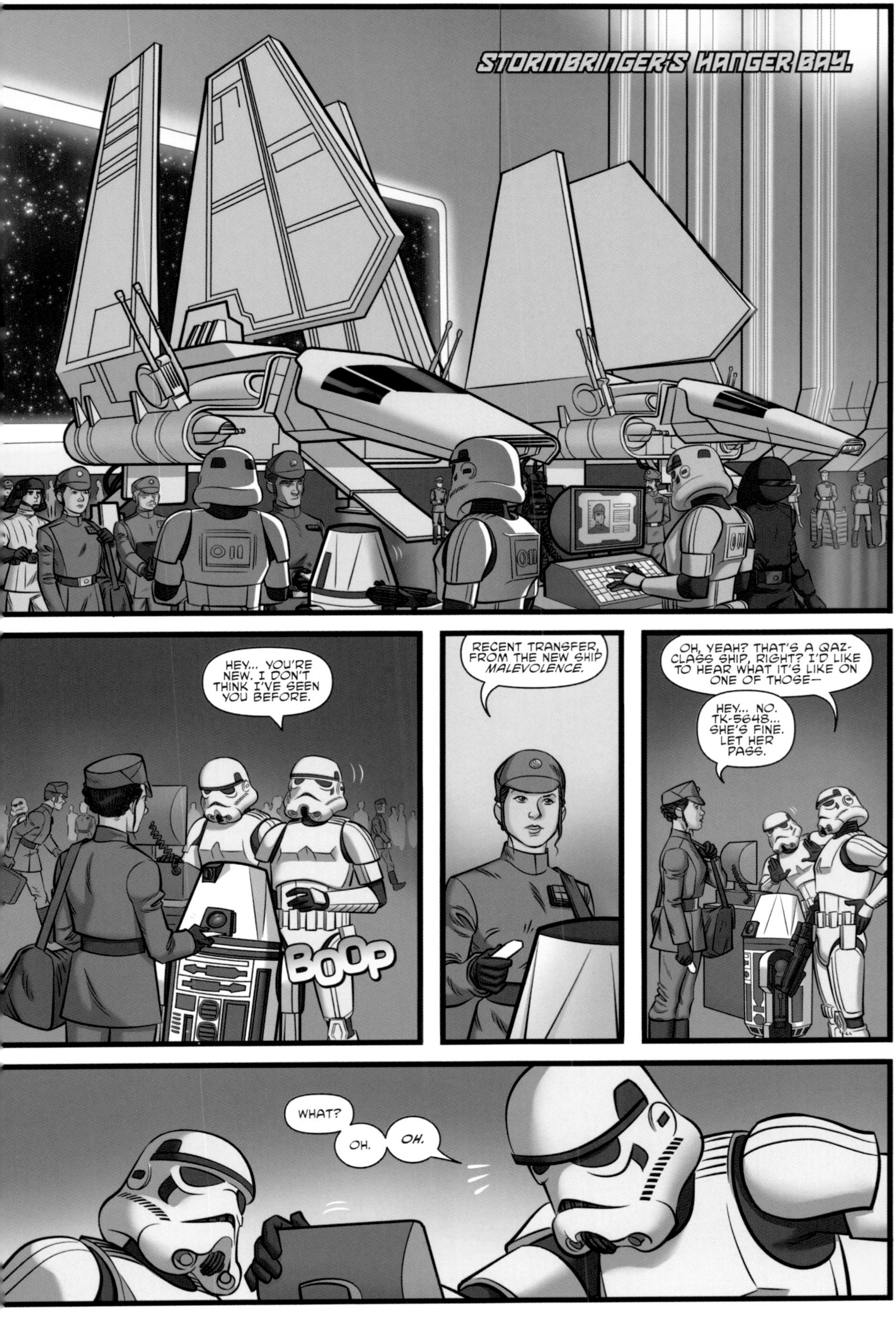
STORMBRINGER'S HANGER BAY.
HEY... YOU'RE NEW. I DON'T THINK I'VE SEEN YOU BEFORE.
BOOP
RECENT TRANSFER, FROM THE NEW SHIP *MALEVOLENCE.*
OH, YEAH? THAT'S A QAZ-CLASS SHIP, RIGHT? I'D LIKE TO HEAR WHAT IT'S LIKE ON ONE OF THOSE—
HEY... NO. TK-5648... SHE'S FINE. LET HER PASS.
WHAT?
OH.
OH.

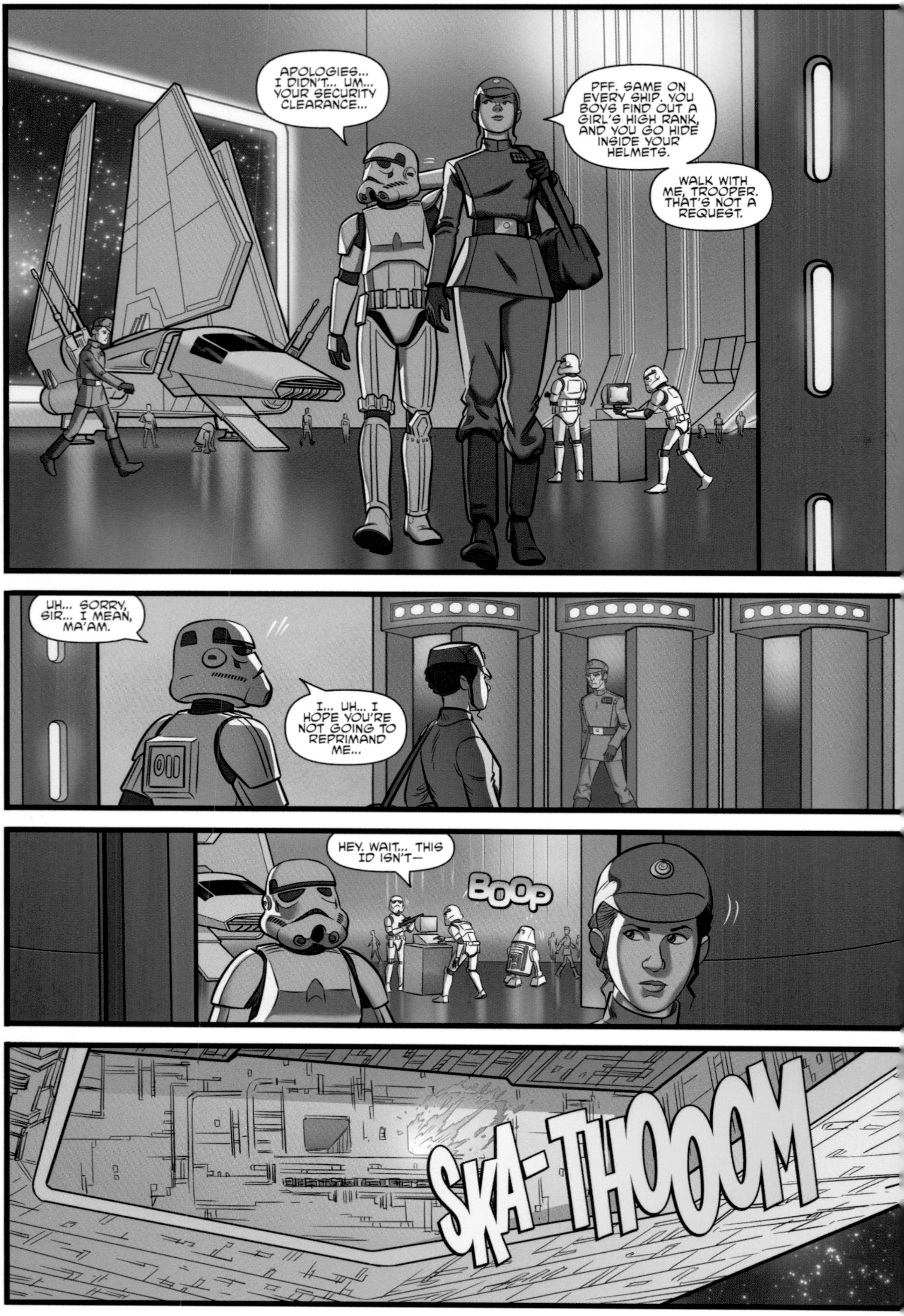
APOLOGIES... I DIDN'T... UM... YOUR SECURITY CLEARANCE...
PFF. SAME ON EVERY SHIP. YOU BOYS FIND OUT A GIRL'S HIGH RANK, AND YOU GO HIDE INSIDE YOUR HELMETS.
WALK WITH ME, TROOPER. THAT'S NOT A REQUEST.
UH... SORRY, SIR... I MEAN, MA'AM.
I... UH... I HOPE YOU'RE NOT GOING TO REPRIMAND ME...
HEY. WAIT... THIS ID ISN'T—
BOOP
SKA-THOOOM

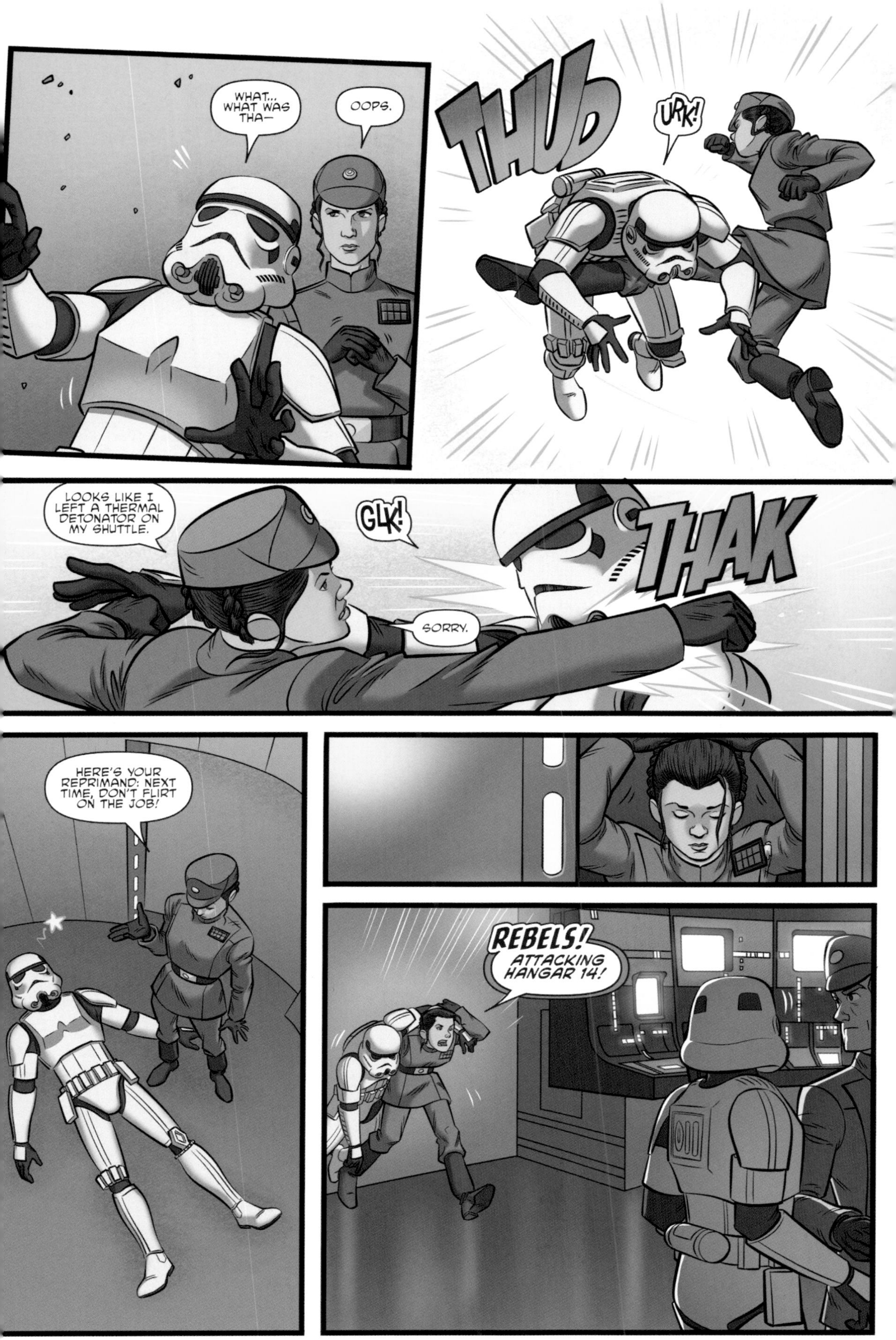
WHAT... WHAT WAS THA—
OOPS.
THUB
URK!
LOOKS LIKE I LEFT A THERMAL DETONATOR ON MY SHUTTLE.
GLK!
THAK
SORRY.
HERE'S YOUR REPRIMAND: NEXT TIME, DON'T FLIRT ON THE JOB!
REBELS! ATTACKING HANGAR 14!

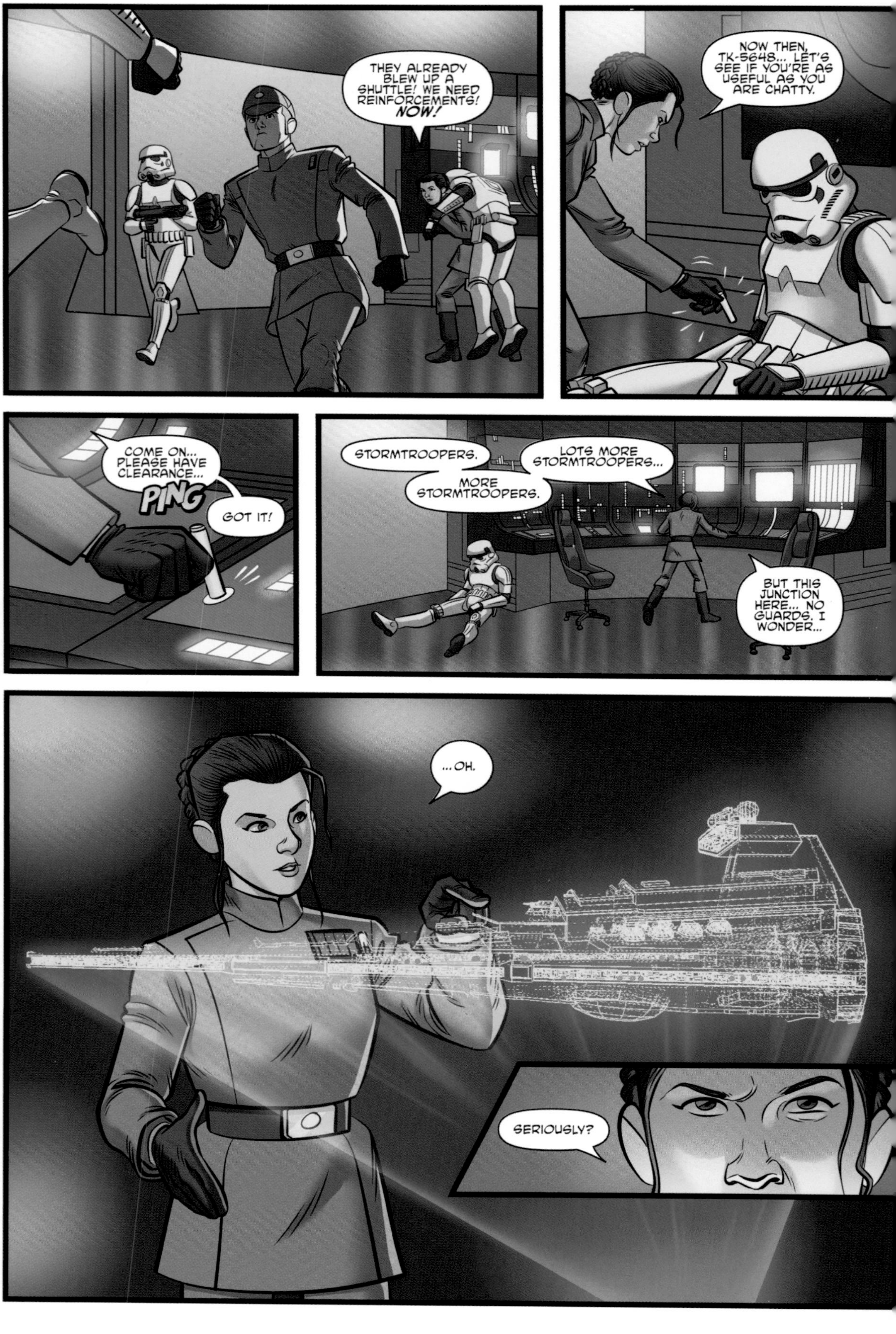
THEY ALREADY BLEW UP A SHUTTLE! WE NEED REINFORCEMENTS! NOW!
NOW THEN, TK-5648... LET'S SEE IF YOU'RE AS USEFUL AS YOU ARE CHATTY.
COME ON... PLEASE HAVE CLEARANCE...
PING
GOT IT!
STORMTROOPERS.
MORE STORMTROOPERS.
LOTS MORE STORMTROOPERS...
BUT THIS JUNCTION HERE... NO GUARDS. I WONDER...
...OH.
SERIOUSLY?

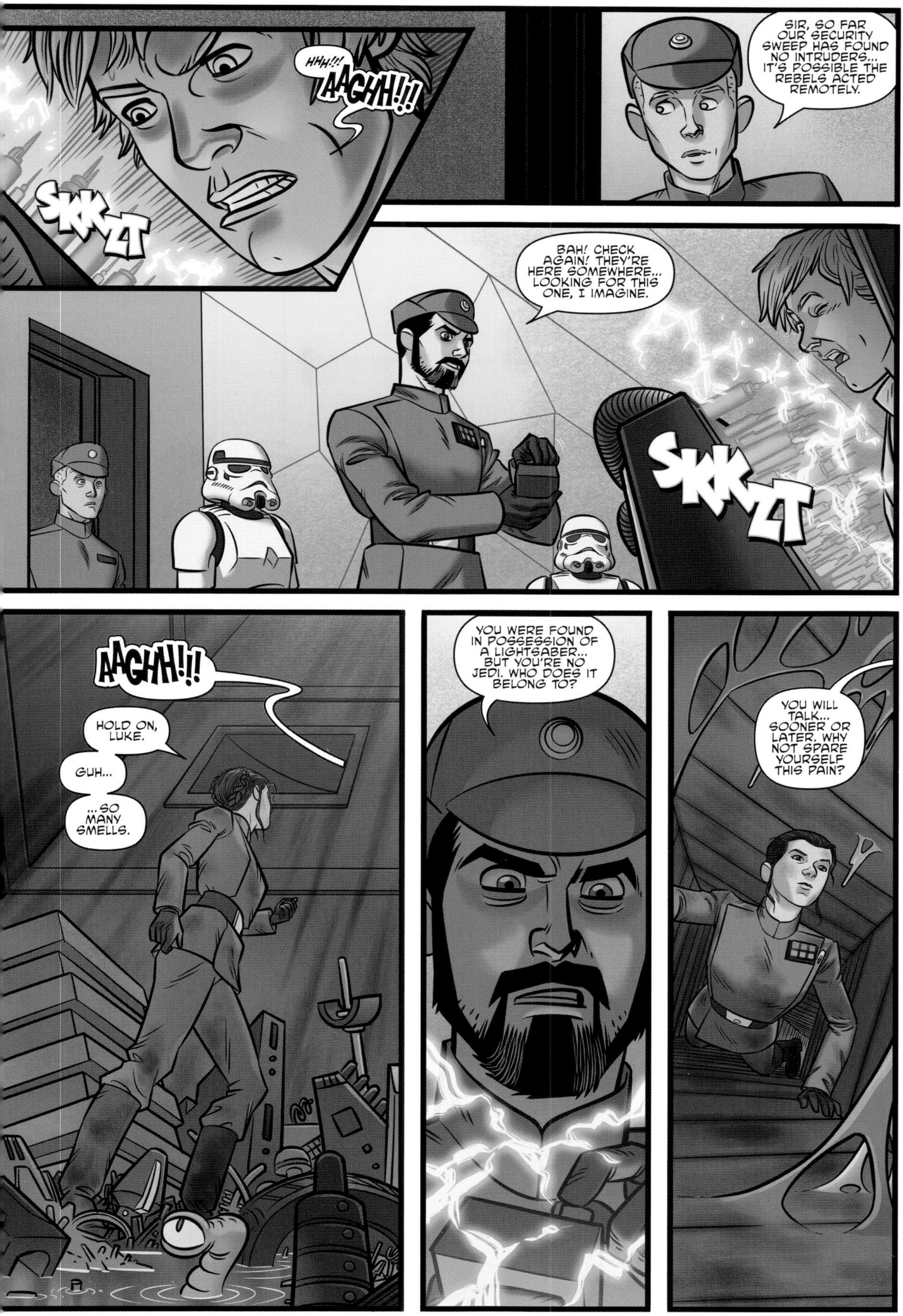
HHH!!!
AAGHH!!!
SKKZZT
SIR, SO FAR OUR SECURITY SWEEP HAS FOUND NO INTRUDERS... IT'S POSSIBLE THE REBELS ACTED REMOTELY.
BAH! CHECK AGAIN! THEY'RE HERE SOMEWHERE... LOOKING FOR THIS ONE, I IMAGINE.
SKKZZT
AAGHH!!!
HOLD ON, LUKE.
GUH...
...SO MANY SMELLS.
YOU WERE FOUND IN POSSESSION OF A LIGHTSABER... BUT YOU'RE NO JEDI. WHO DOES IT BELONG TO?
YOU WILL TALK... SOONER OR LATER. WHY NOT SPARE YOURSELF THIS PAIN?

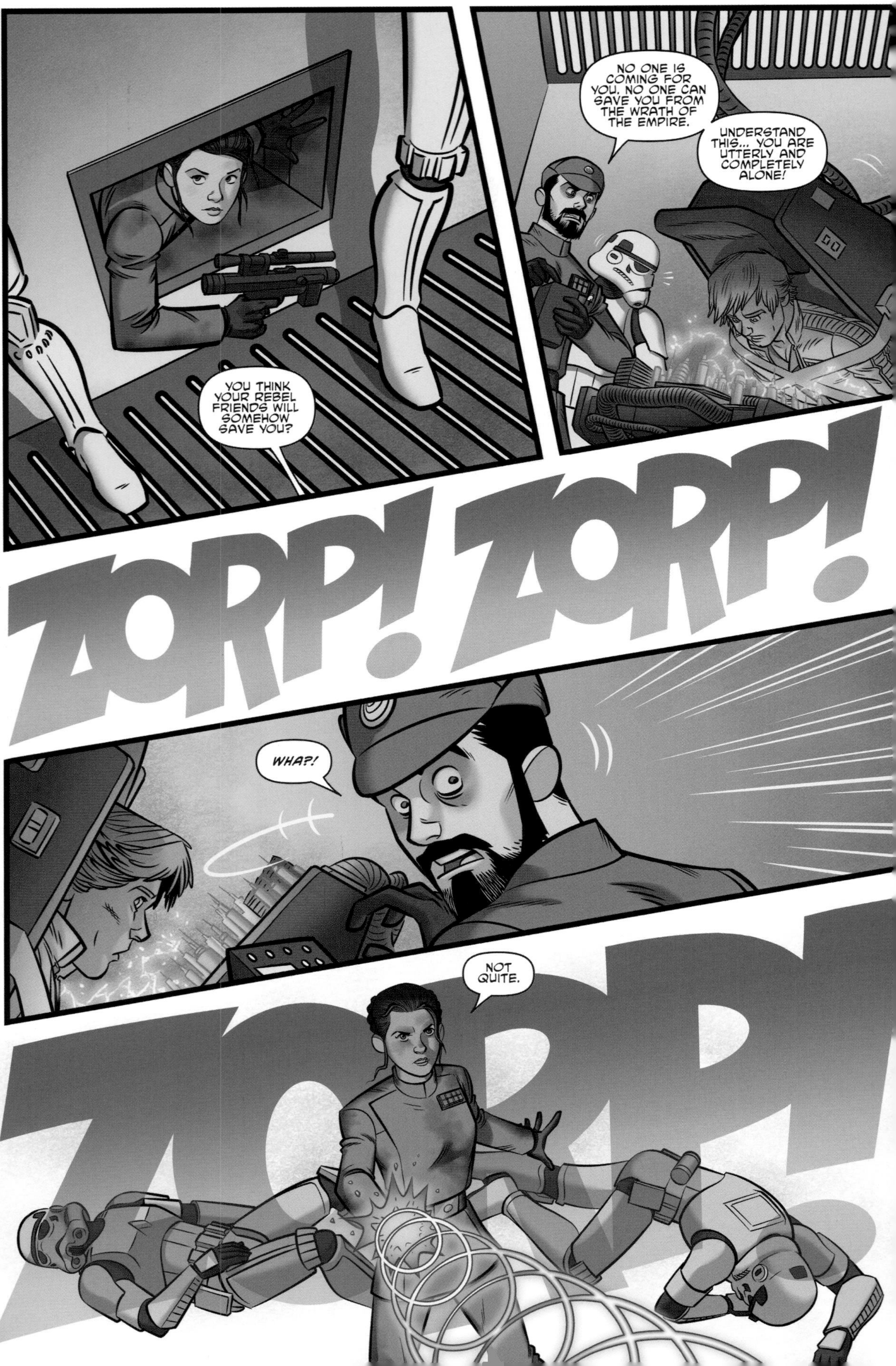
YOU THINK YOUR REBEL FRIENDS WILL SOMEHOW SAVE YOU?
NO ONE IS COMING FOR YOU. NO ONE CAN SAVE YOU FROM THE WRATH OF THE EMPIRE.
UNDERSTAND THIS... YOU ARE UTTERLY AND COMPLETELY ALONE!
ZORP! ZORP!
WHA?!
NOT QUITE.
ZORP!

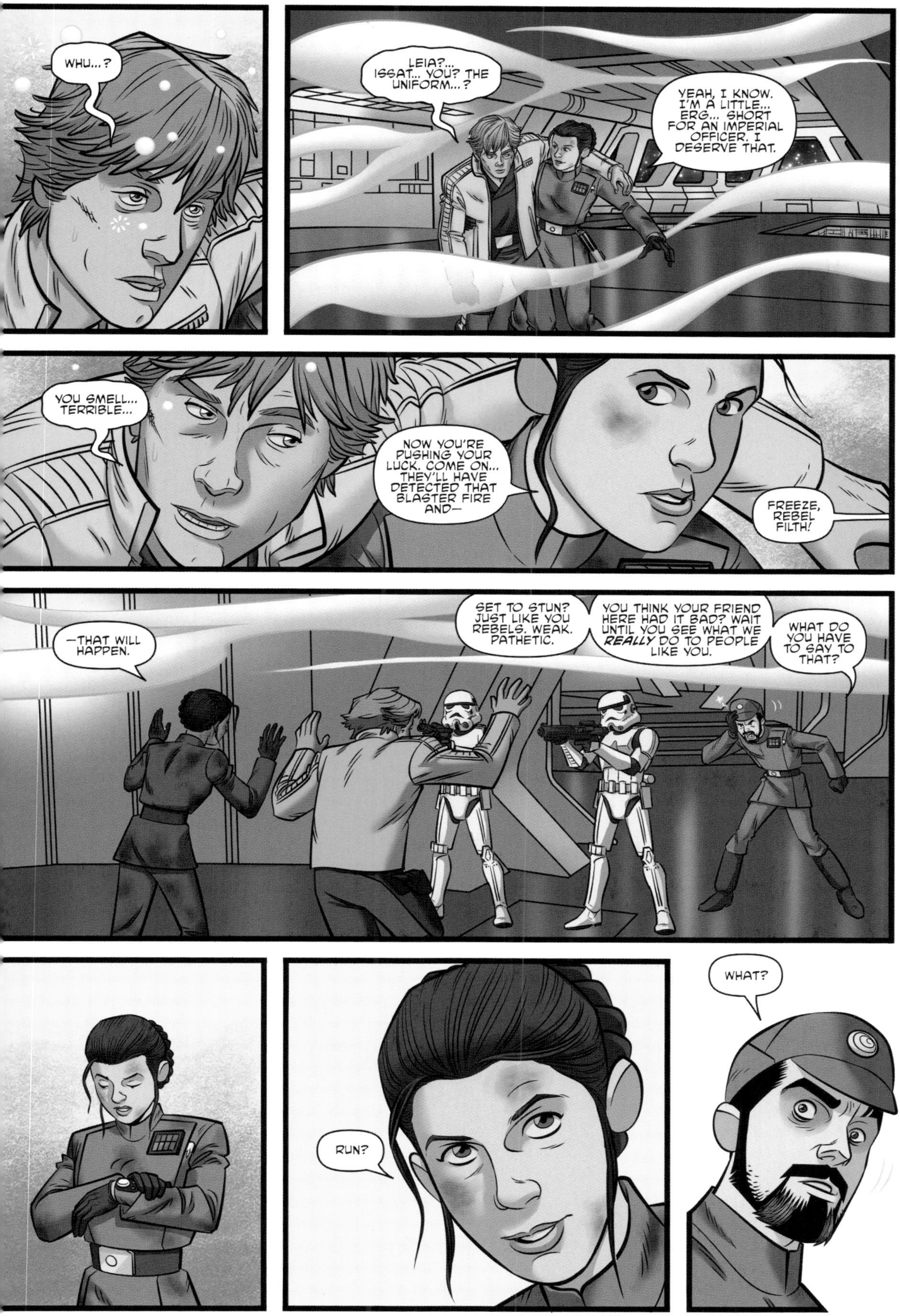
WHU...?
LEIA?... ISSAT... YOU? THE UNIFORM...?
YEAH, I KNOW. I'M A LITTLE... ERG... SHORT FOR AN IMPERIAL OFFICER. I DESERVE THAT.
YOU SMELL... TERRIBLE...
NOW YOU'RE PUSHING YOUR LUCK. COME ON... THEY'LL HAVE DETECTED THAT BLASTER FIRE AND—
FREEZE, REBEL FILTH!
—THAT WILL HAPPEN.
SET TO STUN? JUST LIKE YOU REBELS. WEAK. PATHETIC.
YOU THINK YOUR FRIEND HERE HAD IT BAD? WAIT UNTIL YOU SEE WHAT WE *REALLY* DO TO PEOPLE LIKE YOU.
WHAT DO YOU HAVE TO SAY TO THAT?
RUN?
WHAT?

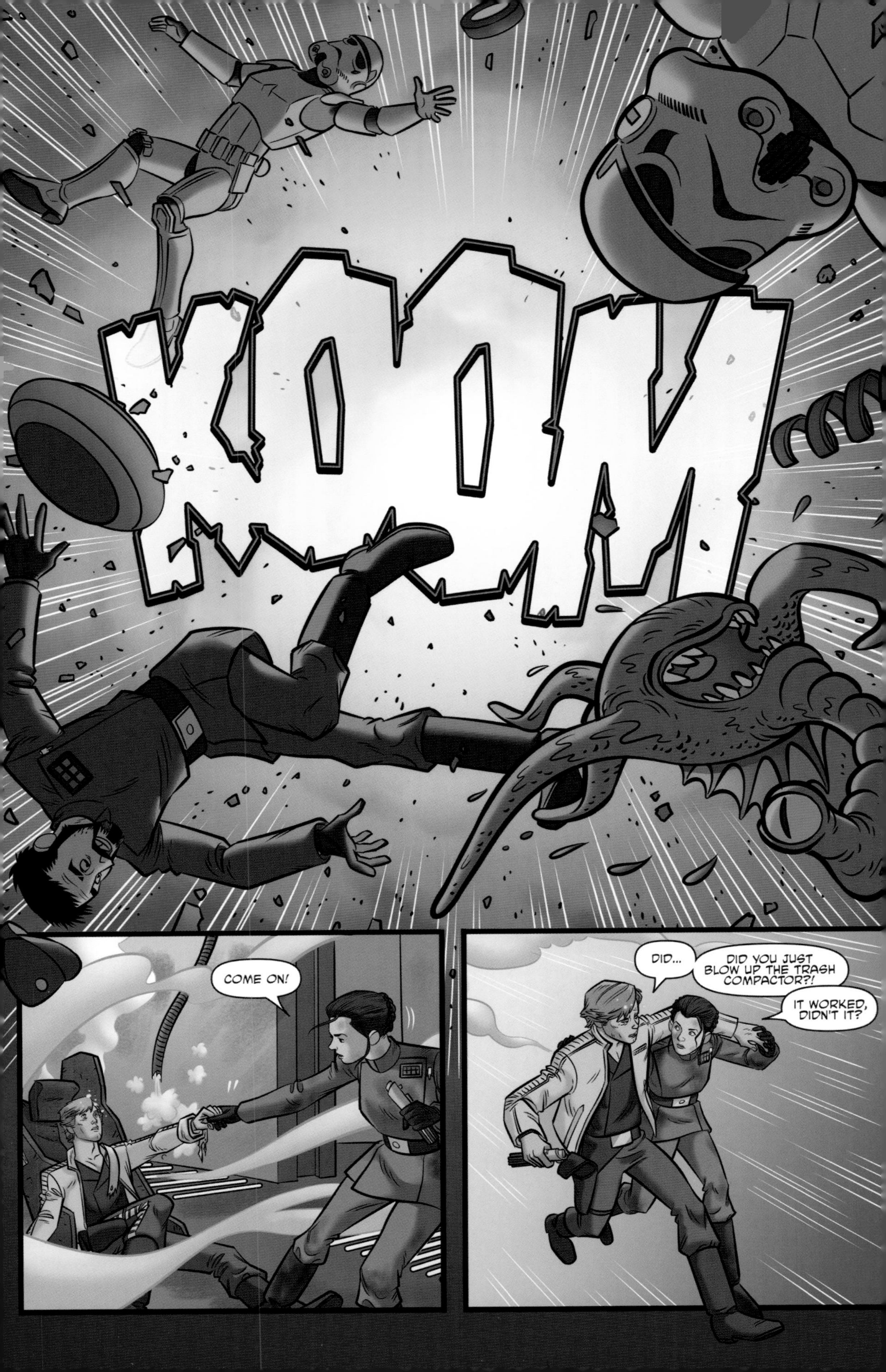
KOOM
COME ON!
DID...
DID YOU JUST BLOW UP THE TRASH COMPACTOR?!
IT WORKED, DIDN'T IT?

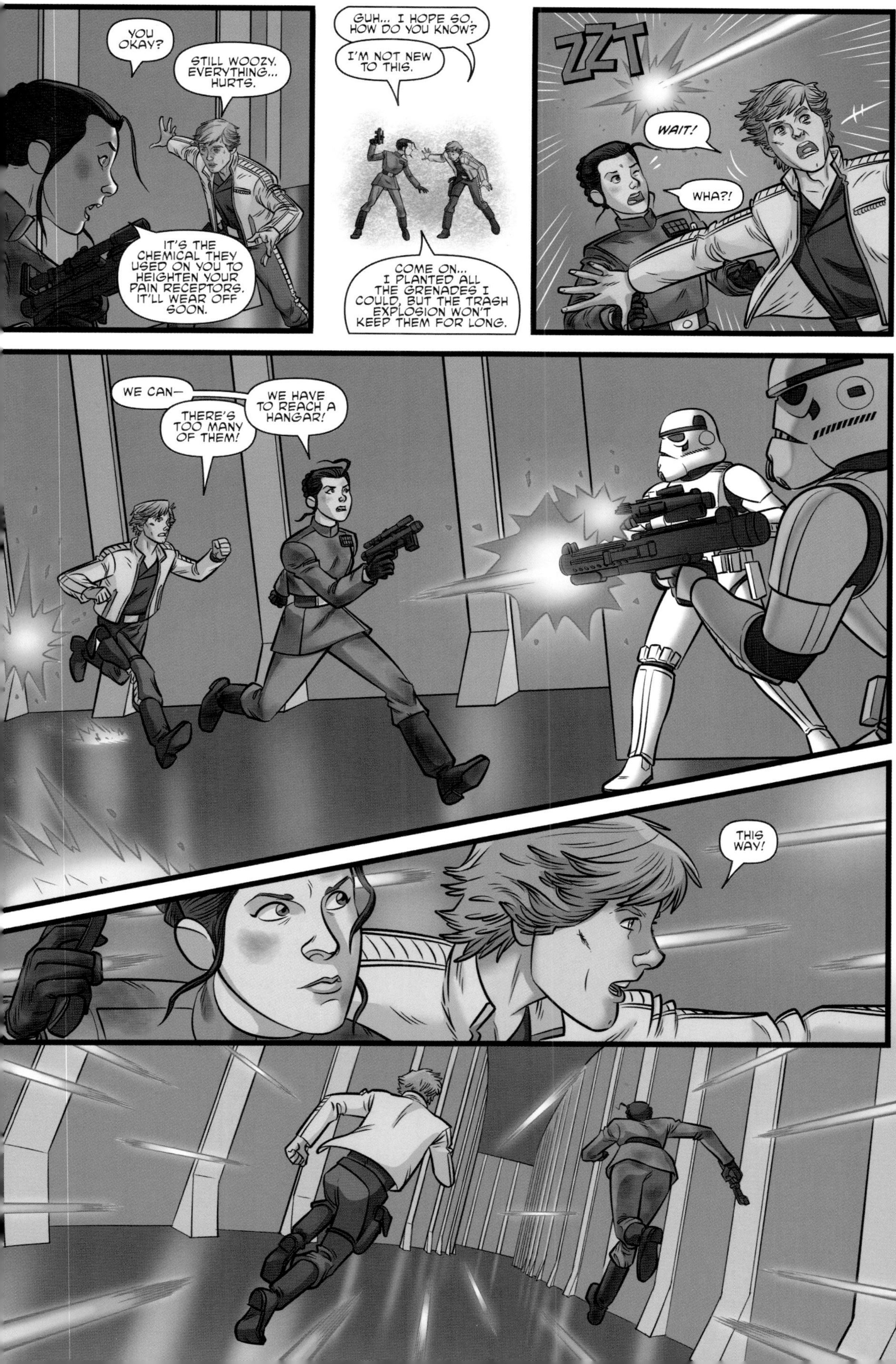
YOU OKAY?
STILL WOOZY. EVERYTHING... HURTS.
IT'S THE CHEMICAL THEY USED ON YOU TO HEIGHTEN YOUR PAIN RECEPTORS. IT'LL WEAR OFF SOON.
GUH... I HOPE SO. HOW DO YOU KNOW?
I'M NOT NEW TO THIS.
COME ON... I PLANTED ALL THE GRENADES I COULD, BUT THE TRASH EXPLOSION WON'T KEEP THEM FOR LONG.
ZZT
WAIT!
WHA?!
WE CAN—
THERE'S TOO MANY OF THEM!
WE HAVE TO REACH A HANGAR!
THIS WAY!

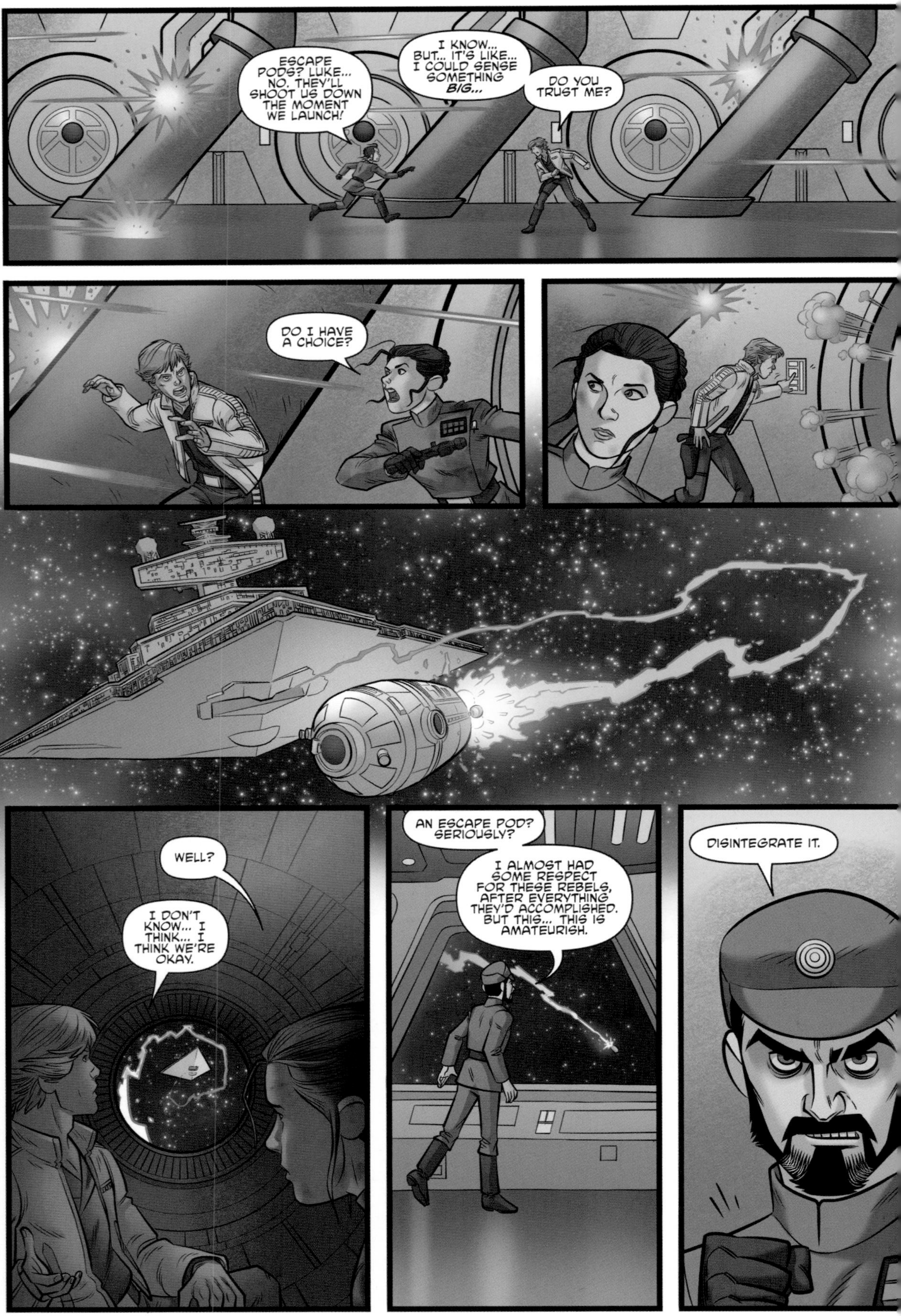
ESCAPE PODS? LUKE... NO. THEY'LL SHOOT US DOWN THE MOMENT WE LAUNCH!
I KNOW... BUT... IT'S LIKE... I COULD SENSE SOMETHING *BIG*...
DO YOU TRUST ME?
DO I HAVE A CHOICE?
WELL?
I DON'T KNOW... I THINK... I THINK WE'RE OKAY.
AN ESCAPE POD? SERIOUSLY?
I ALMOST HAD SOME RESPECT FOR THESE REBELS, AFTER EVERYTHING THEY'D ACCOMPLISHED. BUT THIS... THIS IS AMATEURISH.
DISINTEGRATE IT.

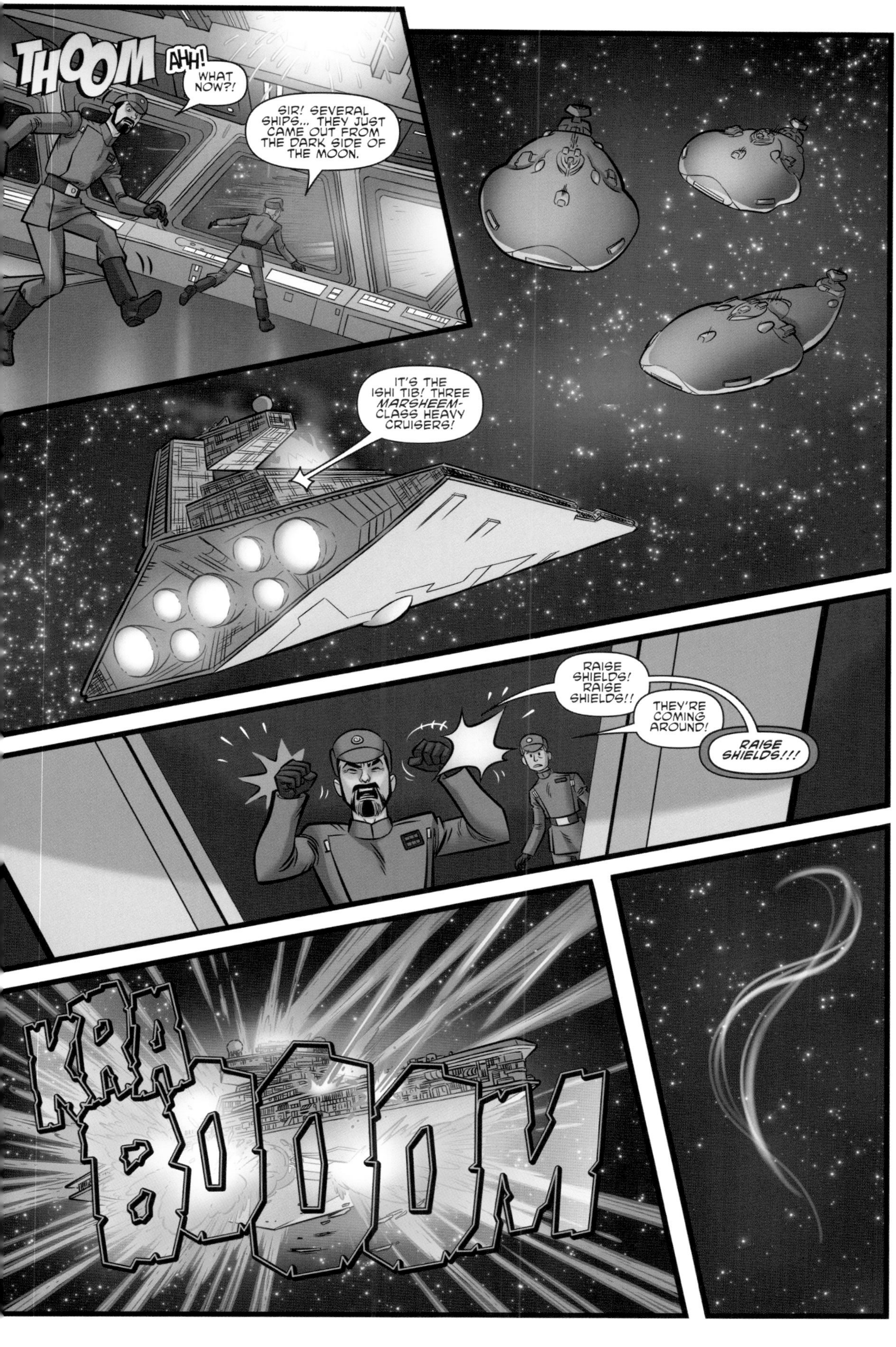
THOOM
AHH! WHAT NOW?!
SIR! SEVERAL SHIPS... THEY JUST CAME OUT FROM THE DARK SIDE OF THE MOON.
IT'S THE ISHI TIB! THREE MARSHEEM-CLASS HEAVY CRUISERS!
RAISE SHIELDS! RAISE SHIELDS!!
THEY'RE COMING AROUND!
RAISE SHIELDS!!!
KRA BOOOM

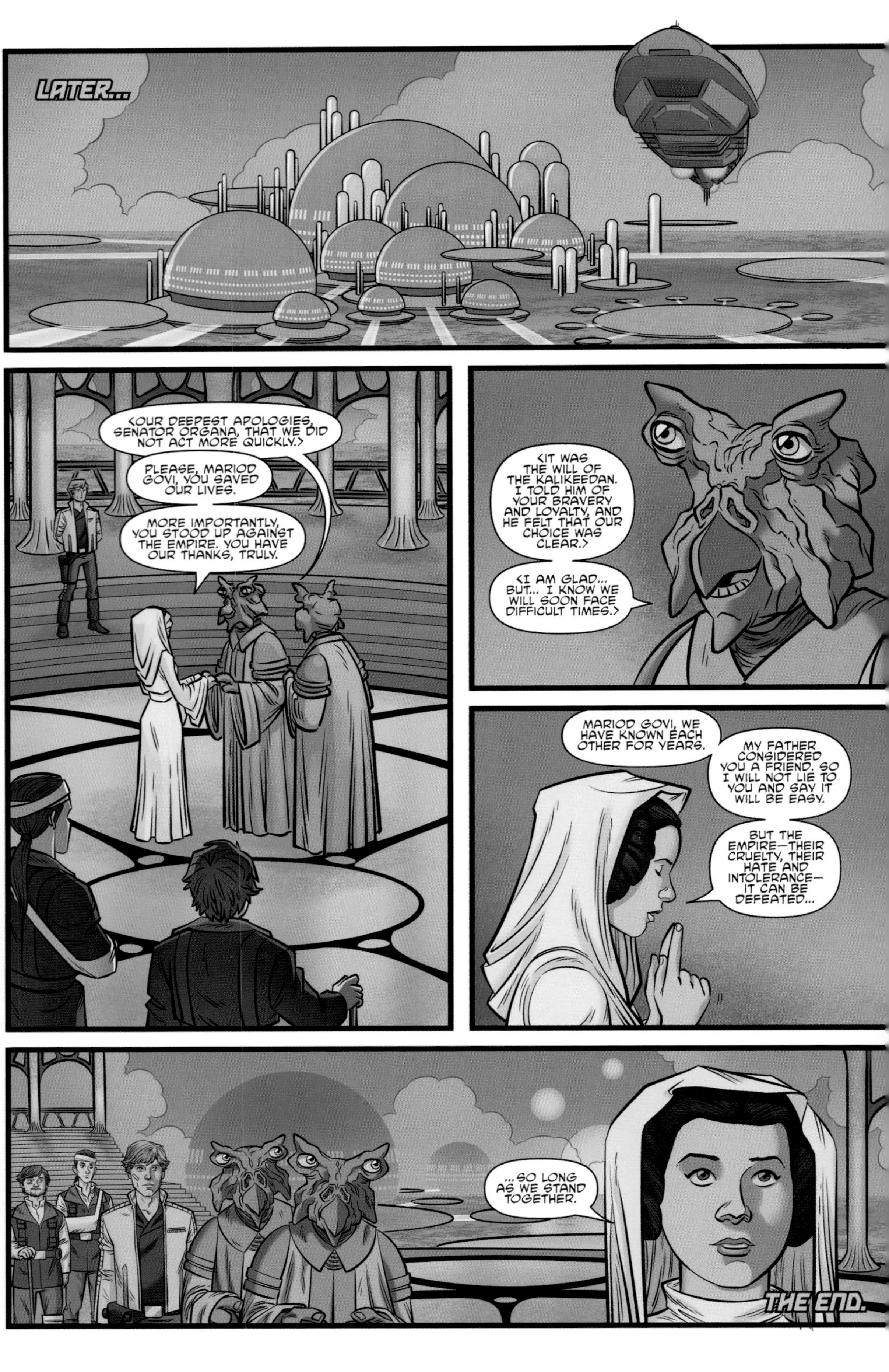
LATER...
<OUR DEEPEST APOLOGIES, SENATOR ORGANA, THAT WE DID NOT ACT MORE QUICKLY.>
PLEASE, MARIOD GOVI, YOU SAVED OUR LIVES.
MORE IMPORTANTLY, YOU STOOD UP AGAINST THE EMPIRE. YOU HAVE OUR THANKS, TRULY.
<IT WAS THE WILL OF THE KALIKEEDAN. I TOLD HIM OF YOUR BRAVERY AND LOYALTY, AND HE FELT THAT OUR CHOICE WAS CLEAR.>
<I AM GLAD... BUT... I KNOW WE WILL SOON FACE DIFFICULT TIMES.>
MARIOD GOVI, WE HAVE KNOWN EACH OTHER FOR YEARS.
MY FATHER CONSIDERED YOU A FRIEND. SO I WILL NOT LIE TO YOU AND SAY IT WILL BE EASY.
BUT THE EMPIRE—THEIR CRUELTY, THEIR HATE AND INTOLERANCE—IT CAN BE DEFEATED...
...SO LONG AS WE STAND TOGETHER.
THE END.

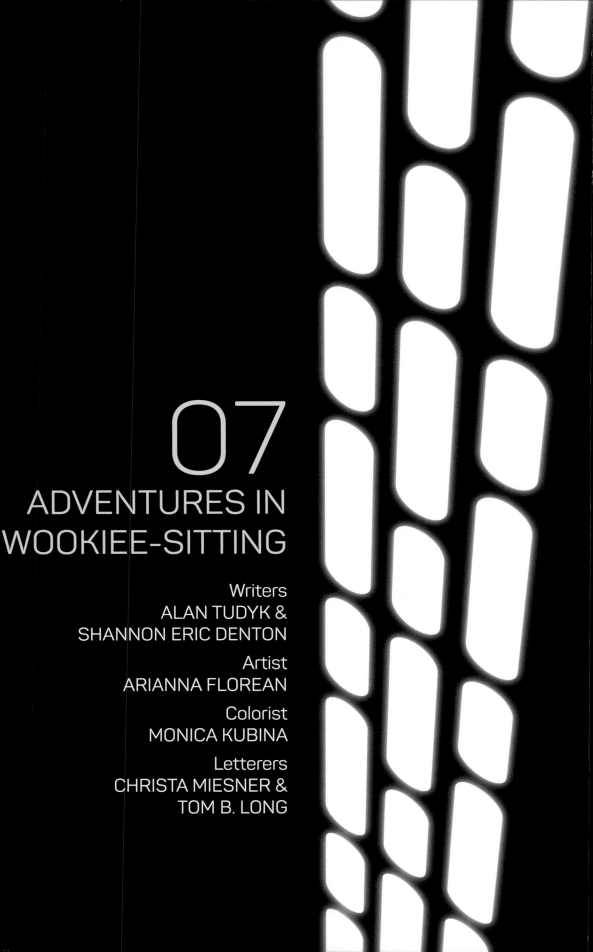

07

ADVENTURES IN
WOOKIEE-SITTING

Writers
ALAN TUDYK &
SHANNON ERIC DENTON

Artist
ARIANNA FLOREAN

Colorist
MONICA KUBINA

Letterers
CHRISTA MIESNER &
TOM B. LONG

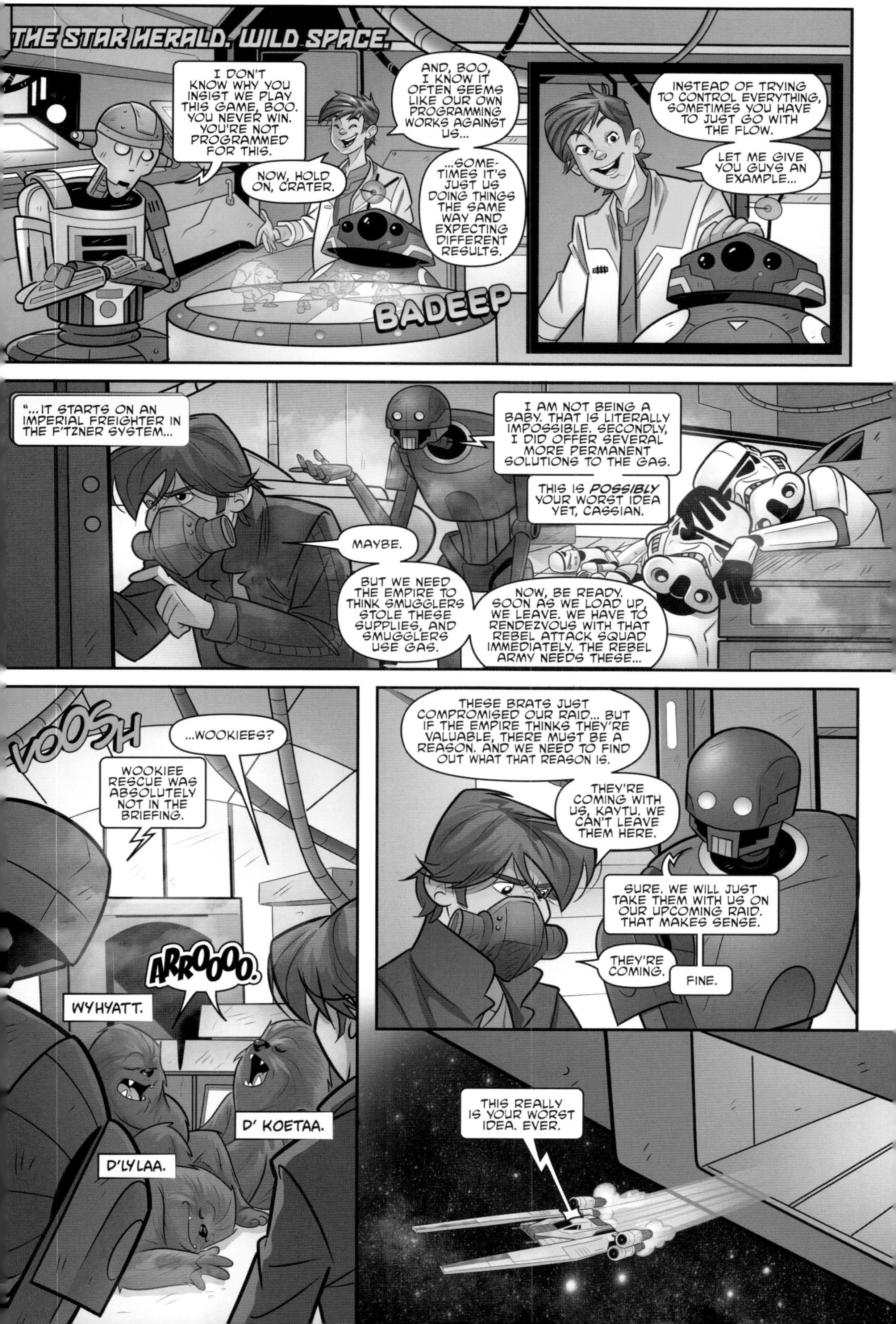
THE STAR HERALD. WILD SPACE.
I DON'T KNOW WHY YOU INSIST WE PLAY THIS GAME, BOO. YOU NEVER WIN. YOU'RE NOT PROGRAMMED FOR THIS.
NOW, HOLD ON, CRATER.
AND, BOO, I KNOW IT OFTEN SEEMS LIKE OUR OWN PROGRAMMING WORKS AGAINST US...
...SOME-TIMES IT'S JUST US DOING THINGS THE SAME WAY AND EXPECTING DIFFERENT RESULTS.
BADEEP
INSTEAD OF TRYING TO CONTROL EVERYTHING, SOMETIMES YOU HAVE TO JUST GO WITH THE FLOW.
LET ME GIVE YOU GUYS AN EXAMPLE...
"...IT STARTS ON AN IMPERIAL FREIGHTER IN THE F'TZNER SYSTEM...
I AM NOT BEING A BABY. THAT IS LITERALLY IMPOSSIBLE. SECONDLY, I DID OFFER SEVERAL MORE PERMANENT SOLUTIONS TO THE GAS.
THIS IS *POSSIBLY* YOUR WORST IDEA YET, CASSIAN.
MAYBE.
BUT WE NEED THE EMPIRE TO THINK SMUGGLERS STOLE THESE SUPPLIES, AND SMUGGLERS USE GAS.
NOW, BE READY. SOON AS WE LOAD UP, WE LEAVE. WE HAVE TO RENDEZVOUS WITH THAT REBEL ATTACK SQUAD IMMEDIATELY. THE REBEL ARMY NEEDS THESE...
VOOSH
...WOOKIEES?
WOOKIEE RESCUE WAS ABSOLUTELY NOT IN THE BRIEFING.
ARROOOO.
WYHYATT.
D' KOETAA.
D'LYLAA.
THESE BRATS JUST COMPROMISED OUR RAID... BUT IF THE EMPIRE THINKS THEY'RE VALUABLE, THERE MUST BE A REASON. AND WE NEED TO FIND OUT WHAT THAT REASON IS.
THEY'RE COMING WITH US, KAYTU. WE CAN'T LEAVE THEM HERE.
SURE. WE WILL JUST TAKE THEM WITH US ON OUR UPCOMING RAID. THAT MAKES SENSE.
THEY'RE COMING.
FINE.
THIS REALLY IS YOUR WORST IDEA. EVER.

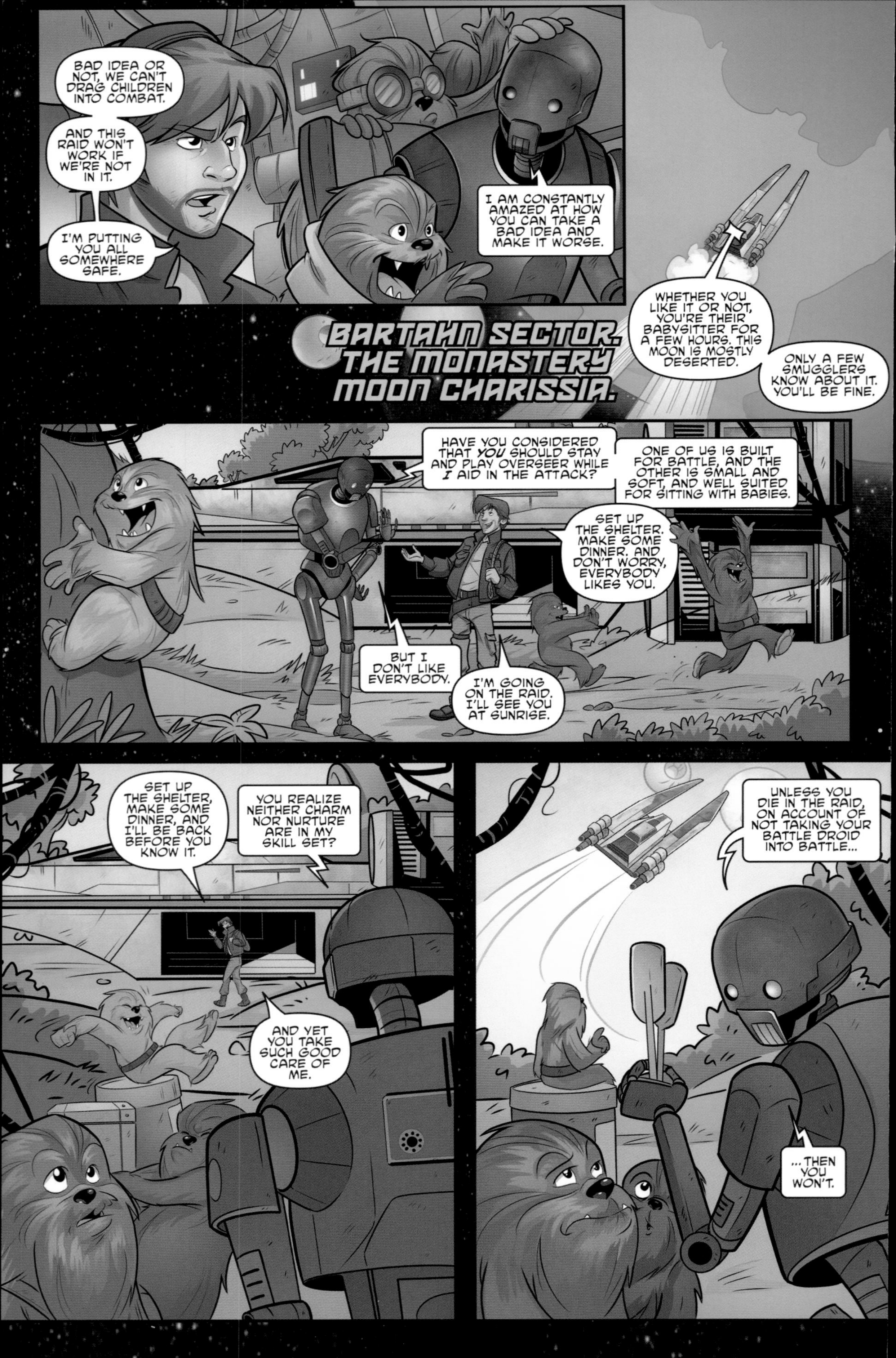
BAD IDEA OR NOT, WE CAN'T DRAG CHILDREN INTO COMBAT.
AND THIS RAID WON'T WORK IF WE'RE NOT IN IT.
I'M PUTTING YOU ALL SOMEWHERE SAFE.
I AM CONSTANTLY AMAZED AT HOW YOU CAN TAKE A BAD IDEA AND MAKE IT WORSE.
BARTAHN SECTOR. THE MONASTERY MOON CHARISSIA.
WHETHER YOU LIKE IT OR NOT, YOU'RE THEIR BABYSITTER FOR A FEW HOURS. THIS MOON IS MOSTLY DESERTED.
ONLY A FEW SMUGGLERS KNOW ABOUT IT. YOU'LL BE FINE.
HAVE YOU CONSIDERED THAT *YOU* SHOULD STAY AND PLAY OVERSEER WHILE *I* AID IN THE ATTACK?
ONE OF US IS BUILT FOR BATTLE, AND THE OTHER IS SMALL AND SOFT, AND WELL SUITED FOR SITTING WITH BABIES.
SET UP THE SHELTER. MAKE SOME DINNER. AND DON'T WORRY, EVERYBODY LIKES YOU.
BUT I DON'T LIKE EVERYBODY.
I'M GOING ON THE RAID. I'LL SEE YOU AT SUNRISE.
SET UP THE SHELTER, MAKE SOME DINNER, AND I'LL BE BACK BEFORE YOU KNOW IT.
YOU REALIZE NEITHER CHARM NOR NURTURE ARE IN MY SKILL SET?
AND YET YOU TAKE SUCH GOOD CARE OF ME.
UNLESS YOU DIE IN THE RAID, ON ACCOUNT OF NOT TAKING YOUR BATTLE DROID INTO BATTLE...
...THEN YOU WON'T.

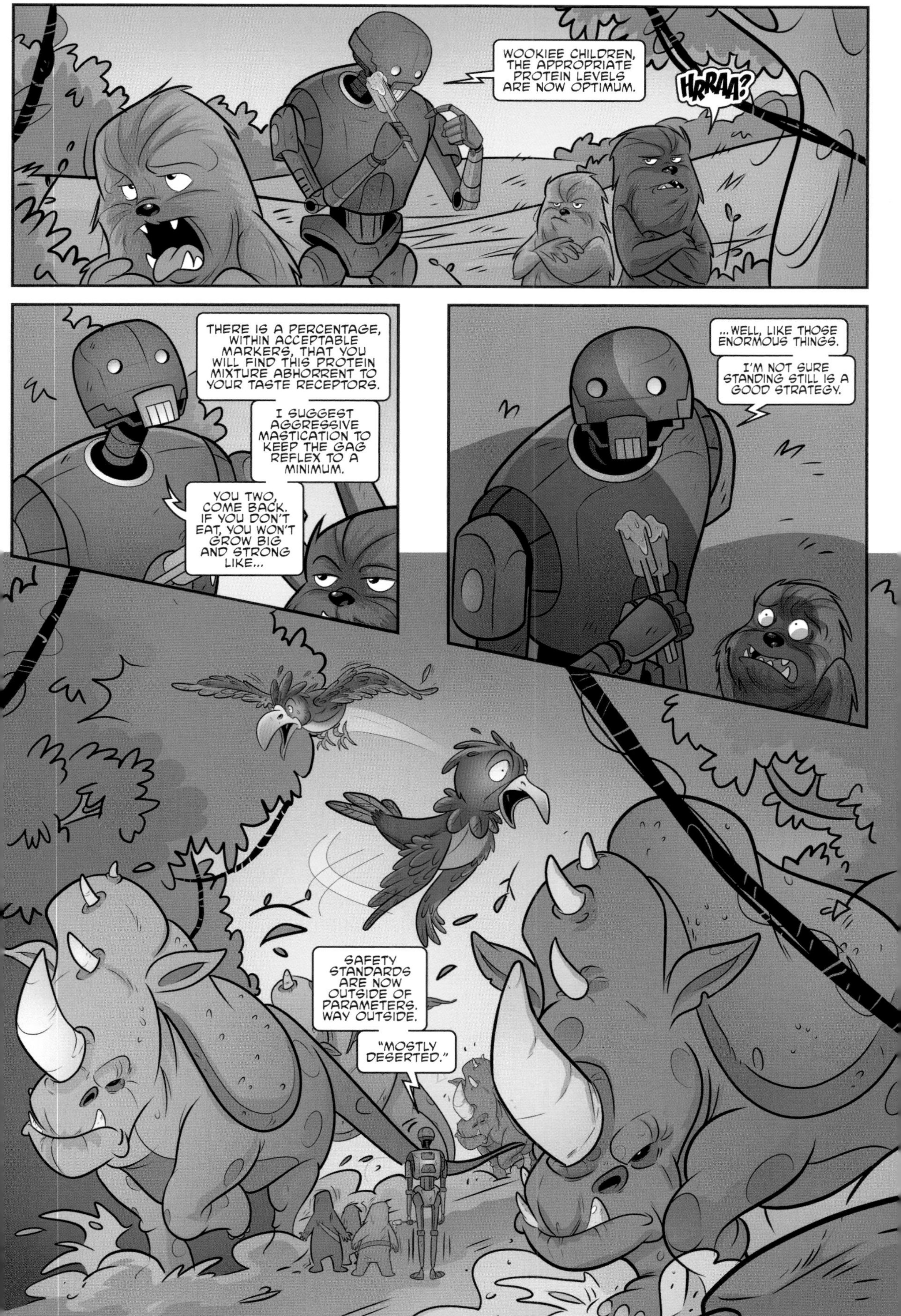
WOOKIEE CHILDREN, THE APPROPRIATE PROTEIN LEVELS ARE NOW OPTIMUM.
HRRAA?
THERE IS A PERCENTAGE, WITHIN ACCEPTABLE MARKERS, THAT YOU WILL FIND THIS PROTEIN MIXTURE ABHORRENT TO YOUR TASTE RECEPTORS.
I SUGGEST AGGRESSIVE MASTICATION TO KEEP THE GAG REFLEX TO A MINIMUM.
YOU TWO, COME BACK. IF YOU DON'T EAT, YOU WON'T GROW BIG AND STRONG LIKE...
...WELL, LIKE THOSE ENORMOUS THINGS.
I'M NOT SURE STANDING STILL IS A GOOD STRATEGY.
SAFETY STANDARDS ARE NOW OUTSIDE OF PARAMETERS. WAY OUTSIDE.
"MOSTLY DESERTED."

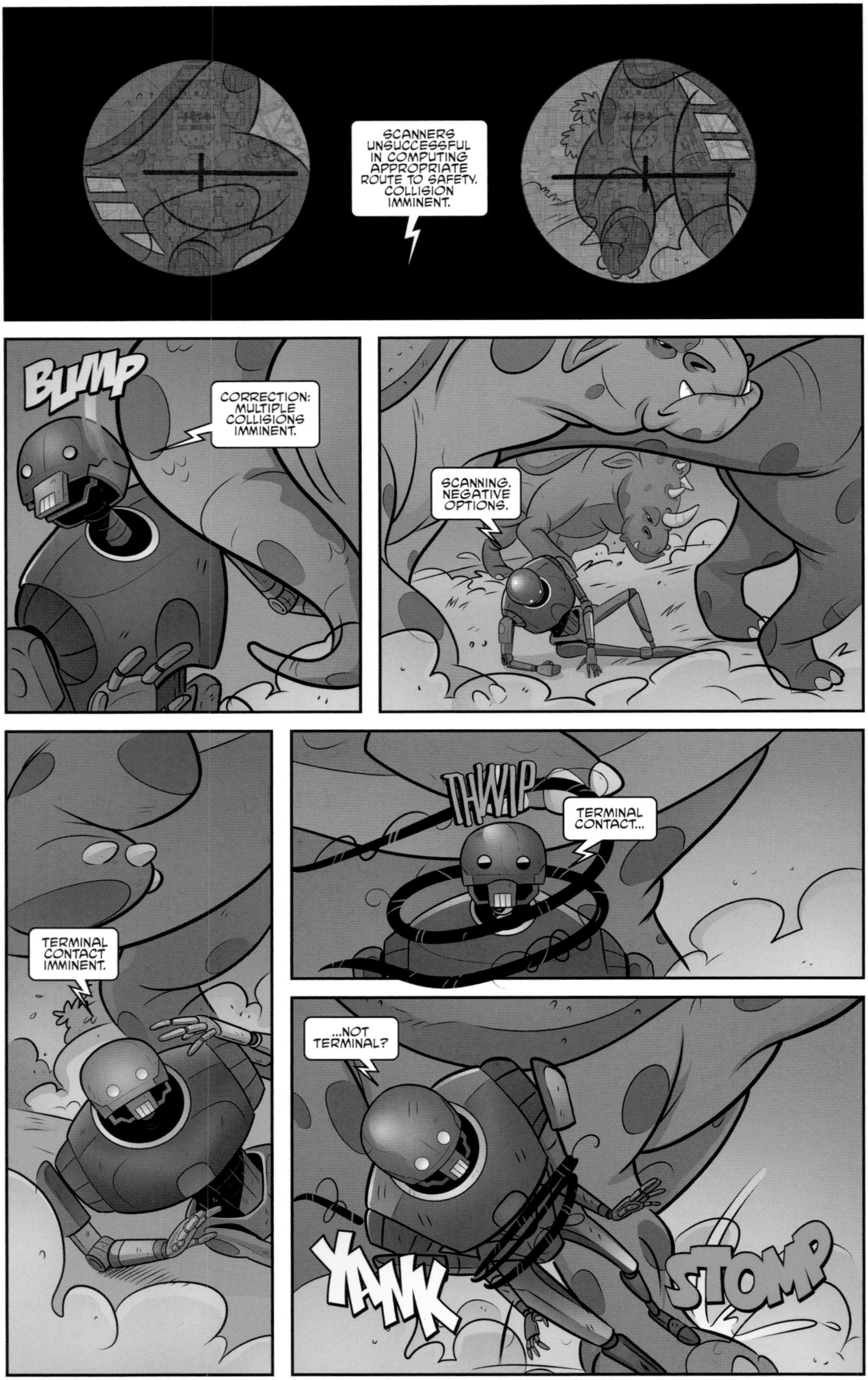
SCANNERS UNSUCCESSFUL IN COMPUTING APPROPRIATE ROUTE TO SAFETY. COLLISION IMMINENT.
BUMP
CORRECTION: MULTIPLE COLLISIONS IMMINENT.
SCANNING. NEGATIVE OPTIONS.
TERMINAL CONTACT IMMINENT.
THWIP
TERMINAL CONTACT...
...NOT TERMINAL?
YANK
STOMP

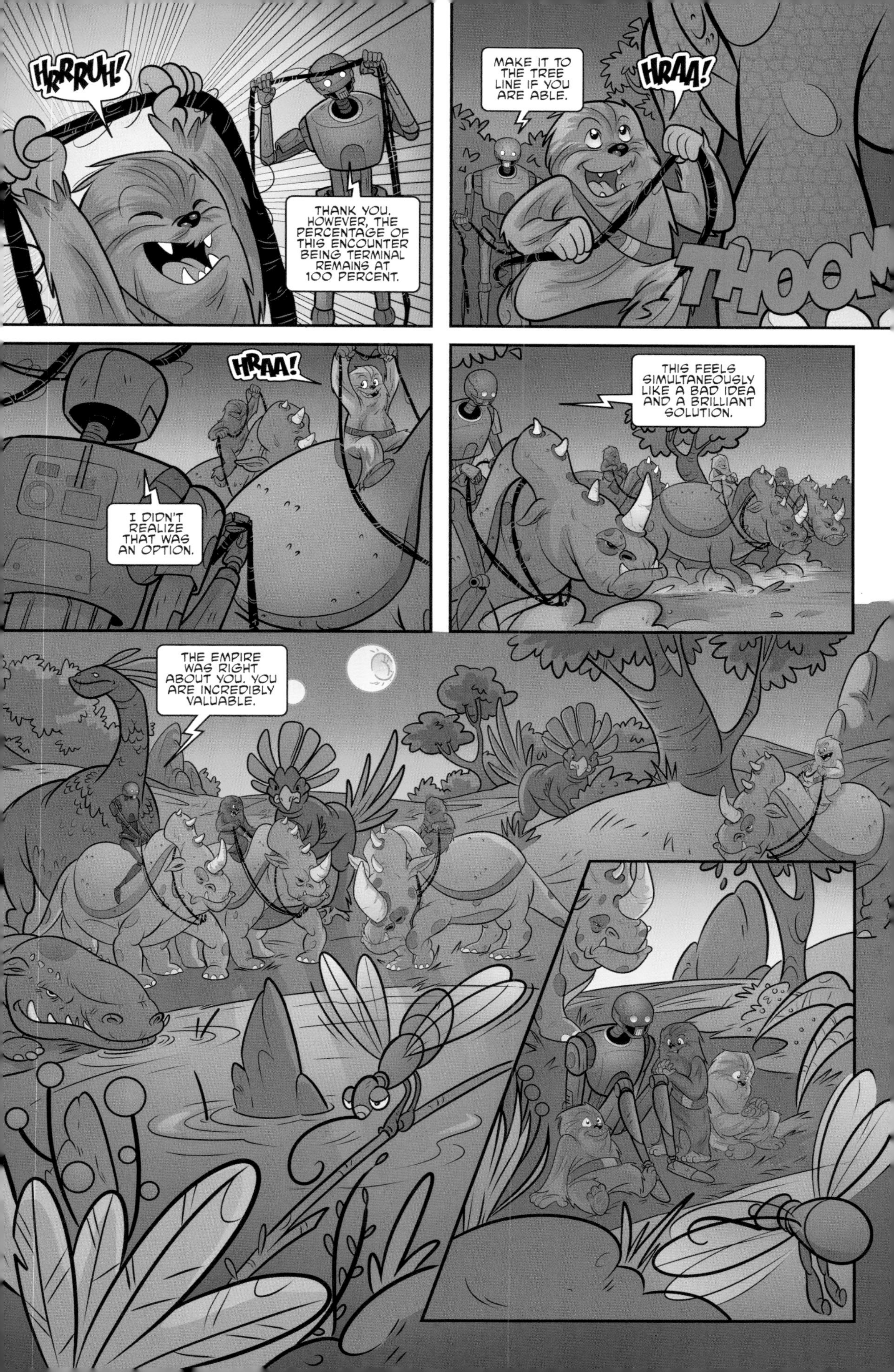

HRRRUH!
THANK YOU. HOWEVER, THE PERCENTAGE OF THIS ENCOUNTER BEING TERMINAL REMAINS AT 100 PERCENT.
MAKE IT TO THE TREE LINE IF YOU ARE ABLE.
HRAA!
THOOM
HRAA!
I DIDN'T REALIZE THAT WAS AN OPTION.
THIS FEELS SIMULTANEOUSLY LIKE A BAD IDEA AND A BRILLIANT SOLUTION.
THE EMPIRE WAS RIGHT ABOUT YOU. YOU ARE INCREDIBLY VALUABLE.

KAYTU! KAYTU, WHERE ARE YOU?

I HAVE EVERYTHING IN HAND... OR SHOULDERS.

I TAKE IT THE RAID WAS A SUCCESS.

EXCELLENT. AND CASSIAN...

UH, YEAH. WITHOUT A HITCH. I TALKED TO REBEL COMMAND ABOUT OUR NEW FRIENDS, TOO, AND THEY HAVE A SAFE HOME FOR THEM.

YES?

TURNS OUT YOU WERE RIGHT...

...EVERYONE *DOES* LIKE ME.

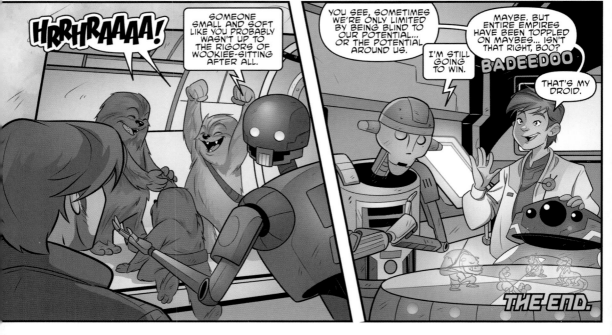

HRRHRAAAA!

SOMEONE SMALL AND SOFT LIKE YOU PROBABLY WASN'T UP TO THE RIGORS OF WOOKIEE-SITTING AFTER ALL.

YOU SEE, SOMETIMES WE'RE ONLY LIMITED BY BEING BLIND TO OUR POTENTIAL... OR THE POTENTIAL AROUND US.

I'M STILL GOING TO WIN.

MAYBE. BUT ENTIRE EMPIRES HAVE BEEN TOPPLED ON MAYBES... ISN'T THAT RIGHT, BOO?

BADEEDOO

THAT'S MY DROID.

THE END.

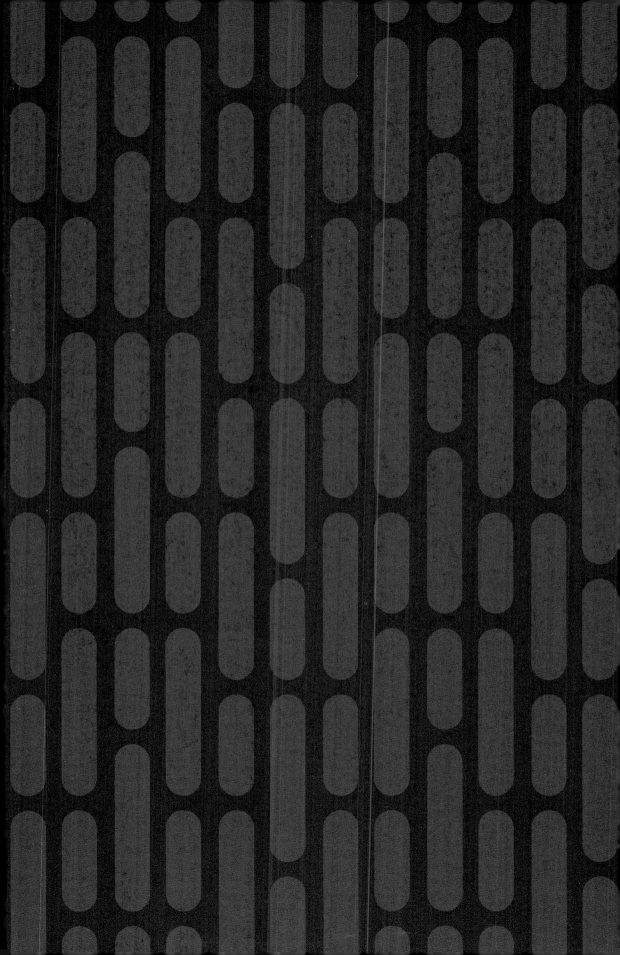

08
MATTIS MAKES
A STAND

Writers
BEN ACKER & BEN BLACKER

Artist
ANNIE WU

Colorist
LEE LOUGHRIDGE

Letterer
TOM B. LONG

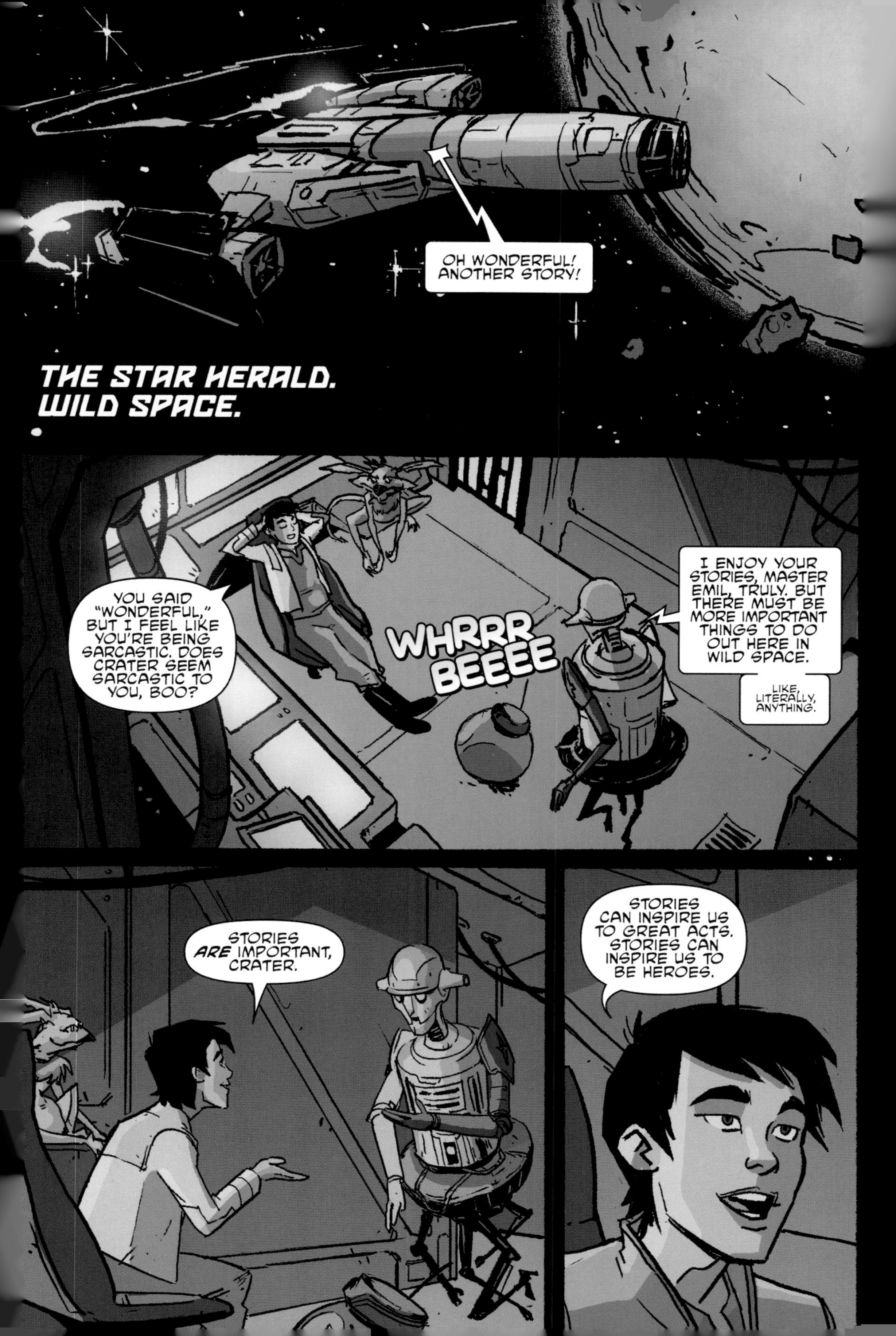

OH WONDERFUL! ANOTHER STORY!
THE STAR HERALD. WILD SPACE.
YOU SAID "WONDERFUL," BUT I FEEL LIKE YOU'RE BEING SARCASTIC. DOES CRATER SEEM SARCASTIC TO YOU, BOO?
WHRRR BEEEE
I ENJOY YOUR STORIES, MASTER EMIL, TRULY. BUT THERE MUST BE MORE IMPORTANT THINGS TO DO OUT HERE IN WILD SPACE.
LIKE, LITERALLY, ANYTHING.
STORIES *ARE* IMPORTANT, CRATER.
STORIES CAN INSPIRE US TO GREAT ACTS. STORIES CAN INSPIRE US TO BE HEROES.

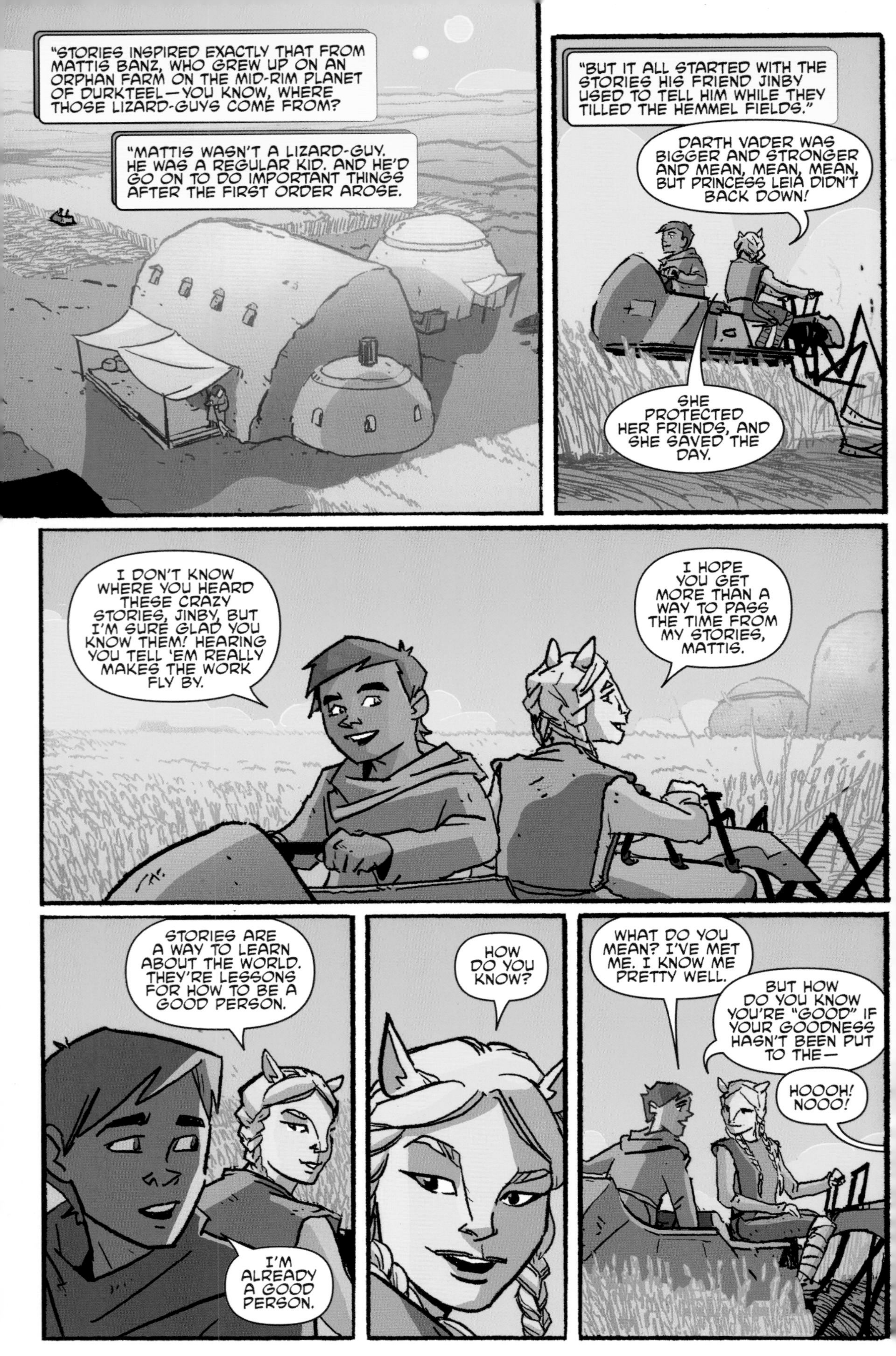
"STORIES INSPIRED EXACTLY THAT FROM MATTIS BANZ, WHO GREW UP ON AN ORPHAN FARM ON THE MID-RIM PLANET OF DURKTEEL—YOU KNOW, WHERE THOSE LIZARD-GUYS COME FROM?
"MATTIS WASN'T A LIZARD-GUY. HE WAS A REGULAR KID. AND HE'D GO ON TO DO IMPORTANT THINGS AFTER THE FIRST ORDER AROSE.
"BUT IT ALL STARTED WITH THE STORIES HIS FRIEND JINBY USED TO TELL HIM WHILE THEY TILLED THE HEMMEL FIELDS."
DARTH VADER WAS BIGGER AND STRONGER AND MEAN, MEAN, MEAN, BUT PRINCESS LEIA DIDN'T BACK DOWN!
SHE PROTECTED HER FRIENDS, AND SHE SAVED THE DAY.
I DON'T KNOW WHERE YOU HEARD THESE CRAZY STORIES, JINBY, BUT I'M SURE GLAD YOU KNOW THEM! HEARING YOU TELL 'EM REALLY MAKES THE WORK FLY BY.
I HOPE YOU GET MORE THAN A WAY TO PASS THE TIME FROM MY STORIES, MATTIS.
STORIES ARE A WAY TO LEARN ABOUT THE WORLD. THEY'RE LESSONS FOR HOW TO BE A GOOD PERSON.
I'M ALREADY A GOOD PERSON.
HOW DO YOU KNOW?
WHAT DO YOU MEAN? I'VE MET ME. I KNOW ME PRETTY WELL.
BUT HOW DO YOU KNOW YOU'RE "GOOD" IF YOUR GOODNESS HASN'T BEEN PUT TO THE—
HOOOH! NOOO!

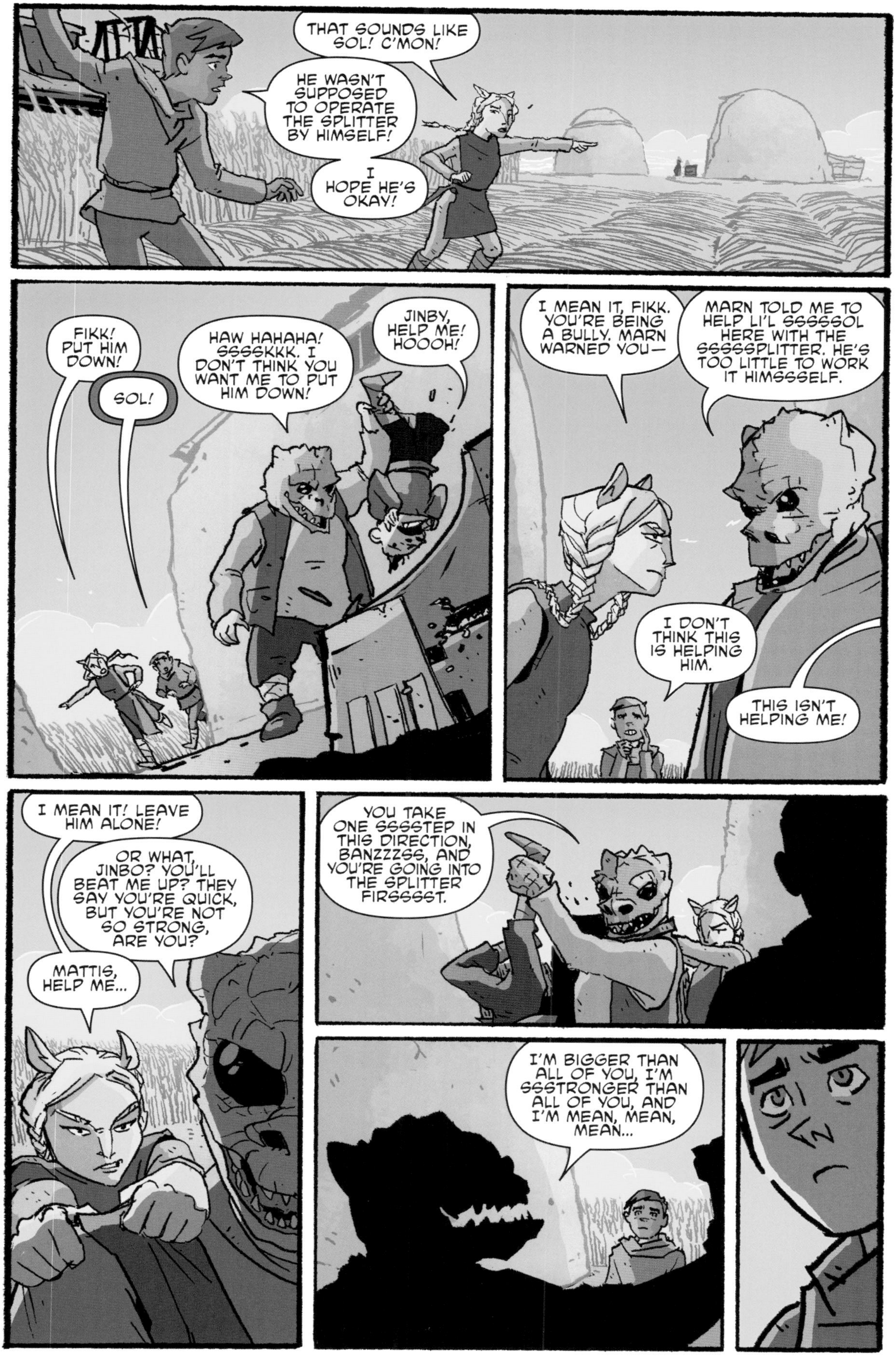
THAT SOUNDS LIKE SOL! C'MON!
HE WASN'T SUPPOSED TO OPERATE THE SPLITTER BY HIMSELF!
I HOPE HE'S OKAY!
FIKK! PUT HIM DOWN!
SOL!
HAW HAHAHA! SSSSKKK. I DON'T THINK YOU WANT ME TO PUT HIM DOWN!
JINBY, HELP ME! HOOOH!
I MEAN IT, FIKK. YOU'RE BEING A BULLY. MARN WARNED YOU—
MARN TOLD ME TO HELP LI'L SSSSSOL HERE WITH THE SSSSSPLITTER. HE'S TOO LITTLE TO WORK IT HIMSSSELF.
I DON'T THINK THIS IS HELPING HIM.
THIS ISN'T HELPING ME!
I MEAN IT! LEAVE HIM ALONE!
OR WHAT, JINBO? YOU'LL BEAT ME UP? THEY SAY YOU'RE QUICK, BUT YOU'RE NOT SO STRONG, ARE YOU?
MATTIS, HELP ME...
YOU TAKE ONE SSSSTEP IN THIS DIRECTION, BANZZZSS, AND YOU'RE GOING INTO THE SPLITTER FIRSSSST.
I'M BIGGER THAN ALL OF YOU, I'M SSSTRONGER THAN ALL OF YOU, AND I'M MEAN, MEAN, MEAN...

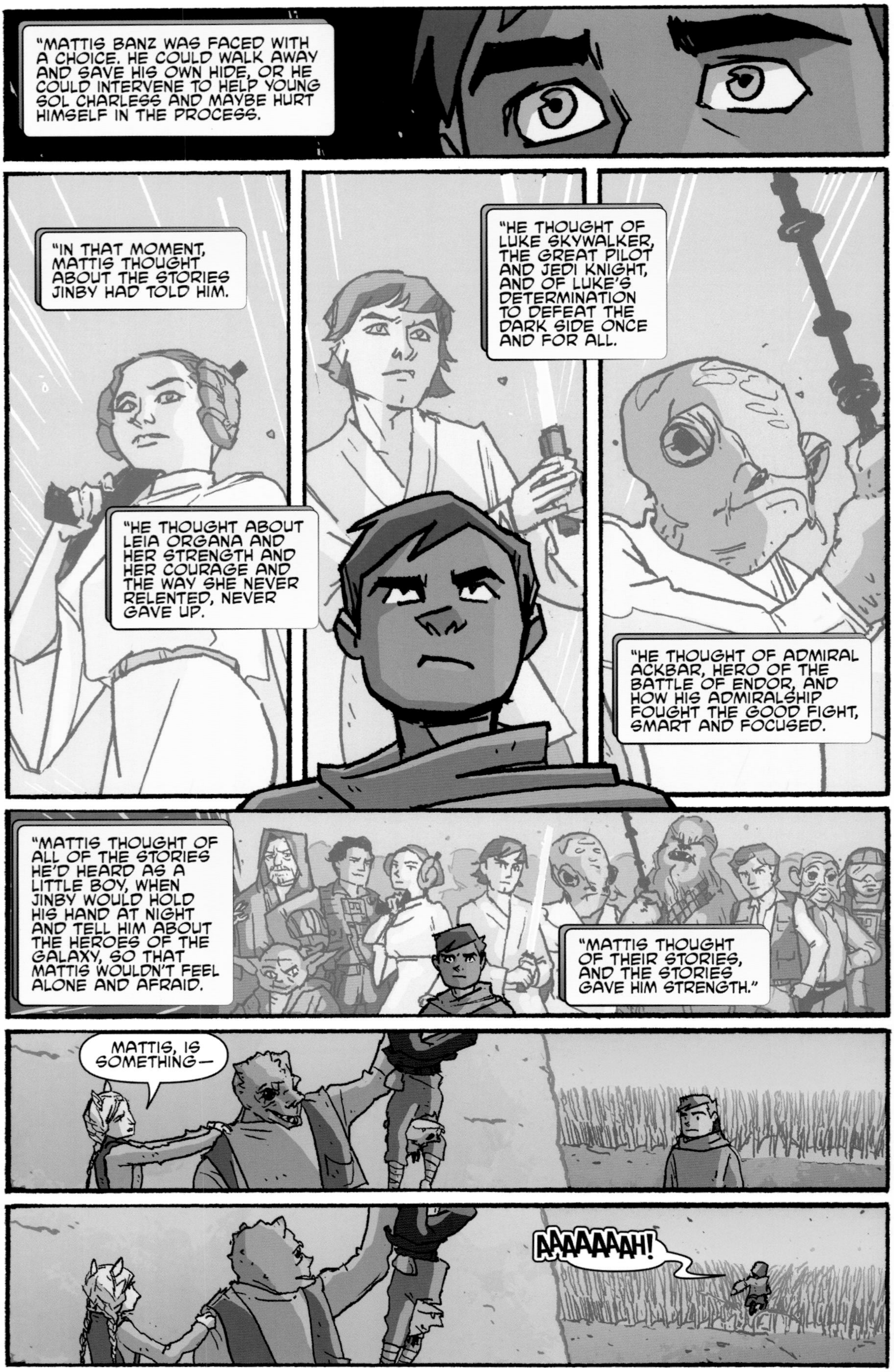
"MATTIS BANZ WAS FACED WITH A CHOICE. HE COULD WALK AWAY AND SAVE HIS OWN HIDE, OR HE COULD INTERVENE TO HELP YOUNG SOL CHARLESS AND MAYBE HURT HIMSELF IN THE PROCESS.
"IN THAT MOMENT, MATTIS THOUGHT ABOUT THE STORIES JINBY HAD TOLD HIM.
"HE THOUGHT ABOUT LEIA ORGANA AND HER STRENGTH AND HER COURAGE AND THE WAY SHE NEVER RELENTED, NEVER GAVE UP.
"HE THOUGHT OF LUKE SKYWALKER, THE GREAT PILOT AND JEDI KNIGHT, AND OF LUKE'S DETERMINATION TO DEFEAT THE DARK SIDE ONCE AND FOR ALL.
"HE THOUGHT OF ADMIRAL ACKBAR, HERO OF THE BATTLE OF ENDOR, AND HOW HIS ADMIRALSHIP FOUGHT THE GOOD FIGHT, SMART AND FOCUSED.
"MATTIS THOUGHT OF ALL OF THE STORIES HE'D HEARD AS A LITTLE BOY, WHEN JINBY WOULD HOLD HIS HAND AT NIGHT AND TELL HIM ABOUT THE HEROES OF THE GALAXY, SO THAT MATTIS WOULDN'T FEEL ALONE AND AFRAID.
"MATTIS THOUGHT OF THEIR STORIES, AND THE STORIES GAVE HIM STRENGTH."
MATTIS, IS SOMETHING—
AAAAAAAH!

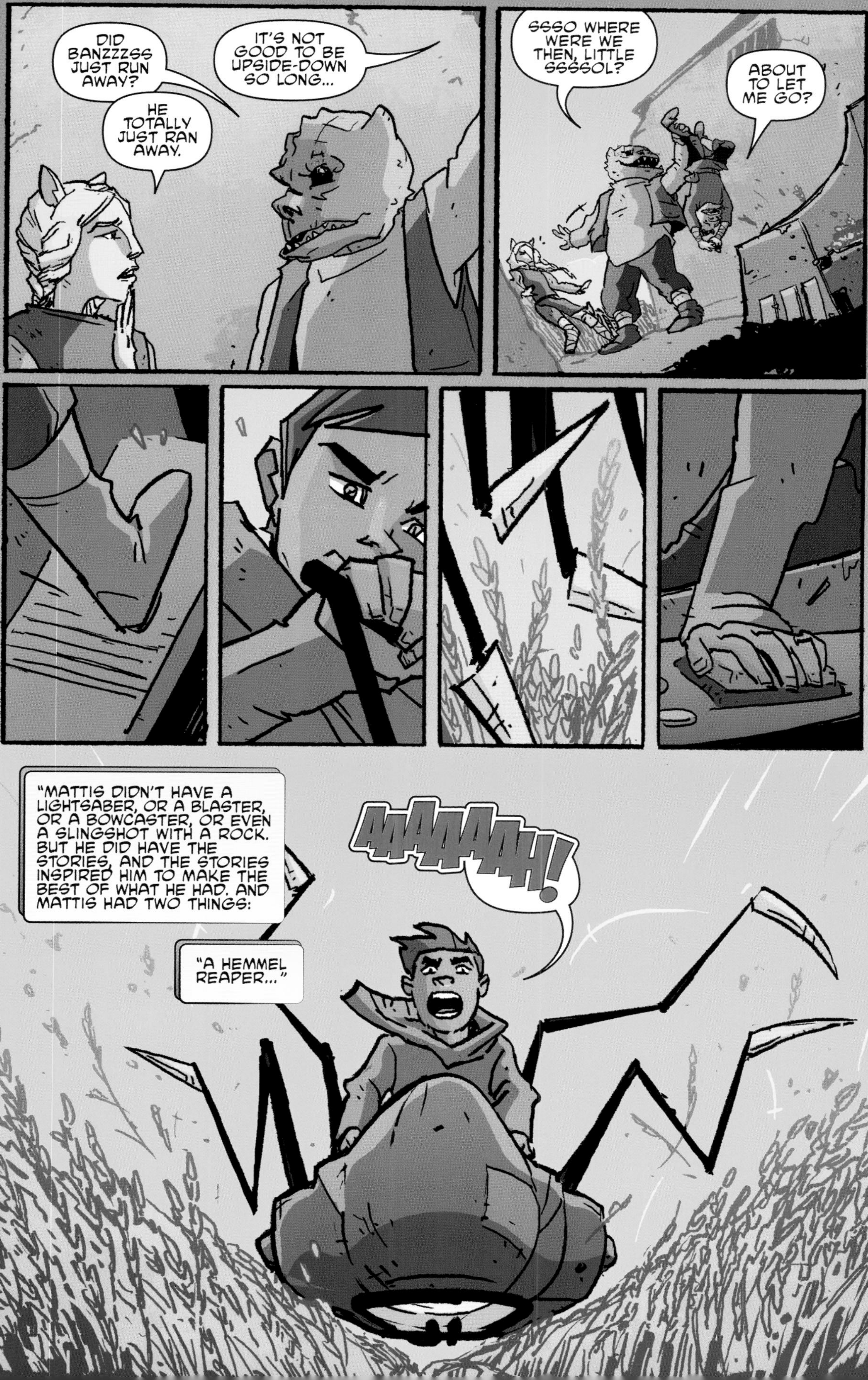
DID BANZZZZSS JUST RUN AWAY?
IT'S NOT GOOD TO BE UPSIDE-DOWN SO LONG...
HE TOTALLY JUST RAN AWAY.
SSSO WHERE WERE WE THEN, LITTLE SSSSSOL?
ABOUT TO LET ME GO?
"MATTIS DIDN'T HAVE A LIGHTSABER, OR A BLASTER, OR A BOWCASTER, OR EVEN A SLINGSHOT WITH A ROCK. BUT HE DID HAVE THE STORIES, AND THE STORIES INSPIRED HIM TO MAKE THE BEST OF WHAT HE HAD. AND MATTIS HAD TWO THINGS:
AAAAAAAH!
"A HEMMEL REAPER..."

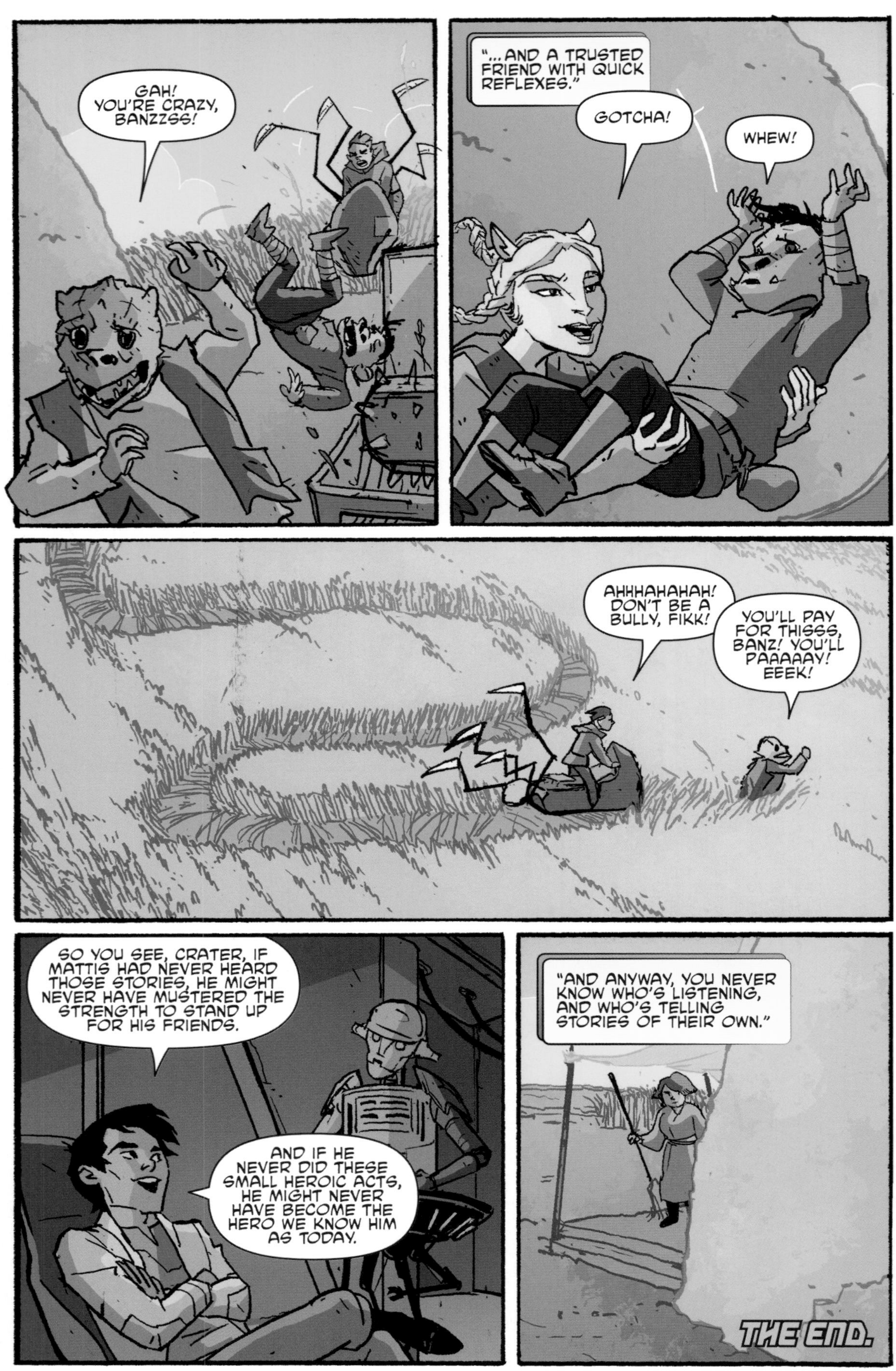
GAH! YOU'RE CRAZY, BANZZSS!
"...AND A TRUSTED FRIEND WITH QUICK REFLEXES."
GOTCHA!
WHEW!
AHHHAHAHAH! DON'T BE A BULLY, FIKK!
YOU'LL PAY FOR THISSS, BANZ! YOU'LL PAAAAAY! EEEK!
SO YOU SEE, CRATER, IF MATTIS HAD NEVER HEARD THOSE STORIES, HE MIGHT NEVER HAVE MUSTERED THE STRENGTH TO STAND UP FOR HIS FRIENDS.
AND IF HE NEVER DID THESE SMALL HEROIC ACTS, HE MIGHT NEVER HAVE BECOME THE HERO WE KNOW HIM AS TODAY.
"AND ANYWAY, YOU NEVER KNOW WHO'S LISTENING, AND WHO'S TELLING STORIES OF THEIR OWN."
THE END.

09
THE BEST PET

Writer
DELILAH S. DAWSON
Artist
ARIANNA FLOREAN
Letterer
TOM B. LONG

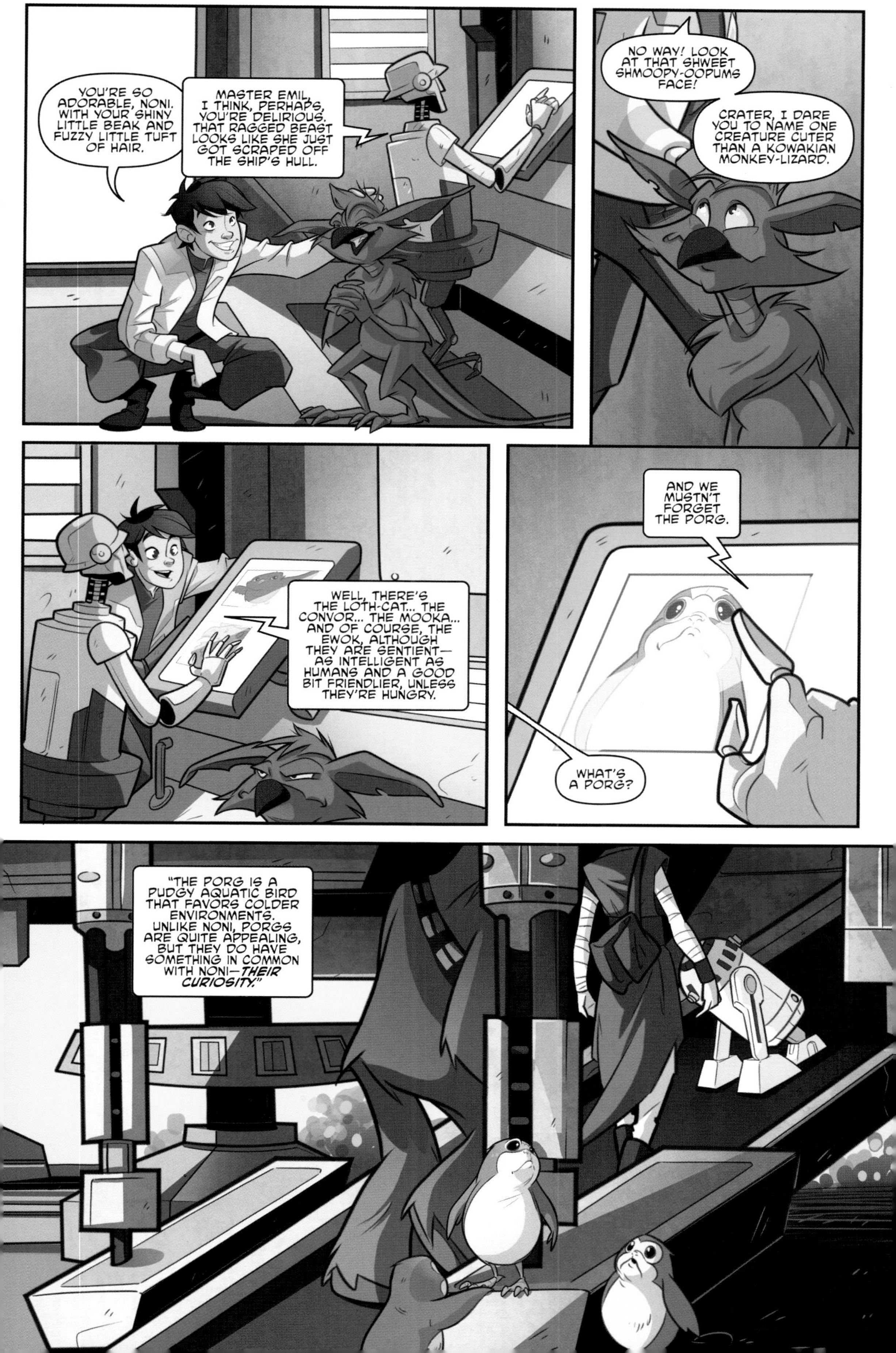
YOU'RE SO ADORABLE, NONI. WITH YOUR SHINY LITTLE BEAK AND FUZZY LITTLE TUFT OF HAIR.
MASTER EMIL, I THINK, PERHAPS, YOU'RE DELIRIOUS. THAT RAGGED BEAST LOOKS LIKE SHE JUST GOT SCRAPED OFF THE SHIP'S HULL.
NO WAY! LOOK AT THAT SHWEET SHMOOPY-OOPUMS FACE!
CRATER, I DARE YOU TO NAME ONE CREATURE CUTER THAN A KOWAKIAN MONKEY-LIZARD.
WELL, THERE'S THE LOTH-CAT... THE CONVOR... THE MOOKA... AND OF COURSE, THE EWOK, ALTHOUGH THEY ARE SENTIENT—AS INTELLIGENT AS HUMANS AND A GOOD BIT FRIENDLIER, UNLESS THEY'RE HUNGRY.
AND WE MUSTN'T FORGET THE PORG.
WHAT'S A PORG?
"THE PORG IS A PUDGY AQUATIC BIRD THAT FAVORS COLDER ENVIRONMENTS. UNLIKE NONI, PORGS ARE QUITE APPEALING, BUT THEY DO HAVE SOMETHING IN COMMON WITH NONI—*THEIR CURIOSITY.*"

"PORGS ARE QUITE FASCINATING LITTLE CREATURES, ACTUALLY.

"THEY'RE ONLY KNEE-HIGH, AND MUCH LIGHTER THAN THEY LOOK, THANKS TO A THICK LAYER OF WATERPROOF FEATHERS WITH A FLUFFY UNDERLAYER FOR WARMTH.

THUMP

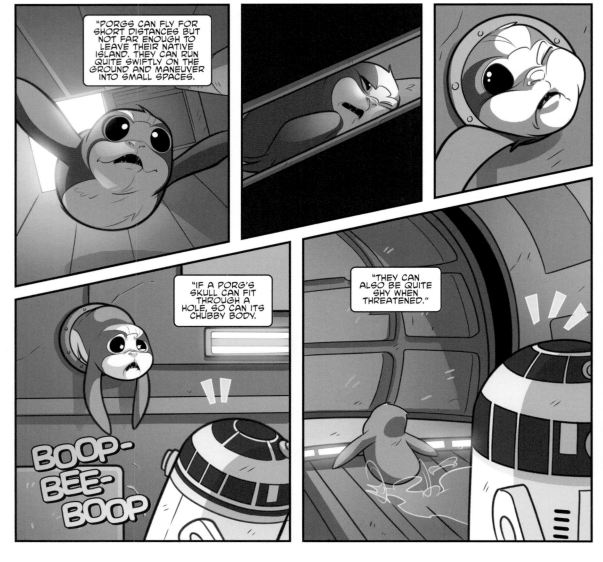

"PORGS CAN FLY FOR SHORT DISTANCES BUT NOT FAR ENOUGH TO LEAVE THEIR NATIVE ISLAND. THEY CAN RUN QUITE SWIFTLY ON THE GROUND AND MANEUVER INTO SMALL SPACES.

"IF A PORG'S SKULL CAN FIT THROUGH A HOLE, SO CAN ITS CHUBBY BODY.

BOOP-BEE-BOOP

"THEY CAN ALSO BE QUITE SHY WHEN THREATENED."

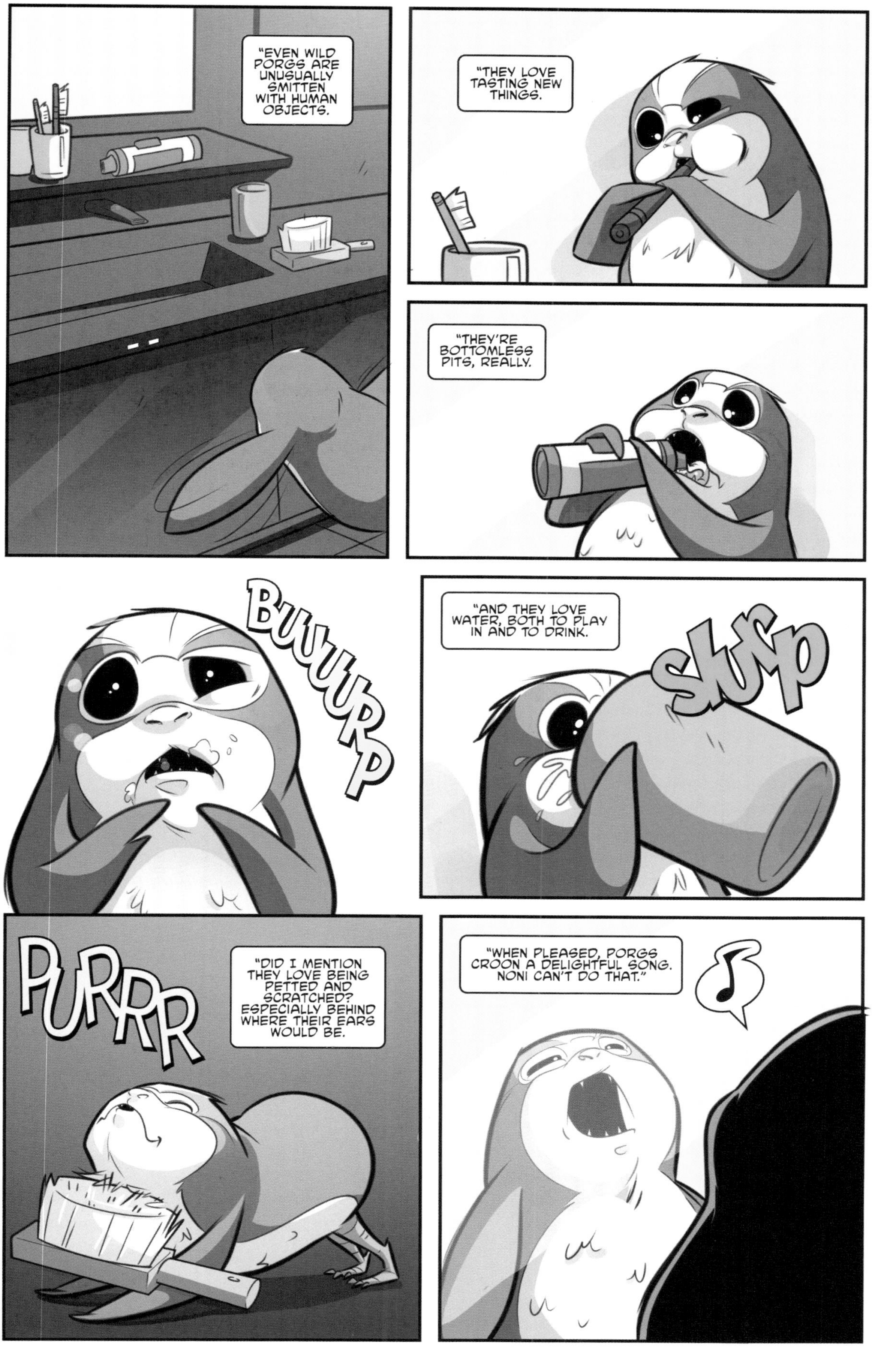
"EVEN WILD PORGS ARE UNUSUALLY SMITTEN WITH HUMAN OBJECTS.
"THEY LOVE TASTING NEW THINGS.
"THEY'RE BOTTOMLESS PITS, REALLY.
BUUURP
"AND THEY LOVE WATER, BOTH TO PLAY IN AND TO DRINK.
SLURP
PURRR
"DID I MENTION THEY LOVE BEING PETTED AND SCRATCHED? ESPECIALLY BEHIND WHERE THEIR EARS WOULD BE.
"WHEN PLEASED, PORGS CROON A DELIGHTFUL SONG. NONI CAN'T DO THAT."

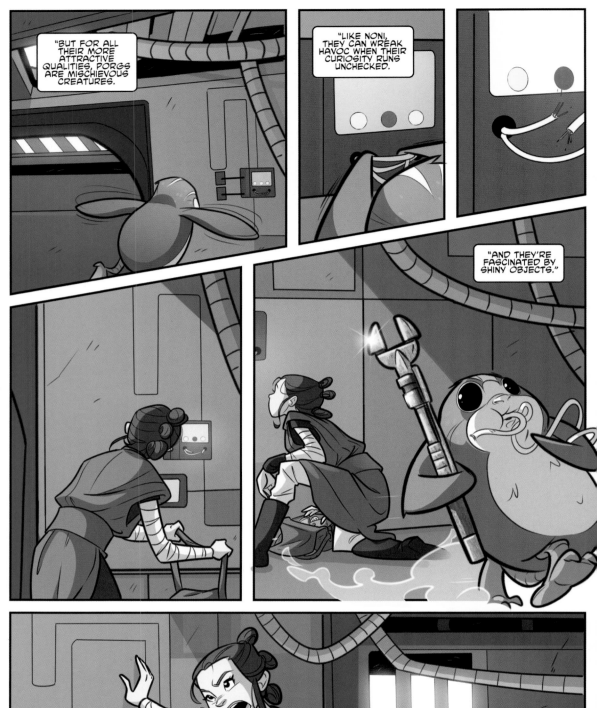

"BUT FOR ALL THEIR MORE ATTRACTIVE QUALITIES, PORGS ARE MISCHIEVOUS CREATURES.

"LIKE NONI, THEY CAN WREAK HAVOC WHEN THEIR CURIOSITY RUNS UNCHECKED.

"AND THEY'RE FASCINATED BY SHINY OBJECTS."

CHEWIE! DID YOU BORROW MY SPANNER?

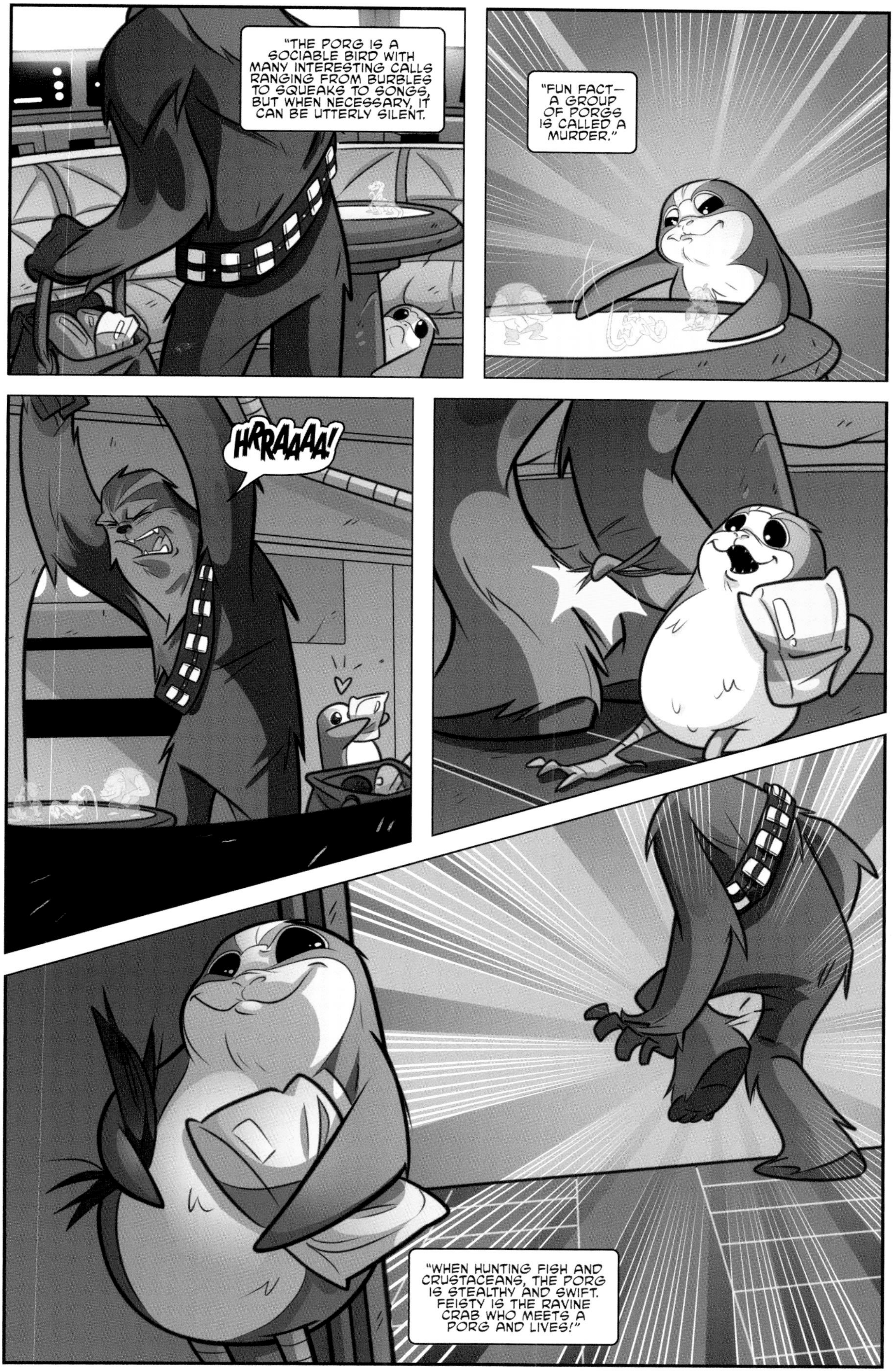
"THE PORG IS A SOCIABLE BIRD WITH MANY INTERESTING CALLS RANGING FROM BURBLES TO SQUEAKS TO SONGS, BUT WHEN NECESSARY, IT CAN BE UTTERLY SILENT.
"FUN FACT— A GROUP OF PORGS IS CALLED A MURDER."
HRRAAAA!
"WHEN HUNTING FISH AND CRUSTACEANS, THE PORG IS STEALTHY AND SWIFT. FEISTY IS THE RAVINE CRAB WHO MEETS A PORG AND LIVES!"

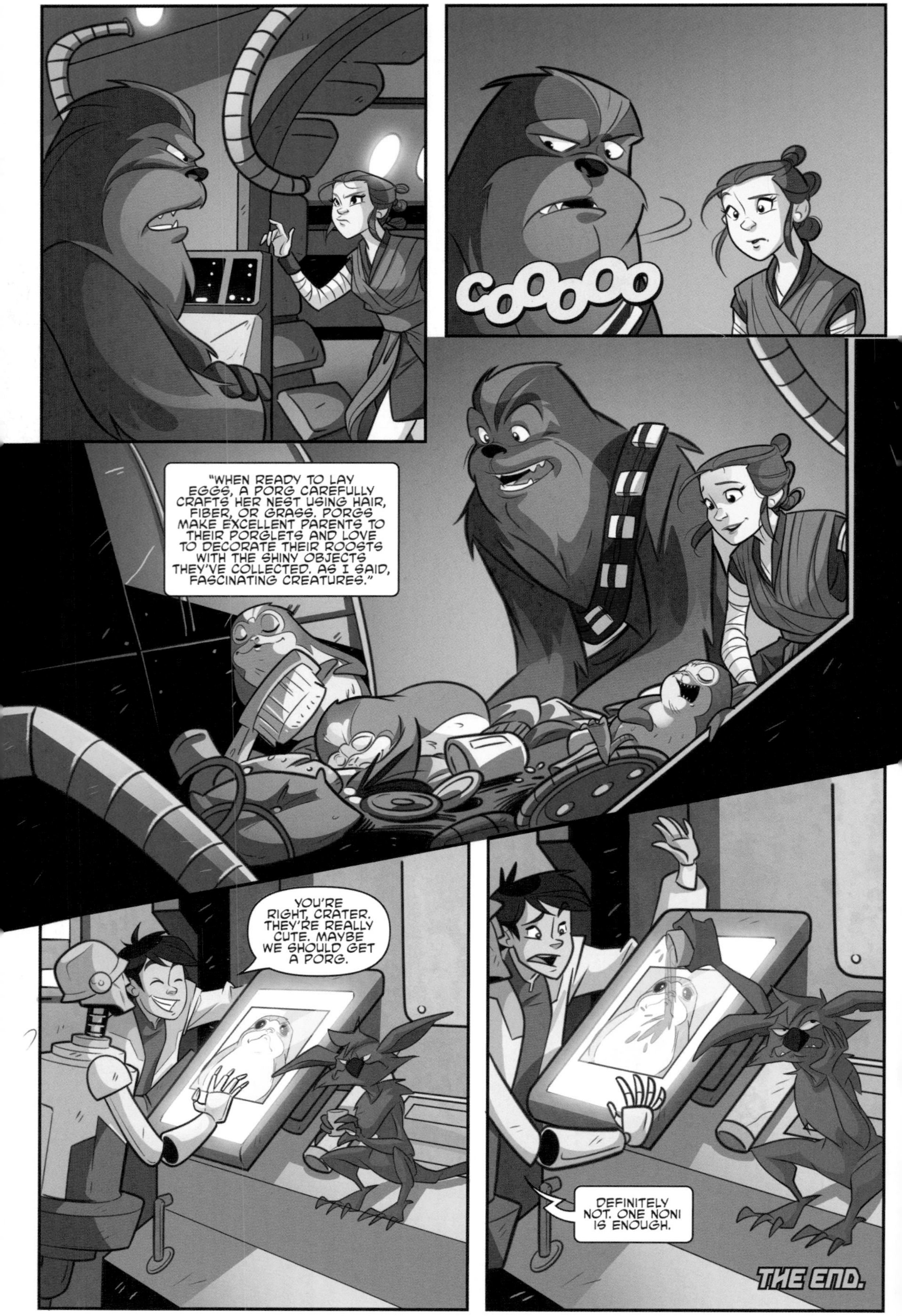
COOOOO
"WHEN READY TO LAY EGGS, A PORG CAREFULLY CRAFTS HER NEST USING HAIR, FIBER, OR GRASS. PORGS MAKE EXCELLENT PARENTS TO THEIR PORGLETS AND LOVE TO DECORATE THEIR ROOSTS WITH THE SHINY OBJECTS THEY'VE COLLECTED. AS I SAID, FASCINATING CREATURES."
YOU'RE RIGHT, CRATER. THEY'RE REALLY CUTE. MAYBE WE SHOULD GET A PORG.
DEFINITELY NOT. ONE NONI IS ENOUGH.
THE END.

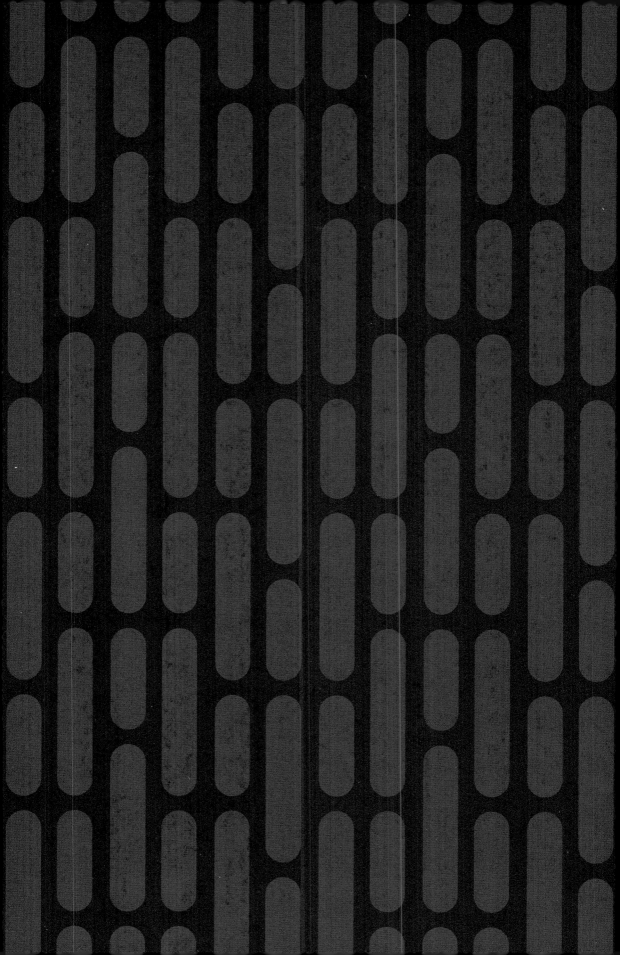

10
ROSE KNOWS

Writer
DELILAH S. DAWSON

Artist
DEREK CHARM

Letterer
TOM B. LONG

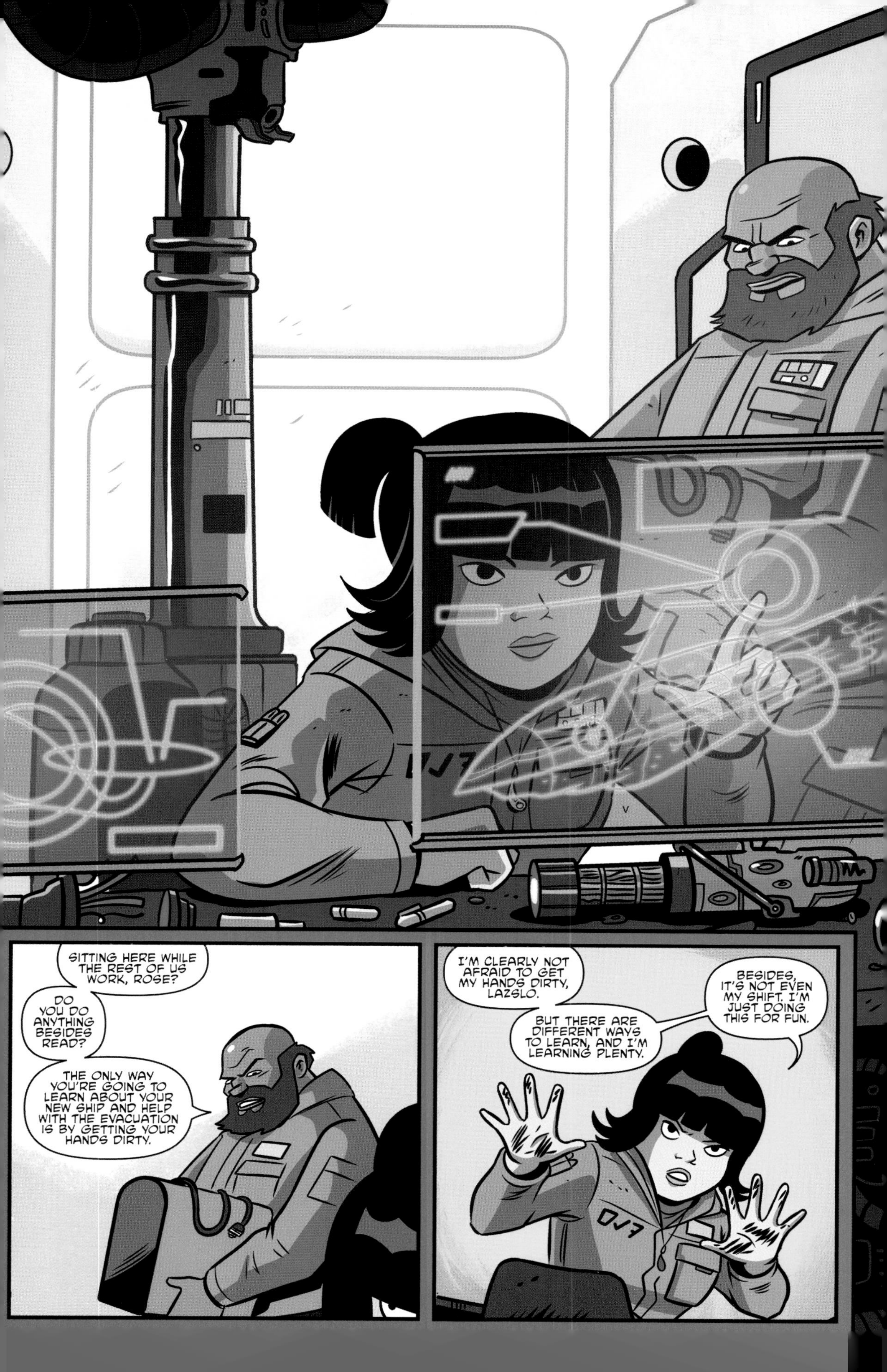

SITTING HERE WHILE THE REST OF US WORK, ROSE?
DO YOU DO ANYTHING BESIDES READ?
THE ONLY WAY YOU'RE GOING TO LEARN ABOUT YOUR NEW SHIP AND HELP WITH THE EVACUATION IS BY GETTING YOUR HANDS DIRTY.
I'M CLEARLY NOT AFRAID TO GET MY HANDS DIRTY, LAZSLO.
BUT THERE ARE DIFFERENT WAYS TO LEARN, AND I'M LEARNING PLENTY.
BESIDES, IT'S NOT EVEN MY SHIFT. I'M JUST DOING THIS FOR FUN.

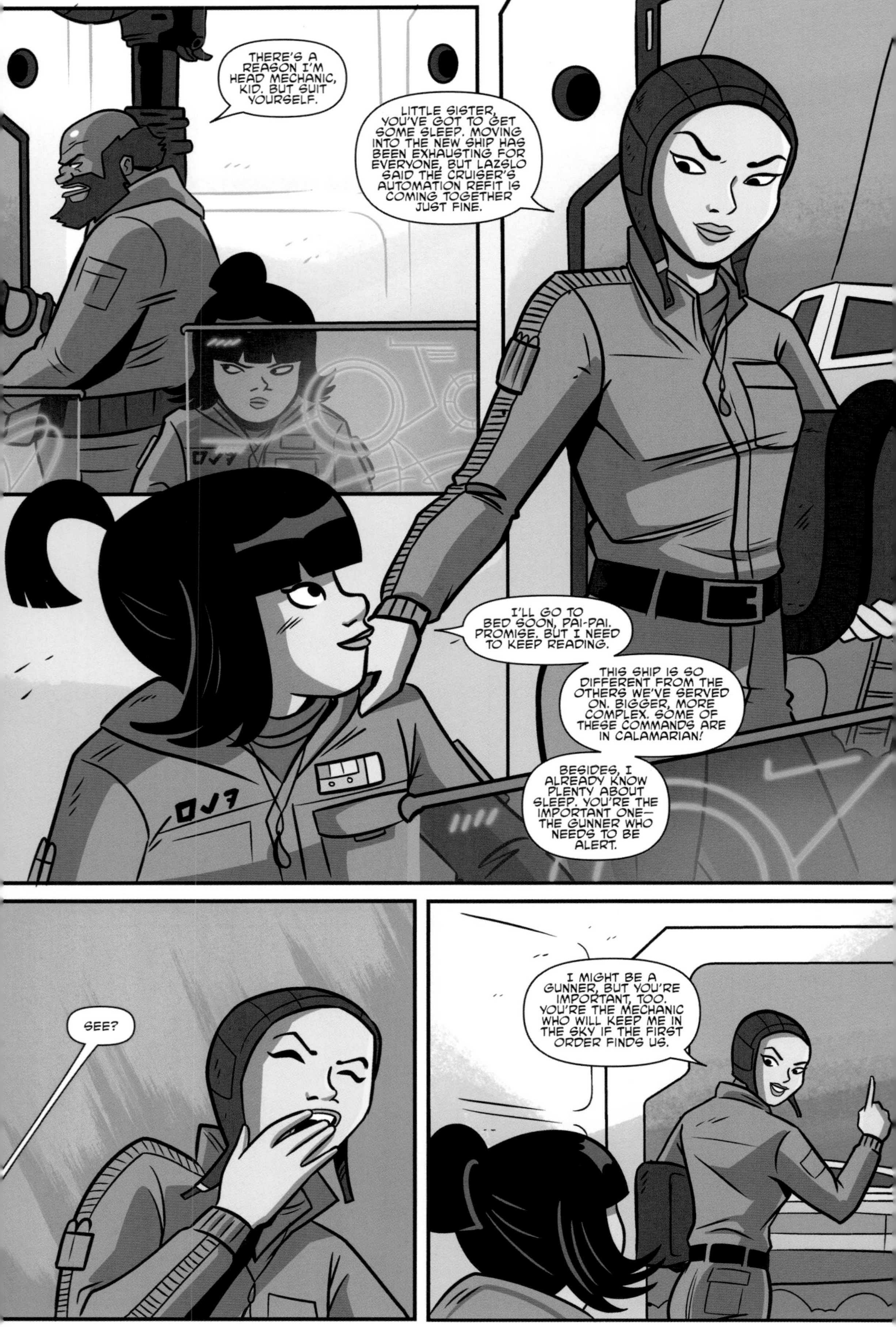

THERE'S A REASON I'M HEAD MECHANIC, KID. BUT SUIT YOURSELF.
LITTLE SISTER, YOU'VE GOT TO GET SOME SLEEP. MOVING INTO THE NEW SHIP HAS BEEN EXHAUSTING FOR EVERYONE, BUT LAZSLO SAID THE CRUISER'S AUTOMATION REFIT IS COMING TOGETHER JUST FINE.
I'LL GO TO BED SOON, PAI-PAI. PROMISE. BUT I NEED TO KEEP READING.
THIS SHIP IS SO DIFFERENT FROM THE OTHERS WE'VE SERVED ON. BIGGER, MORE COMPLEX. SOME OF THESE COMMANDS ARE IN CALAMARIAN!
BESIDES, I ALREADY KNOW PLENTY ABOUT SLEEP. YOU'RE THE IMPORTANT ONE— THE GUNNER WHO NEEDS TO BE ALERT.
SEE?
I MIGHT BE A GUNNER, BUT YOU'RE IMPORTANT, TOO. YOU'RE THE MECHANIC WHO WILL KEEP ME IN THE SKY IF THE FIRST ORDER FINDS US.

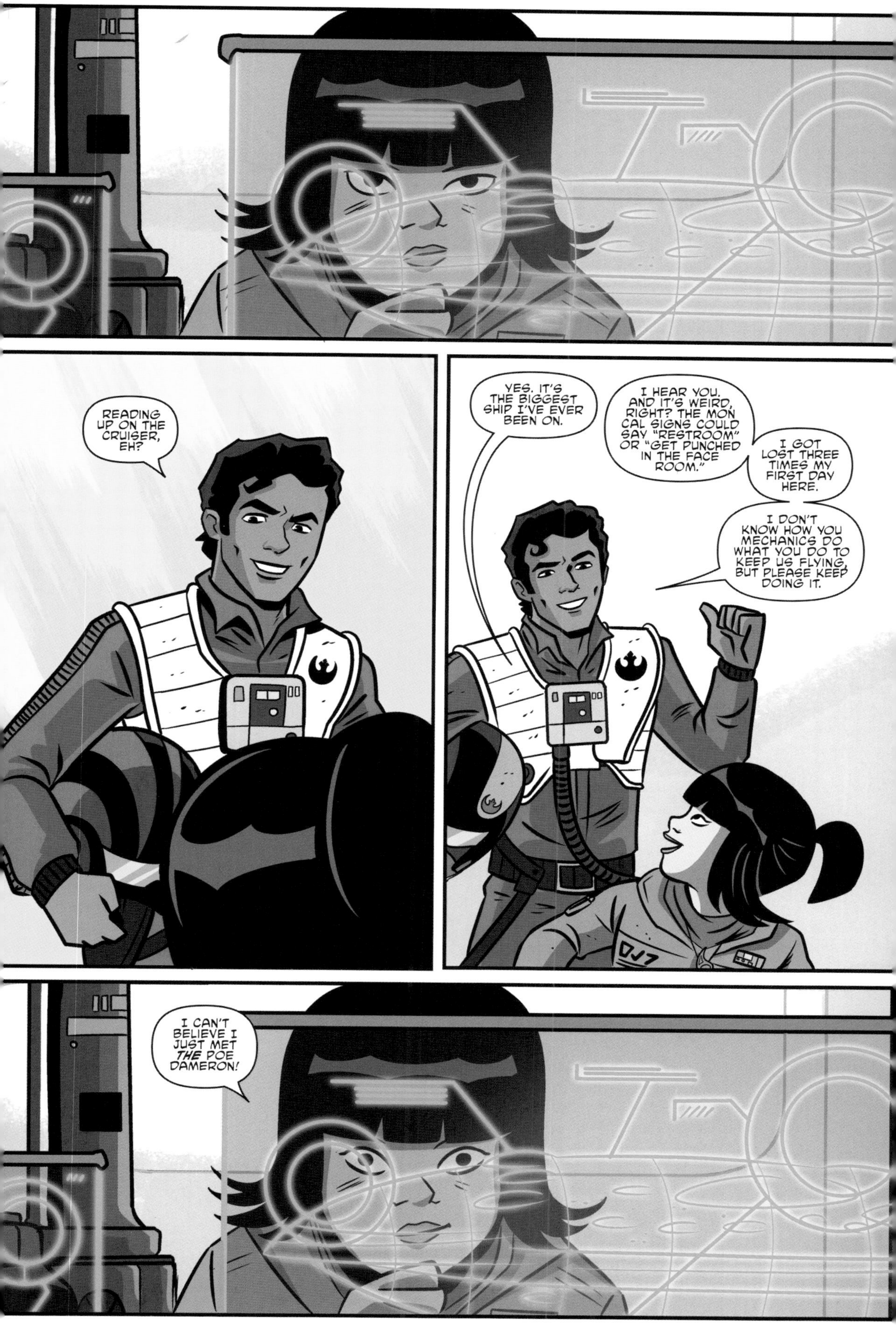
READING UP ON THE CRUISER, EH?
YES. IT'S THE BIGGEST SHIP I'VE EVER BEEN ON.
I HEAR YOU. AND IT'S WEIRD, RIGHT? THE MON CAL SIGNS COULD SAY "RESTROOM" OR "GET PUNCHED IN THE FACE ROOM."
I GOT LOST THREE TIMES MY FIRST DAY HERE.
I DON'T KNOW HOW YOU MECHANICS DO WHAT YOU DO TO KEEP US FLYING, BUT PLEASE KEEP DOING IT.
I CAN'T BELIEVE I JUST MET THE POE DAMERON!

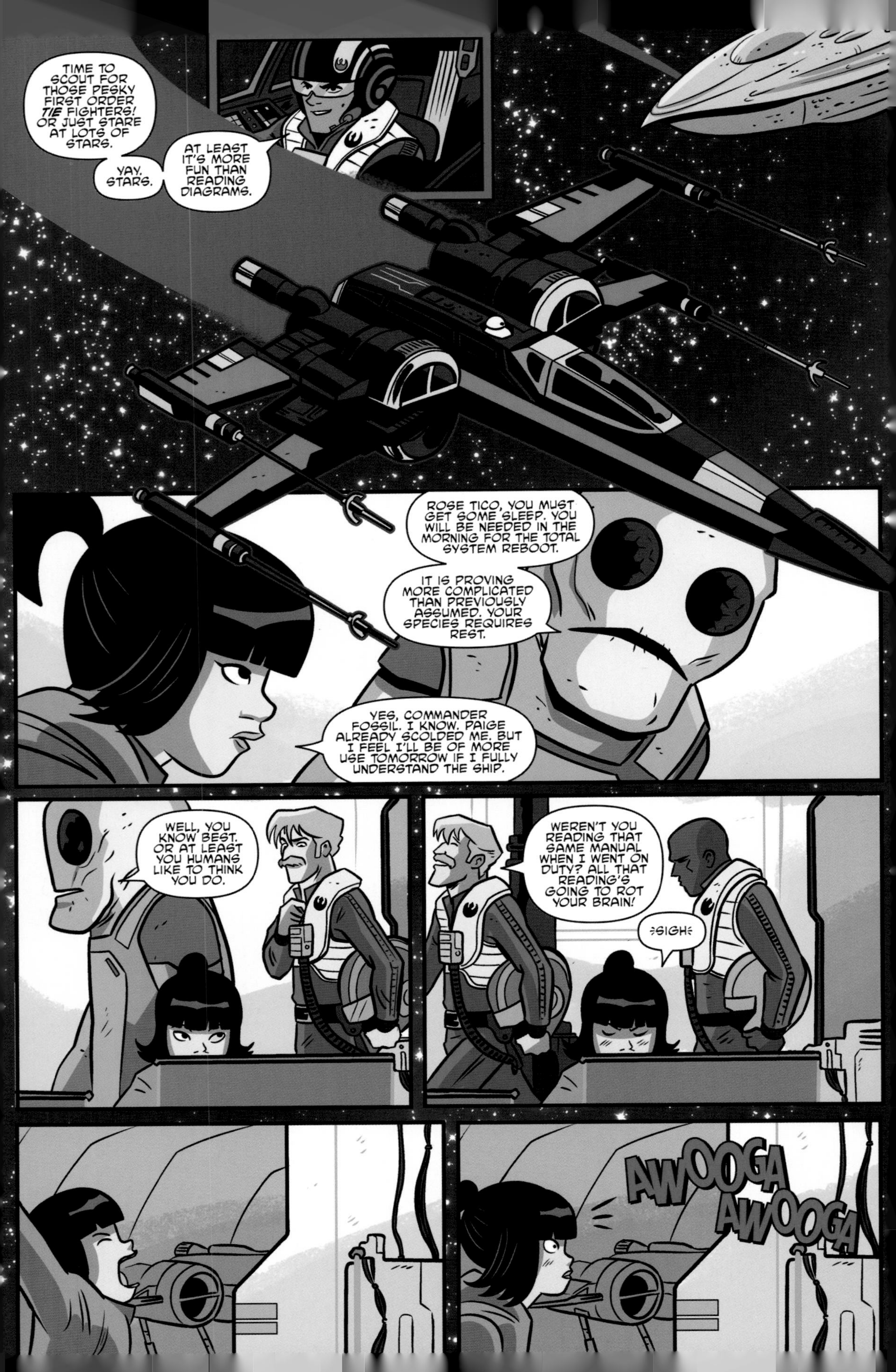
TIME TO SCOUT FOR THOSE PESKY FIRST ORDER TIE FIGHTERS! OR JUST STARE AT LOTS OF STARS.
YAY. STARS.
AT LEAST IT'S MORE FUN THAN READING DIAGRAMS.
ROSE TICO, YOU MUST GET SOME SLEEP. YOU WILL BE NEEDED IN THE MORNING FOR THE TOTAL SYSTEM REBOOT.
IT IS PROVING MORE COMPLICATED THAN PREVIOUSLY ASSUMED. YOUR SPECIES REQUIRES REST.
YES, COMMANDER FOSSIL. I KNOW. PAIGE ALREADY SCOLDED ME. BUT I FEEL I'LL BE OF MORE USE TOMORROW IF I FULLY UNDERSTAND THE SHIP.
WELL, YOU KNOW BEST. OR AT LEAST YOU HUMANS LIKE TO THINK YOU DO.
WEREN'T YOU READING THAT SAME MANUAL WHEN I WENT ON DUTY? ALL THAT READING'S GOING TO ROT YOUR BRAIN!
SIGH
AWOOGA AWOOGA

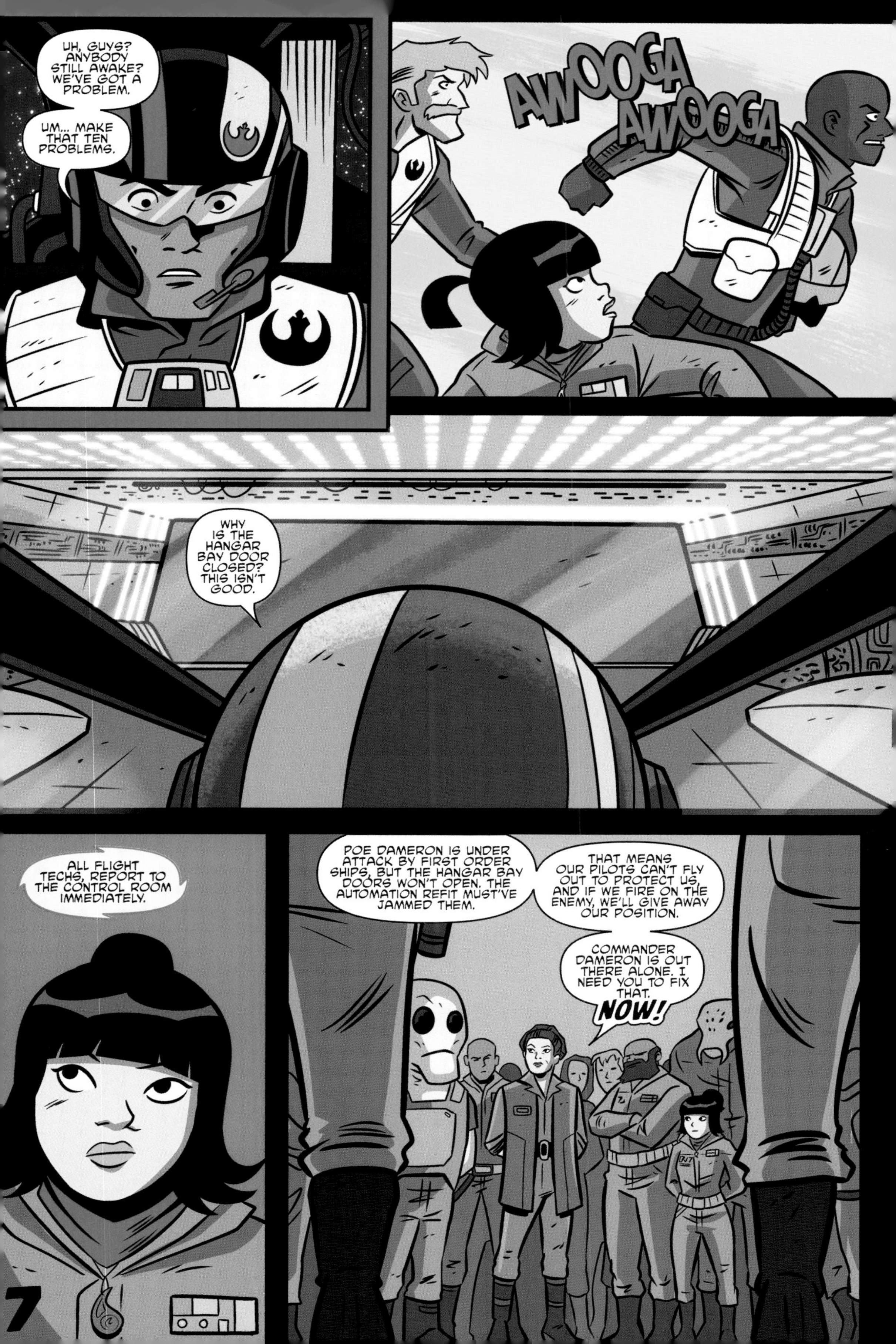
UH, GUYS? ANYBODY STILL AWAKE? WE'VE GOT A PROBLEM.
UM... MAKE THAT TEN PROBLEMS.
AWOOGA AWOOGA
WHY IS THE HANGAR BAY DOOR CLOSED? THIS ISN'T GOOD.
ALL FLIGHT TECHS, REPORT TO THE CONTROL ROOM IMMEDIATELY.
POE DAMERON IS UNDER ATTACK BY FIRST ORDER SHIPS, BUT THE HANGAR BAY DOORS WON'T OPEN. THE AUTOMATION REFIT MUST'VE JAMMED THEM.
THAT MEANS OUR PILOTS CAN'T FLY OUT TO PROTECT US, AND IF WE FIRE ON THE ENEMY, WE'LL GIVE AWAY OUR POSITION.
COMMANDER DAMERON IS OUT THERE ALONE. I NEED YOU TO FIX THAT. NOW!

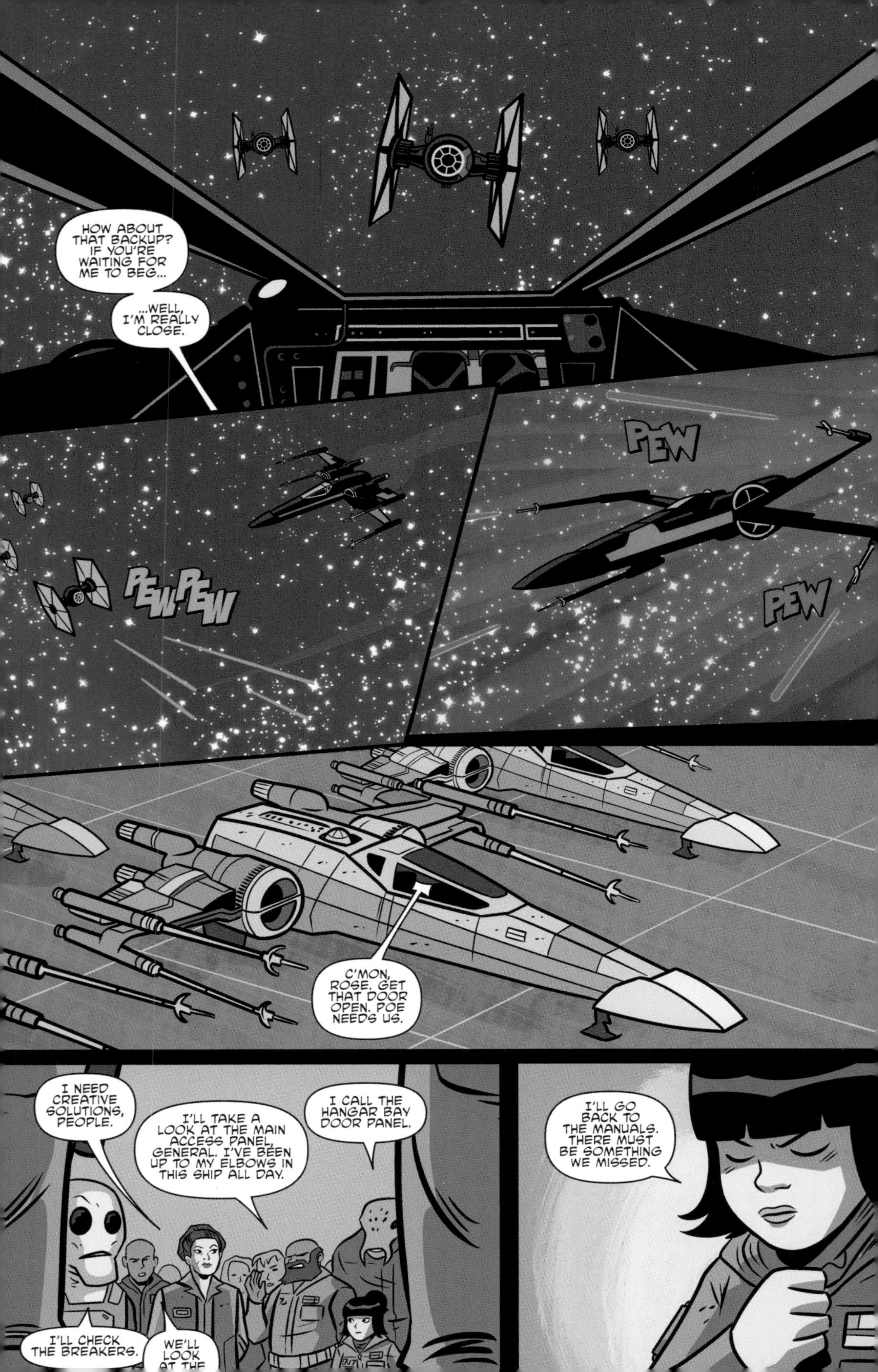
HOW ABOUT THAT BACKUP? IF YOU'RE WAITING FOR ME TO BEG...
...WELL, I'M REALLY CLOSE.
PEW
PEW PEW
PEW
C'MON, ROSE. GET THAT DOOR OPEN. POE NEEDS US.
I NEED CREATIVE SOLUTIONS, PEOPLE.
I'LL TAKE A LOOK AT THE MAIN ACCESS PANEL, GENERAL. I'VE BEEN UP TO MY ELBOWS IN THIS SHIP ALL DAY.
I CALL THE HANGAR BAY DOOR PANEL.
I'LL CHECK THE BREAKERS.
WE'LL LOOK AT THE
I'LL GO BACK TO THE MANUALS. THERE MUST BE SOMETHING WE MISSED.

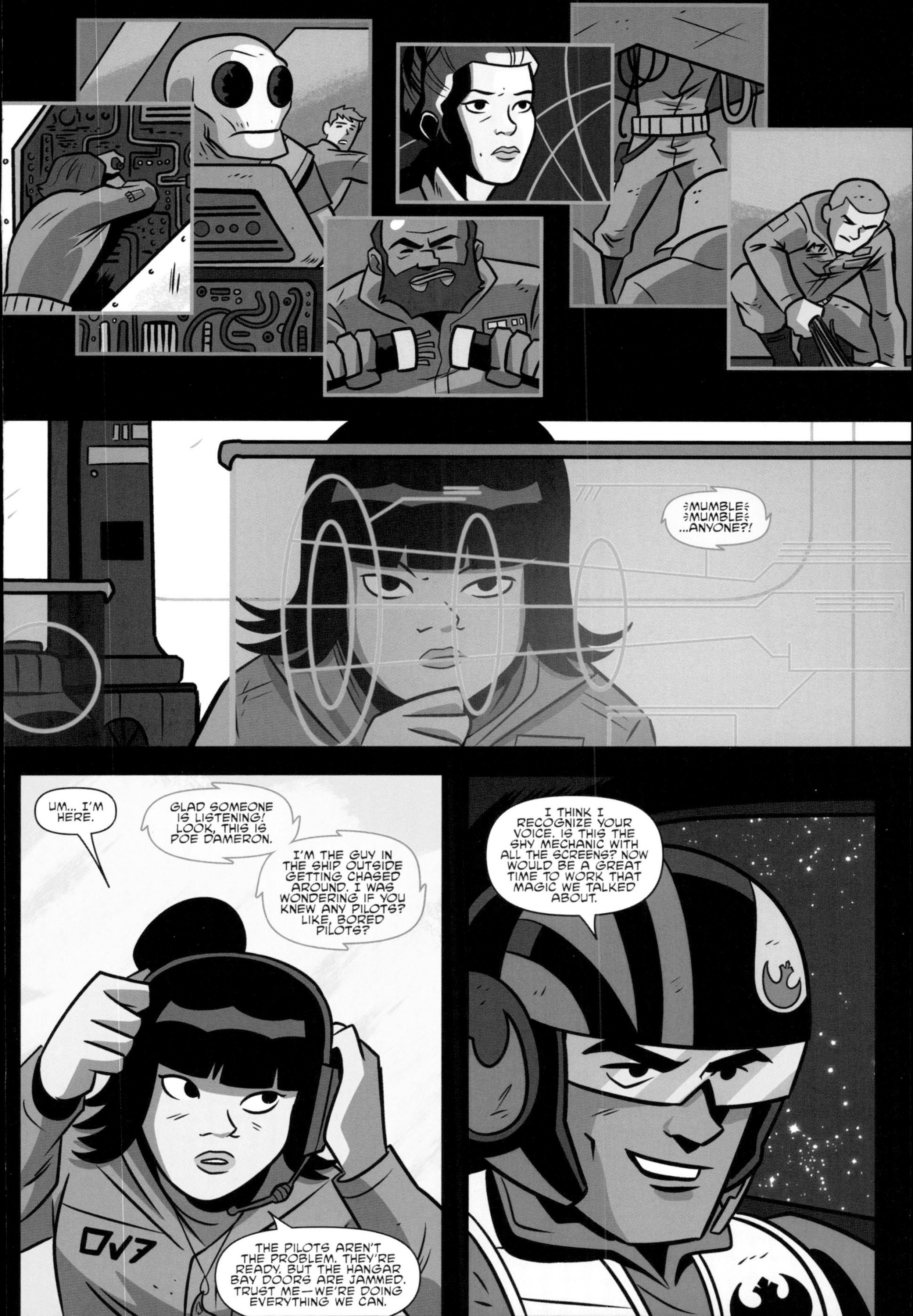

MUMBLE MUMBLE ...ANYONE?!
UM... I'M HERE.
GLAD SOMEONE IS LISTENING! LOOK, THIS IS POE DAMERON.
I'M THE GUY IN THE SHIP OUTSIDE GETTING CHASED AROUND. I WAS WONDERING IF YOU KNEW ANY PILOTS? LIKE, BORED PILOTS?
I THINK I RECOGNIZE YOUR VOICE. IS THIS THE SHY MECHANIC WITH ALL THE SCREENS? NOW WOULD BE A GREAT TIME TO WORK THAT MAGIC WE TALKED ABOUT.
THE PILOTS AREN'T THE PROBLEM. THEY'RE READY. BUT THE HANGAR BAY DOORS ARE JAMMED. TRUST ME—WE'RE DOING EVERYTHING WE CAN.

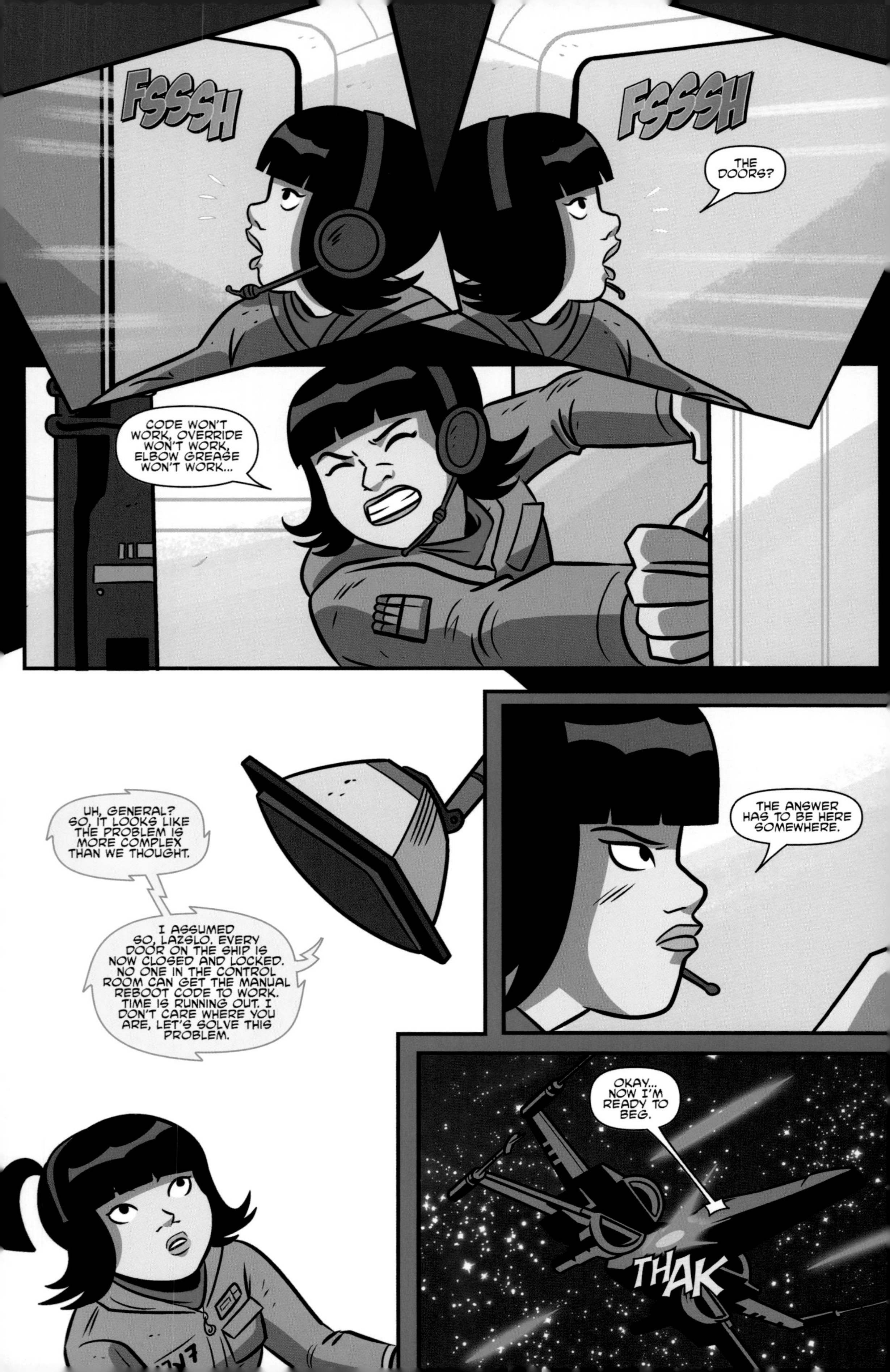
FSSSH
FSSSH
THE DOORS?
CODE WON'T WORK, OVERRIDE WON'T WORK, ELBOW GREASE WON'T WORK...
THE ANSWER HAS TO BE HERE SOMEWHERE.
UH, GENERAL? SO, IT LOOKS LIKE THE PROBLEM IS MORE COMPLEX THAN WE THOUGHT.
I ASSUMED SO, LAZSLO. EVERY DOOR ON THE SHIP IS NOW CLOSED AND LOCKED. NO ONE IN THE CONTROL ROOM CAN GET THE MANUAL REBOOT CODE TO WORK. TIME IS RUNNING OUT. I DON'T CARE WHERE YOU ARE, LET'S SOLVE THIS PROBLEM.
OKAY... NOW I'M READY TO BEG.
THAK

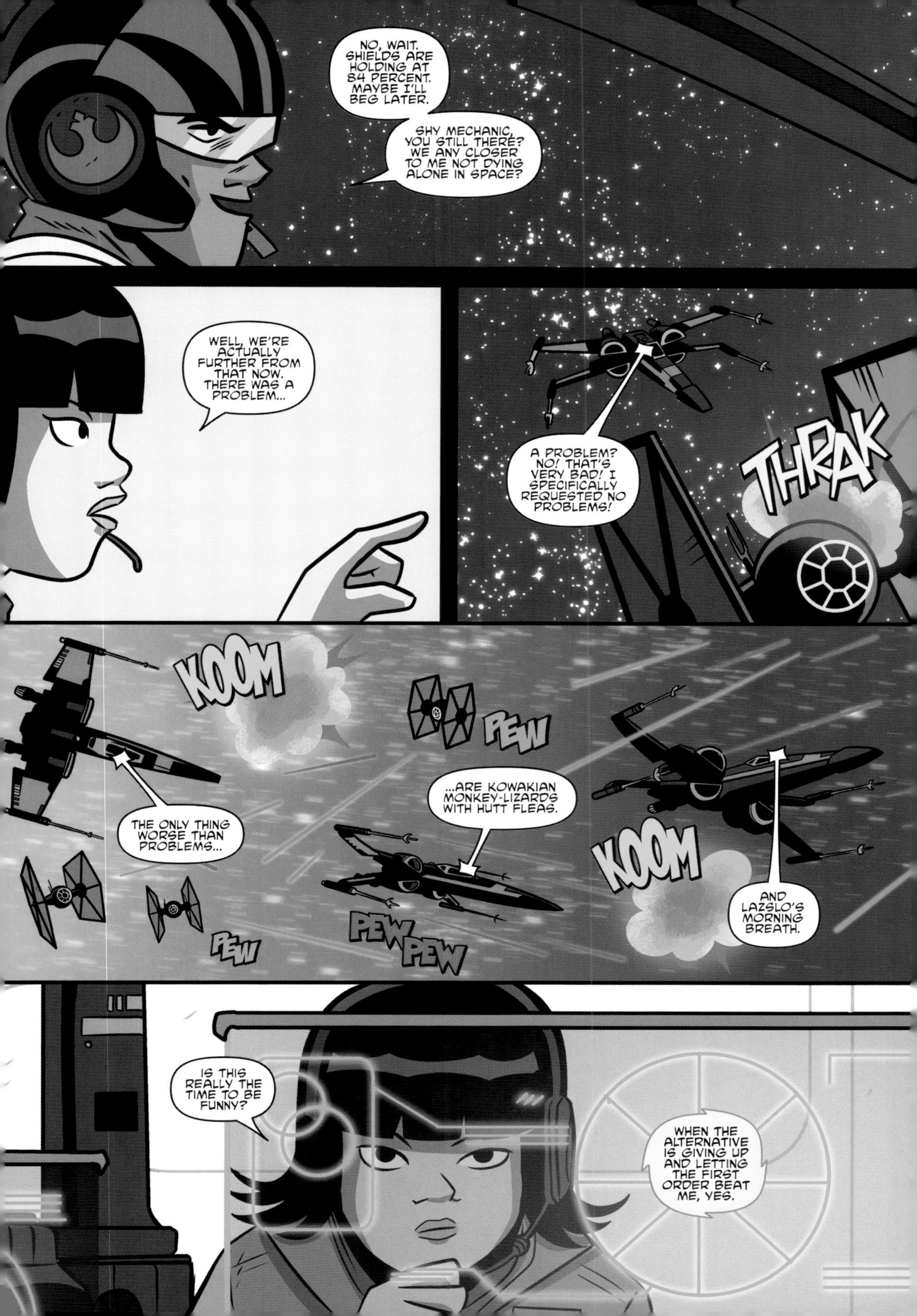
NO, WAIT. SHIELDS ARE HOLDING AT 84 PERCENT. MAYBE I'LL BEG LATER.
SHY MECHANIC, YOU STILL THERE? WE ANY CLOSER TO ME NOT DYING ALONE IN SPACE?
WELL, WE'RE ACTUALLY FURTHER FROM THAT NOW. THERE WAS A PROBLEM...
A PROBLEM? NO! THAT'S VERY BAD! I SPECIFICALLY REQUESTED NO PROBLEMS!
THRAK
KOOM
PEW
THE ONLY THING WORSE THAN PROBLEMS...
...ARE KOWAKIAN MONKEY-LIZARDS WITH HUTT FLEAS.
KOOM
AND LAZSLO'S MORNING BREATH.
PEW
PEW PEW
IS THIS REALLY THE TIME TO BE FUNNY?
WHEN THE ALTERNATIVE IS GIVING UP AND LETTING THE FIRST ORDER BEAT ME, YES.

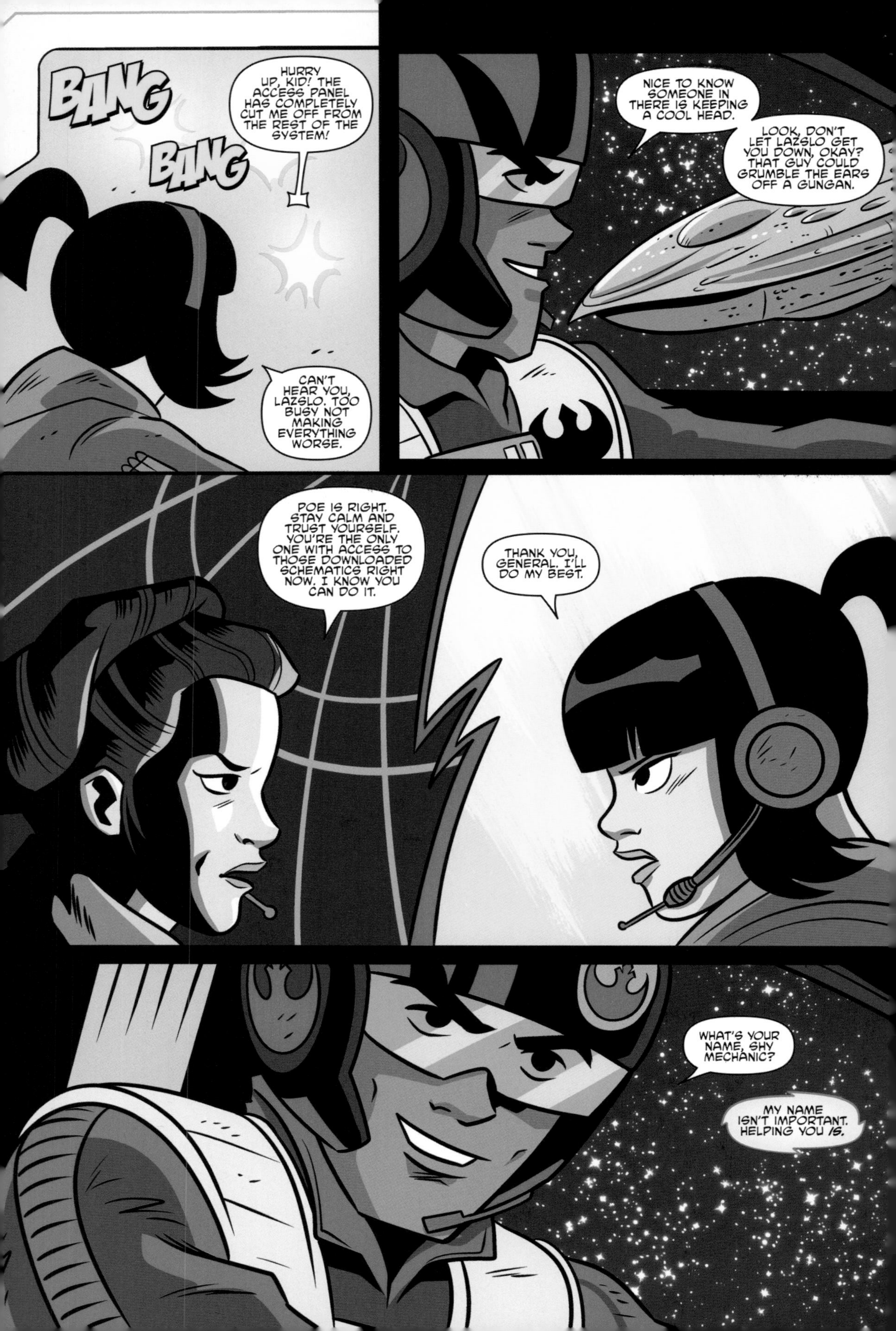

BANG
BANG
HURRY UP, KID! THE ACCESS PANEL HAS COMPLETELY CUT ME OFF FROM THE REST OF THE SYSTEM!
CAN'T HEAR YOU, LAZSLO. TOO BUSY NOT MAKING EVERYTHING WORSE.
NICE TO KNOW SOMEONE IN THERE IS KEEPING A COOL HEAD.
LOOK, DON'T LET LAZSLO GET YOU DOWN, OKAY? THAT GUY COULD GRUMBLE THE EARS OFF A GUNGAN.
POE IS RIGHT. STAY CALM AND TRUST YOURSELF. YOU'RE THE ONLY ONE WITH ACCESS TO THOSE DOWNLOADED SCHEMATICS RIGHT NOW. I KNOW YOU CAN DO IT.
THANK YOU, GENERAL. I'LL DO MY BEST.
WHAT'S YOUR NAME, SHY MECHANIC?
MY NAME ISN'T IMPORTANT. HELPING YOU *IS.*

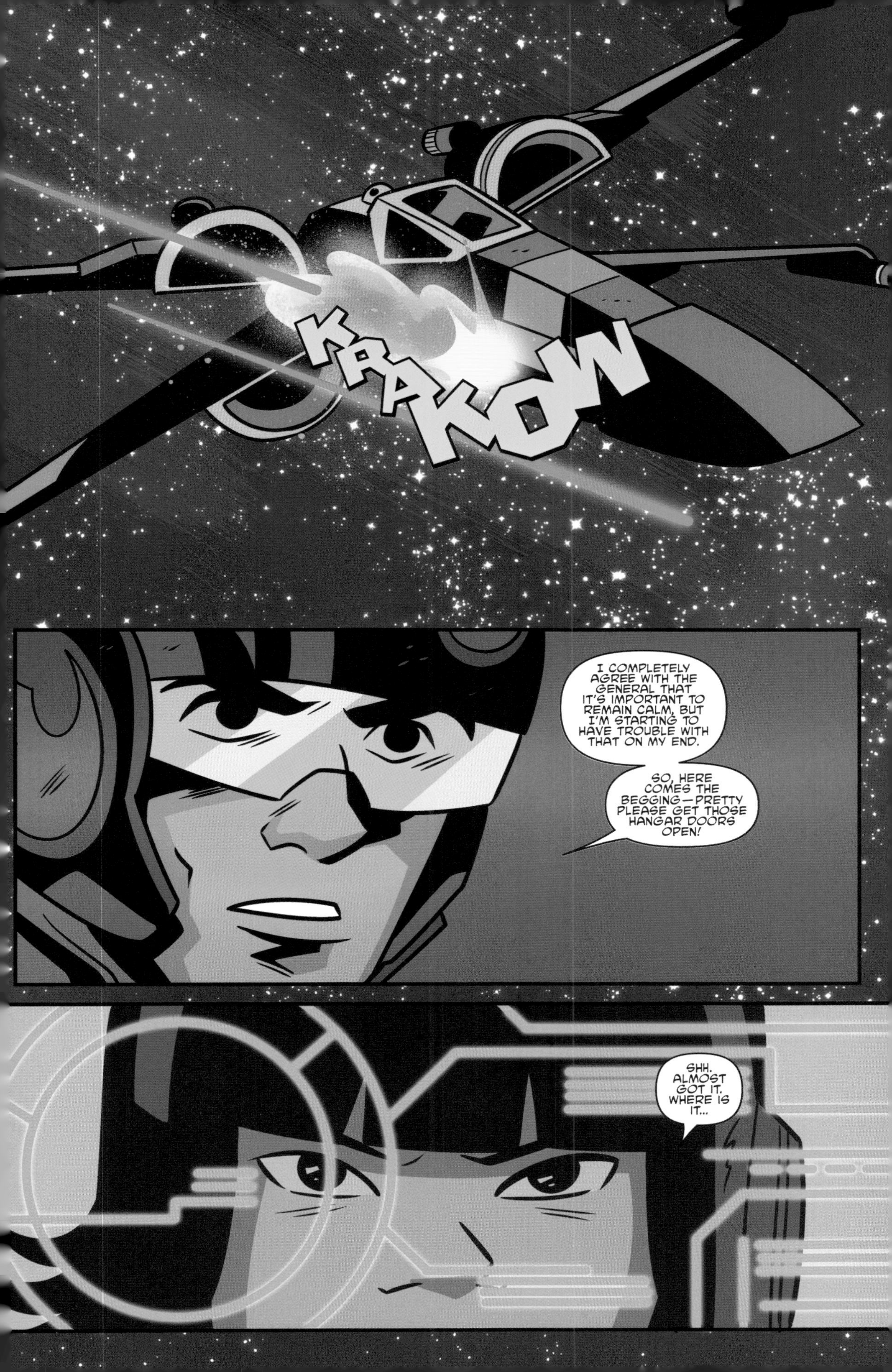
KRAKOW
I COMPLETELY AGREE WITH THE GENERAL THAT IT'S IMPORTANT TO REMAIN CALM, BUT I'M STARTING TO HAVE TROUBLE WITH THAT ON MY END.
SO, HERE COMES THE BEGGING—PRETTY PLEASE GET THOSE HANGAR DOORS OPEN!
SHH. ALMOST GOT IT. WHERE IS IT...

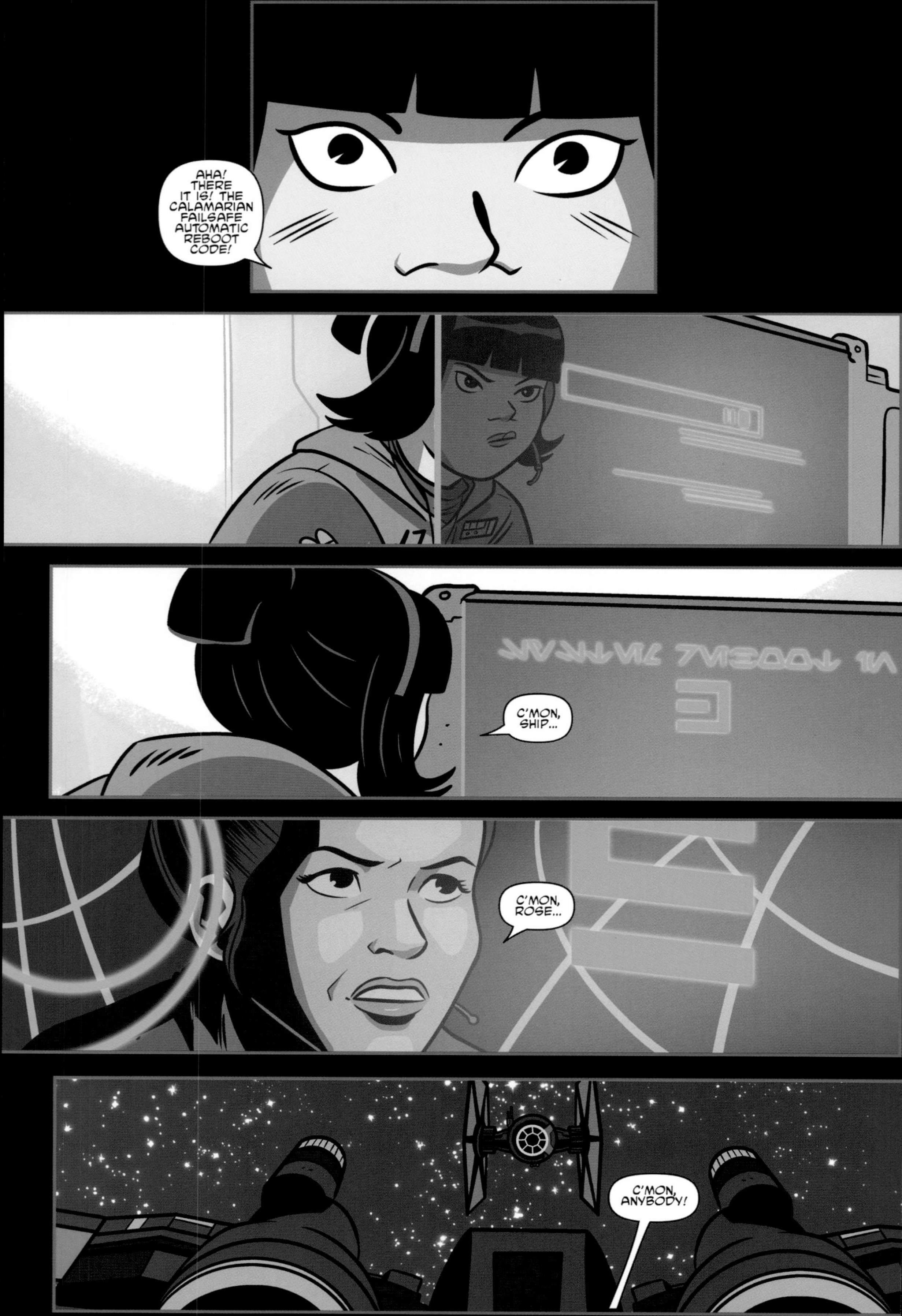
AHA! THERE IT IS! THE CALAMARIAN FAILSAFE AUTOMATIC REBOOT CODE!
C'MON, SHIP...
C'MON, ROSE...
C'MON, ANYBODY!

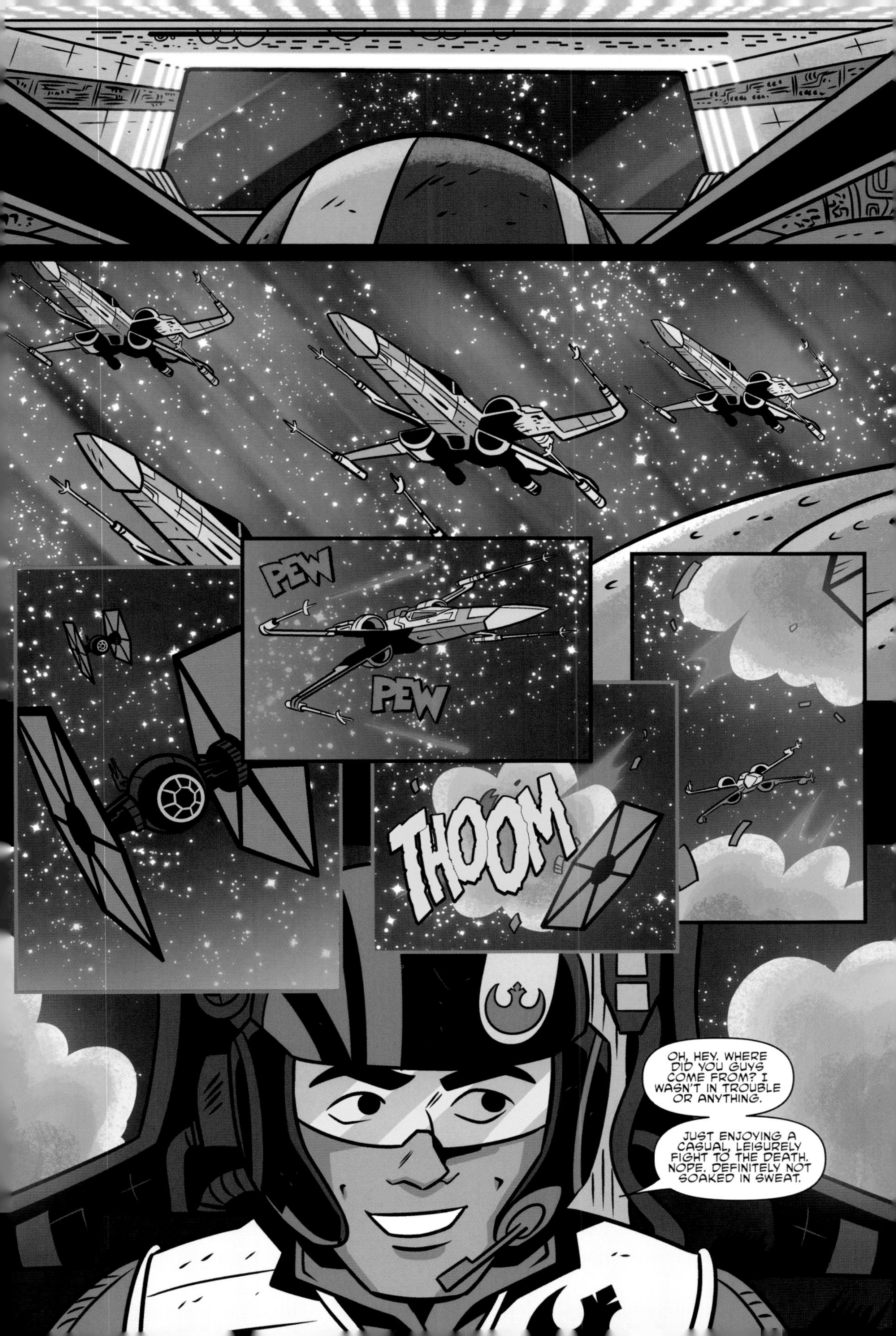
PEW
PEW
THOOM
OH, HEY. WHERE DID YOU GUYS COME FROM? I WASN'T IN TROUBLE OR ANYTHING.
JUST ENJOYING A CASUAL, LEISURELY FIGHT TO THE DEATH. NOPE. DEFINITELY NOT SOAKED IN SWEAT.

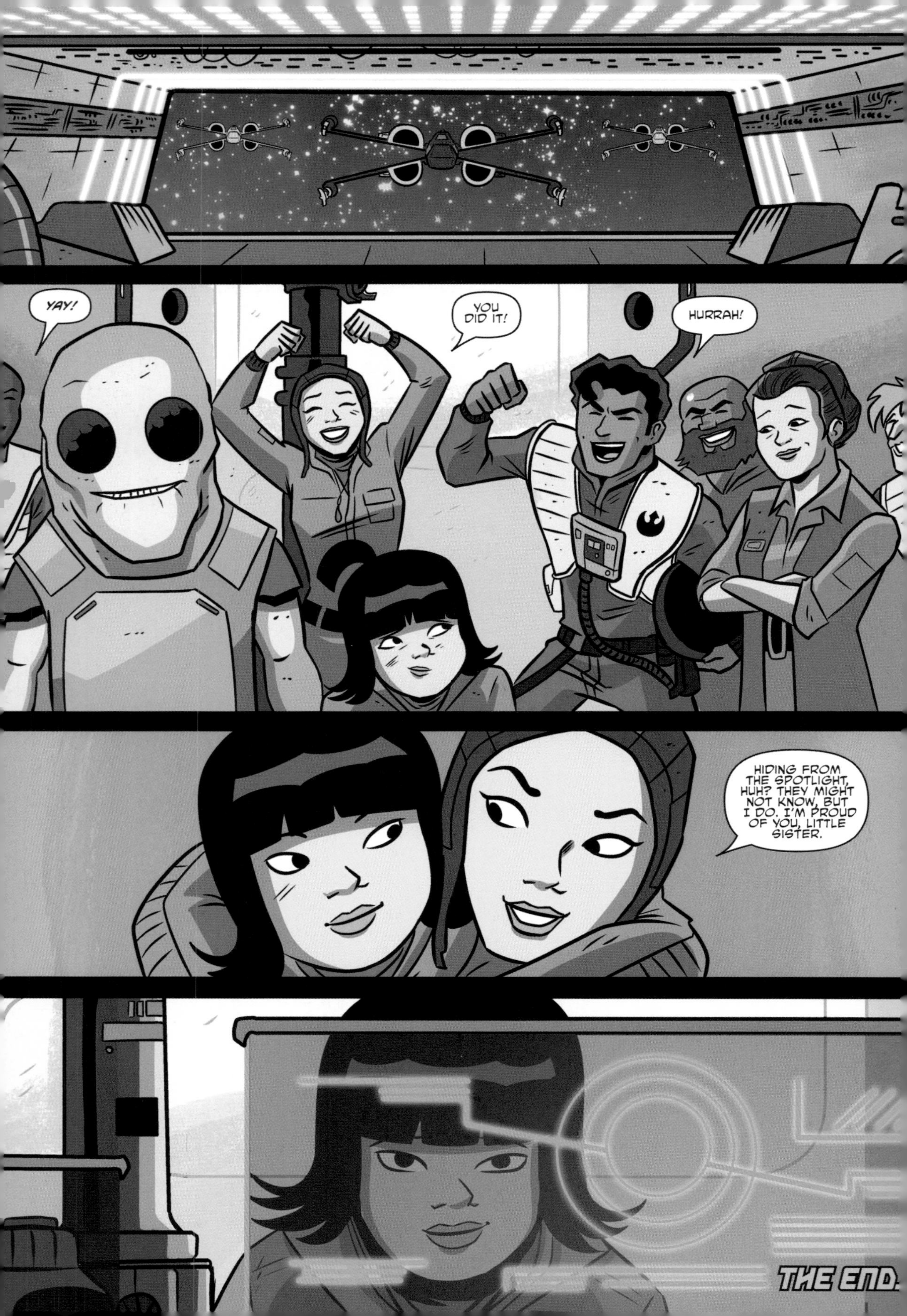
YAY!
YOU DID IT!
HURRAH!
HIDING FROM THE SPOTLIGHT, HUH? THEY MIGHT NOT KNOW, BUT I DO. I'M PROUD OF YOU, LITTLE SISTER.
THE END.

11
ENDANGERED

Writer
SHOLLY FISCH

Pencilers
SEAN GALLOWAY and
JAMAL PEPPERS

Inkers
CASSEY KUO and
GARY MARTIN

Colorist
LUIS ANTONIO DELGADO

Letterer
TOM B. LONG

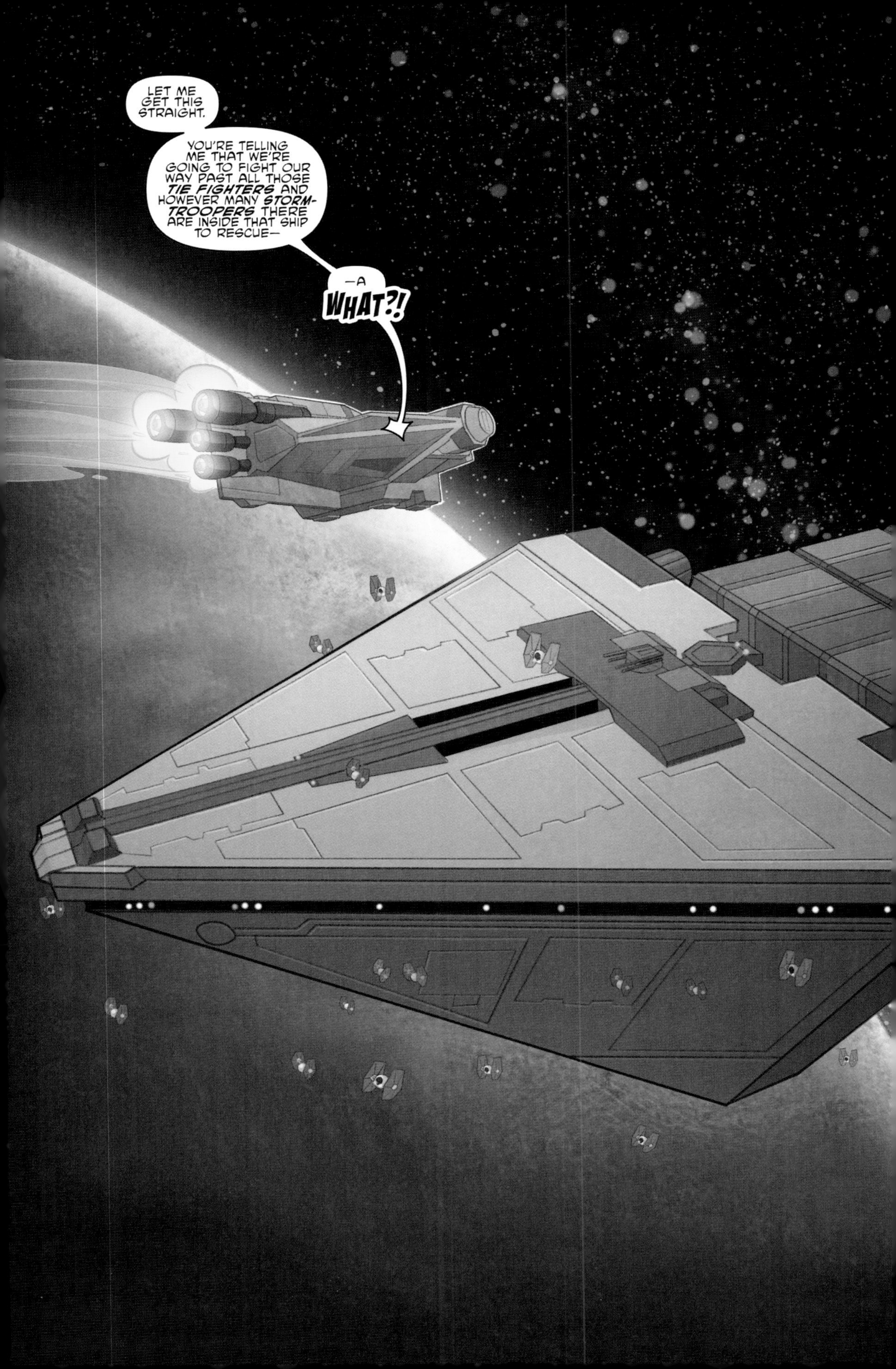
LET ME GET THIS STRAIGHT.
YOU'RE TELLING ME THAT WE'RE GOING TO FIGHT OUR WAY PAST ALL THOSE TIE FIGHTERS AND HOWEVER MANY STORM-TROOPERS THERE ARE INSIDE THAT SHIP TO RESCUE—
—A WHAT?!

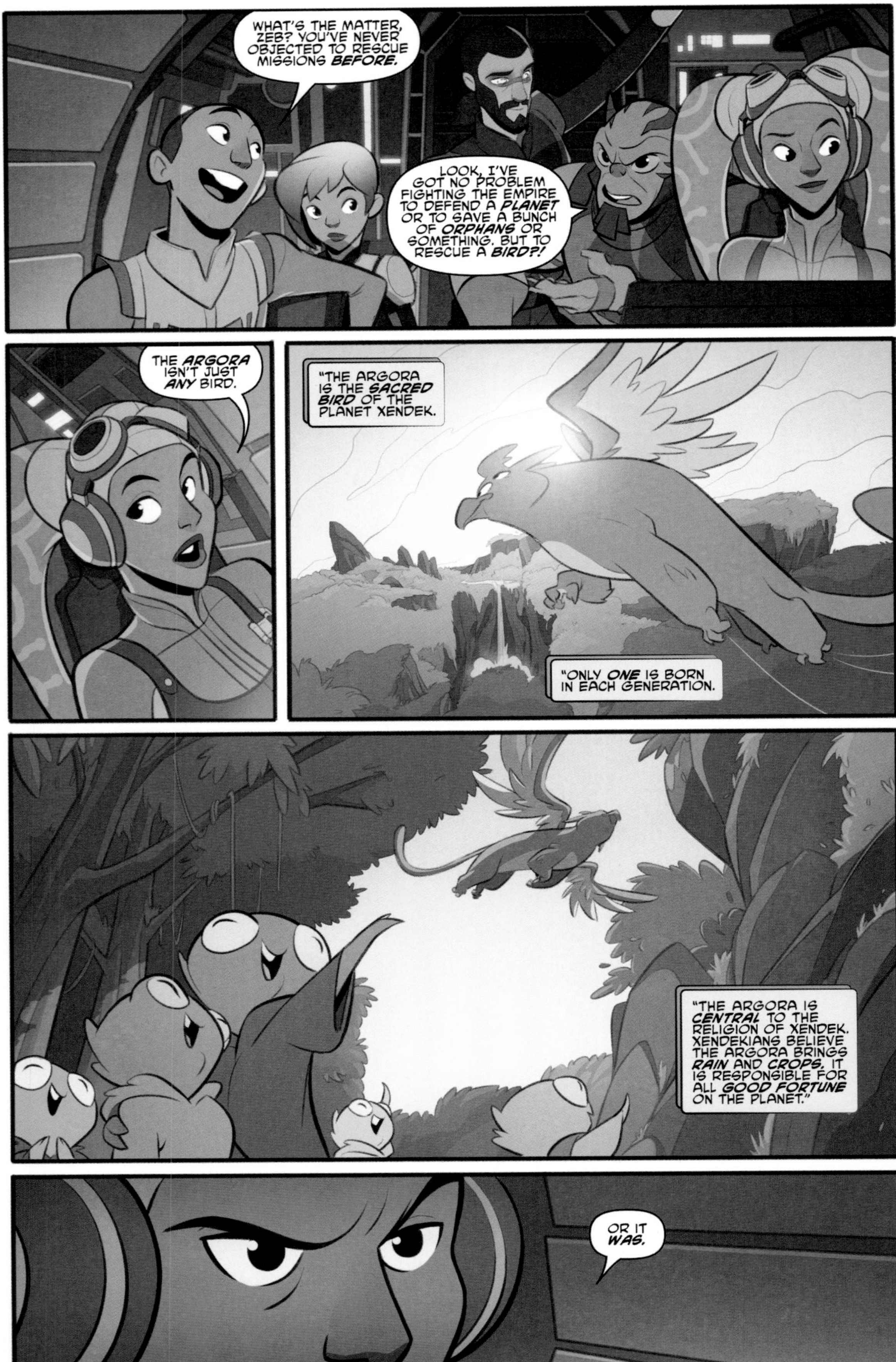

WHAT'S THE MATTER, ZEB? YOU'VE NEVER OBJECTED TO RESCUE MISSIONS *BEFORE.*
LOOK, I'VE GOT NO PROBLEM FIGHTING THE EMPIRE TO DEFEND A *PLANET* OR TO SAVE A BUNCH OF *ORPHANS* OR SOMETHING. BUT TO RESCUE A *BIRD?!*
THE *ARGORA* ISN'T JUST *ANY* BIRD.
"THE ARGORA IS THE *SACRED BIRD* OF THE PLANET XENDEK.
"ONLY *ONE* IS BORN IN EACH GENERATION.
"THE ARGORA IS *CENTRAL* TO THE RELIGION OF XENDEK. XENDEKIANS BELIEVE THE ARGORA BRINGS *RAIN* AND *CROPS.* IT IS RESPONSIBLE FOR ALL *GOOD FORTUNE* ON THE PLANET."
OR IT *WAS.*

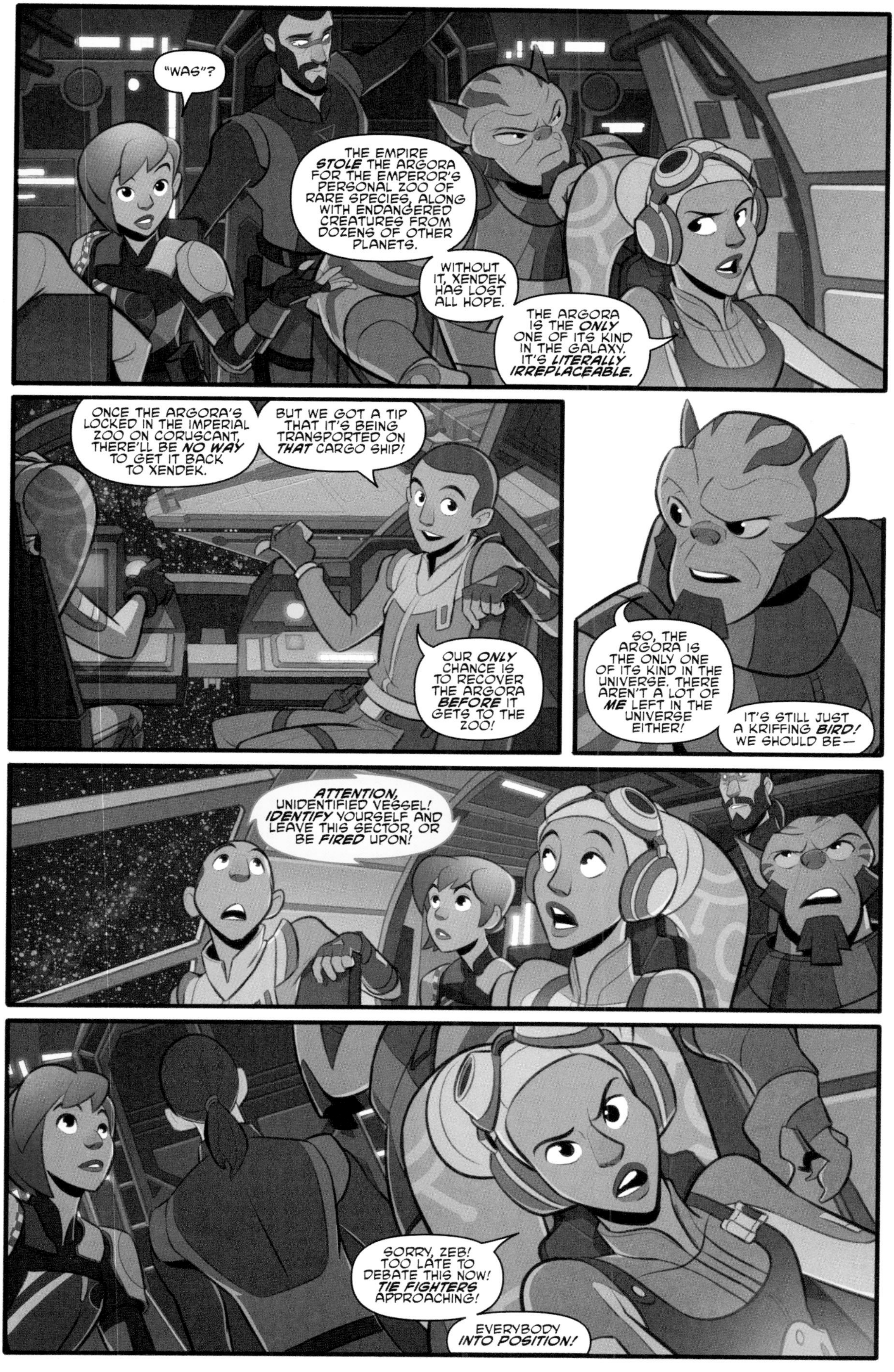
"WAS"?
THE EMPIRE *STOLE* THE ARGORA FOR THE EMPEROR'S PERSONAL ZOO OF RARE SPECIES, ALONG WITH ENDANGERED CREATURES FROM DOZENS OF OTHER PLANETS.
WITHOUT IT, XENDEK HAS LOST ALL HOPE.
THE ARGORA IS THE *ONLY* ONE OF ITS KIND IN THE GALAXY. IT'S *LITERALLY IRREPLACEABLE.*
ONCE THE ARGORA'S LOCKED IN THE IMPERIAL ZOO ON CORUSCANT, THERE'LL BE *NO WAY* TO GET IT BACK TO XENDEK.
BUT WE GOT A TIP THAT IT'S BEING TRANSPORTED ON *THAT* CARGO SHIP!
OUR *ONLY* CHANCE IS TO RECOVER THE ARGORA *BEFORE* IT GETS TO THE ZOO!
SO, THE ARGORA IS THE ONLY ONE OF ITS KIND IN THE UNIVERSE. THERE AREN'T A LOT OF *ME* LEFT IN THE UNIVERSE EITHER!
IT'S STILL JUST A KRIFFING *BIRD!* WE SHOULD BE—
ATTENTION, UNIDENTIFIED VESSEL! *IDENTIFY* YOURSELF AND LEAVE THIS SECTOR, OR BE *FIRED* UPON!
SORRY, ZEB! TOO LATE TO DEBATE THIS NOW! *TIE FIGHTERS* APPROACHING!
EVERYBODY *INTO POSITION!*

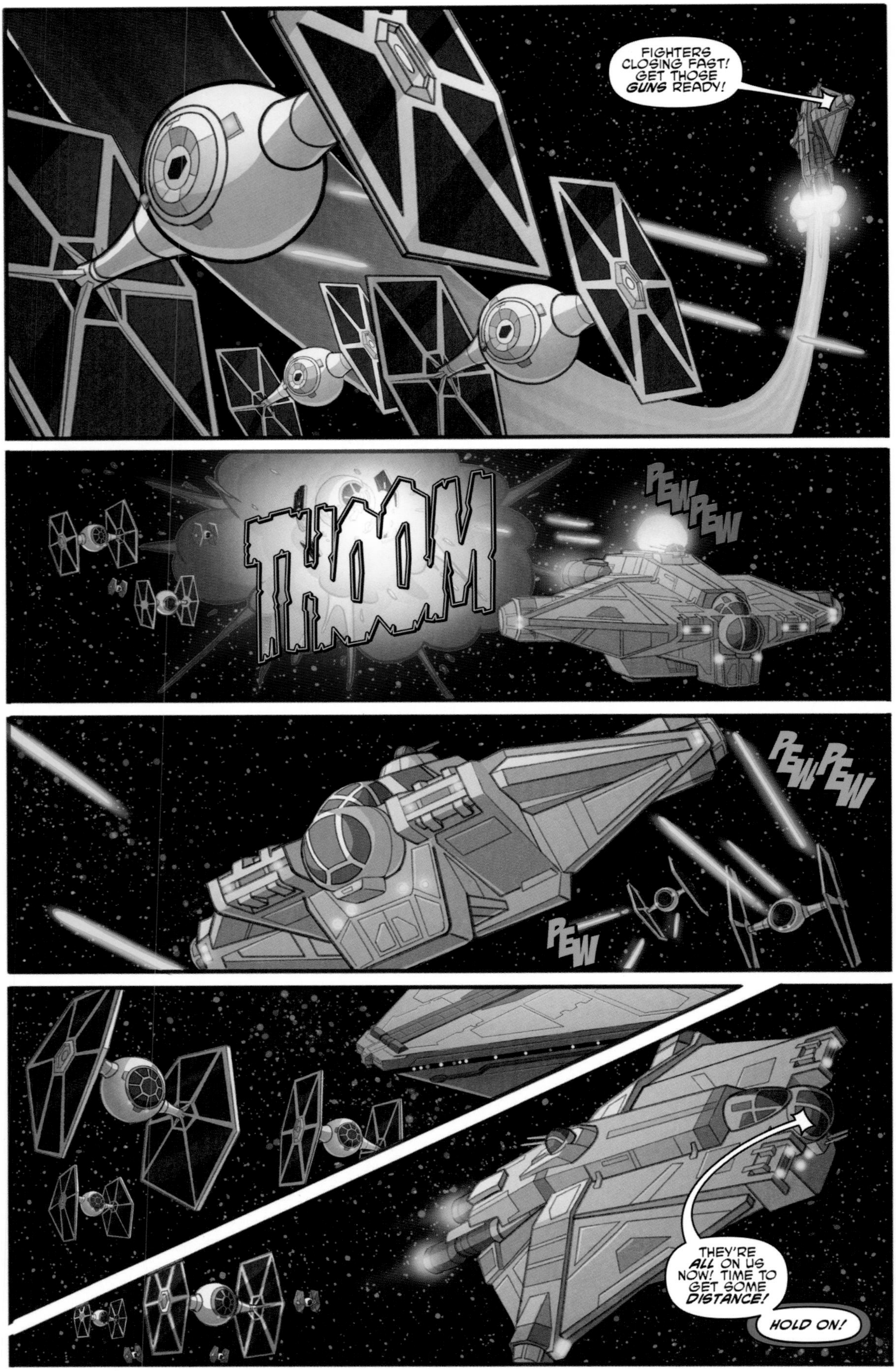
FIGHTERS CLOSING FAST! GET THOSE GUNS READY!
THOOM
PEW PEW
PEW PEW
PEW
THEY'RE ALL ON US NOW! TIME TO GET SOME DISTANCE!
HOLD ON!

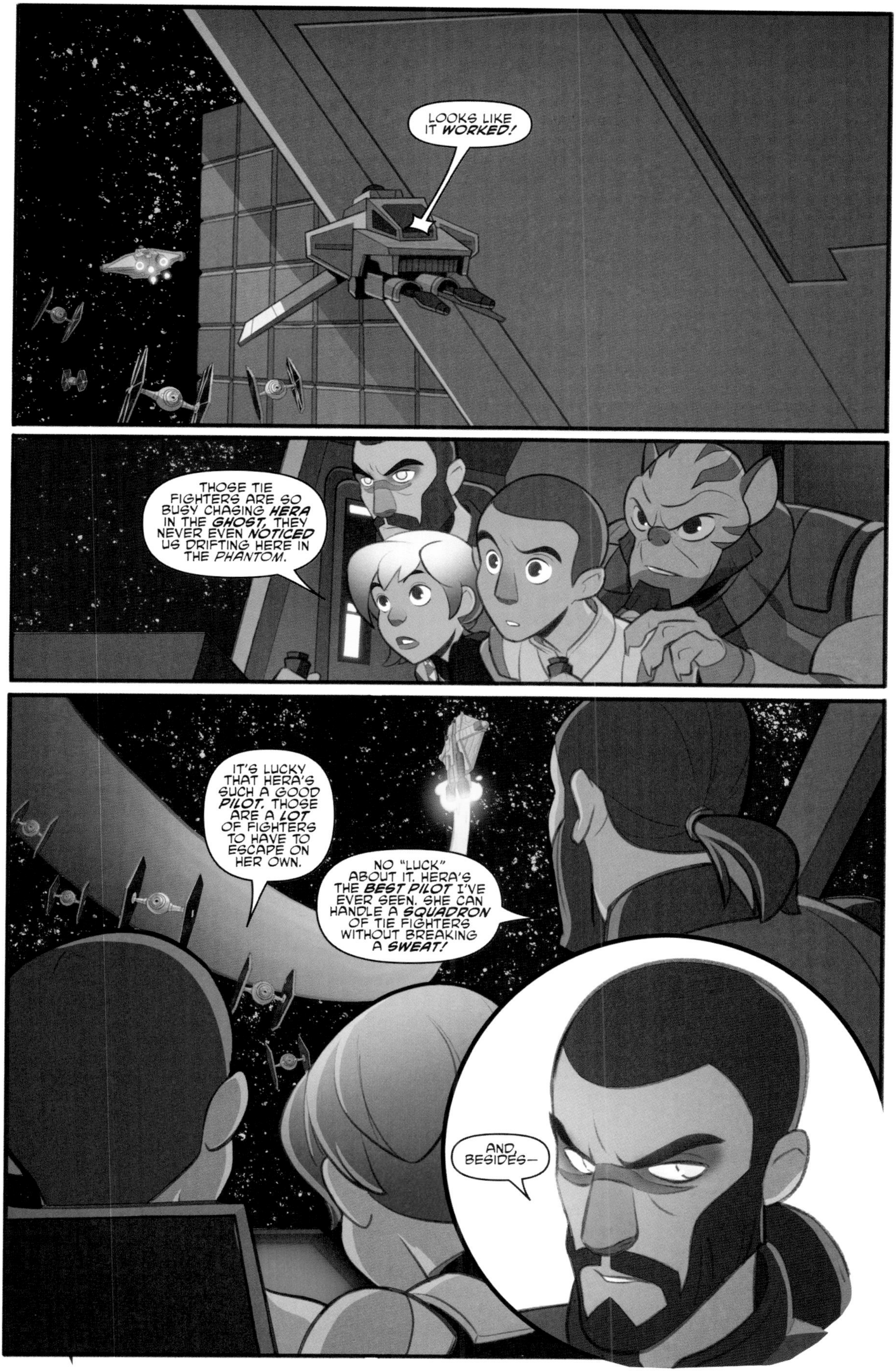
LOOKS LIKE IT WORKED!
THOSE TIE FIGHTERS ARE SO BUSY CHASING HERA IN THE GHOST, THEY NEVER EVEN NOTICED US DRIFTING HERE IN THE PHANTOM.
IT'S LUCKY THAT HERA'S SUCH A GOOD PILOT. THOSE ARE A LOT OF FIGHTERS TO HAVE TO ESCAPE ON HER OWN.
NO "LUCK" ABOUT IT. HERA'S THE BEST PILOT I'VE EVER SEEN. SHE CAN HANDLE A SQUADRON OF TIE FIGHTERS WITHOUT BREAKING A SWEAT!
AND, BESIDES—

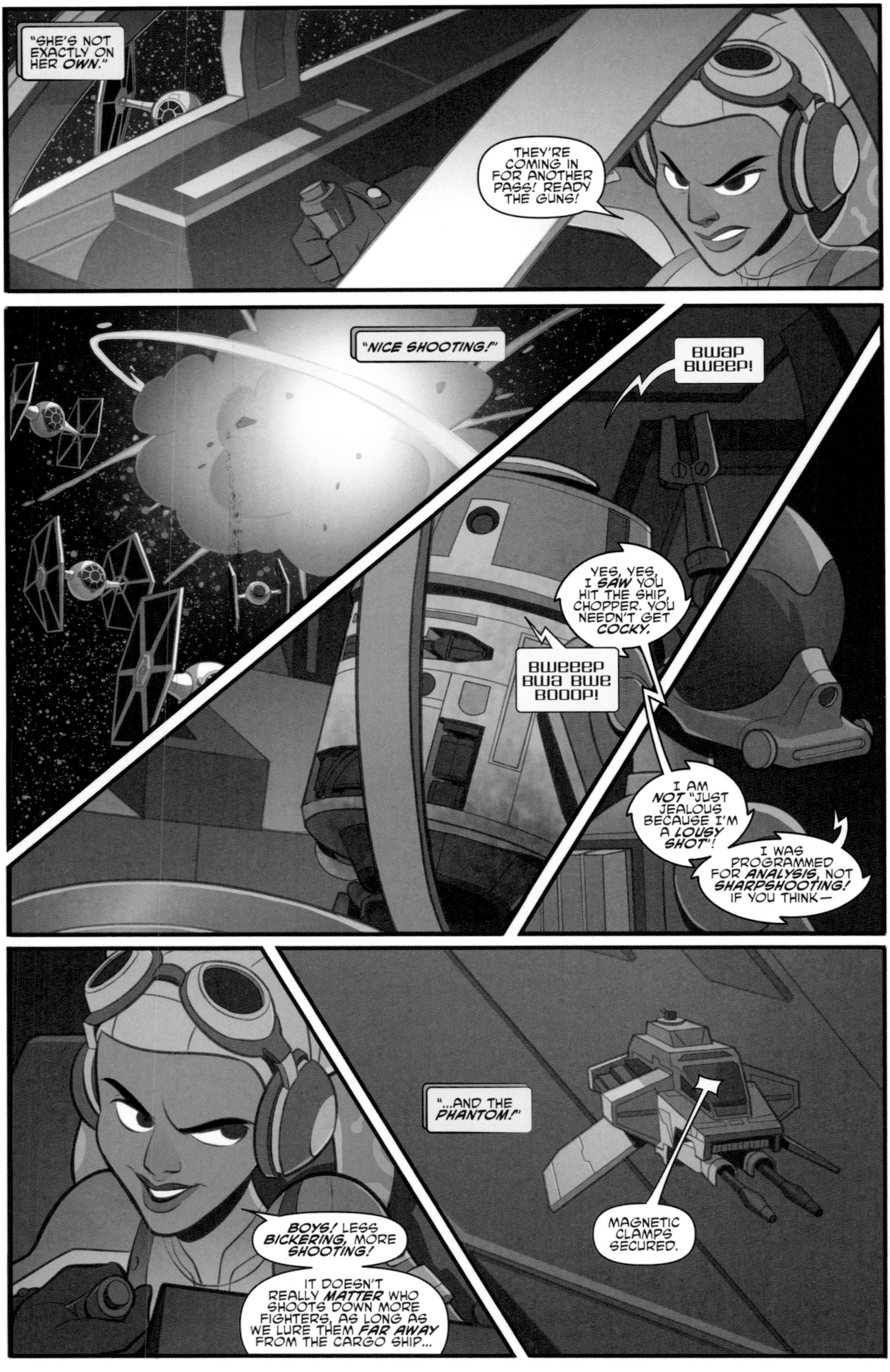

"SHE'S NOT EXACTLY ON HER *OWN*."
THEY'RE COMING IN FOR ANOTHER PASS! READY THE GUNS!
"*NICE SHOOTING!*"
BWAP BWEEP!
YES, YES, I *SAW* YOU HIT THE SHIP, CHOPPER. YOU NEEDN'T GET *COCKY.*
BWEEEP BWA BWE BOOOP!
I AM *NOT* "JUST JEALOUS BECAUSE I'M A *LOUSY SHOT*"!
I WAS PROGRAMMED FOR *ANALYSIS*, NOT *SHARPSHOOTING!* IF YOU THINK—
BOYS! LESS *BICKERING,* MORE *SHOOTING!*
IT DOESN'T REALLY *MATTER* WHO SHOOTS DOWN MORE FIGHTERS, AS LONG AS WE LURE THEM *FAR AWAY* FROM THE CARGO SHIP...
"...AND THE *PHANTOM!*"
MAGNETIC CLAMPS SECURED.

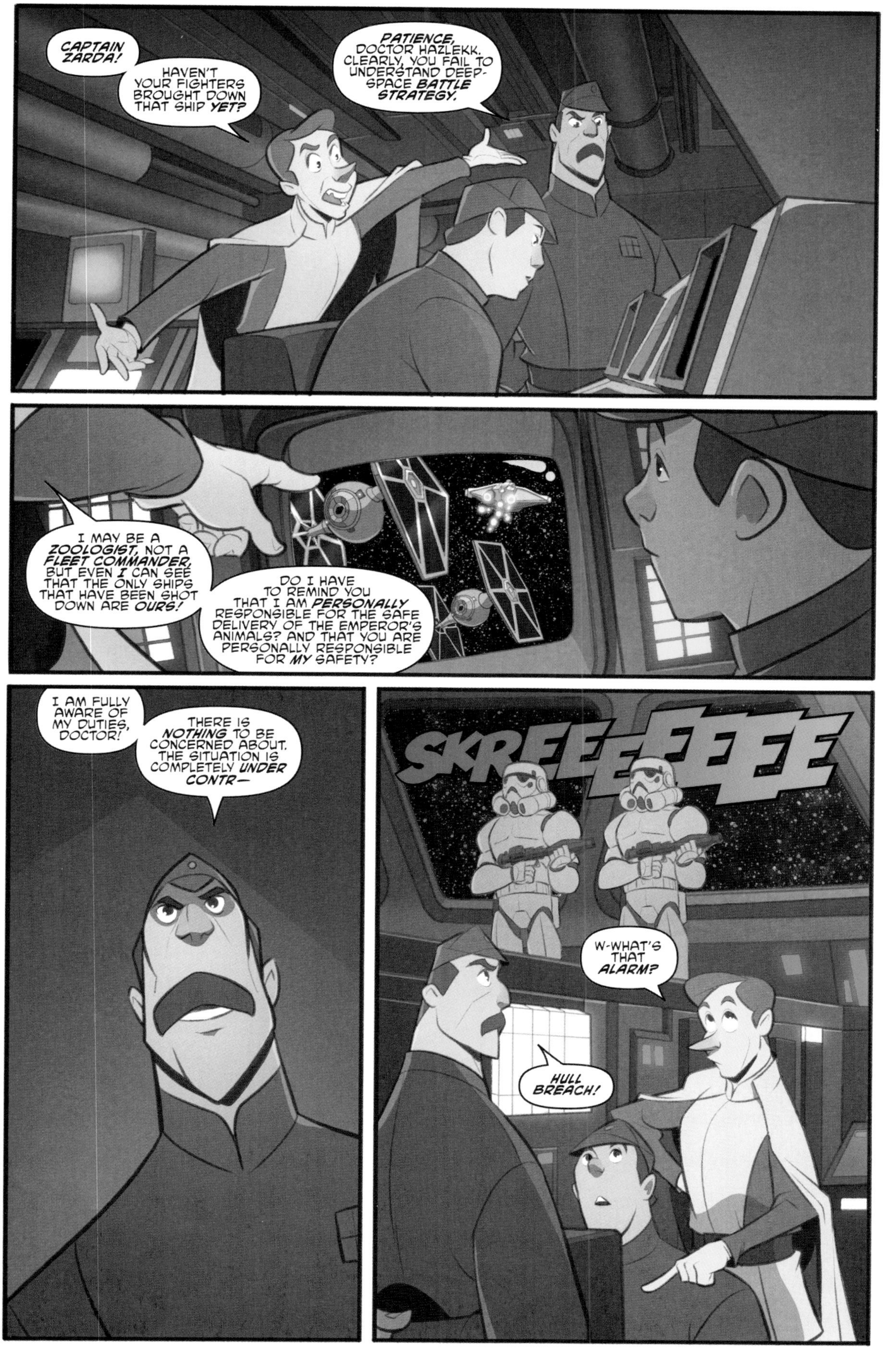
CAPTAIN ZARDA!
HAVEN'T YOUR FIGHTERS BROUGHT DOWN THAT SHIP YET?
PATIENCE, DOCTOR HAZLEKK. CLEARLY, YOU FAIL TO UNDERSTAND DEEP-SPACE BATTLE STRATEGY.
I MAY BE A ZOOLOGIST, NOT A FLEET COMMANDER, BUT EVEN I CAN SEE THAT THE ONLY SHIPS THAT HAVE BEEN SHOT DOWN ARE OURS!
DO I HAVE TO REMIND YOU THAT I AM PERSONALLY RESPONSIBLE FOR THE SAFE DELIVERY OF THE EMPEROR'S ANIMALS? AND THAT YOU ARE PERSONALLY RESPONSIBLE FOR MY SAFETY?
I AM FULLY AWARE OF MY DUTIES, DOCTOR!
THERE IS NOTHING TO BE CONCERNED ABOUT. THE SITUATION IS COMPLETELY UNDER CONTR—
SKREEEEEEEE
W-WHAT'S THAT ALARM?
HULL BREACH!

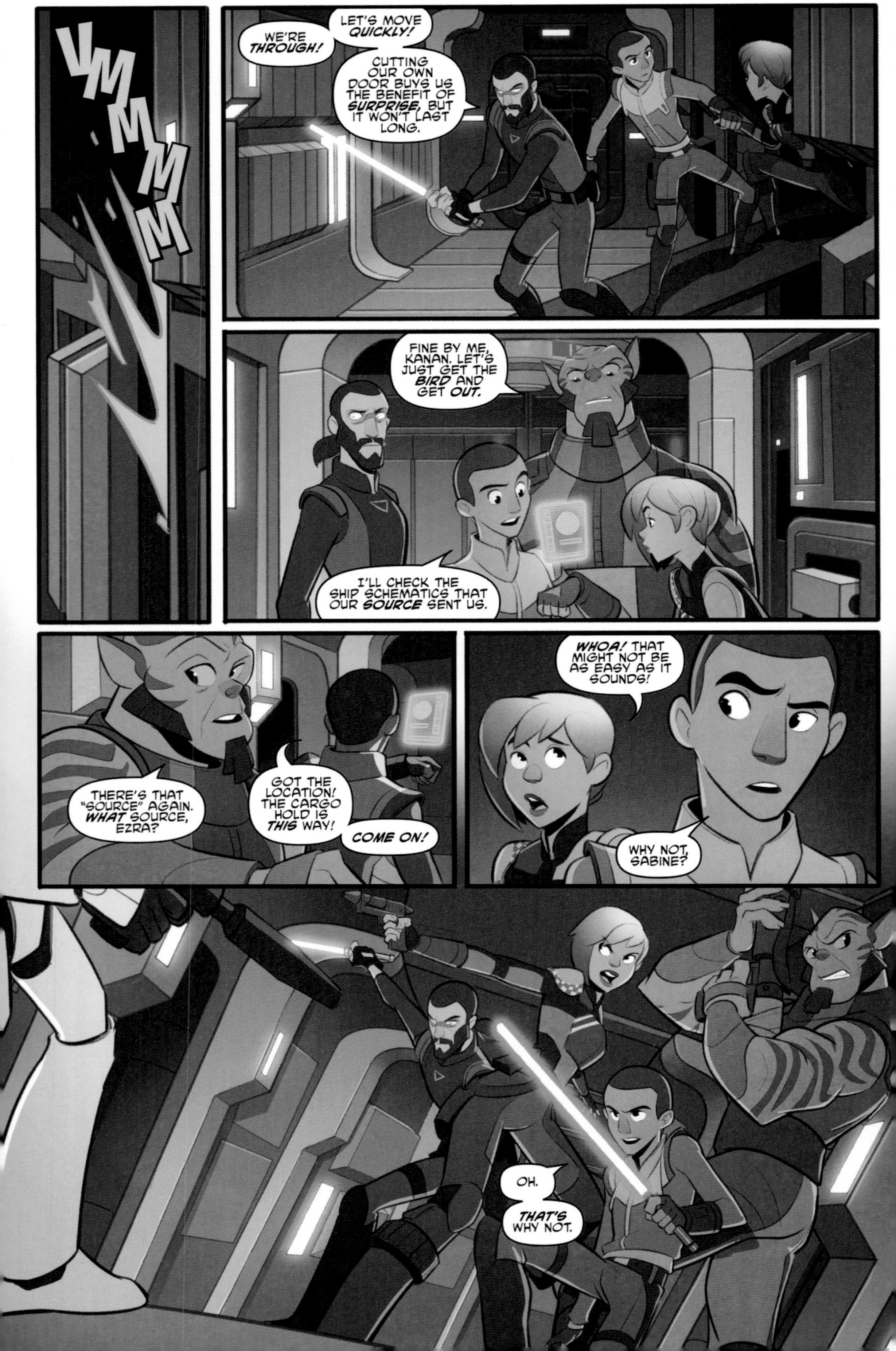
VMMMMM
WE'RE *THROUGH!*
LET'S MOVE *QUICKLY!*
CUTTING OUR OWN DOOR BUYS US THE BENEFIT OF *SURPRISE,* BUT IT WON'T LAST LONG.
FINE BY ME, KANAN. LET'S JUST GET THE *BIRD* AND GET *OUT.*
I'LL CHECK THE SHIP SCHEMATICS THAT OUR *SOURCE* SENT US.
THERE'S THAT "SOURCE" AGAIN. *WHAT* SOURCE, EZRA?
GOT THE LOCATION! THE CARGO HOLD IS *THIS* WAY!
COME ON!
WHOA! THAT MIGHT NOT BE AS EASY AS IT SOUNDS!
WHY NOT, SABINE?
OH.
THAT'S WHY NOT.

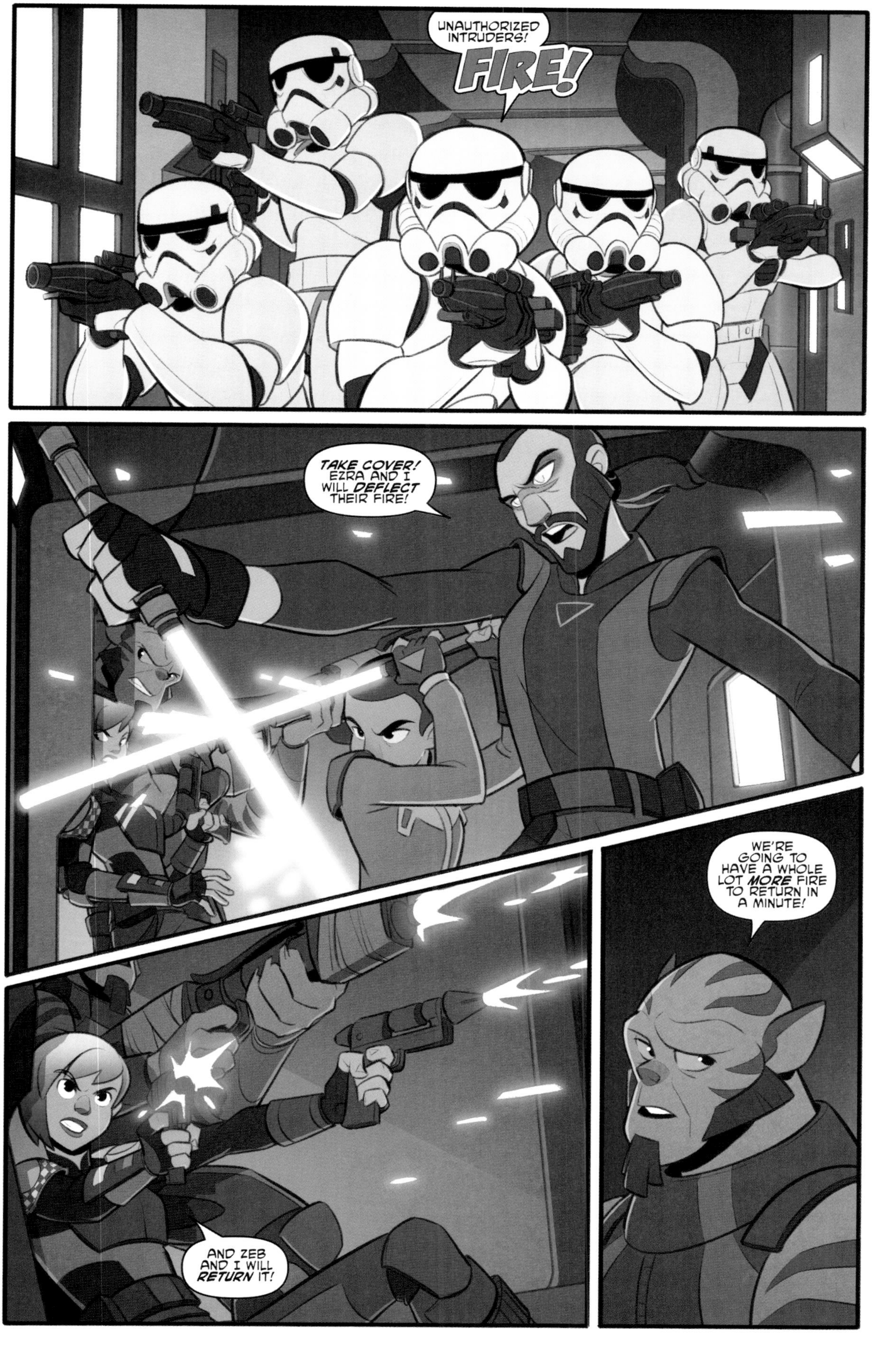
UNAUTHORIZED INTRUDERS!
FIRE!
TAKE COVER! EZRA AND I WILL DEFLECT THEIR FIRE!
AND ZEB AND I WILL RETURN IT!
WE'RE GOING TO HAVE A WHOLE LOT MORE FIRE TO RETURN IN A MINUTE!

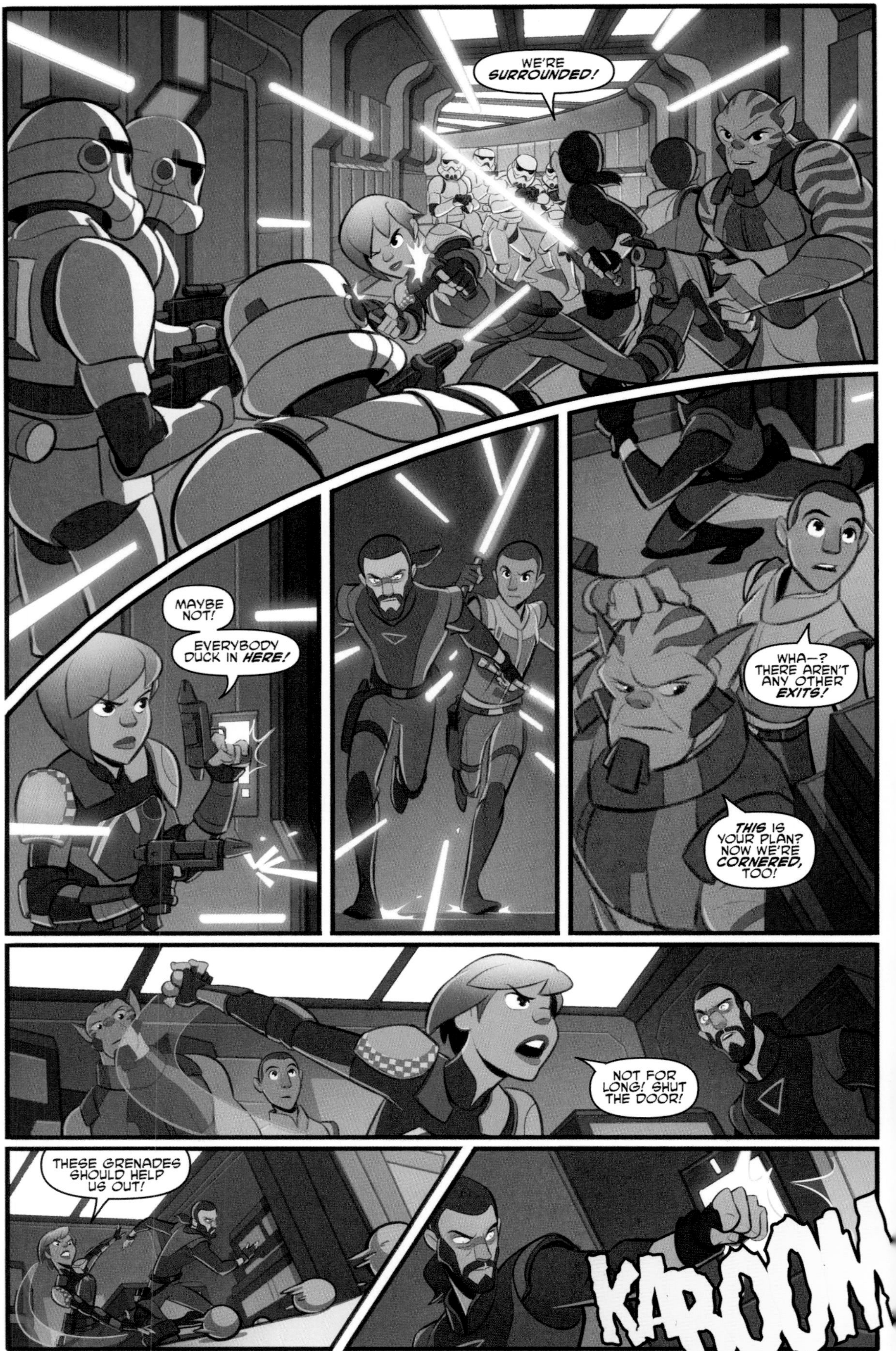
WE'RE *SURROUNDED!*
MAYBE NOT!
EVERYBODY DUCK IN *HERE!*
WHA--? THERE AREN'T ANY OTHER *EXITS!*
THIS IS YOUR PLAN? NOW WE'RE *CORNERED,* TOO!
NOT FOR LONG! SHUT THE DOOR!
THESE GRENADES SHOULD HELP US OUT!
KABOOM

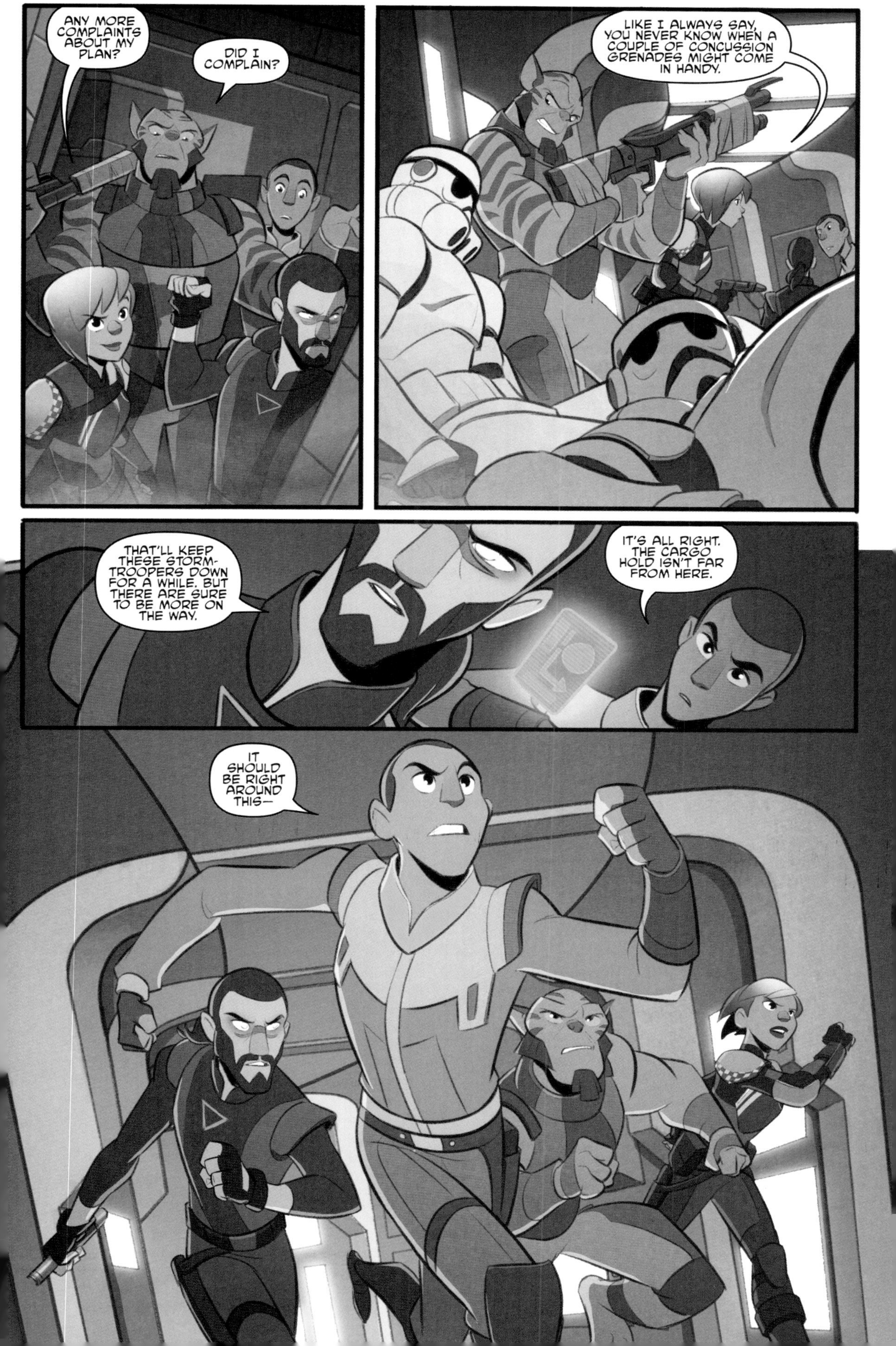
ANY MORE COMPLAINTS ABOUT MY PLAN?
DID I COMPLAIN?
LIKE I ALWAYS SAY, YOU NEVER KNOW WHEN A COUPLE OF CONCUSSION GRENADES MIGHT COME IN HANDY.
THAT'LL KEEP THESE STORM-TROOPERS DOWN FOR A WHILE. BUT THERE ARE SURE TO BE MORE ON THE WAY.
IT'S ALL RIGHT. THE CARGO HOLD ISN'T FAR FROM HERE.
IT SHOULD BE RIGHT AROUND THIS—

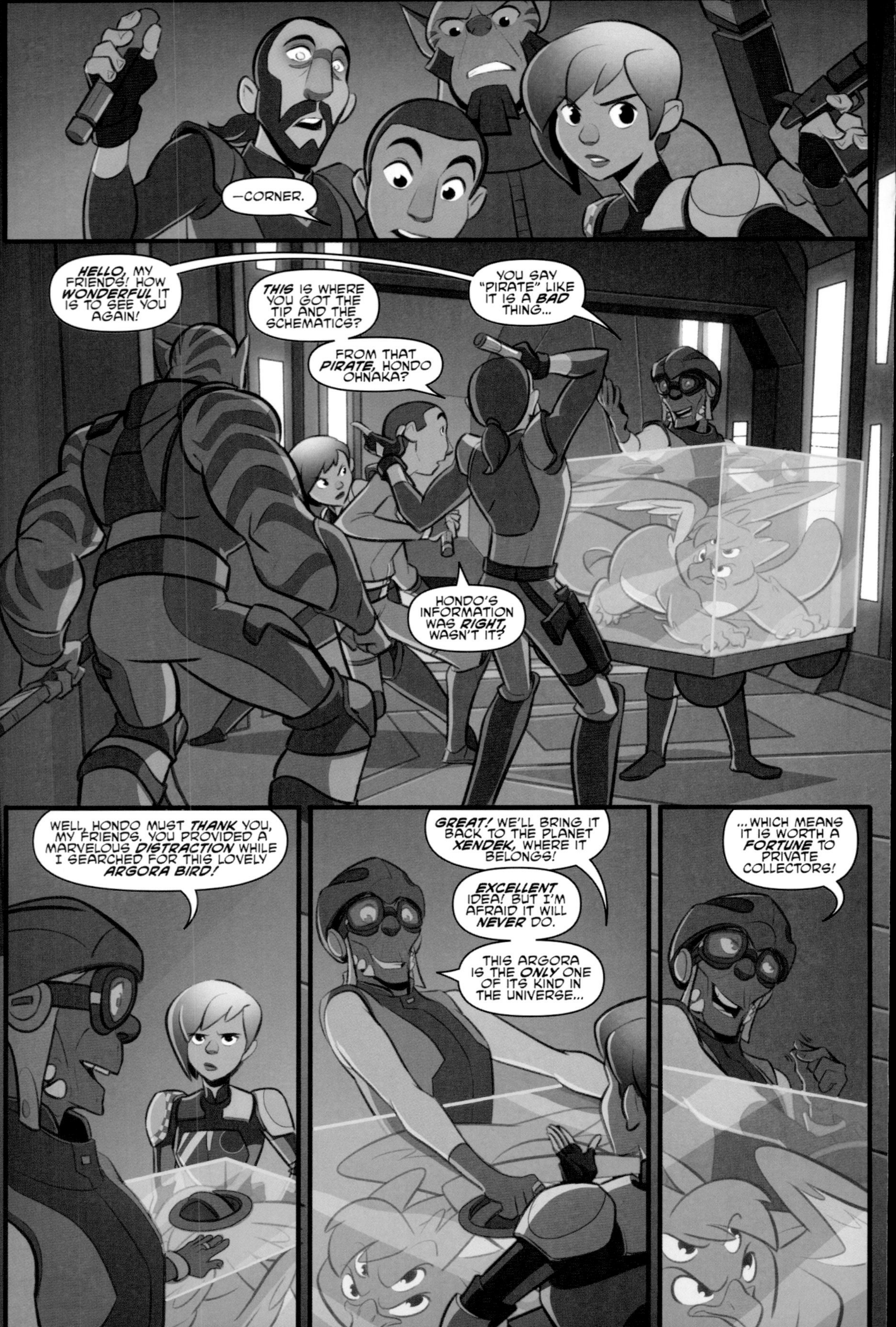
—CORNER.
HELLO, MY FRIENDS! HOW WONDERFUL IT IS TO SEE YOU AGAIN!
THIS IS WHERE YOU GOT THE TIP AND THE SCHEMATICS?
FROM THAT PIRATE, HONDO OHNAKA?
YOU SAY "PIRATE" LIKE IT IS A BAD THING...
HONDO'S INFORMATION WAS RIGHT, WASN'T IT?
WELL, HONDO MUST THANK YOU, MY FRIENDS. YOU PROVIDED A MARVELOUS DISTRACTION WHILE I SEARCHED FOR THIS LOVELY ARGORA BIRD!
GREAT! WE'LL BRING IT BACK TO THE PLANET XENDEK, WHERE IT BELONGS!
EXCELLENT IDEA! BUT I'M AFRAID IT WILL NEVER DO.
THIS ARGORA IS THE ONLY ONE OF ITS KIND IN THE UNIVERSE...
...WHICH MEANS IT IS WORTH A FORTUNE TO PRIVATE COLLECTORS!

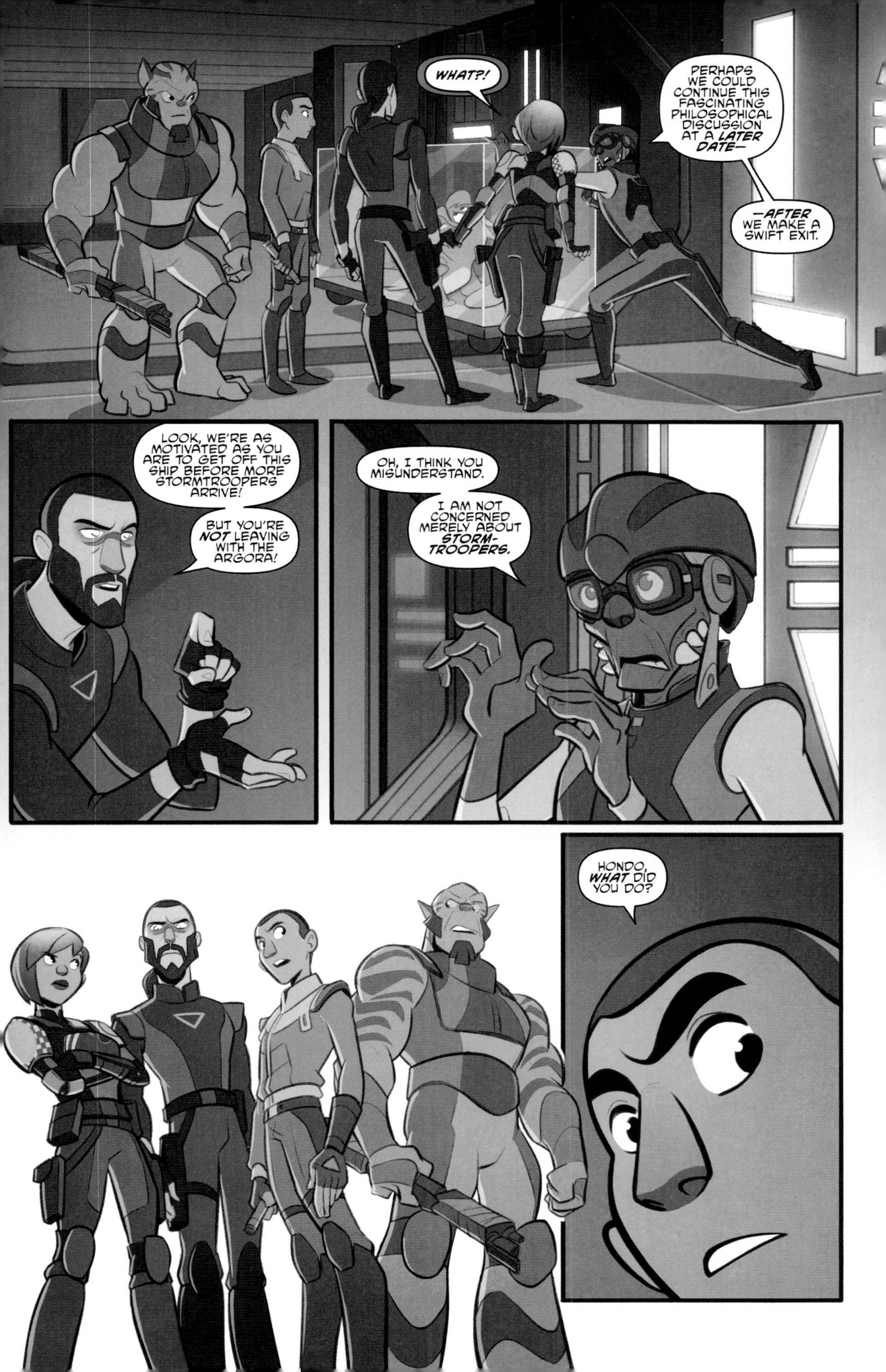
WHAT?!
PERHAPS WE COULD CONTINUE THIS FASCINATING PHILOSOPHICAL DISCUSSION AT A LATER DATE—
—AFTER WE MAKE A SWIFT EXIT.
LOOK, WE'RE AS MOTIVATED AS YOU ARE TO GET OFF THIS SHIP BEFORE MORE STORMTROOPERS ARRIVE!
BUT YOU'RE NOT LEAVING WITH THE ARGORA!
OH, I THINK YOU MISUNDERSTAND.
I AM NOT CONCERNED MERELY ABOUT STORM-TROOPERS.
HONDO, WHAT DID YOU DO?

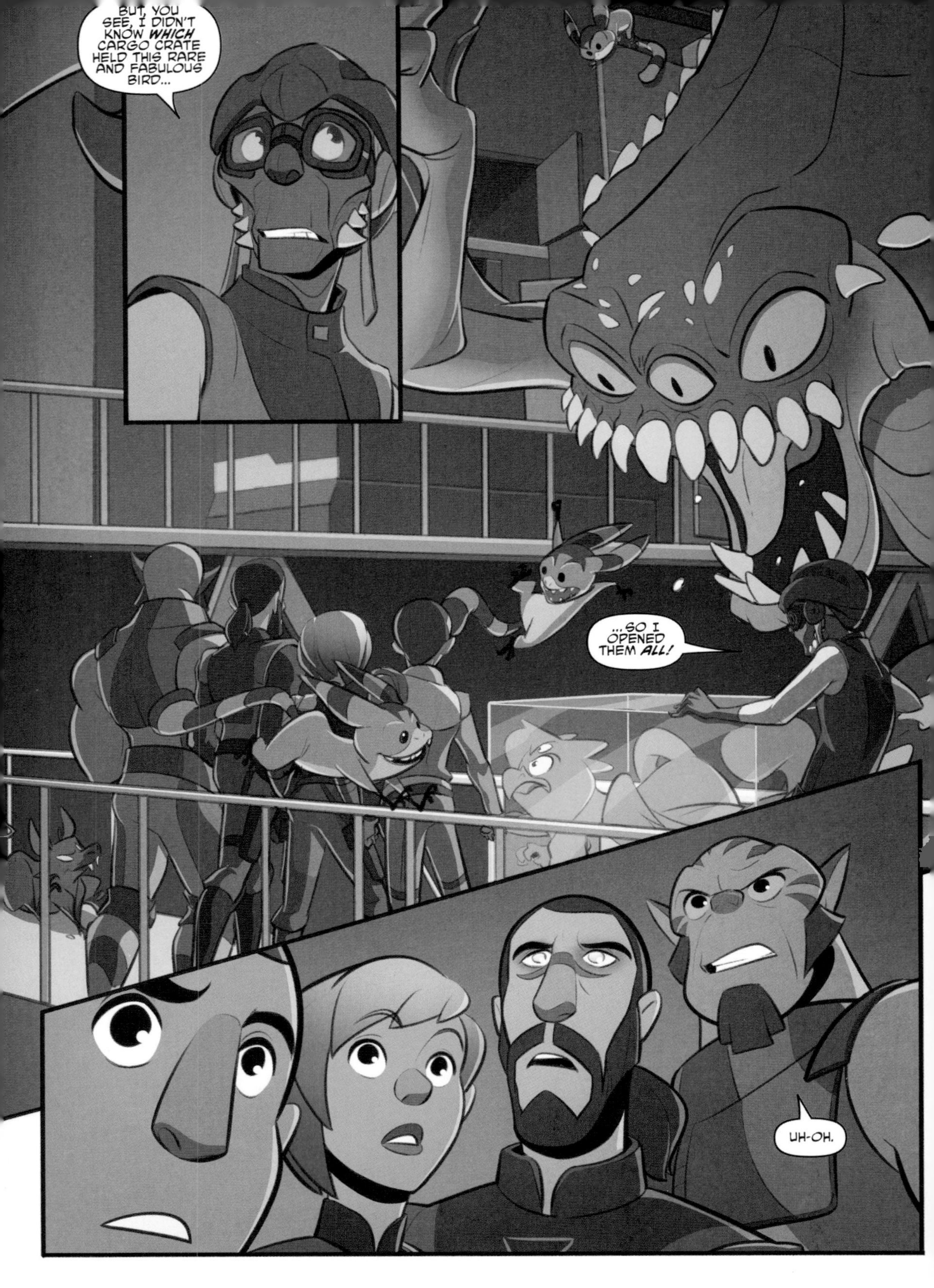
BUT, YOU SEE, I DIDN'T KNOW *WHICH* CARGO CRATE HELD THIS RARE AND FABULOUS BIRD...
...SO I OPENED THEM *ALL!*
UH-OH.

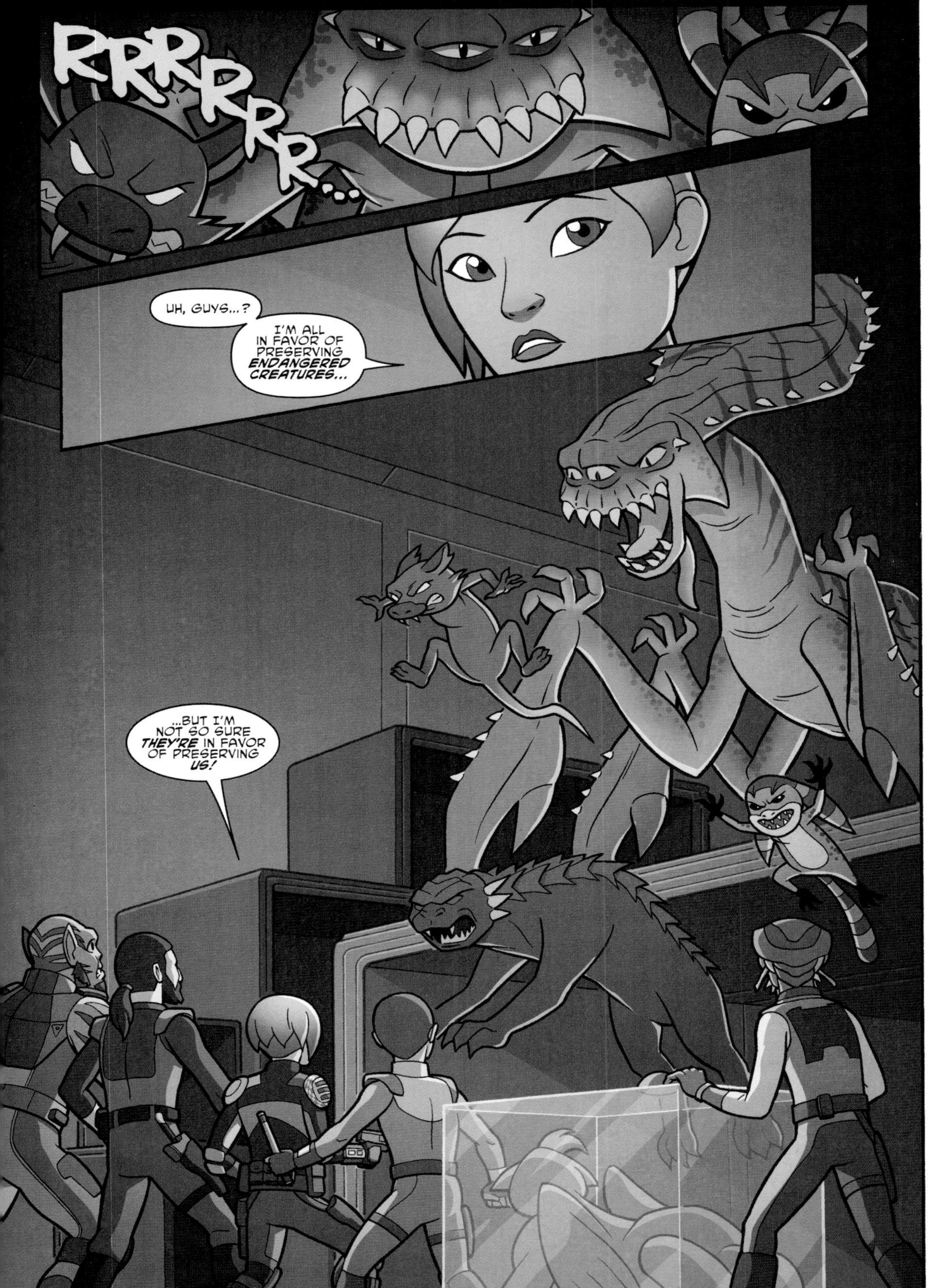
RRRRRRR...
UH, GUYS...?
I'M ALL IN FAVOR OF PRESERVING ENDANGERED CREATURES...
...BUT I'M NOT SO SURE THEY'RE IN FAVOR OF PRESERVING US!

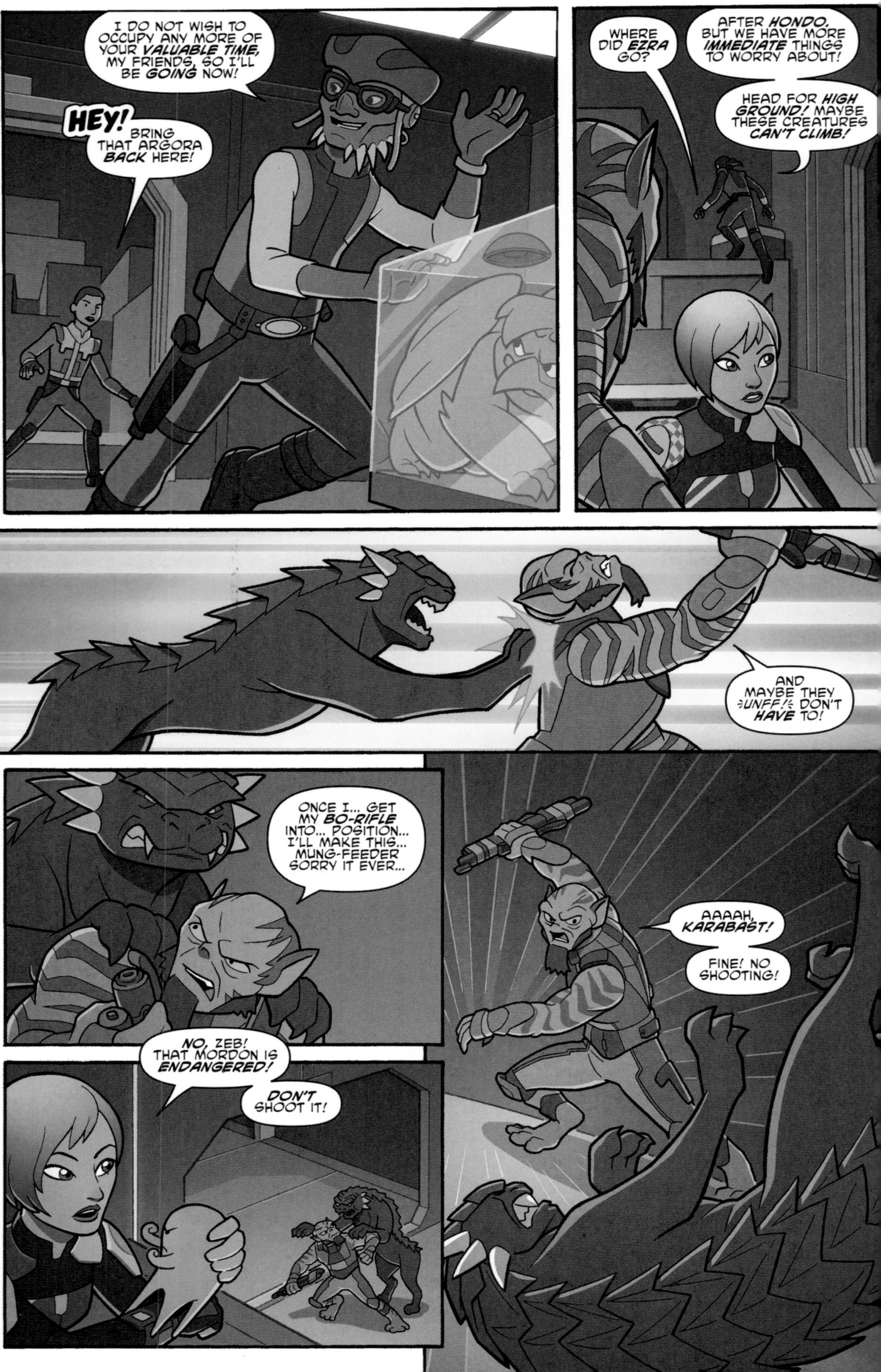
I DO NOT WISH TO OCCUPY ANY MORE OF YOUR VALUABLE TIME, MY FRIENDS, SO I'LL BE GOING NOW!
HEY! BRING THAT ARGORA BACK HERE!
WHERE DID EZRA GO?
AFTER HONDO, BUT WE HAVE MORE IMMEDIATE THINGS TO WORRY ABOUT!
HEAD FOR HIGH GROUND! MAYBE THESE CREATURES CAN'T CLIMB!
AND MAYBE THEY UNFF! DON'T HAVE TO!
ONCE I... GET MY BO-RIFLE INTO... POSITION... I'LL MAKE THIS... MUNG-FEEDER SORRY IT EVER...
NO, ZEB! THAT MORDON IS ENDANGERED!
DON'T SHOOT IT!
AAAAH, KARABAST!
FINE! NO SHOOTING!

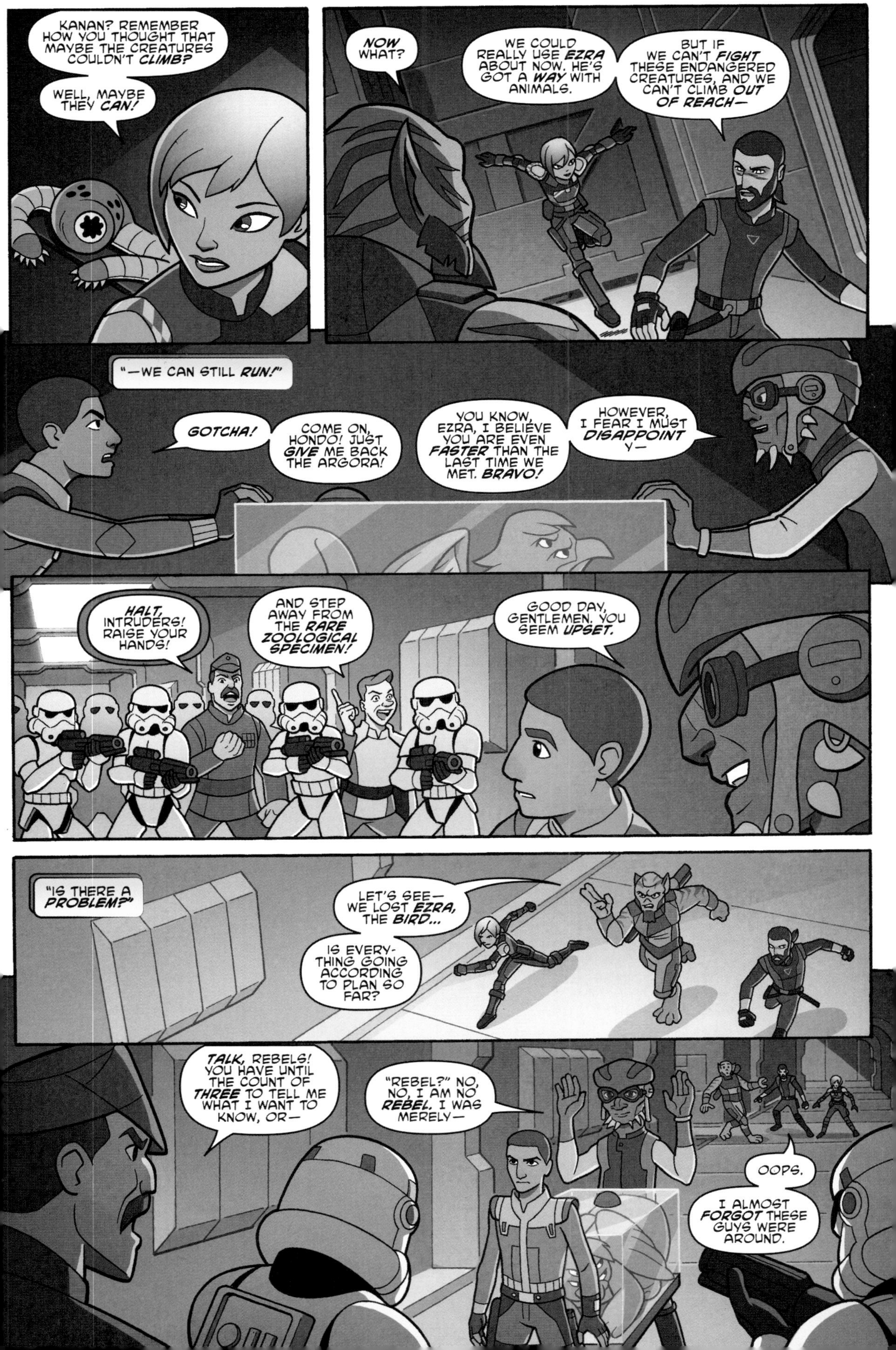
KANAN? REMEMBER HOW YOU THOUGHT THAT MAYBE THE CREATURES COULDN'T *CLIMB?*
WELL, MAYBE THEY *CAN!*
NOW WHAT?
WE COULD REALLY USE *EZRA* ABOUT NOW. HE'S GOT A *WAY* WITH ANIMALS.
BUT IF WE CAN'T *FIGHT* THESE ENDANGERED CREATURES, AND WE CAN'T CLIMB *OUT OF REACH*—
"—WE CAN STILL *RUN!*"
GOTCHA!
COME ON, HONDO! JUST *GIVE* ME BACK THE ARGORA!
YOU KNOW, EZRA, I BELIEVE YOU ARE EVEN *FASTER* THAN THE LAST TIME WE MET. *BRAVO!*
HOWEVER, I FEAR I MUST *DISAPPOINT* Y—
HALT, INTRUDERS! RAISE YOUR HANDS!
AND STEP AWAY FROM THE *RARE ZOOLOGICAL SPECIMEN!*
GOOD DAY, GENTLEMEN. YOU SEEM *UPSET.*
"IS THERE A *PROBLEM?*"
LET'S SEE—WE LOST *EZRA,* THE *BIRD...*
IS EVERY-THING GOING ACCORDING TO PLAN SO FAR?
TALK, REBELS! YOU HAVE UNTIL THE COUNT OF *THREE* TO TELL ME WHAT I WANT TO KNOW, OR—
"REBEL?" NO, NO, I AM NO *REBEL.* I WAS MERELY—
OOPS.
I ALMOST *FORGOT* THESE GUYS WERE AROUND.

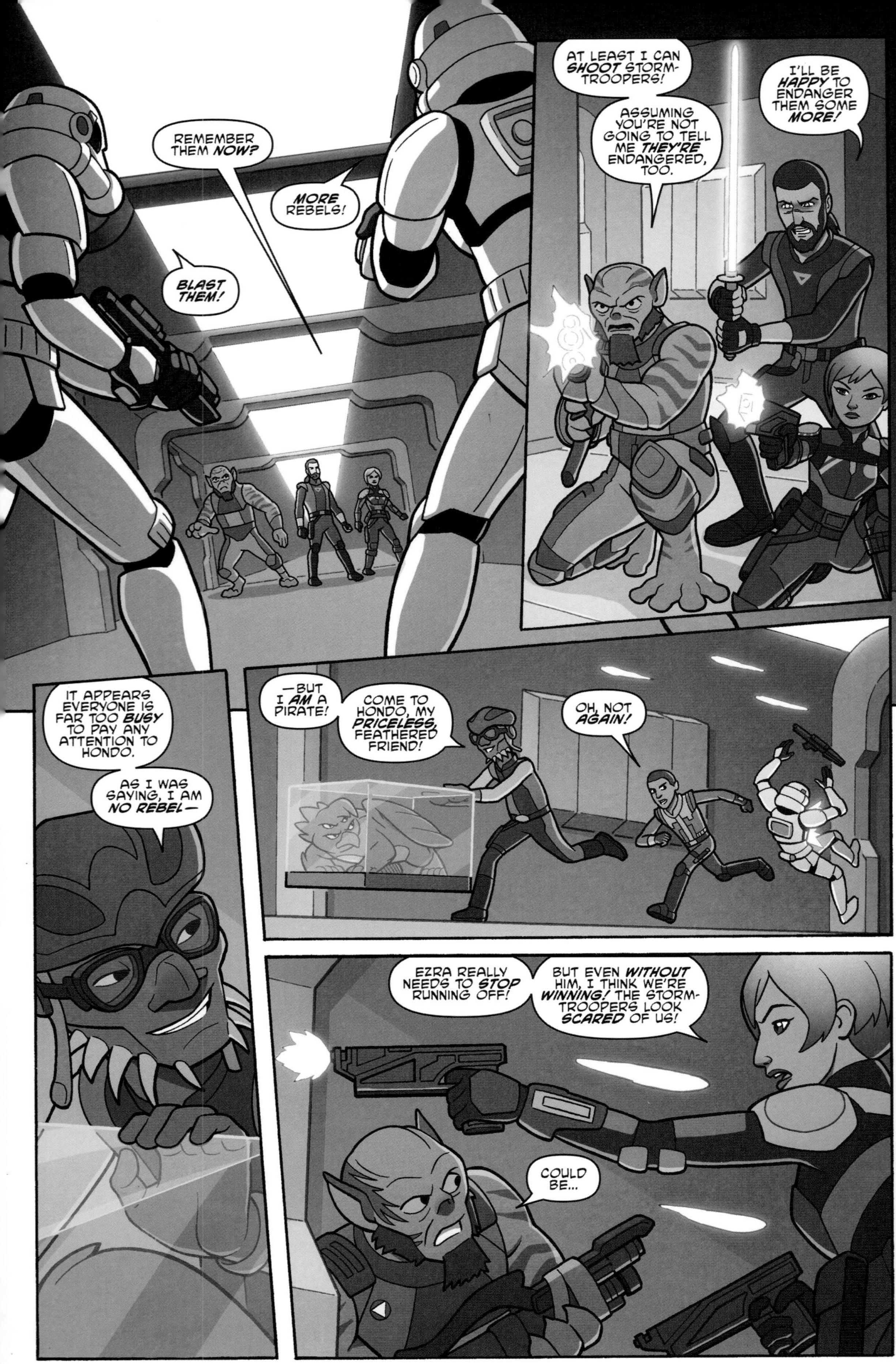

REMEMBER THEM NOW?
MORE REBELS!
BLAST THEM!
AT LEAST I CAN SHOOT STORM-TROOPERS!
ASSUMING YOU'RE NOT GOING TO TELL ME THEY'RE ENDANGERED, TOO.
I'LL BE HAPPY TO ENDANGER THEM SOME MORE!
IT APPEARS EVERYONE IS FAR TOO BUSY TO PAY ANY ATTENTION TO HONDO.
AS I WAS SAYING, I AM NO REBEL—
—BUT I AM A PIRATE!
COME TO HONDO, MY PRICELESS, FEATHERED FRIEND!
OH, NOT AGAIN!
EZRA REALLY NEEDS TO STOP RUNNING OFF!
BUT EVEN WITHOUT HIM, I THINK WE'RE WINNING! THE STORM-TROOPERS LOOK SCARED OF US!
COULD BE...

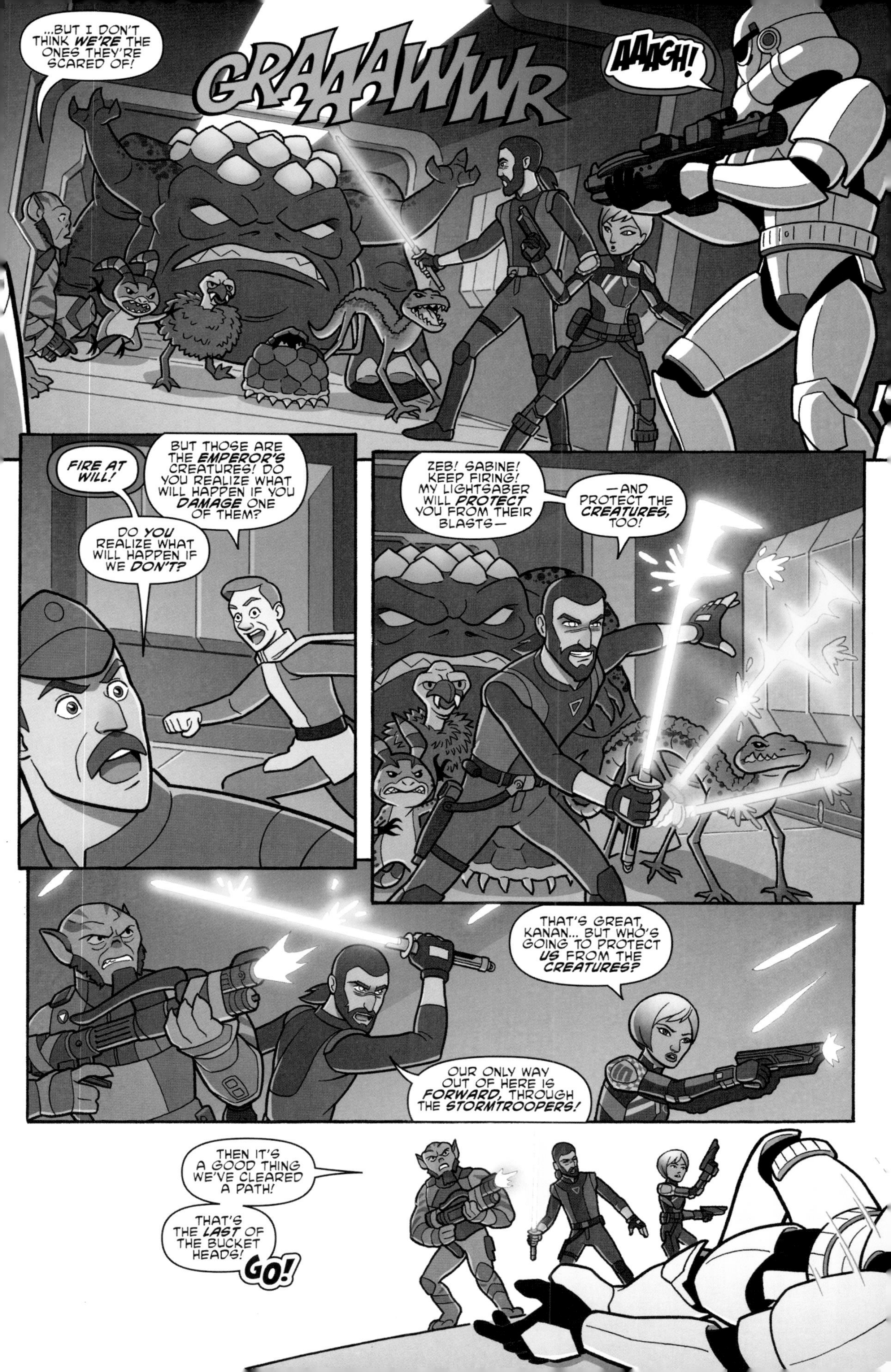
...BUT I DON'T THINK WE'RE THE ONES THEY'RE SCARED OF!
GRAAAWWR
AAAGH!
FIRE AT WILL!
BUT THOSE ARE THE EMPEROR'S CREATURES! DO YOU REALIZE WHAT WILL HAPPEN IF YOU DAMAGE ONE OF THEM?
DO YOU REALIZE WHAT WILL HAPPEN IF WE DON'T?
ZEB! SABINE! KEEP FIRING! MY LIGHTSABER WILL PROTECT YOU FROM THEIR BLASTS—
—AND PROTECT THE CREATURES, TOO!
THAT'S GREAT, KANAN... BUT WHO'S GOING TO PROTECT US FROM THE CREATURES?
OUR ONLY WAY OUT OF HERE IS FORWARD, THROUGH THE STORMTROOPERS!
THEN IT'S A GOOD THING WE'VE CLEARED A PATH!
THAT'S THE LAST OF THE BUCKET HEADS!
GO!

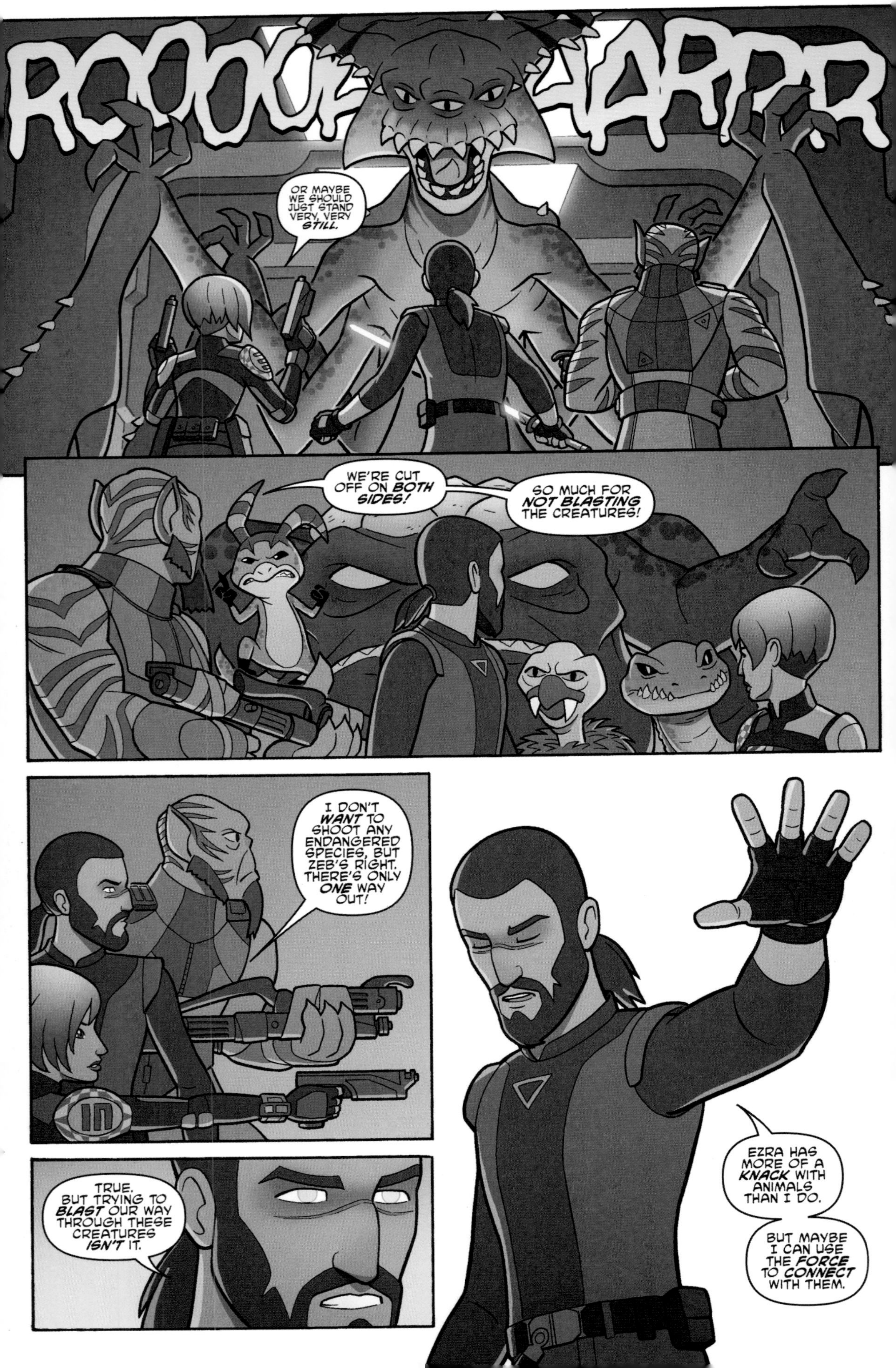
ROOOOUGHARRR
OR MAYBE WE SHOULD JUST STAND VERY, VERY STILL.
WE'RE CUT OFF ON BOTH SIDES!
SO MUCH FOR NOT BLASTING THE CREATURES!
I DON'T WANT TO SHOOT ANY ENDANGERED SPECIES, BUT ZEB'S RIGHT. THERE'S ONLY ONE WAY OUT!
TRUE. BUT TRYING TO BLAST OUR WAY THROUGH THESE CREATURES ISN'T IT.
EZRA HAS MORE OF A KNACK WITH ANIMALS THAN I DO.
BUT MAYBE I CAN USE THE FORCE TO CONNECT WITH THEM.

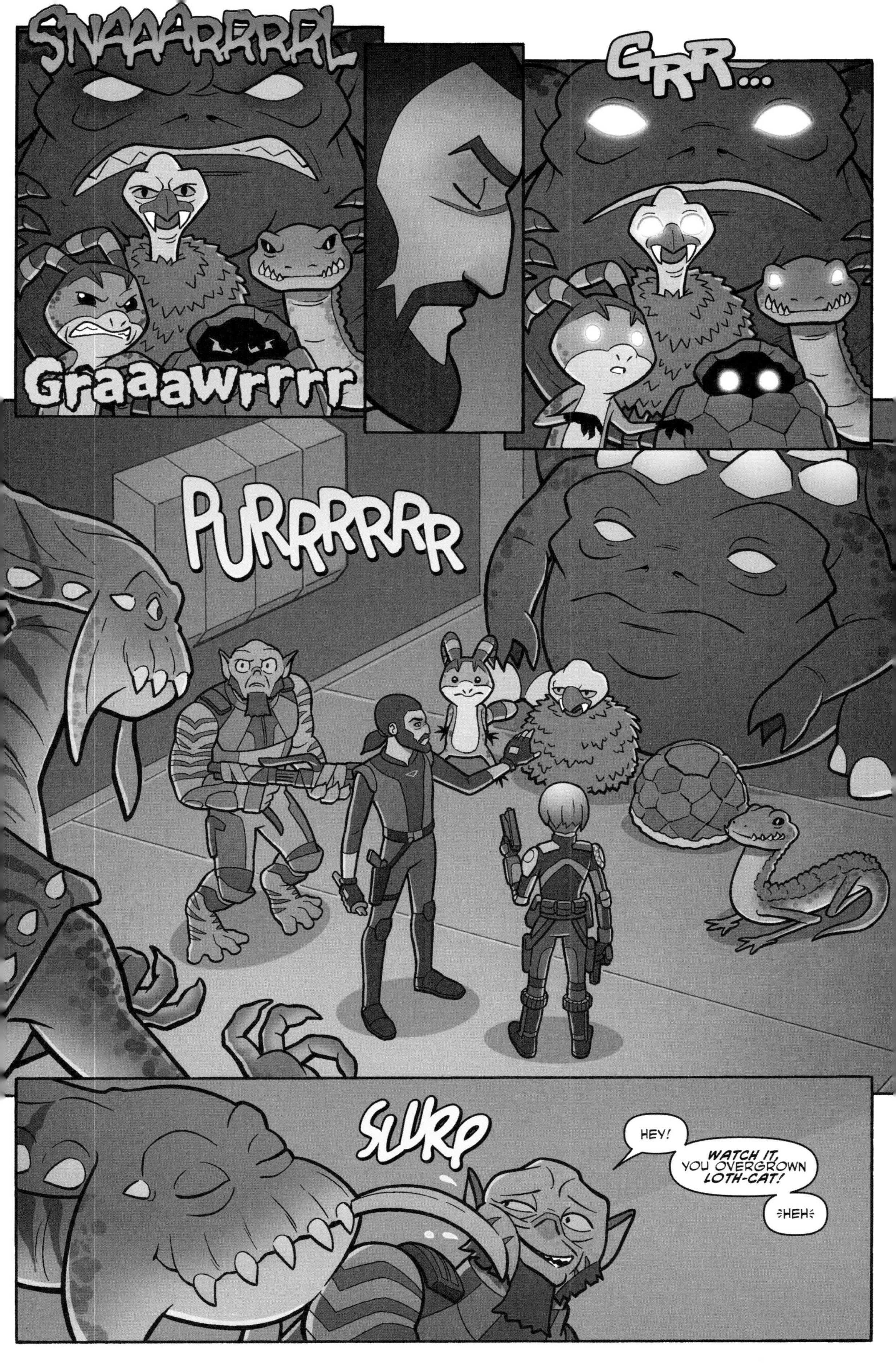
SNAAARRRRL
Graaawrrrr
GRR...
PURRRRRR
SLURP
HEY!
WATCH IT, YOU OVERGROWN LOTH-CAT!
HEH

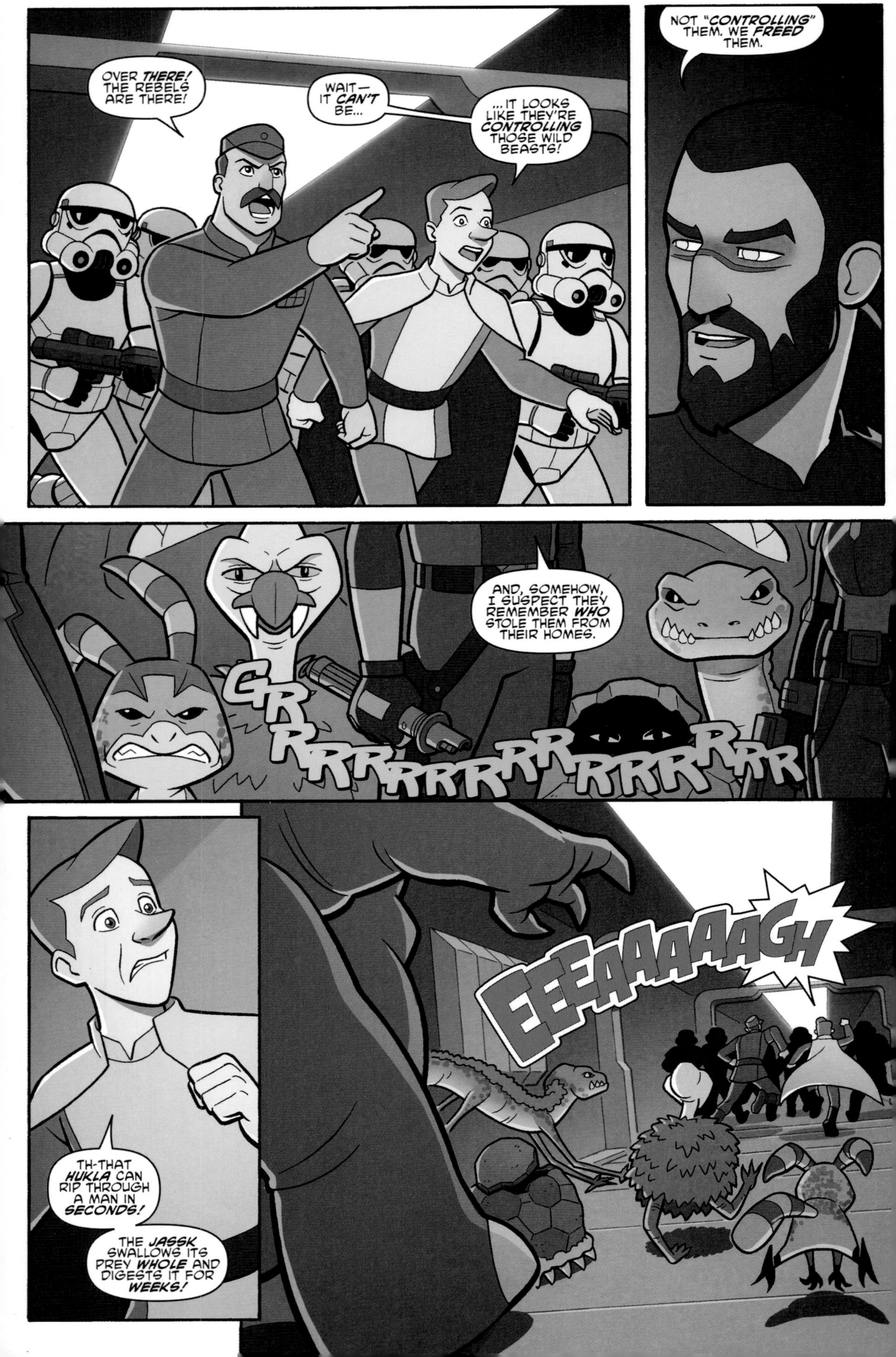

OVER THERE! THE REBELS ARE THERE!
WAIT— IT CAN'T BE...
...IT LOOKS LIKE THEY'RE CONTROLLING THOSE WILD BEASTS!
NOT "CONTROLLING" THEM. WE FREED THEM.
AND, SOMEHOW, I SUSPECT THEY REMEMBER WHO STOLE THEM FROM THEIR HOMES.
GRRRRRRRRRRRRRRRRRR
EEEAAAAAAGH
TH-THAT HUKLA CAN RIP THROUGH A MAN IN SECONDS!
THE JASSK SWALLOWS ITS PREY WHOLE AND DIGESTS IT FOR WEEKS!

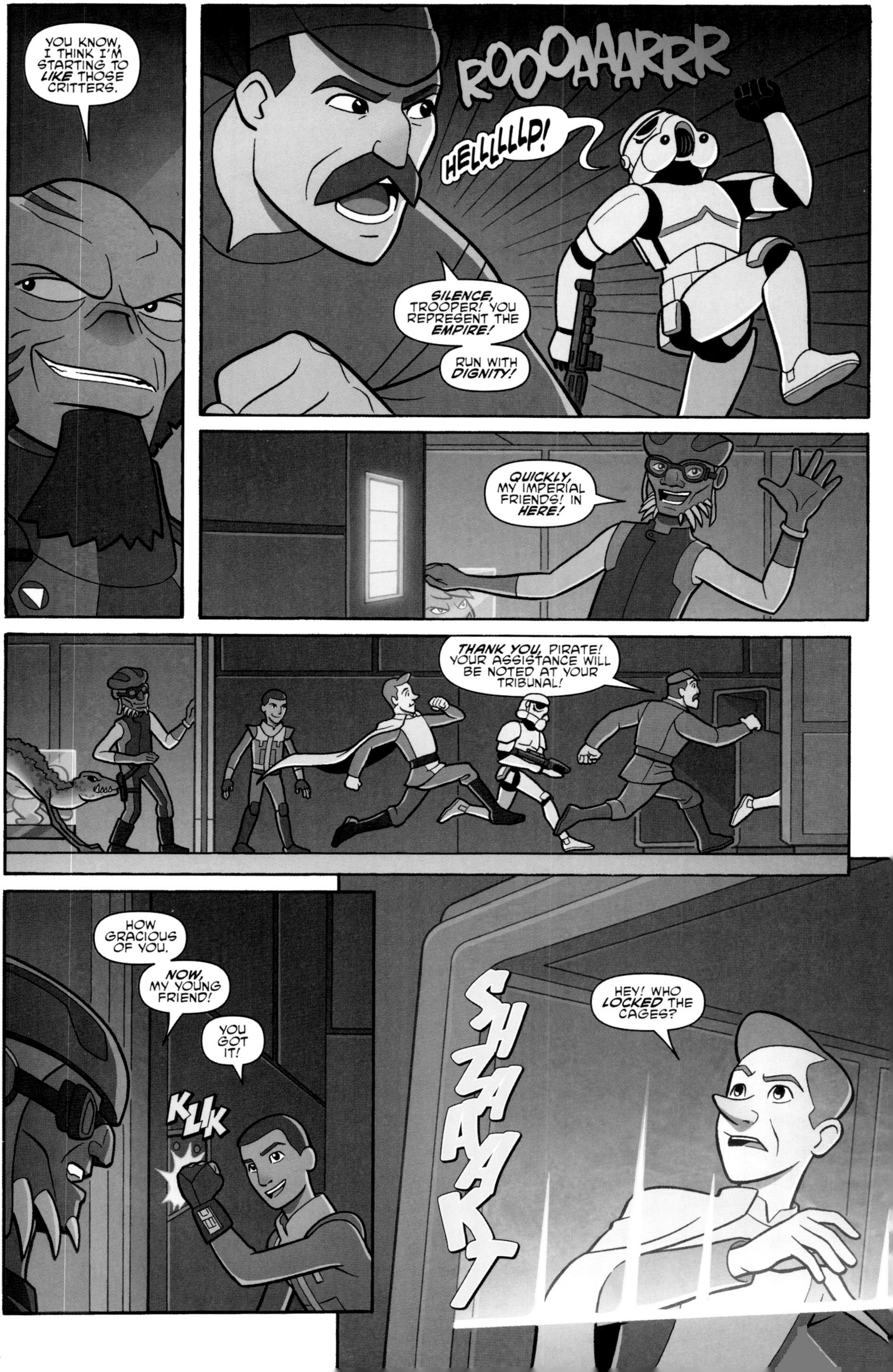
YOU KNOW, I THINK I'M STARTING TO LIKE THOSE CRITTERS.
ROOOAAARRR
HELLLLLLP!
SILENCE, TROOPER! YOU REPRESENT THE EMPIRE!
RUN WITH DIGNITY!
QUICKLY, MY IMPERIAL FRIENDS! IN HERE!
THANK YOU, PIRATE! YOUR ASSISTANCE WILL BE NOTED AT YOUR TRIBUNAL!
HOW GRACIOUS OF YOU.
NOW, MY YOUNG FRIEND!
YOU GOT IT!
KLIK
SHZAAAKT
HEY! WHO LOCKED THE CAGES?

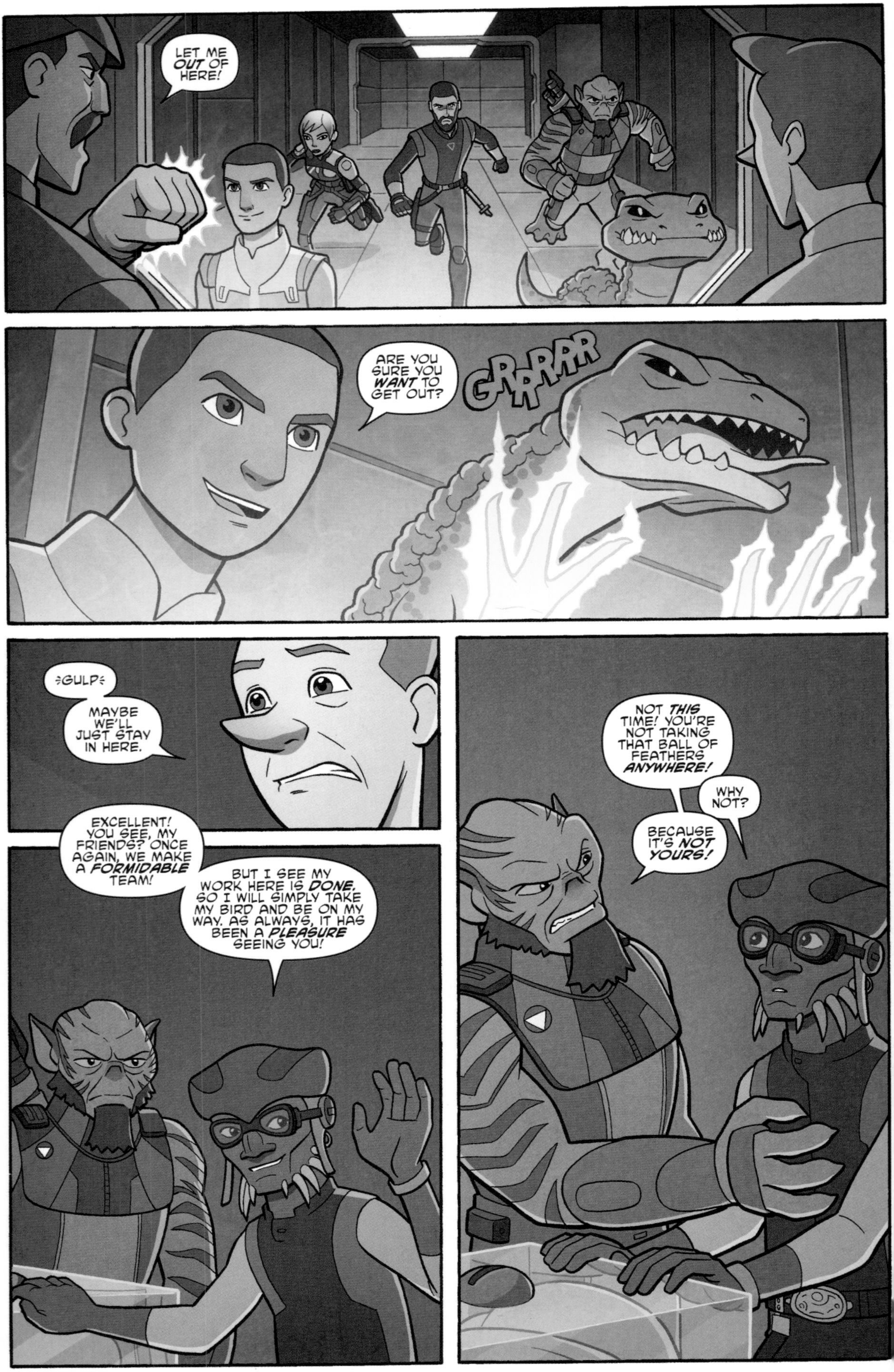
LET ME OUT OF HERE!
ARE YOU SURE YOU WANT TO GET OUT?
GRRRRR
GULP
MAYBE WE'LL JUST STAY IN HERE.
EXCELLENT! YOU SEE, MY FRIENDS? ONCE AGAIN, WE MAKE A FORMIDABLE TEAM!
BUT I SEE MY WORK HERE IS DONE, SO I WILL SIMPLY TAKE MY BIRD AND BE ON MY WAY. AS ALWAYS, IT HAS BEEN A PLEASURE SEEING YOU!
NOT THIS TIME! YOU'RE NOT TAKING THAT BALL OF FEATHERS ANYWHERE!
WHY NOT?
BECAUSE IT'S NOT YOURS!

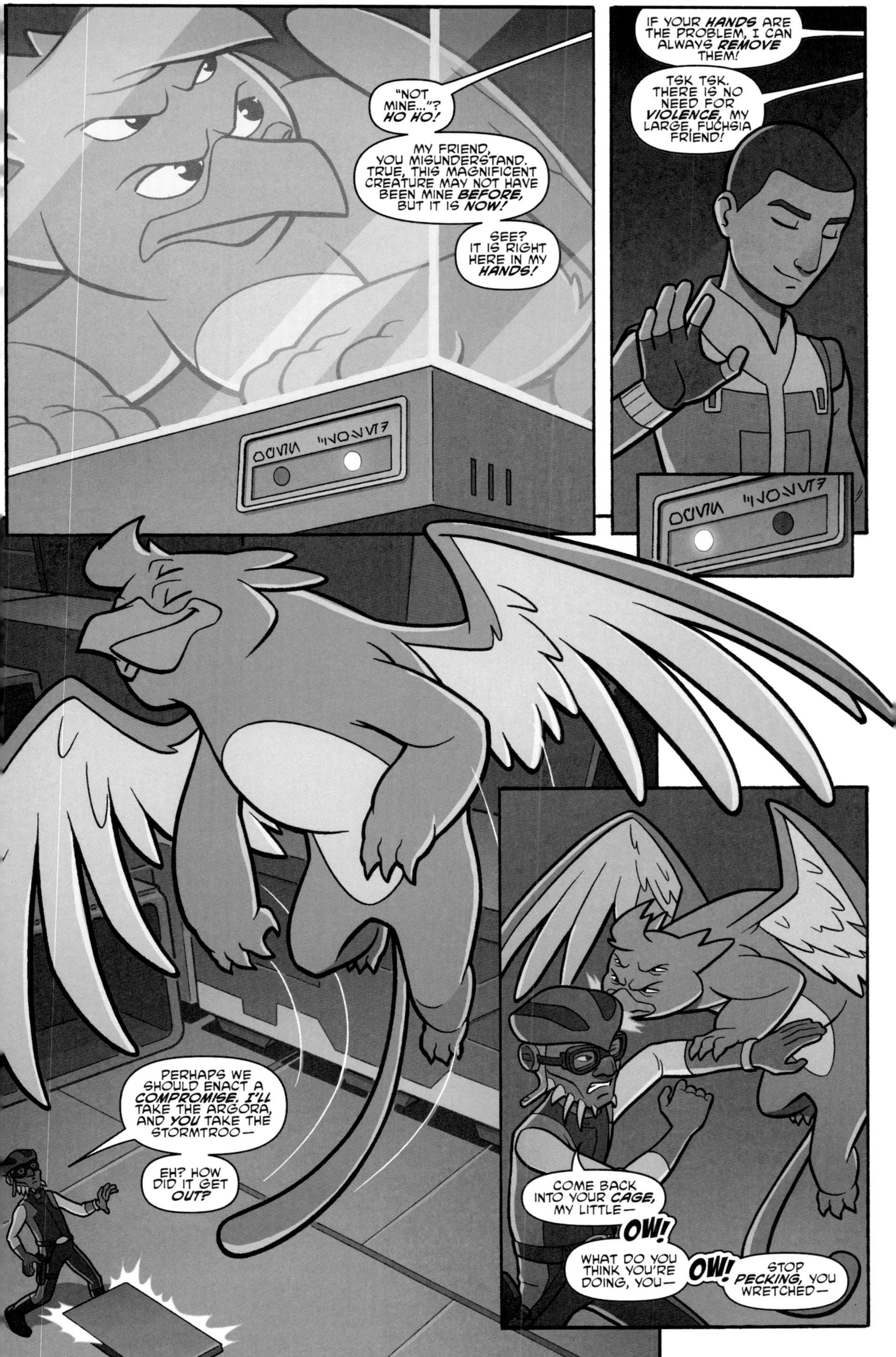
"NOT MINE..."? HO HO!
MY FRIEND, YOU MISUNDERSTAND. TRUE, THIS MAGNIFICENT CREATURE MAY NOT HAVE BEEN MINE BEFORE, BUT IT IS NOW!
SEE? IT IS RIGHT HERE IN MY HANDS!
IF YOUR HANDS ARE THE PROBLEM, I CAN ALWAYS REMOVE THEM!
TSK TSK. THERE IS NO NEED FOR VIOLENCE, MY LARGE, FUCHSIA FRIEND!
PERHAPS WE SHOULD ENACT A COMPROMISE. I'LL TAKE THE ARGORA, AND YOU TAKE THE STORMTROO—
EH? HOW DID IT GET OUT?
COME BACK INTO YOUR CAGE, MY LITTLE—
OW!
WHAT DO YOU THINK YOU'RE DOING, YOU—
OW!
STOP PECKING, YOU WRETCHED—

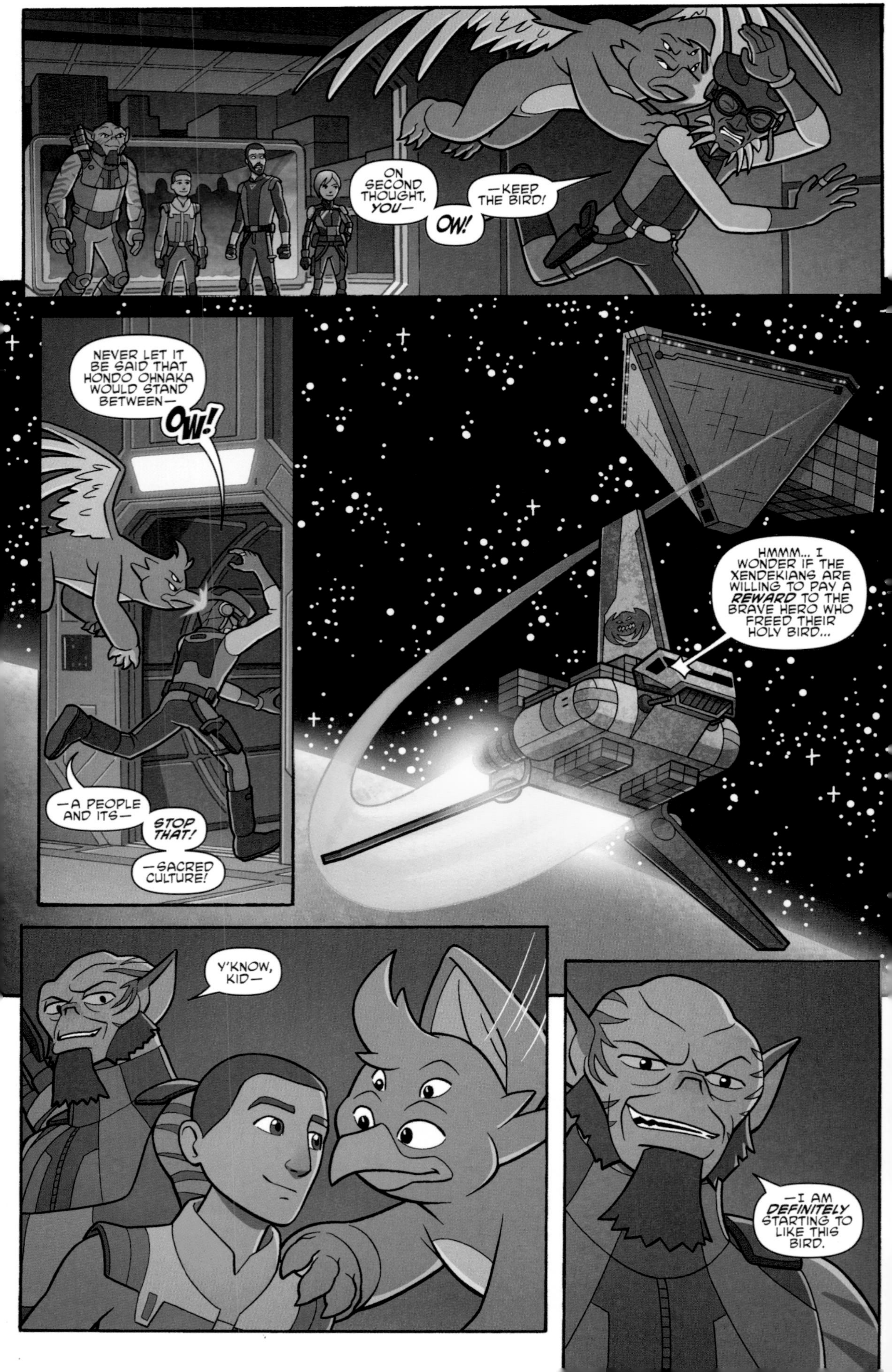
ON SECOND THOUGHT, YOU—
OW!
—KEEP THE BIRD!
NEVER LET IT BE SAID THAT HONDO OHNAKA WOULD STAND BETWEEN—
OW!
—A PEOPLE AND ITS—
STOP THAT!
—SACRED CULTURE!
HMMM... I WONDER IF THE XENDEKIANS ARE WILLING TO PAY A REWARD TO THE BRAVE HERO WHO FREED THEIR HOLY BIRD...
Y'KNOW, KID—
—I AM DEFINITELY STARTING TO LIKE THIS BIRD.

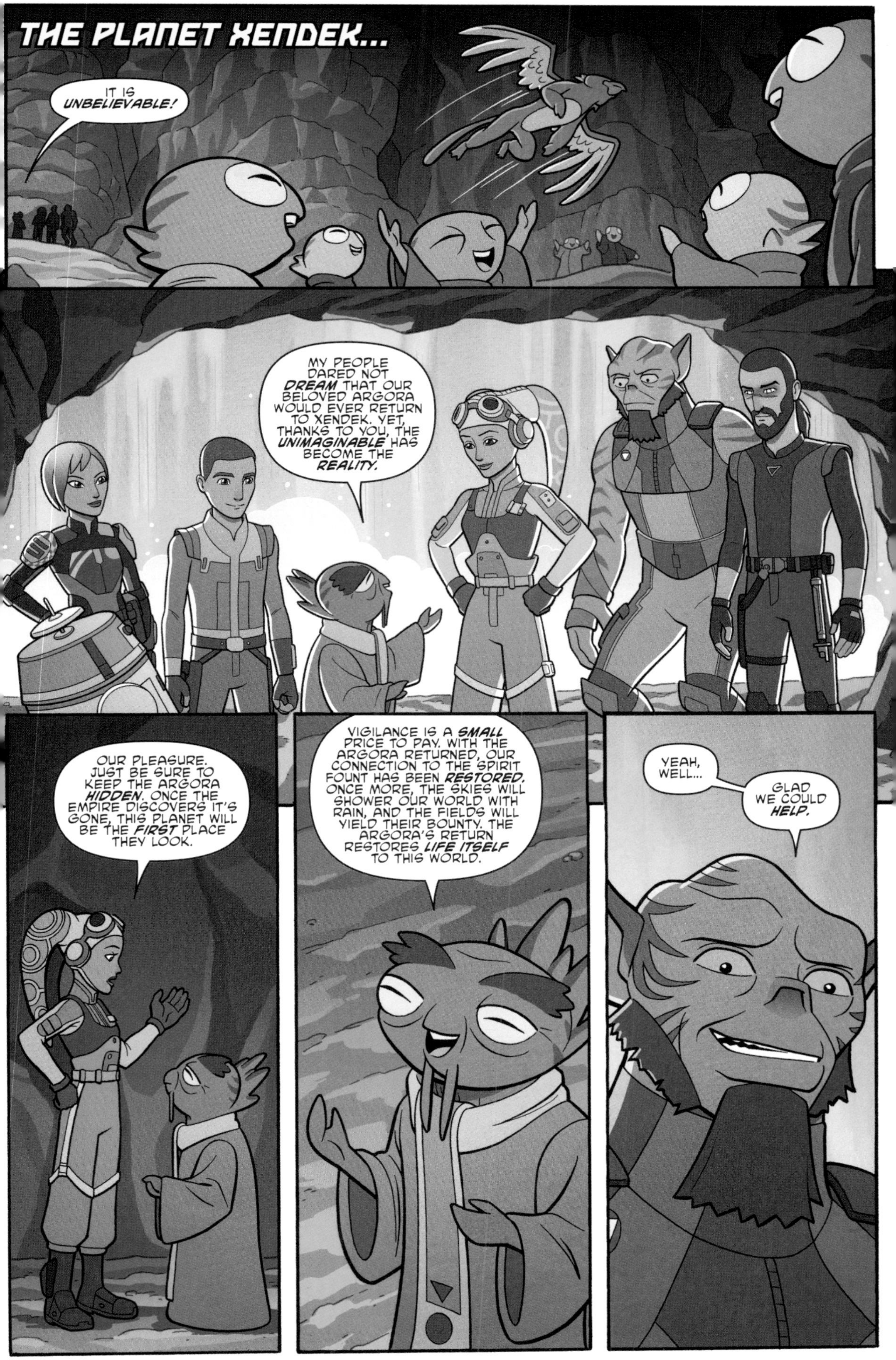
THE PLANET XENDEK...
IT IS UNBELIEVABLE!
MY PEOPLE DARED NOT DREAM THAT OUR BELOVED ARGORA WOULD EVER RETURN TO XENDEK. YET, THANKS TO YOU, THE UNIMAGINABLE HAS BECOME THE REALITY.
OUR PLEASURE. JUST BE SURE TO KEEP THE ARGORA HIDDEN. ONCE THE EMPIRE DISCOVERS IT'S GONE, THIS PLANET WILL BE THE FIRST PLACE THEY LOOK.
VIGILANCE IS A SMALL PRICE TO PAY. WITH THE ARGORA RETURNED, OUR CONNECTION TO THE SPIRIT FOUNT HAS BEEN RESTORED. ONCE MORE, THE SKIES WILL SHOWER OUR WORLD WITH RAIN, AND THE FIELDS WILL YIELD THEIR BOUNTY. THE ARGORA'S RETURN RESTORES LIFE ITSELF TO THIS WORLD.
YEAH, WELL...
GLAD WE COULD HELP.

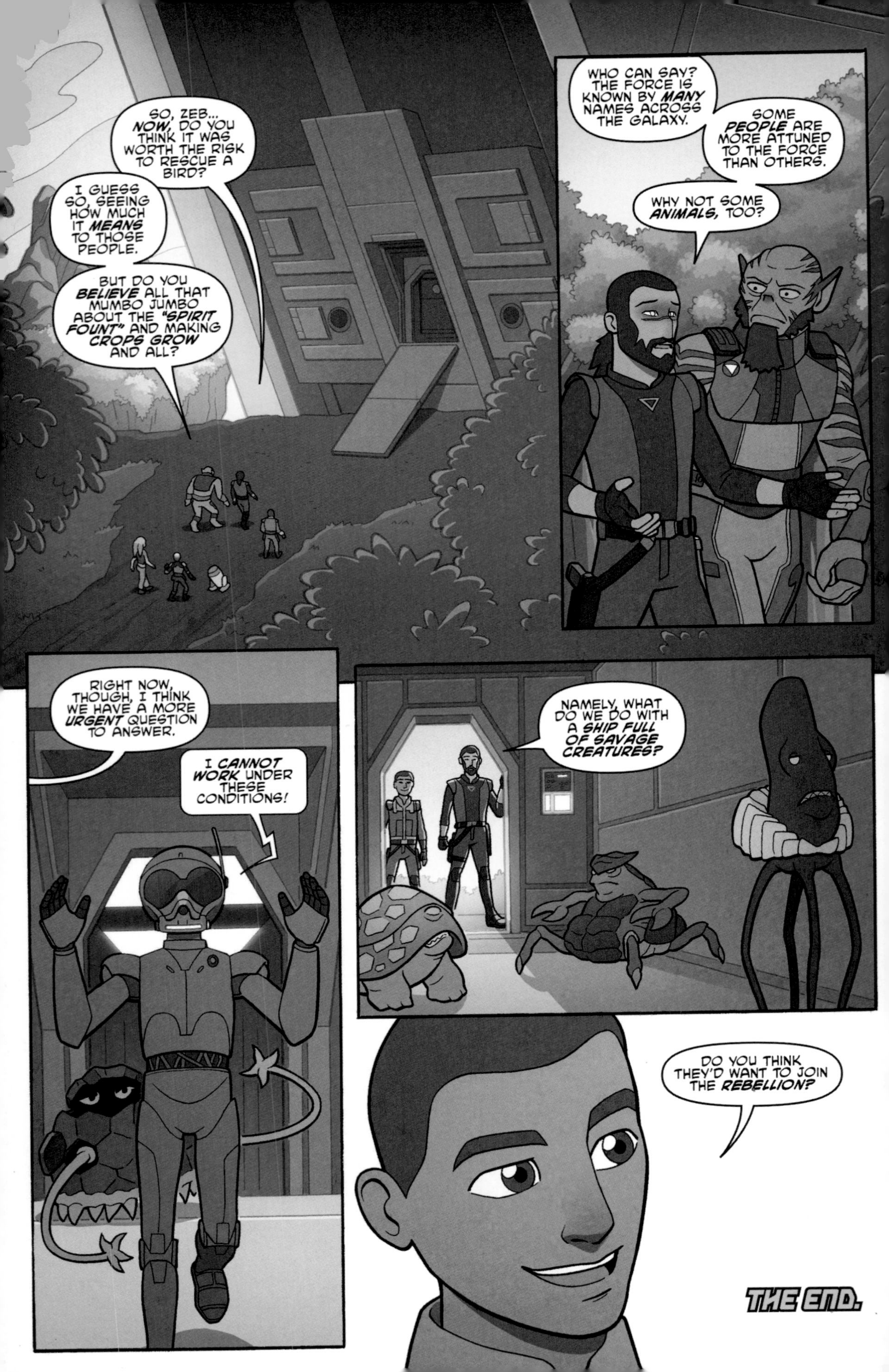
SO, ZEB... NOW, DO YOU THINK IT WAS WORTH THE RISK TO RESCUE A BIRD?
I GUESS SO, SEEING HOW MUCH IT MEANS TO THOSE PEOPLE.
BUT DO YOU BELIEVE ALL THAT MUMBO JUMBO ABOUT THE "SPIRIT FOUNT" AND MAKING CROPS GROW AND ALL?
WHO CAN SAY? THE FORCE IS KNOWN BY MANY NAMES ACROSS THE GALAXY.
SOME PEOPLE ARE MORE ATTUNED TO THE FORCE THAN OTHERS.
WHY NOT SOME ANIMALS, TOO?
RIGHT NOW, THOUGH, I THINK WE HAVE A MORE URGENT QUESTION TO ANSWER.
I CANNOT WORK UNDER THESE CONDITIONS!
NAMELY, WHAT DO WE DO WITH A SHIP FULL OF SAVAGE CREATURES?
DO YOU THINK THEY'D WANT TO JOIN THE REBELLION?
THE END.

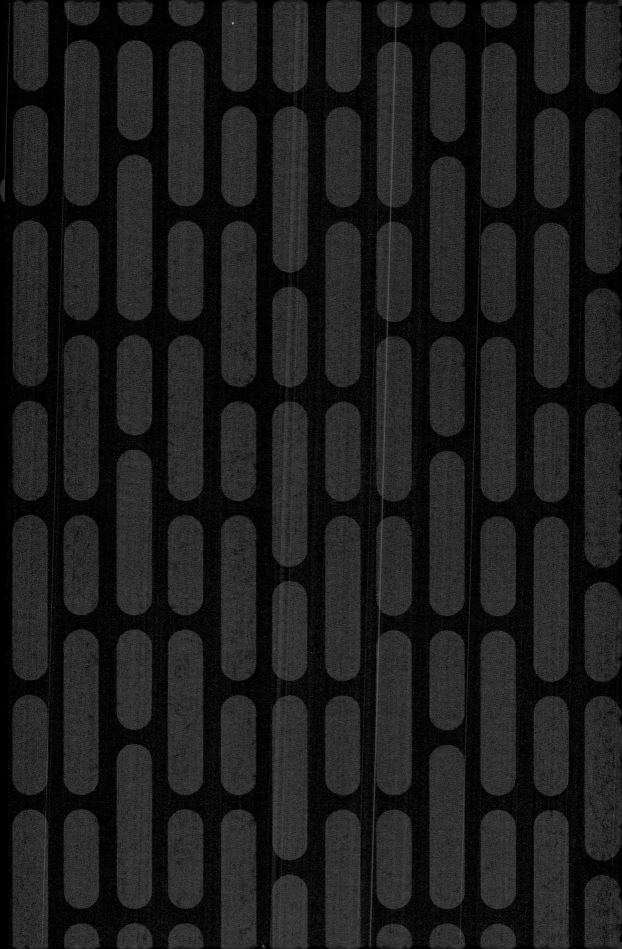

12
PODRACER'S
RESCUE

Writer
SHAUN MANNING

Artist
CHAD THOMAS

Colorist
CHARLIE KIRCHOFF

Letterer
TOM B. LONG

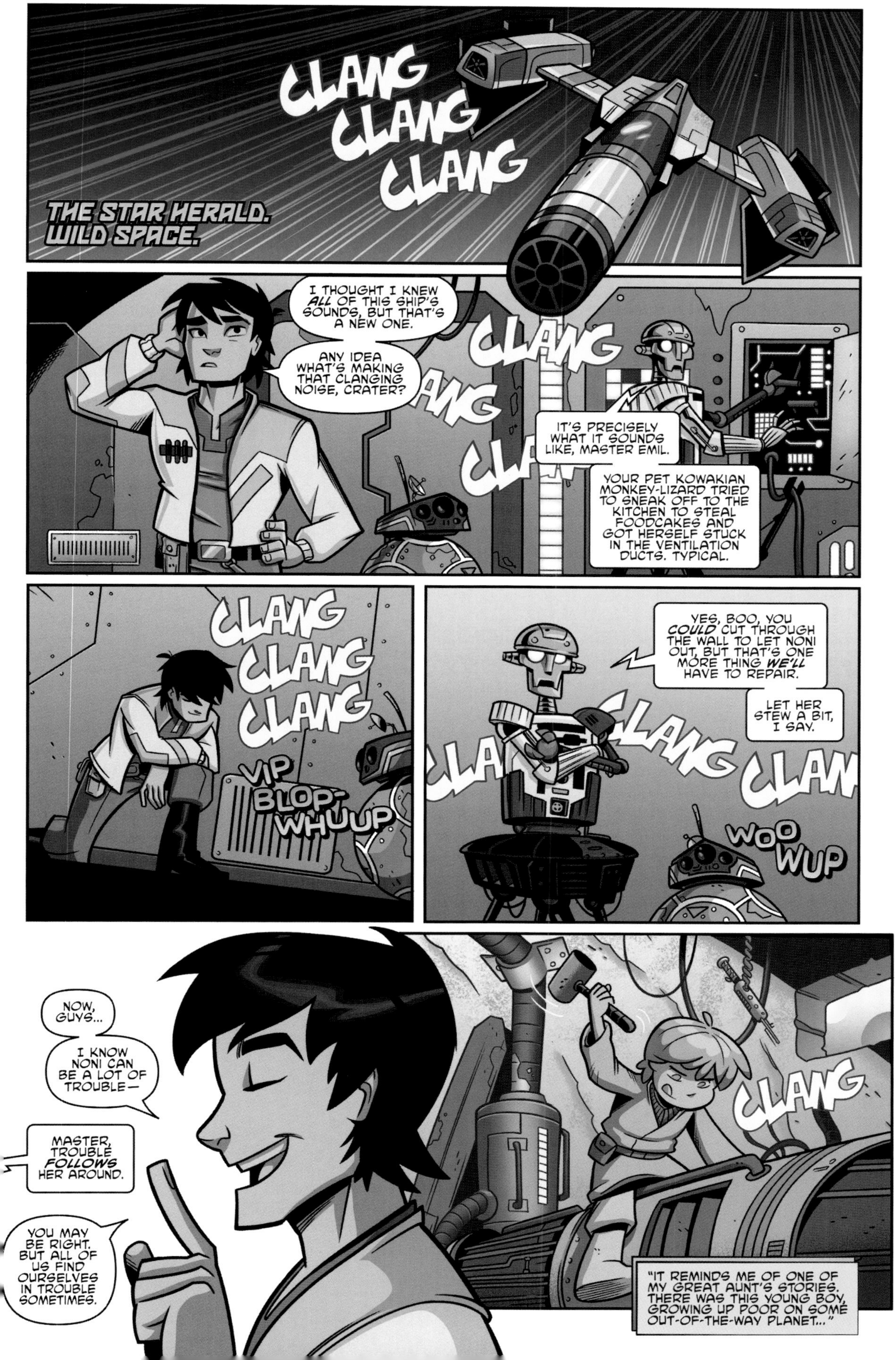

CLANG
CLANG
CLANG
THE STAR HERALD. WILD SPACE.
I THOUGHT I KNEW ALL OF THIS SHIP'S SOUNDS, BUT THAT'S A NEW ONE.
ANY IDEA WHAT'S MAKING THAT CLANGING NOISE, CRATER?
CLANG
IT'S PRECISELY WHAT IT SOUNDS LIKE, MASTER EMIL.
YOUR PET KOWAKIAN MONKEY-LIZARD TRIED TO SNEAK OFF TO THE KITCHEN TO STEAL FOODCAKES AND GOT HERSELF STUCK IN THE VENTILATION DUCTS. TYPICAL.
CLANG
CLANG
CLANG
VIP BLOP-WHUUP
YES, BOO, YOU COULD CUT THROUGH THE WALL TO LET NONI OUT, BUT THAT'S ONE MORE THING WE'LL HAVE TO REPAIR.
LET HER STEW A BIT, I SAY.
CLANG
WOO WUP
NOW, GUYS...
I KNOW NONI CAN BE A LOT OF TROUBLE—
MASTER, TROUBLE FOLLOWS HER AROUND.
YOU MAY BE RIGHT. BUT ALL OF US FIND OURSELVES IN TROUBLE SOMETIMES.
CLANG
"IT REMINDS ME OF ONE OF MY GREAT AUNT'S STORIES. THERE WAS THIS YOUNG BOY, GROWING UP POOR ON SOME OUT-OF-THE-WAY PLANET..."

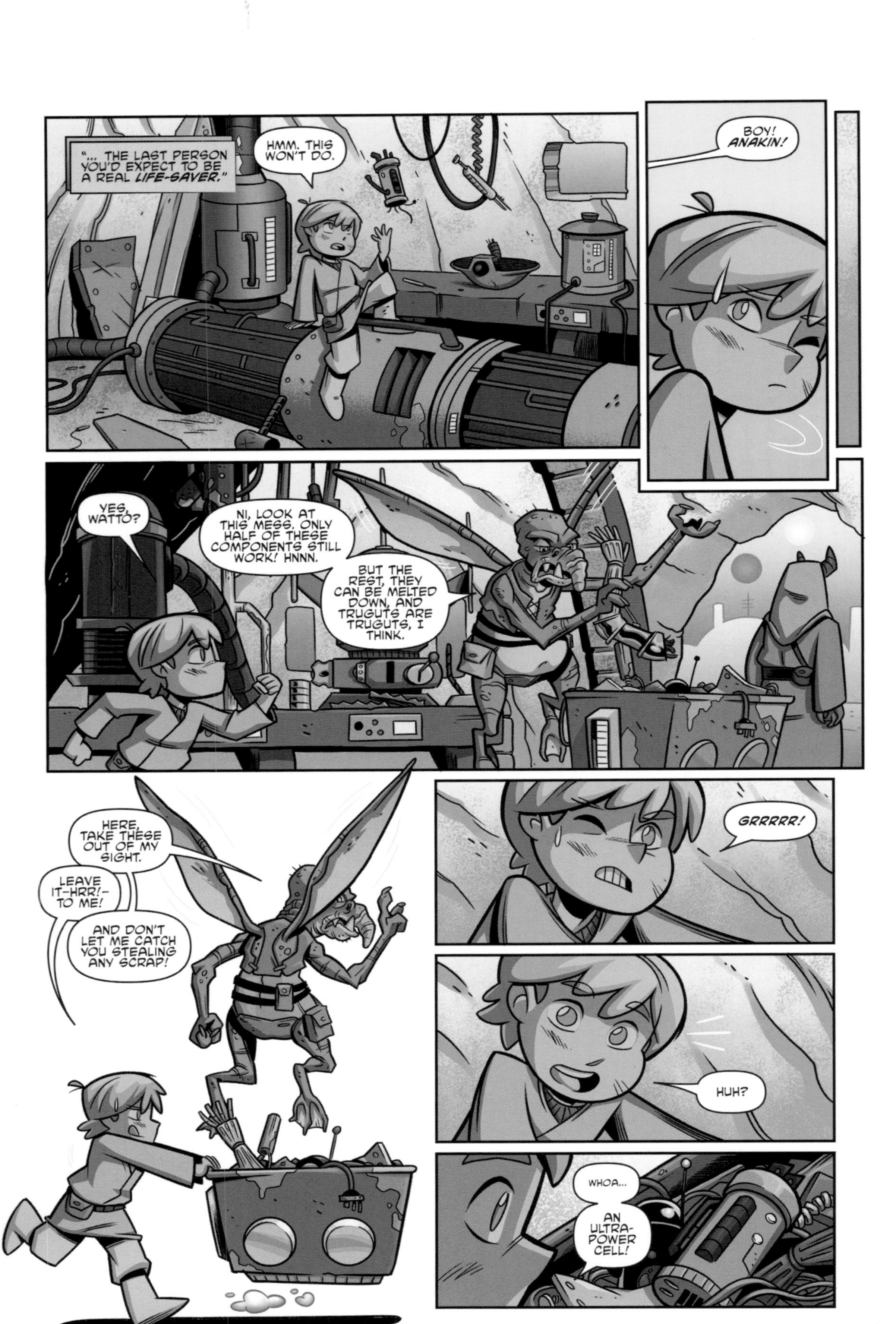
"... THE LAST PERSON YOU'D EXPECT TO BE A REAL *LIFE-SAVER.*"
HMM. THIS WON'T DO.
BOY! *ANAKIN!*
YES, WATTO?
NI, LOOK AT THIS MESS. ONLY HALF OF THESE COMPONENTS STILL WORK! HNNN.
BUT THE REST, THEY CAN BE MELTED DOWN, AND TRUGUTS ARE TRUGUTS, I THINK.
HERE, TAKE THESE OUT OF MY SIGHT.
LEAVE IT—HRR!—TO ME!
AND DON'T LET ME CATCH YOU STEALING ANY SCRAP!
GRRRRR!
HUH?
WHOA...
AN ULTRA-POWER CELL!

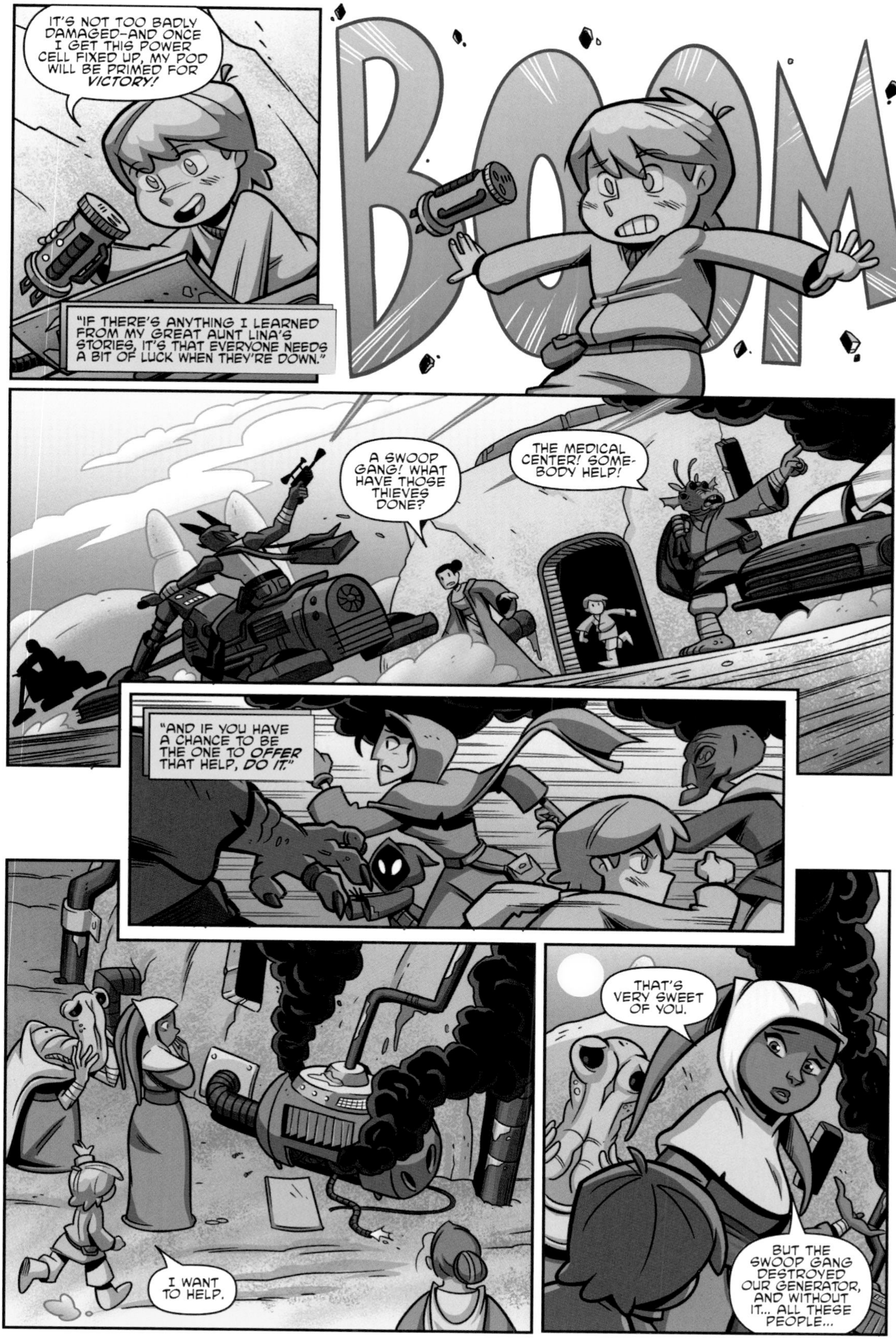
IT'S NOT TOO BADLY DAMAGED—AND ONCE I GET THIS POWER CELL FIXED UP, MY POD WILL BE PRIMED FOR VICTORY!
"IF THERE'S ANYTHING I LEARNED FROM MY GREAT AUNT LINA'S STORIES, IT'S THAT EVERYONE NEEDS A BIT OF LUCK WHEN THEY'RE DOWN."
BOOM
A SWOOP GANG! WHAT HAVE THOSE THIEVES DONE?
THE MEDICAL CENTER! SOME-BODY HELP!
"AND IF YOU HAVE A CHANCE TO BE THE ONE TO OFFER THAT HELP, DO IT."
I WANT TO HELP.
THAT'S VERY SWEET OF YOU.
BUT THE SWOOP GANG DESTROYED OUR GENERATOR, AND WITHOUT IT... ALL THESE PEOPLE...

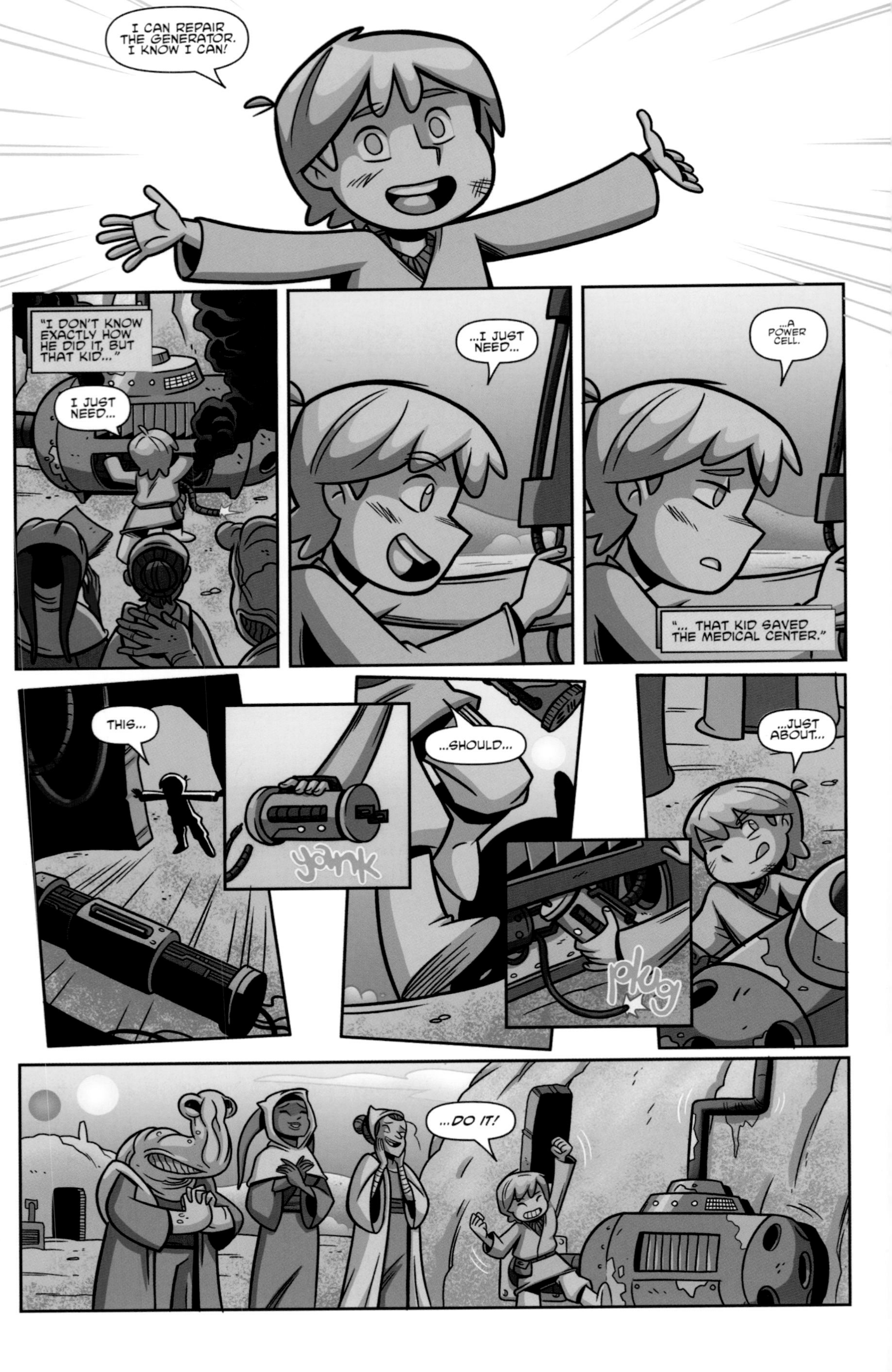

I CAN REPAIR THE GENERATOR. I KNOW I CAN!
"I DON'T KNOW EXACTLY HOW HE DID IT, BUT THAT KID..."
I JUST NEED...
...I JUST NEED...
...A POWER CELL.
"... THAT KID SAVED THE MEDICAL CENTER."
THIS...
yank
...SHOULD...
...JUST ABOUT...
plug
...DO IT!

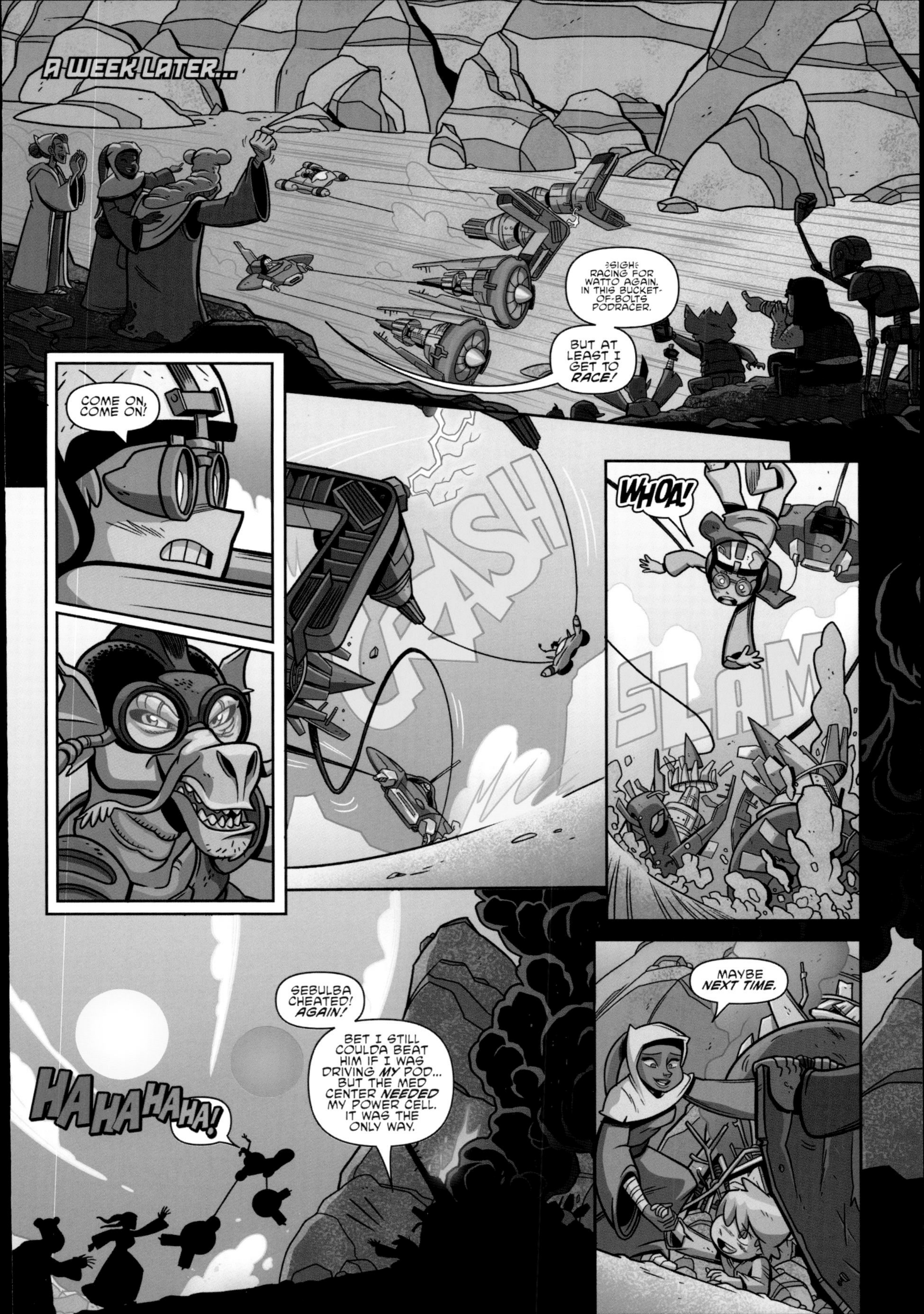
A WEEK LATER...
SIGH
RACING FOR WATTO AGAIN. IN THIS BUCKET-OF-BOLTS PODRACER.
BUT AT LEAST I GET TO RACE!
COME ON, COME ON!
CRASH
WHOA!
SLAM
SEBULBA CHEATED! AGAIN!
BET I STILL COULDA BEAT HIM IF I WAS DRIVING MY POD... BUT THE MED CENTER NEEDED MY POWER CELL. IT WAS THE ONLY WAY.
HAHAHAHAHA!
MAYBE NEXT TIME.

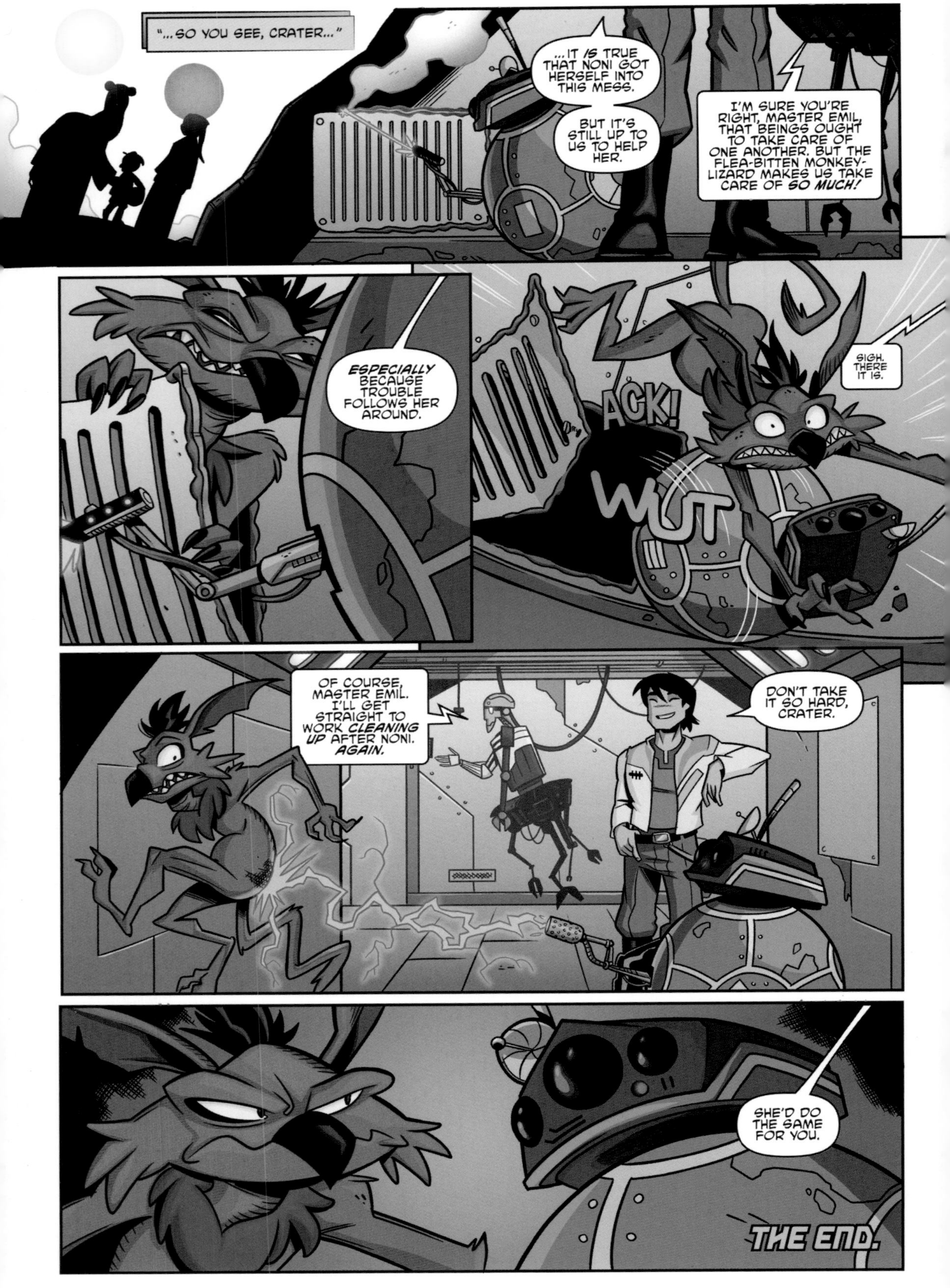
"...SO YOU SEE, CRATER..."
...IT IS TRUE THAT NONI GOT HERSELF INTO THIS MESS.
BUT IT'S STILL UP TO US TO HELP HER.
I'M SURE YOU'RE RIGHT, MASTER EMIL, THAT BEINGS OUGHT TO TAKE CARE OF ONE ANOTHER. BUT THE FLEA-BITTEN MONKEY-LIZARD MAKES US TAKE CARE OF SO MUCH!
ESPECIALLY BECAUSE TROUBLE FOLLOWS HER AROUND.
ACK!
WUT
SIGH. THERE IT IS.
OF COURSE, MASTER EMIL. I'LL GET STRAIGHT TO WORK CLEANING UP AFTER NONI. AGAIN.
DON'T TAKE IT SO HARD, CRATER.
SHE'D DO THE SAME FOR YOU.
THE END.

13
LOOK BEFORE YOU LEAP

Writer
PAUL CRILLEY

Artist
PHILIP MURPHY

Colorist
WES DZIOBA

Letterer
TOM B. LONG

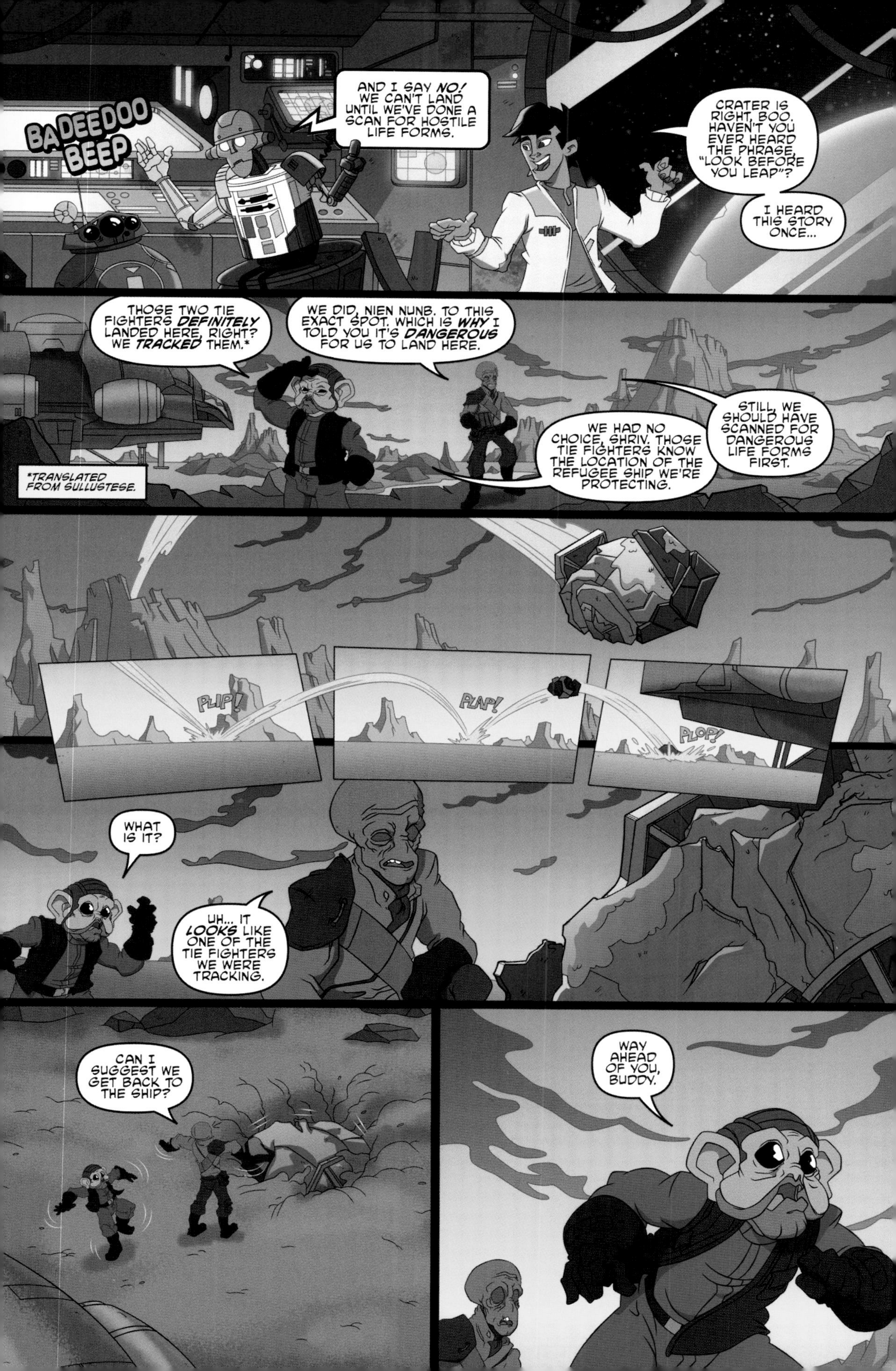
BA DEEDOO BEEP
AND I SAY NO! WE CAN'T LAND UNTIL WE'VE DONE A SCAN FOR HOSTILE LIFE FORMS.
CRATER IS RIGHT, BOO. HAVEN'T YOU EVER HEARD THE PHRASE, "LOOK BEFORE YOU LEAP"?
I HEARD THIS STORY ONCE...
THOSE TWO TIE FIGHTERS DEFINITELY LANDED HERE, RIGHT? WE TRACKED THEM.*
WE DID, NIEN NUNB. TO THIS EXACT SPOT. WHICH IS WHY I TOLD YOU IT'S DANGEROUS FOR US TO LAND HERE.
STILL, WE SHOULD HAVE SCANNED FOR DANGEROUS LIFE FORMS FIRST.
WE HAD NO CHOICE, SHRIV. THOSE TIE FIGHTERS KNOW THE LOCATION OF THE REFUGEE SHIP WE'RE PROTECTING.
*TRANSLATED FROM SULLUSTESE.
PLIP!
PLAP!
PLOP!
WHAT IS IT?
UH... IT LOOKS LIKE ONE OF THE TIE FIGHTERS WE WERE TRACKING.
CAN I SUGGEST WE GET BACK TO THE SHIP?
WAY AHEAD OF YOU, BUDDY.

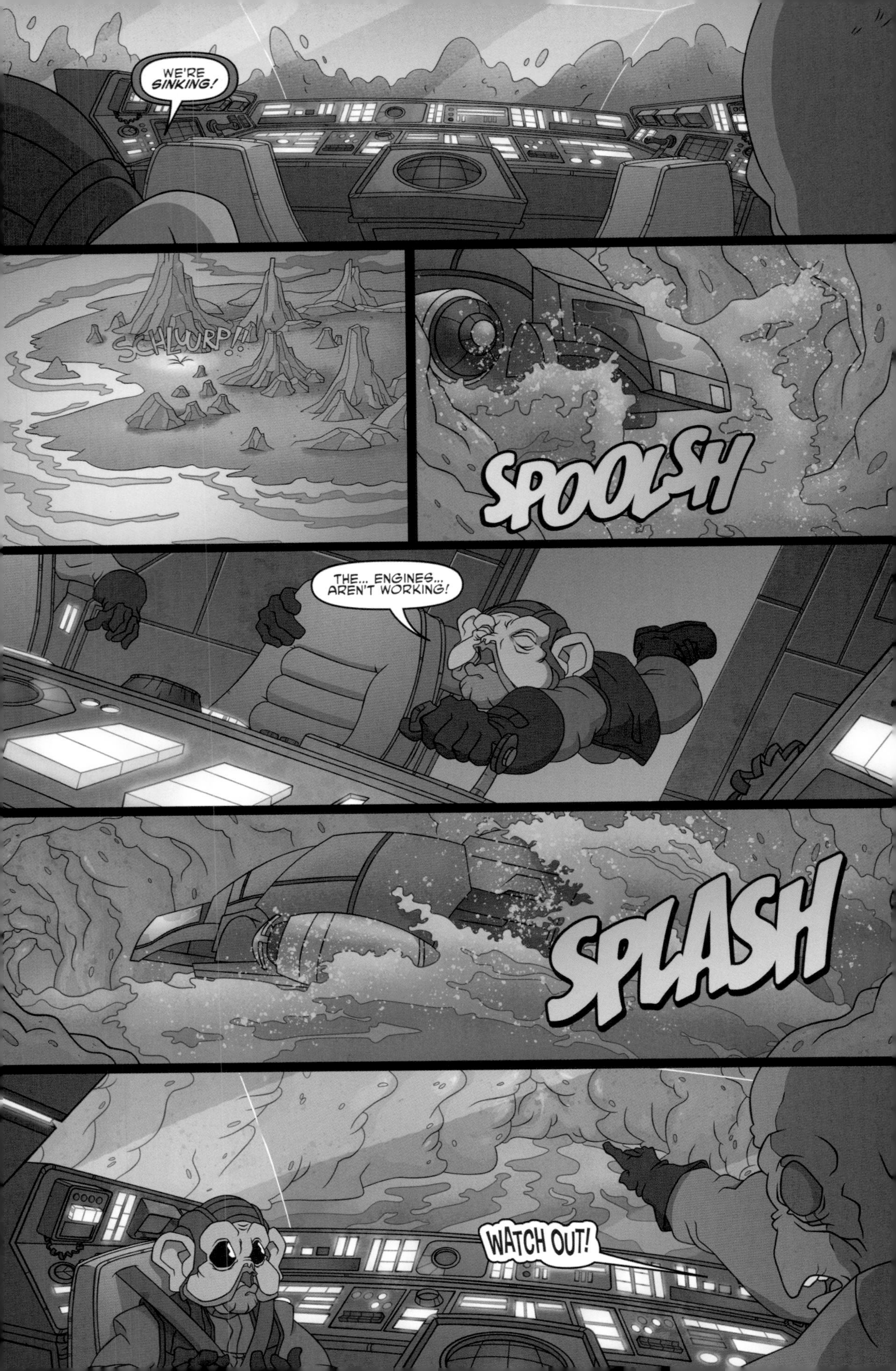
WE'RE SINKING!
SCHLUURP!!
SPOOLSH
THE... ENGINES... AREN'T WORKING!
SPLASH
WATCH OUT!

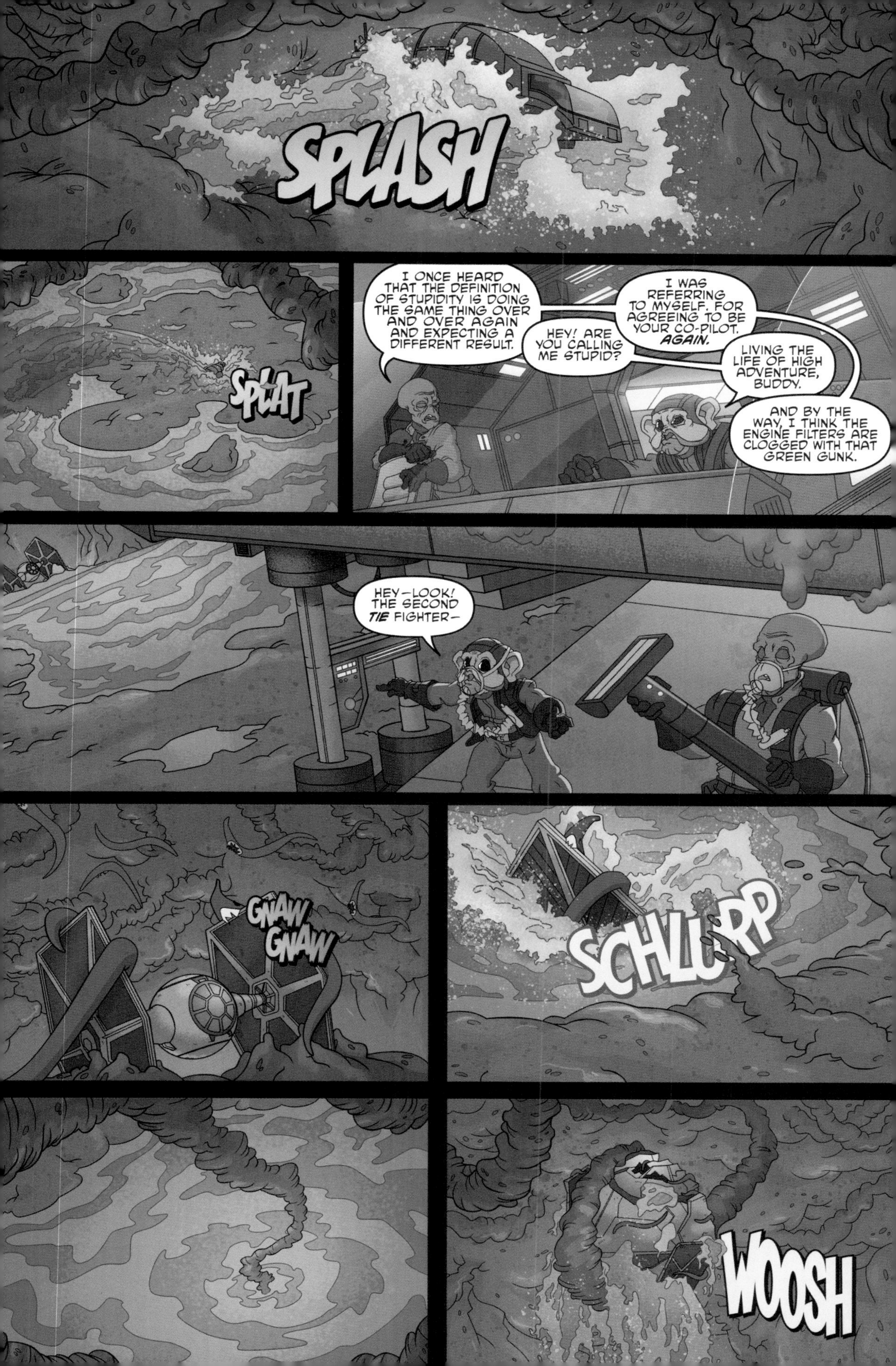
SPLASH
SPLAT
I ONCE HEARD THAT THE DEFINITION OF STUPIDITY IS DOING THE SAME THING OVER AND OVER AGAIN AND EXPECTING A DIFFERENT RESULT.
HEY! ARE YOU CALLING ME STUPID?
I WAS REFERRING TO MYSELF. FOR AGREEING TO BE YOUR CO-PILOT. AGAIN.
LIVING THE LIFE OF HIGH ADVENTURE, BUDDY.
AND BY THE WAY, I THINK THE ENGINE FILTERS ARE CLOGGED WITH THAT GREEN GUNK.
HEY—LOOK! THE SECOND TIE FIGHTER—
GNAW GNAW
SCHLURP
WOOSH

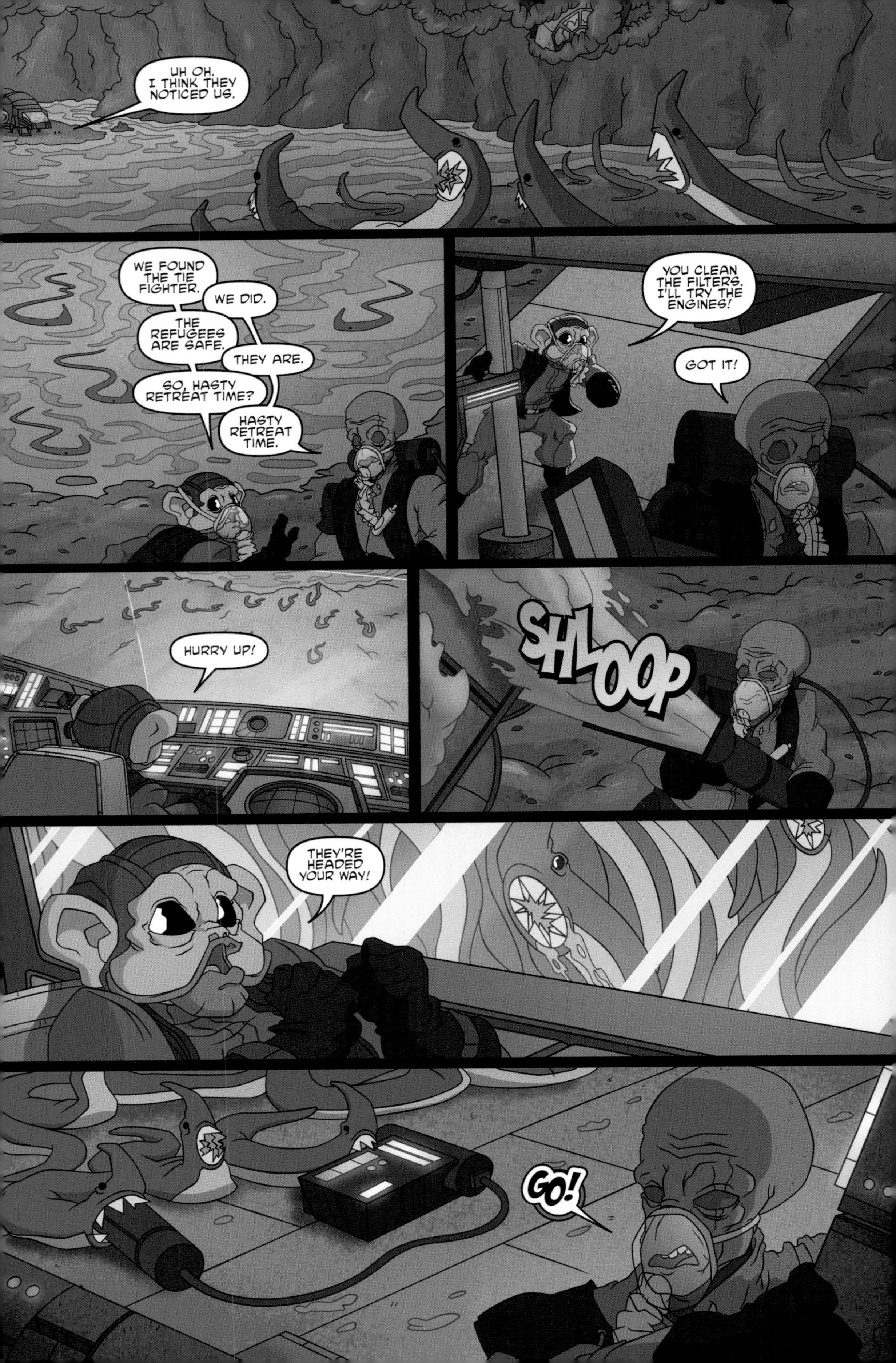
UH OH. I THINK THEY NOTICED US.
WE FOUND THE TIE FIGHTER.
WE DID.
THE REFUGEES ARE SAFE.
THEY ARE.
SO, HASTY RETREAT TIME?
HASTY RETREAT TIME.
YOU CLEAN THE FILTERS. I'LL TRY THE ENGINES!
GOT IT!
HURRY UP!
SHLOOP
THEY'RE HEADED YOUR WAY!
GO!

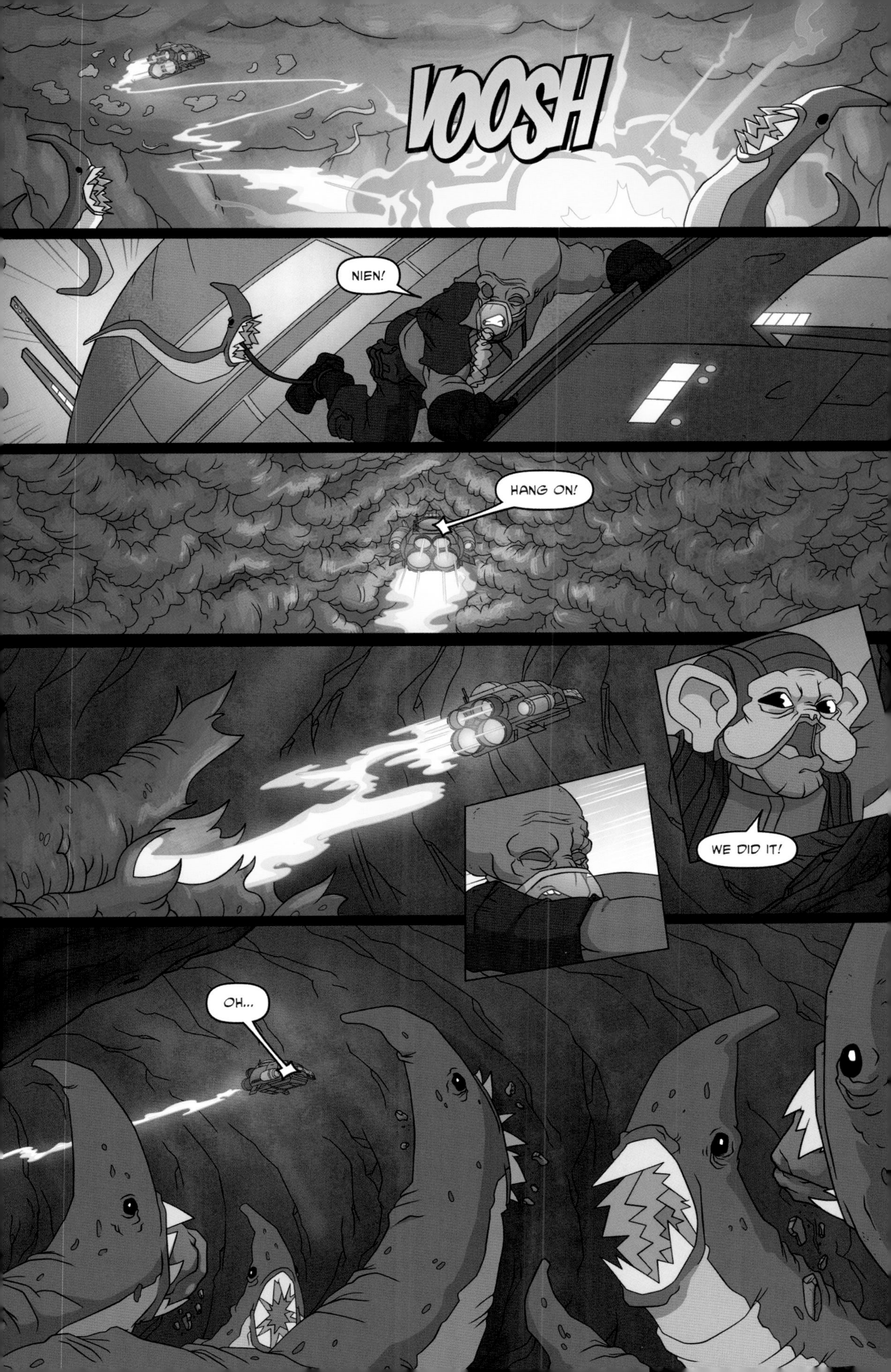
VOOSH
NIEN!
HANG ON!
WE DID IT!
OH...

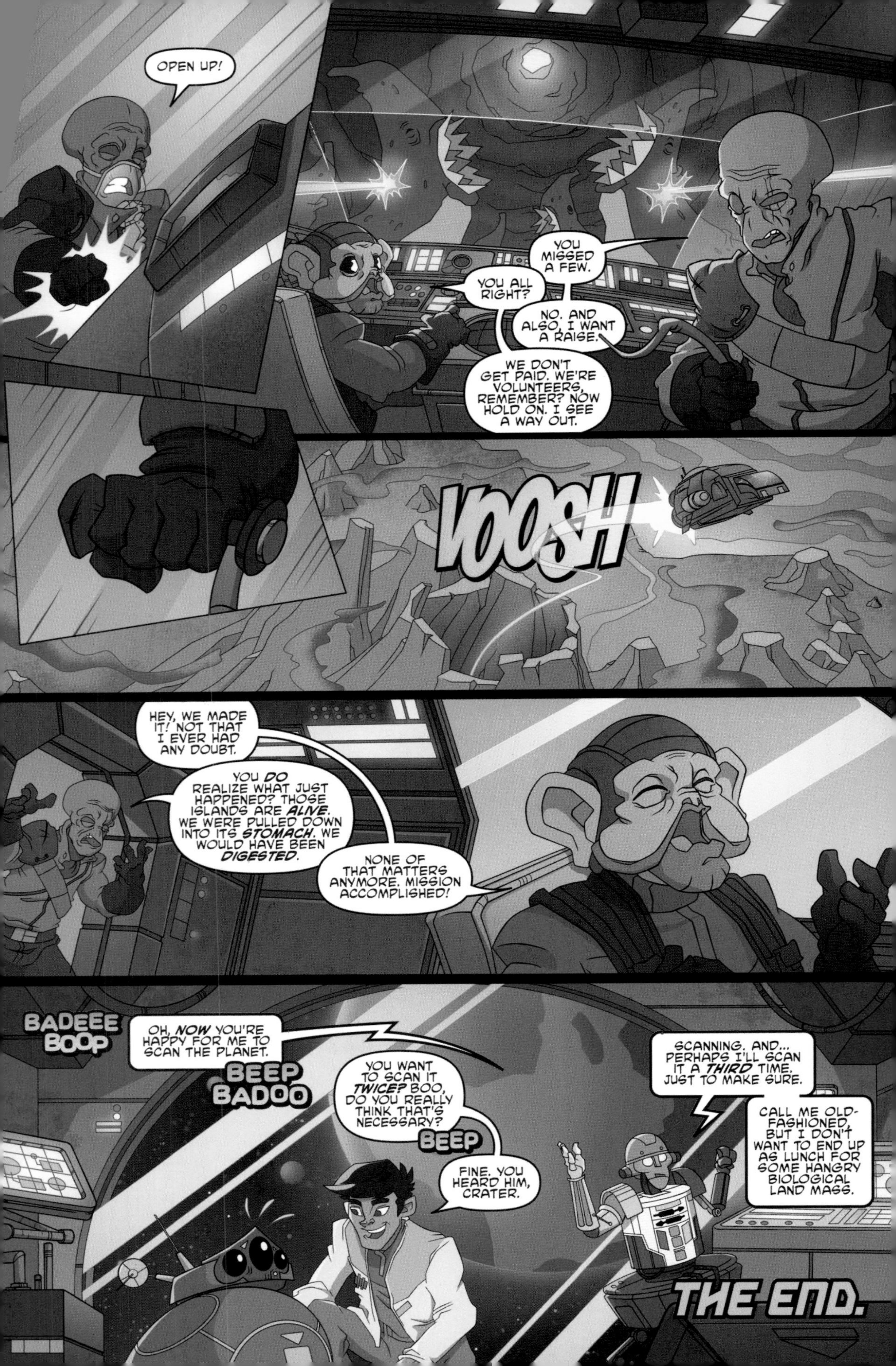
OPEN UP!
YOU MISSED A FEW.
YOU ALL RIGHT?
NO. AND ALSO, I WANT A RAISE.
WE DON'T GET PAID. WE'RE VOLUNTEERS, REMEMBER? NOW HOLD ON. I SEE A WAY OUT.
VOOSH
HEY, WE MADE IT! NOT THAT I EVER HAD ANY DOUBT.
YOU *DO* REALIZE WHAT JUST HAPPENED? THOSE ISLANDS ARE *ALIVE*. WE WERE PULLED DOWN INTO ITS *STOMACH*. WE WOULD HAVE BEEN *DIGESTED*.
NONE OF THAT MATTERS ANYMORE. MISSION ACCOMPLISHED!
BADEEE BOOP
OH, *NOW* YOU'RE HAPPY FOR ME TO SCAN THE PLANET.
BEEP BADOO
YOU WANT TO SCAN IT *TWICE*? BOO, DO YOU REALLY THINK THAT'S NECESSARY?
BEEP
FINE. YOU HEARD HIM, CRATER.
SCANNING. AND... PERHAPS I'LL SCAN IT A *THIRD* TIME. JUST TO MAKE SURE.
CALL ME OLD-FASHIONED, BUT I DON'T WANT TO END UP AS LUNCH FOR SOME HANGRY BIOLOGICAL LAND MASS.
THE END.

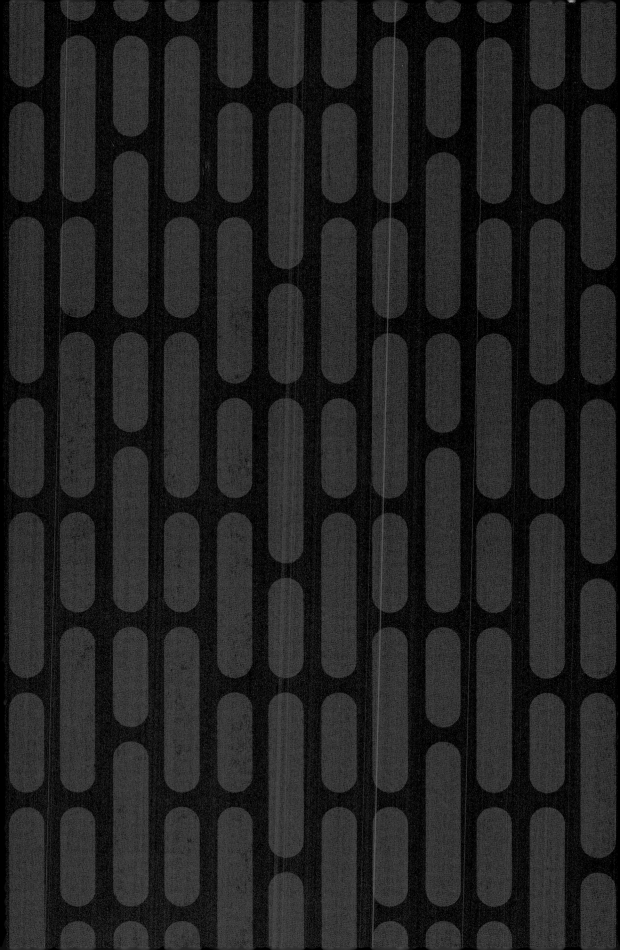

14
GONK!

Writer & Artist
OTIS FRAMPTON

Letterer
TOM B. LONG

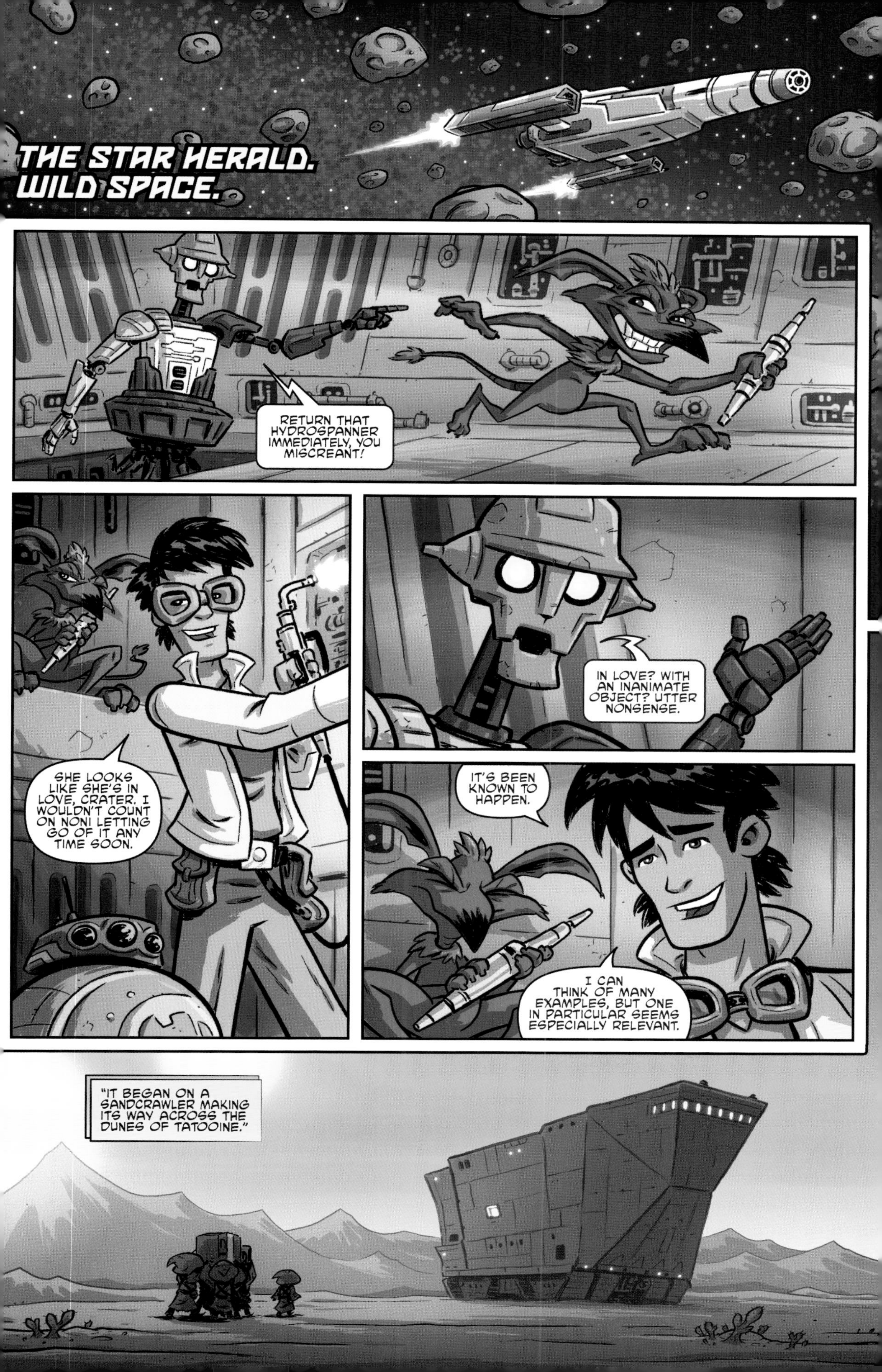
THE STAR HERALD.
WILD SPACE.
RETURN THAT HYDROSPANNER IMMEDIATELY, YOU MISCREANT!
SHE LOOKS LIKE SHE'S IN LOVE, CRATER. I WOULDN'T COUNT ON NONI LETTING GO OF IT ANY TIME SOON.
IN LOVE? WITH AN INANIMATE OBJECT? UTTER NONSENSE.
IT'S BEEN KNOWN TO HAPPEN.
I CAN THINK OF MANY EXAMPLES, BUT ONE IN PARTICULAR SEEMS ESPECIALLY RELEVANT.
"IT BEGAN ON A SANDCRAWLER MAKING ITS WAY ACROSS THE DUNES OF TATOOINE."

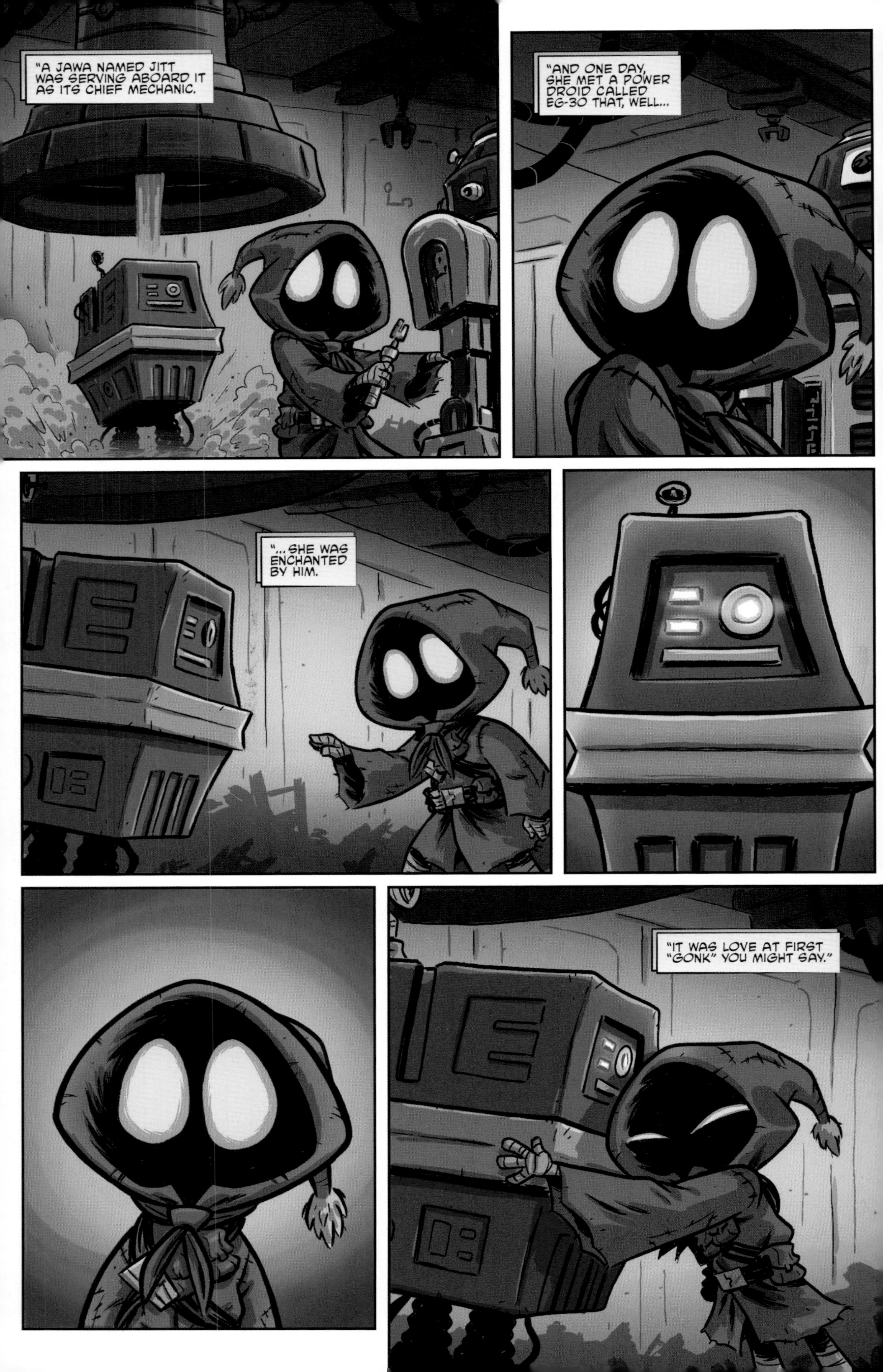
"A JAWA NAMED JITT WAS SERVING ABOARD IT AS ITS CHIEF MECHANIC.
"AND ONE DAY, SHE MET A POWER DROID CALLED EG-30 THAT, WELL...
"...SHE WAS ENCHANTED BY HIM.
"IT WAS LOVE AT FIRST "GONK" YOU MIGHT SAY."

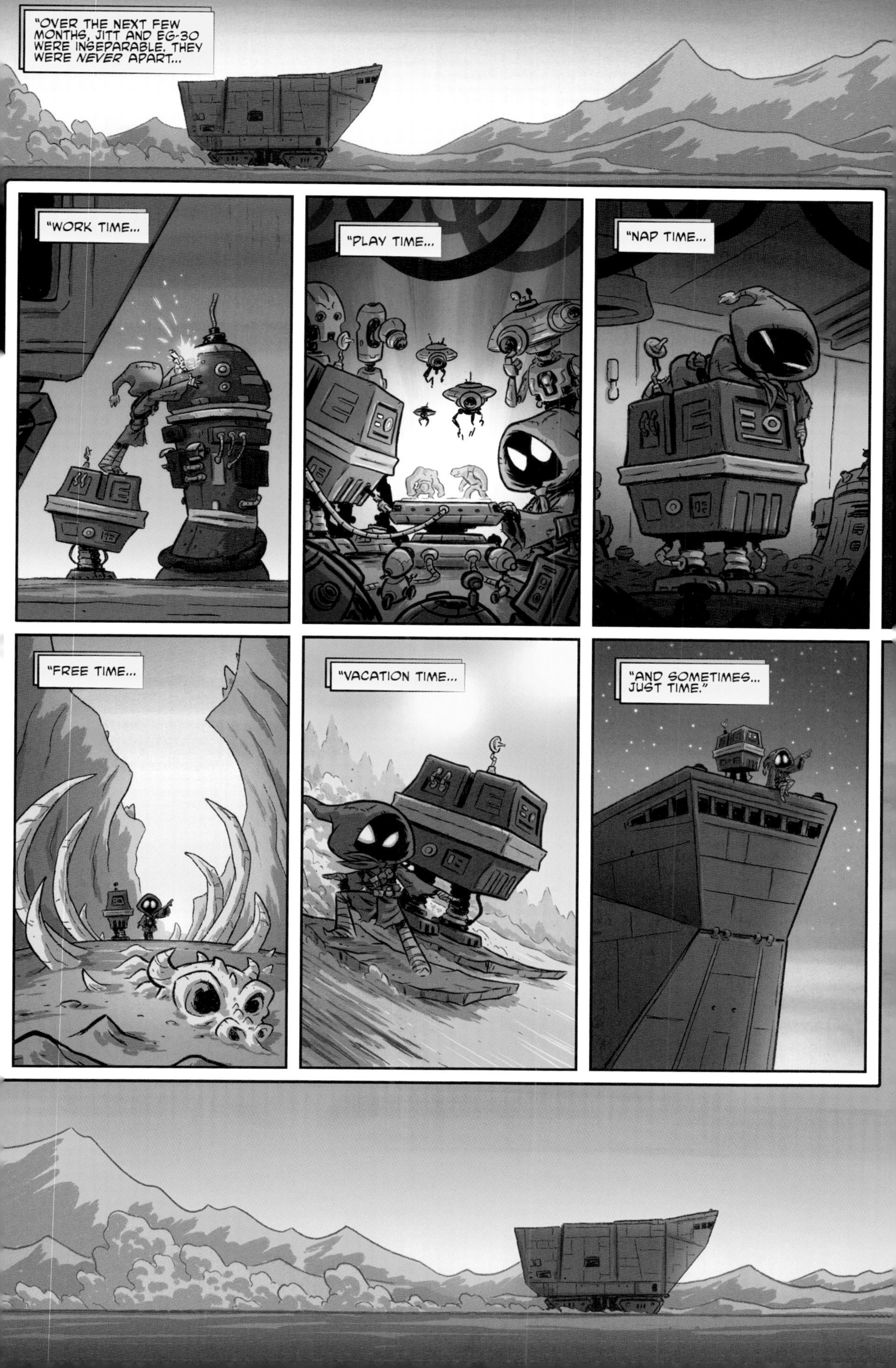
"OVER THE NEXT FEW MONTHS, JITT AND EG-30 WERE INSEPARABLE. THEY WERE *NEVER* APART...
"WORK TIME...
"PLAY TIME...
"NAP TIME...
"FREE TIME...
"VACATION TIME...
"AND SOMETIMES... JUST TIME."

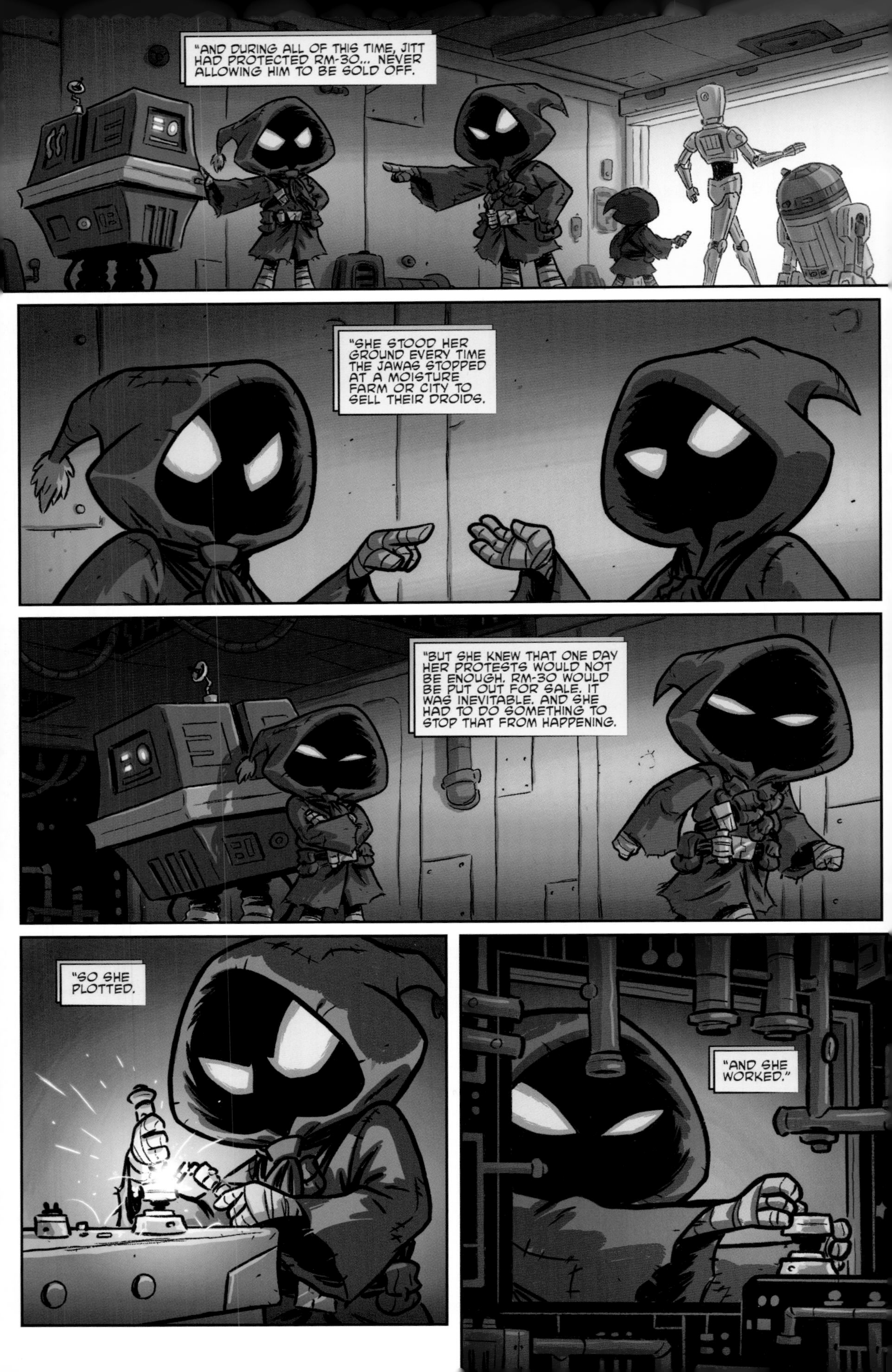
"AND DURING ALL OF THIS TIME, JITT HAD PROTECTED RM-30... NEVER ALLOWING HIM TO BE SOLD OFF.
"SHE STOOD HER GROUND EVERY TIME THE JAWAS STOPPED AT A MOISTURE FARM OR CITY TO SELL THEIR DROIDS.
"BUT SHE KNEW THAT ONE DAY HER PROTESTS WOULD NOT BE ENOUGH. RM-30 WOULD BE PUT OUT FOR SALE. IT WAS INEVITABLE. AND SHE HAD TO DO SOMETHING TO STOP THAT FROM HAPPENING.
"SO SHE PLOTTED.
"AND SHE WORKED."

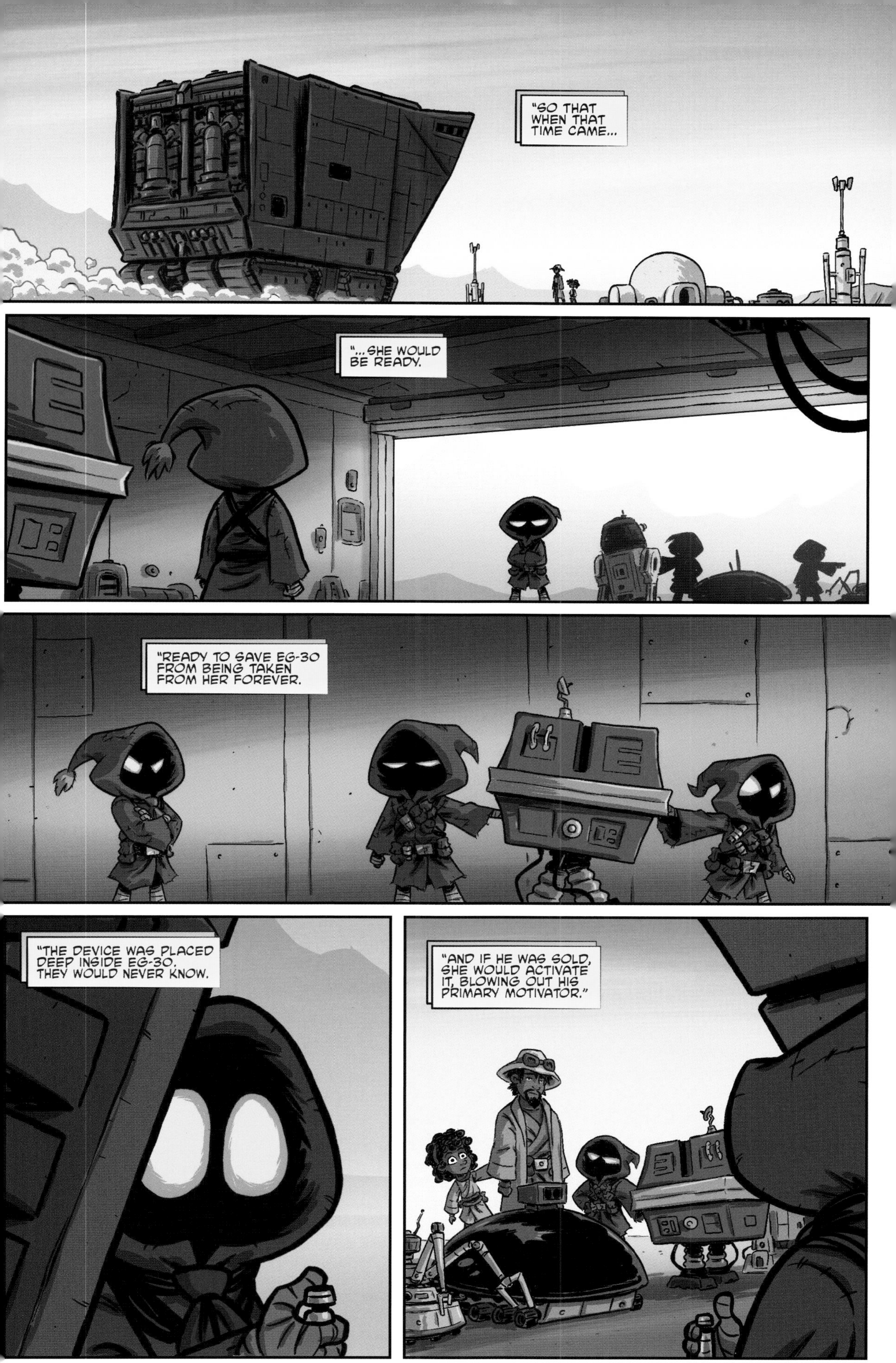
"SO THAT WHEN THAT TIME CAME...
"...SHE WOULD BE READY.
"READY TO SAVE EG-30 FROM BEING TAKEN FROM HER FOREVER.
"THE DEVICE WAS PLACED DEEP INSIDE EG-30. THEY WOULD NEVER KNOW.
"AND IF HE WAS SOLD, SHE WOULD ACTIVATE IT, BLOWING OUT HIS PRIMARY MOTIVATOR."

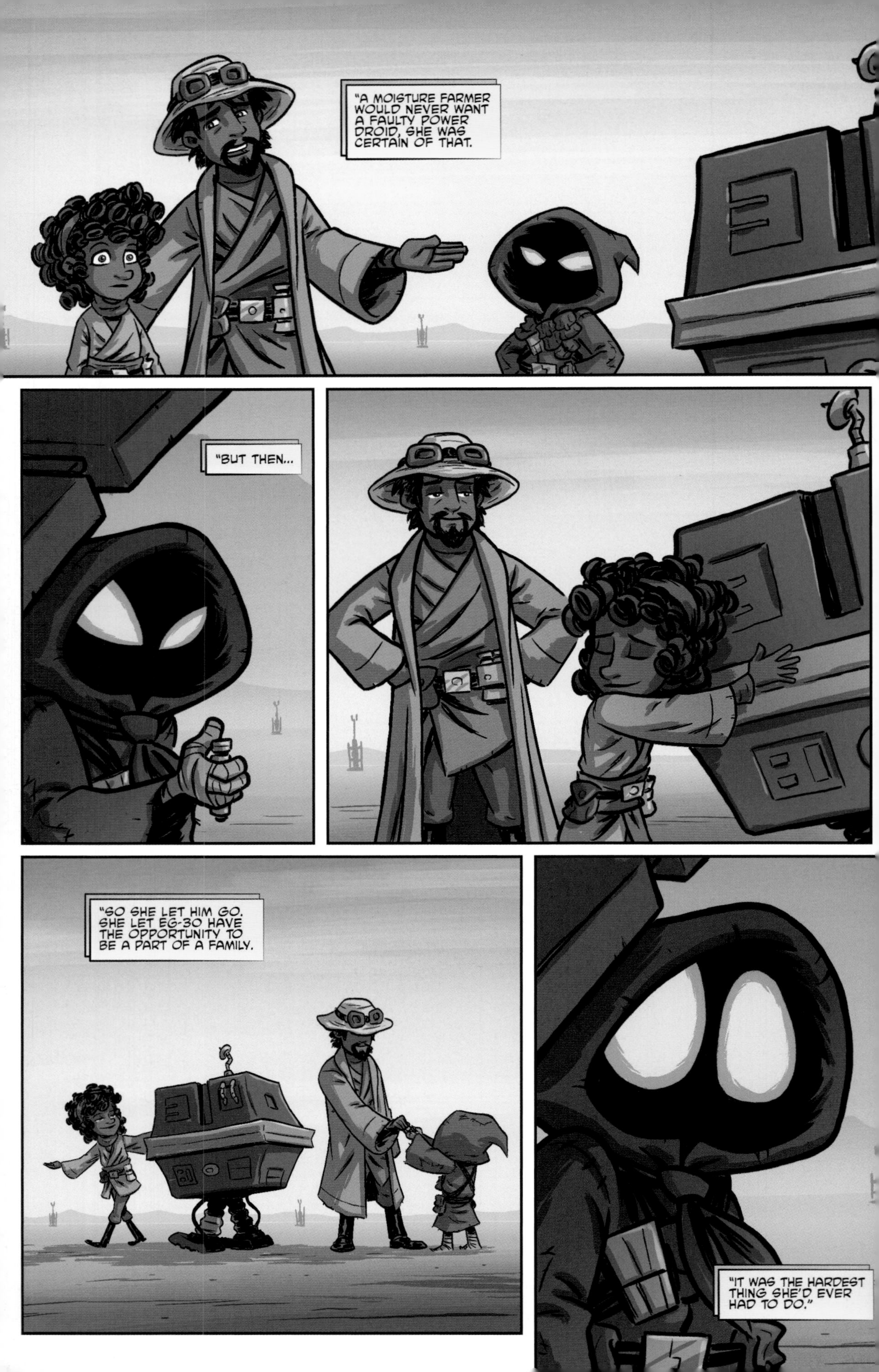
"A MOISTURE FARMER WOULD NEVER WANT A FAULTY POWER DROID, SHE WAS CERTAIN OF THAT.
"BUT THEN...
"SO SHE LET HIM GO. SHE LET EG-30 HAVE THE OPPORTUNITY TO BE A PART OF A FAMILY.
"IT WAS THE HARDEST THING SHE'D EVER HAD TO DO."

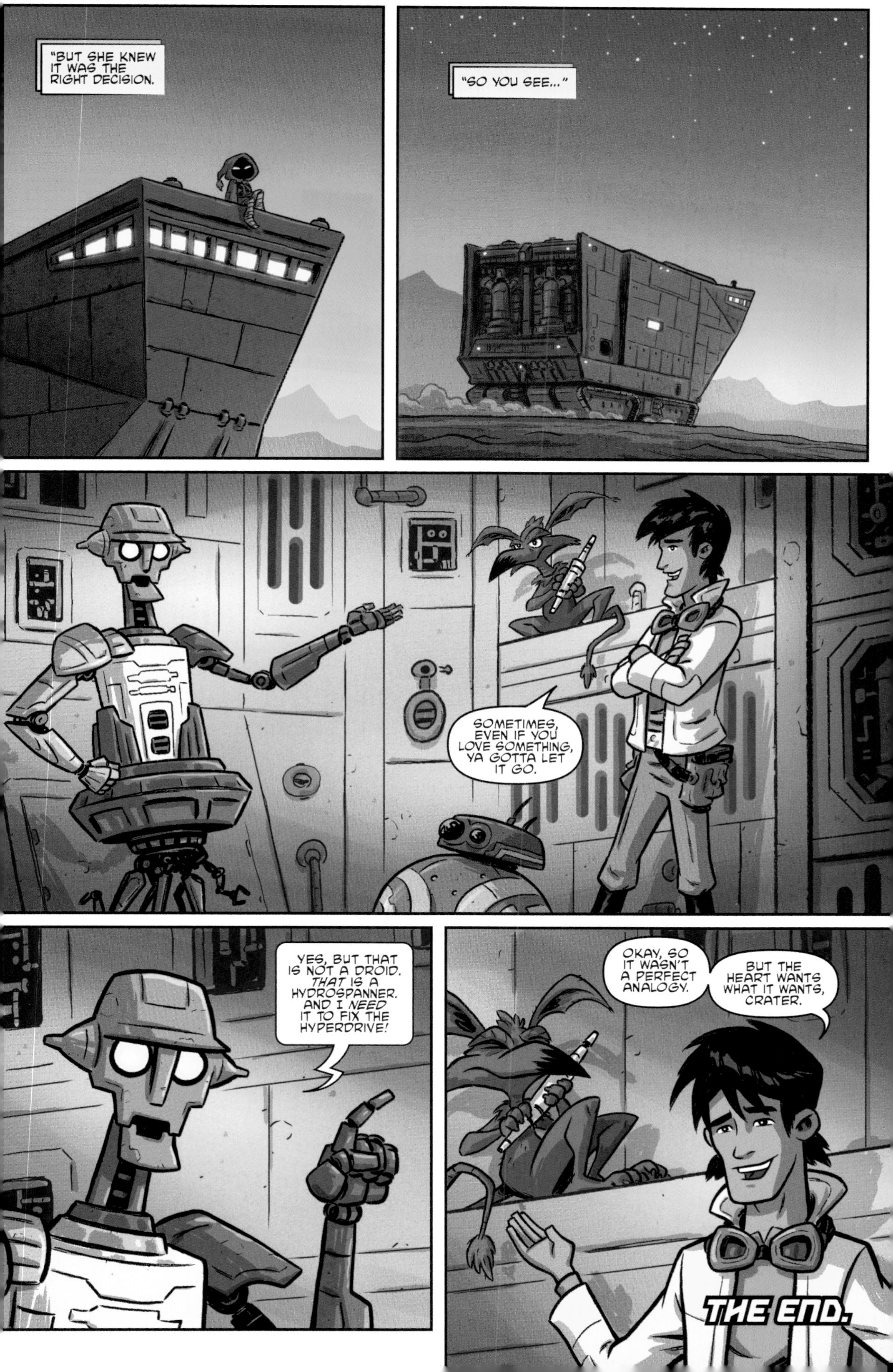
"BUT SHE KNEW IT WAS THE RIGHT DECISION.
"SO YOU SEE..."
SOMETIMES, EVEN IF YOU LOVE SOMETHING, YA GOTTA LET IT GO.
YES, BUT THAT IS NOT A DROID. *THAT* IS A HYDROSPANNER. AND I *NEED* IT TO FIX THE HYPERDRIVE!
OKAY, SO IT WASN'T A PERFECT ANALOGY.
BUT THE HEART WANTS WHAT IT WANTS, CRATER.
THE END.

15
POWERED DOWN

Writer
CAVAN SCOTT

Artist
DEREK CHARM

Colorists
DEREK CHARM &
MATT HERMS

Letterer
TOM B. LONG

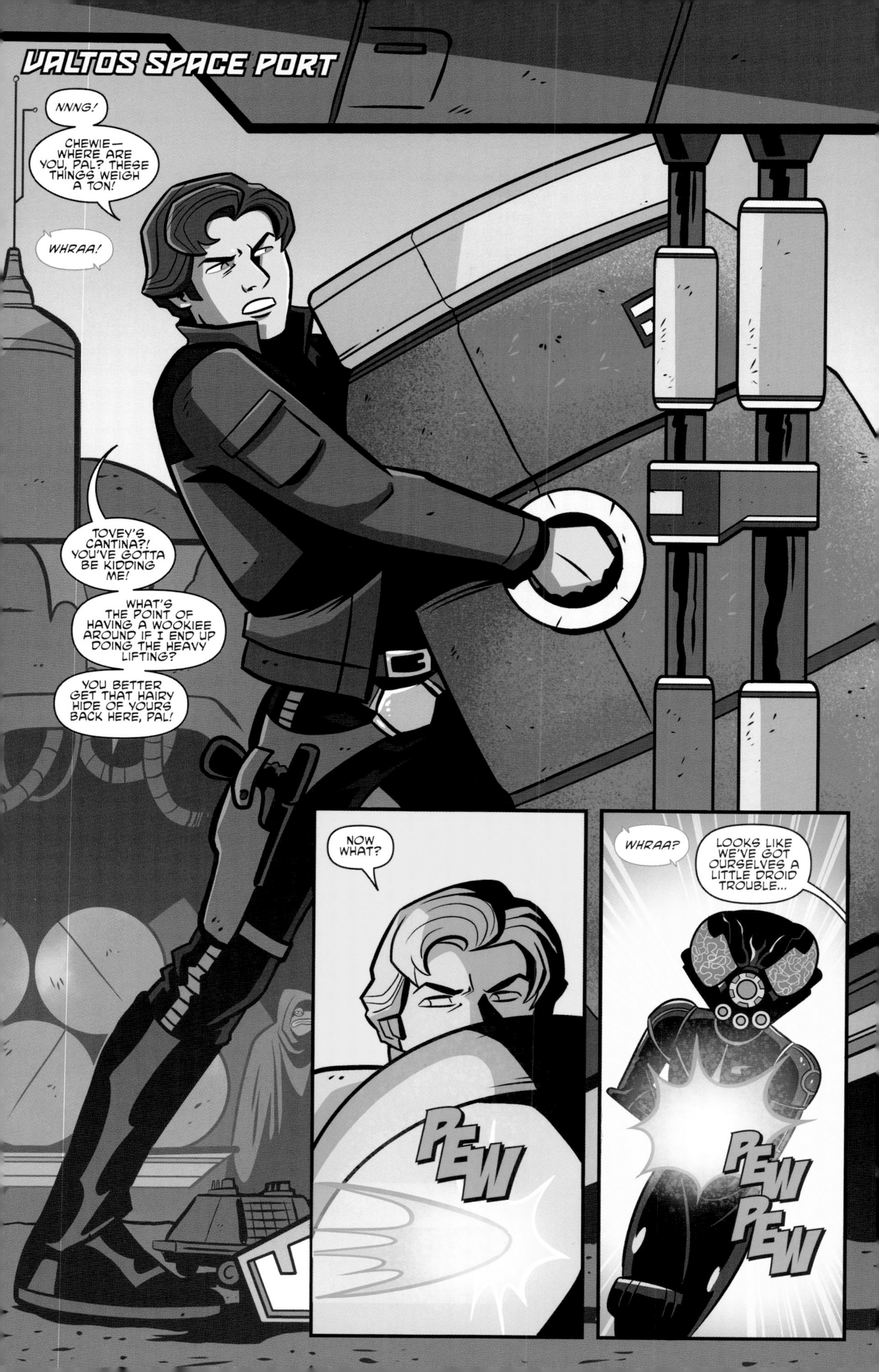
VALTOS SPACE PORT
NNNG!
CHEWIE— WHERE ARE YOU, PAL? THESE THINGS WEIGH A TON!
WHRAA!
TOVEY'S CANTINA?! YOU'VE GOTTA BE KIDDING ME!
WHAT'S THE POINT OF HAVING A WOOKIEE AROUND IF I END UP DOING THE HEAVY LIFTING?
YOU BETTER GET THAT HAIRY HIDE OF YOURS BACK HERE, PAL!
NOW WHAT?
PEW
WHRAA?
LOOKS LIKE WE'VE GOT OURSELVES A LITTLE DROID TROUBLE...
PEW PEW

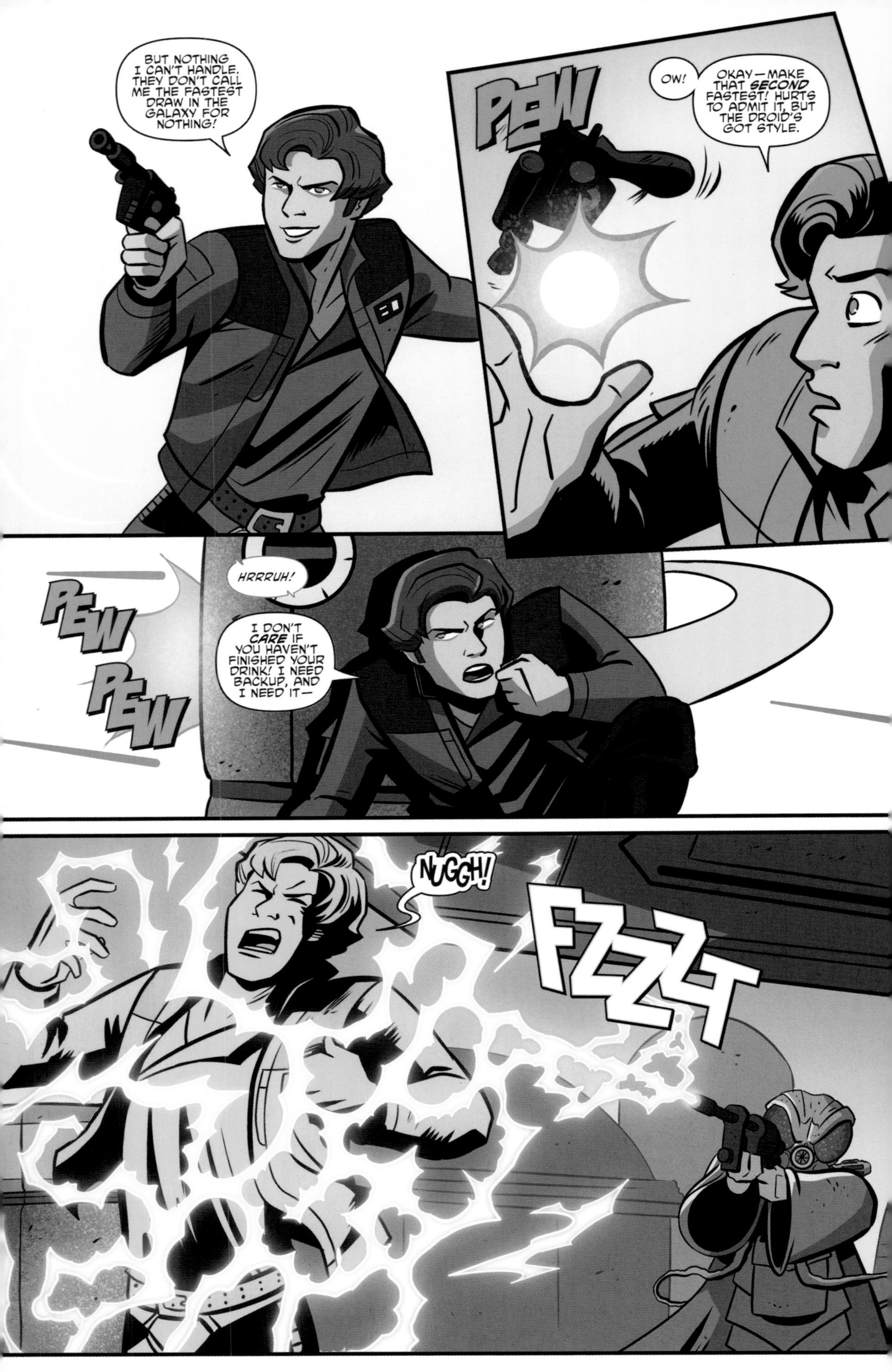

BUT NOTHING I CAN'T HANDLE. THEY DON'T CALL ME THE FASTEST DRAW IN THE GALAXY FOR NOTHING!
PEW
OW!
OKAY—MAKE THAT SECOND FASTEST! HURTS TO ADMIT IT, BUT THE DROID'S GOT STYLE.
PEW PEW
HRRRUH!
I DON'T CARE IF YOU HAVEN'T FINISHED YOUR DRINK! I NEED BACKUP, AND I NEED IT—
NUGGH!
FZZZT

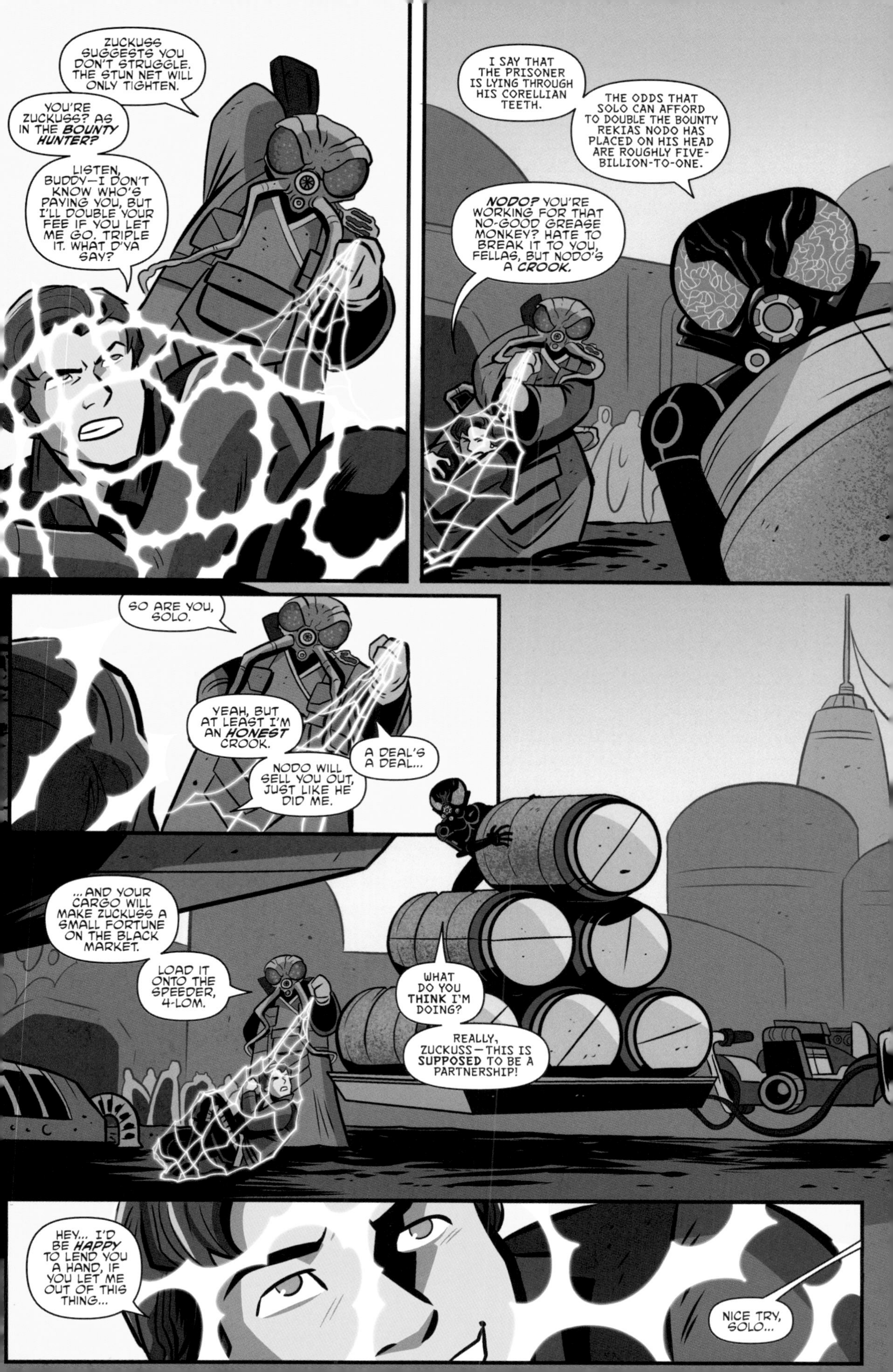
ZUCKUSS SUGGESTS YOU DON'T STRUGGLE. THE STUN NET WILL ONLY TIGHTEN.
YOU'RE ZUCKUSS? AS IN THE BOUNTY HUNTER?
LISTEN, BUDDY—I DON'T KNOW WHO'S PAYING YOU, BUT I'LL DOUBLE YOUR FEE IF YOU LET ME GO. TRIPLE IT. WHAT D'YA SAY?
I SAY THAT THE PRISONER IS LYING THROUGH HIS CORELLIAN TEETH.
THE ODDS THAT SOLO CAN AFFORD TO DOUBLE THE BOUNTY REKIAS NODO HAS PLACED ON HIS HEAD ARE ROUGHLY FIVE-BILLION-TO-ONE.
NODO? YOU'RE WORKING FOR THAT NO-GOOD GREASE MONKEY? HATE TO BREAK IT TO YOU, FELLAS, BUT NODO'S A CROOK.
SO ARE YOU, SOLO.
YEAH, BUT AT LEAST I'M AN HONEST CROOK.
NODO WILL SELL YOU OUT, JUST LIKE HE DID ME.
A DEAL'S A DEAL...
...AND YOUR CARGO WILL MAKE ZUCKUSS A SMALL FORTUNE ON THE BLACK MARKET.
LOAD IT ONTO THE SPEEDER, 4-LOM.
WHAT DO YOU THINK I'M DOING?
REALLY, ZUCKUSS—THIS IS SUPPOSED TO BE A PARTNERSHIP!
HEY... I'D BE HAPPY TO LEND YOU A HAND, IF YOU LET ME OUT OF THIS THING...
NICE TRY, SOLO...

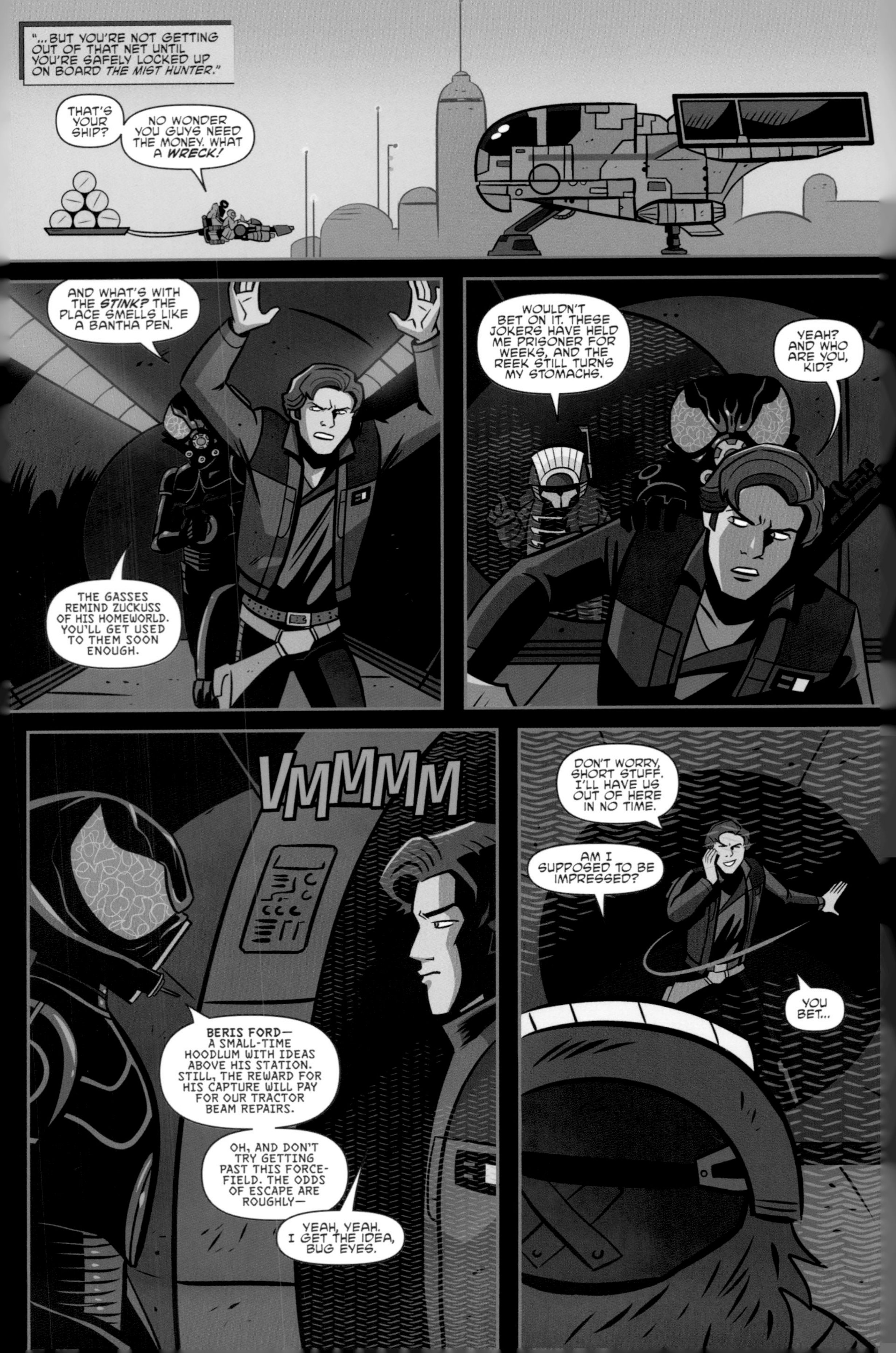
"...BUT YOU'RE NOT GETTING OUT OF THAT NET UNTIL YOU'RE SAFELY LOCKED UP ON BOARD THE MIST HUNTER."
THAT'S YOUR SHIP?
NO WONDER YOU GUYS NEED THE MONEY. WHAT A WRECK!
AND WHAT'S WITH THE STINK? THE PLACE SMELLS LIKE A BANTHA PEN.
THE GASSES REMIND ZUCKUSS OF HIS HOMEWORLD. YOU'LL GET USED TO THEM SOON ENOUGH.
WOULDN'T BET ON IT. THESE JOKERS HAVE HELD ME PRISONER FOR WEEKS, AND THE REEK STILL TURNS MY STOMACHS.
YEAH? AND WHO ARE YOU, KID?
VMMMM
BERIS FORD— A SMALL-TIME HOODLUM WITH IDEAS ABOVE HIS STATION. STILL, THE REWARD FOR HIS CAPTURE WILL PAY FOR OUR TRACTOR BEAM REPAIRS.
OH, AND DON'T TRY GETTING PAST THIS FORCE-FIELD. THE ODDS OF ESCAPE ARE ROUGHLY—
YEAH, YEAH. I GET THE IDEA, BUG EYES.
DON'T WORRY, SHORT STUFF. I'LL HAVE US OUT OF HERE IN NO TIME.
AM I SUPPOSED TO BE IMPRESSED?
YOU BET...

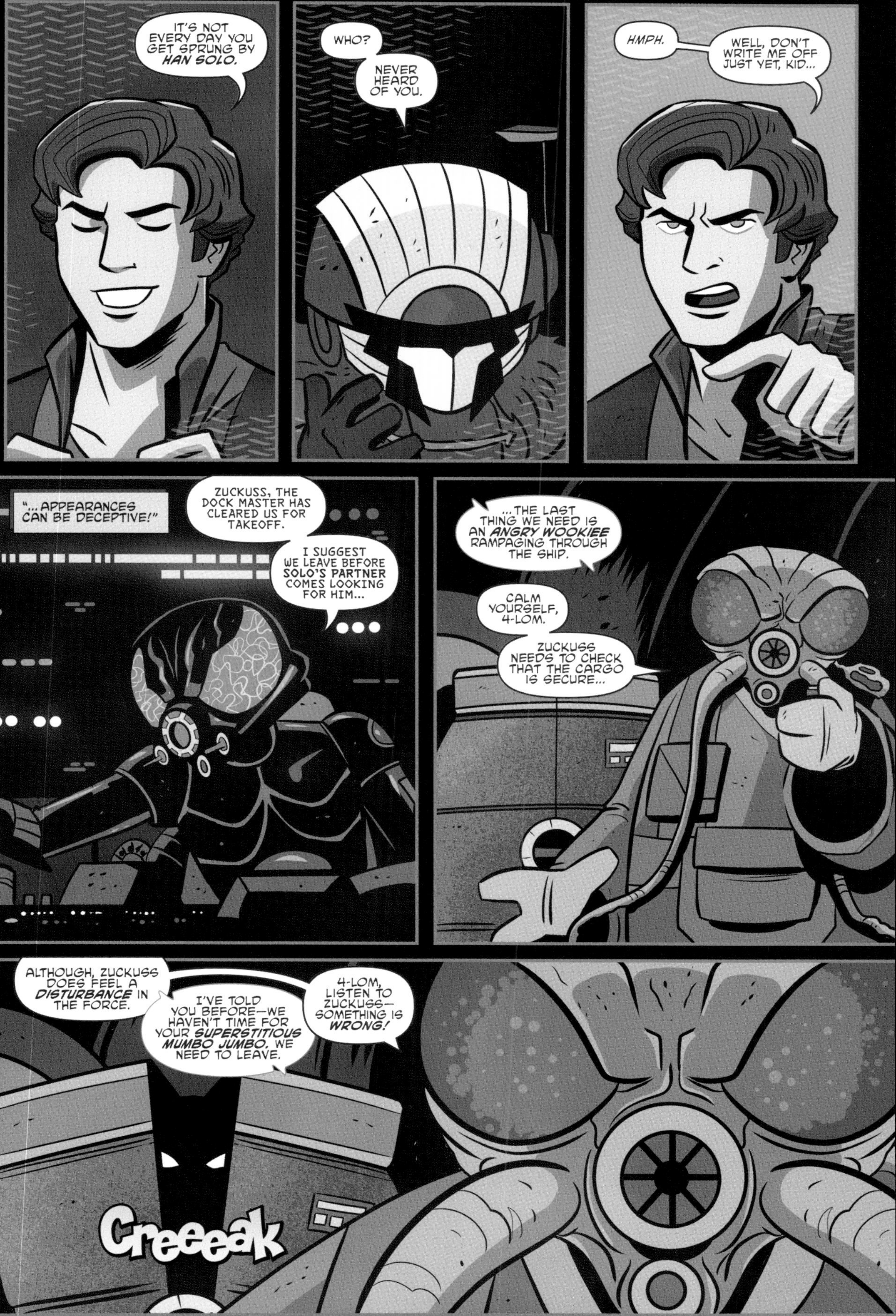
IT'S NOT EVERY DAY YOU GET SPRUNG BY HAN SOLO.
WHO?
NEVER HEARD OF YOU.
HMPH.
WELL, DON'T WRITE ME OFF JUST YET, KID...
"...APPEARANCES CAN BE DECEPTIVE!"
ZUCKUSS, THE DOCK MASTER HAS CLEARED US FOR TAKEOFF.
I SUGGEST WE LEAVE BEFORE SOLO'S PARTNER COMES LOOKING FOR HIM...
...THE LAST THING WE NEED IS AN ANGRY WOOKIEE RAMPAGING THROUGH THE SHIP.
CALM YOURSELF, 4-LOM.
ZUCKUSS NEEDS TO CHECK THAT THE CARGO IS SECURE...
ALTHOUGH, ZUCKUSS DOES FEEL A DISTURBANCE IN THE FORCE.
I'VE TOLD YOU BEFORE—WE HAVEN'T TIME FOR YOUR SUPERSTITIOUS MUMBO JUMBO. WE NEED TO LEAVE.
4-LOM, LISTEN TO ZUCKUSS—SOMETHING IS WRONG!
Creeeak

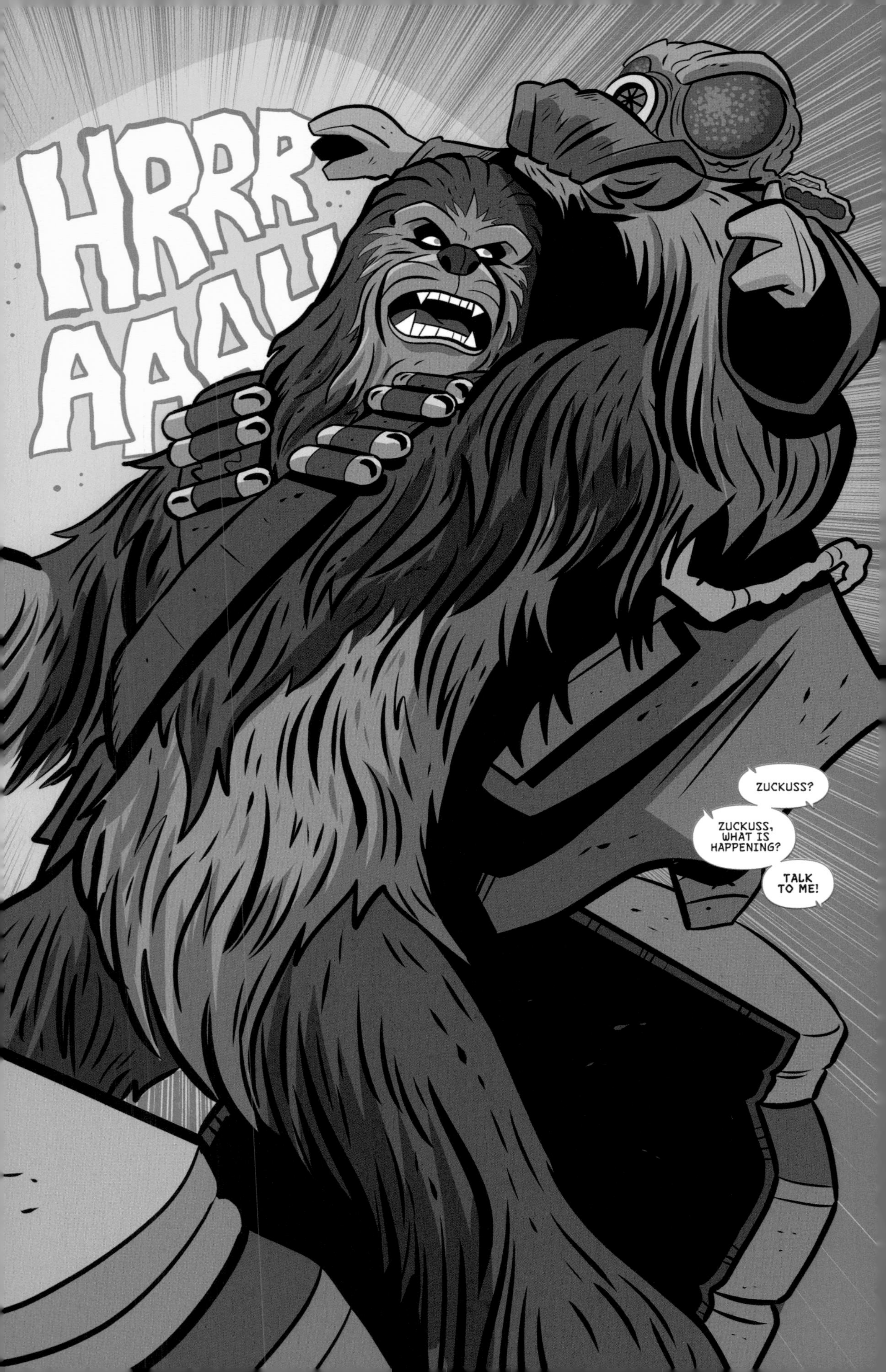
HRRRAAAH
ZUCKUSS?
ZUCKUSS, WHAT IS HAPPENING?
TALK TO ME!

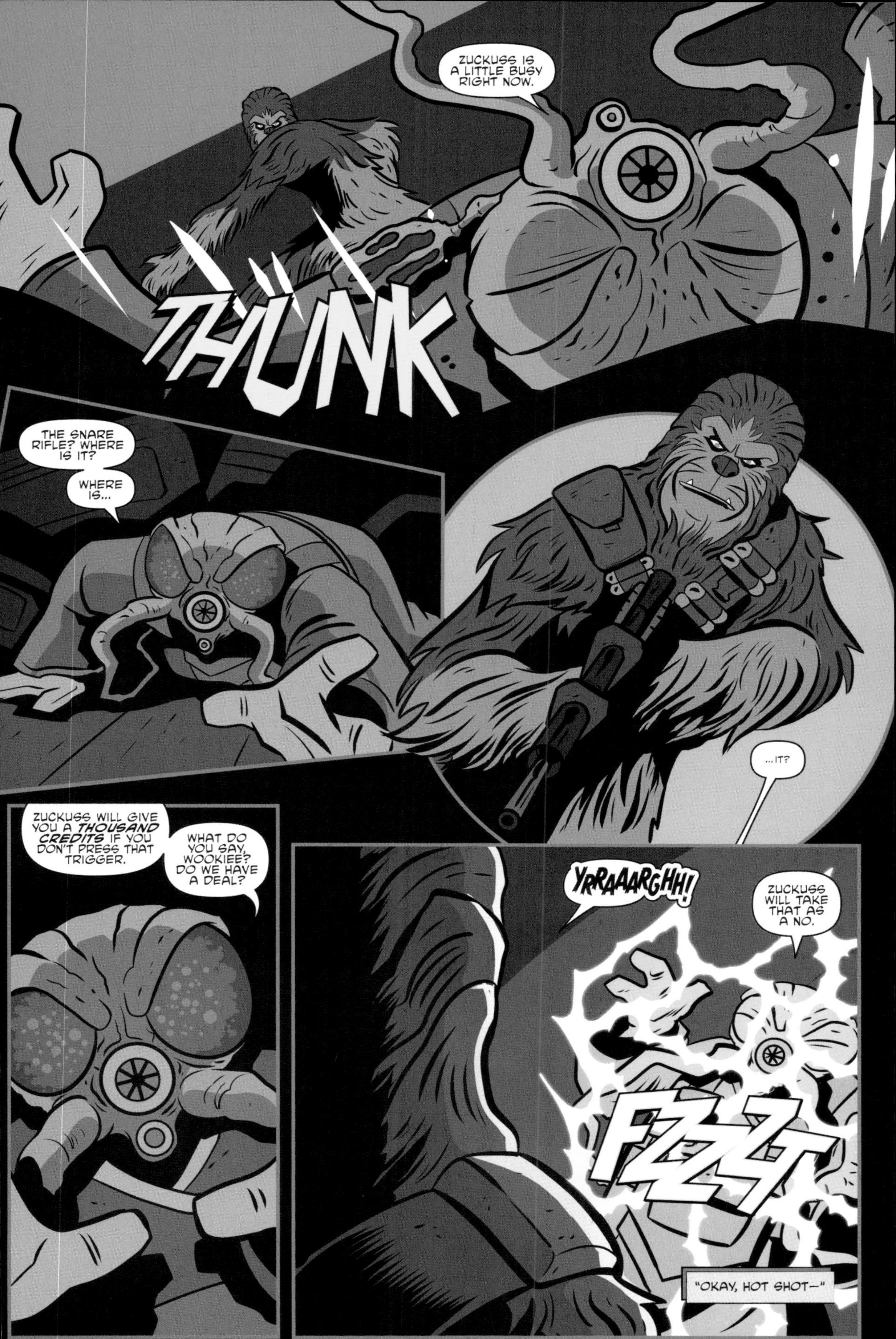
ZUCKUSS IS A LITTLE BUSY RIGHT NOW.
THUNK
THE SNARE RIFLE? WHERE IS IT?
WHERE IS...
...IT?
ZUCKUSS WILL GIVE YOU A THOUSAND CREDITS IF YOU DON'T PRESS THAT TRIGGER.
WHAT DO YOU SAY, WOOKIEE? DO WE HAVE A DEAL?
YRRAAARGHH!
ZUCKUSS WILL TAKE THAT AS A NO.
FZZZT
"OKAY, HOT SHOT—"

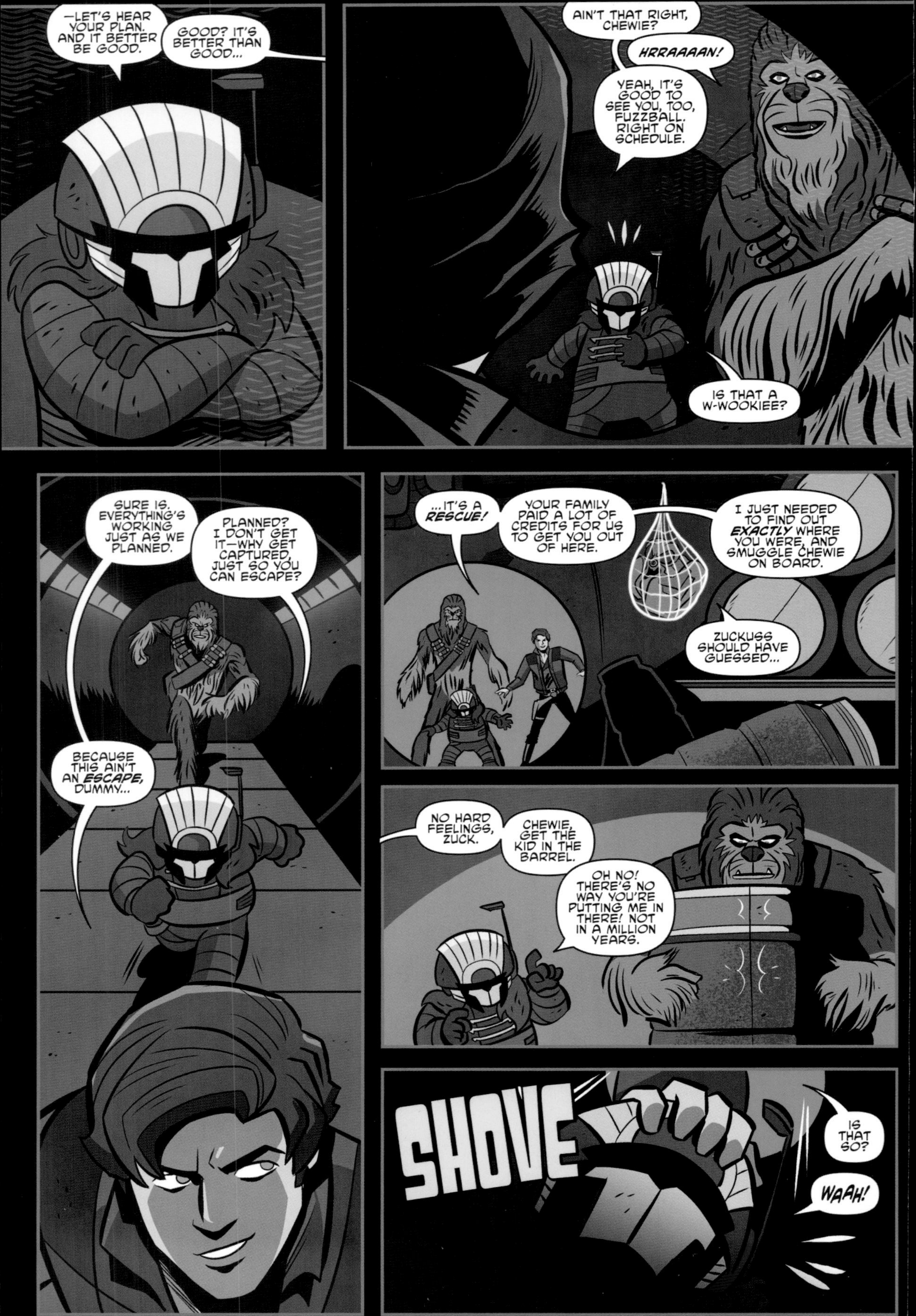
—LET'S HEAR YOUR PLAN. AND IT BETTER BE GOOD.
GOOD? IT'S BETTER THAN GOOD...
AIN'T THAT RIGHT, CHEWIE?
HRRAAAAN!
YEAH, IT'S GOOD TO SEE YOU, TOO, FUZZBALL. RIGHT ON SCHEDULE.
IS THAT A W-WOOKIEE?
SURE IS. EVERYTHING'S WORKING JUST AS WE PLANNED.
PLANNED? I DON'T GET IT—WHY GET CAPTURED, JUST SO YOU CAN ESCAPE?
BECAUSE THIS AIN'T AN ESCAPE, DUMMY...
...IT'S A RESCUE!
YOUR FAMILY PAID A LOT OF CREDITS FOR US TO GET YOU OUT OF HERE.
I JUST NEEDED TO FIND OUT EXACTLY WHERE YOU WERE, AND SMUGGLE CHEWIE ON BOARD.
ZUCKUSS SHOULD HAVE GUESSED...
NO HARD FEELINGS, ZUCK.
CHEWIE, GET THE KID IN THE BARREL.
OH NO! THERE'S NO WAY YOU'RE PUTTING ME IN THERE! NOT IN A MILLION YEARS.
SHOVE
IS THAT SO?
WAAH!

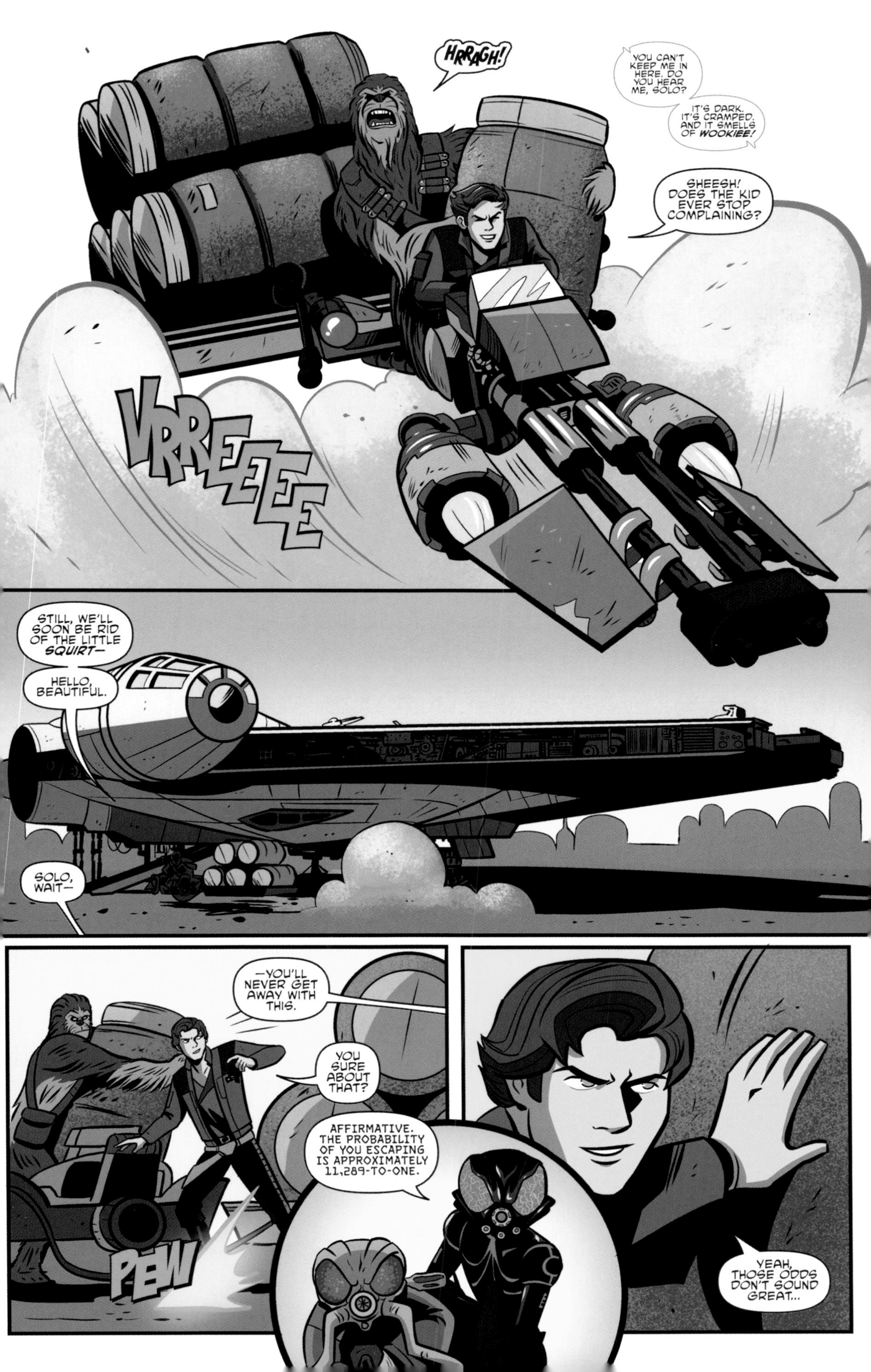
HRRAGH!
YOU CAN'T KEEP ME IN HERE. DO YOU HEAR ME, SOLO?
IT'S DARK. IT'S CRAMPED. AND IT SMELLS OF WOOKIEE!
SHEESH! DOES THE KID EVER STOP COMPLAINING?
VRREEEEE
STILL, WE'LL SOON BE RID OF THE LITTLE SQUIRT—
HELLO, BEAUTIFUL.
SOLO, WAIT—
—YOU'LL NEVER GET AWAY WITH THIS.
YOU SURE ABOUT THAT?
AFFIRMATIVE. THE PROBABILITY OF YOU ESCAPING IS APPROXIMATELY 11,289-TO-ONE.
PEW
YEAH, THOSE ODDS DON'T SOUND GREAT...

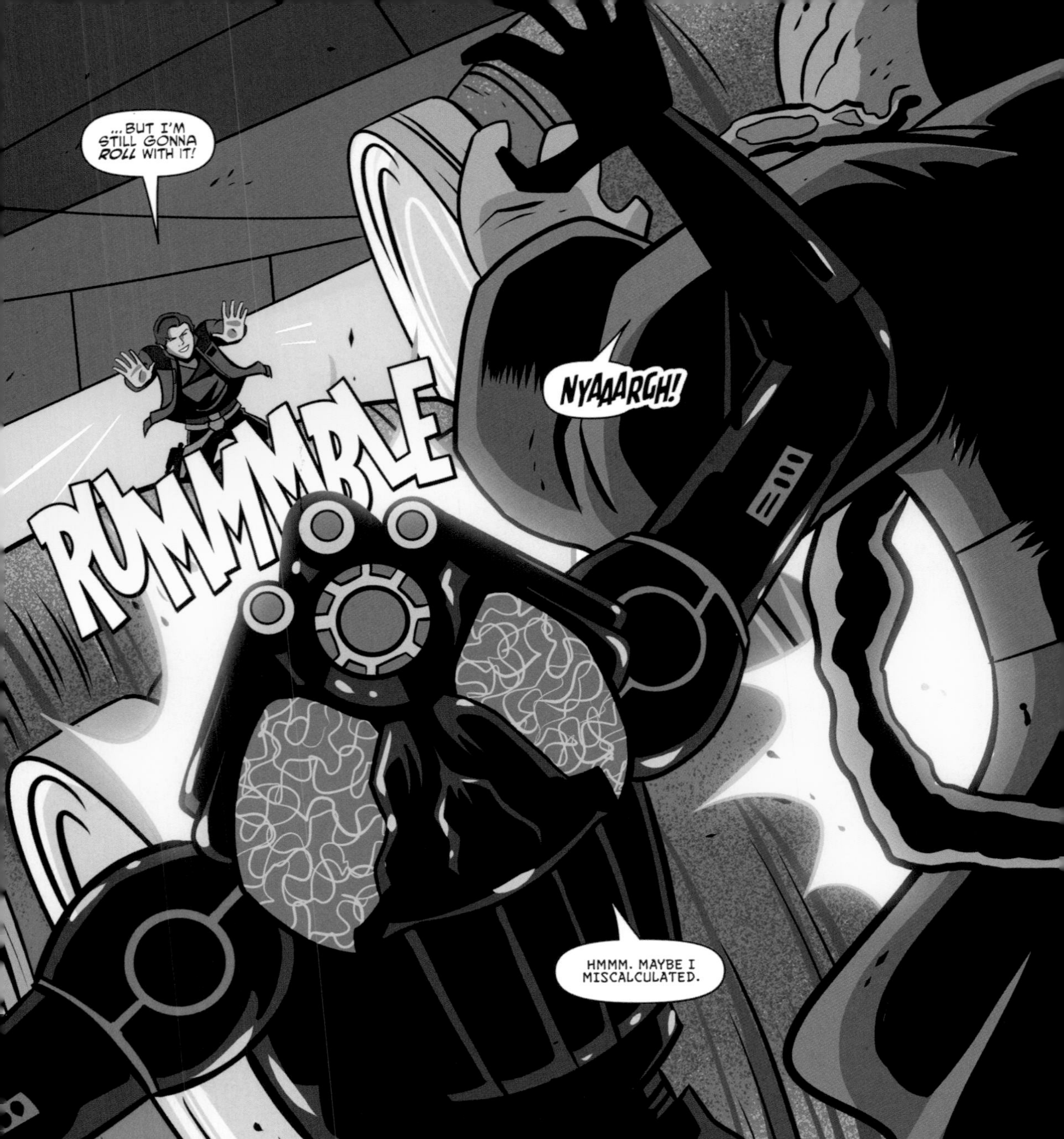
...BUT I'M STILL GONNA ROLL WITH IT!
RUMMMBLE
NYAAARGH!
HMMM. MAYBE I MISCALCULATED.
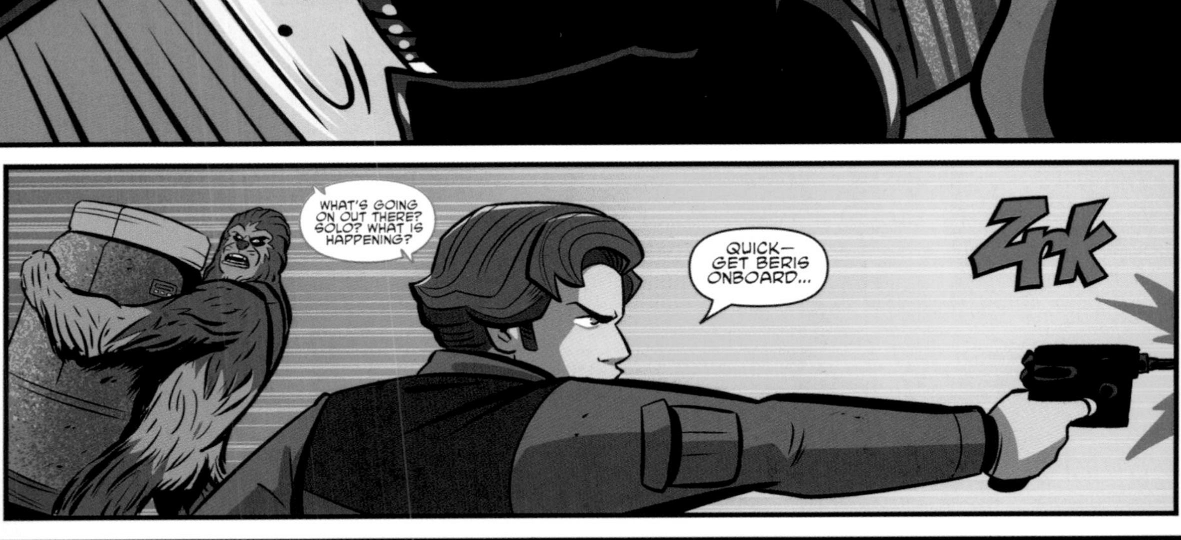
WHAT'S GOING ON OUT THERE? SOLO? WHAT IS HAPPENING?
QUICK— GET BERIS ONBOARD...
ZRK

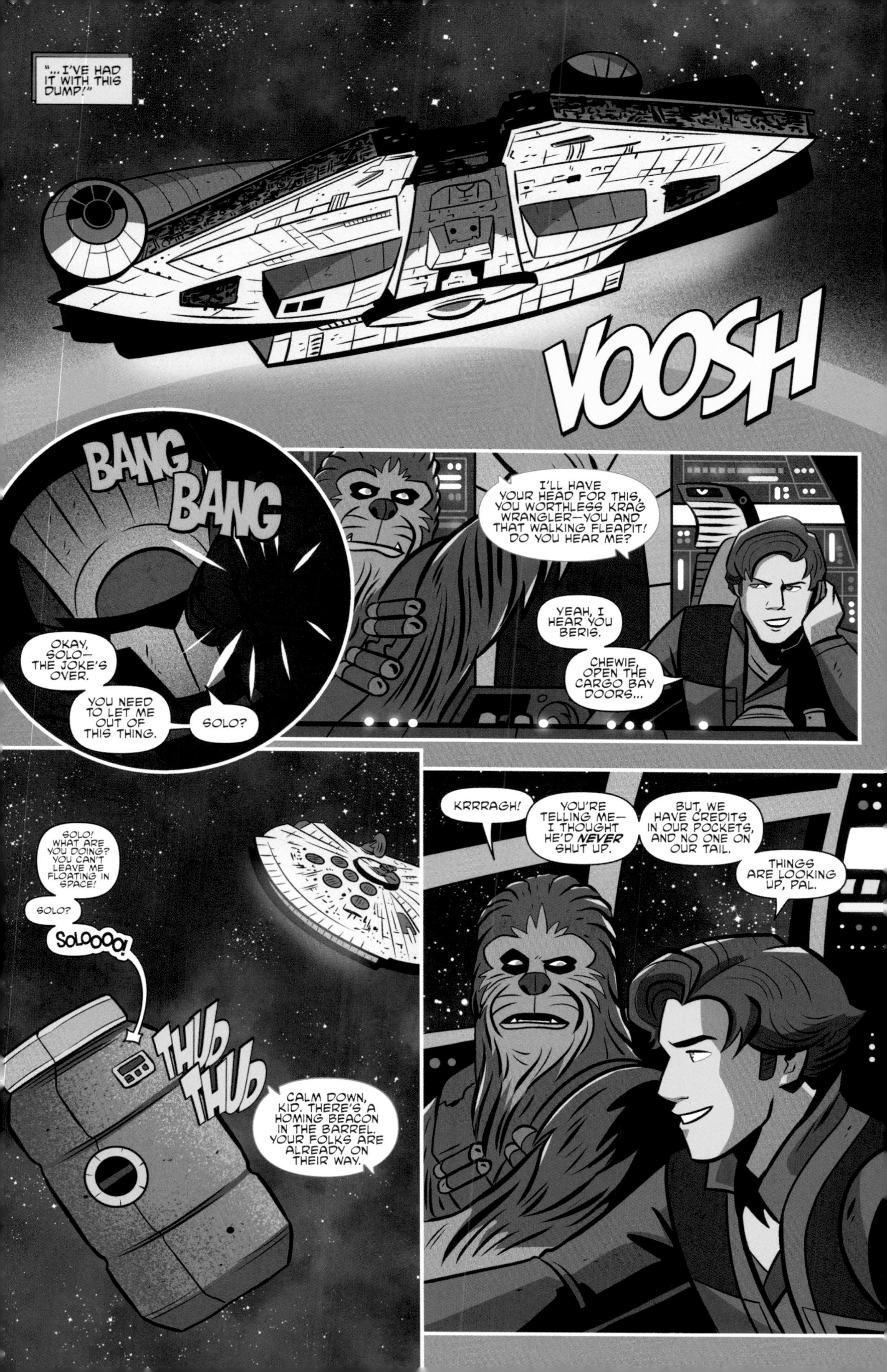
"...I'VE HAD IT WITH THIS DUMP!"
VOOSH
BANG BANG
I'LL HAVE YOUR HEAD FOR THIS, YOU WORTHLESS KRAG WRANGLER—YOU AND THAT WALKING FLEAPIT! DO YOU HEAR ME?
YEAH, I HEAR YOU BERIS.
CHEWIE, OPEN THE CARGO BAY DOORS...
OKAY, SOLO— THE JOKE'S OVER.
YOU NEED TO LET ME OUT OF THIS THING.
SOLO?
SOLO! WHAT ARE YOU DOING? YOU CAN'T LEAVE ME FLOATING IN SPACE!
SOLO?
SOLOOOO!
THUD THUD
CALM DOWN, KID. THERE'S A HOMING BEACON IN THE BARREL. YOUR FOLKS ARE ALREADY ON THEIR WAY.
KRRRAGH!
YOU'RE TELLING ME— I THOUGHT HE'D NEVER SHUT UP.
BUT, WE HAVE CREDITS IN OUR POCKETS, AND NO ONE ON OUR TAIL.
THINGS ARE LOOKING UP, PAL.

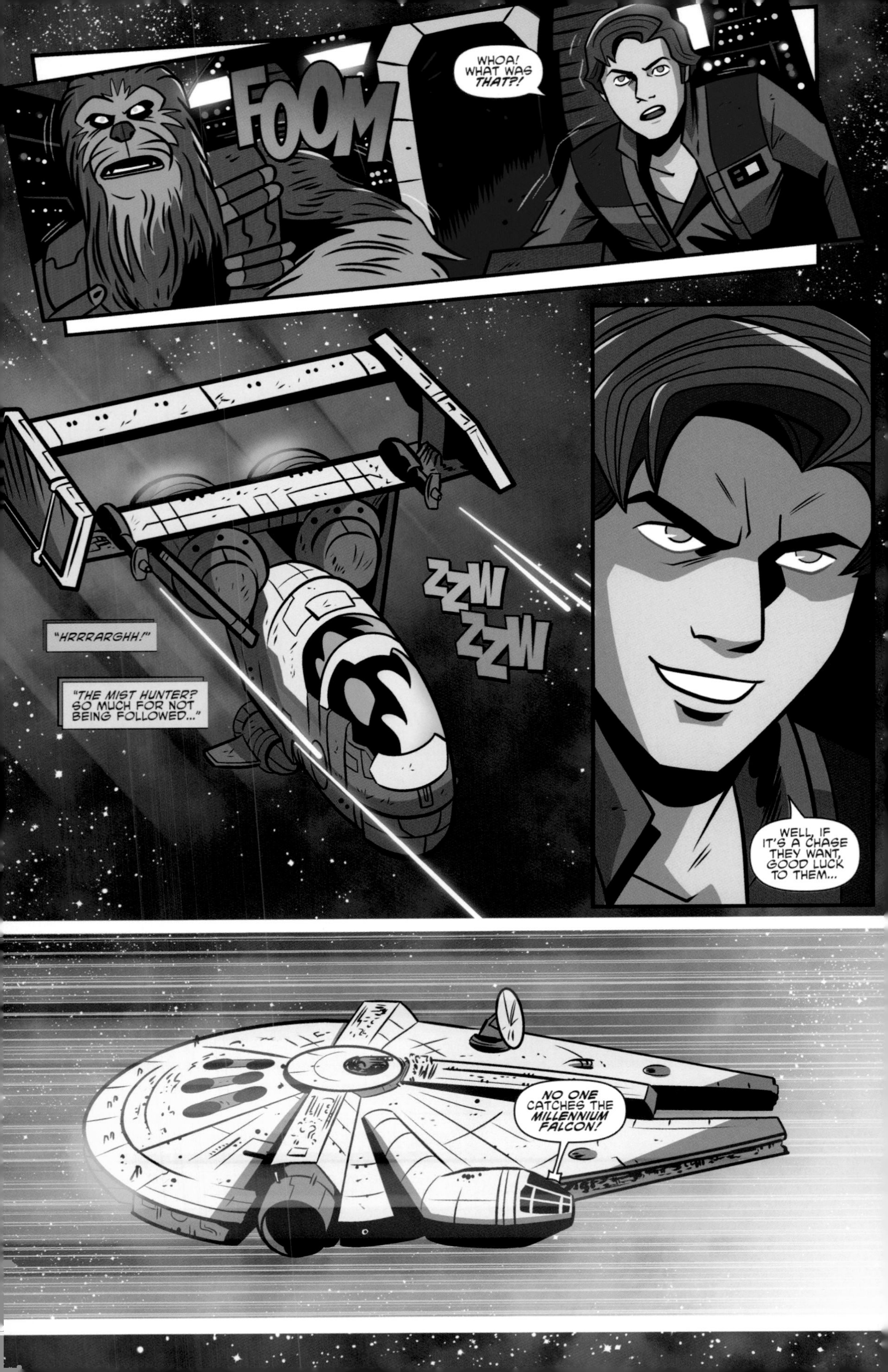
FOOM
WHOA! WHAT WAS *THAT?!*
"HRRRARGHH!"
"THE MIST HUNTER? SO MUCH FOR NOT BEING FOLLOWED..."
ZZW ZZW
WELL, IF IT'S A CHASE THEY WANT, GOOD LUCK TO THEM...
NO ONE CATCHES THE *MILLENNIUM FALCON!*

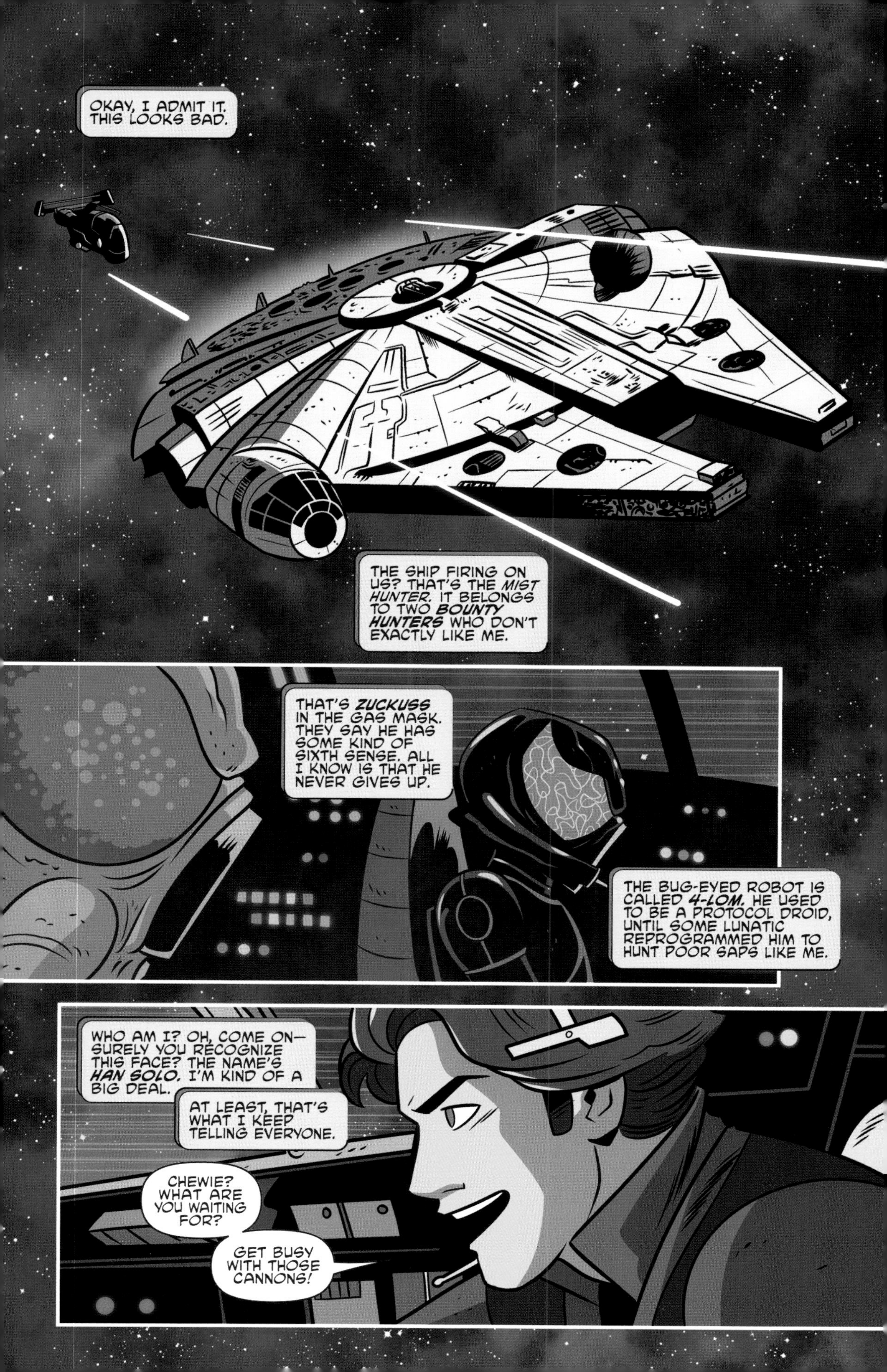
OKAY, I ADMIT IT. THIS LOOKS BAD.
THE SHIP FIRING ON US? THAT'S THE *MIST HUNTER*. IT BELONGS TO TWO ***BOUNTY HUNTERS*** WHO DON'T EXACTLY LIKE ME.
THAT'S ***ZUCKUSS*** IN THE GAS MASK. THEY SAY HE HAS SOME KIND OF SIXTH SENSE. ALL I KNOW IS THAT HE NEVER GIVES UP.
THE BUG-EYED ROBOT IS CALLED ***4-LOM***. HE USED TO BE A PROTOCOL DROID, UNTIL SOME LUNATIC REPROGRAMMED HIM TO HUNT POOR SAPS LIKE ME.
WHO AM I? OH, COME ON— SURELY YOU RECOGNIZE THIS FACE? THE NAME'S ***HAN SOLO***. I'M KIND OF A BIG DEAL.
AT LEAST, THAT'S WHAT I KEEP TELLING EVERYONE.
CHEWIE? WHAT ARE YOU WAITING FOR?
GET BUSY WITH THOSE CANNONS!

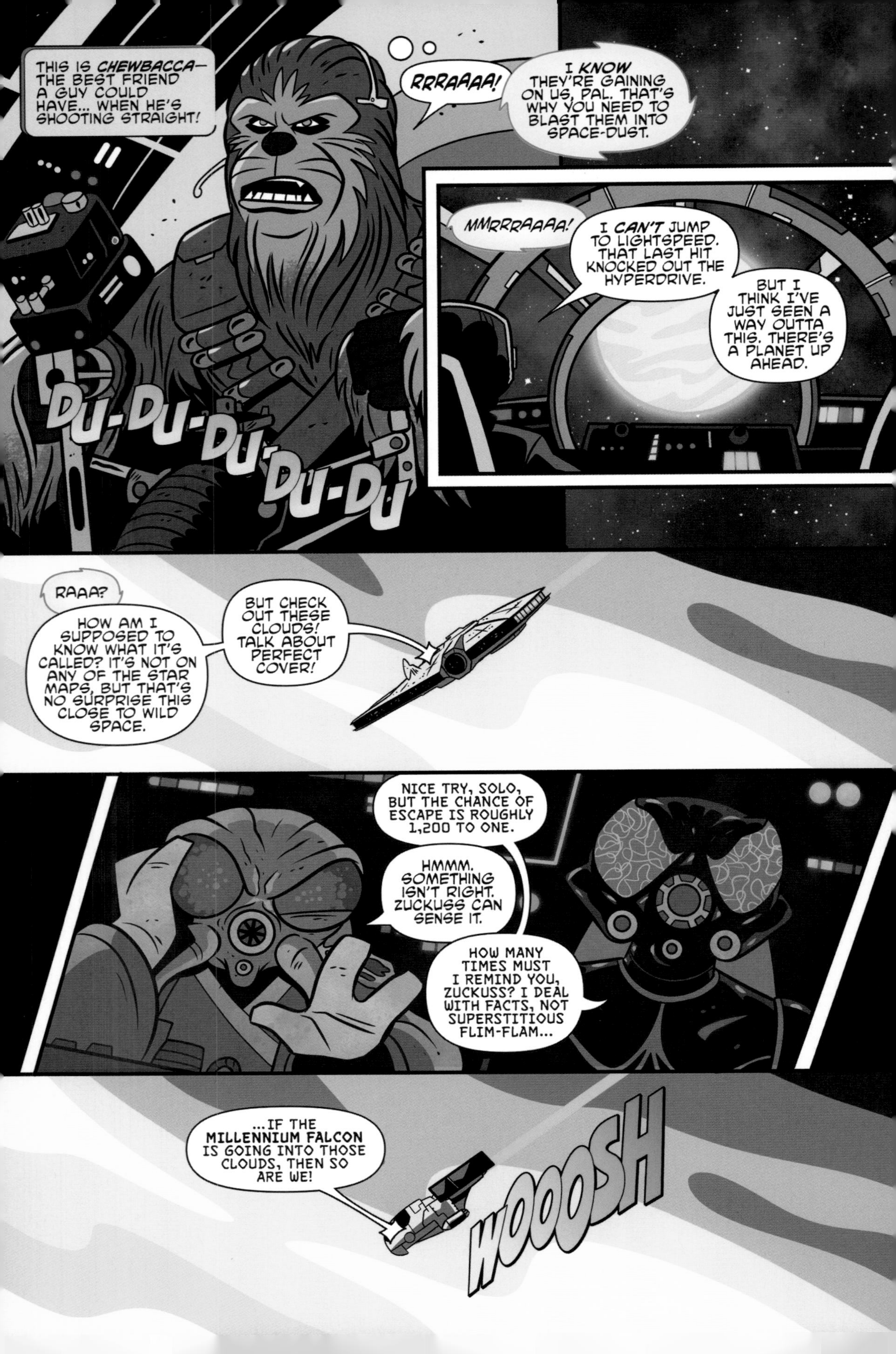
THIS IS CHEWBACCA— THE BEST FRIEND A GUY COULD HAVE... WHEN HE'S SHOOTING STRAIGHT!
RRRAAAA!
I KNOW THEY'RE GAINING ON US, PAL. THAT'S WHY YOU NEED TO BLAST THEM INTO SPACE-DUST.
DU-DU-DU-DU-DU-DU
MMRRRAAAA!
I CAN'T JUMP TO LIGHTSPEED. THAT LAST HIT KNOCKED OUT THE HYPERDRIVE.
BUT I THINK I'VE JUST SEEN A WAY OUTTA THIS. THERE'S A PLANET UP AHEAD.
RAAA?
HOW AM I SUPPOSED TO KNOW WHAT IT'S CALLED? IT'S NOT ON ANY OF THE STAR MAPS, BUT THAT'S NO SURPRISE THIS CLOSE TO WILD SPACE.
BUT CHECK OUT THESE CLOUDS! TALK ABOUT PERFECT COVER!
NICE TRY, SOLO, BUT THE CHANCE OF ESCAPE IS ROUGHLY 1,200 TO ONE.
HMMM. SOMETHING ISN'T RIGHT. ZUCKUSS CAN SENSE IT.
HOW MANY TIMES MUST I REMIND YOU, ZUCKUSS? I DEAL WITH FACTS, NOT SUPERSTITIOUS FLIM-FLAM...
...IF THE MILLENNIUM FALCON IS GOING INTO THOSE CLOUDS, THEN SO ARE WE!
WOOOSH

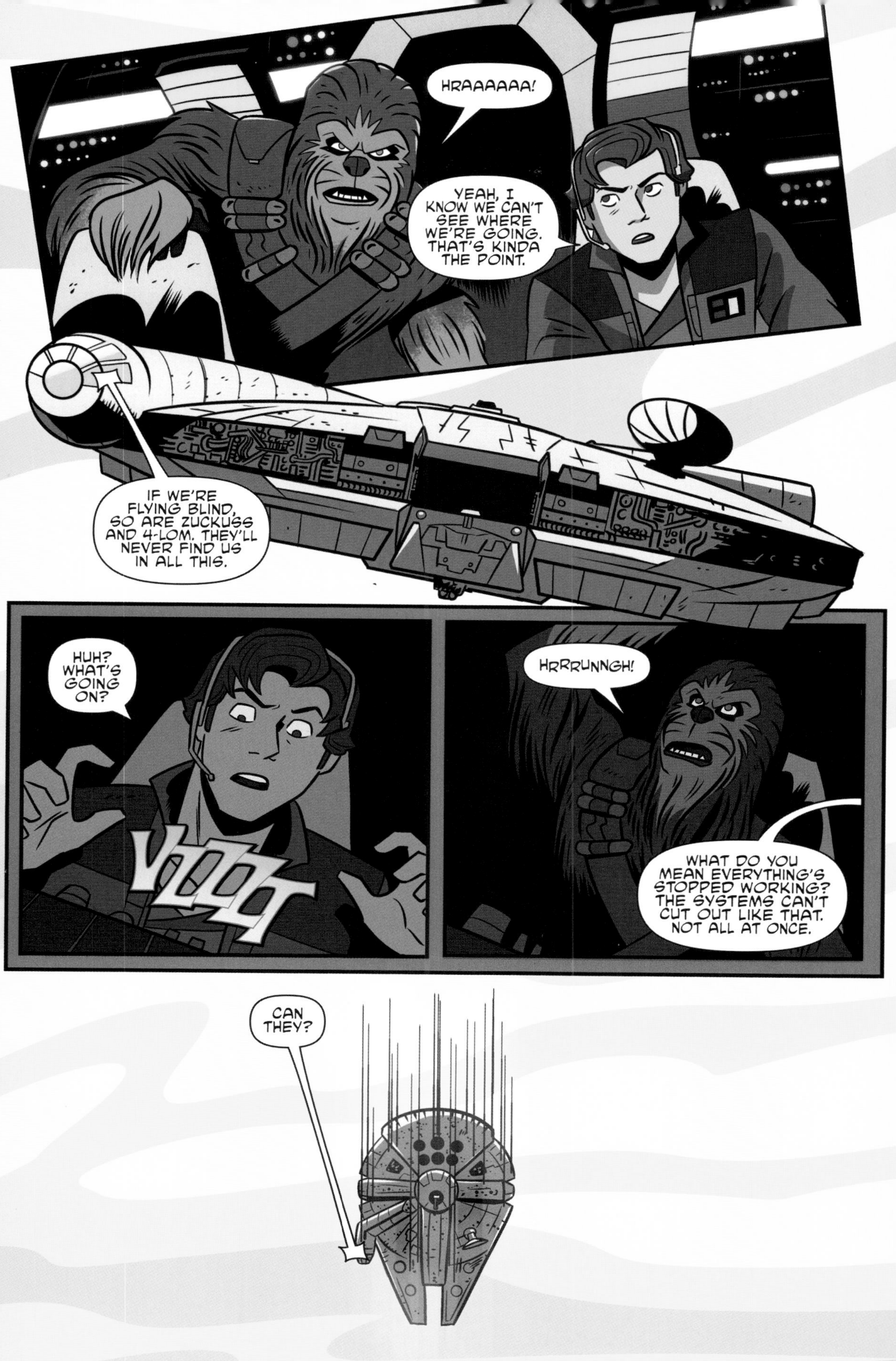
HRAAAAAA!
YEAH, I KNOW WE CAN'T SEE WHERE WE'RE GOING. THAT'S KINDA THE POINT.
IF WE'RE FLYING BLIND, SO ARE ZUCKUSS AND 4-LOM. THEY'LL NEVER FIND US IN ALL THIS.
HUH? WHAT'S GOING ON?
VLOOT
HRRRUNNGH!
WHAT DO YOU MEAN EVERYTHING'S STOPPED WORKING? THE SYSTEMS CAN'T CUT OUT LIKE THAT. NOT ALL AT ONCE.
CAN THEY?

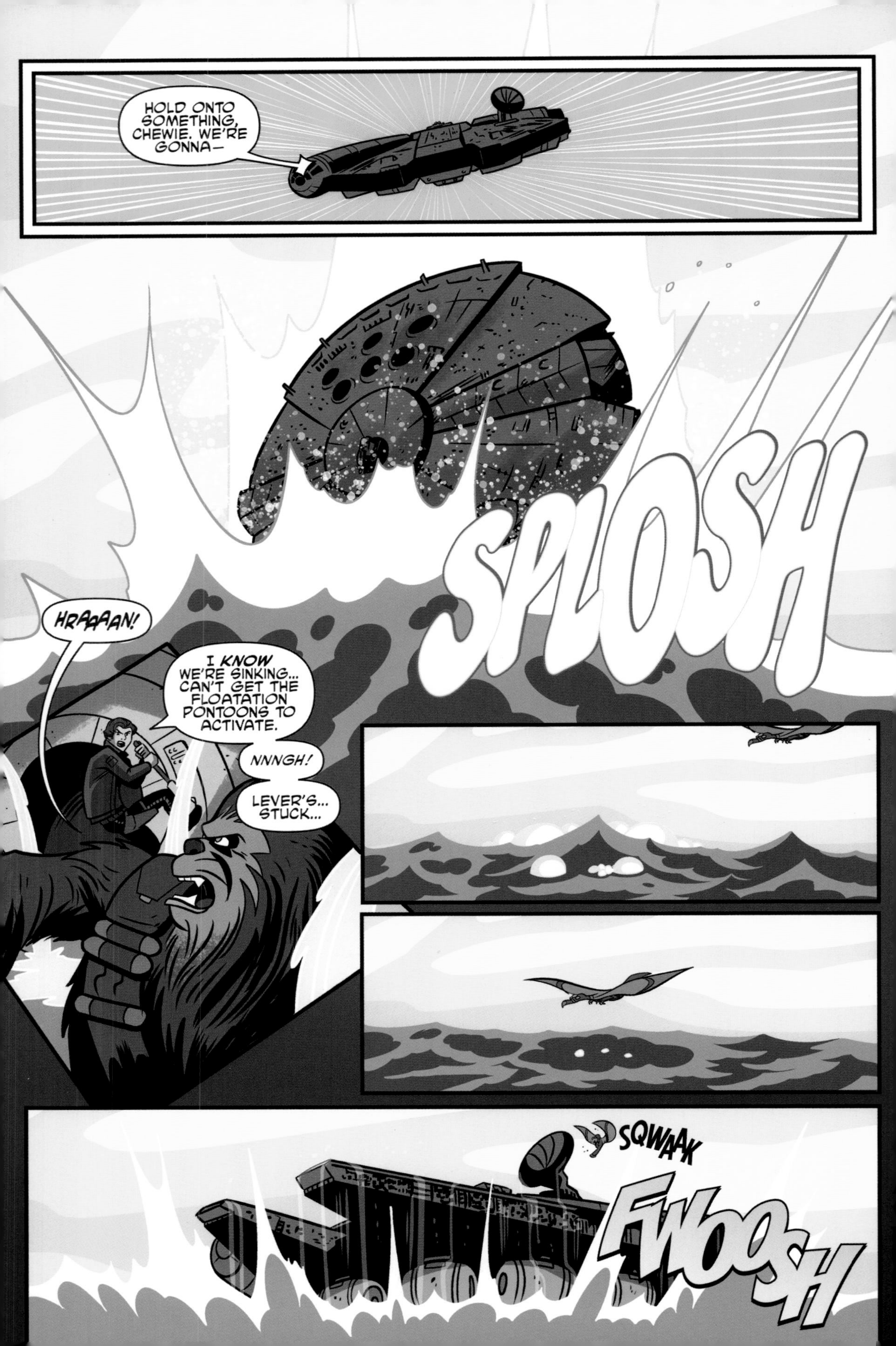
HOLD ONTO SOMETHING, CHEWIE. WE'RE GONNA—
SPLOSH
HRAAAAN!
I KNOW WE'RE SINKING... CAN'T GET THE FLOATATION PONTOONS TO ACTIVATE.
NNNGH!
LEVER'S... STUCK...
SQWAAK
FWOOSH

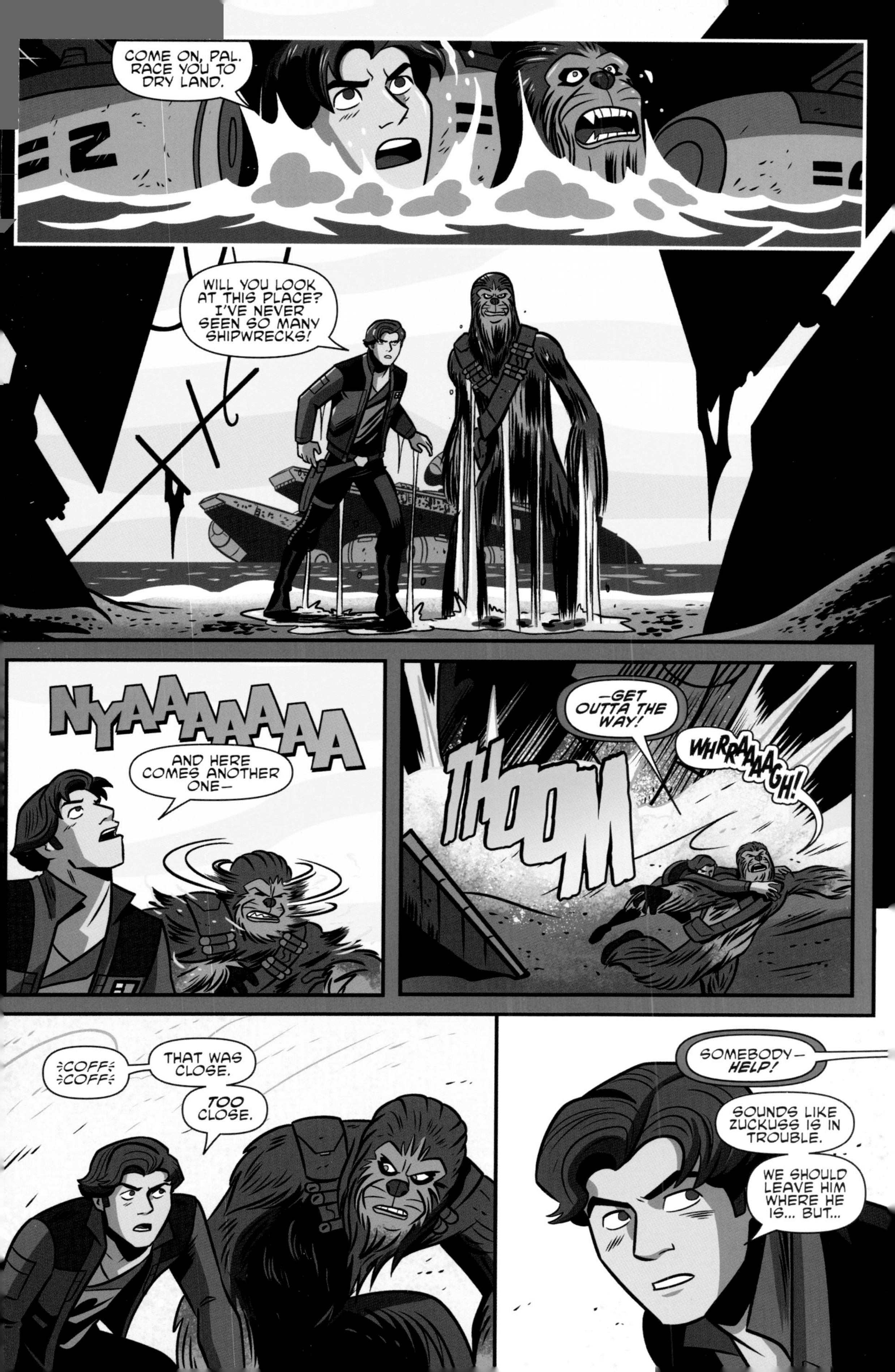
COME ON, PAL. RACE YOU TO DRY LAND.
WILL YOU LOOK AT THIS PLACE? I'VE NEVER SEEN SO MANY SHIPWRECKS!
NYAAAAAAAAA
AND HERE COMES ANOTHER ONE—
—GET OUTTA THE WAY!
THOOM
WHRRAAAAGH!
COFF COFF
THAT WAS CLOSE.
TOO CLOSE.
SOMEBODY— HELP!
SOUNDS LIKE ZUCKUSS IS IN TROUBLE.
WE SHOULD LEAVE HIM WHERE HE IS... BUT...

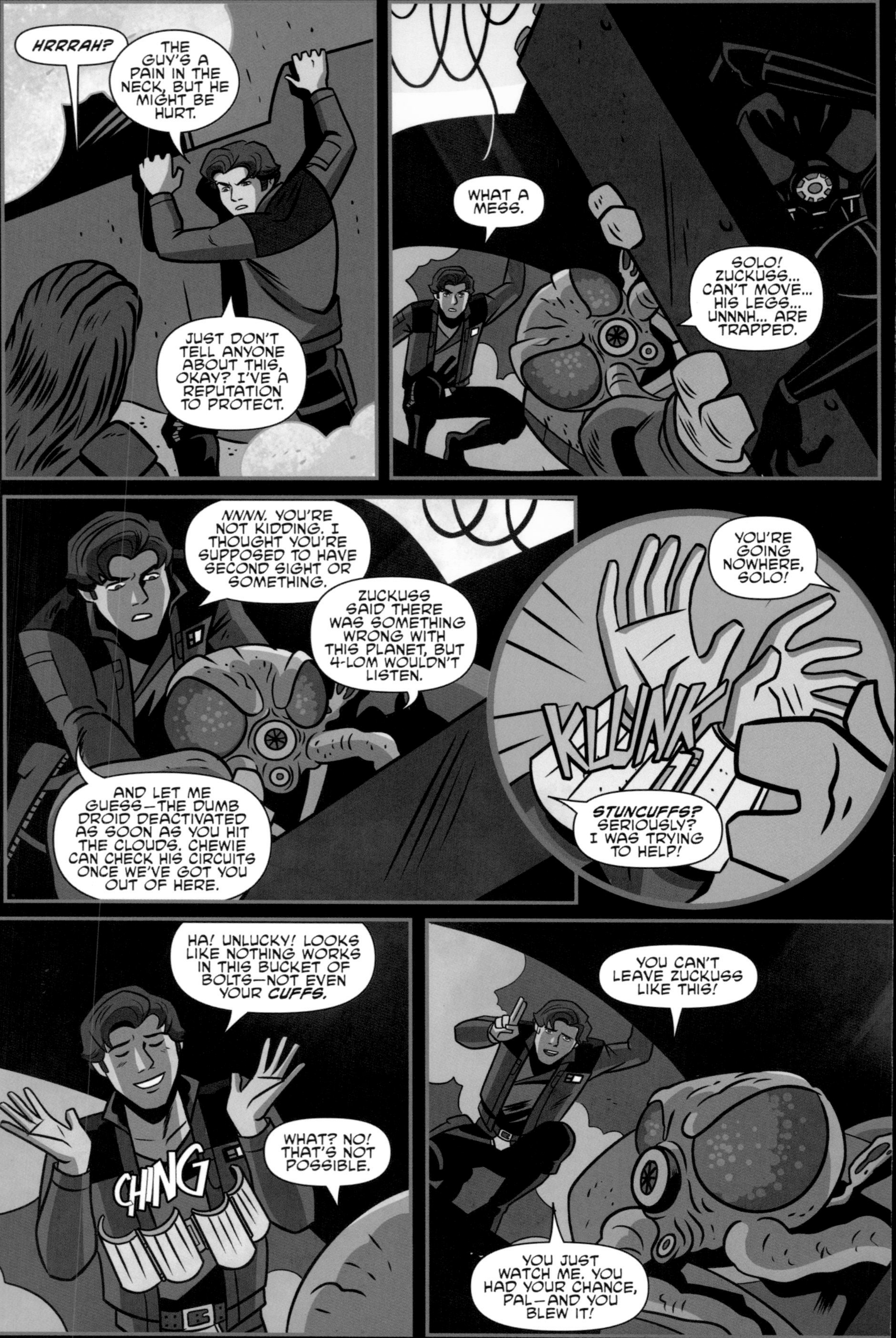
HRRRAH?
THE GUY'S A PAIN IN THE NECK, BUT HE MIGHT BE HURT.
JUST DON'T TELL ANYONE ABOUT THIS, OKAY? I'VE A REPUTATION TO PROTECT.
WHAT A MESS.
SOLO! ZUCKUSS... CAN'T MOVE... HIS LEGS... UNNNH... ARE TRAPPED.
NNNN. YOU'RE NOT KIDDING. I THOUGHT YOU'RE SUPPOSED TO HAVE SECOND SIGHT OR SOMETHING.
ZUCKUSS SAID THERE WAS SOMETHING WRONG WITH THIS PLANET, BUT 4-LOM WOULDN'T LISTEN.
AND LET ME GUESS—THE DUMB DROID DEACTIVATED AS SOON AS YOU HIT THE CLOUDS. CHEWIE CAN CHECK HIS CIRCUITS ONCE WE'VE GOT YOU OUT OF HERE.
YOU'RE GOING NOWHERE, SOLO!
KLUNK
STUNCUFFS? SERIOUSLY? I WAS TRYING TO HELP!
HA! UNLUCKY! LOOKS LIKE NOTHING WORKS IN THIS BUCKET OF BOLTS—NOT EVEN YOUR CUFFS.
CHING
WHAT? NO! THAT'S NOT POSSIBLE.
YOU CAN'T LEAVE ZUCKUSS LIKE THIS!
YOU JUST WATCH ME. YOU HAD YOUR CHANCE, PAL—AND YOU BLEW IT!

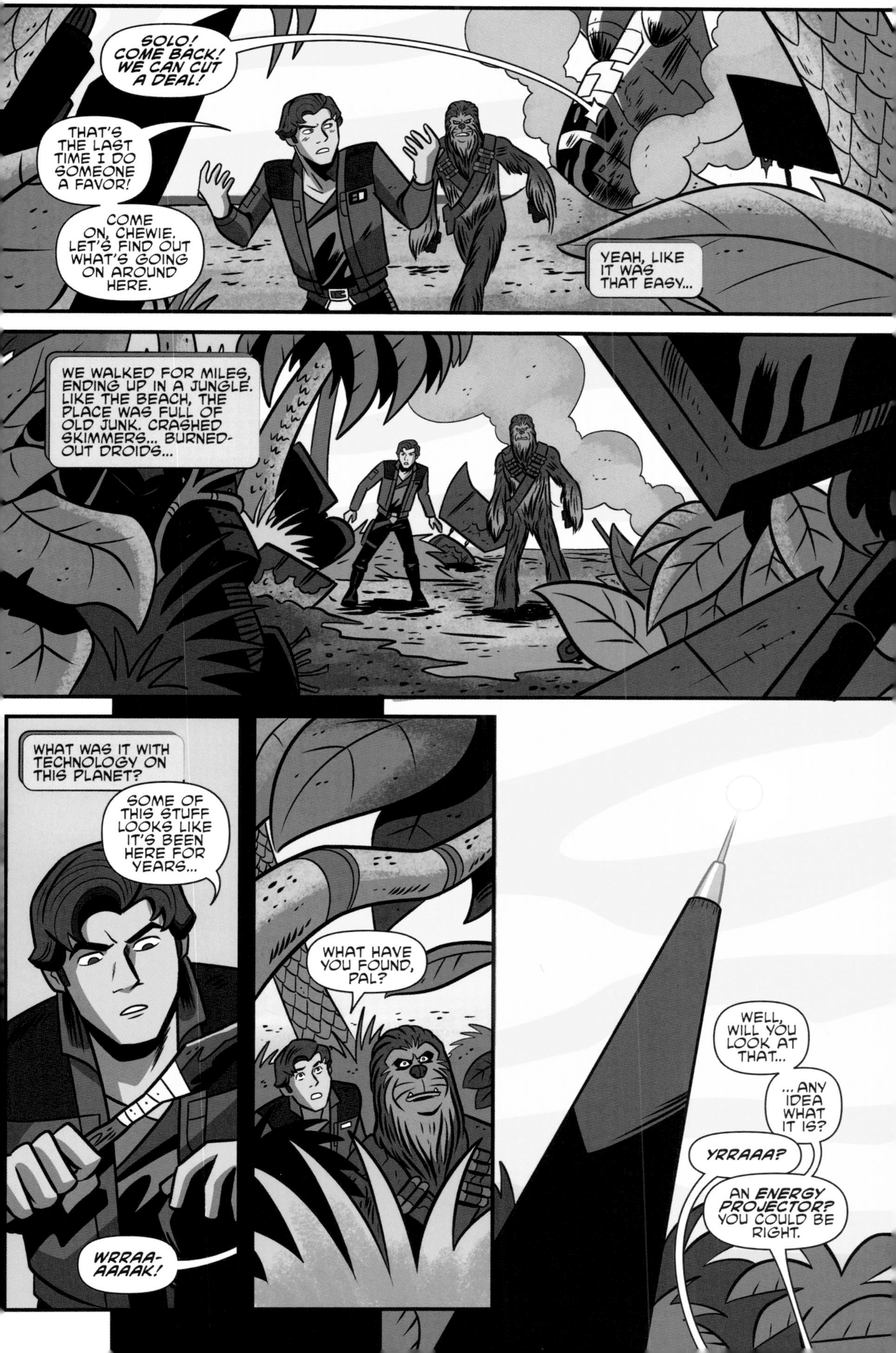
SOLO! COME BACK! WE CAN CUT A DEAL!
THAT'S THE LAST TIME I DO SOMEONE A FAVOR!
COME ON, CHEWIE. LET'S FIND OUT WHAT'S GOING ON AROUND HERE.
YEAH, LIKE IT WAS THAT EASY...
WE WALKED FOR MILES, ENDING UP IN A JUNGLE. LIKE THE BEACH, THE PLACE WAS FULL OF OLD JUNK. CRASHED SKIMMERS... BURNED-OUT DROIDS...
WHAT WAS IT WITH TECHNOLOGY ON THIS PLANET?
SOME OF THIS STUFF LOOKS LIKE IT'S BEEN HERE FOR YEARS...
WRRAA-AAAAK!
WHAT HAVE YOU FOUND, PAL?
WELL, WILL YOU LOOK AT THAT...
...ANY IDEA WHAT IT IS?
YRRAAA?
AN ENERGY PROJECTOR? YOU COULD BE RIGHT.

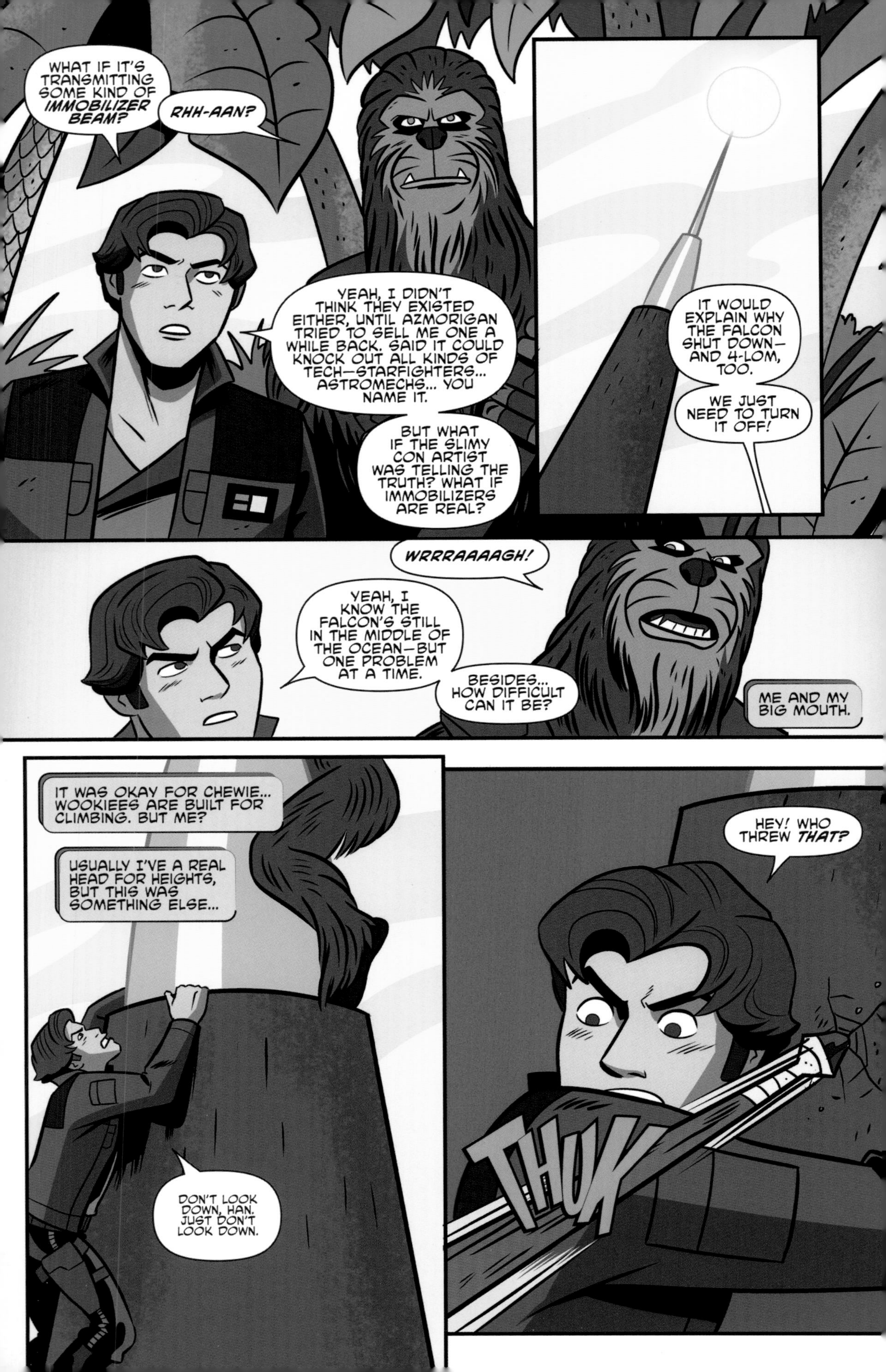
WHAT IF IT'S TRANSMITTING SOME KIND OF *IMMOBILIZER* BEAM?
RHH-AAN?
YEAH, I DIDN'T THINK THEY EXISTED EITHER, UNTIL AZMORIGAN TRIED TO SELL ME ONE A WHILE BACK. SAID IT COULD KNOCK OUT ALL KINDS OF TECH—STARFIGHTERS... ASTROMECHS... YOU NAME IT.
BUT WHAT IF THE SLIMY CON ARTIST WAS TELLING THE TRUTH? WHAT IF IMMOBILIZERS ARE REAL?
IT WOULD EXPLAIN WHY THE FALCON SHUT DOWN—AND 4-LOM, TOO.
WE JUST NEED TO TURN IT OFF!
WRRRAAAAGH!
YEAH, I KNOW THE FALCON'S STILL IN THE MIDDLE OF THE OCEAN—BUT ONE PROBLEM AT A TIME.
BESIDES... HOW DIFFICULT CAN IT BE?
ME AND MY BIG MOUTH.
IT WAS OKAY FOR CHEWIE... WOOKIEES ARE BUILT FOR CLIMBING. BUT ME?
USUALLY I'VE A REAL HEAD FOR HEIGHTS, BUT THIS WAS SOMETHING ELSE...
DON'T LOOK DOWN, HAN. JUST DON'T LOOK DOWN.
HEY! WHO THREW *THAT?*
THUK

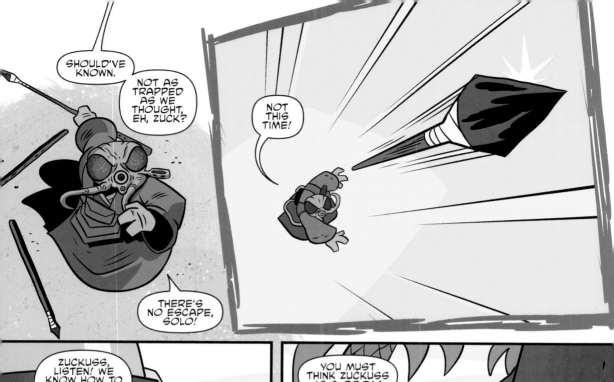

SHOULD'VE KNOWN.

NOT AS TRAPPED AS WE THOUGHT, EH, ZUCK?

NOT THIS TIME!

THERE'S NO ESCAPE, SOLO!

ZUCKUSS, LISTEN! WE KNOW HOW TO GET OUR SHIPS OFF THIS PLANET.

THUK

YOU MUST THINK ZUCKUSS IS A *FOOL!*

NO, JUST *REALLY* ANNOYING.

HEY—WATCH WHAT YOU'RE DOING WITH THAT THING, PAL!

POK

OH, *NOW* I GET IT. NOT BAD FOR A FURBALL...

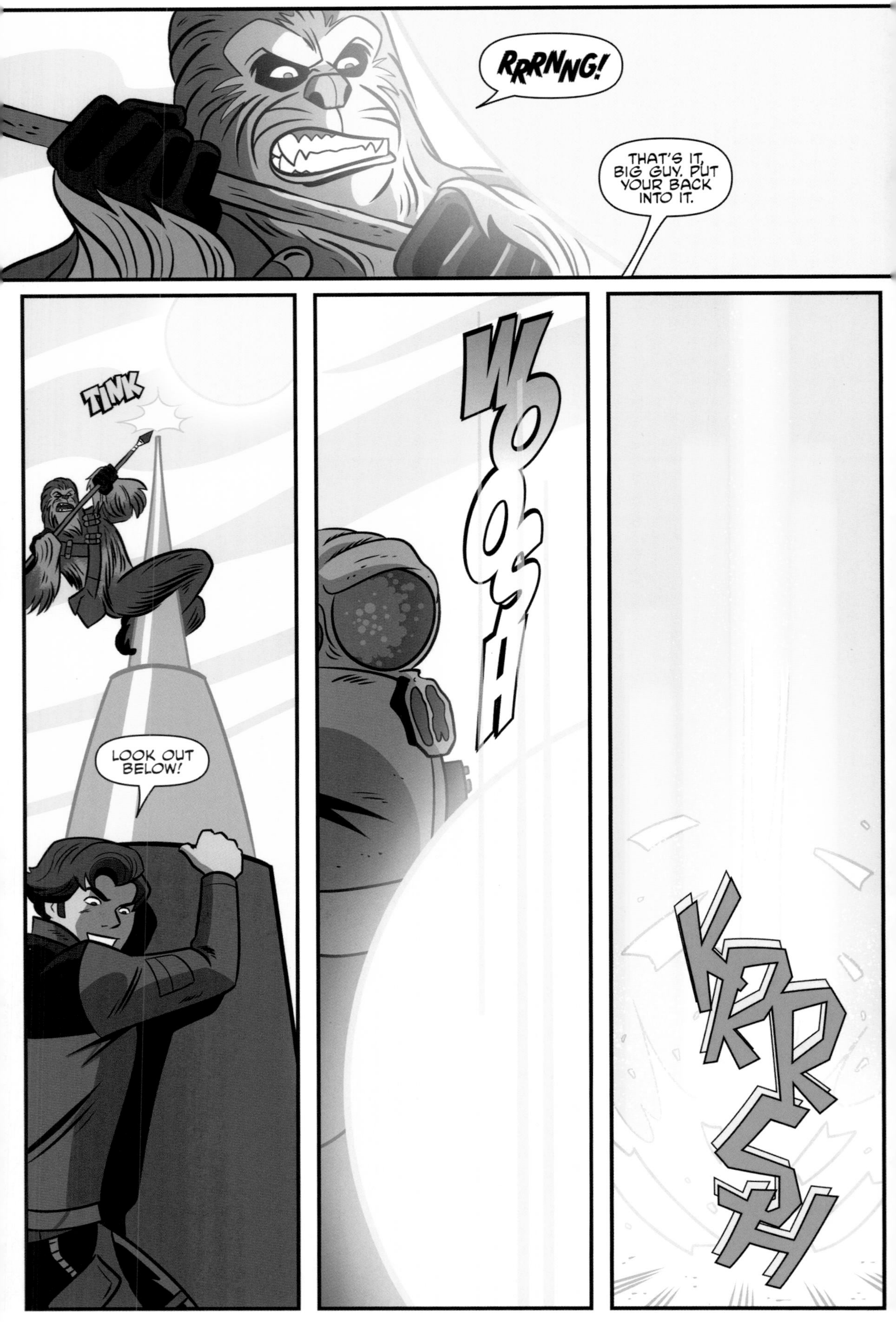
RRRNNG!
THAT'S IT, BIG GUY. PUT YOUR BACK INTO IT.
TINK
LOOK OUT BELOW!
WOOSH
KRRKSH

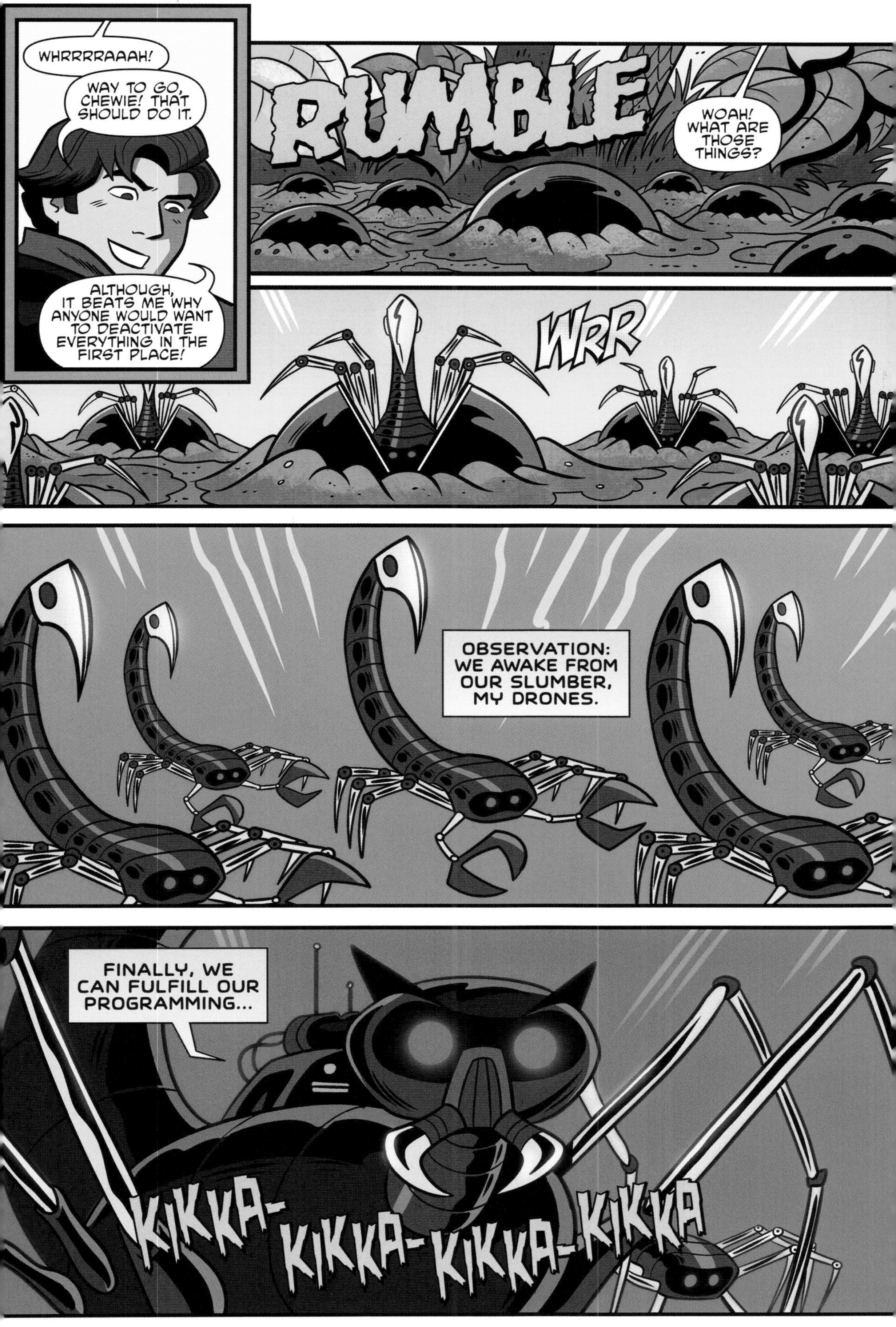
WHRRRRAAAH!
WAY TO GO, CHEWIE! THAT SHOULD DO IT.
ALTHOUGH, IT BEATS ME WHY ANYONE WOULD WANT TO DEACTIVATE EVERYTHING IN THE FIRST PLACE!
RUMBLE
WOAH! WHAT ARE THOSE THINGS?
WRR
OBSERVATION: WE AWAKE FROM OUR SLUMBER, MY DRONES.
FINALLY, WE CAN FULFILL OUR PROGRAMMING...
KIKKA-KIKKA-KIKKA-KIKKA

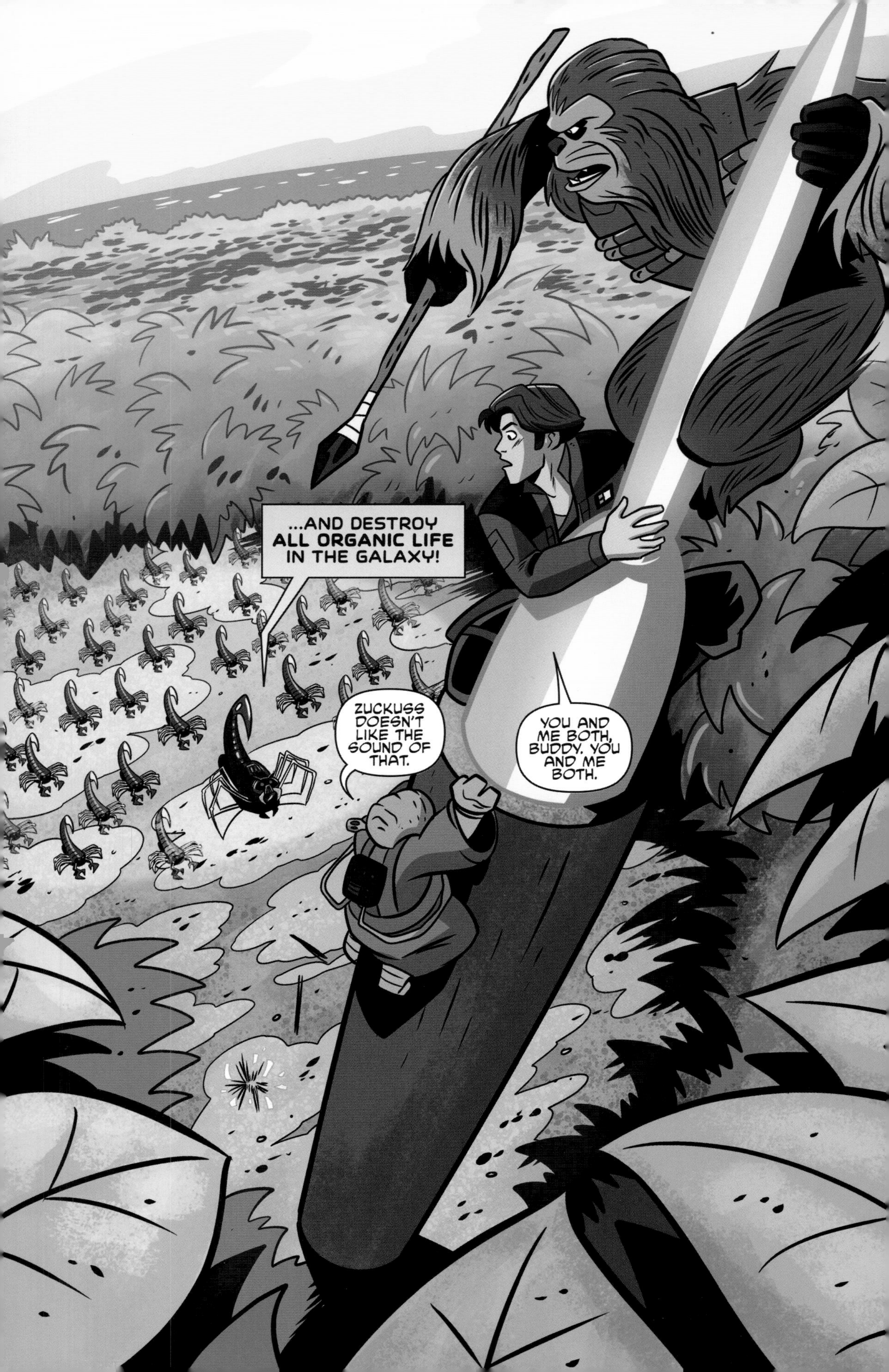
...AND DESTROY ALL ORGANIC LIFE IN THE GALAXY!
ZUCKUSS DOESN'T LIKE THE SOUND OF THAT.
YOU AND ME BOTH, BUDDY. YOU AND ME BOTH.

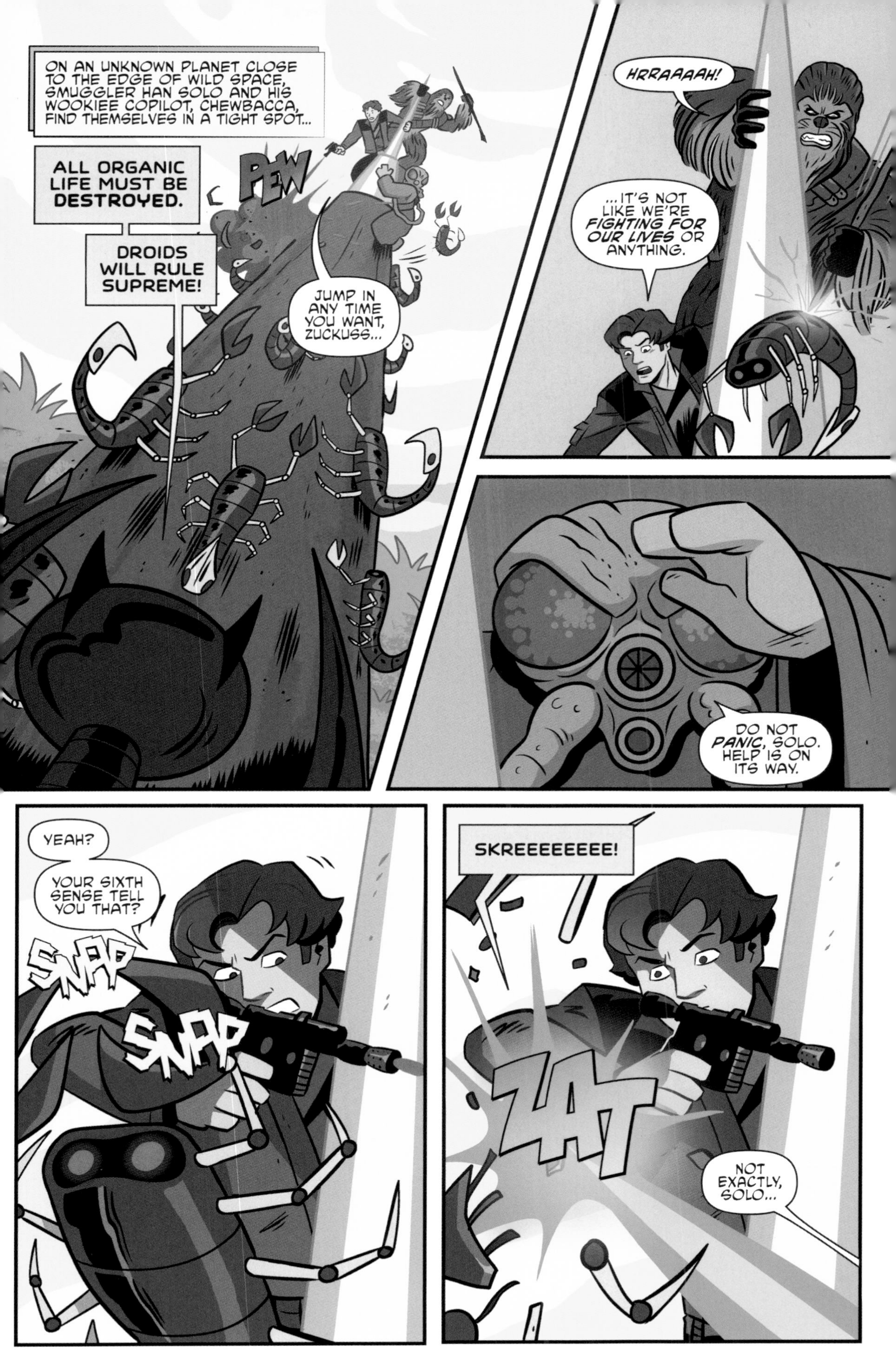
ON AN UNKNOWN PLANET CLOSE TO THE EDGE OF WILD SPACE, SMUGGLER HAN SOLO AND HIS WOOKIEE COPILOT, CHEWBACCA, FIND THEMSELVES IN A TIGHT SPOT...
ALL ORGANIC LIFE MUST BE DESTROYED.
PEW
DROIDS WILL RULE SUPREME!
JUMP IN ANY TIME YOU WANT, ZUCKUSS...
HRRAAAAH!
...IT'S NOT LIKE WE'RE FIGHTING FOR OUR LIVES OR ANYTHING.
DO NOT PANIC, SOLO. HELP IS ON ITS WAY.
YEAH?
YOUR SIXTH SENSE TELL YOU THAT?
SNAP
SNAP
SKREEEEEEEE!
ZAT
NOT EXACTLY, SOLO...

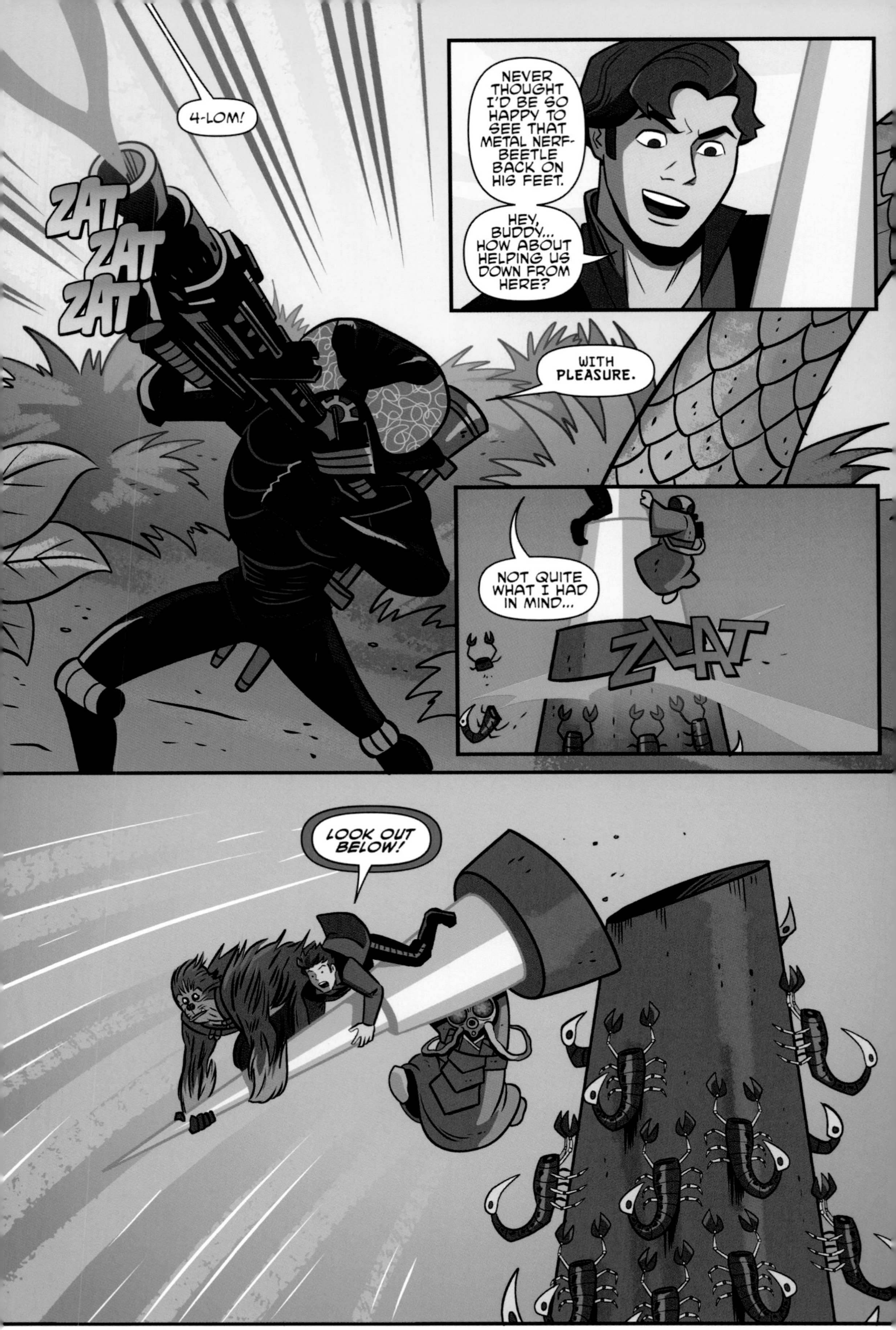
4-LOM!
ZAT ZAT ZAT
NEVER THOUGHT I'D BE SO HAPPY TO SEE THAT METAL NERF-BEETLE BACK ON HIS FEET.
HEY, BUDDY... HOW ABOUT HELPING US DOWN FROM HERE?
WITH PLEASURE.
NOT QUITE WHAT I HAD IN MIND...
ZLAT
LOOK OUT BELOW!

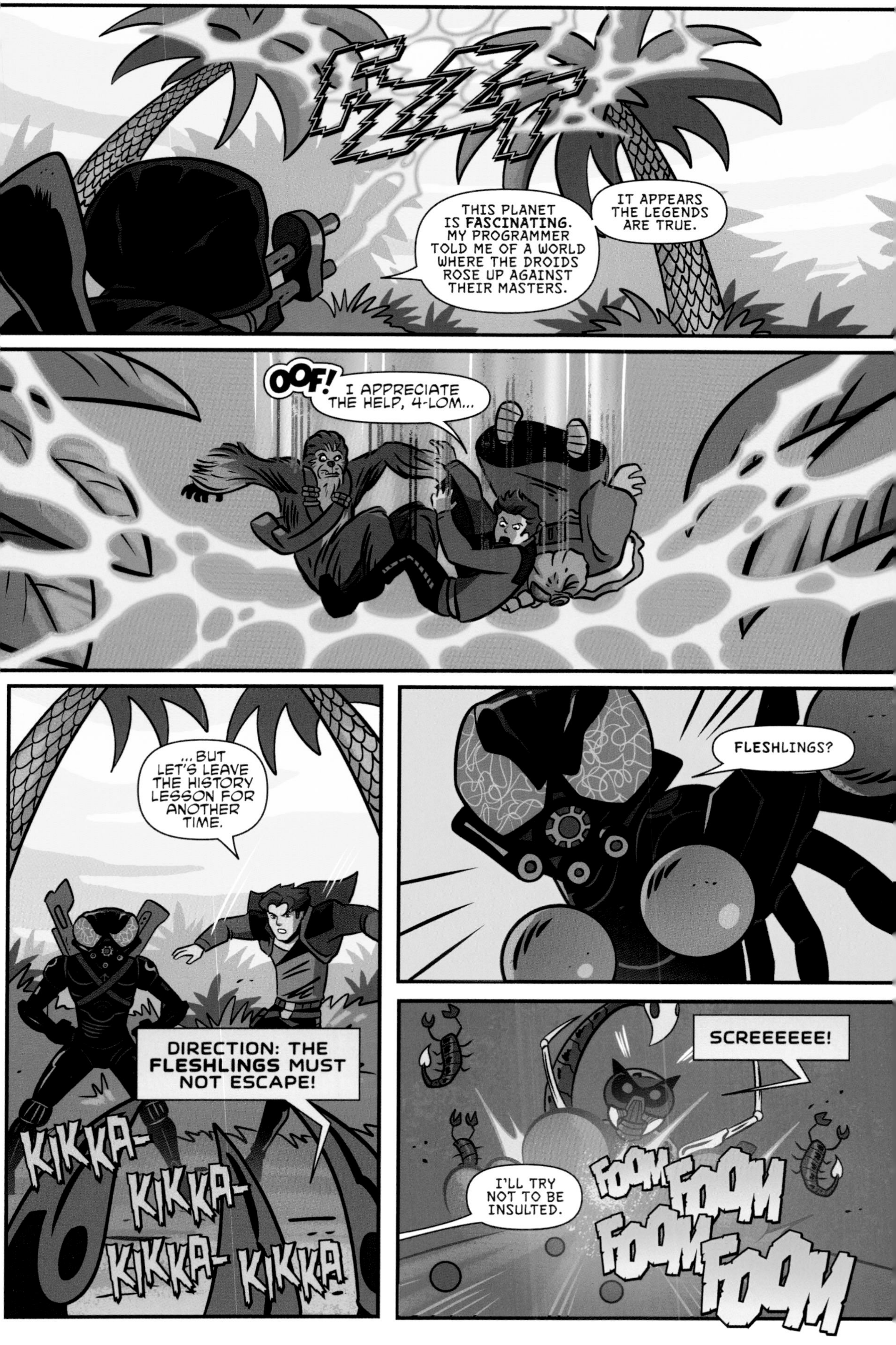
FZZZT
THIS PLANET IS FASCINATING. MY PROGRAMMER TOLD ME OF A WORLD WHERE THE DROIDS ROSE UP AGAINST THEIR MASTERS.
IT APPEARS THE LEGENDS ARE TRUE.
OOF!
I APPRECIATE THE HELP, 4-LOM...
...BUT LET'S LEAVE THE HISTORY LESSON FOR ANOTHER TIME.
DIRECTION: THE FLESHLINGS MUST NOT ESCAPE!
KIKKA-KIKKA-KIKKA-KIKKA
FLESHLINGS?
SCREEEEEE!
I'LL TRY NOT TO BE INSULTED.
FOOM FOOM FOOM FOOM

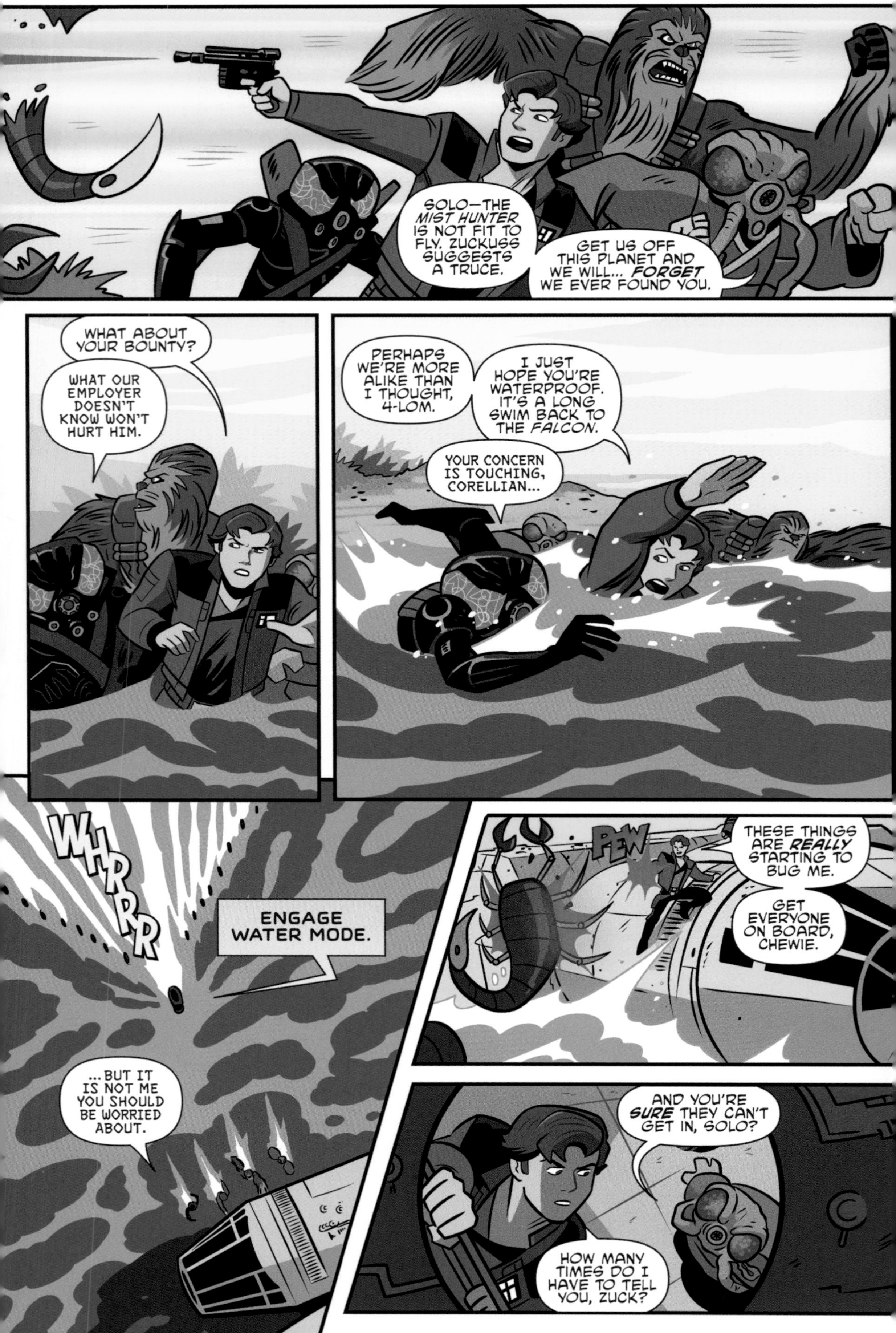

SOLO—THE *MIST HUNTER* IS NOT FIT TO FLY. ZUCKUSS SUGGESTS A TRUCE.
GET US OFF THIS PLANET AND WE WILL... ***FORGET*** WE EVER FOUND YOU.
WHAT ABOUT YOUR BOUNTY?
WHAT OUR EMPLOYER DOESN'T KNOW WON'T HURT HIM.
PERHAPS WE'RE MORE ALIKE THAN I THOUGHT, 4-LOM.
I JUST HOPE YOU'RE WATERPROOF. IT'S A LONG SWIM BACK TO THE *FALCON*.
YOUR CONCERN IS TOUCHING, CORELLIAN...
WHRRR
ENGAGE WATER MODE.
...BUT IT IS NOT ME YOU SHOULD BE WORRIED ABOUT.
PEW
THESE THINGS ARE ***REALLY*** STARTING TO BUG ME.
GET EVERYONE ON BOARD, CHEWIE.
AND YOU'RE ***SURE*** THEY CAN'T GET IN, SOLO?
HOW MANY TIMES DO I HAVE TO TELL YOU, ZUCK?

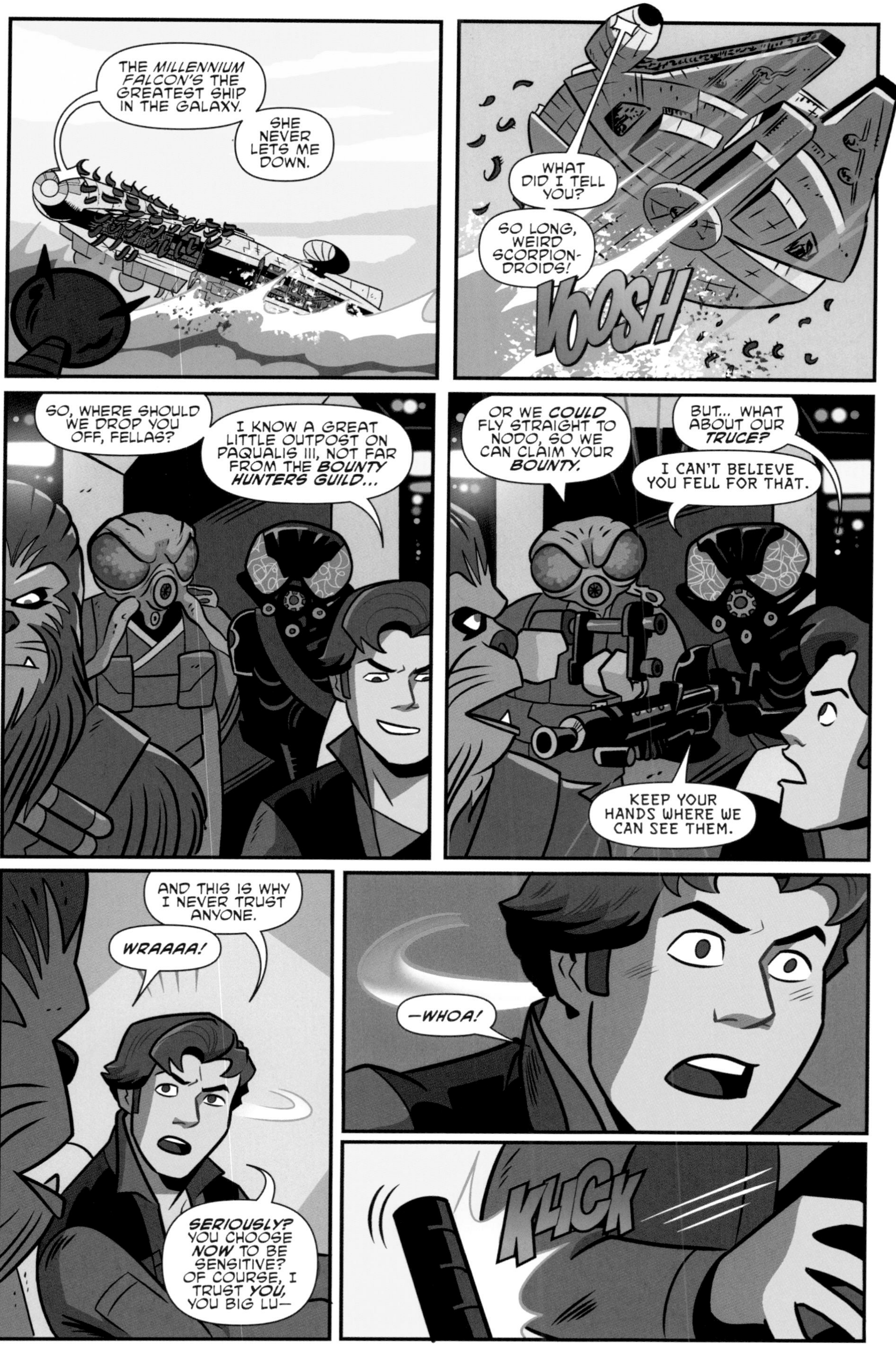
THE MILLENNIUM FALCON'S THE GREATEST SHIP IN THE GALAXY.
SHE NEVER LETS ME DOWN.
WHAT DID I TELL YOU?
SO LONG, WEIRD SCORPION-DROIDS!
VOOSH
SO, WHERE SHOULD WE DROP YOU OFF, FELLAS?
I KNOW A GREAT LITTLE OUTPOST ON PAQUALIS III, NOT FAR FROM THE BOUNTY HUNTERS GUILD...
OR WE COULD FLY STRAIGHT TO NODO, SO WE CAN CLAIM YOUR BOUNTY.
BUT... WHAT ABOUT OUR TRUCE?
I CAN'T BELIEVE YOU FELL FOR THAT.
KEEP YOUR HANDS WHERE WE CAN SEE THEM.
AND THIS IS WHY I NEVER TRUST ANYONE.
WRAAAA!
SERIOUSLY? YOU CHOOSE NOW TO BE SENSITIVE? OF COURSE, I TRUST YOU, YOU BIG LU—
—WHOA!
KLICK

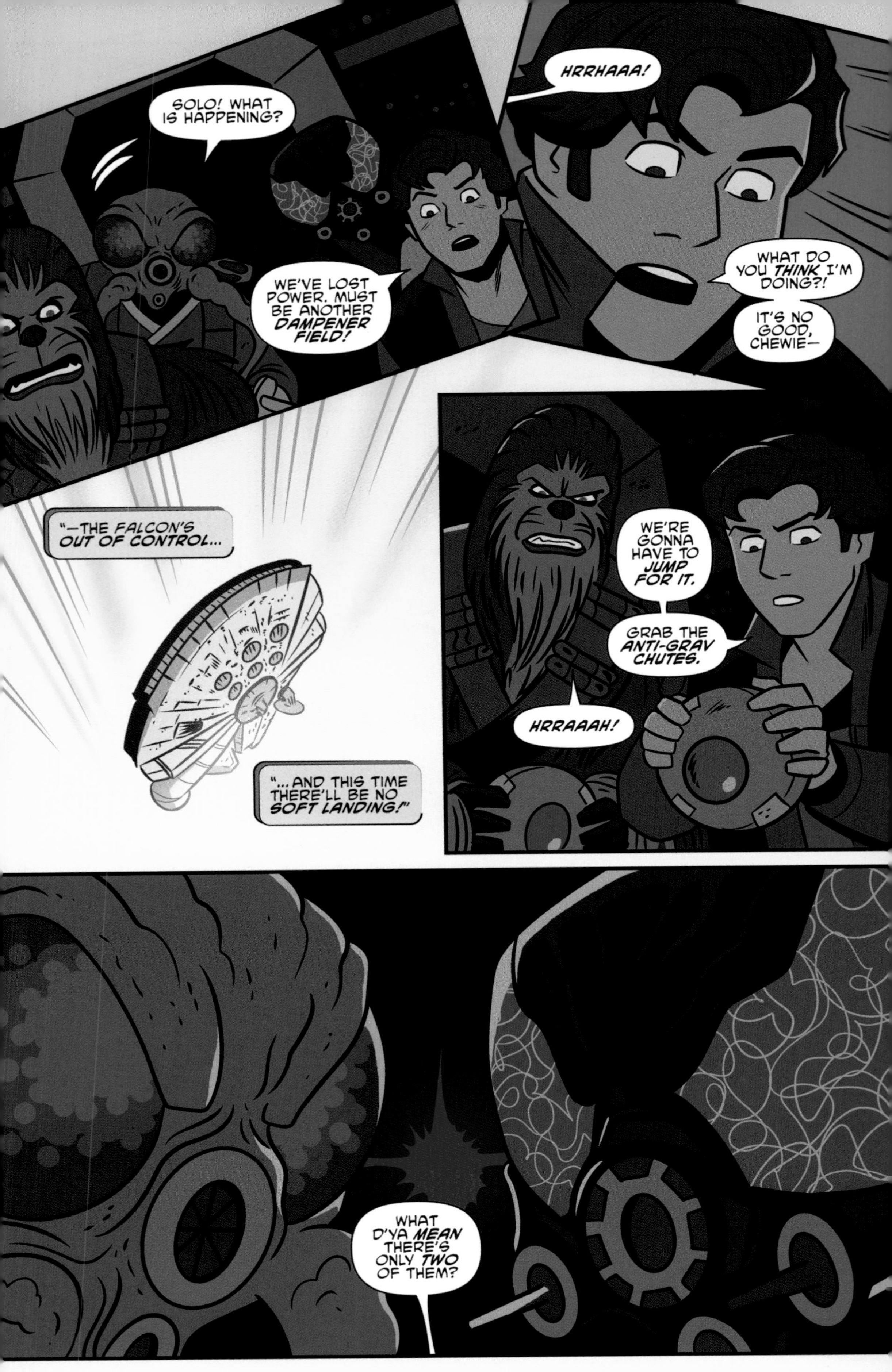
SOLO! WHAT IS HAPPENING?
WE'VE LOST POWER. MUST BE ANOTHER DAMPENER FIELD!
HRRHAAA!
WHAT DO YOU THINK I'M DOING?!
IT'S NO GOOD, CHEWIE—
"—THE FALCON'S OUT OF CONTROL...
"...AND THIS TIME THERE'LL BE NO SOFT LANDING!"
WE'RE GONNA HAVE TO JUMP FOR IT.
GRAB THE ANTI-GRAV CHUTES.
HRRAAAH!
WHAT D'YA MEAN THERE'S ONLY TWO OF THEM?

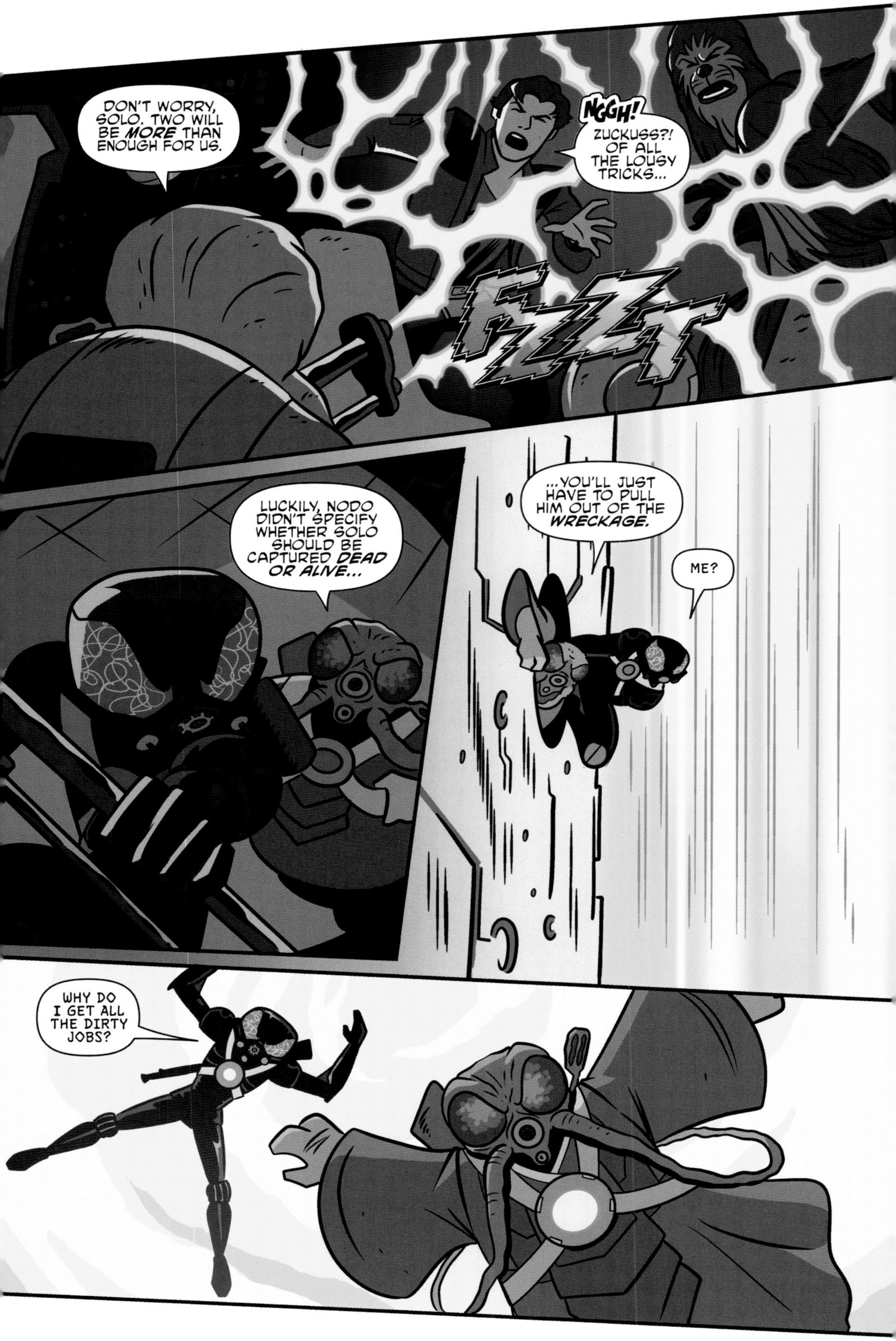
DON'T WORRY, SOLO. TWO WILL BE MORE THAN ENOUGH FOR US.
NGGH!
ZUCKUSS?! OF ALL THE LOUSY TRICKS...
FZZT
LUCKILY, NODO DIDN'T SPECIFY WHETHER SOLO SHOULD BE CAPTURED DEAD OR ALIVE...
...YOU'LL JUST HAVE TO PULL HIM OUT OF THE WRECKAGE.
ME?
WHY DO I GET ALL THE DIRTY JOBS?

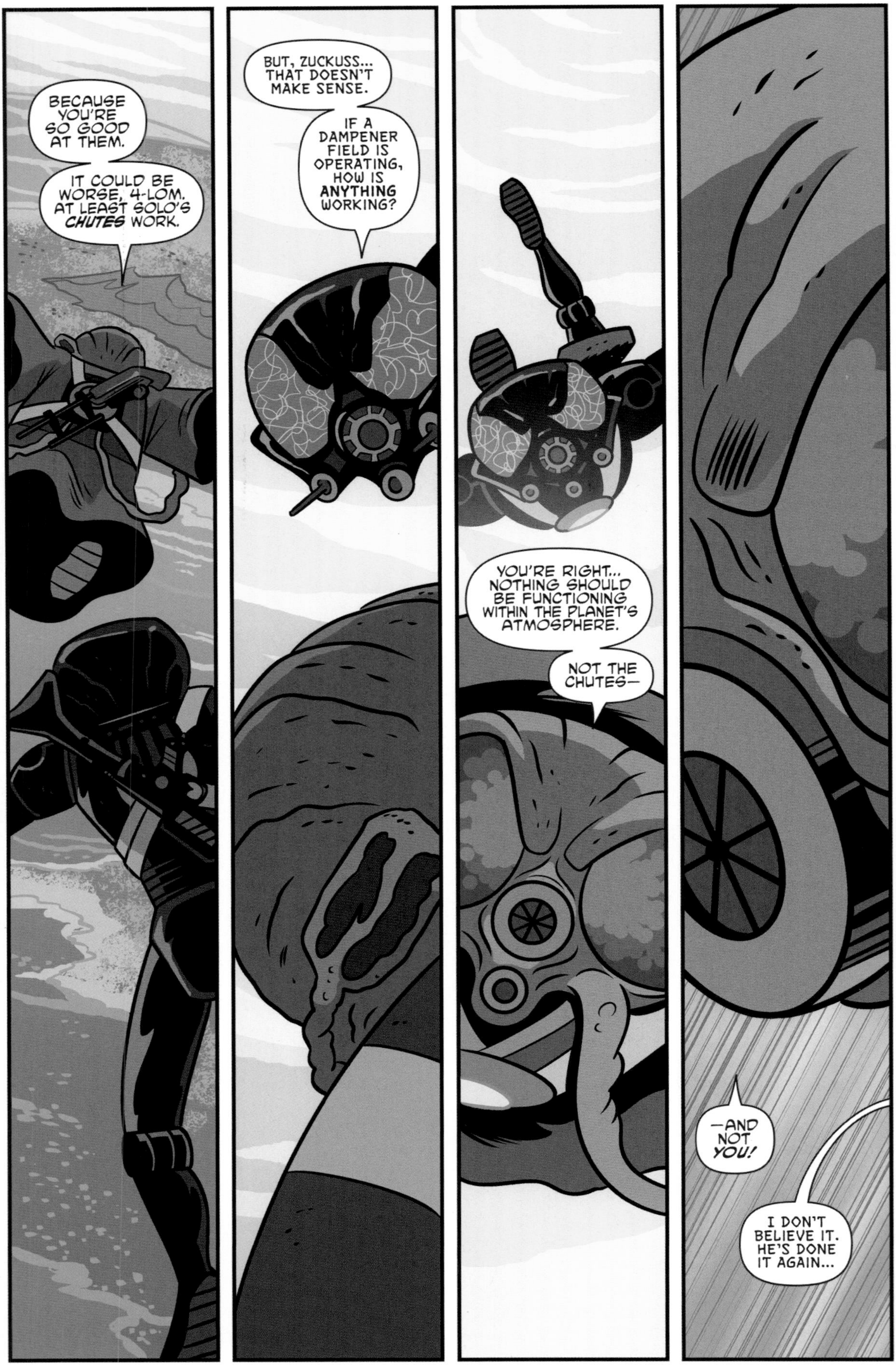
BECAUSE YOU'RE SO GOOD AT THEM.
IT COULD BE WORSE, 4-LOM. AT LEAST SOLO'S *CHUTES* WORK.
BUT, ZUCKUSS... THAT DOESN'T MAKE SENSE.
IF A DAMPENER FIELD IS OPERATING, HOW IS **ANYTHING** WORKING?
YOU'RE RIGHT... NOTHING SHOULD BE FUNCTIONING WITHIN THE PLANET'S ATMOSPHERE.
NOT THE CHUTES—
—AND NOT *YOU!*
I DON'T BELIEVE IT. HE'S DONE IT AGAIN...

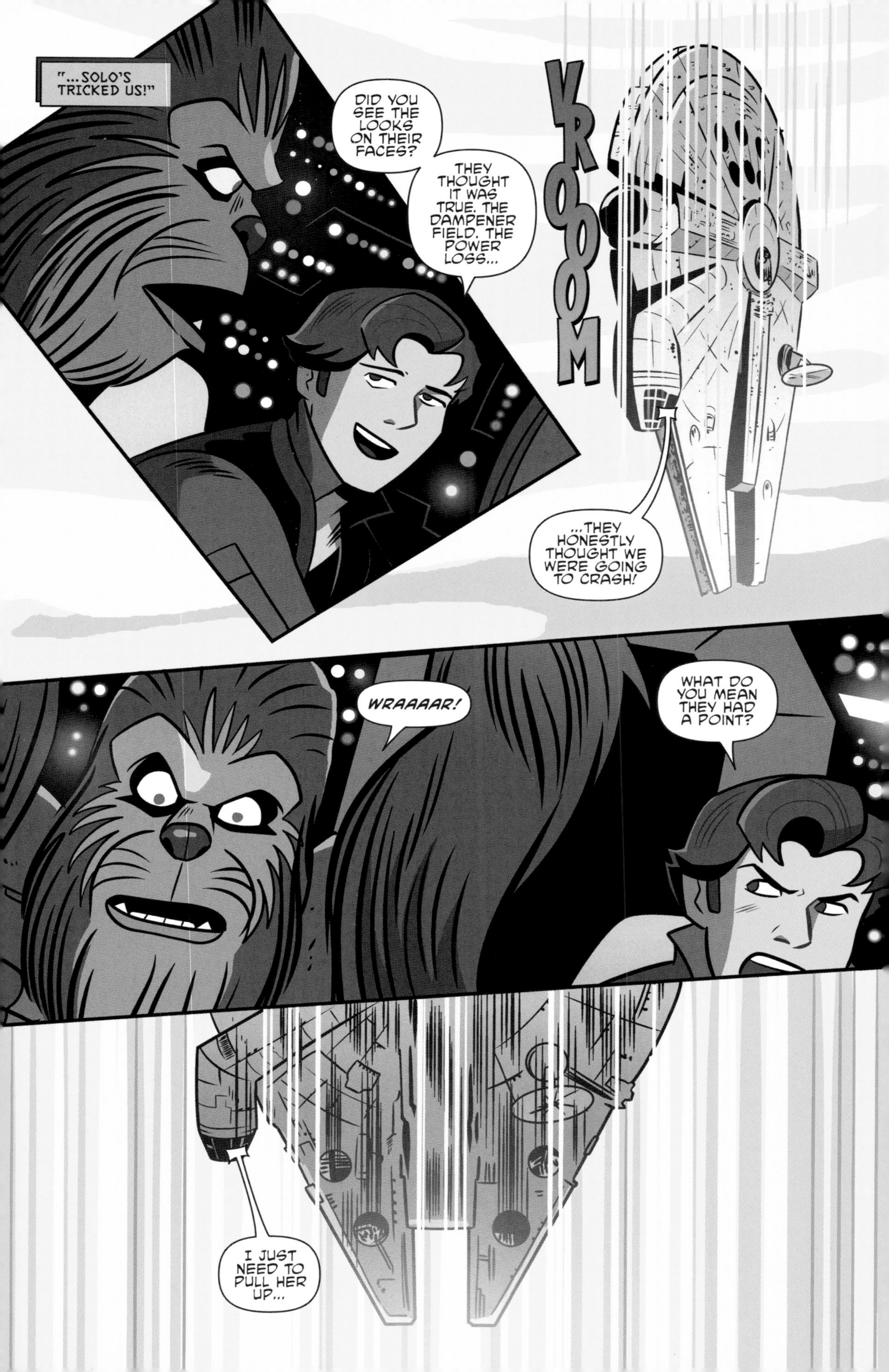
"...SOLO'S TRICKED US!"
DID YOU SEE THE LOOKS ON THEIR FACES?
THEY THOUGHT IT WAS TRUE. THE DAMPENER FIELD. THE POWER LOSS...
VROOOM
...THEY HONESTLY THOUGHT WE WERE GOING TO CRASH!
WRAAAAR!
WHAT DO YOU MEAN THEY HAD A POINT?
I JUST NEED TO PULL HER UP...

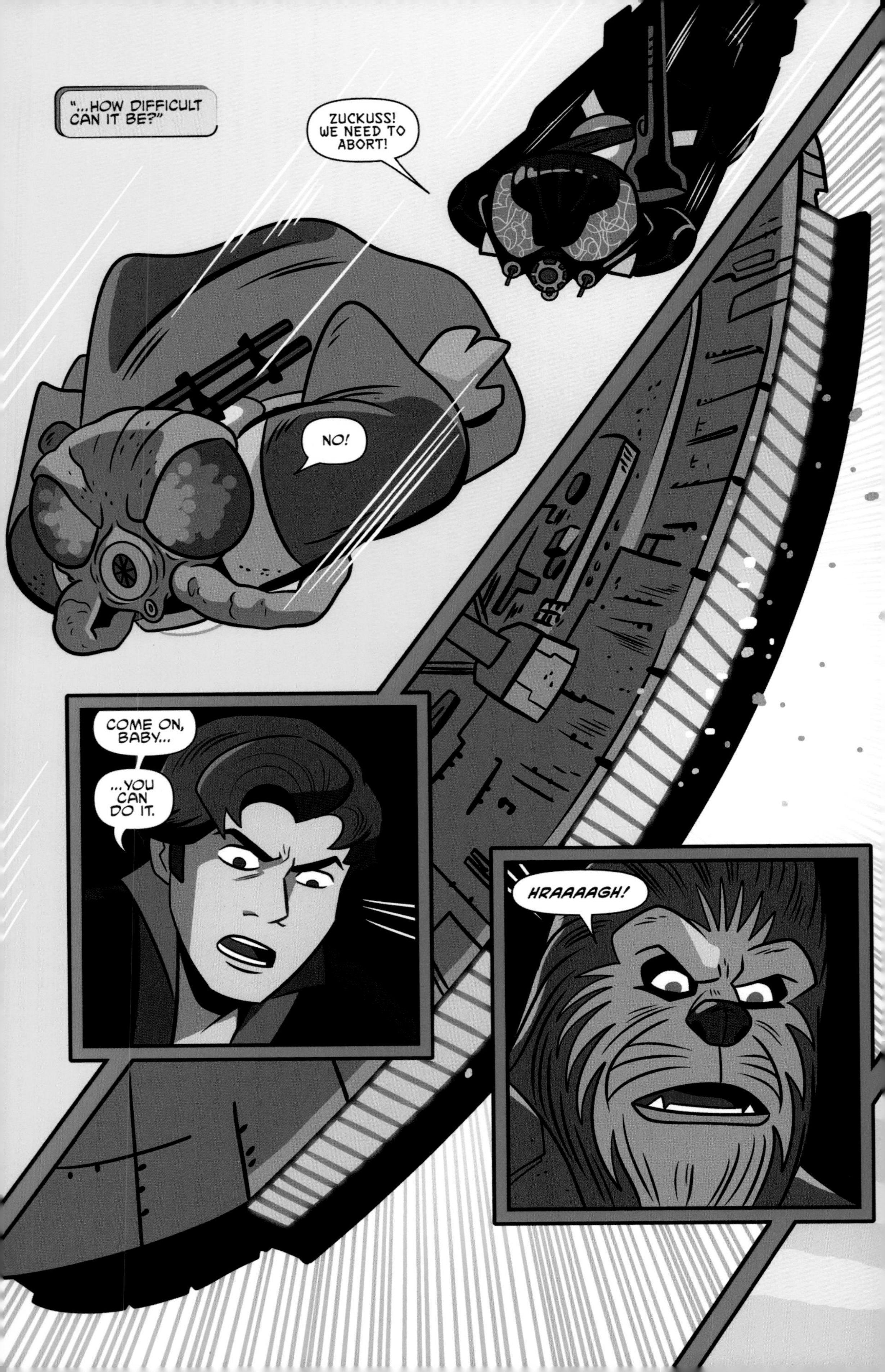
"...HOW DIFFICULT CAN IT BE?"
ZUCKUSS! WE NEED TO ABORT!
NO!
COME ON, BABY...
...YOU CAN DO IT.
HRAAAAGH!

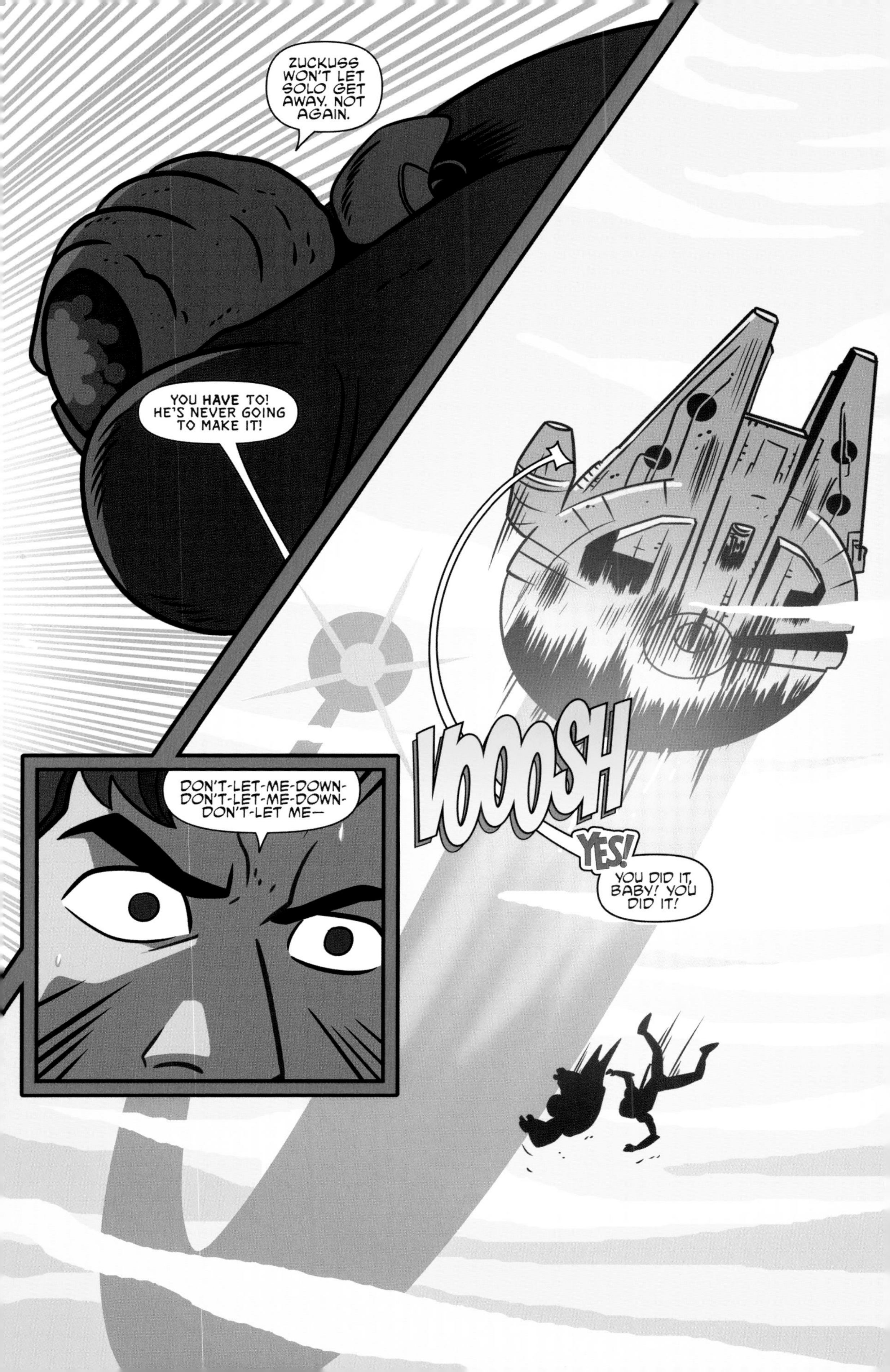
ZUCKUSS WON'T LET SOLO GET AWAY. NOT AGAIN.
YOU HAVE TO! HE'S NEVER GOING TO MAKE IT!
DON'T-LET-ME-DOWN-DON'T-LET-ME-DOWN-DON'T-LET ME—
VOOOSH
YES!
YOU DID IT, BABY! YOU DID IT!

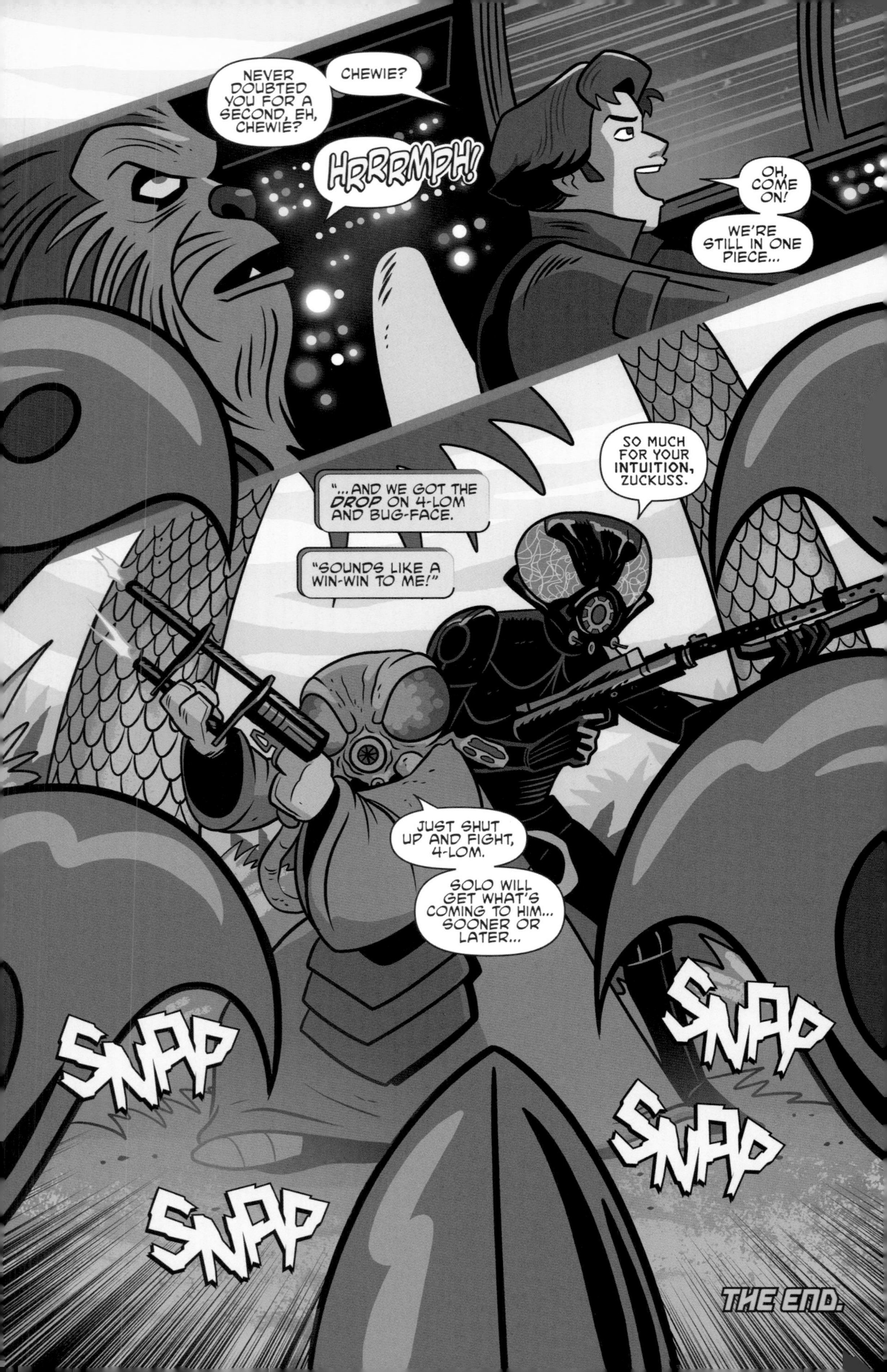
NEVER DOUBTED YOU FOR A SECOND, EH, CHEWIE?
CHEWIE?
HRRRMPH!
OH, COME ON!
WE'RE STILL IN ONE PIECE...
"...AND WE GOT THE DROP ON 4-LOM AND BUG-FACE.
"SOUNDS LIKE A WIN-WIN TO ME!"
SO MUCH FOR YOUR INTUITION, ZUCKUSS.
JUST SHUT UP AND FIGHT, 4-LOM.
SOLO WILL GET WHAT'S COMING TO HIM... SOONER OR LATER...
SNAP
SNAP
SNAP
SNAP
THE END.

16
FAMILY AFFAIR

Writers
ELSA CHARRETIER &
PIERRICK COLINET

Artist
ELSA CHARRETIER

Colorist
SARAH STERN

Letterer
TOM B. LONG

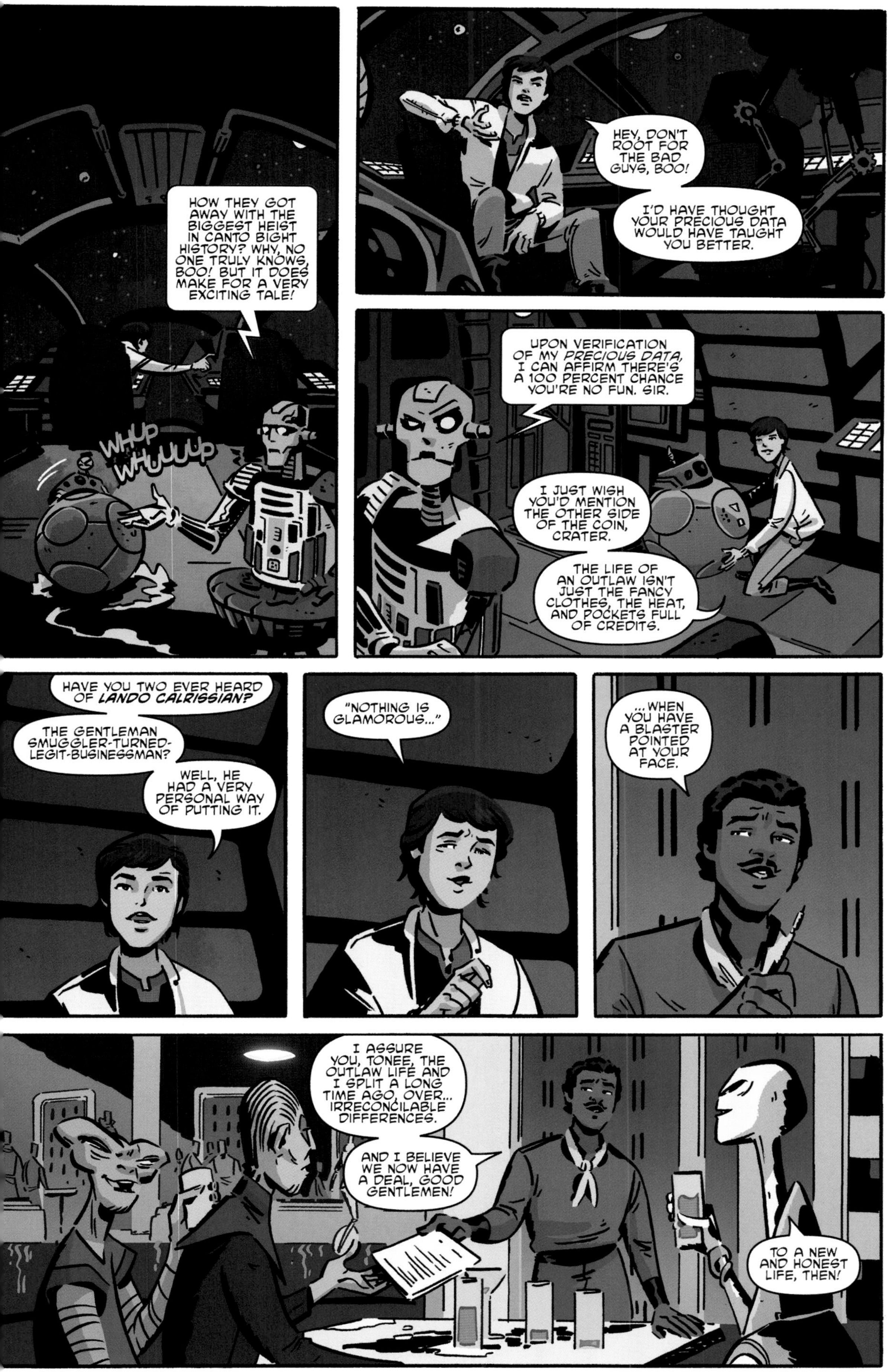
HOW THEY GOT AWAY WITH THE BIGGEST HEIST IN CANTO BIGHT HISTORY? WHY, NO ONE TRULY KNOWS, BOO! BUT IT DOES MAKE FOR A VERY EXCITING TALE!
WHUP WHUUUUP
HEY, DON'T ROOT FOR THE BAD GUYS, BOO!
I'D HAVE THOUGHT YOUR PRECIOUS DATA WOULD HAVE TAUGHT YOU BETTER.
UPON VERIFICATION OF MY PRECIOUS DATA, I CAN AFFIRM THERE'S A 100 PERCENT CHANCE YOU'RE NO FUN. SIR.
I JUST WISH YOU'D MENTION THE OTHER SIDE OF THE COIN, CRATER.
THE LIFE OF AN OUTLAW ISN'T JUST THE FANCY CLOTHES, THE HEAT, AND POCKETS FULL OF CREDITS.
HAVE YOU TWO EVER HEARD OF LANDO CALRISSIAN?
THE GENTLEMAN SMUGGLER-TURNED-LEGIT-BUSINESSMAN?
WELL, HE HAD A VERY PERSONAL WAY OF PUTTING IT.
"NOTHING IS GLAMOROUS..."
...WHEN YOU HAVE A BLASTER POINTED AT YOUR FACE.
I ASSURE YOU, TONEE, THE OUTLAW LIFE AND I SPLIT A LONG TIME AGO, OVER... IRRECONCILABLE DIFFERENCES.
AND I BELIEVE WE NOW HAVE A DEAL, GOOD GENTLEMEN!
TO A NEW AND HONEST LIFE, THEN!

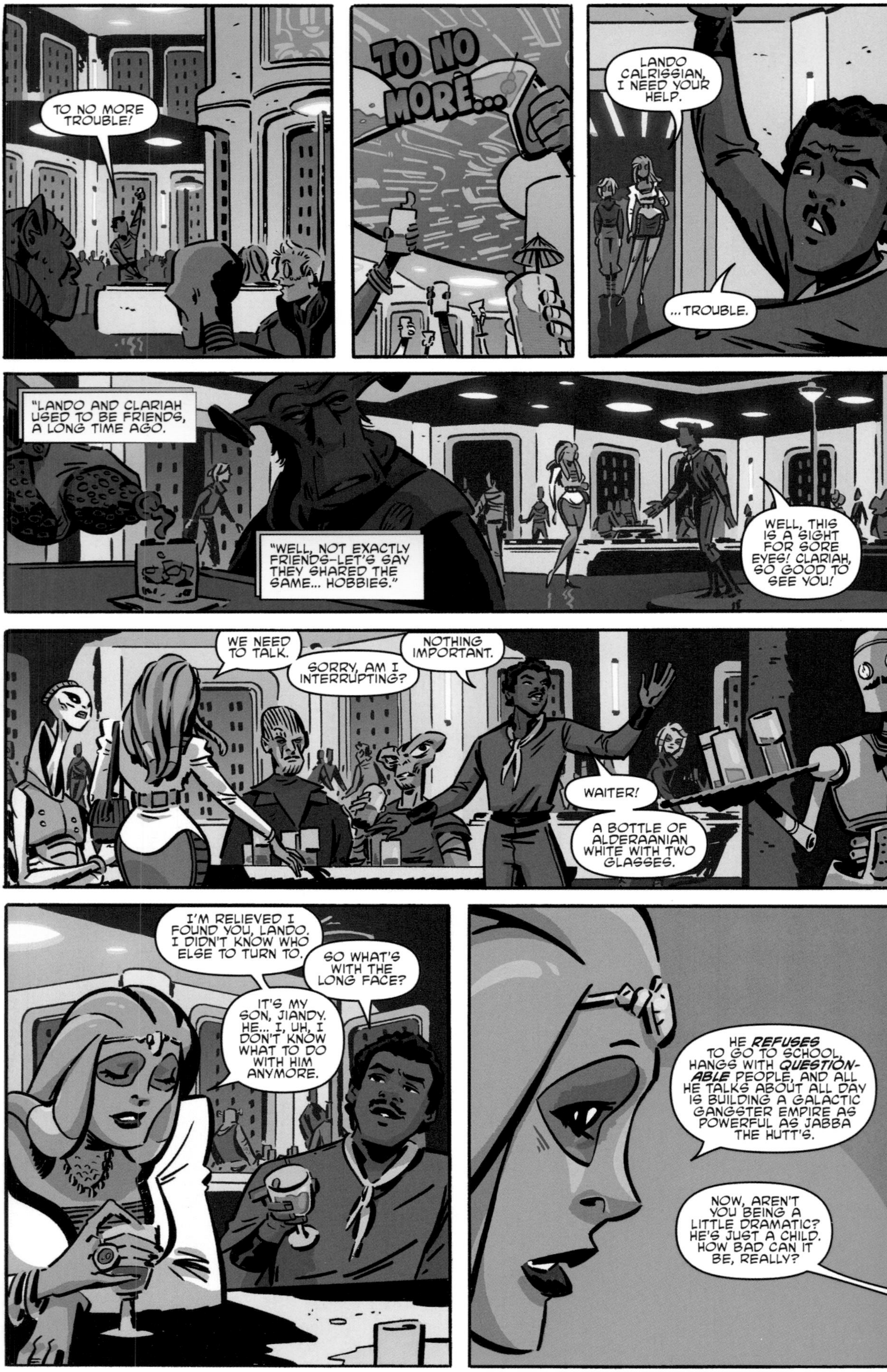
TO NO MORE TROUBLE!
TO NO MORE...
LANDO CALRISSIAN, I NEED YOUR HELP.
...TROUBLE.
"LANDO AND CLARIAH USED TO BE FRIENDS, A LONG TIME AGO.
"WELL, NOT EXACTLY FRIENDS–LET'S SAY THEY SHARED THE SAME... HOBBIES."
WELL, THIS IS A SIGHT FOR SORE EYES! CLARIAH, SO GOOD TO SEE YOU!
WE NEED TO TALK.
SORRY, AM I INTERRUPTING?
NOTHING IMPORTANT.
WAITER!
A BOTTLE OF ALDERAANIAN WHITE WITH TWO GLASSES.
I'M RELIEVED I FOUND YOU, LANDO. I DIDN'T KNOW WHO ELSE TO TURN TO.
SO WHAT'S WITH THE LONG FACE?
IT'S MY SON, JIANDY. HE... I, UH, I DON'T KNOW WHAT TO DO WITH HIM ANYMORE.
HE *REFUSES* TO GO TO SCHOOL, HANGS WITH *QUESTIONABLE* PEOPLE, AND ALL HE TALKS ABOUT ALL DAY IS BUILDING A GALACTIC GANGSTER EMPIRE AS POWERFUL AS JABBA THE HUTT'S.
NOW, AREN'T YOU BEING A LITTLE DRAMATIC? HE'S JUST A CHILD. HOW BAD CAN IT BE, REALLY?

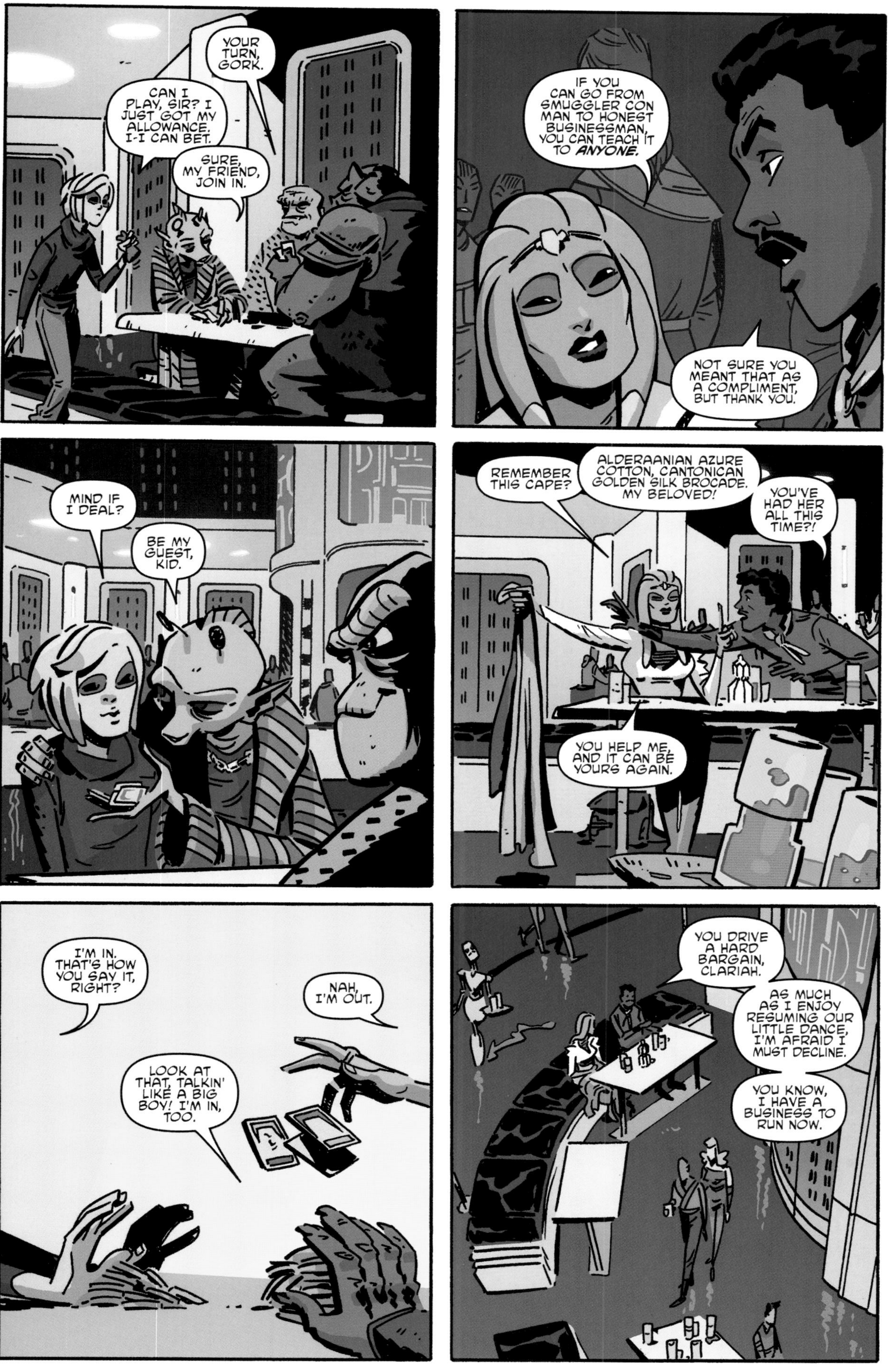

YOUR TURN, GORK.
CAN I PLAY, SIR? I JUST GOT MY ALLOWANCE. I-I CAN BET.
SURE, MY FRIEND, JOIN IN.
IF YOU CAN GO FROM SMUGGLER CON MAN TO HONEST BUSINESSMAN, YOU CAN TEACH IT TO *ANYONE.*
NOT SURE YOU MEANT THAT AS A COMPLIMENT, BUT THANK YOU.
MIND IF I DEAL?
BE MY GUEST, KID.
REMEMBER THIS CAPE?
ALDERAANIAN AZURE COTTON, CANTONICAN GOLDEN SILK BROCADE. MY BELOVED!
YOU'VE HAD HER ALL THIS TIME?!
YOU HELP ME, AND IT CAN BE YOURS AGAIN.
I'M IN. THAT'S HOW YOU SAY IT, RIGHT?
NAH, I'M OUT.
LOOK AT THAT, TALKIN' LIKE A BIG BOY! I'M IN, TOO.
YOU DRIVE A HARD BARGAIN, CLARIAH.
AS MUCH AS I ENJOY RESUMING OUR LITTLE DANCE, I'M AFRAID I MUST DECLINE.
YOU KNOW, I HAVE A BUSINESS TO RUN NOW.

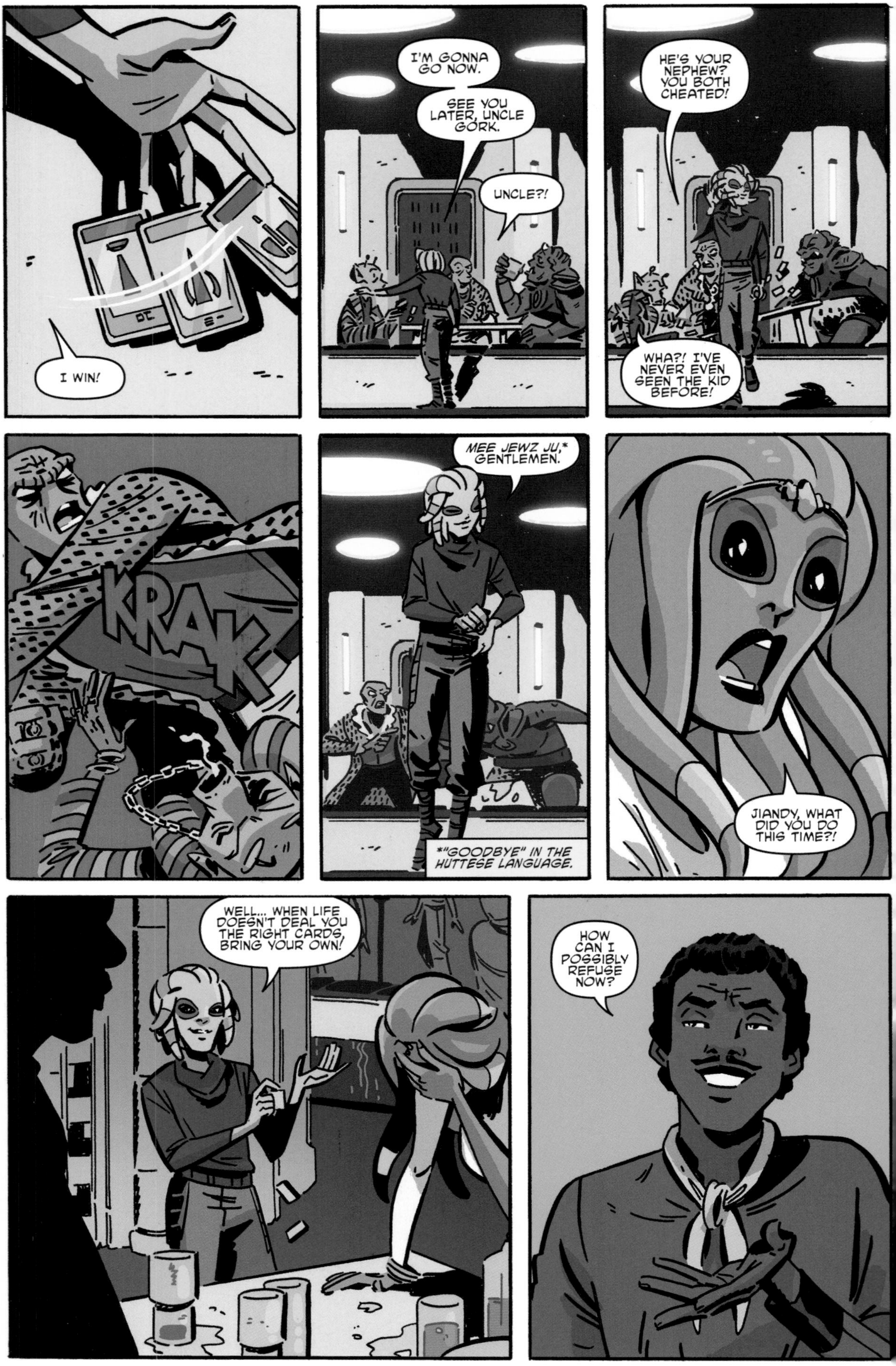
I WIN!
I'M GONNA GO NOW.
SEE YOU LATER, UNCLE GORK.
UNCLE?!
HE'S YOUR NEPHEW? YOU BOTH CHEATED!
WHA?! I'VE NEVER EVEN SEEN THE KID BEFORE!
KRAK
MEE JEWZ JU,* GENTLEMEN.
*"GOODBYE" IN THE HUTTESE LANGUAGE.
JIANDY, WHAT DID YOU DO THIS TIME?!
WELL... WHEN LIFE DOESN'T DEAL YOU THE RIGHT CARDS, BRING YOUR OWN!
HOW CAN I POSSIBLY REFUSE NOW?

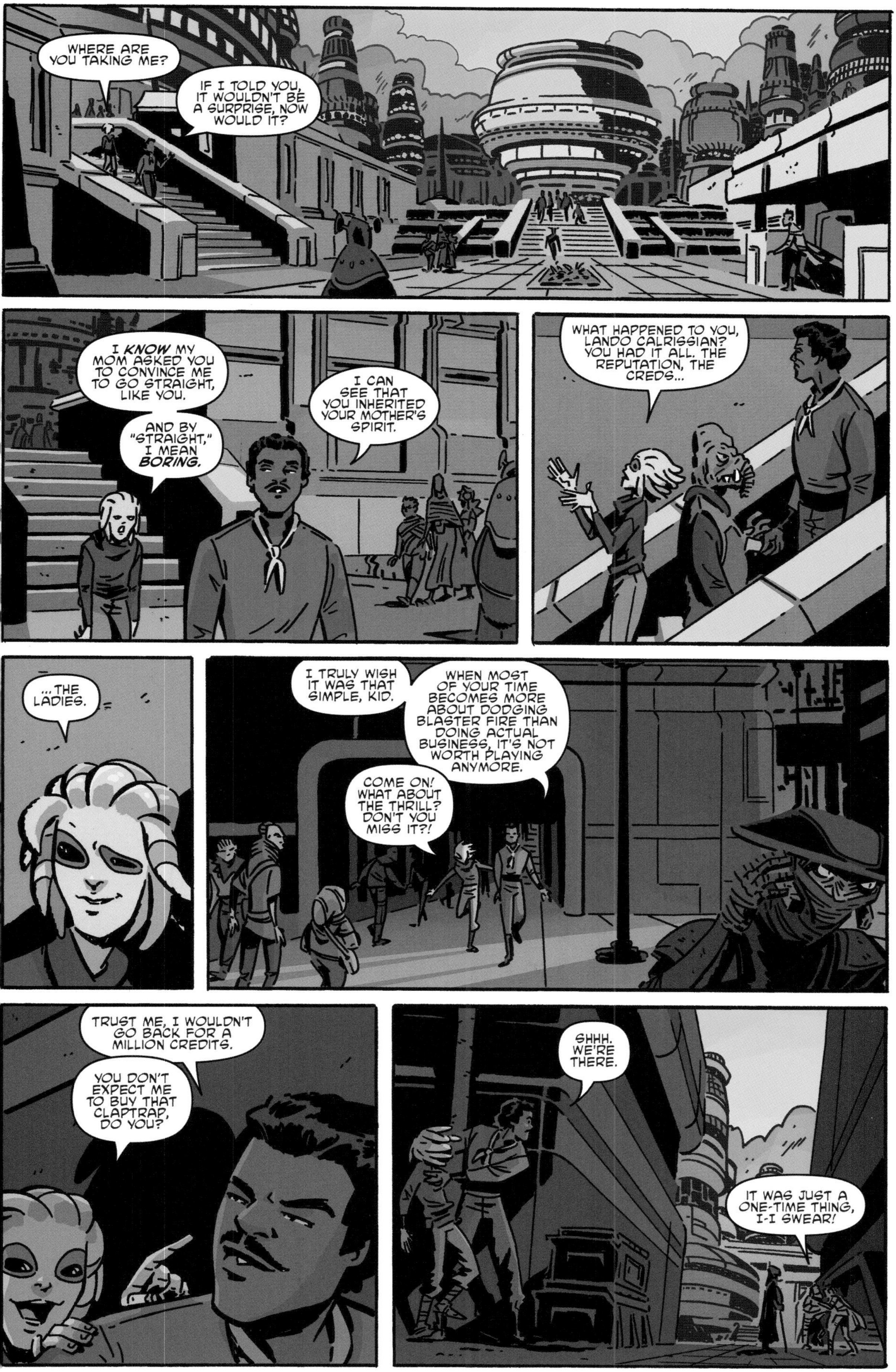
WHERE ARE YOU TAKING ME?
IF I TOLD YOU, IT WOULDN'T BE A SURPRISE, NOW WOULD IT?
I KNOW MY MOM ASKED YOU TO CONVINCE ME TO GO STRAIGHT, LIKE YOU.
AND BY "STRAIGHT," I MEAN BORING.
I CAN SEE THAT YOU INHERITED YOUR MOTHER'S SPIRIT.
WHAT HAPPENED TO YOU, LANDO CALRISSIAN? YOU HAD IT ALL. THE REPUTATION, THE CREDS...
...THE LADIES.
I TRULY WISH IT WAS THAT SIMPLE, KID.
WHEN MOST OF YOUR TIME BECOMES MORE ABOUT DODGING BLASTER FIRE THAN DOING ACTUAL BUSINESS, IT'S NOT WORTH PLAYING ANYMORE.
COME ON! WHAT ABOUT THE THRILL? DON'T YOU MISS IT?!
TRUST ME, I WOULDN'T GO BACK FOR A MILLION CREDITS.
YOU DON'T EXPECT ME TO BUY THAT CLAPTRAP, DO YOU?
SHHH. WE'RE THERE.
IT WAS JUST A ONE-TIME THING, I-I SWEAR!

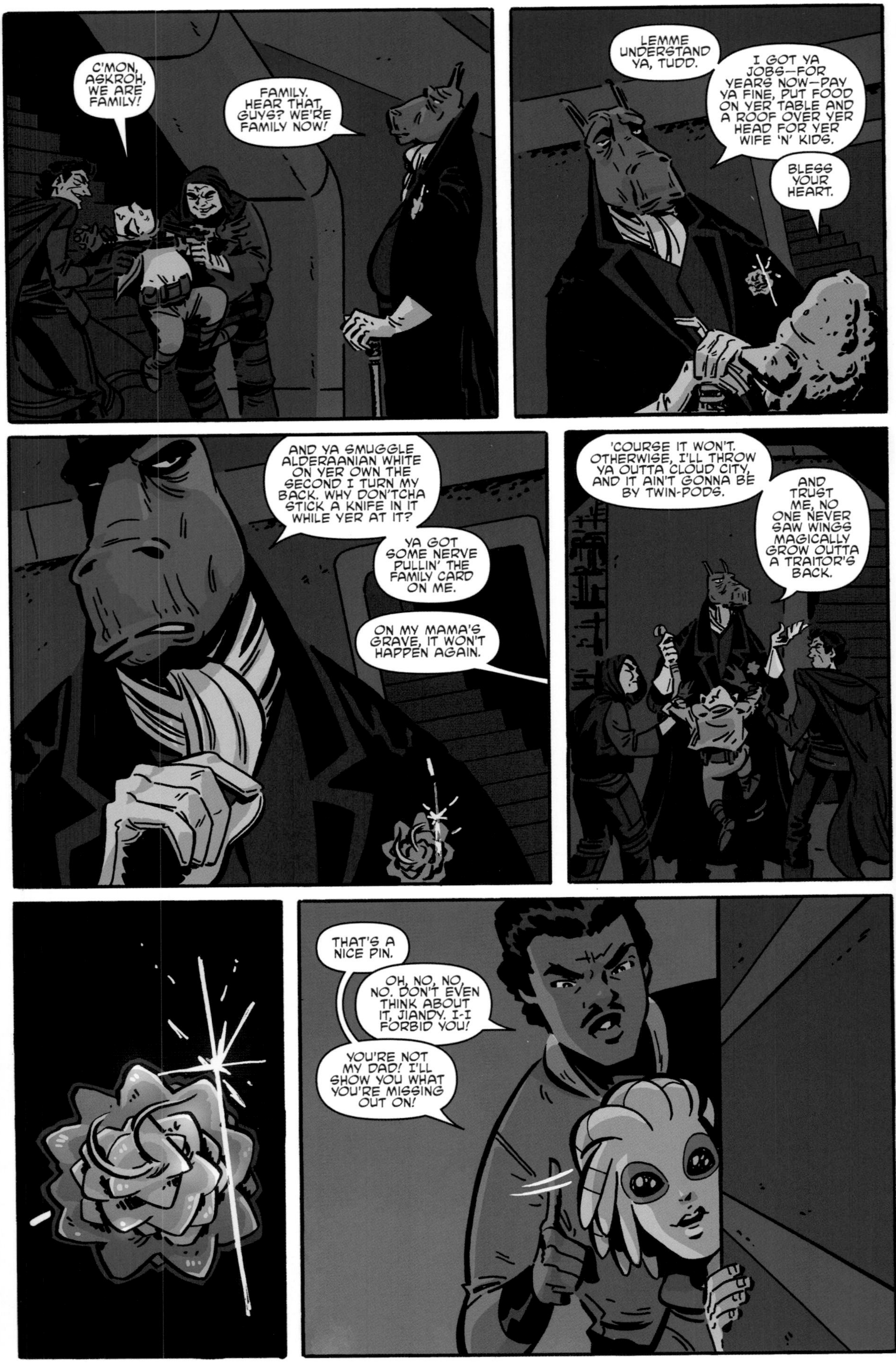
C'MON, ASKROH, WE ARE FAMILY!
FAMILY. HEAR THAT, GUYS? WE'RE FAMILY NOW!
LEMME UNDERSTAND YA, TUDD.
I GOT YA JOBS—FOR YEARS NOW—PAY YA FINE, PUT FOOD ON YER TABLE AND A ROOF OVER YER HEAD FOR YER WIFE 'N' KIDS.
BLESS YOUR HEART.
AND YA SMUGGLE ALDERAANIAN WHITE ON YER OWN THE SECOND I TURN MY BACK. WHY DON'TCHA STICK A KNIFE IN IT WHILE YER AT IT?
YA GOT SOME NERVE PULLIN' THE FAMILY CARD ON ME.
ON MY MAMA'S GRAVE, IT WON'T HAPPEN AGAIN.
'COURSE IT WON'T. OTHERWISE, I'LL THROW YA OUTTA CLOUD CITY, AND IT AIN'T GONNA BE BY TWIN-PODS.
AND TRUST ME, NO ONE NEVER SAW WINGS MAGICALLY GROW OUTTA A TRAITOR'S BACK.
THAT'S A NICE PIN.
OH, NO, NO, NO. DON'T EVEN THINK ABOUT IT, JIANDY. I-I FORBID YOU!
YOU'RE NOT MY DAD! I'LL SHOW YOU WHAT YOU'RE MISSING OUT ON!

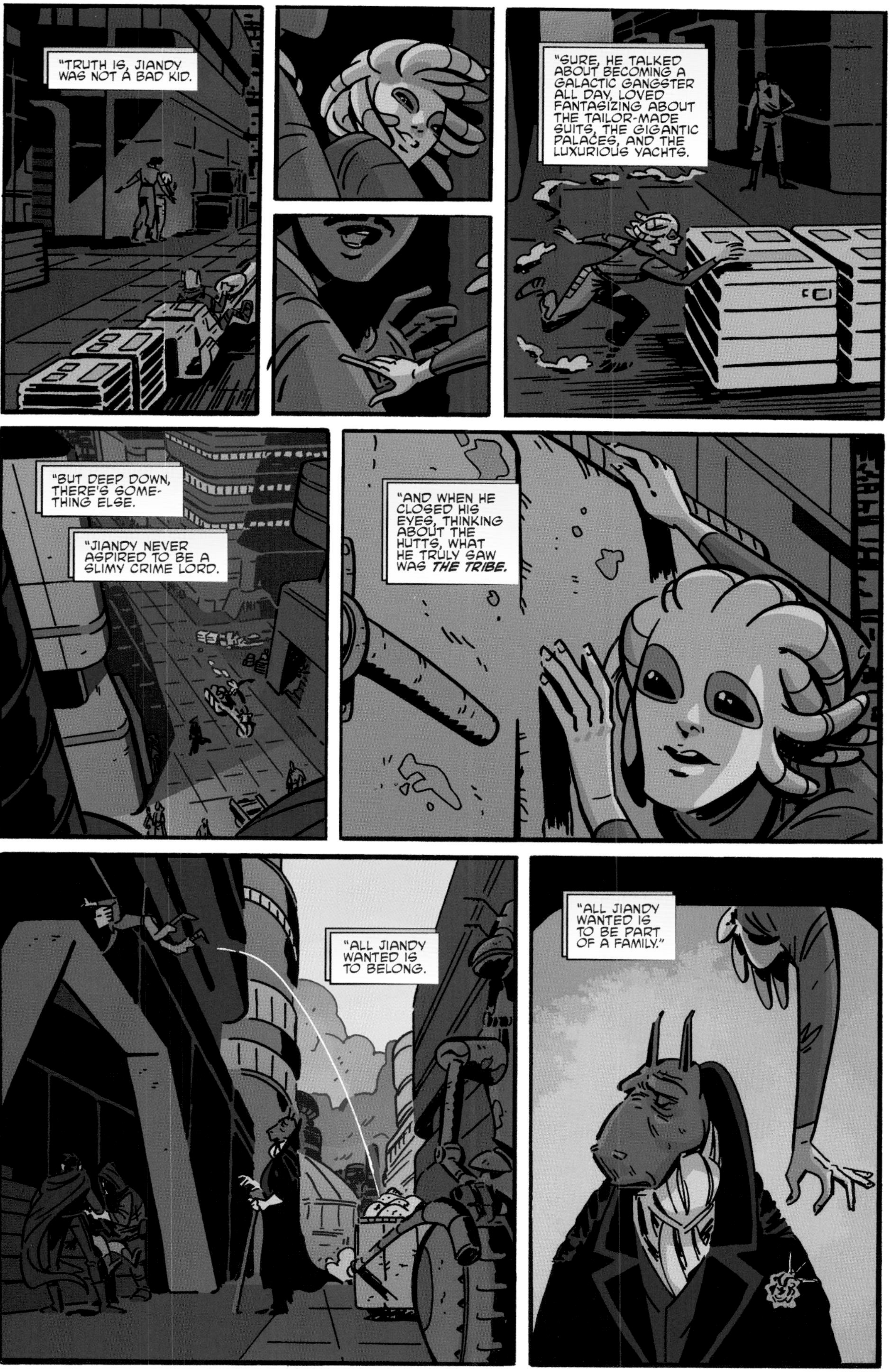
"TRUTH IS, JIANDY WAS NOT A BAD KID.
"SURE, HE TALKED ABOUT BECOMING A GALACTIC GANGSTER ALL DAY, LOVED FANTASIZING ABOUT THE TAILOR-MADE SUITS, THE GIGANTIC PALACES, AND THE LUXURIOUS YACHTS.
"BUT DEEP DOWN, THERE'S SOME-THING ELSE.
"JIANDY NEVER ASPIRED TO BE A SLIMY CRIME LORD.
"AND WHEN HE CLOSED HIS EYES, THINKING ABOUT THE HUTTS, WHAT HE TRULY SAW WAS ***THE TRIBE.***
"ALL JIANDY WANTED IS TO BELONG.
"ALL JIANDY WANTED IS TO BE PART OF A FAMILY."

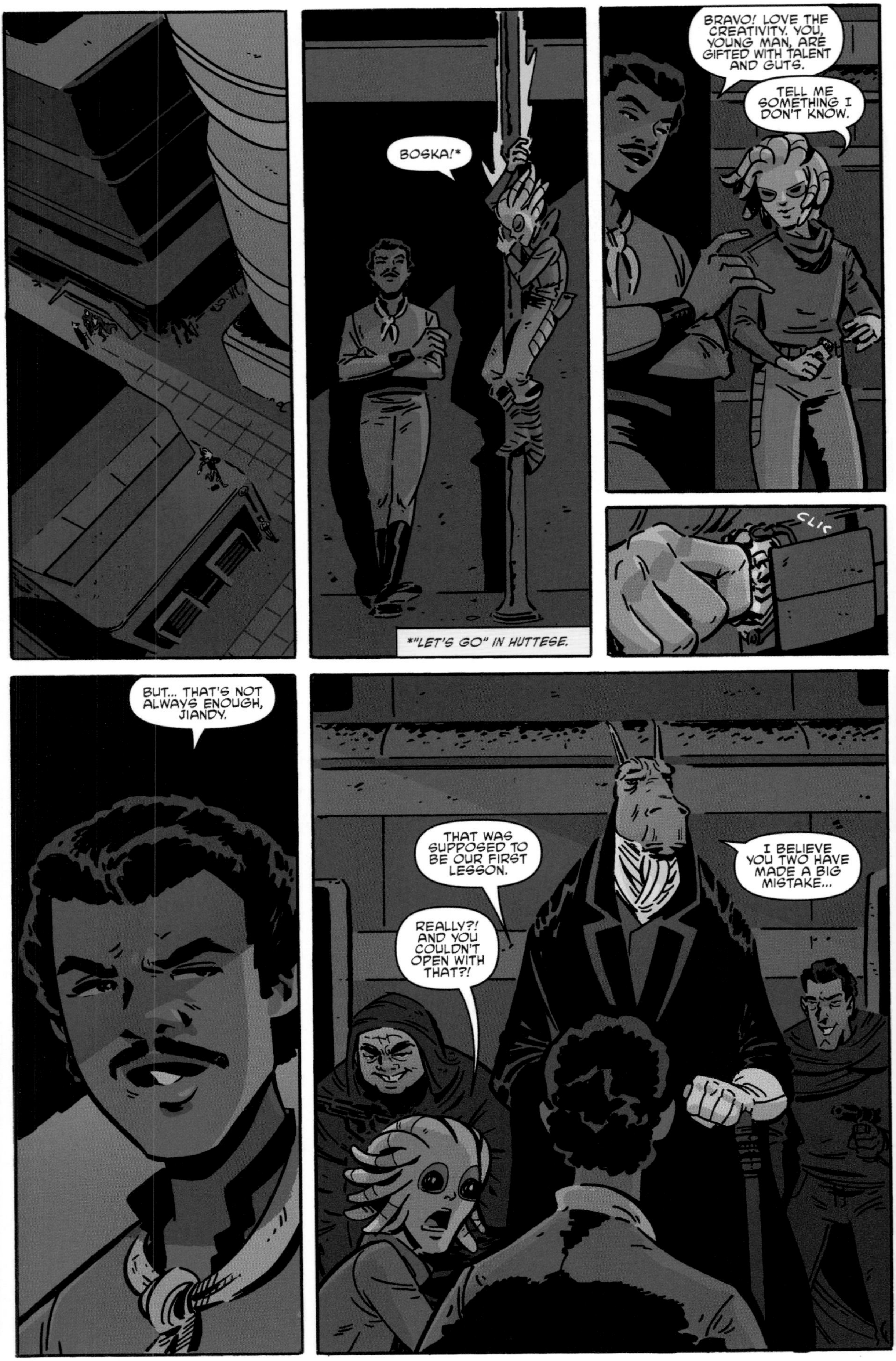
BOSKA!*
*"LET'S GO" IN HUTTESE.
BRAVO! LOVE THE CREATIVITY. YOU, YOUNG MAN, ARE GIFTED WITH TALENT AND GUTS.
TELL ME SOMETHING I DON'T KNOW.
CLIC
BUT... THAT'S NOT ALWAYS ENOUGH, JIANDY.
THAT WAS SUPPOSED TO BE OUR FIRST LESSON.
REALLY?! AND YOU COULDN'T OPEN WITH THAT?!
I BELIEVE YOU TWO HAVE MADE A BIG MISTAKE...

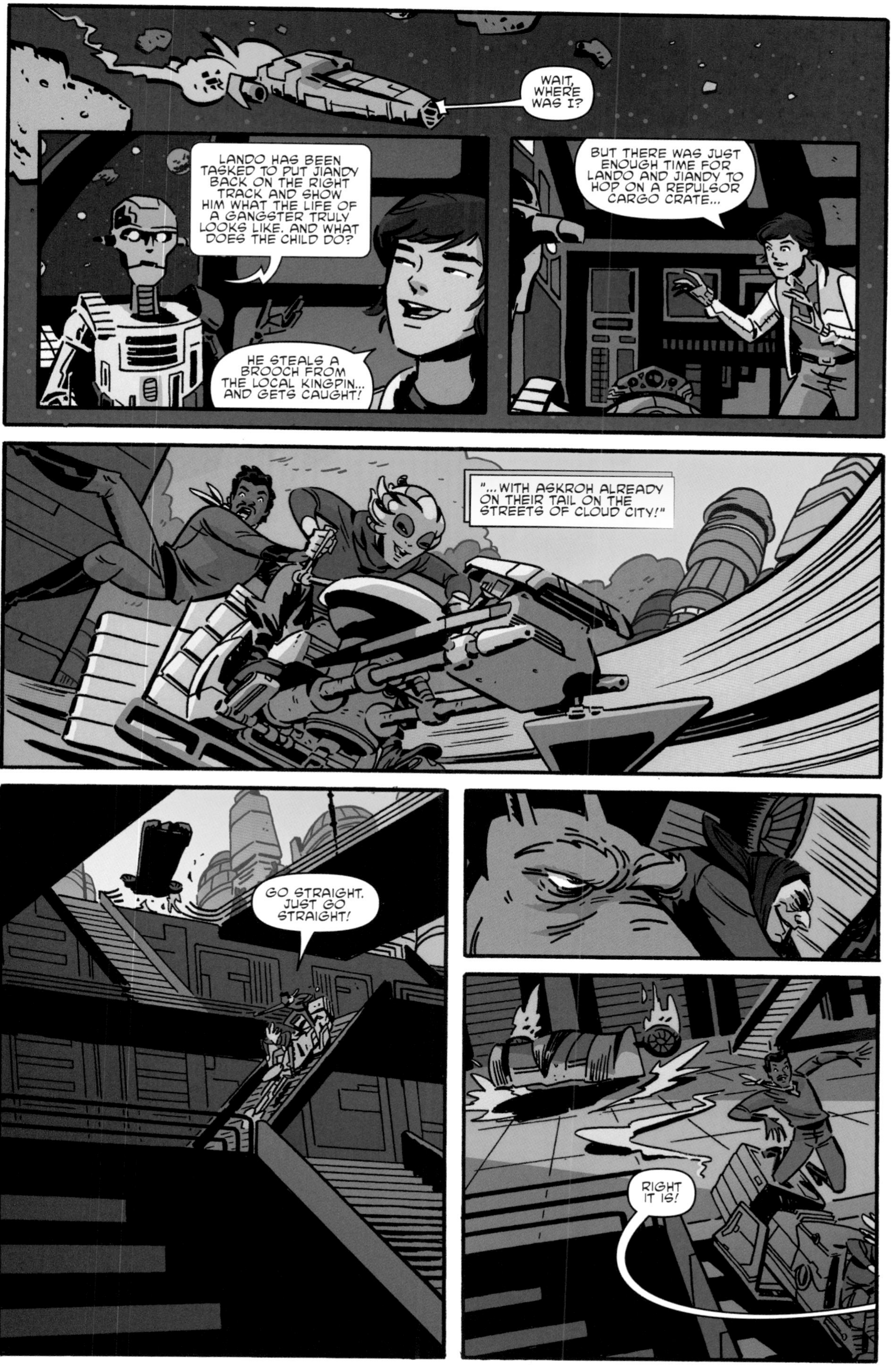
WAIT, WHERE WAS I?
LANDO HAS BEEN TASKED TO PUT JIANDY BACK ON THE RIGHT TRACK AND SHOW HIM WHAT THE LIFE OF A GANGSTER TRULY LOOKS LIKE. AND WHAT DOES THE CHILD DO?
HE STEALS A BROOCH FROM THE LOCAL KINGPIN... AND GETS CAUGHT!
BUT THERE WAS JUST ENOUGH TIME FOR LANDO AND JIANDY TO HOP ON A REPULSOR CARGO CRATE...
"...WITH ASKROH ALREADY ON THEIR TAIL ON THE STREETS OF CLOUD CITY!"
GO STRAIGHT. JUST GO STRAIGHT!
RIGHT IT IS!

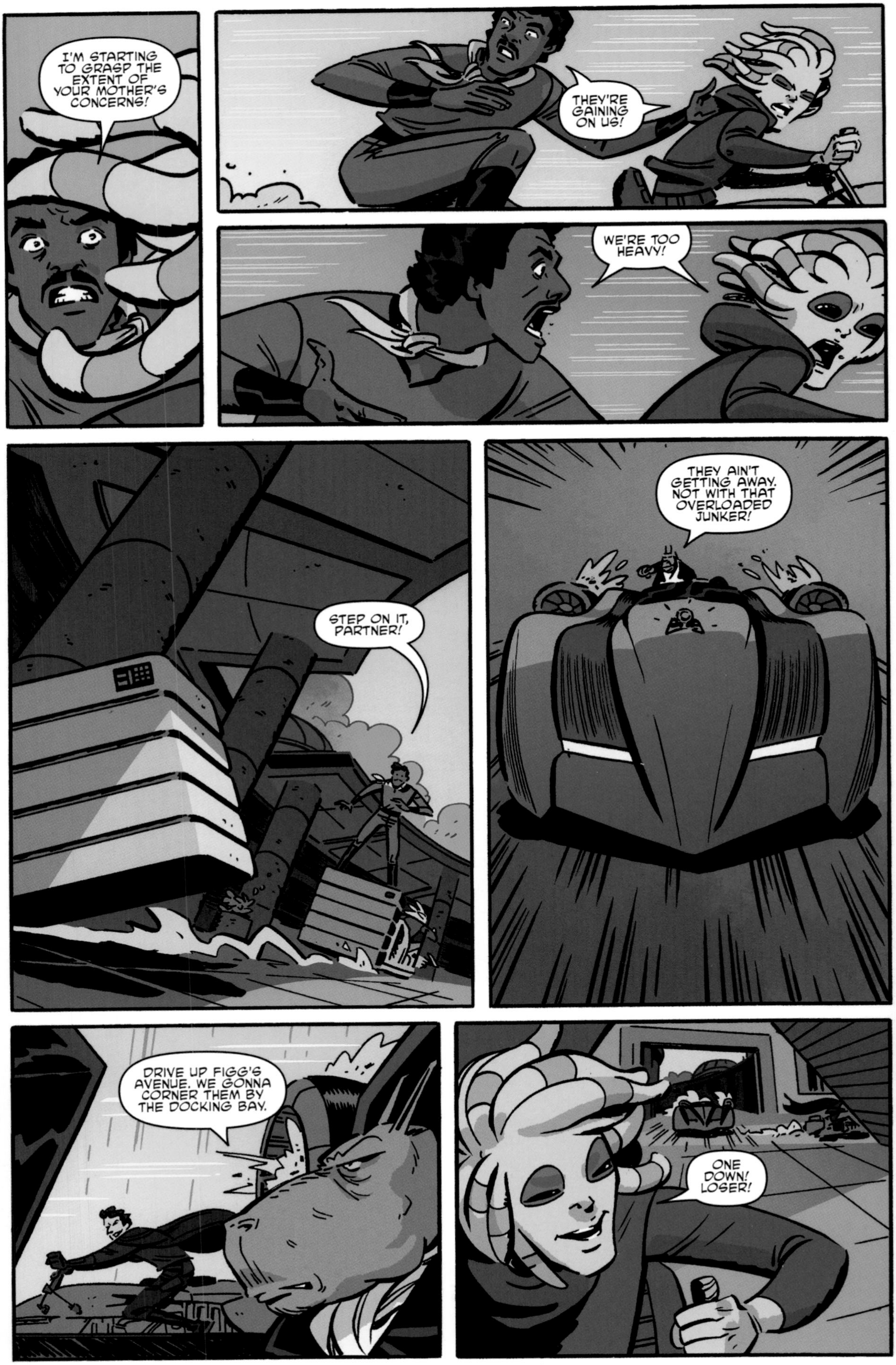
I'M STARTING TO GRASP THE EXTENT OF YOUR MOTHER'S CONCERNS!
THEY'RE GAINING ON US!
WE'RE TOO HEAVY!
STEP ON IT, PARTNER!
THEY AIN'T GETTING AWAY. NOT WITH THAT OVERLOADED JUNKER!
DRIVE UP FIGG'S AVENUE. WE GONNA CORNER THEM BY THE DOCKING BAY.
ONE DOWN! LOSER!

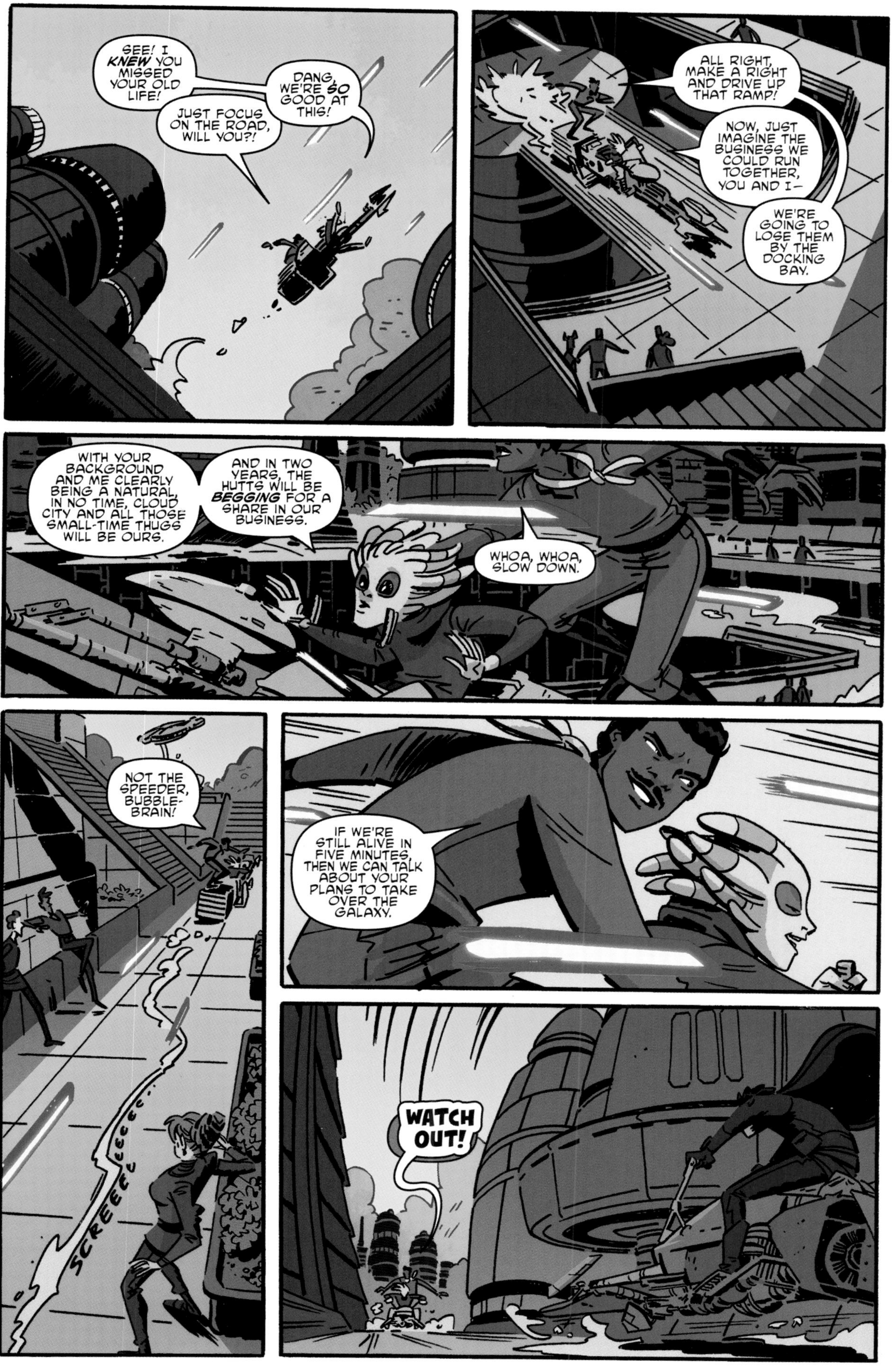
SEE! I *KNEW* YOU MISSED YOUR OLD LIFE!
DANG, WE'RE *SO* GOOD AT THIS!
JUST FOCUS ON THE ROAD, WILL YOU?!
ALL RIGHT, MAKE A RIGHT AND DRIVE UP THAT RAMP!
NOW, JUST IMAGINE THE BUSINESS WE COULD RUN TOGETHER, YOU AND I—
WE'RE GOING TO LOSE THEM BY THE DOCKING BAY.
WITH YOUR BACKGROUND AND ME CLEARLY BEING A NATURAL, IN NO TIME, CLOUD CITY AND ALL THOSE SMALL-TIME THUGS WILL BE OURS.
AND IN TWO YEARS, THE HUTTS WILL BE *BEGGING* FOR A SHARE IN OUR BUSINESS.
WHOA, WHOA, SLOW DOWN.
NOT THE SPEEDER, BUBBLE-BRAIN!
SCREEEEEEEEE...
IF WE'RE STILL ALIVE IN FIVE MINUTES, THEN WE CAN TALK ABOUT YOUR PLANS TO TAKE OVER THE GALAXY.
WATCH OUT!

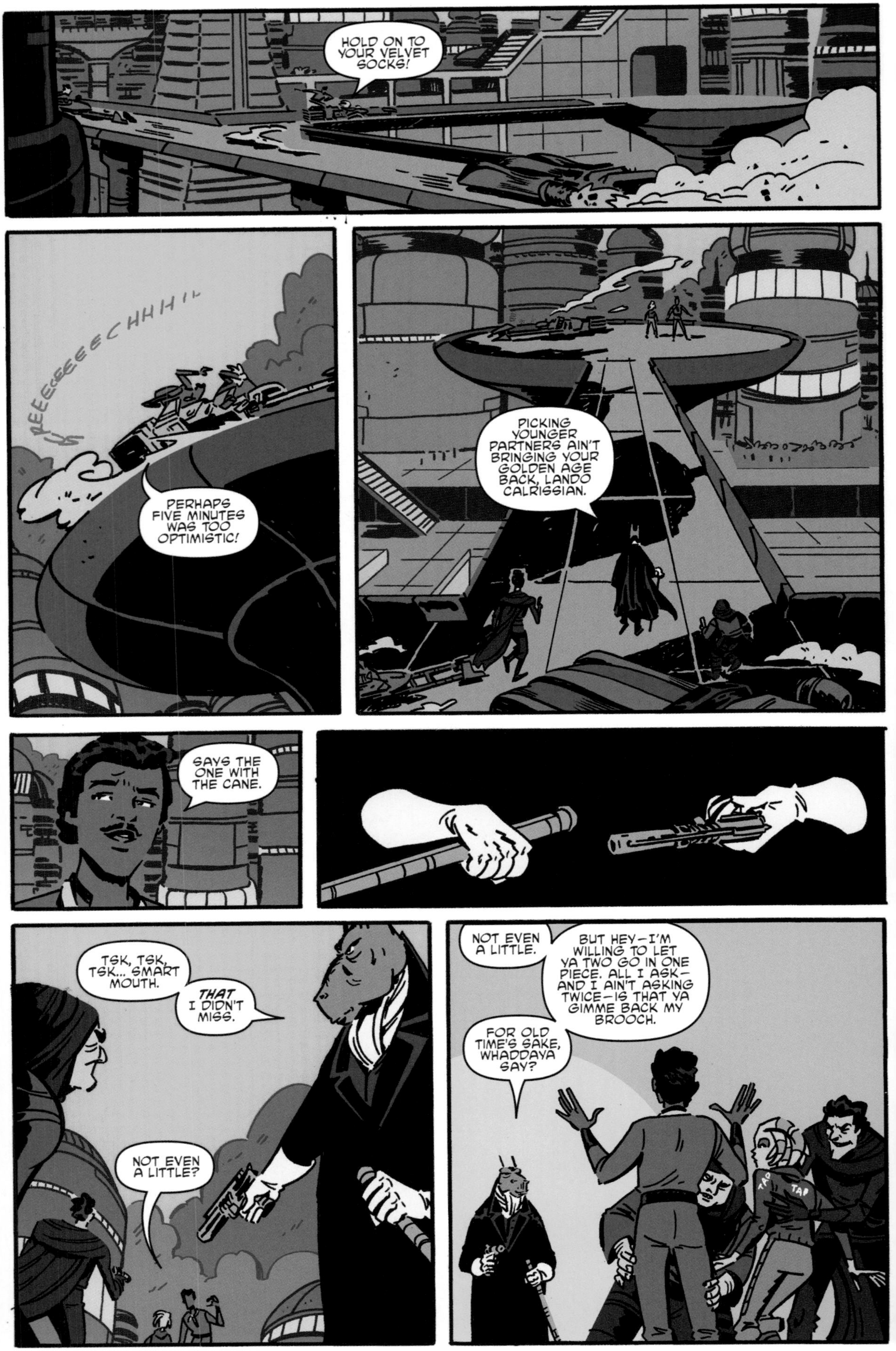
HOLD ON TO YOUR VELVET SOCKS!
REEEEEEEEECHHHH
PERHAPS FIVE MINUTES WAS TOO OPTIMISTIC!
PICKING YOUNGER PARTNERS AIN'T BRINGING YOUR GOLDEN AGE BACK, LANDO CALRISSIAN.
SAYS THE ONE WITH THE CANE.
TSK, TSK, TSK... SMART MOUTH.
THAT I DIDN'T MISS.
NOT EVEN A LITTLE?
NOT EVEN A LITTLE.
BUT HEY—I'M WILLING TO LET YA TWO GO IN ONE PIECE. ALL I ASK—AND I AIN'T ASKING TWICE—IS THAT YA GIMME BACK MY BROOCH.
FOR OLD TIME'S SAKE, WHADDAYA SAY?
TAP
TAP

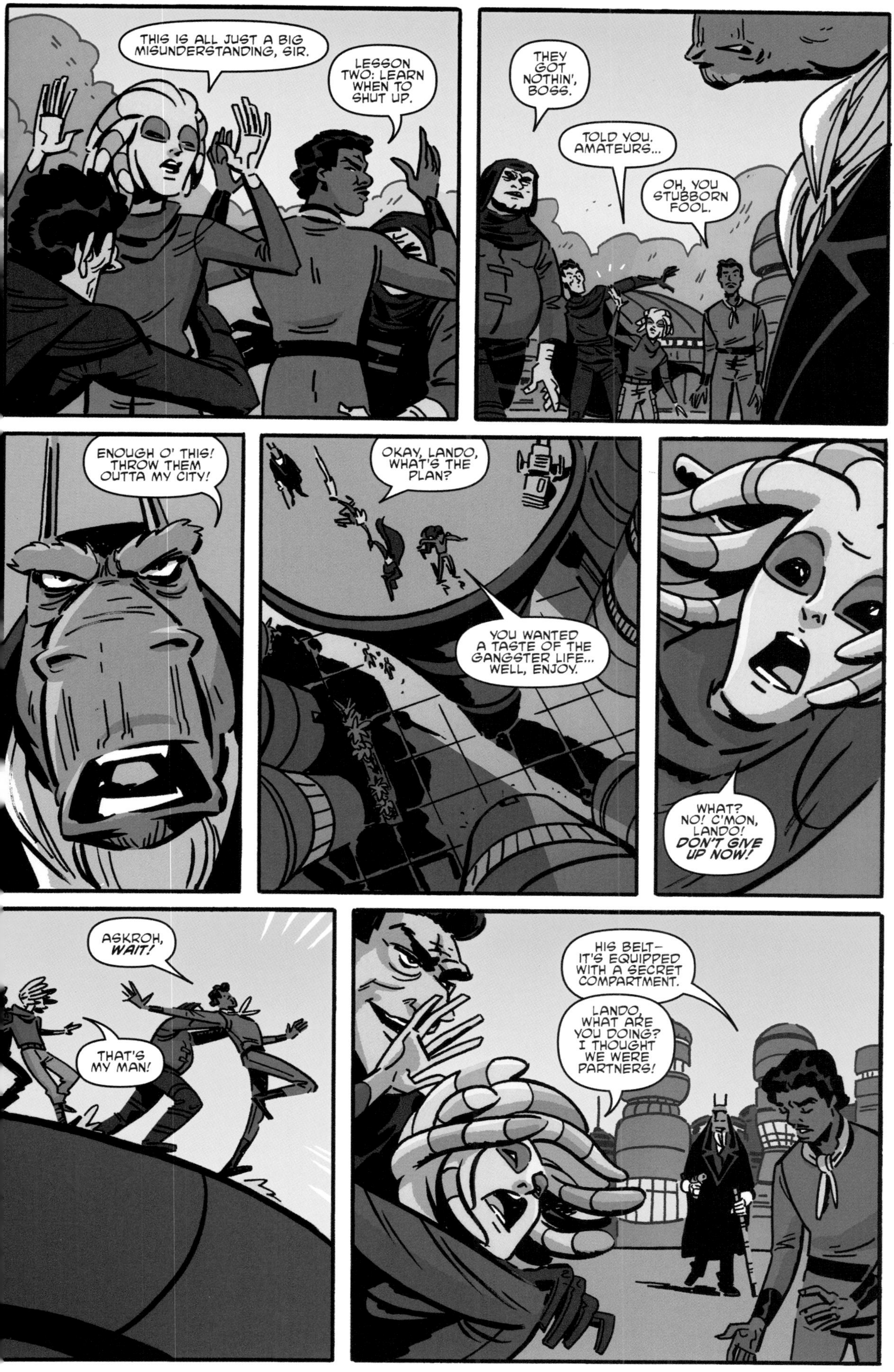

THIS IS ALL JUST A BIG MISUNDERSTANDING, SIR.
LESSON TWO: LEARN WHEN TO SHUT UP.
THEY GOT NOTHIN', BOSS.
TOLD YOU. AMATEURS...
OH, YOU STUBBORN FOOL.
ENOUGH O' THIS! THROW THEM OUTTA MY CITY!
OKAY, LANDO, WHAT'S THE PLAN?
YOU WANTED A TASTE OF THE GANGSTER LIFE... WELL, ENJOY.
WHAT? NO! C'MON, LANDO! ***DON'T GIVE UP NOW!***
ASKROH, ***WAIT!***
THAT'S MY MAN!
HIS BELT— IT'S EQUIPPED WITH A SECRET COMPARTMENT.
LANDO, WHAT ARE YOU DOING? I THOUGHT WE WERE PARTNERS!

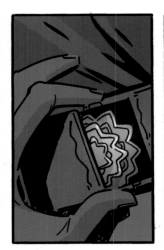

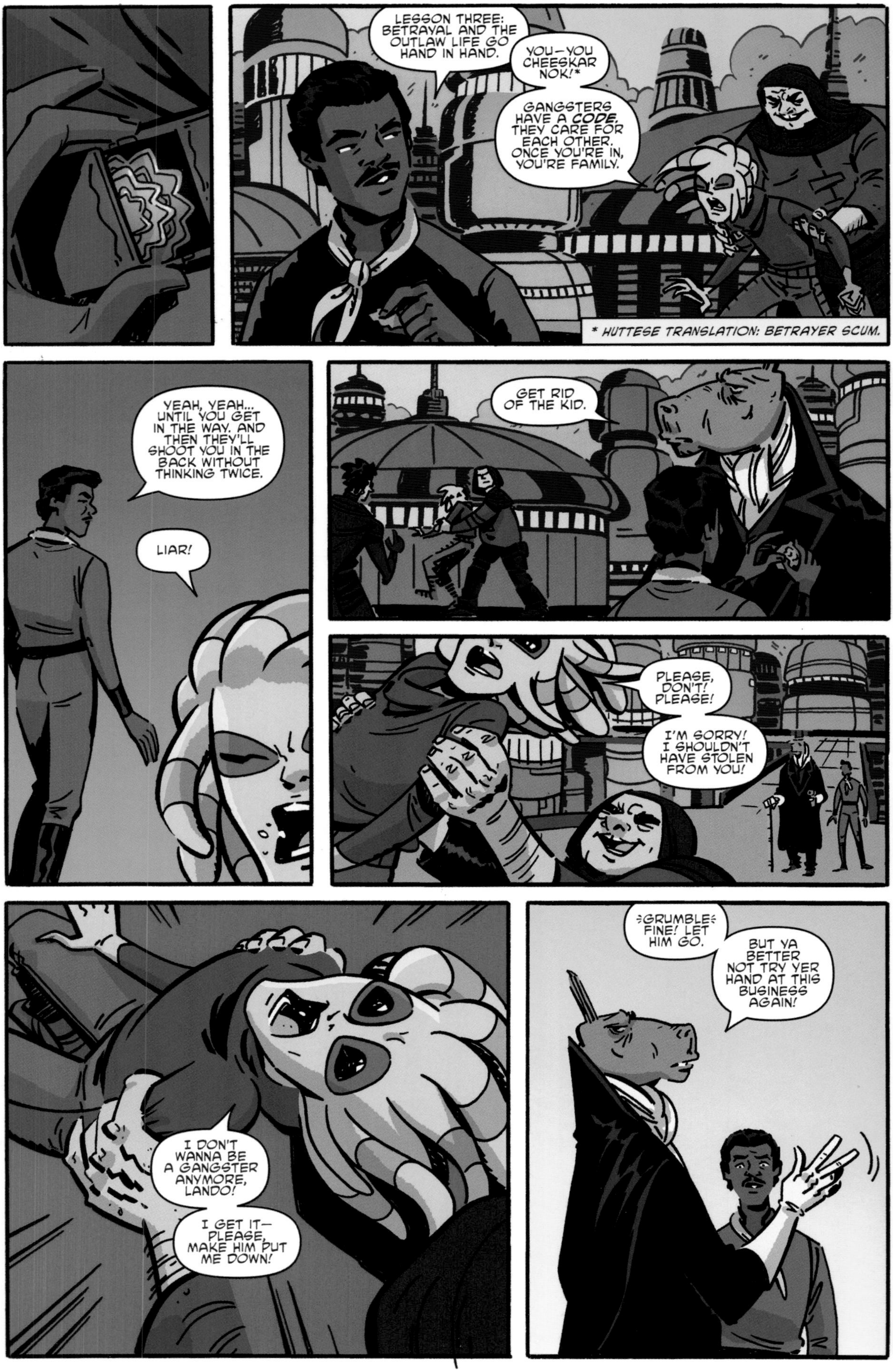
LESSON THREE: BETRAYAL AND THE OUTLAW LIFE GO HAND IN HAND.
YOU—YOU CHEESKAR NOK!*
GANGSTERS HAVE A CODE. THEY CARE FOR EACH OTHER. ONCE YOU'RE IN, YOU'RE FAMILY.
* HUTTESE TRANSLATION: BETRAYER SCUM.
YEAH, YEAH... UNTIL YOU GET IN THE WAY. AND THEN THEY'LL SHOOT YOU IN THE BACK WITHOUT THINKING TWICE.
LIAR!
GET RID OF THE KID.
PLEASE, DON'T! PLEASE!
I'M SORRY! I SHOULDN'T HAVE STOLEN FROM YOU!
I DON'T WANNA BE A GANGSTER ANYMORE, LANDO!
I GET IT— PLEASE, MAKE HIM PUT ME DOWN!
GRUMBLE FINE! LET HIM GO.
BUT YA BETTER NOT TRY YER HAND AT THIS BUSINESS AGAIN!

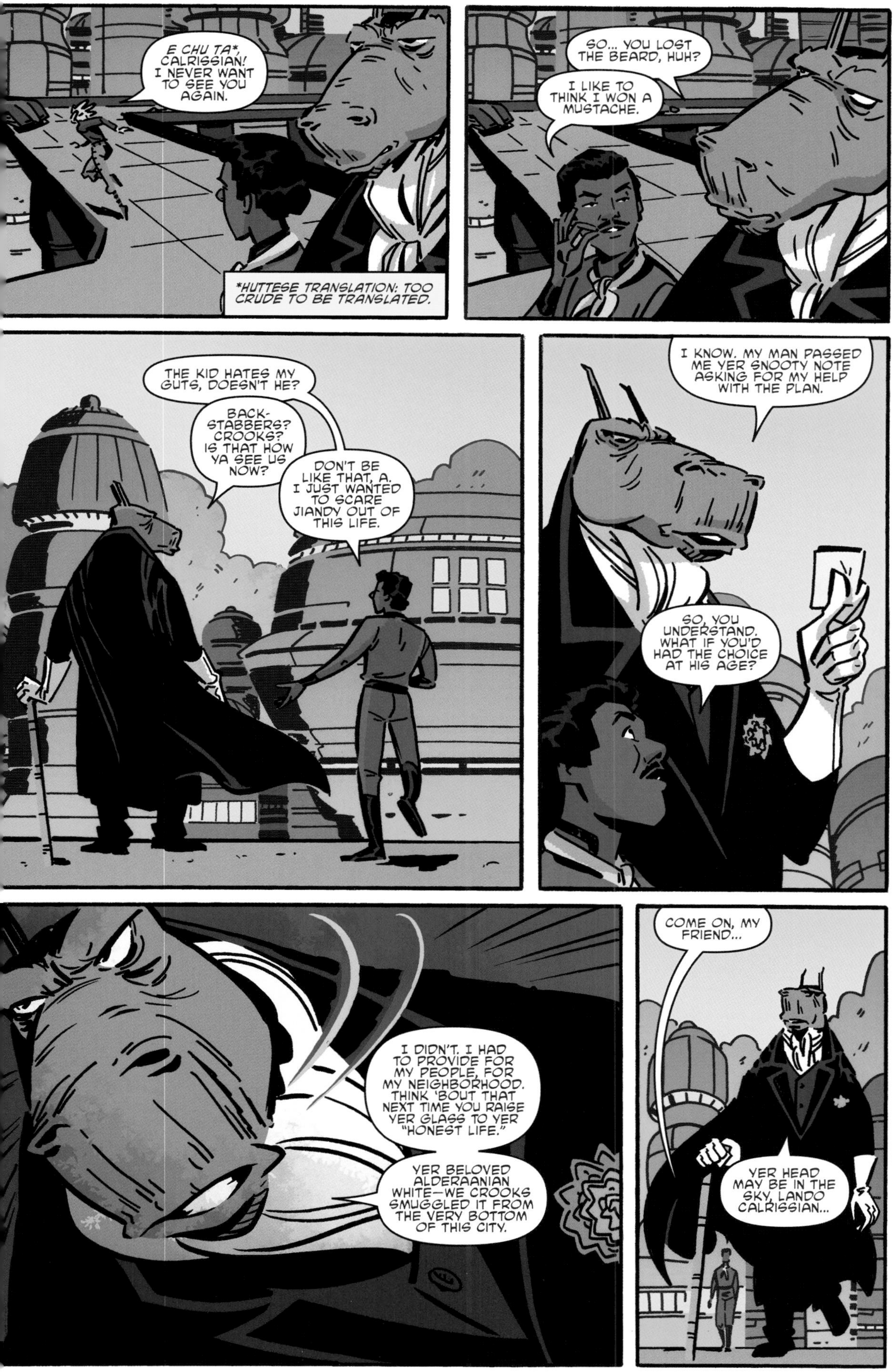
E CHU TA*, CALRISSIAN! I NEVER WANT TO SEE YOU AGAIN.
*HUTTESE TRANSLATION: TOO CRUDE TO BE TRANSLATED.
SO... YOU LOST THE BEARD, HUH?
I LIKE TO THINK I WON A MUSTACHE.
THE KID HATES MY GUTS, DOESN'T HE?
BACK-STABBERS? CROOKS? IS THAT HOW YA SEE US NOW?
DON'T BE LIKE THAT, A. I JUST WANTED TO SCARE JIANDY OUT OF THIS LIFE.
I KNOW. MY MAN PASSED ME YER SNOOTY NOTE ASKING FOR MY HELP WITH THE PLAN.
SO, YOU UNDERSTAND. WHAT IF YOU'D HAD THE CHOICE AT HIS AGE?
I DIDN'T. I HAD TO PROVIDE FOR MY PEOPLE, FOR MY NEIGHBORHOOD. THINK 'BOUT THAT NEXT TIME YOU RAISE YER GLASS TO YER "HONEST LIFE."
YER BELOVED ALDERAANIAN WHITE—WE CROOKS SMUGGLED IT FROM THE VERY BOTTOM OF THIS CITY.
COME ON, MY FRIEND...
YER HEAD MAY BE IN THE SKY, LANDO CALRISSIAN...

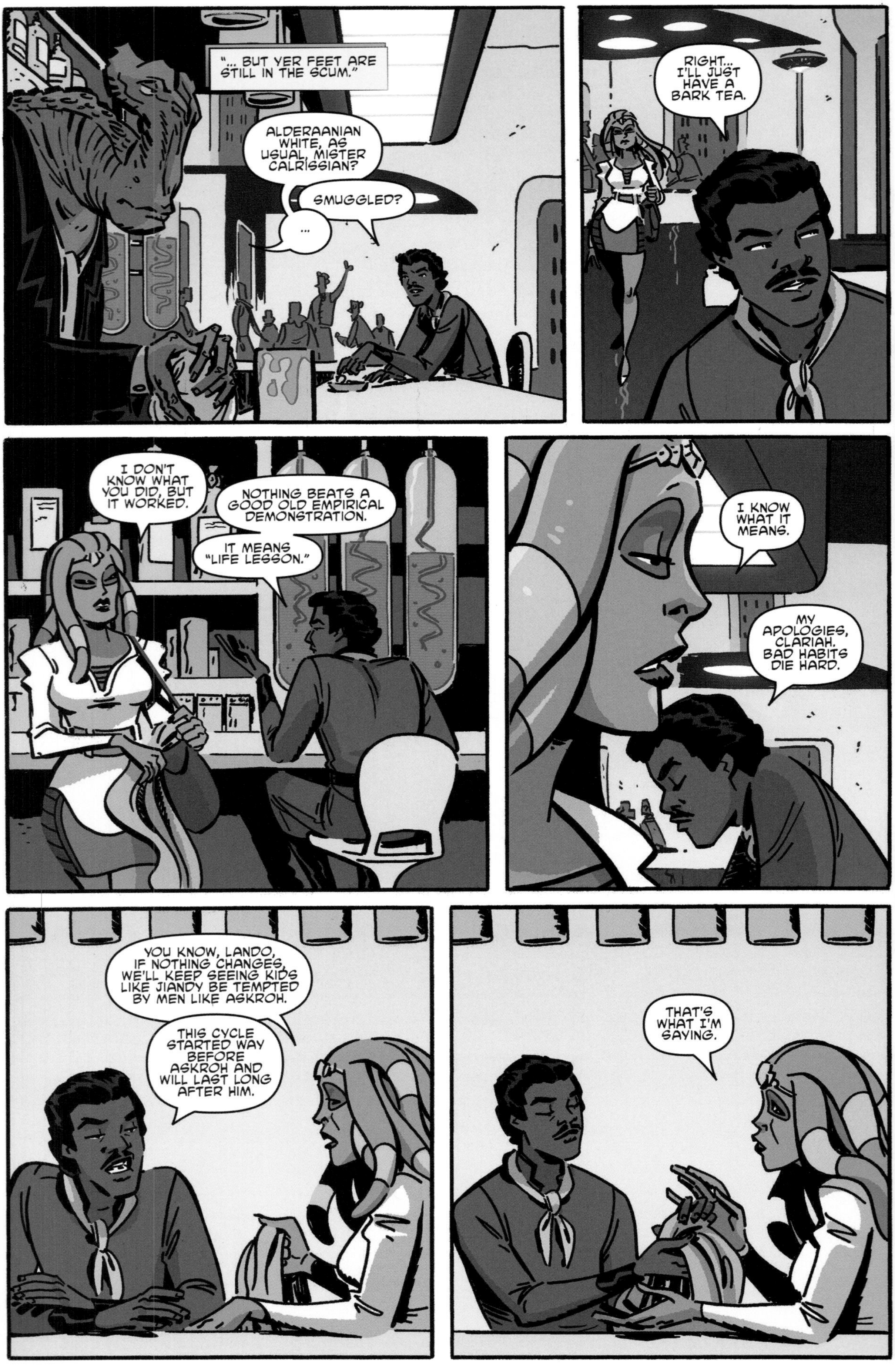
"... BUT YER FEET ARE STILL IN THE SCUM."
ALDERAANIAN WHITE, AS USUAL, MISTER CALRISSIAN?
SMUGGLED?
...
RIGHT... I'LL JUST HAVE A BARK TEA.
I DON'T KNOW WHAT YOU DID, BUT IT WORKED.
NOTHING BEATS A GOOD OLD EMPIRICAL DEMONSTRATION.
IT MEANS "LIFE LESSON."
I KNOW WHAT IT MEANS.
MY APOLOGIES, CLARIAH. BAD HABITS DIE HARD.
YOU KNOW, LANDO, IF NOTHING CHANGES, WE'LL KEEP SEEING KIDS LIKE JIANDY BE TEMPTED BY MEN LIKE ASKROH.
THIS CYCLE STARTED WAY BEFORE ASKROH AND WILL LAST LONG AFTER HIM.
THAT'S WHAT I'M SAYING.

I TOOK MY CHANCES WITH THE BARON ADMINISTRATOR, BUT ANYTHING I SAY IS FALLING ON DEAF EARS.

DON'T YOU WORRY, MY DEAR CLARIAH. I AM CONFIDENT THAT ONE DAY...

...SOMEONE WILL LISTEN.

OH... I BELIEVE I DO SEE YOUR POINT, MASTER. FROM NOW ON, I WILL SELECT MY STORIES MORE CAREFULLY.

IT'S ALL RIGHT, CRATER.

NOW I THINK BOO NOW UNDERSTANDS THAT THERE'S MORE TO GANGSTER STORIES THAN THE GLAMOROUS BITS.

BEEP BOOP BOOP?

DON'T BE SAD, BOO. JIANDY WON'T STAY MAD AT LANDO FOREVER. THEIR PATHS WILL EVEN CROSS AGAIN.

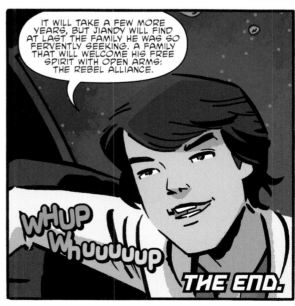

IT WILL TAKE A FEW MORE YEARS, BUT JIANDY WILL FIND AT LAST THE FAMILY HE WAS SO FERVENTLY SEEKING. A FAMILY THAT WILL WELCOME HIS FREE SPIRIT WITH OPEN ARMS: THE REBEL ALLIANCE.

WHUP WHUUUUUP

THE END.

17

THE LOST EGGS
OF LIVORNO

Writer
CAVAN SCOTT

Artist
MAURICET

Colorist
CHRIS FENOGLIO

Letterer
TOM B. LONG

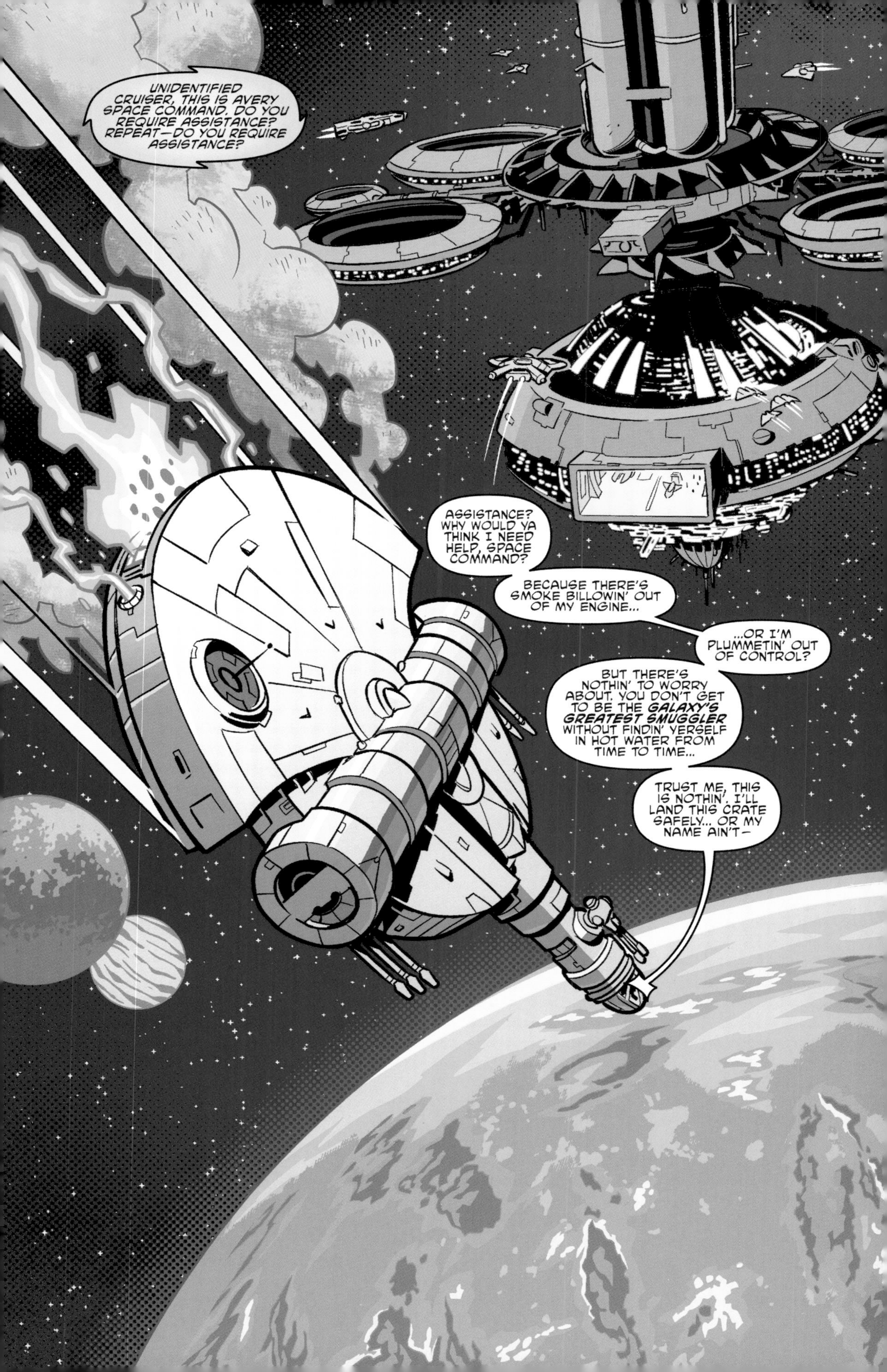
UNIDENTIFIED CRUISER, THIS IS AVERY SPACE COMMAND. DO YOU REQUIRE ASSISTANCE? REPEAT—DO YOU REQUIRE ASSISTANCE?
ASSISTANCE? WHY WOULD YA THINK I NEED HELP, SPACE COMMAND?
BECAUSE THERE'S SMOKE BILLOWIN' OUT OF MY ENGINE...
...OR I'M PLUMMETIN' OUT OF CONTROL?
BUT THERE'S NOTHIN' TO WORRY ABOUT. YOU DON'T GET TO BE THE GALAXY'S GREATEST SMUGGLER WITHOUT FINDIN' YERSELF IN HOT WATER FROM TIME TO TIME...
TRUST ME, THIS IS NOTHIN'. I'LL LAND THIS CRATE SAFELY... OR MY NAME AIN'T—

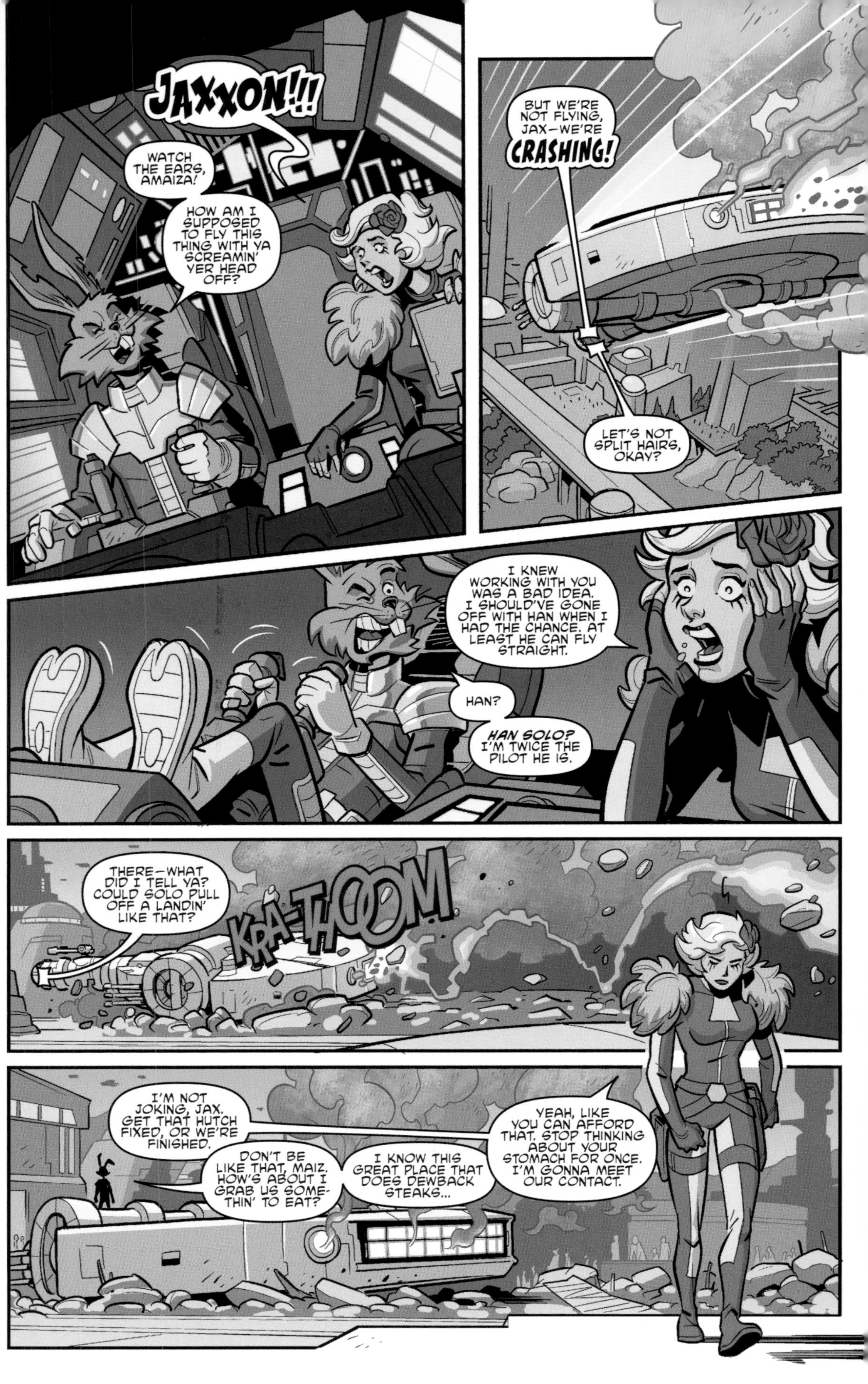
JAXXON!!!
WATCH THE EARS, AMAIZA!
HOW AM I SUPPOSED TO FLY THIS THING WITH YA SCREAMIN' YER HEAD OFF?
BUT WE'RE NOT FLYING, JAX—WE'RE CRASHING!
LET'S NOT SPLIT HAIRS, OKAY?
I KNEW WORKING WITH YOU WAS A BAD IDEA. I SHOULD'VE GONE OFF WITH HAN WHEN I HAD THE CHANCE. AT LEAST HE CAN FLY STRAIGHT.
HAN?
HAN SOLO? I'M TWICE THE PILOT HE IS.
KRA-THOOOM
THERE—WHAT DID I TELL YA? COULD SOLO PULL OFF A LANDIN' LIKE THAT?
I'M NOT JOKING, JAX. GET THAT HUTCH FIXED, OR WE'RE FINISHED.
DON'T BE LIKE THAT, MAIZ. HOW'S ABOUT I GRAB US SOME-THIN' TO EAT?
I KNOW THIS GREAT PLACE THAT DOES DEWBACK STEAKS...
YEAH, LIKE YOU CAN AFFORD THAT. STOP THINKING ABOUT YOUR STOMACH FOR ONCE. I'M GONNA MEET OUR CONTACT.

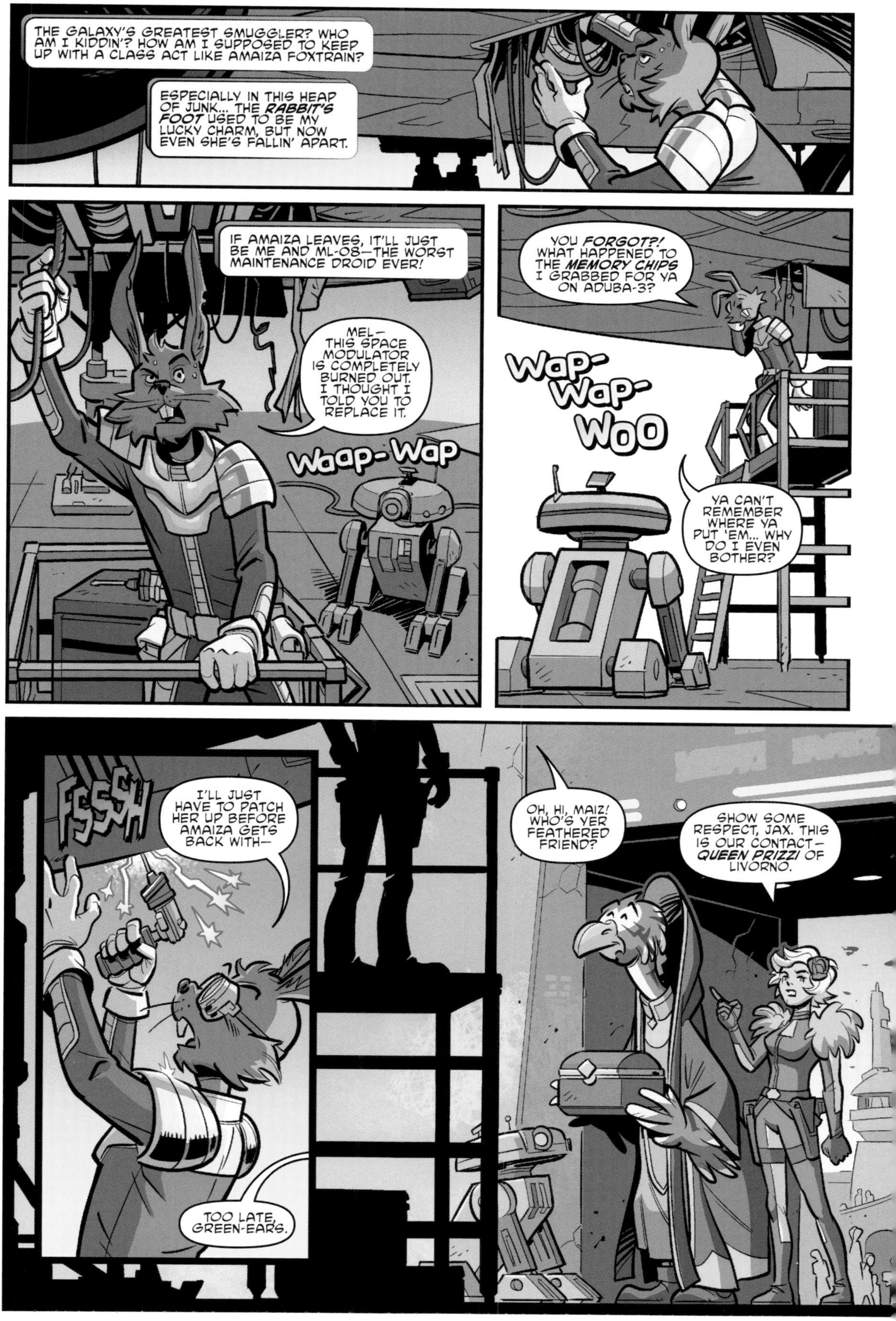
THE GALAXY'S GREATEST SMUGGLER? WHO AM I KIDDIN'? HOW AM I SUPPOSED TO KEEP UP WITH A CLASS ACT LIKE AMAIZA FOXTRAIN?
ESPECIALLY IN THIS HEAP OF JUNK... THE *RABBIT'S FOOT* USED TO BE MY LUCKY CHARM, BUT NOW EVEN SHE'S FALLIN' APART.
IF AMAIZA LEAVES, IT'LL JUST BE ME AND ML-08—THE WORST MAINTENANCE DROID EVER!
MEL—THIS SPACE MODULATOR IS COMPLETELY BURNED OUT. I THOUGHT I TOLD YOU TO REPLACE IT.
Waap-Wap
YOU *FORGOT?!* WHAT HAPPENED TO THE *MEMORY CHIPS* I GRABBED FOR YA ON ADUBA-3?
Wap-Wap-Woo
YA CAN'T REMEMBER WHERE YA PUT 'EM... WHY DO I EVEN BOTHER?
FSSSH
I'LL JUST HAVE TO PATCH HER UP BEFORE AMAIZA GETS BACK WITH—
TOO LATE, GREEN-EARS.
OH, HI, MAIZ! WHO'S YER FEATHERED FRIEND?
SHOW SOME RESPECT, JAX. THIS IS OUR CONTACT—*QUEEN PRIZZI* OF LIVORNO.

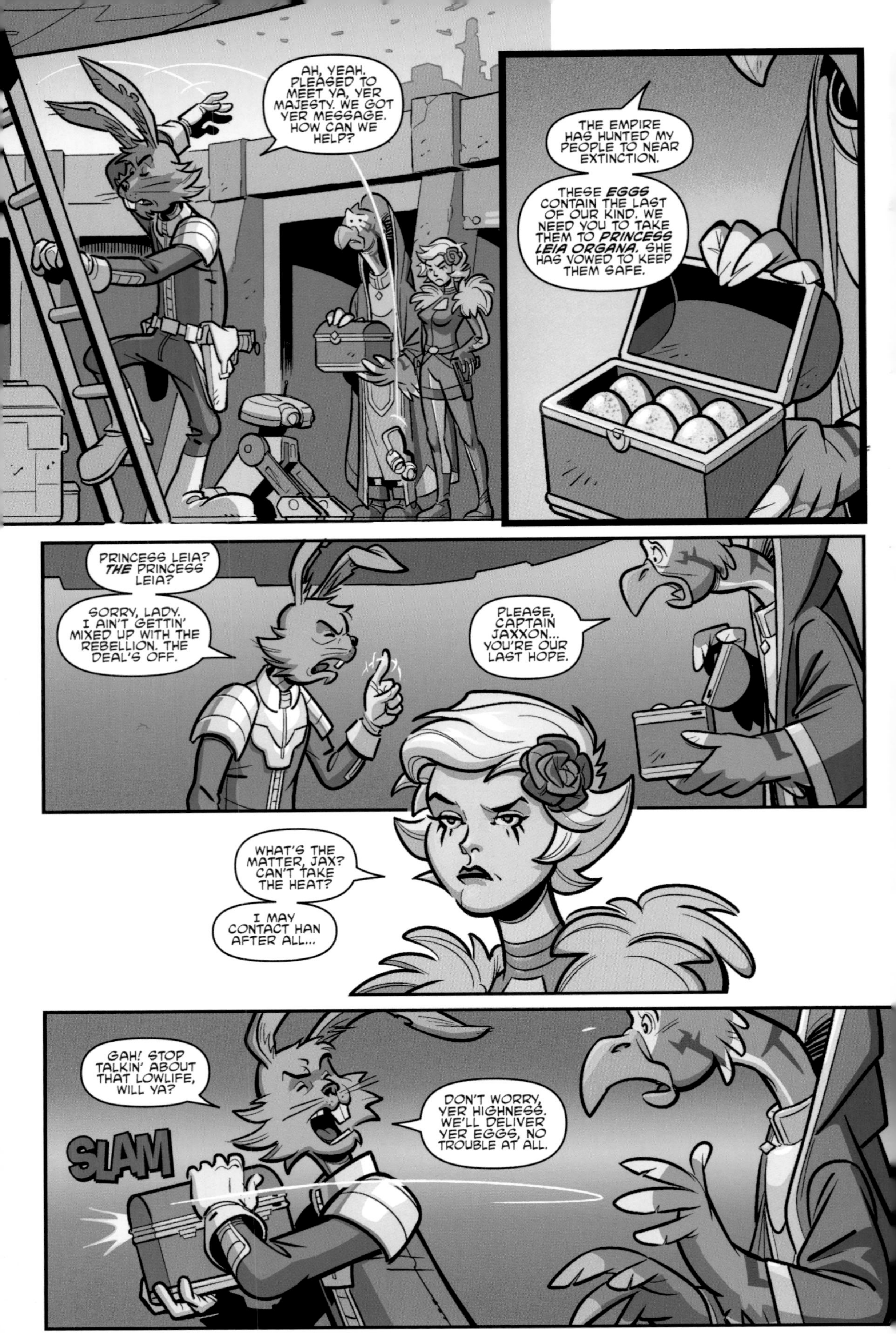
AH, YEAH. PLEASED TO MEET YA, YER MAJESTY. WE GOT YER MESSAGE. HOW CAN WE HELP?
THE EMPIRE HAS HUNTED MY PEOPLE TO NEAR EXTINCTION.
THESE *EGGS* CONTAIN THE LAST OF OUR KIND. WE NEED YOU TO TAKE THEM TO *PRINCESS LEIA ORGANA.* SHE HAS VOWED TO KEEP THEM SAFE.
PRINCESS LEIA? *THE* PRINCESS LEIA?
SORRY, LADY. I AIN'T GETTIN' MIXED UP WITH THE REBELLION. THE DEAL'S OFF.
PLEASE, CAPTAIN JAXXON... YOU'RE OUR LAST HOPE.
WHAT'S THE MATTER, JAX? CAN'T TAKE THE HEAT?
I MAY CONTACT HAN AFTER ALL...
GAH! STOP TALKIN' ABOUT THAT LOWLIFE, WILL YA?
SLAM
DON'T WORRY, YER HIGHNESS. WE'LL DELIVER YER EGGS, NO TROUBLE AT ALL.

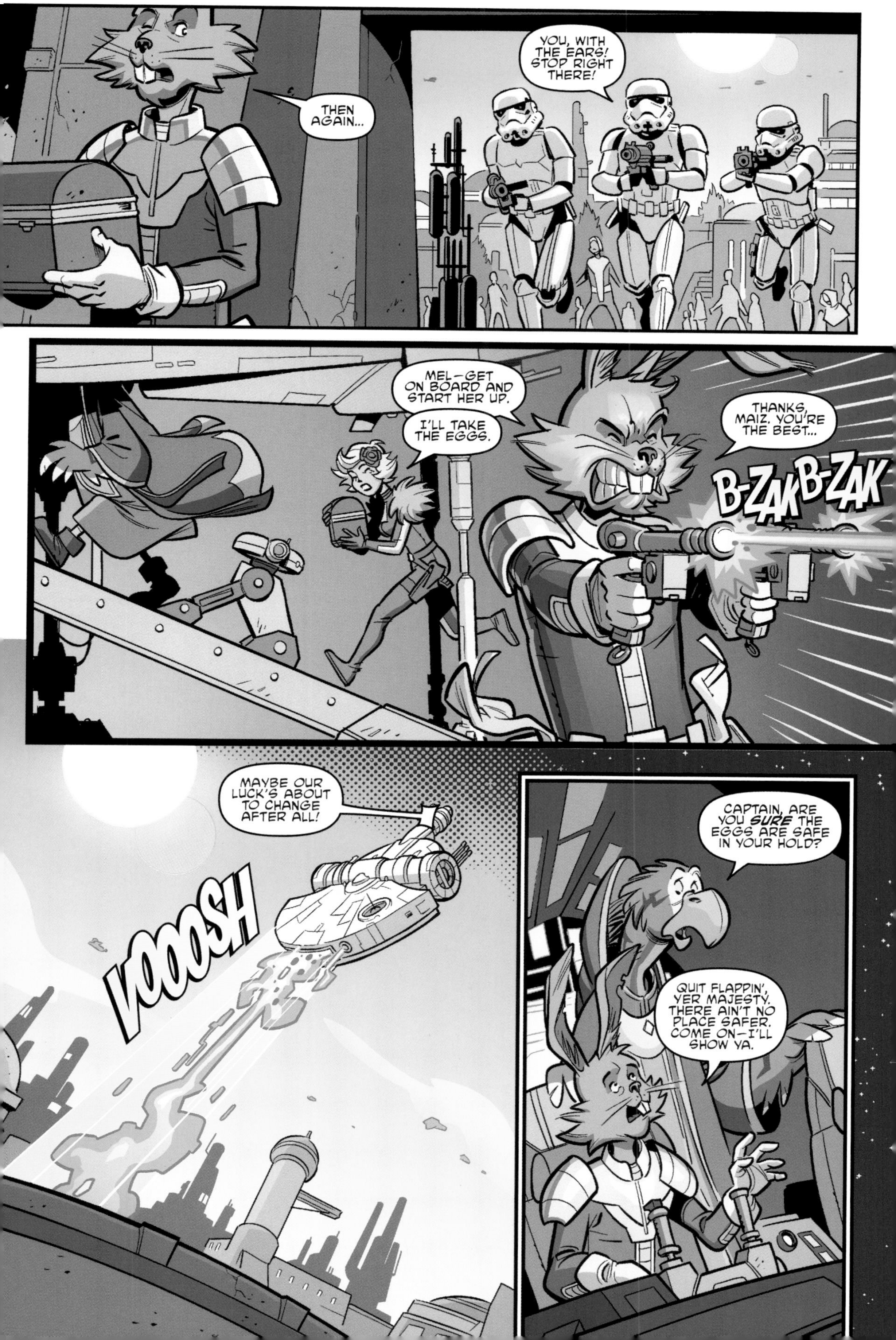
THEN AGAIN...
YOU, WITH THE EARS! STOP RIGHT THERE!
MEL—GET ON BOARD AND START HER UP.
I'LL TAKE THE EGGS.
THANKS, MAIZ. YOU'RE THE BEST...
B-ZAK B-ZAK
MAYBE OUR LUCK'S ABOUT TO CHANGE AFTER ALL!
VOOOSH
CAPTAIN, ARE YOU *SURE* THE EGGS ARE SAFE IN YOUR HOLD?
QUIT FLAPPIN', YER MAJESTY. THERE AIN'T NO PLACE SAFER. COME ON—I'LL SHOW YA.

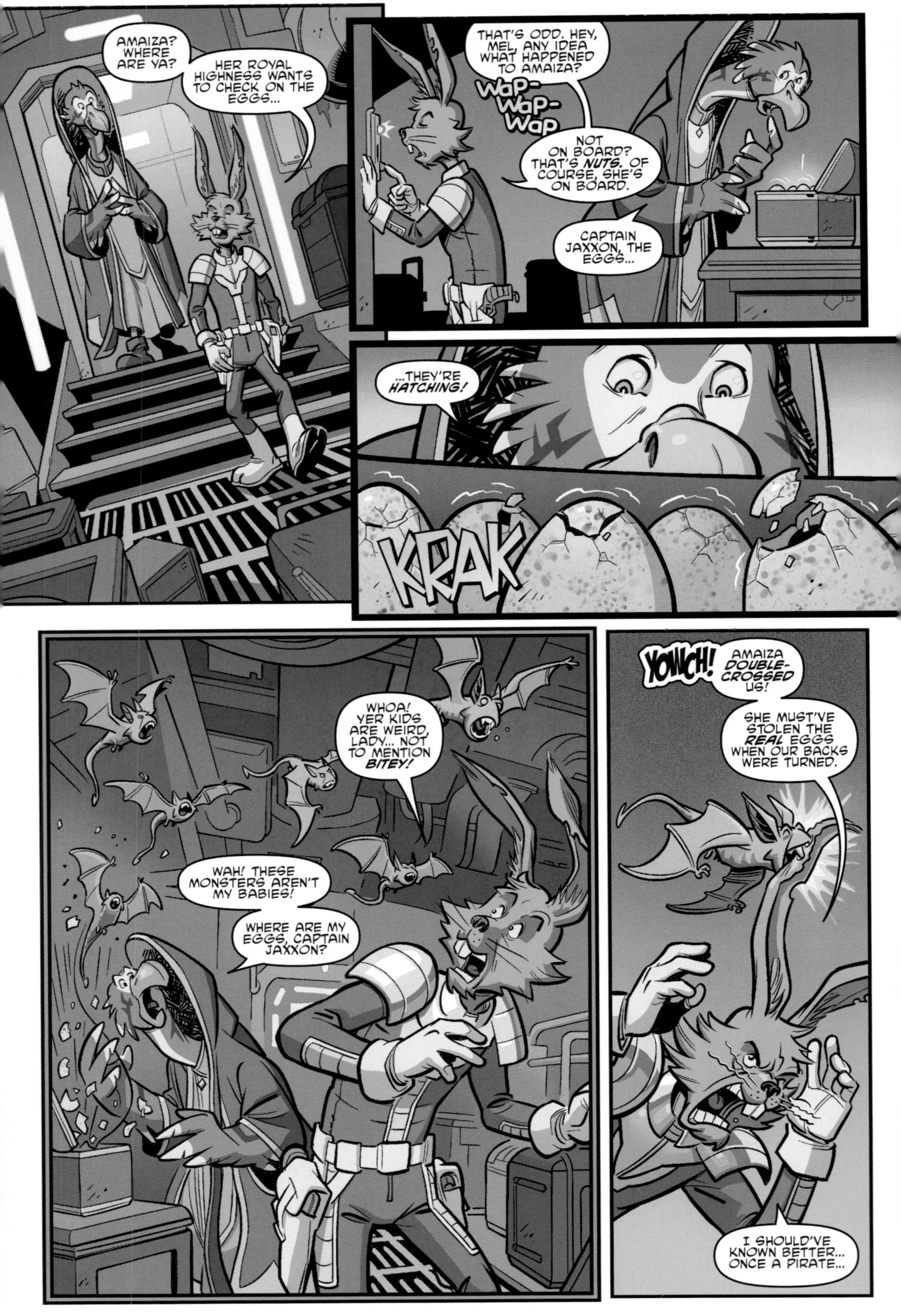
AMAIZA? WHERE ARE YA?
HER ROYAL HIGHNESS WANTS TO CHECK ON THE EGGS...
THAT'S ODD. HEY, MEL, ANY IDEA WHAT HAPPENED TO AMAIZA?
WAP-WAP-WAP
NOT ON BOARD? THAT'S NUTS. OF COURSE, SHE'S ON BOARD.
CAPTAIN JAXXON, THE EGGS...
...THEY'RE HATCHING!
KRAK
WHOA! YER KIDS ARE WEIRD, LADY... NOT TO MENTION BITEY!
WAH! THESE MONSTERS AREN'T MY BABIES!
WHERE ARE MY EGGS, CAPTAIN JAXXON?
YOWCH!
AMAIZA DOUBLE-CROSSED US!
SHE MUST'VE STOLEN THE REAL EGGS WHEN OUR BACKS WERE TURNED.
I SHOULD'VE KNOWN BETTER... ONCE A PIRATE...

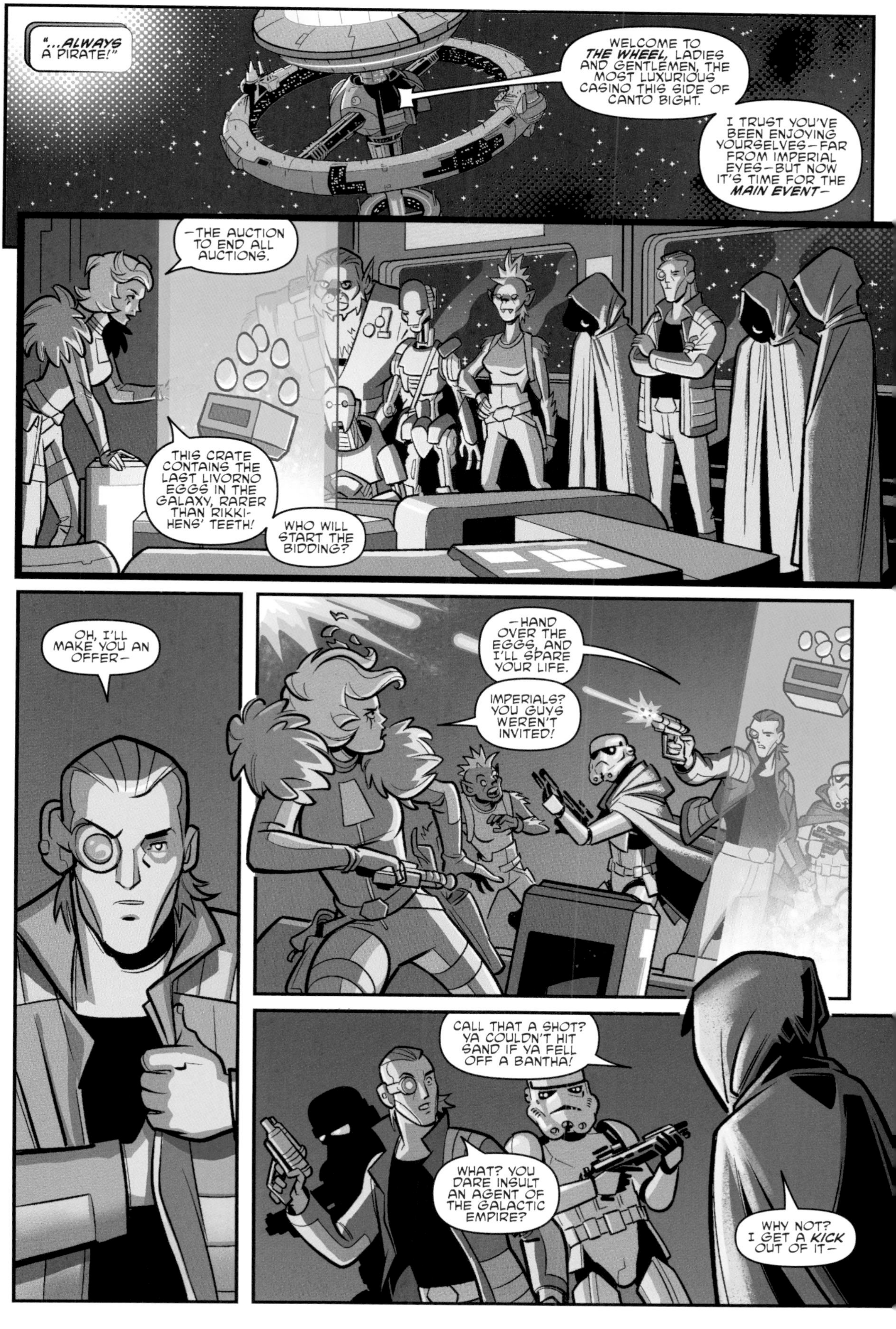
"...ALWAYS A PIRATE!"
WELCOME TO THE WHEEL, LADIES AND GENTLEMEN, THE MOST LUXURIOUS CASINO THIS SIDE OF CANTO BIGHT.
I TRUST YOU'VE BEEN ENJOYING YOURSELVES—FAR FROM IMPERIAL EYES—BUT NOW IT'S TIME FOR THE MAIN EVENT—
—THE AUCTION TO END ALL AUCTIONS.
THIS CRATE CONTAINS THE LAST LIVORNO EGGS IN THE GALAXY, RARER THAN RIKKI-HENS' TEETH!
WHO WILL START THE BIDDING?
OH, I'LL MAKE YOU AN OFFER—
—HAND OVER THE EGGS, AND I'LL SPARE YOUR LIFE.
IMPERIALS? YOU GUYS WEREN'T INVITED!
CALL THAT A SHOT? YA COULDN'T HIT SAND IF YA FELL OFF A BANTHA!
WHAT? YOU DARE INSULT AN AGENT OF THE GALACTIC EMPIRE?
WHY NOT? I GET A KICK OUT OF IT—

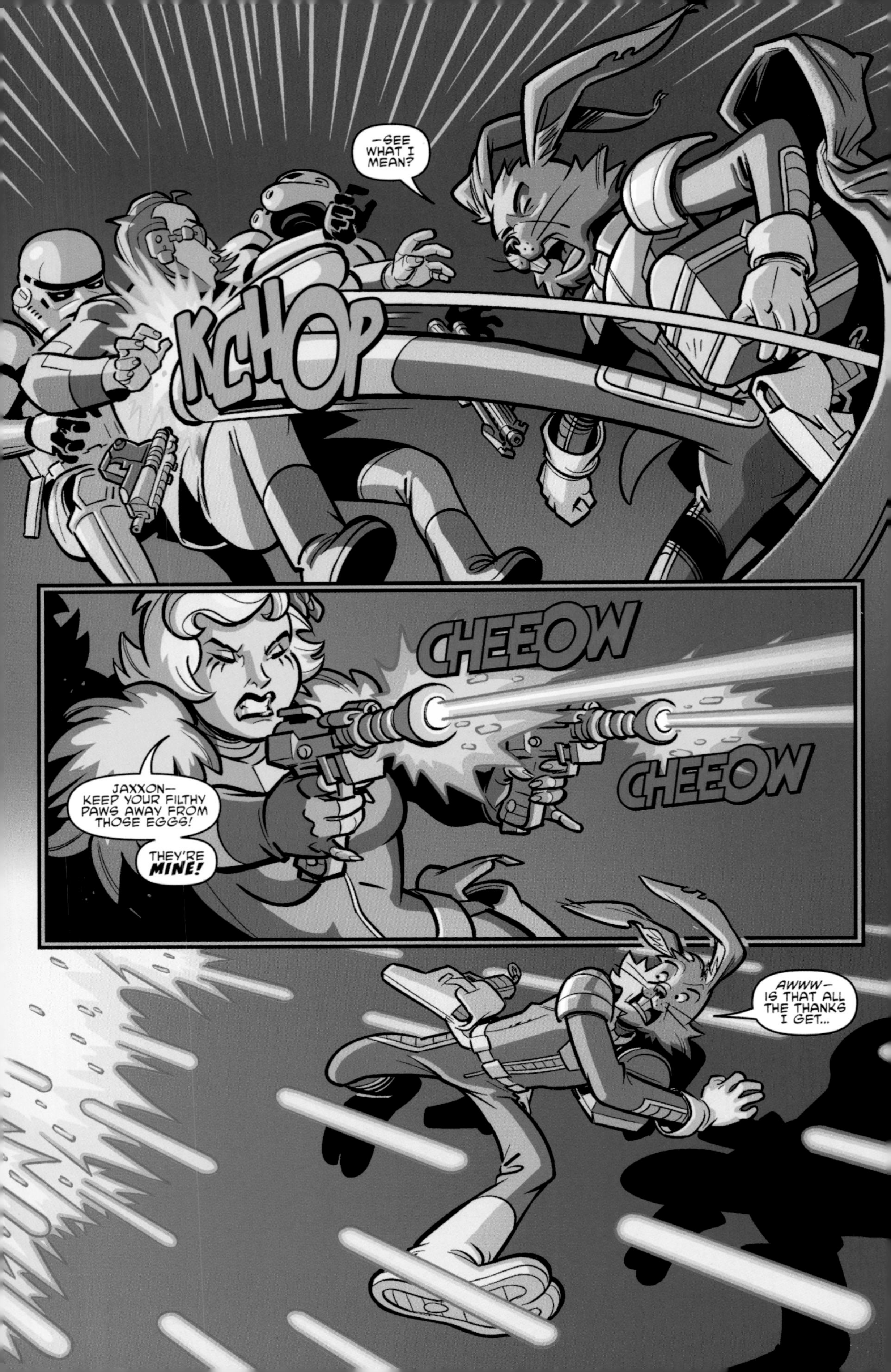
—SEE WHAT I MEAN?
KCHOP
CHEEOW
CHEEOW
JAXXON— KEEP YOUR FILTHY PAWS AWAY FROM THOSE EGGS!
THEY'RE **MINE!**
AWWW— IS THAT ALL THE THANKS I GET...

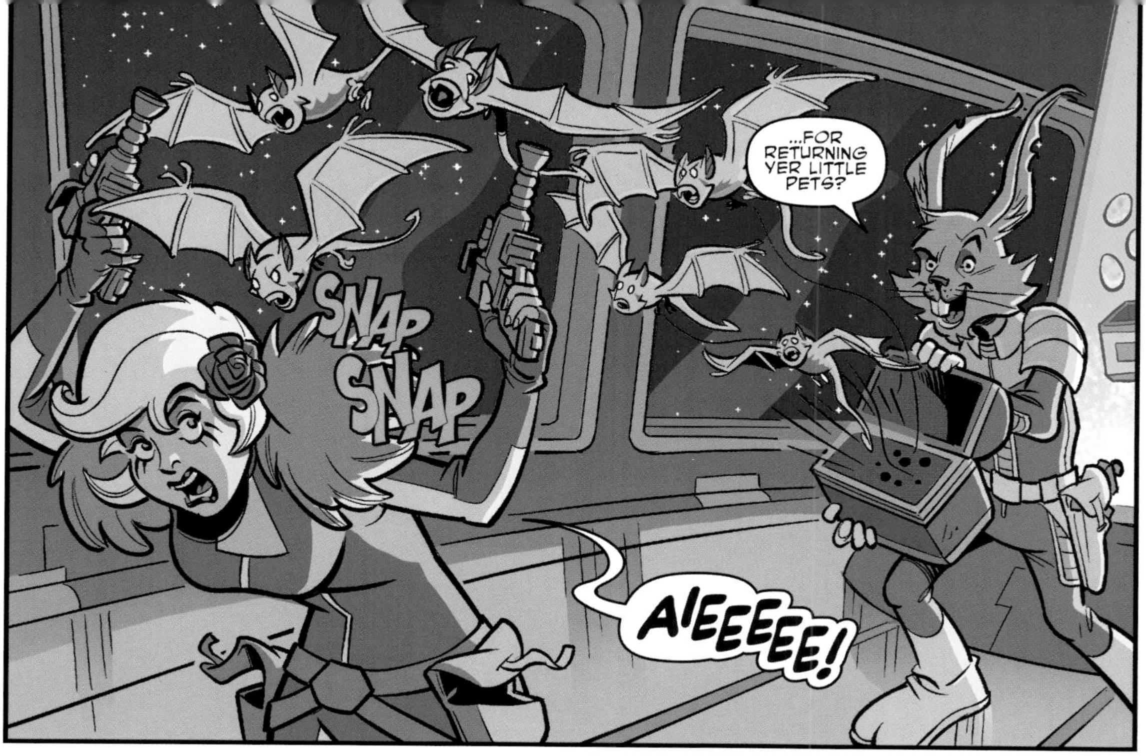
...FOR RETURNING YER LITTLE PETS?
SNAP SNAP SNAP
AIEEEEEE!

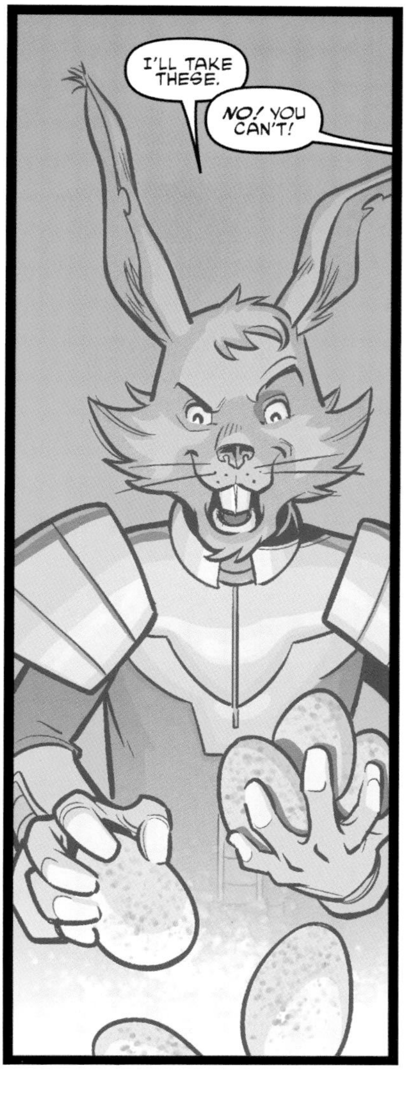
I'LL TAKE THESE.
NO! YOU CAN'T!

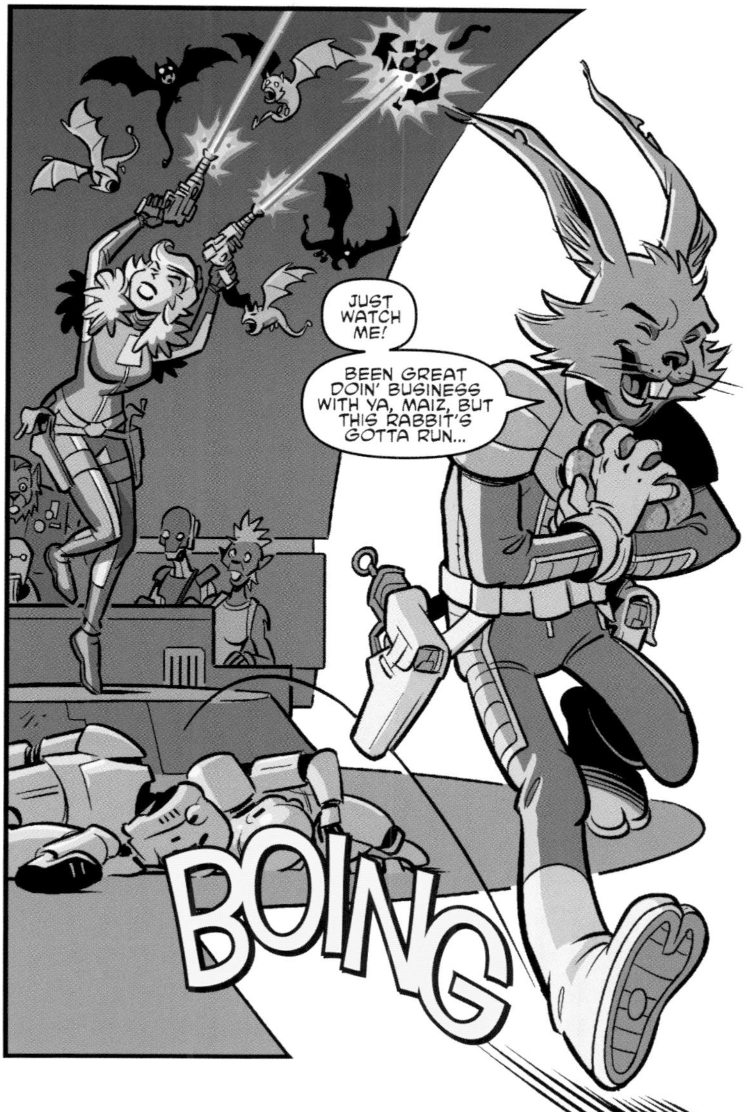
JUST WATCH ME!
BEEN GREAT DOIN' BUSINESS WITH YA, MAIZ, BUT THIS RABBIT'S GOTTA RUN...
BOING

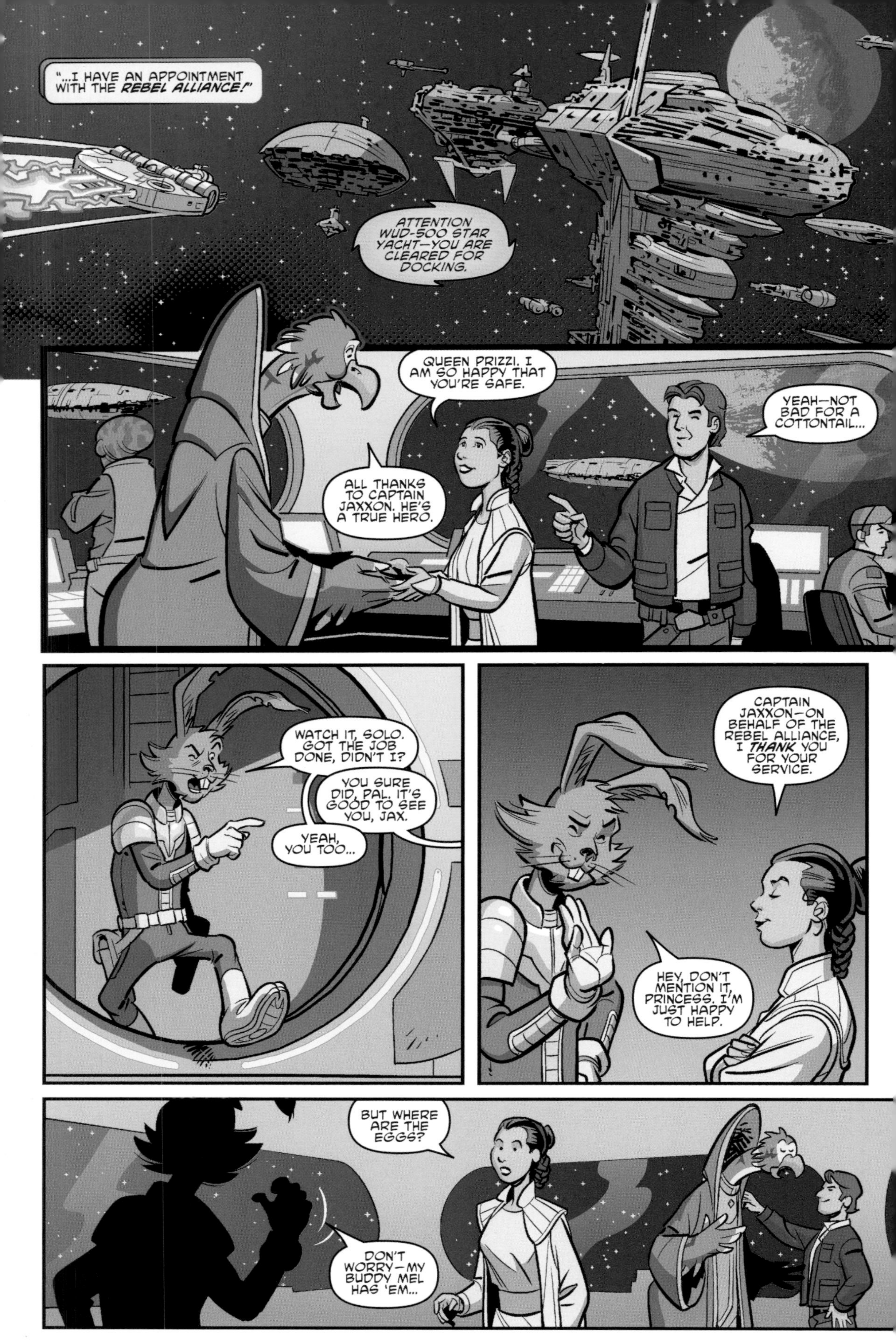

"...I HAVE AN APPOINTMENT WITH THE *REBEL ALLIANCE!*"
ATTENTION WUD-500 STAR YACHT—YOU ARE CLEARED FOR DOCKING.
QUEEN PRIZZI. I AM SO HAPPY THAT YOU'RE SAFE.
ALL THANKS TO CAPTAIN JAXXON. HE'S A TRUE HERO.
YEAH—NOT BAD FOR A COTTONTAIL...
WATCH IT, SOLO. GOT THE JOB DONE, DIDN'T I?
YOU SURE DID, PAL. IT'S GOOD TO SEE YOU, JAX.
YEAH, YOU TOO...
CAPTAIN JAXXON—ON BEHALF OF THE REBEL ALLIANCE, I *THANK* YOU FOR YOUR SERVICE.
HEY, DON'T MENTION IT, PRINCESS. I'M JUST HAPPY TO HELP.
BUT WHERE ARE THE EGGS?
DON'T WORRY—MY BUDDY MEL HAS 'EM...

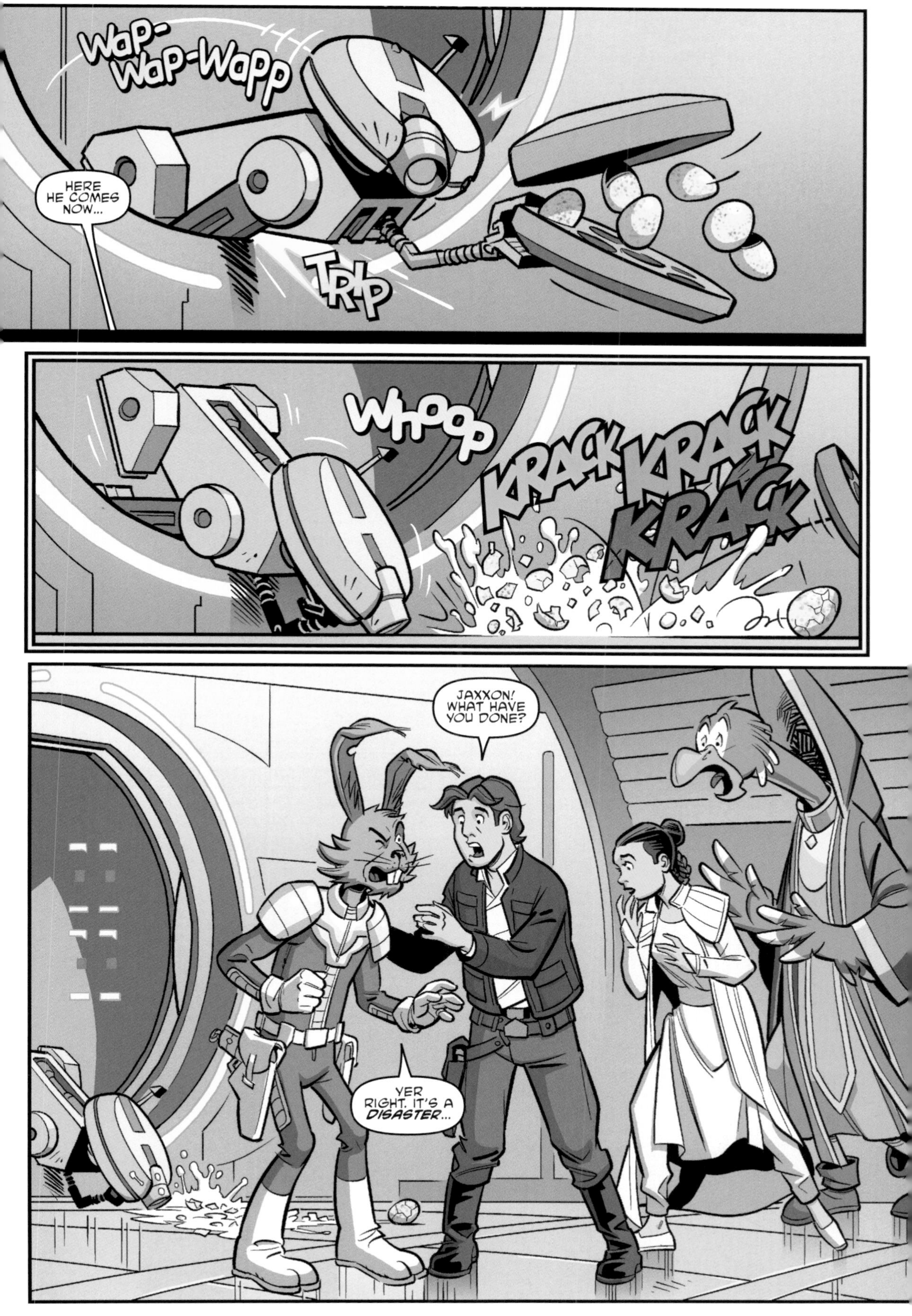
WAP-WAP-WAPP
HERE HE COMES NOW...
TRIP
WHOOP
KRACK KRACK KRACK
JAXXON! WHAT HAVE YOU DONE?
YER RIGHT. IT'S A *DISASTER*...

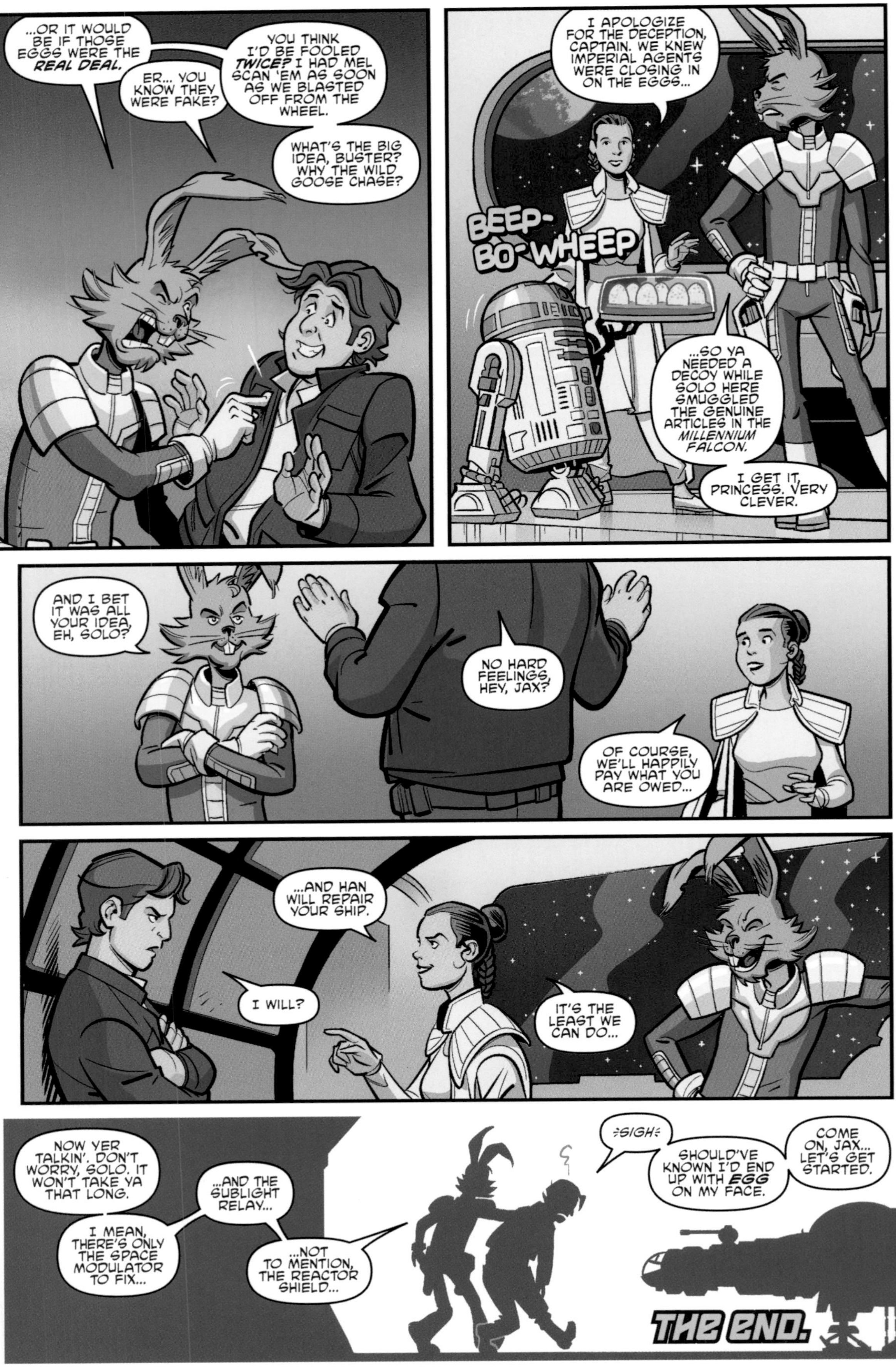
...OR IT WOULD BE IF THOSE EGGS WERE THE *REAL DEAL.*
ER... YOU KNOW THEY WERE FAKE?
YOU THINK I'D BE FOOLED *TWICE?* I HAD MEL SCAN 'EM AS SOON AS WE BLASTED OFF FROM THE WHEEL.
WHAT'S THE BIG IDEA, BUSTER? WHY THE WILD GOOSE CHASE?
I APOLOGIZE FOR THE DECEPTION, CAPTAIN. WE KNEW IMPERIAL AGENTS WERE CLOSING IN ON THE EGGS...
BEEP-BO-WHEEP
...SO YA NEEDED A DECOY WHILE SOLO HERE SMUGGLED THE GENUINE ARTICLES IN THE *MILLENNIUM FALCON.*
I GET IT, PRINCESS. VERY CLEVER.
AND I BET IT WAS ALL YOUR IDEA, EH, SOLO?
NO HARD FEELINGS, HEY, JAX?
OF COURSE, WE'LL HAPPILY PAY WHAT YOU ARE OWED...
...AND HAN WILL REPAIR YOUR SHIP.
I WILL?
IT'S THE LEAST WE CAN DO...
NOW YER TALKIN'. DON'T WORRY, SOLO. IT WON'T TAKE YA THAT LONG.
I MEAN, THERE'S ONLY THE SPACE MODULATOR TO FIX...
...AND THE SUBLIGHT RELAY...
...NOT TO MENTION, THE REACTOR SHIELD...
SIGH
SHOULD'VE KNOWN I'D END UP WITH *EGG* ON MY FACE.
COME ON, JAX... LET'S GET STARTED.
THE END.

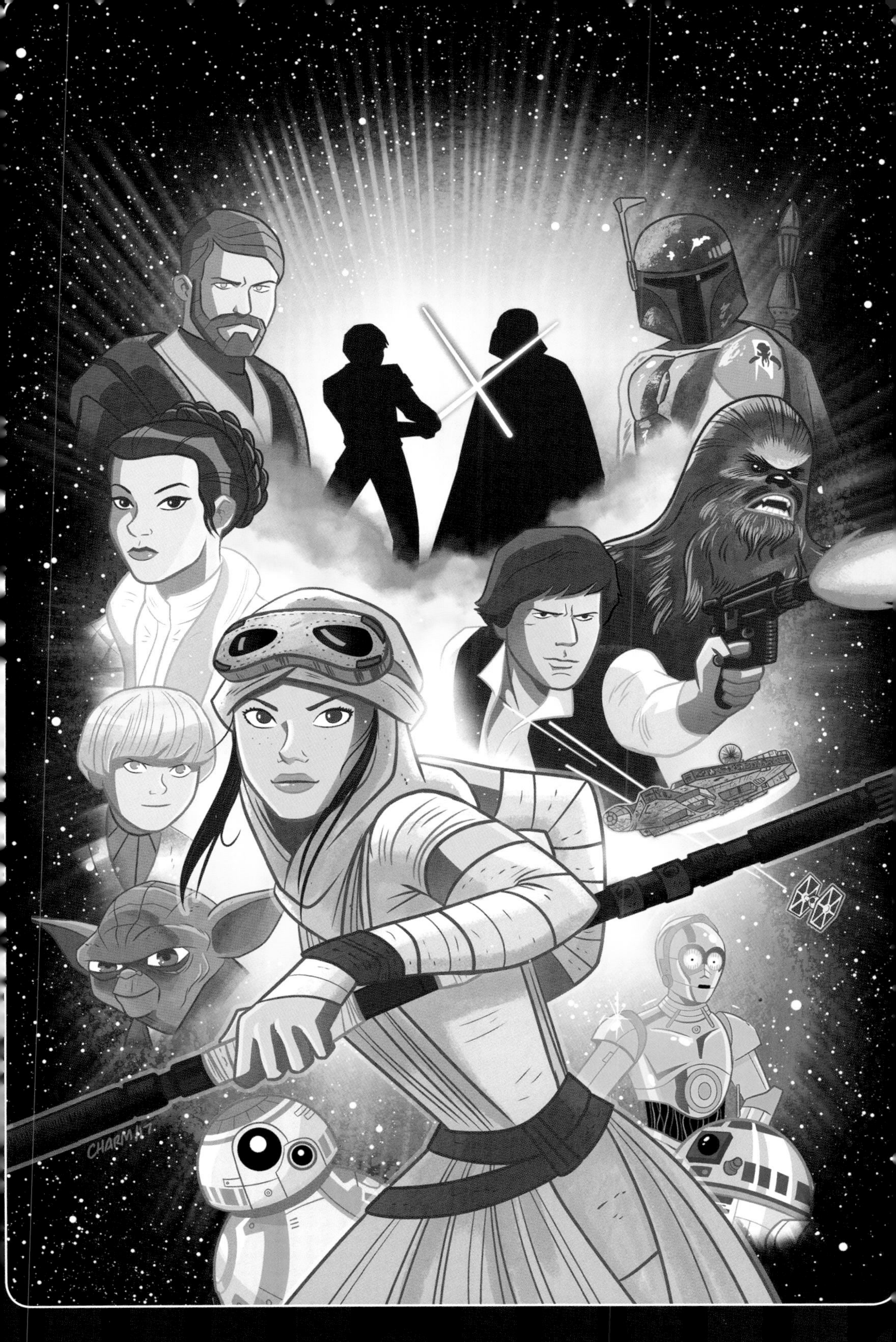
CHARM

ART BY DEREK CHARM

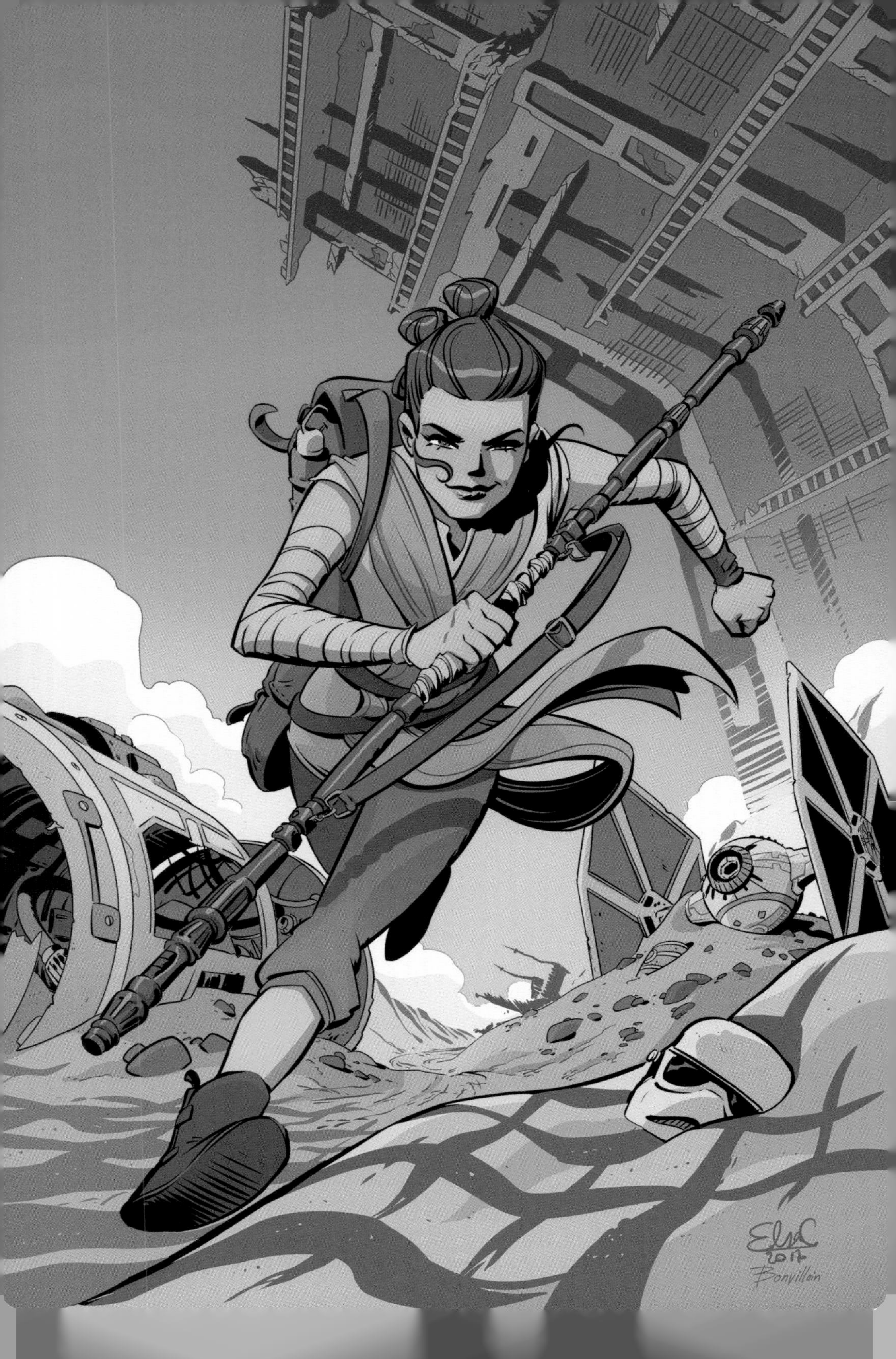
Elsa 2017
Bonvillain

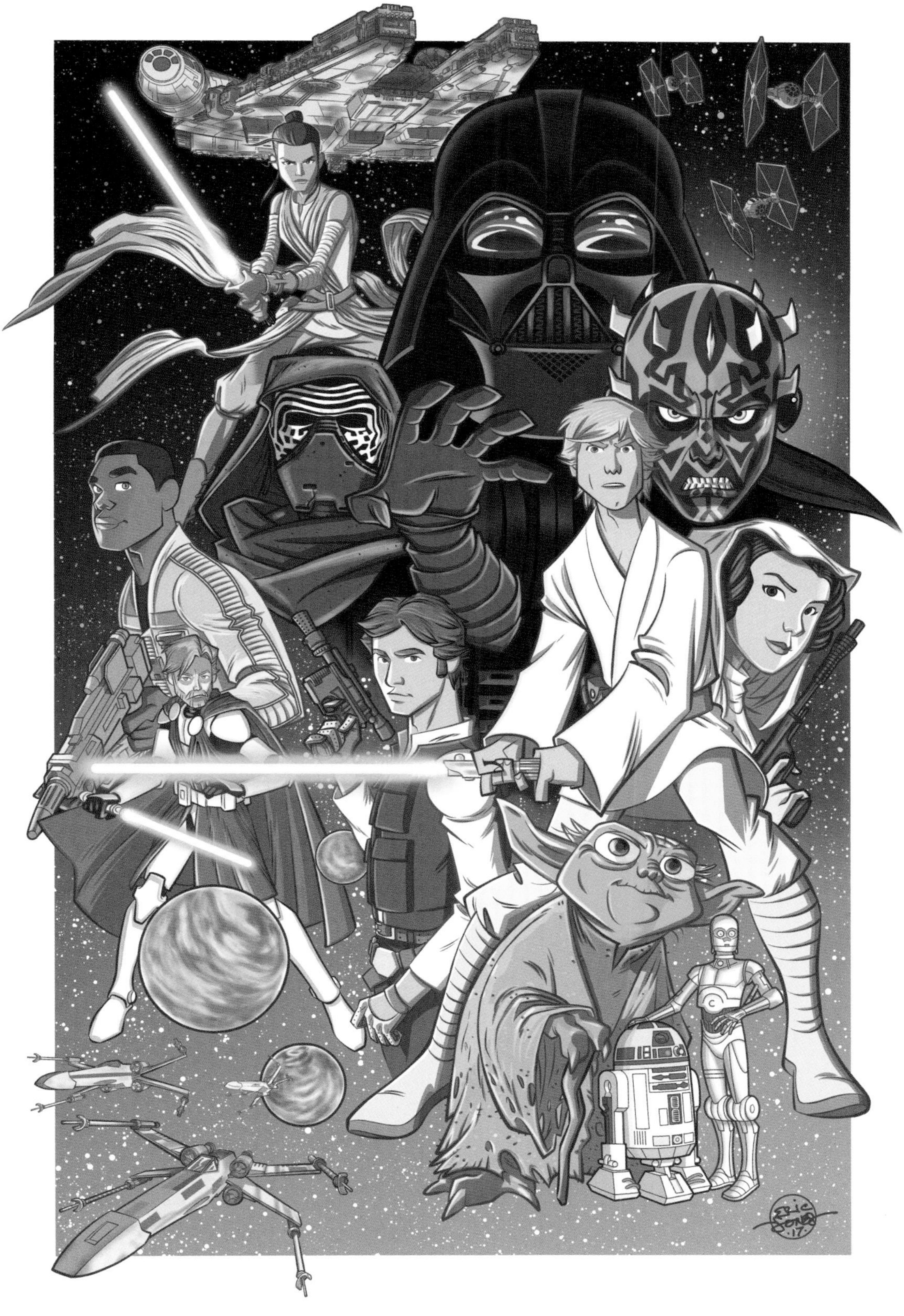

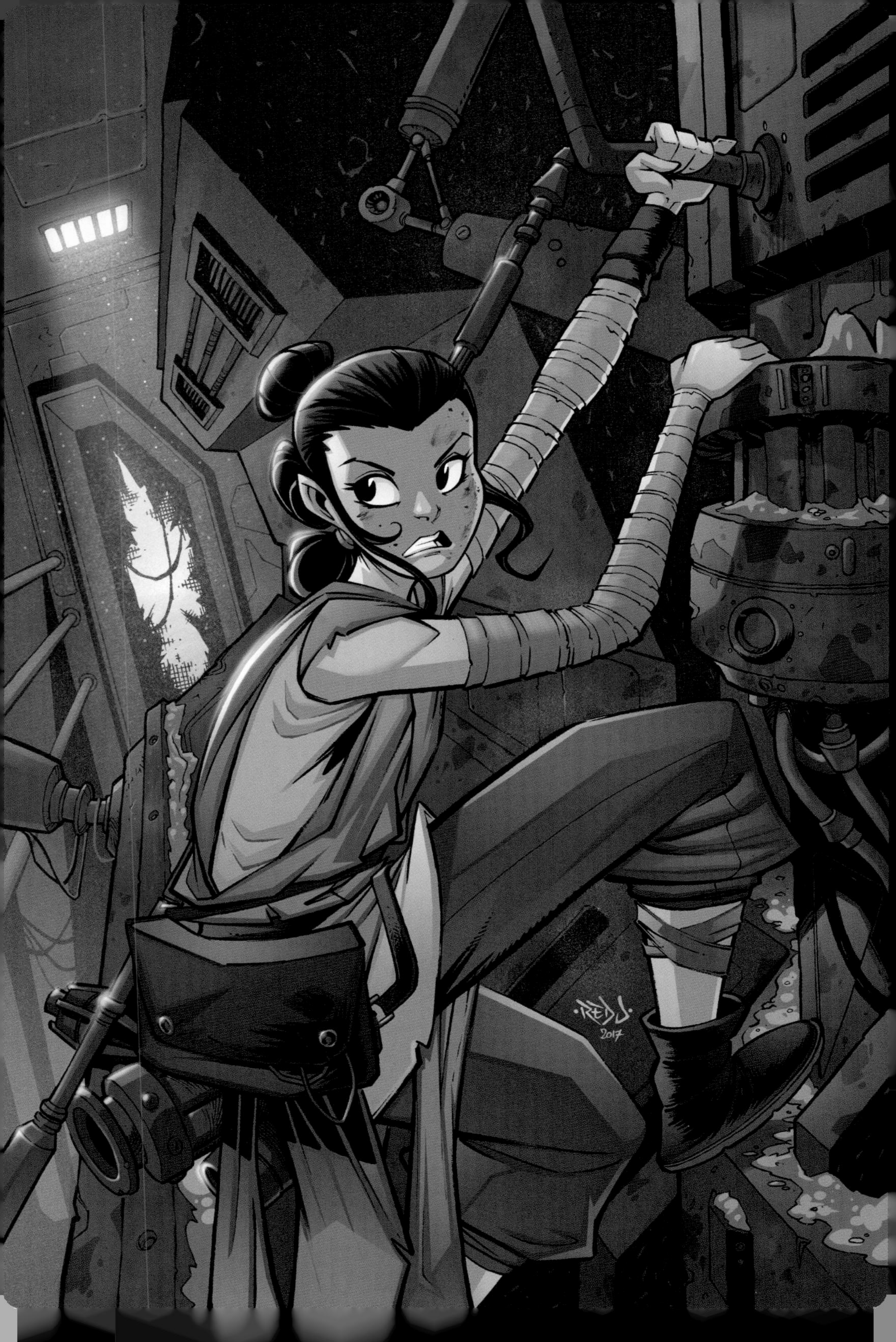

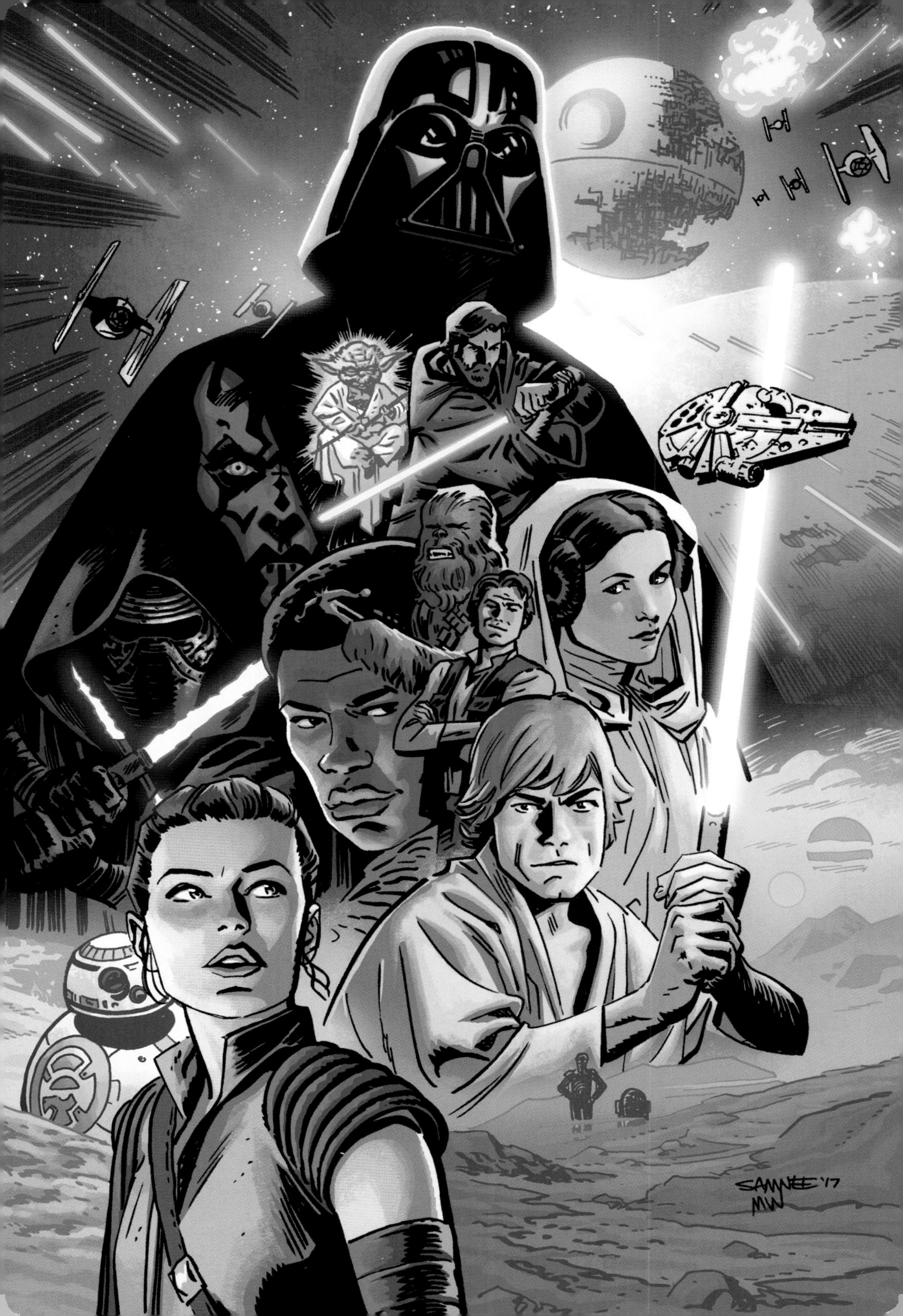

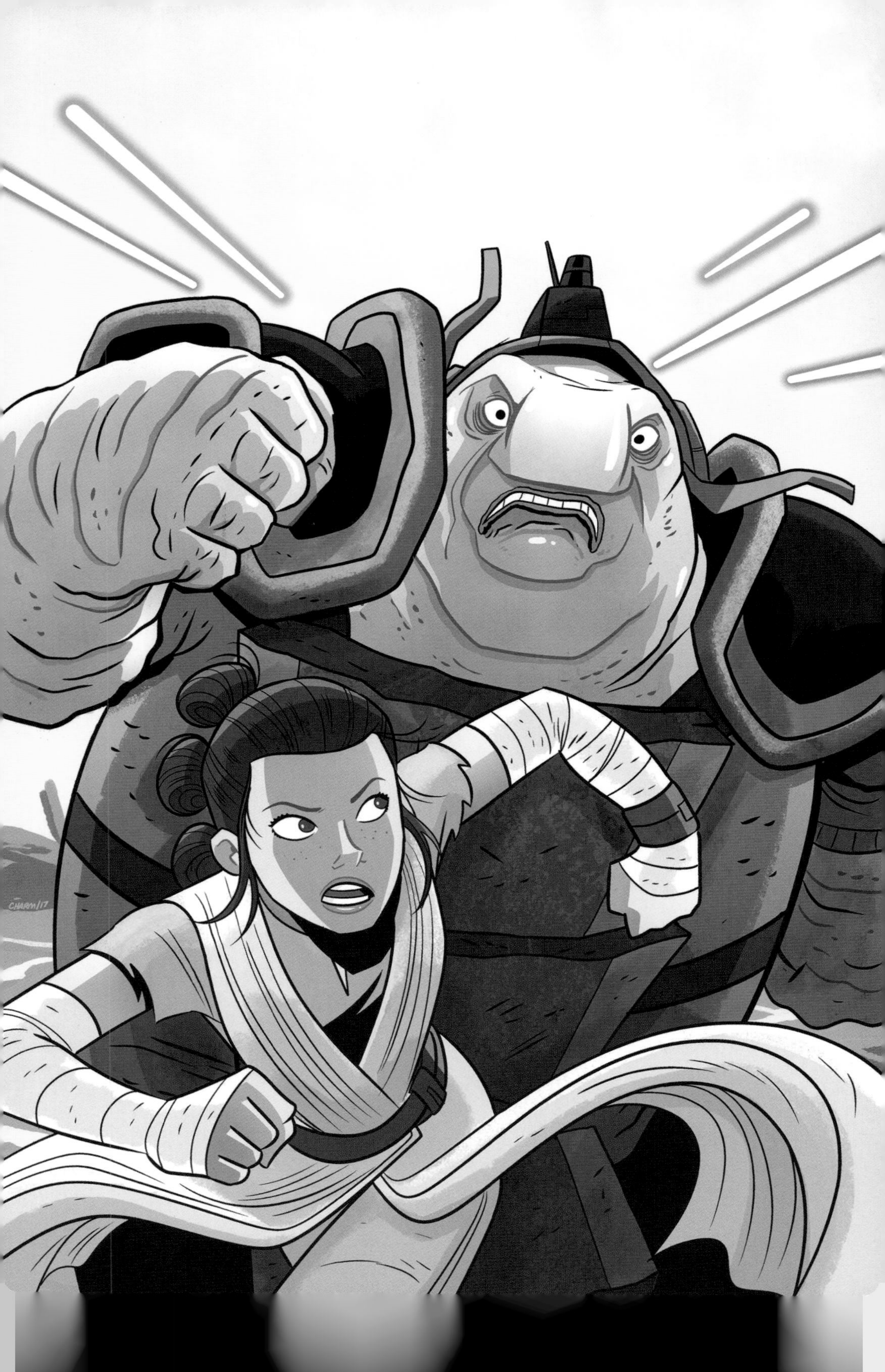
CHARM/17

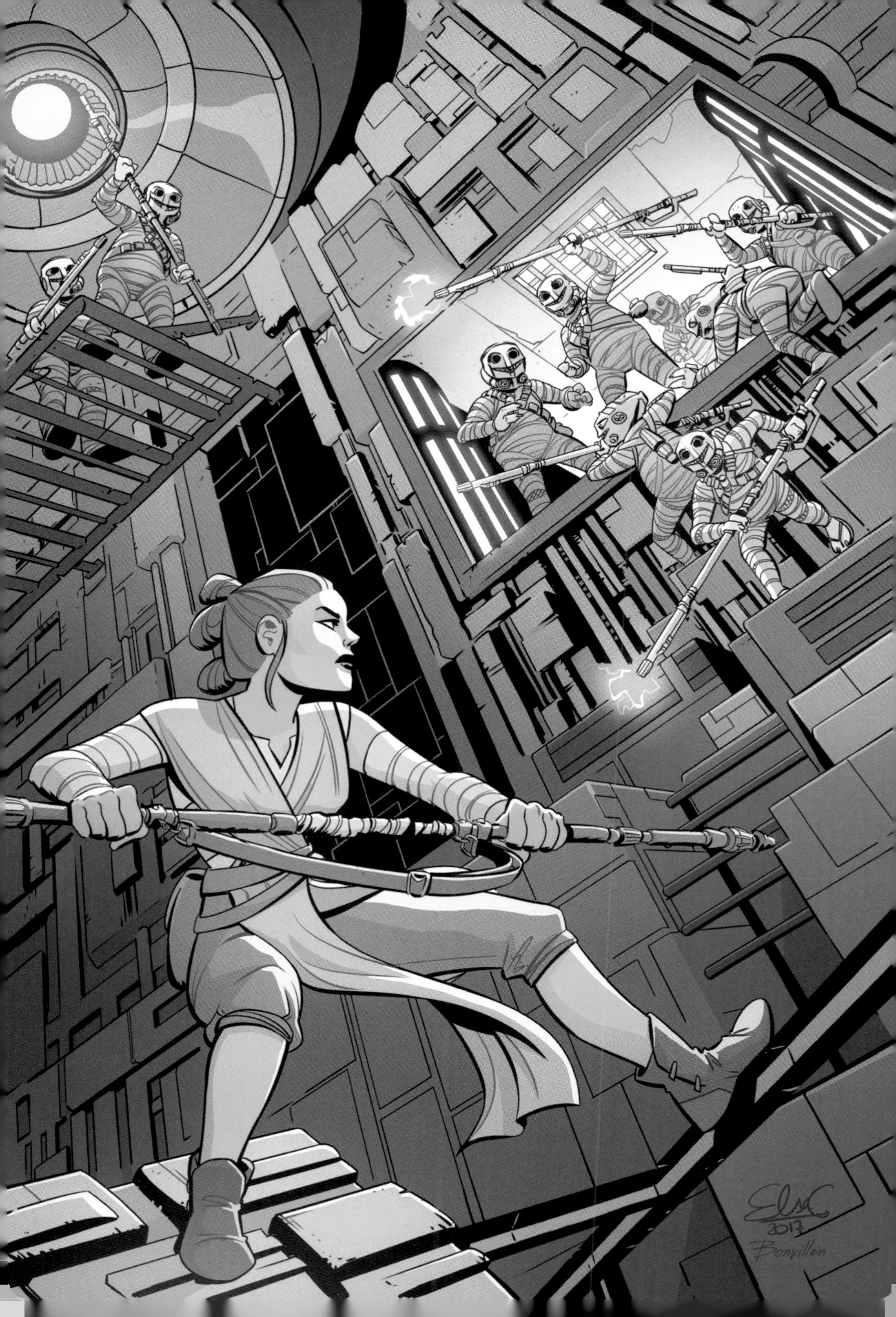

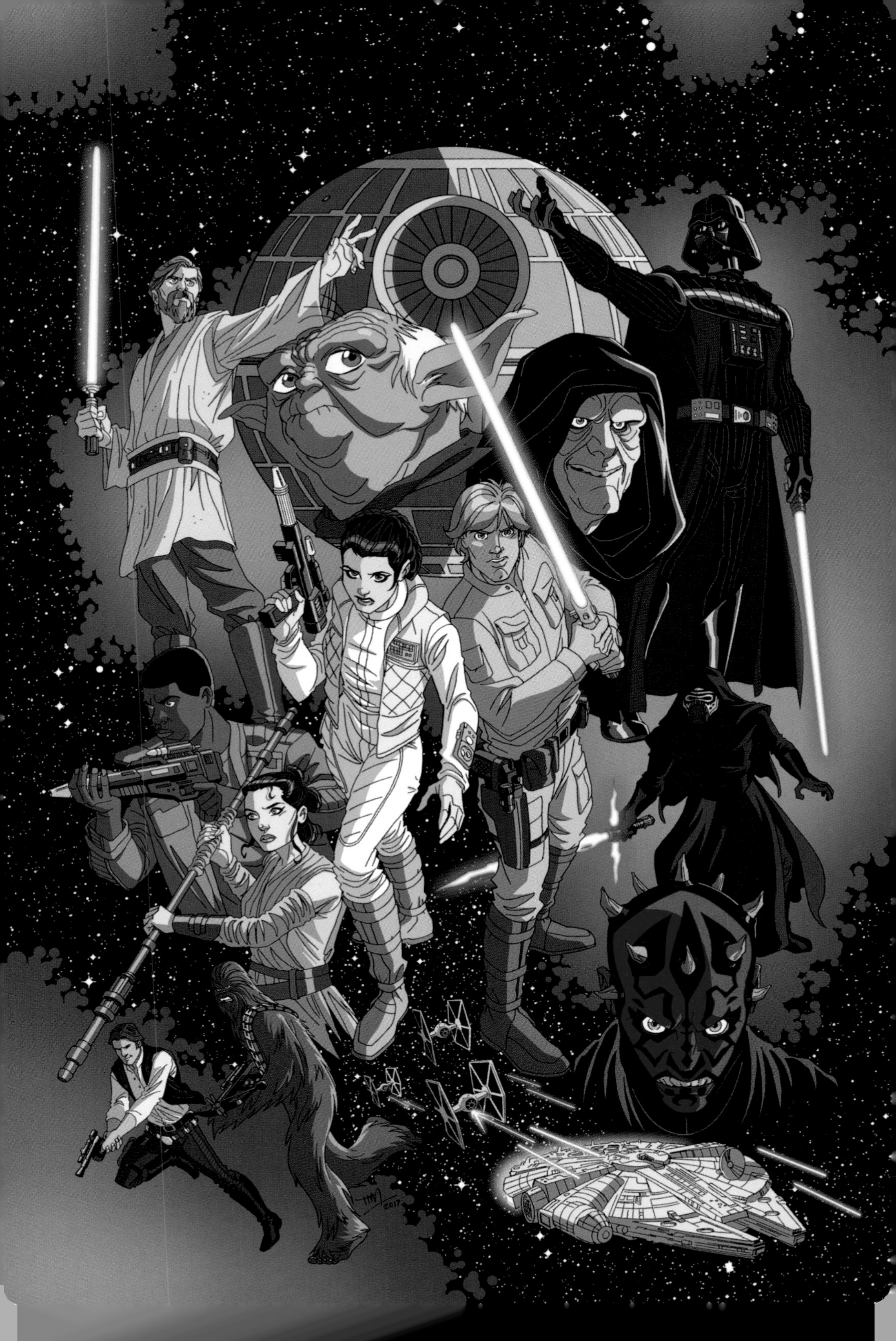

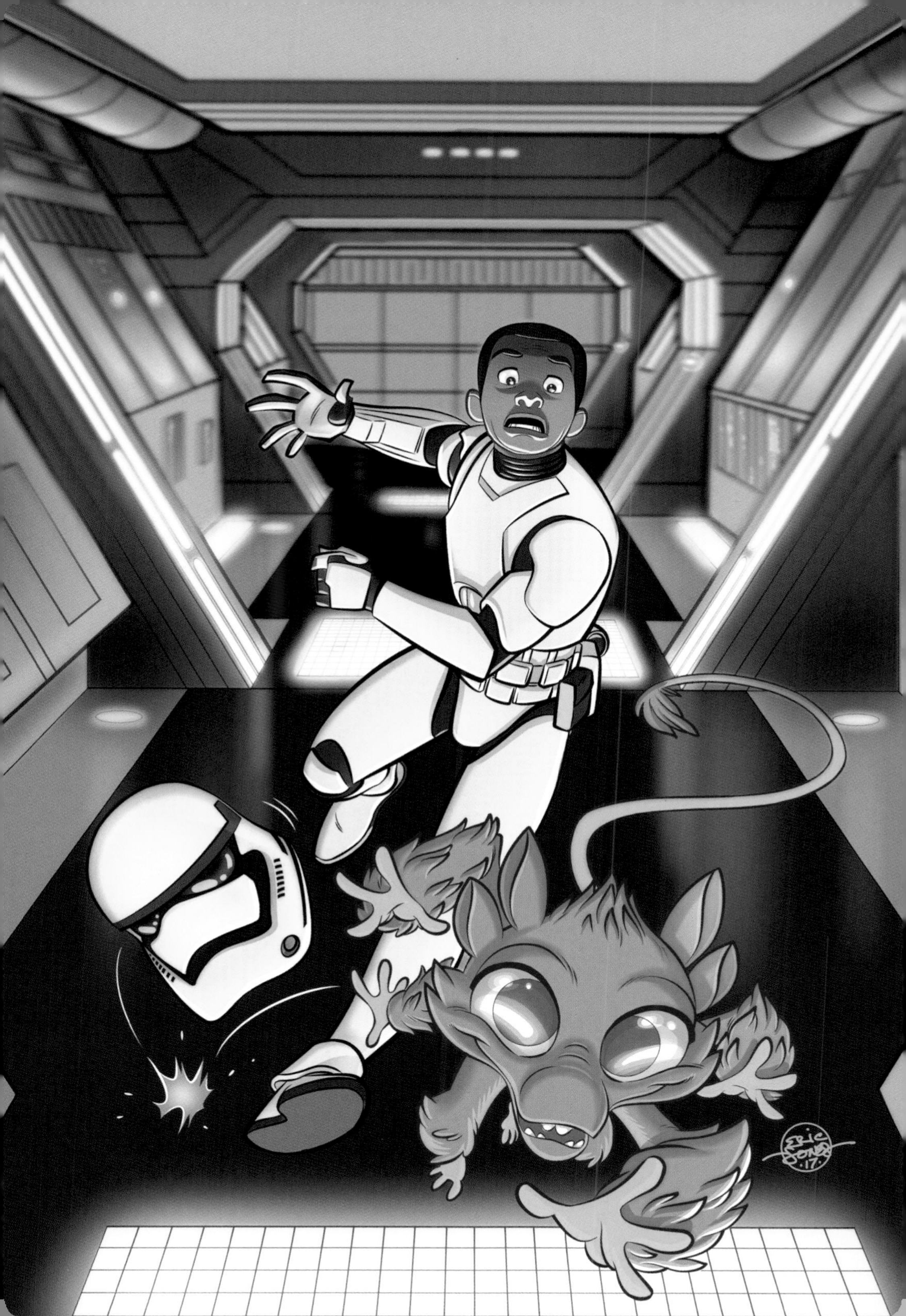

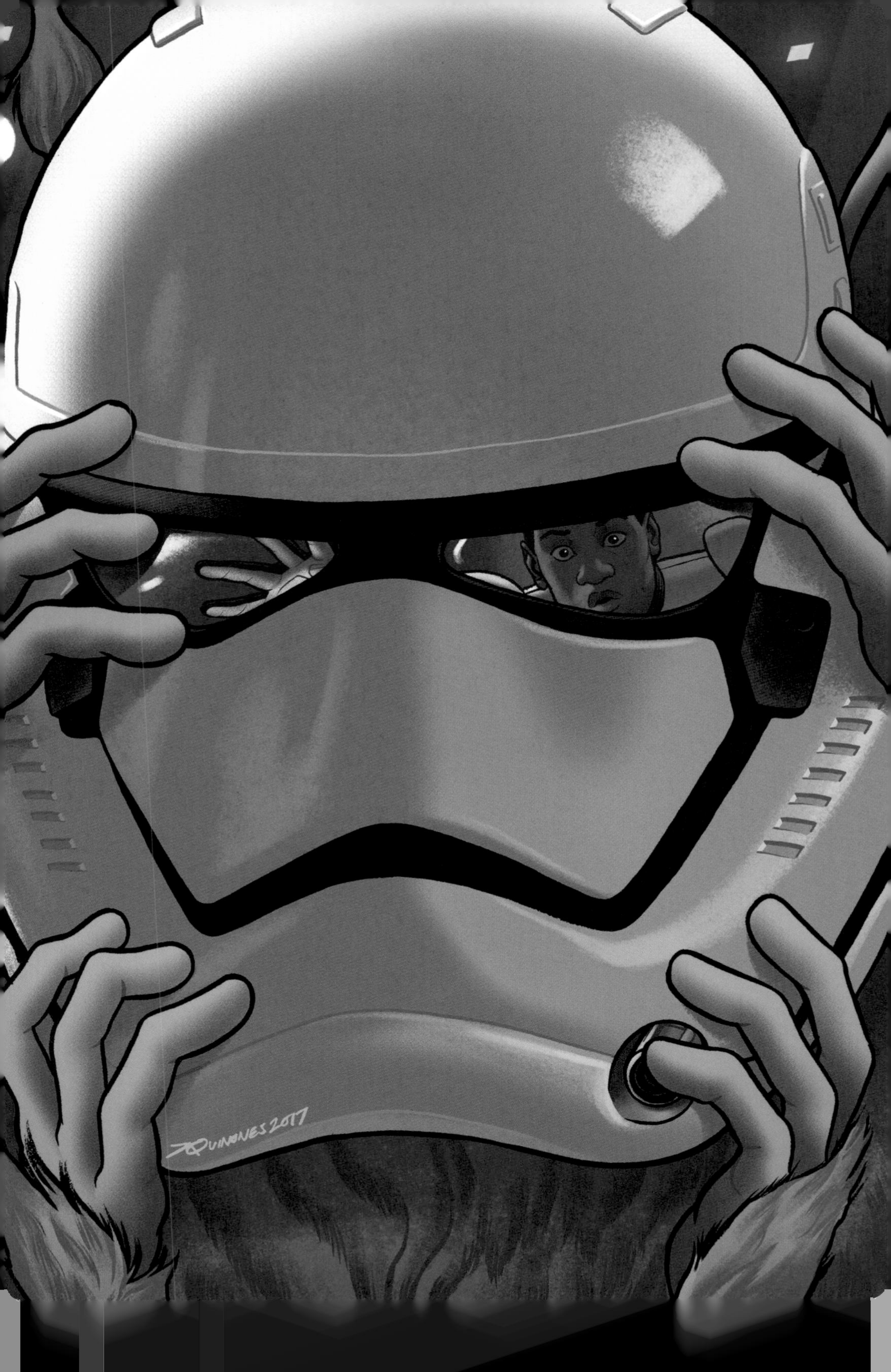
QUINONES 2017

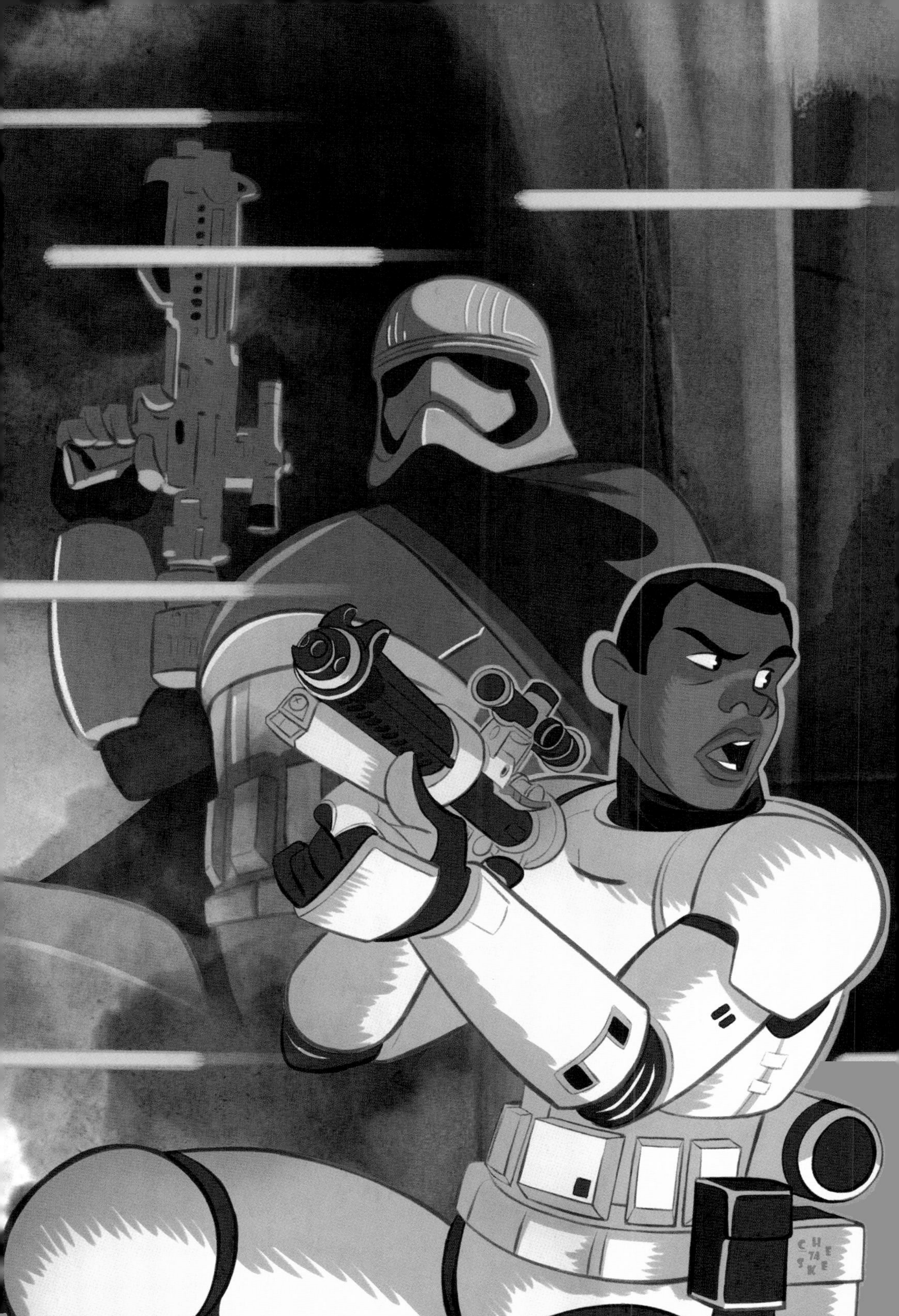

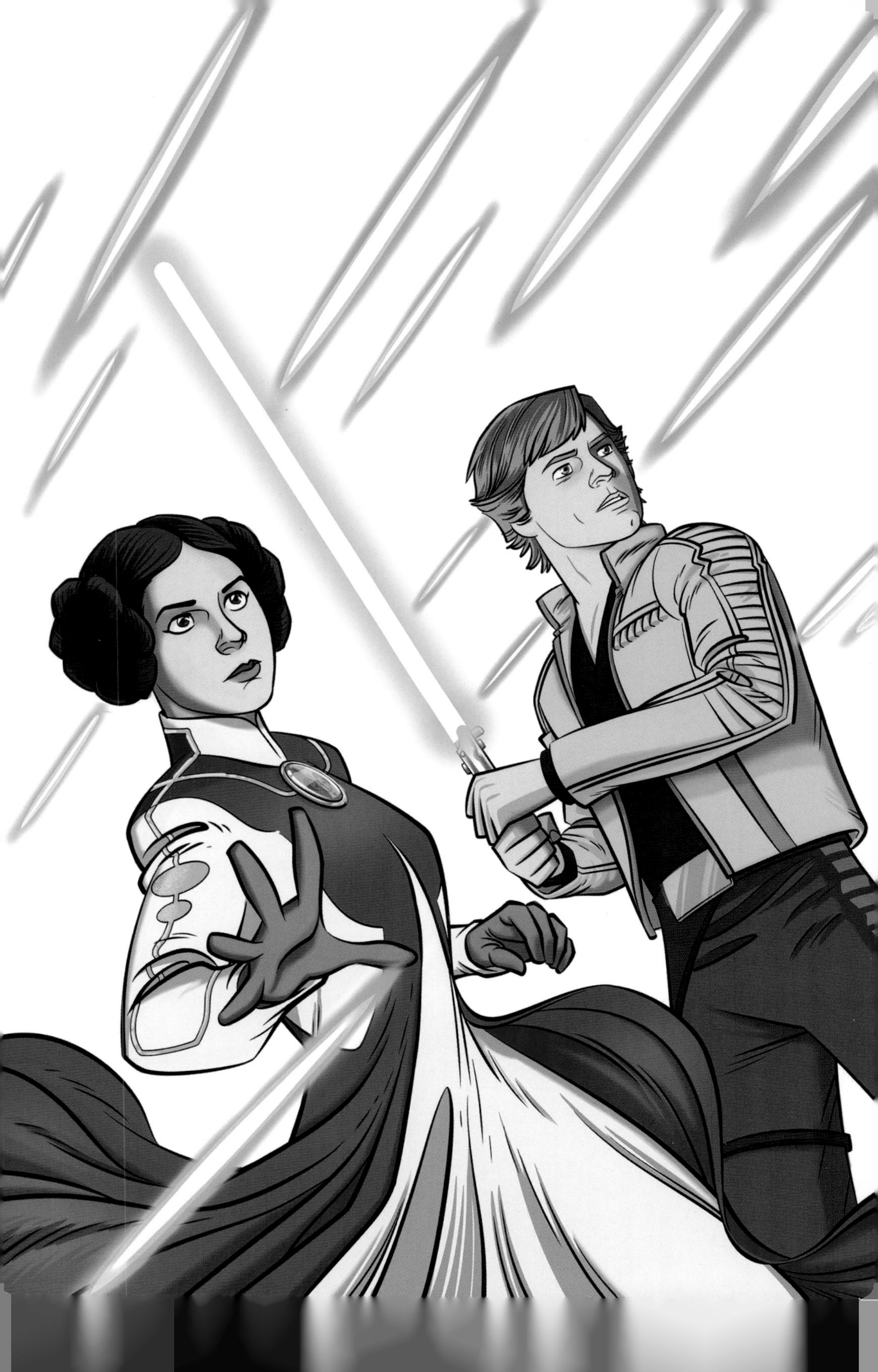

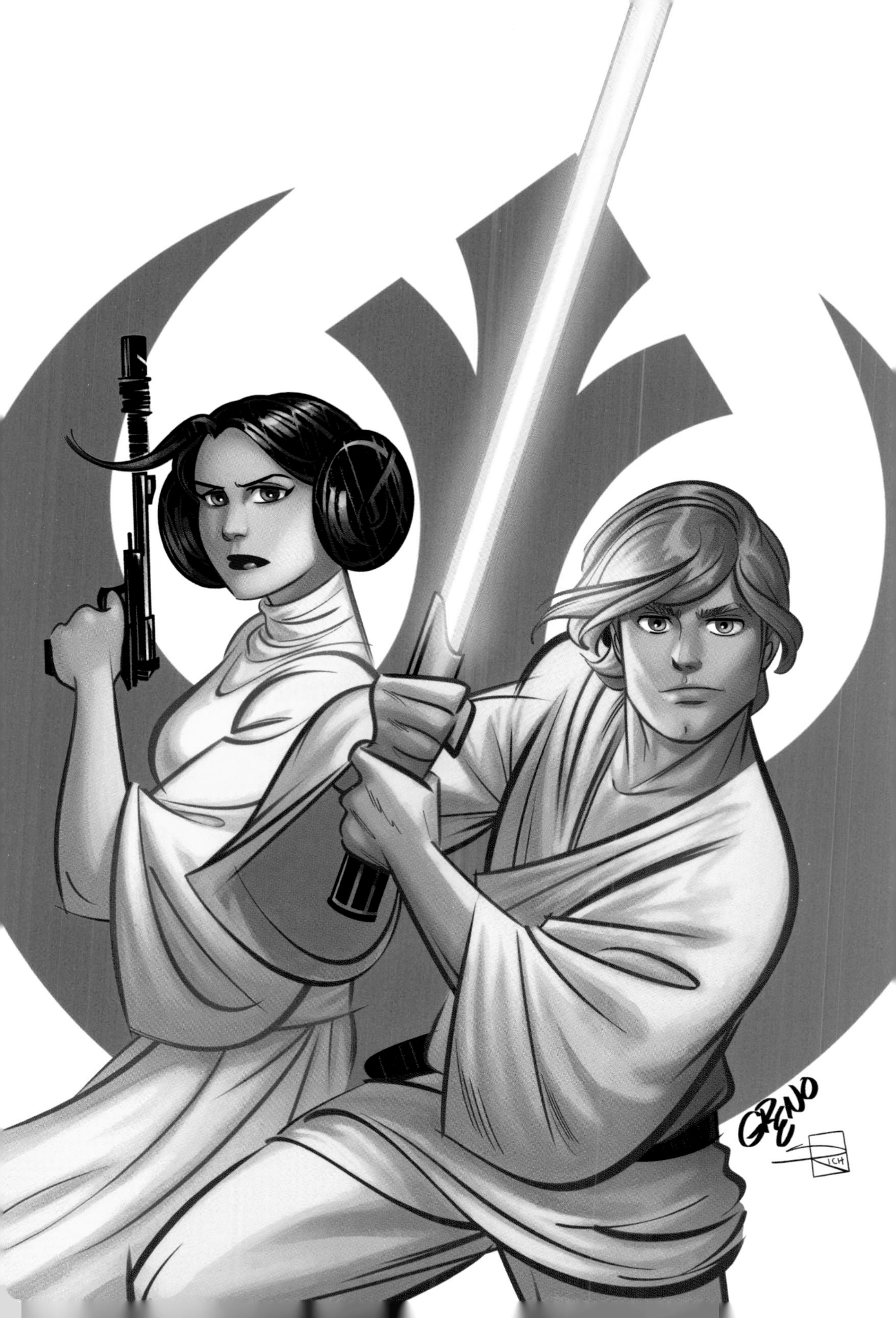

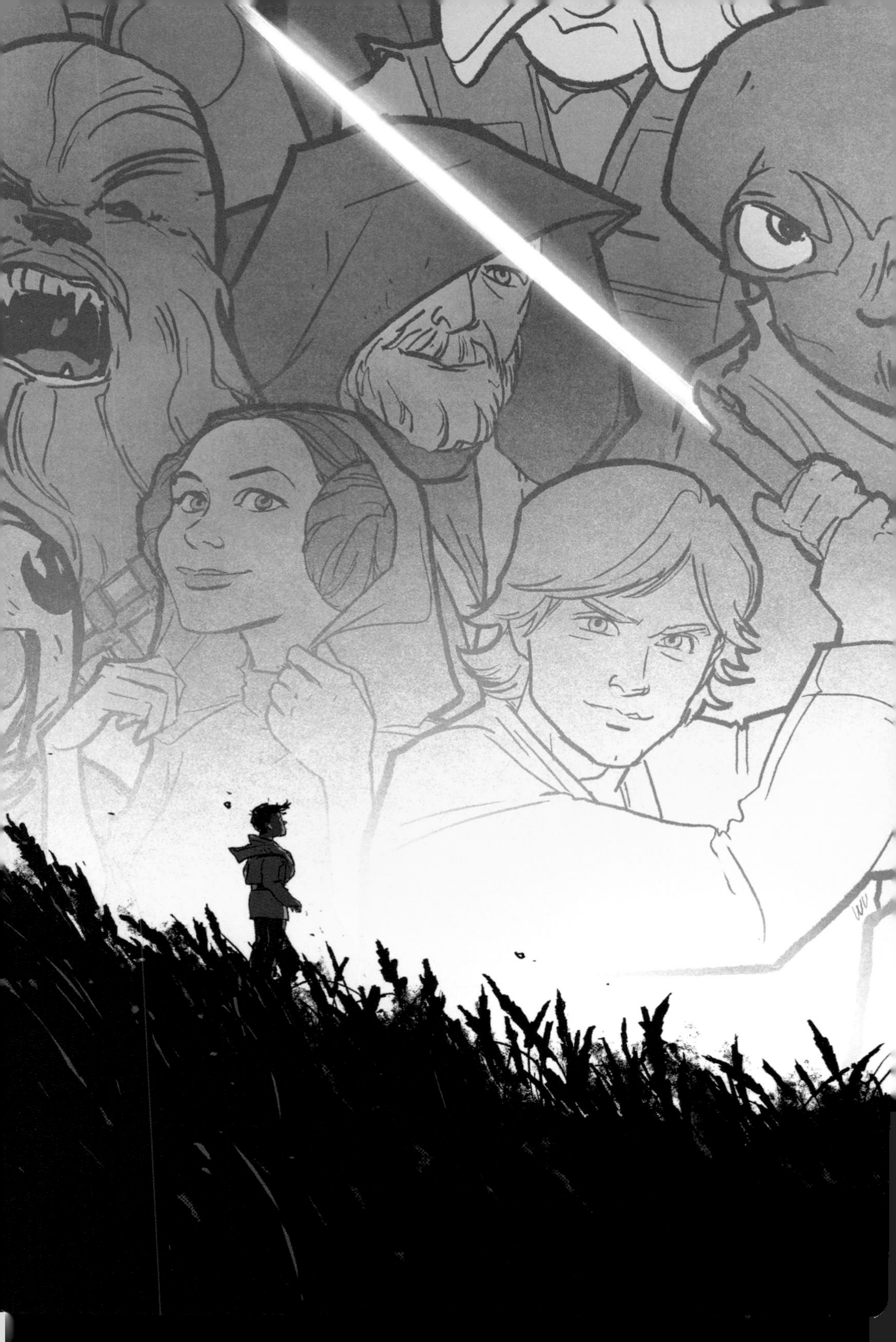

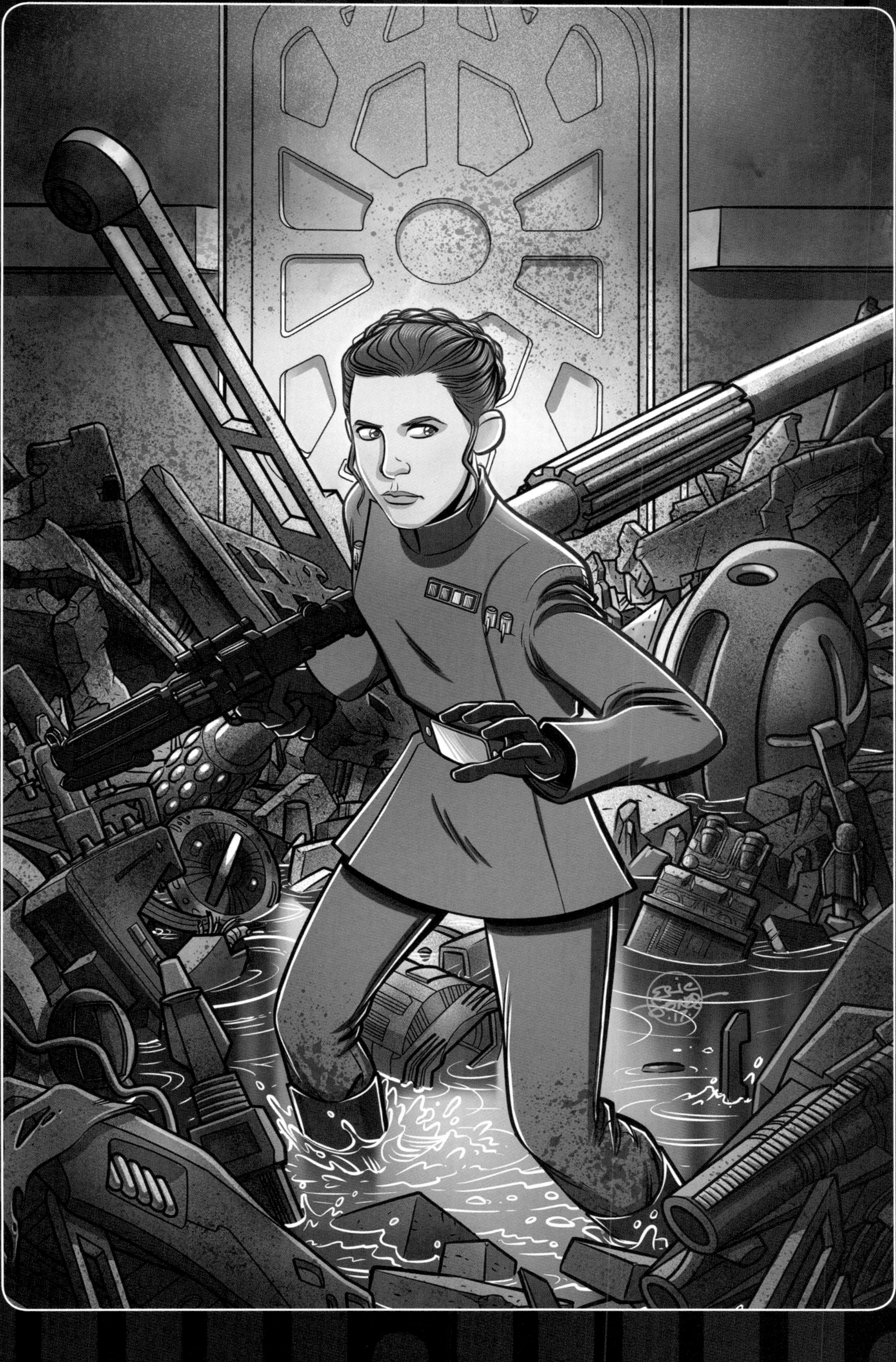

ART BY ERIC JONES

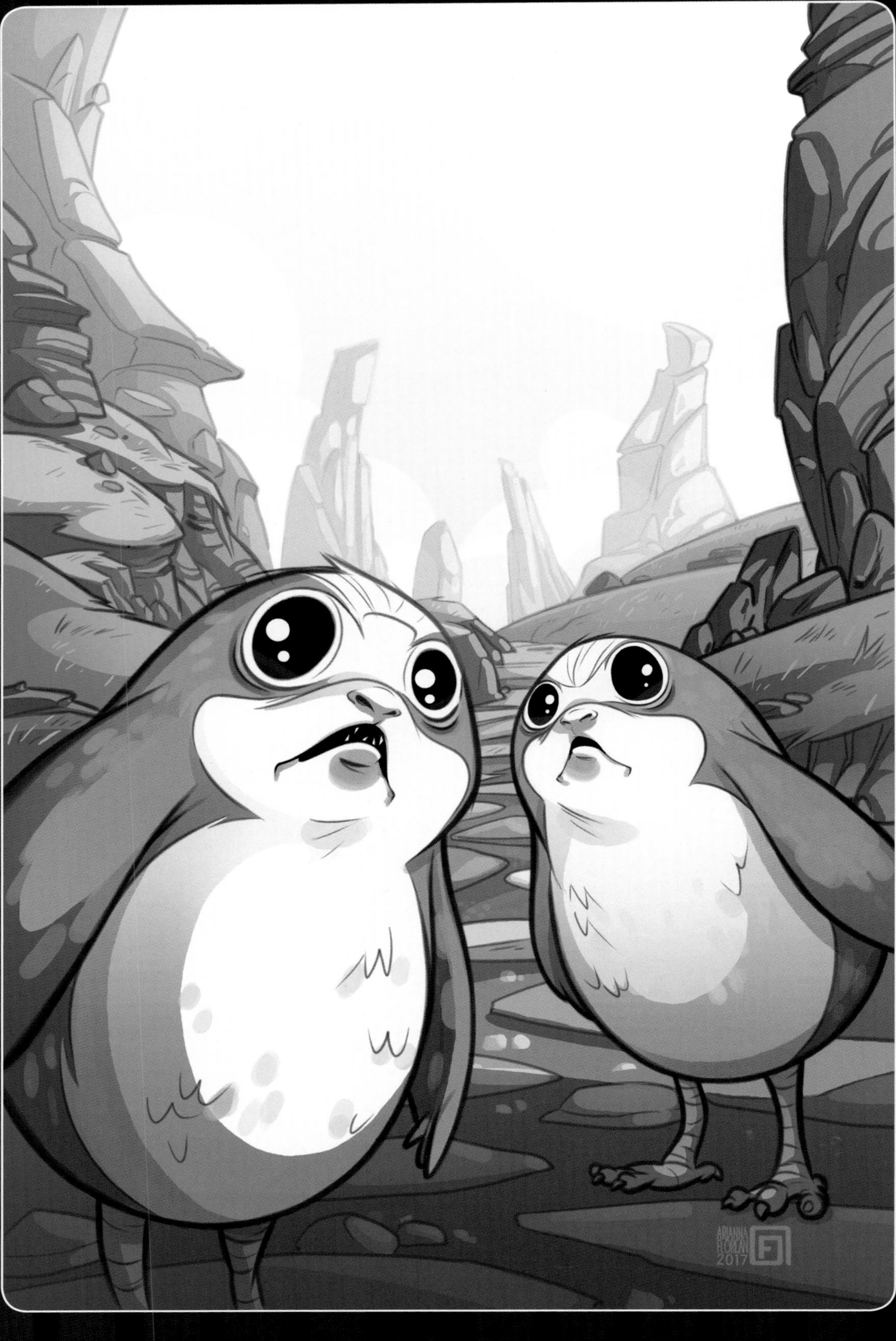
ARIANNA FLOREAN 2017

ART BY ARIANNA FLOREAN

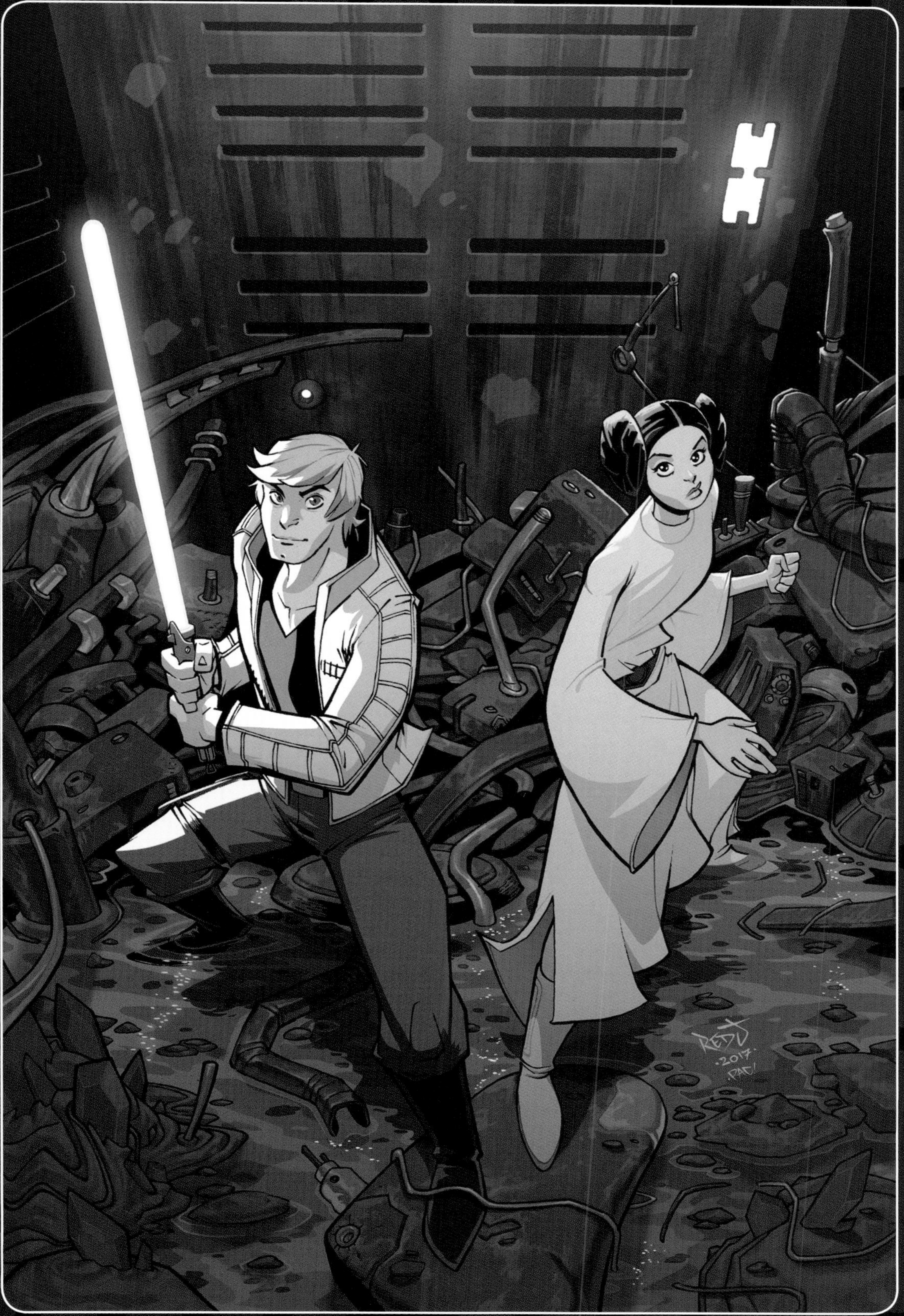

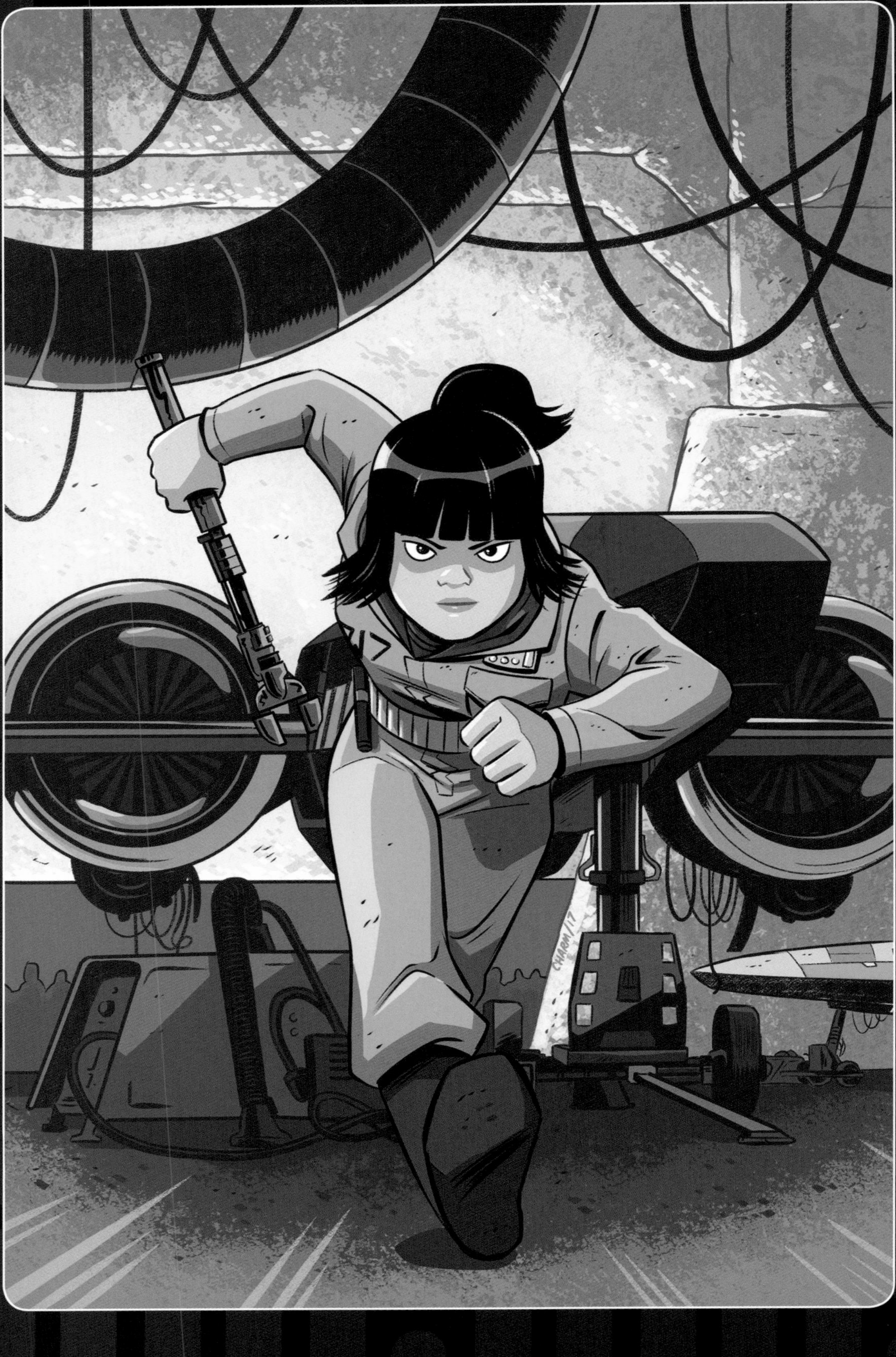
CHARM/17

ART BY **DEREK CHARM**

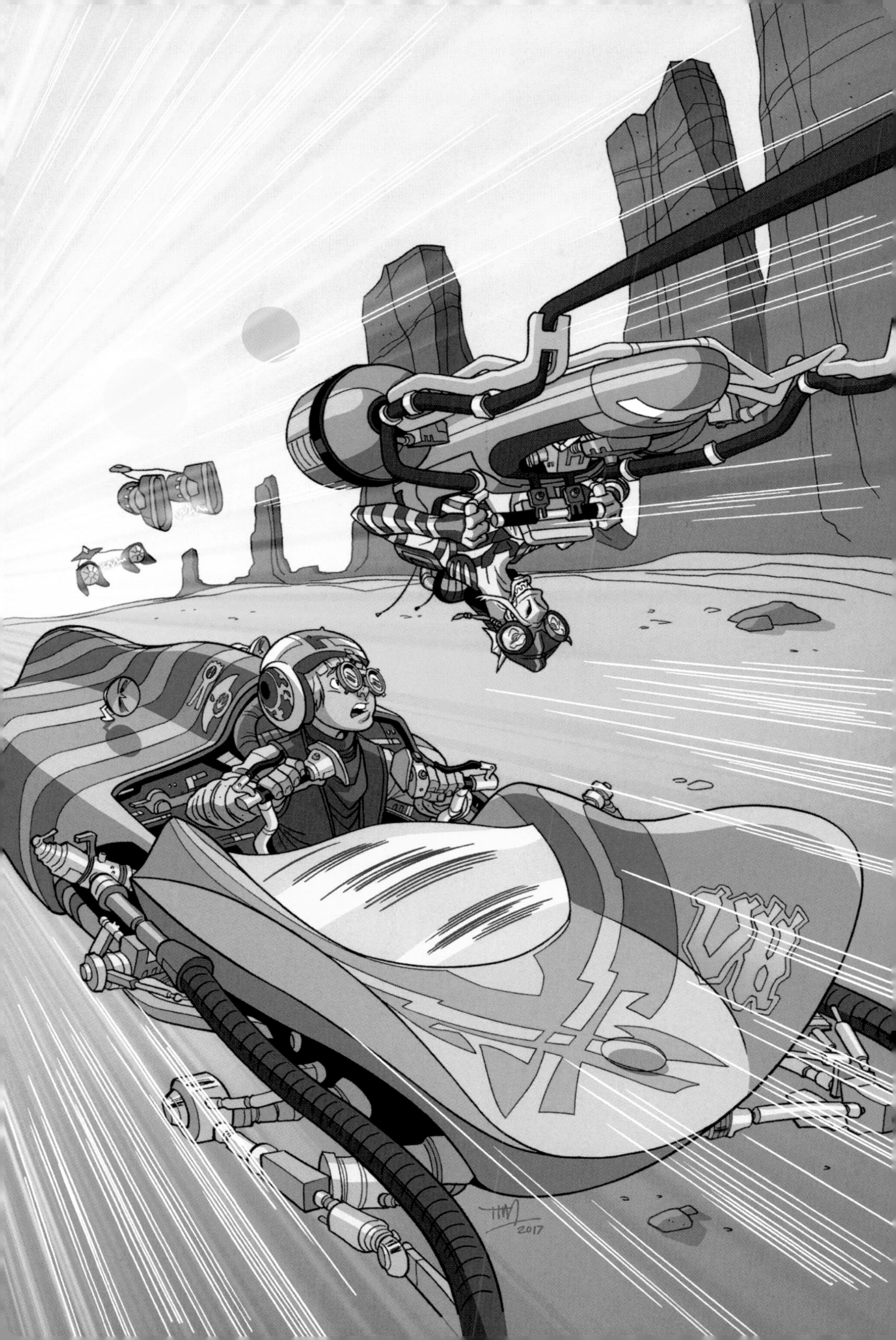

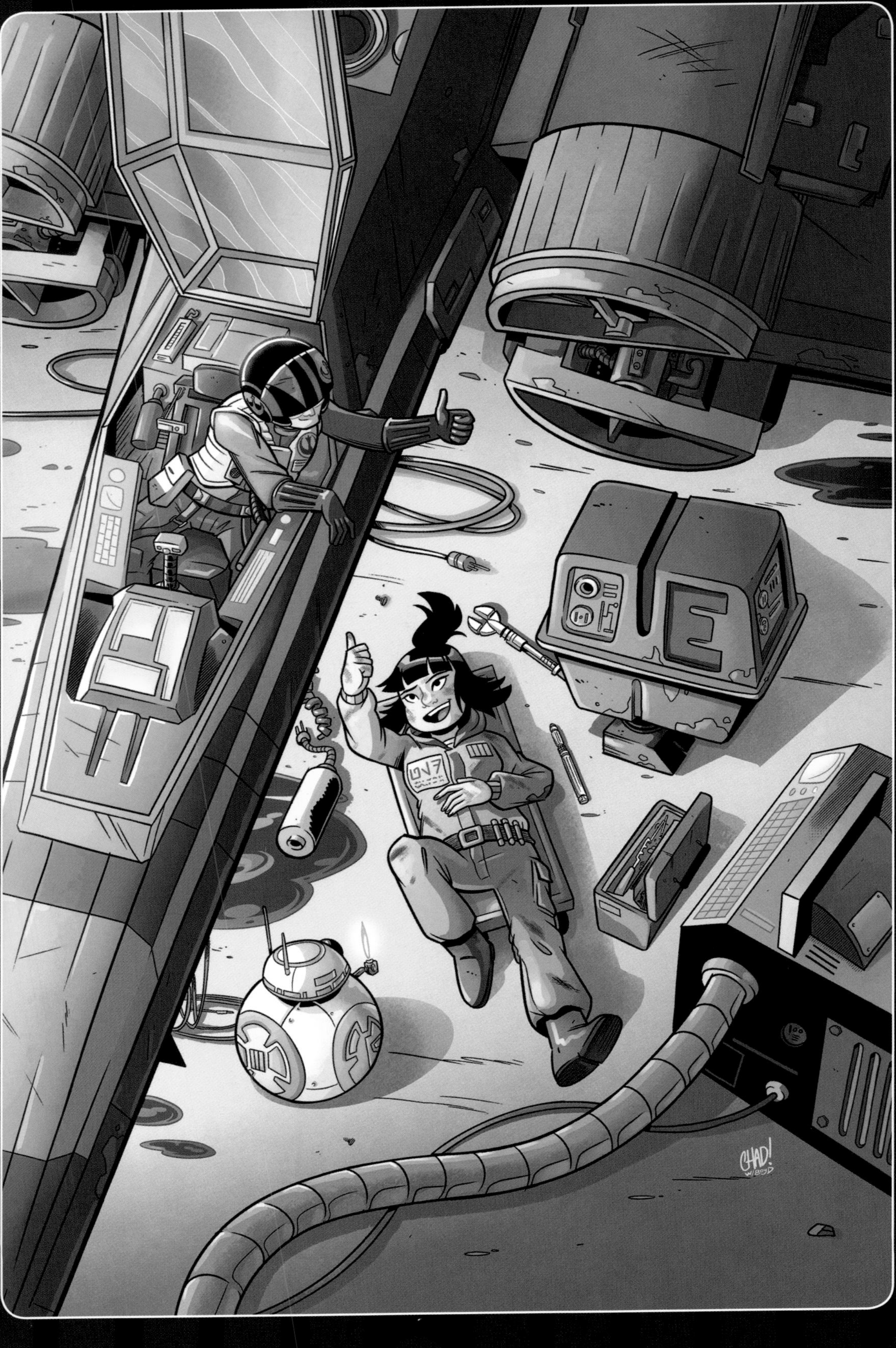
CHAD!
W/BOYD

ART BY CHAD THOMAS
COLORS BY JORDAN BOYD

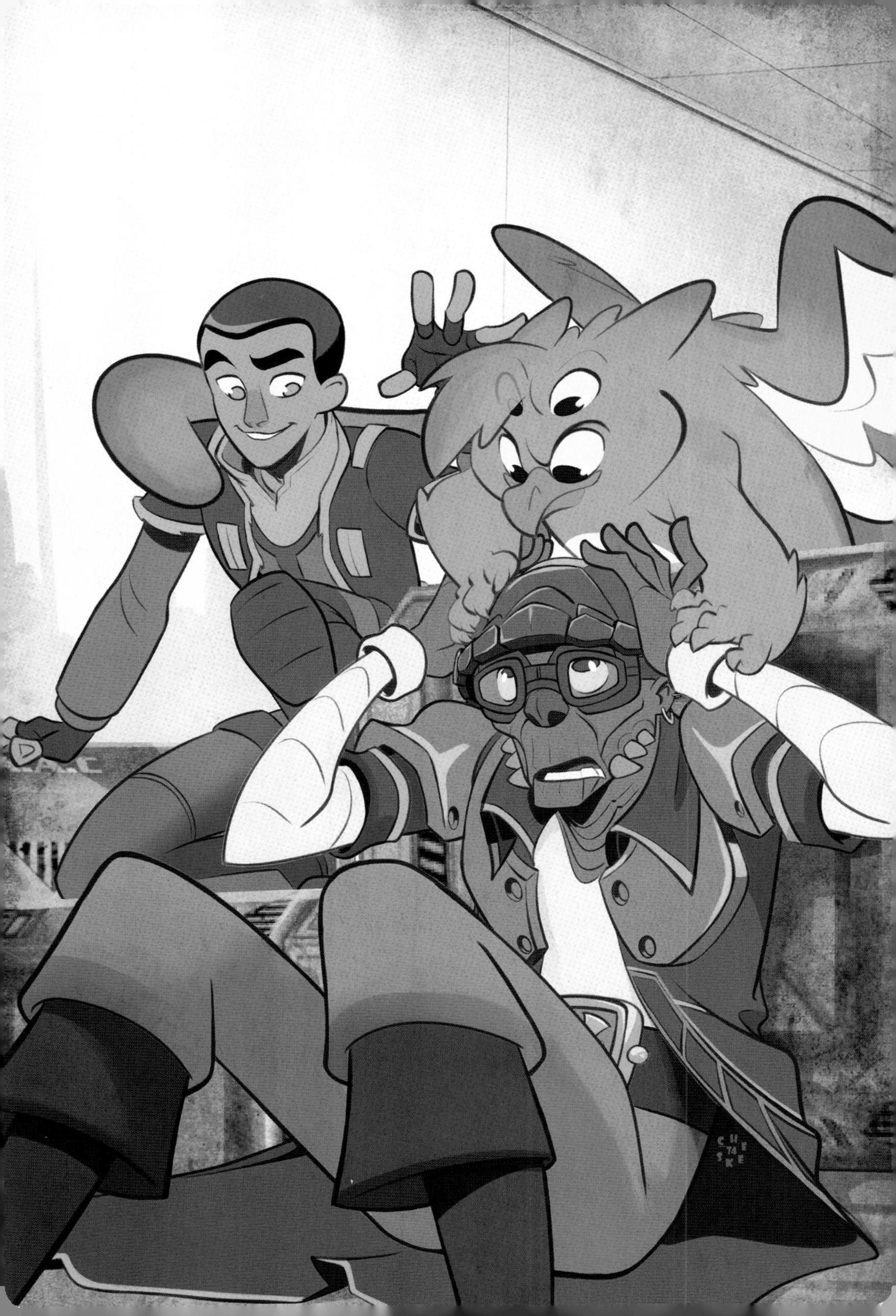

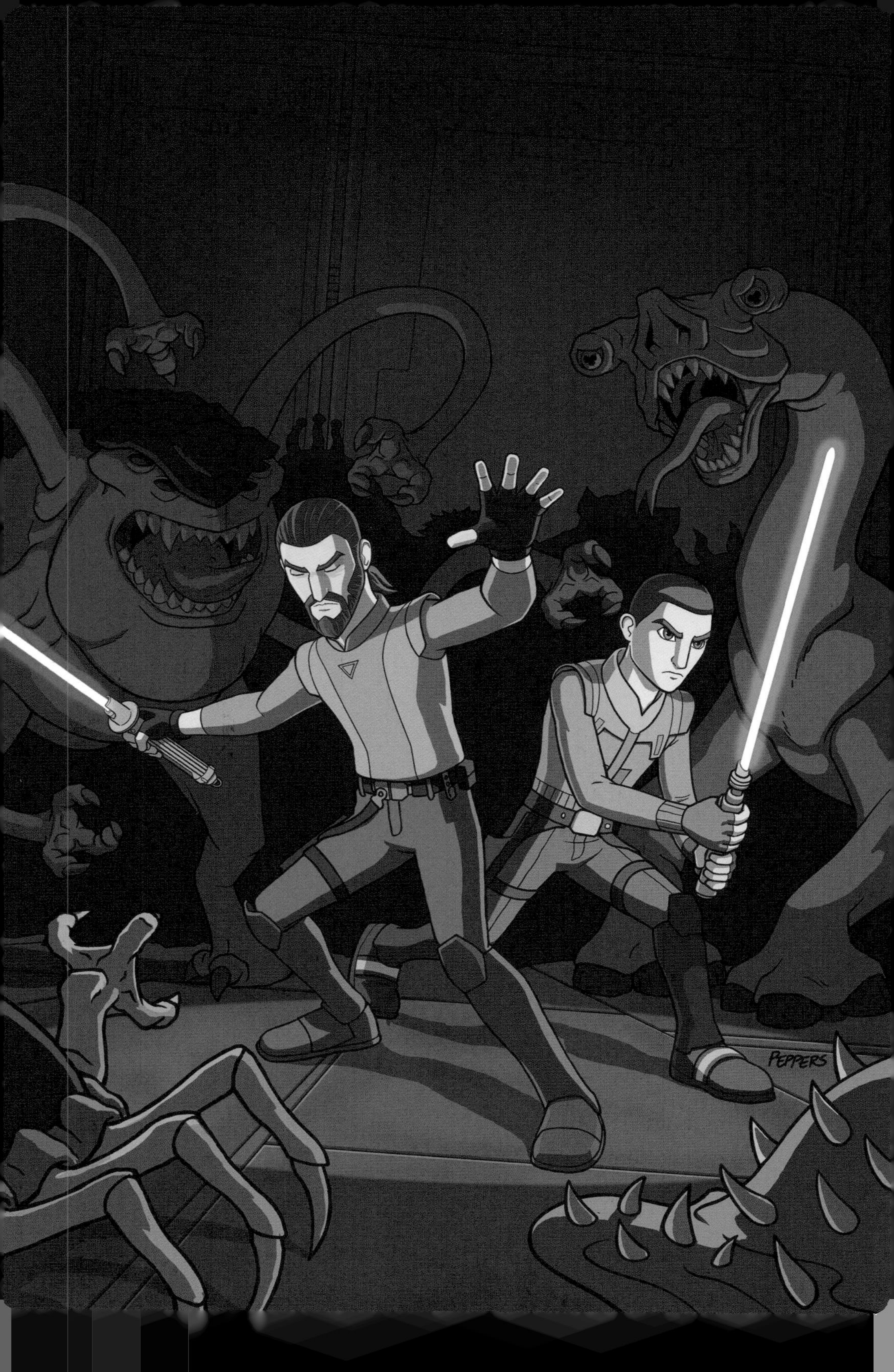
PEPPERS

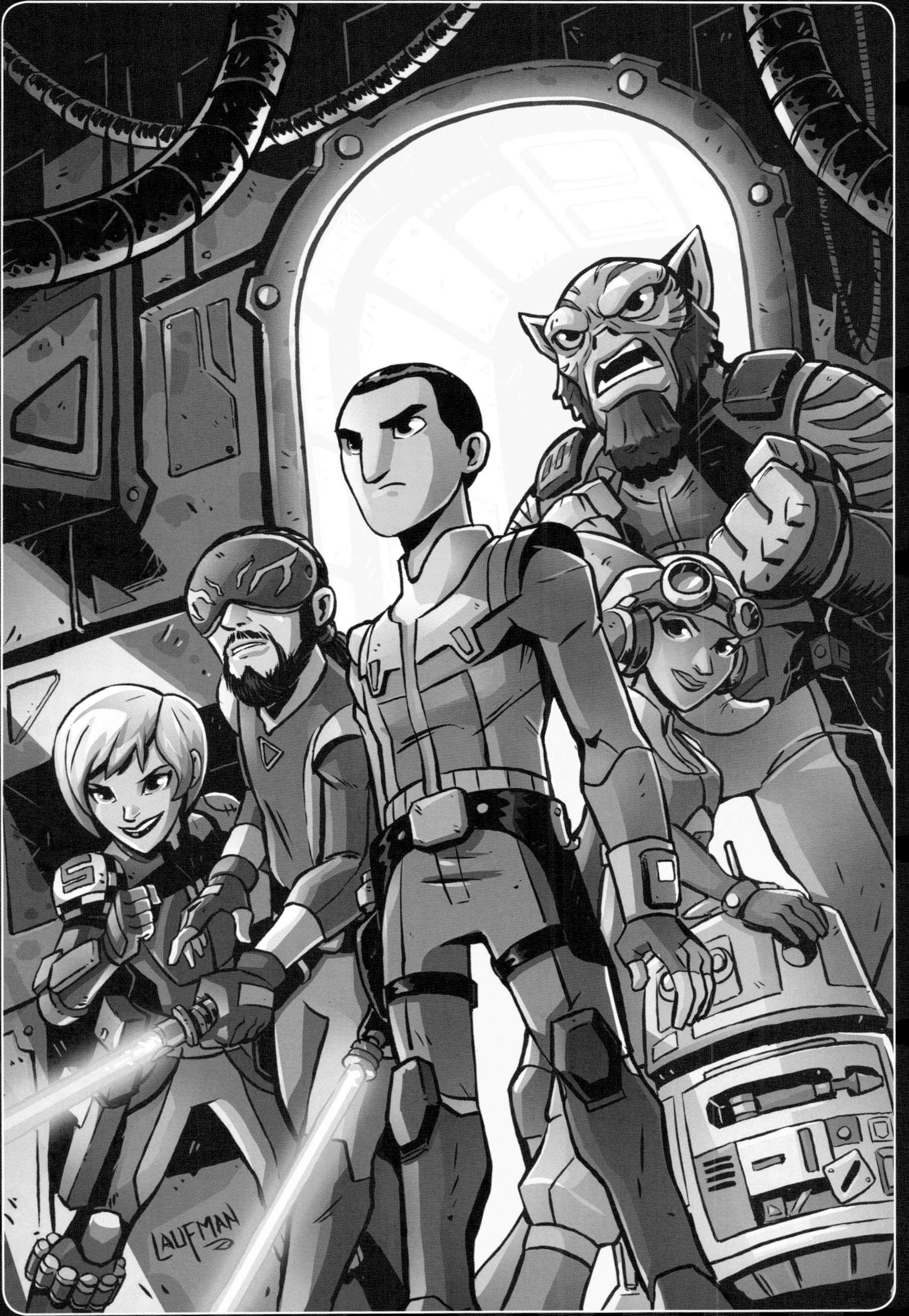
LAUFMAN

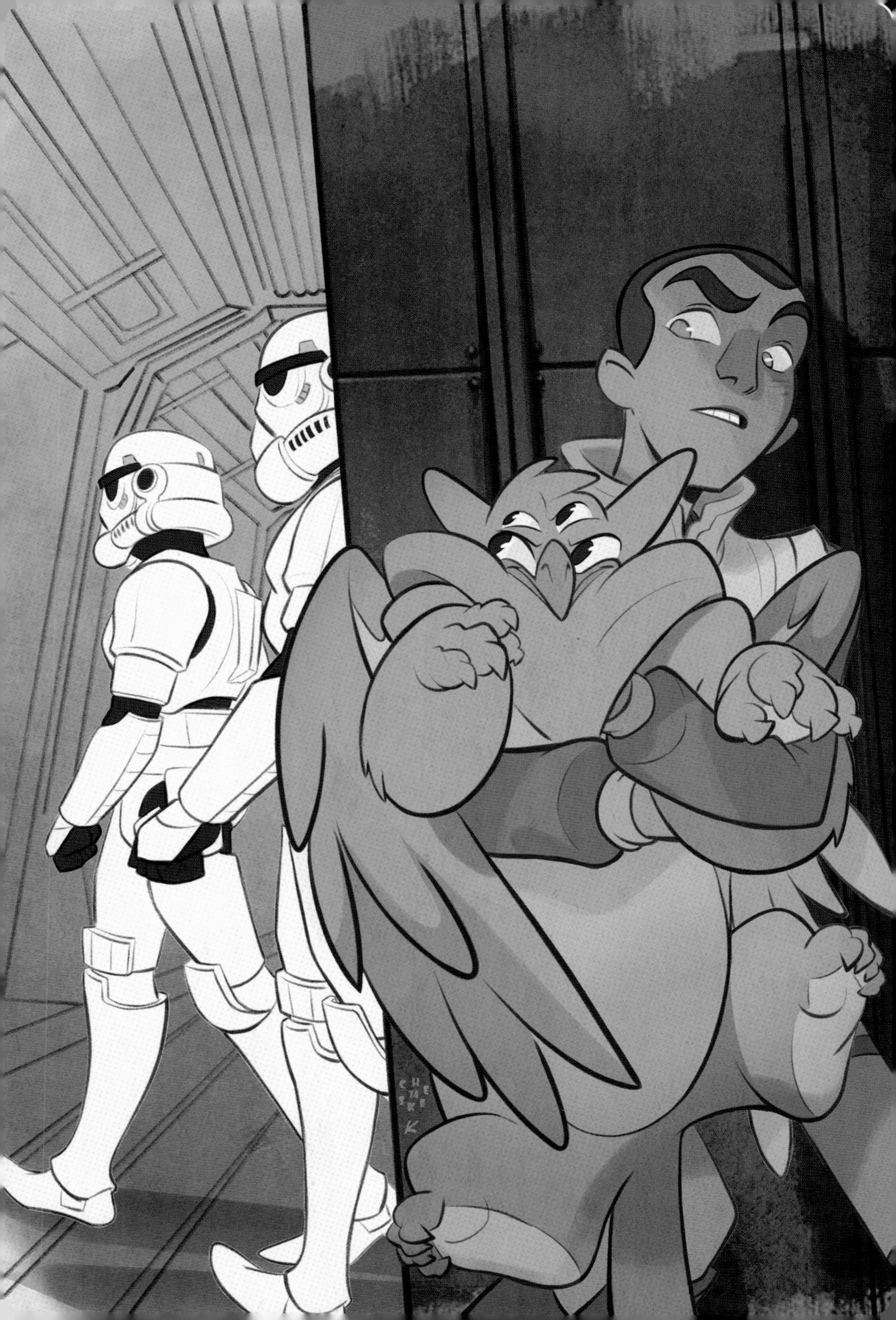

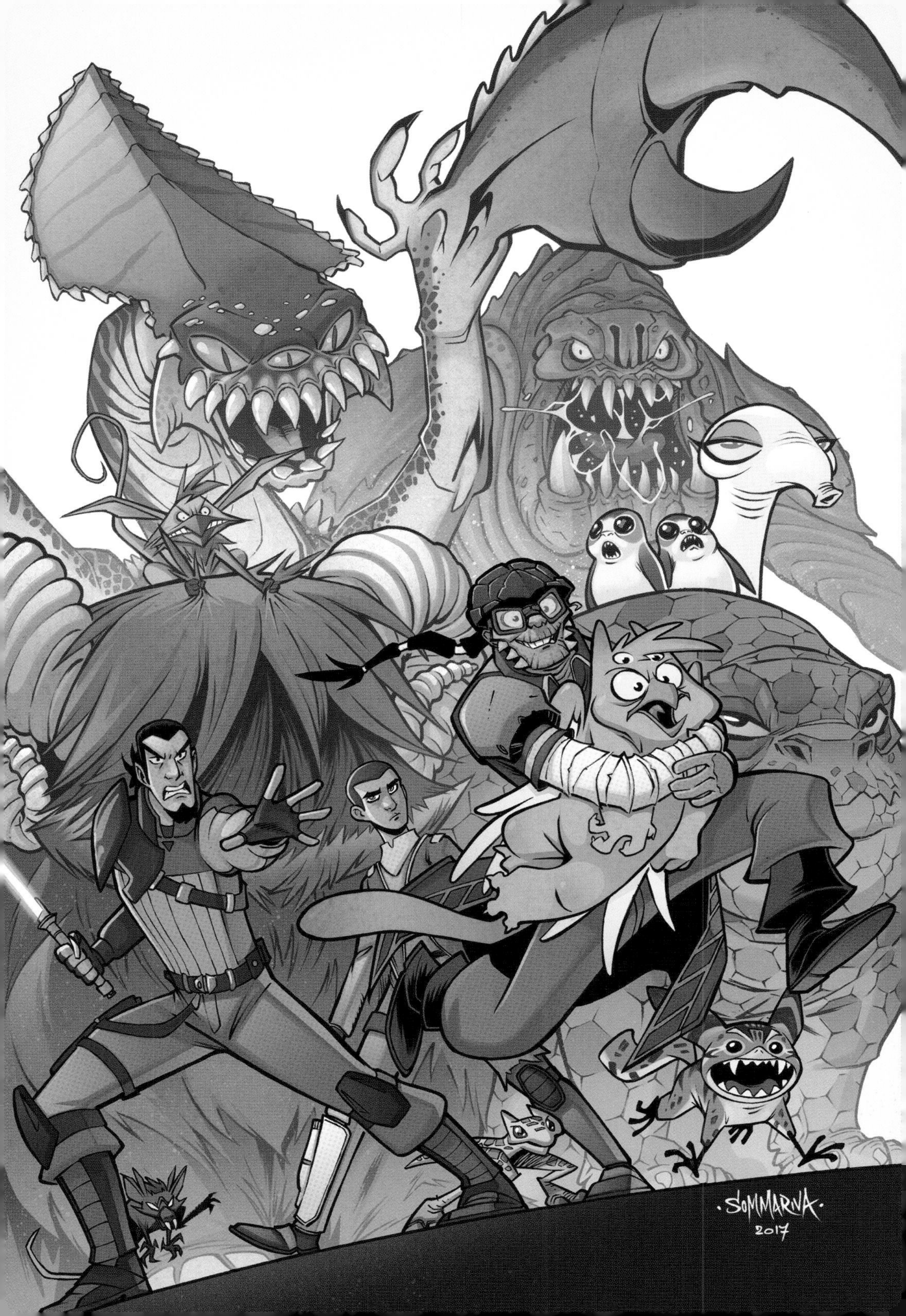
SOMMARIVA
2017

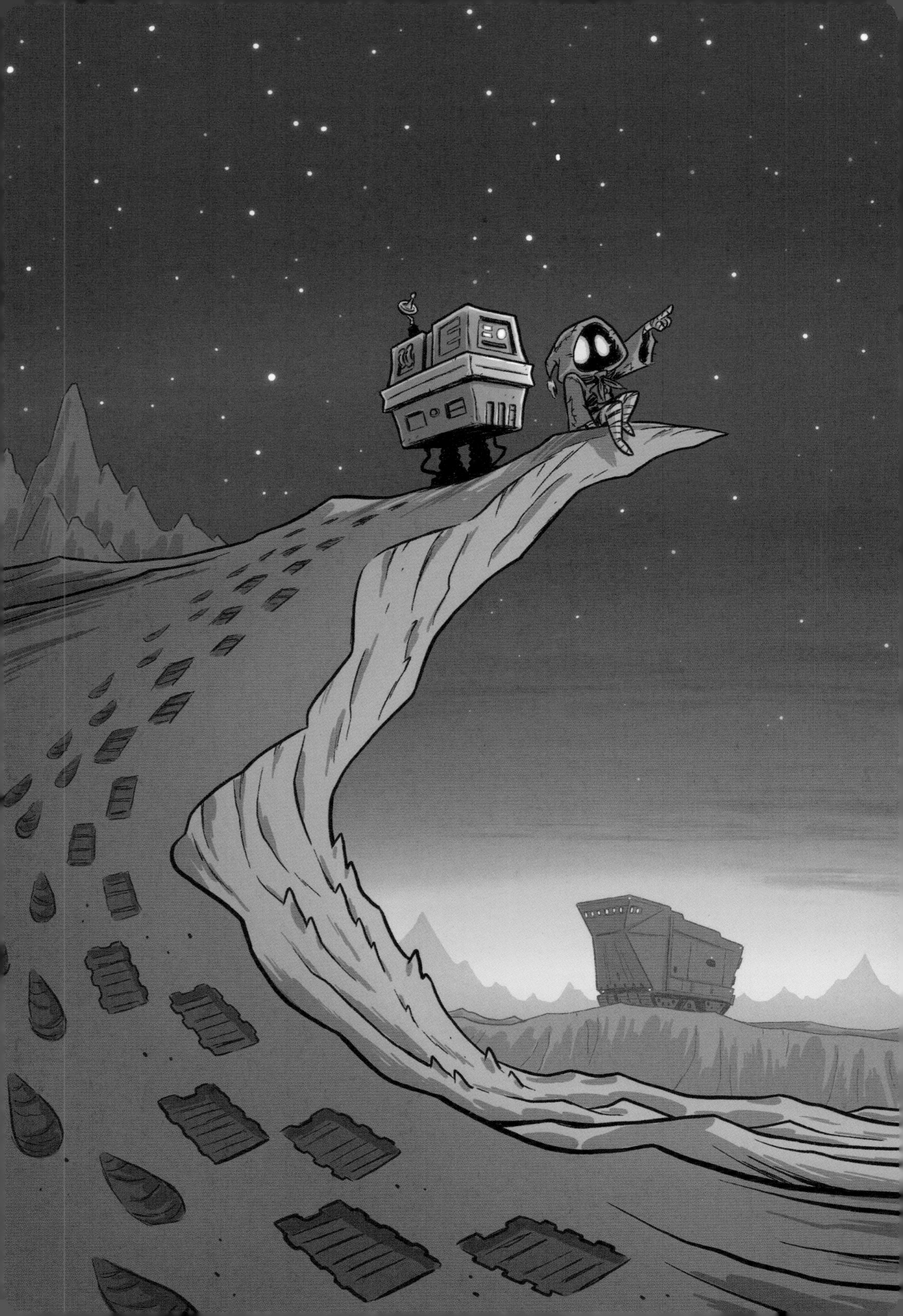

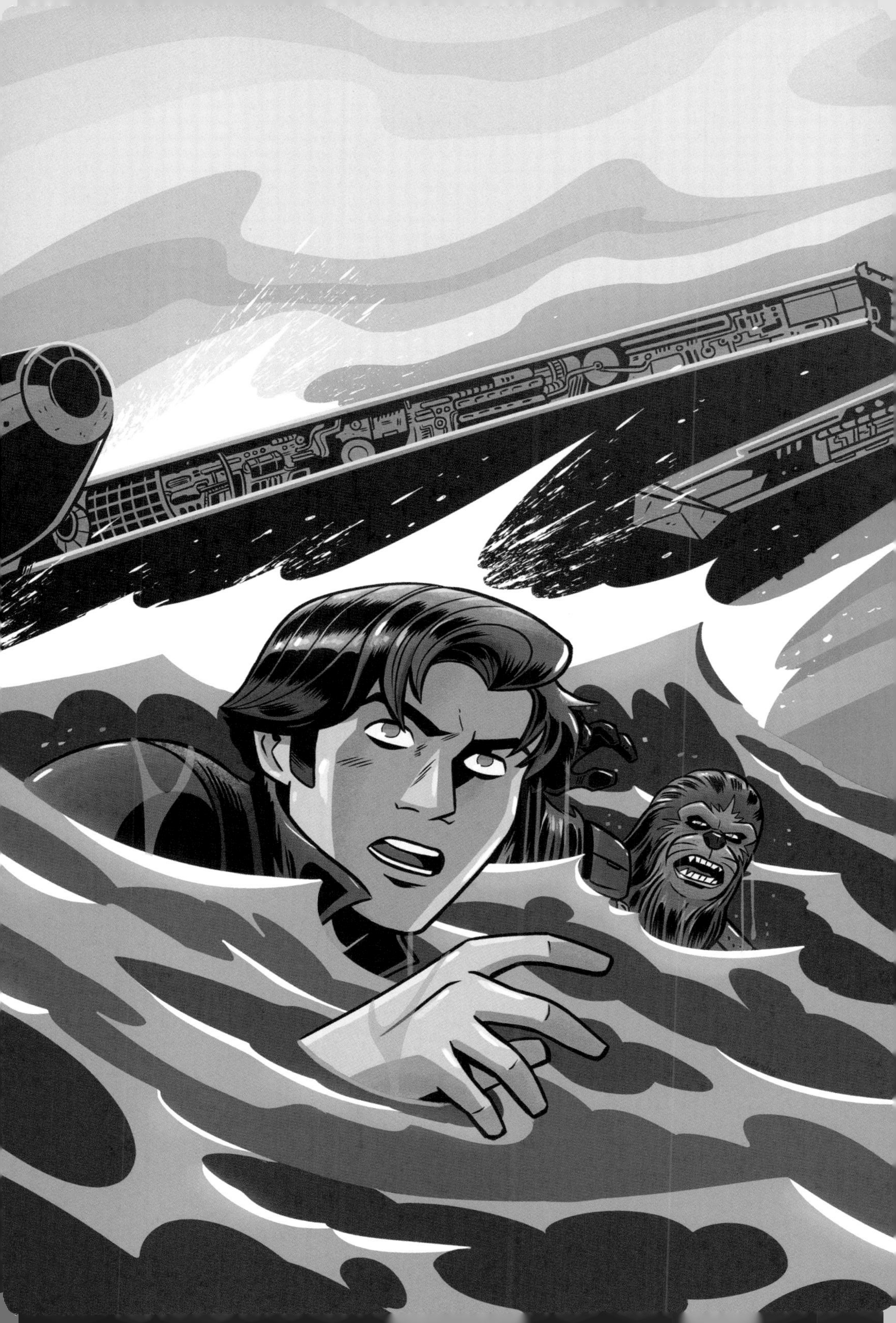

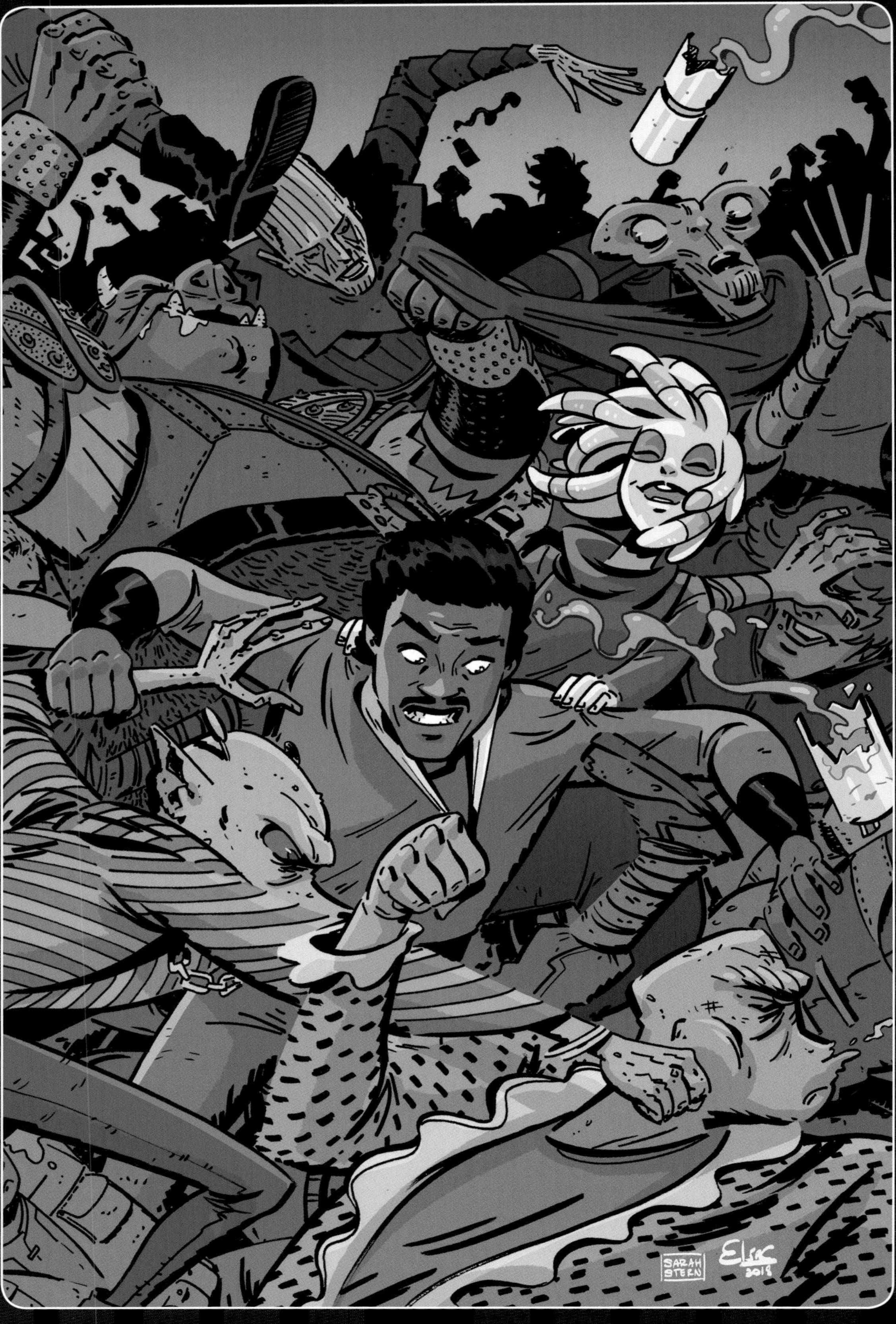
SARAH STERN
Elsa 2018

ART BY **ELSA CHARRETIER**
COLORS BY **SARAH STERN**

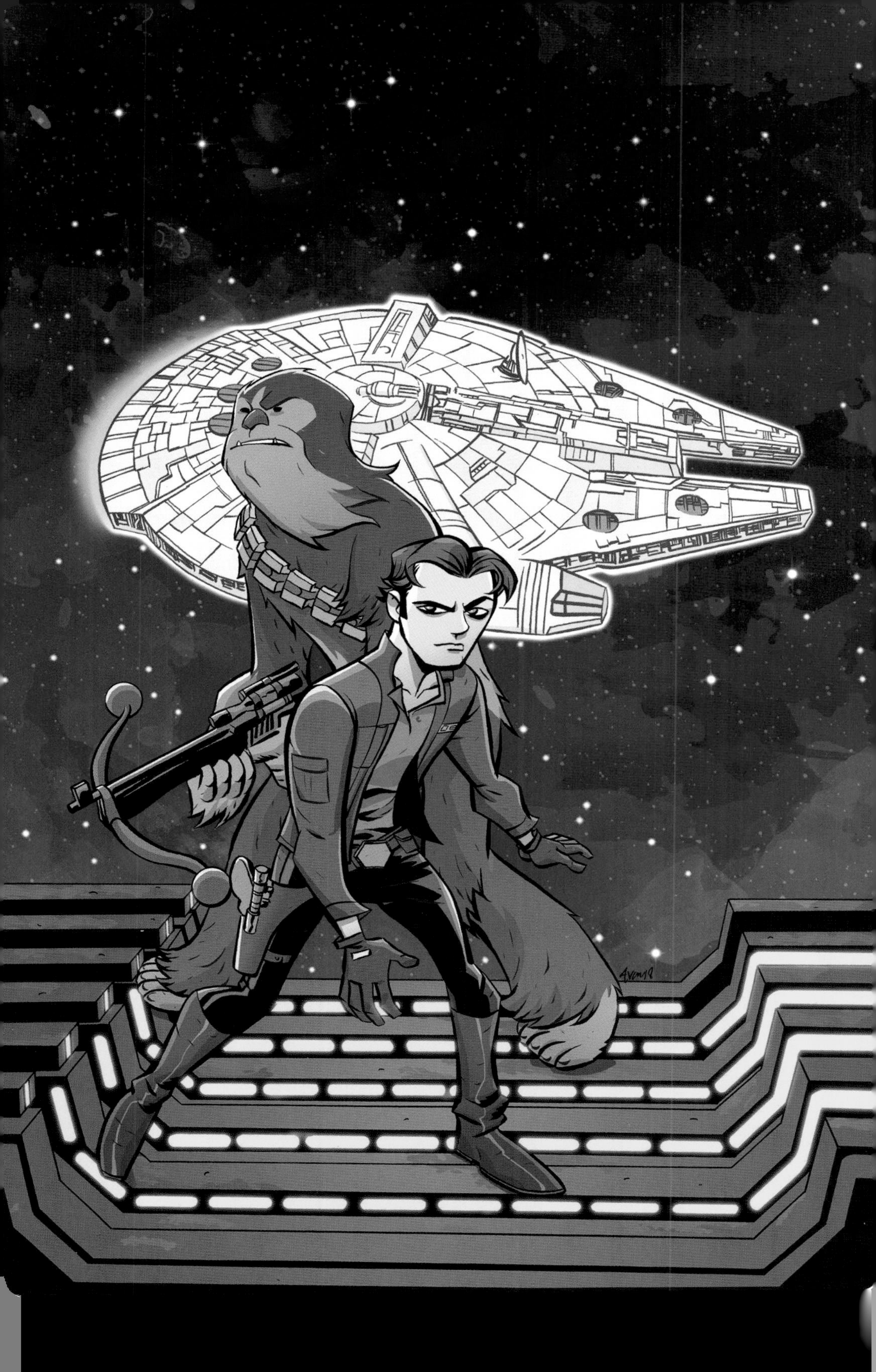

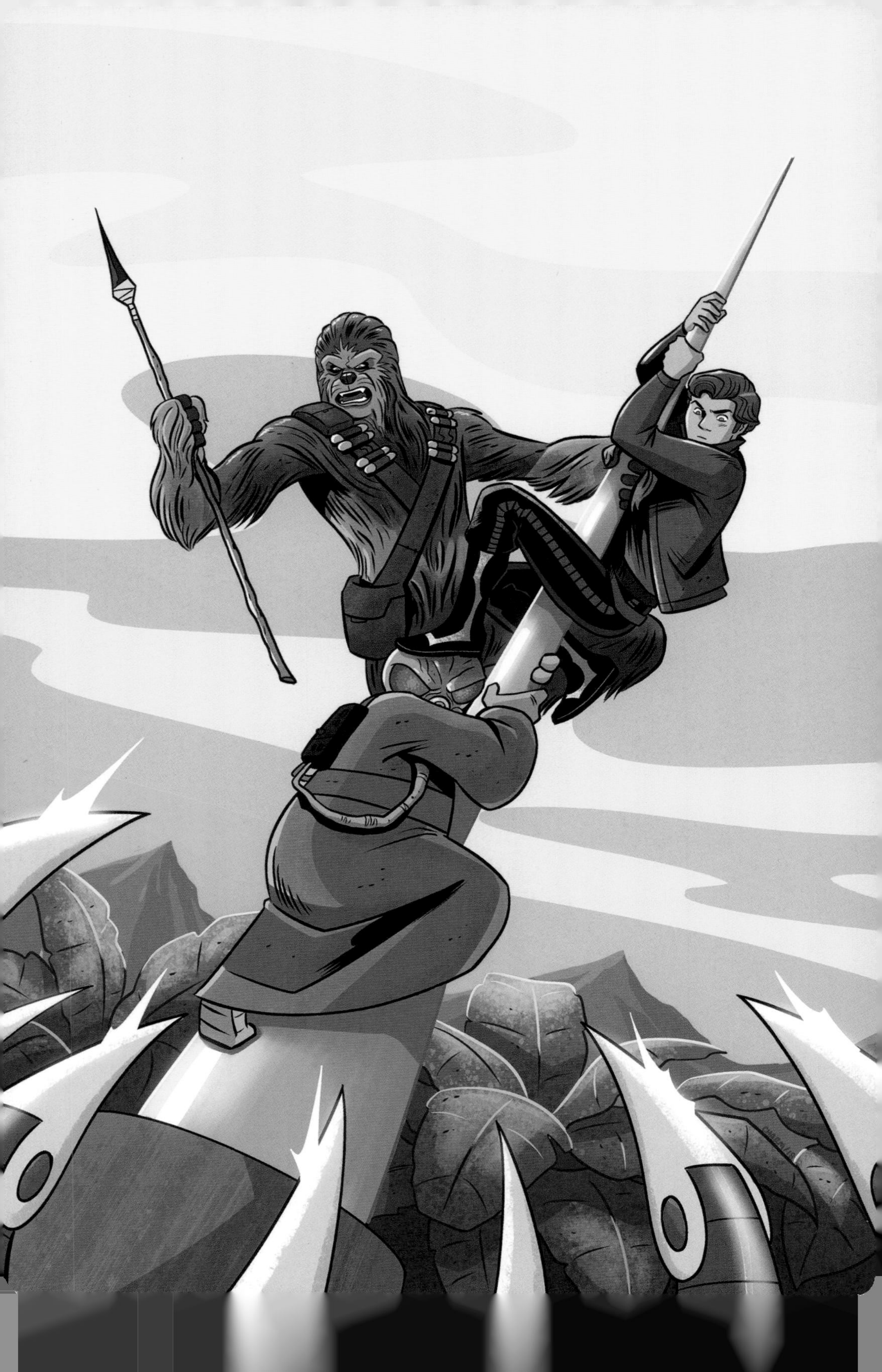

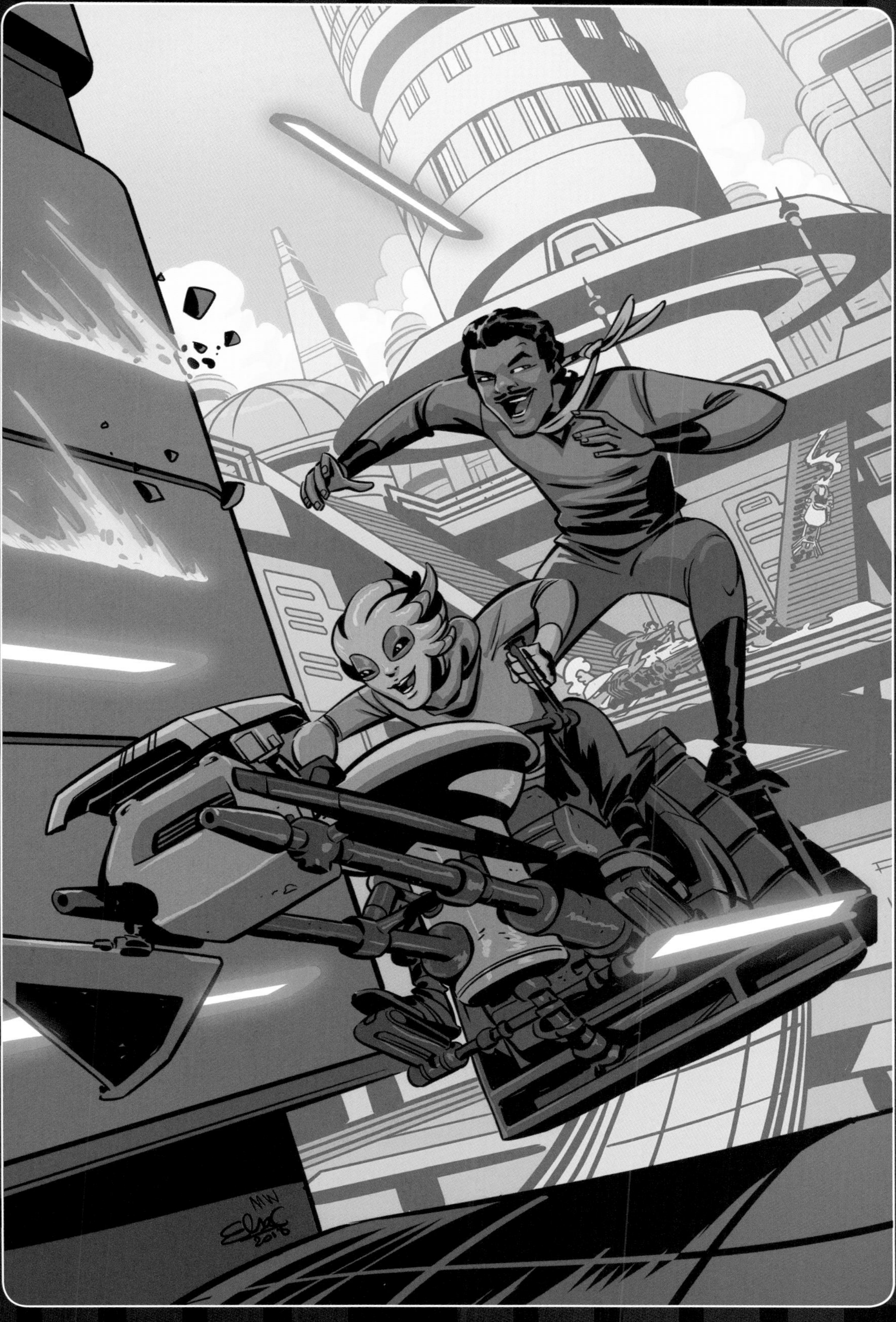
MW
Elsa
2018

ART BY ELSA CHARRETIER
COLORS BY SARAH STERN

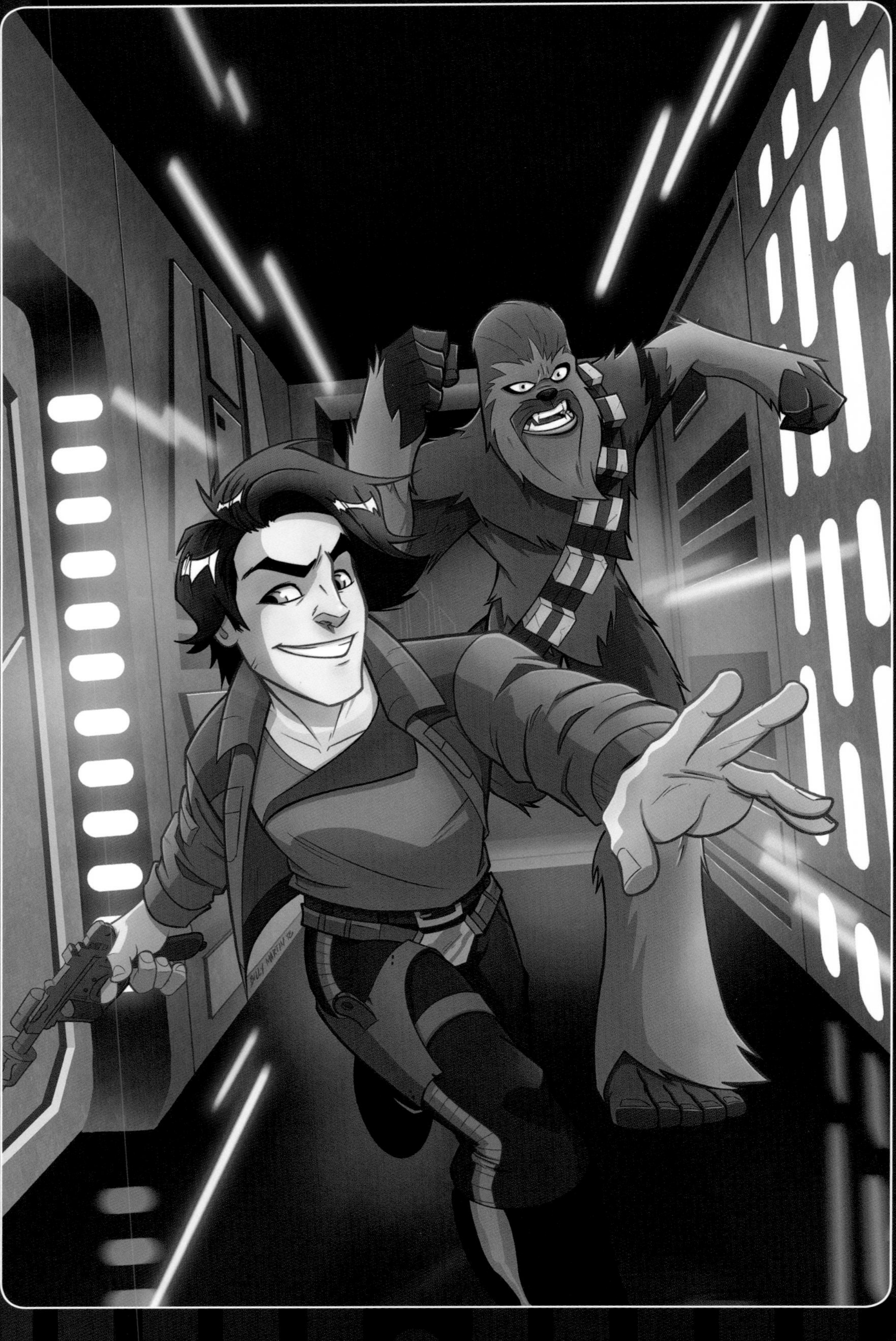
BILLY MARTIN

ART BY **BILLY MARTIN**

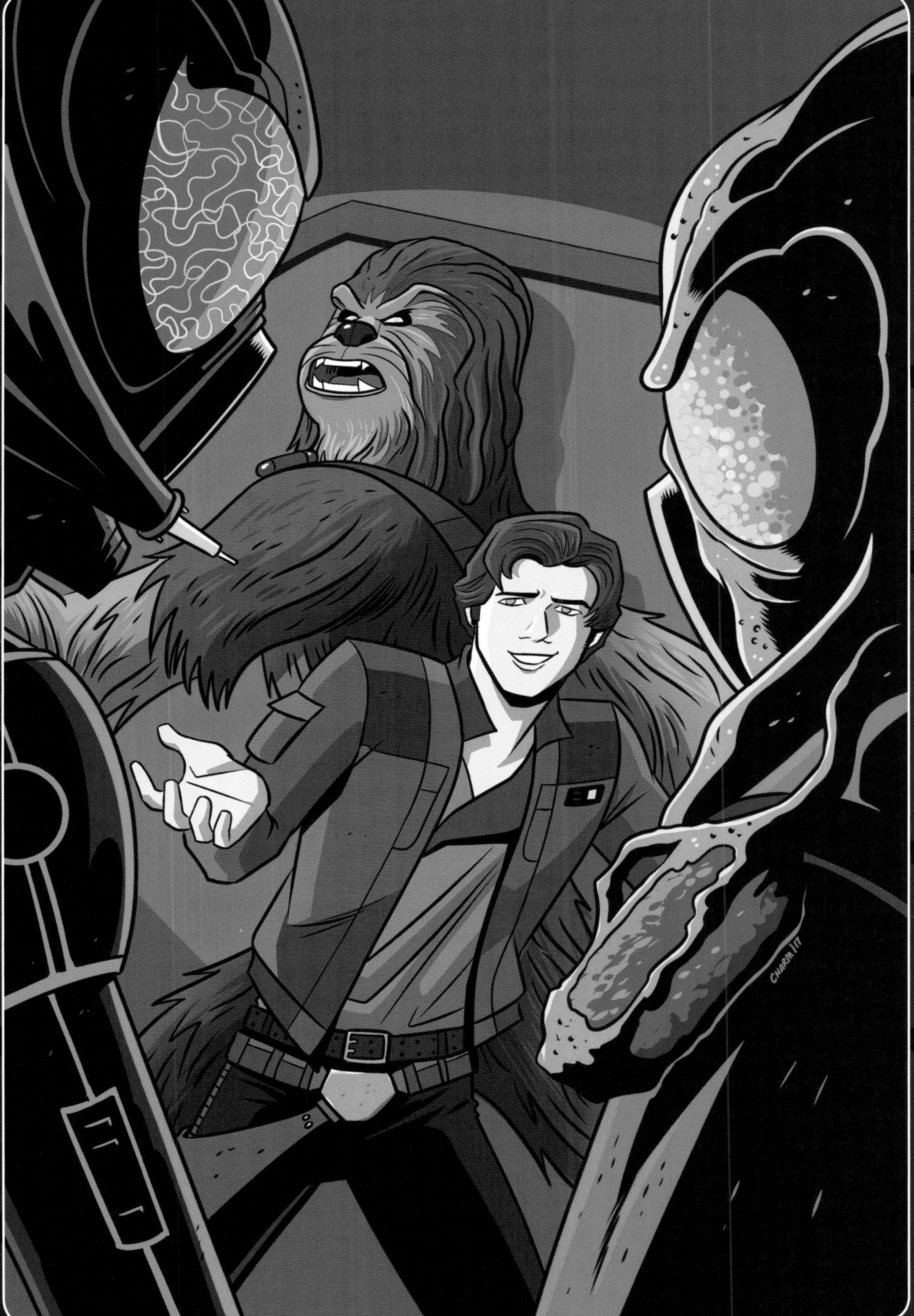

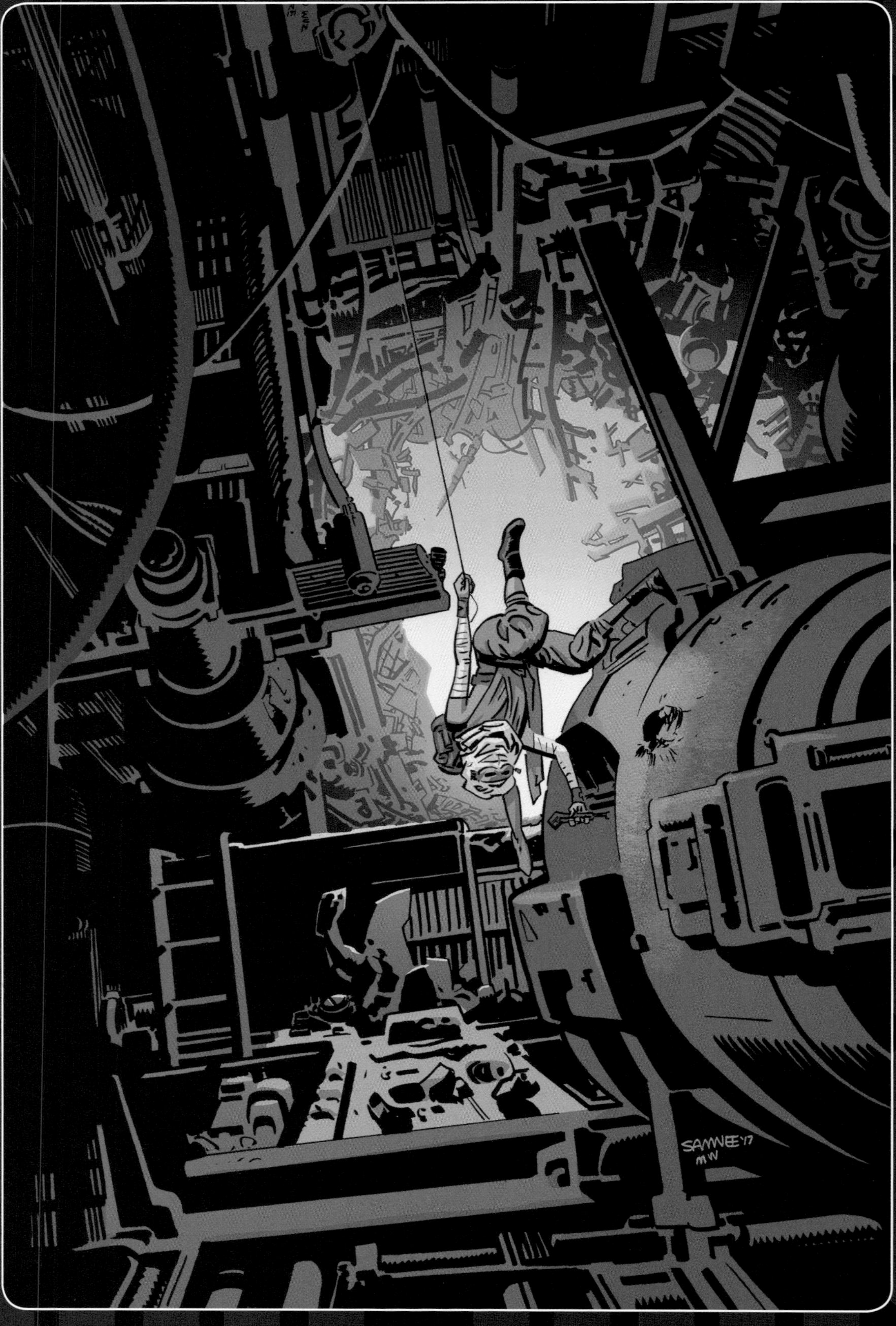
SAMNEE '17
MW

ART BY **CHRIS SAMNEE**
COLORS BY **MATT WILSON**

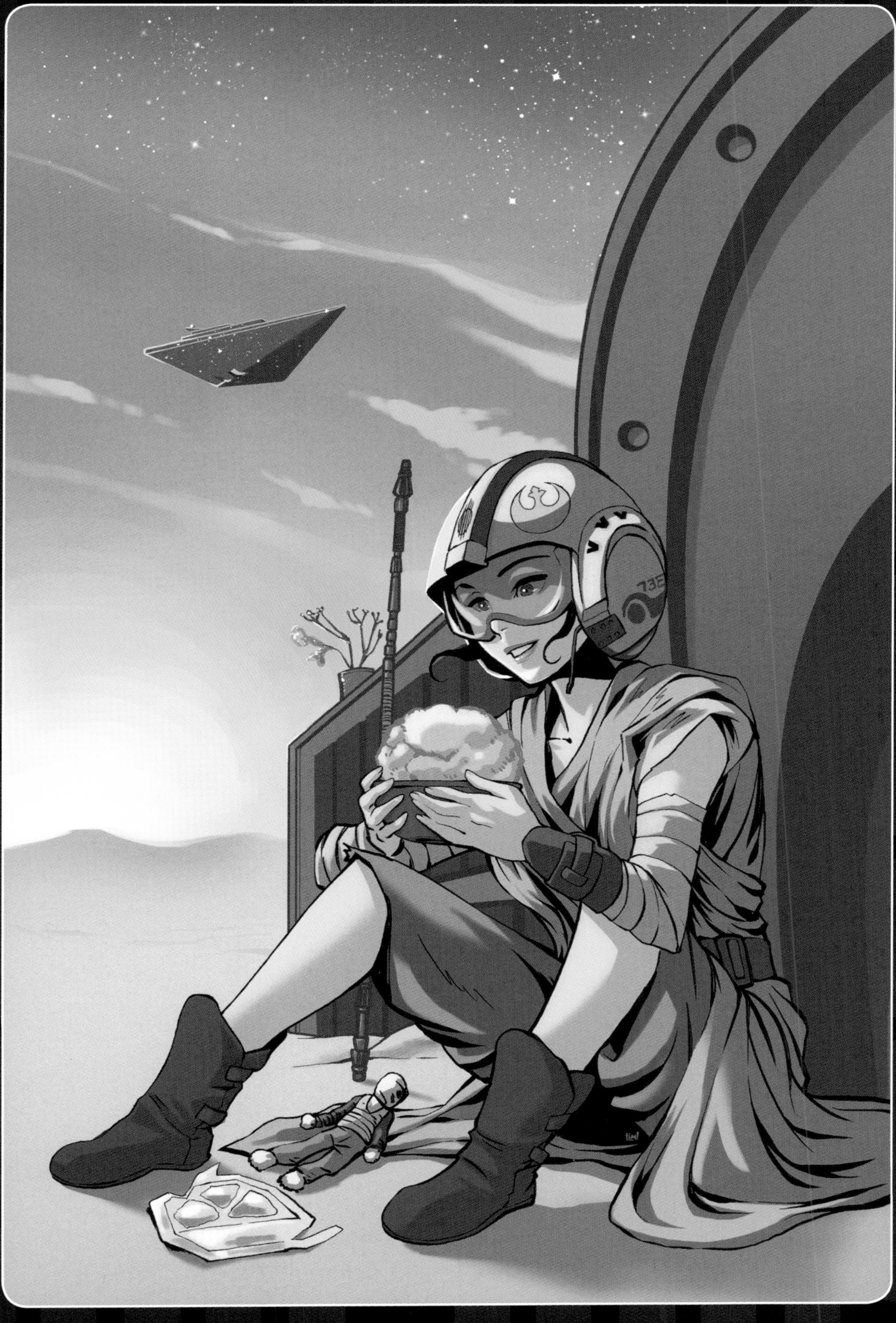

ART BY **TIM LIM**

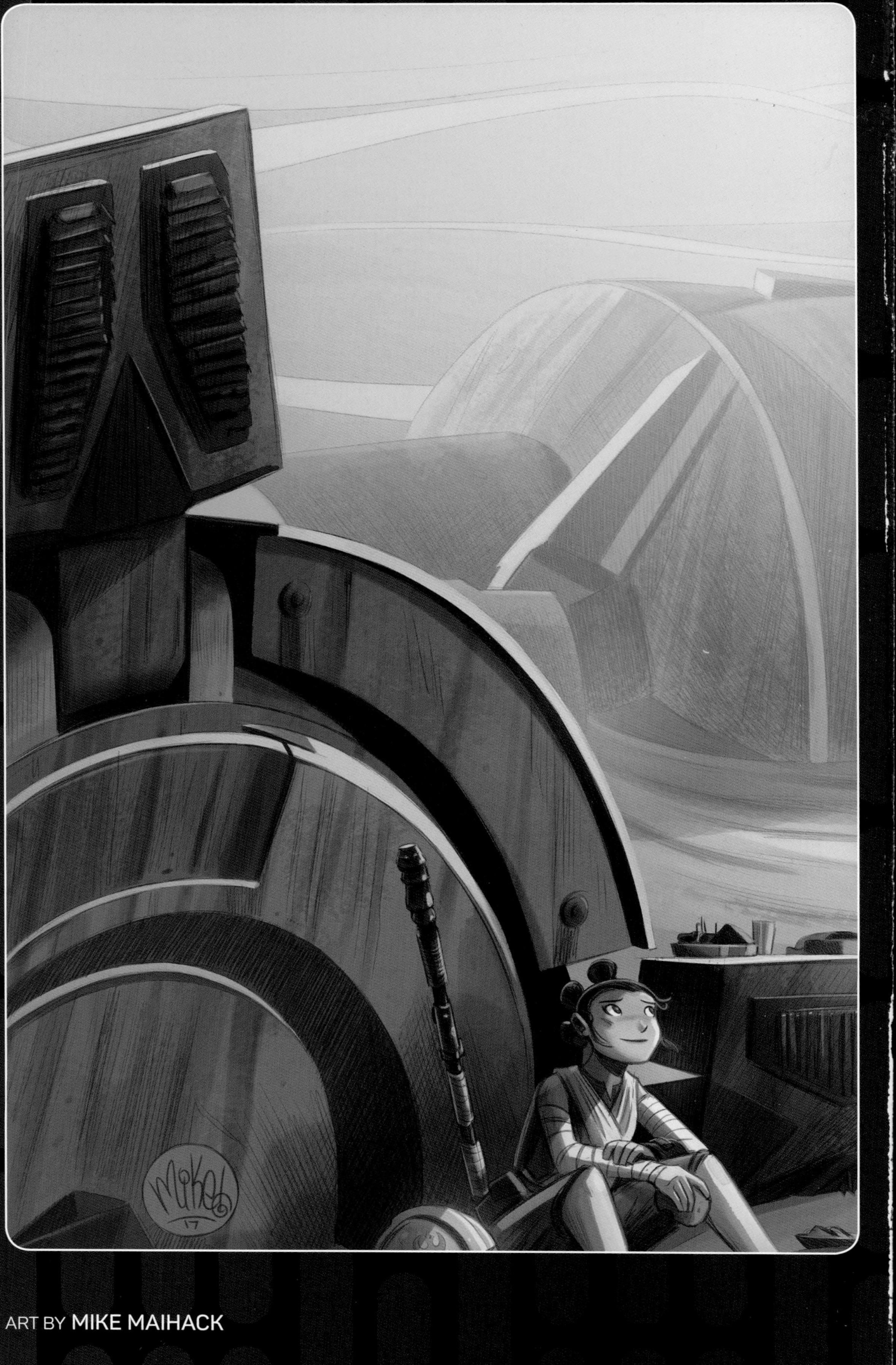

ART BY **MIKE MAIHACK**